frank

Steven Farnworth

Blue Wind Books
Menlo Park, California

First Edition

ISBN-13: 978-0615625089

Published in the United States by Blue Wind Books

Acknowledgements

Writing this book was a five-year journey of dedicated nights, weekends and just about any spare moments I could find. Without the support of my wife and family, as well as the input and early reader feedback from friends and colleagues, this work would not have been possible.

Thank you to my wife and copy editor Suzy Farnworth for the multiple rounds of edits and grammar checking—thank goodness one of us has a clue.

Thank you to Officer Felicia Byars of the Menlo Park PD, Jim Blake, Janice Cheng, Bob Gordon, Ray Martino Jr., David Allen, Dave DeMoss and Scott Stevens for wading through early versions of the manuscripts.

While all the characters and situations are fiction, I've endeavored to put as much first hand experience into the story as possible.

Chapter 1

Time not registering—only darkness.

Sharp drumbeat of taxi drivers pounding away on their horns in the traffic jam over on 15th Street mercilessly beats against my skull. Shouting match erupting between a school bus driver and the driver of a beaten up, white delivery van as they compete to get around a double-parked, brand new 1975 black Cadillac—assholes.

Stuyvesant Park in its late morning glory under the gray sky; weeds pushing up through cracks in the pavement, potholes, dog shit, discarded syringes, empty MD 20-20 pint bottles wrapped in dirty brown paper bags, run down park benches, trash strewn around the park. Rusting iron fences surround fields of dark brown dirt with solitary islands of rich green grass here and there—the few that escaped the daily stampede of high school feet running free after another day in captivity.

Body dreading the thought of going back to school and sitting in that damn classroom for the rest of the day. So much to do in the world and I'm stuck in this awful place.

Fervent prayer—one brief moment God, one moment reliving the elation of surfacing from the deep, cold ocean and taking in that first breath of clean, cool, sea air after a long dive. Eyes closed trying to recapture the freedom of the moment.

Nothing but horns and people yelling at each other—I hate this place.

Gripping a weathered park bench slat as hard as I can. Closing my eyes, flexing my arm and body muscles, holding them tight till they shake in pain. My insides still burning from last night's fight with Dad.

Seeing his mocking face as he comes in to land another body-blow insult, his face twisted in disdain—Mom standing silently in the background in her porcelain beauty. Wishing I could stop reliving this argument again and again in my head.

"Mr. Smart Guy, thinks he knows better than everyone else?"

"Why is nothing ever good enough for you, Dad?"

"You waste your time with those niggers and spics you call your friends, you don't respect nobody, you don't listen to nobody. Look at what you are doing to us! Look at what you are doing to your mother. You don't care about nothin."

"That right? You don't know anything about us!"

"That right, Mr. Big Man? I tell you what, you stand next to them in the subway... they smell."

"You racist..." stepping towards the violent, jagged line I know I'll cross.

"Yeah, well you're gonna turn out to be a loser just like your fag sister! How do you feel about that, Big Man?"

"How can you say that about her, damn you! I'll show you!"

Pain bringing me back—taxi horns blaring away.

"Yo Frankaaay!"

Turning to the voice. Oh no, not now. Not that asshole Leroy.

"There he is, the Great White Mope," smile on his face while he's playing to his audience, the mental midget Thomas Jones following obediently in Leroy's footsteps. Slight relief seeing Alton hustling over across the traffic stacked up on 15th Street. The van's moved up a couple of car lengths, the bus driver still yelling, his face a slightly lighter shade of red.

"My man, Leroy," breathing in, standing up, can't stop the words, "your mother make you that ugly or you got to work at it?"

Shifting over to his side-kick, "Now I know you could talk some shit Thomas Jones, but your dumbass would be stuttering for an hour for you even start making sense," mimicking him when he gets flushed, "ffffffuck, yyyyyou," crossing my arms.

"Mman d'on't be fffuckin with me," his face starting to shake.

"Such a nice day, Leroy, till yo ugly ass showed up."

Moving my body and arms to try and shake out some of the anger building up. "Man, the doctor smack the right end when you came out or did he just whack both to make sure. I can't make sure, can you TJ? We got a ass here, or a face?"

Thomas Jones laughing for a second then getting serious as Leroy flashes anger across his face. "Awfully funny for a man hanging on to school by a thread. White man gots everything in this world and all you can do is fuck it up, that right, Frankaaay? You got any tips?"

"Man, fuck you Leroy, you're just pissed cause I got hot last game in front of the college scouts. Your ass is outta here this year, why don't you just leave. Nobody here that wants to hear your bullshit 'cept his dumb ass," pointing at Thomas Jones.

Can't stop my body—feeling anger building.

"Yo Frank, Leroy," said Alton hustling over from across the park. "You got to knock this shit off. Coach is gonna be pissed if you guys get into it again."

"Hey, it's Uncle Tom Alton here to make peace with the man."

"Leroy, kiss my black ass," called Alton.

"So, what's it like, Leroy?" zeroing in on him. "What's it like to live in a world where you're the only one who counts? Mr. One-on-Five. Mr. Trash-Talking-Motherfucker who never stays after practice working his shots, his moves," looking at him hard. "I know you don't work your passing or your D. You just work your mouth."

"Hey baby, leading scorer!"

"Hey baby," parroting his speech and facial expressions. "Worst shooting percentage, same fucking assists per game as me." He gets closer, chest-to-chest now. "How's that work, huh? A forward with the same number of assists as the point guard, who's only two points per game back from Mr. Scoring Leader?" pushing him back with my chest, can't control this.

Getting in his face, "Let's see, you sit we win. I sit we lose. How does that work, Mr. Chuck-Shot?"

"Mr. Golden Boy. Wants to be the big star. Just like the man, got to have everything."

"I want the team to win, Leroy," he bumps me with his chest, bumping him back. "You want Leroy to win. You've been that way for the last three years, you'll pull that same shit in college."

"Yeah, I'll be doing it at St. John's baby!" he waves an envelope in my face. "Gonna give my ass a scholarship. What you gonna have year after next, Mr. Great White Dope?"

Moving in close to him, Alton putting his hands between us and trying to move us back. "Cool it down," he's looking at Thomas Jones. "This is bullshit, Coach is gonna bench both yo dumb asses."

"The man's talking too much sh'shit Leroy," said Thomas Jones circling.

"You know Mr. One-on-Five, as fucked up as my daddy is, at least I know who my daddy is, you'd have to follow the motherfuckin train tracks to find yours."

His face is turning purple—he's got to start this.

"Man, fuck you! Mister who thinks he knows some shit. I see how your daddy looks at black people, your daddy a racist? Huh?"

Shoving him back. Moving closer.

"My dad's fucked up, Leroy, but I tell you one thing, he knows how to recognize a piece of shit when he sees one and that's what I'm looking at right now."

"So what's your definition of a black man then? You tell me that!" his face starting to waver side to side. "Man with a racist father who thinks he knows so much, thinks he's got some shit cause he takes his five hundred jump shots every day."

Alton steps between us, his strong six-foot three-inch frame creating space. Thomas Jones pushes me from the side. He's starting to get that crazy smile. Bring it on TJ.

"Thomas Jones, you push me again and I will fuck you up."

"Sssshhi, shhit," his body starting to shake.

"Frank, cool it man," Alton holds up his hands to Thomas Jones to get him to back off. Leroy trying to come around to the other side of Alton, "It's your ass if you get into trouble again."

"Mr. Smartass, how's that work, huh? Strike three and you're out," from that shithead Leroy. Pissed that Alton is facing me and pushing me back.

"Alton, why are you telling me to cool it? You know this guy is a piece of shit. Why are you standing with him?"

"I ain't standing with nobody!" he yells at me, his breathing going quickly. "Back the fuck off, Leroy!" He turns back to me while trying to keep his body between us. "You talk about the team winning. You get your ass thrown off the team, how's that gonna help us out, huh? I'm trying to help you man!"

Clenching and unclenching my fists and wishing I could ignore the sweet familiar call of red rage.

"Alton, the big peace maker. Jumping at the beck and call of the man," Leroy moving his hands in waves around Alton.

"You just have to disrespect everyone, Leroy? Alton's about the only thing between you and your little bitch getting another ass whipping," feeling the dark red start to rise. "What? Your mama going to write another nasty letter to the school principal about your getting your ass beat by someone who," looking up at the sky, then at him, "who, that's right, looks just like me?"

"Man, don't stick up for me," said Alton starting to get hot.

"Then butt the fuck out!" trying to move by Alton. He moves, blocking me, Leroy starting to do a little side-to-side dance.

"Listen Frank, you need to cool it, you can't do this. Coach will…"

"I need to cool it?" losing it. "These dickheads come over and started it!"

"And you have to always be the guy that ends it, no matter what?"

"Man, why are you standing with them?"

Voices behind us, "They're fighting again," looking over—asshole tenth grader running back toward school.

"Man, fuck you, what kind a friend are you? You can't see shit," says Alton, his voice getting higher.

"You can't trust the man," Leroy points at me. "Big white ape, big man thinks he's so cool, so smart. You ain't shit you cracker motherfucker!"

"You are shit, Leroy, a big fucking piece of shit," holding my hands wide apart. "It takes two or three flushes to get a piece of shit like you down the toilet," Thomas Jones coming around. "You talk shit about white people and black people, that's just the bullshit you use to get what you want. The only person you care about is yourself. You'll use this dumb motherfucker to cover your ass, no matter if it gets his ass busted up again," Thomas Jones coming in to give me another shove, turning toward him.

Face stinging, seeing Leroy's hand moving back from the slap.

Red flashes in my vision, shoving past Alton, feeling his hands on my body as he tries to grab hold and stop me. Leading left to Leroy's smug face, good contact on the bridge of his nose. Sliding in, circling, feeling Thomas Jones' punches glance off the back of my head. Leroy crying-out in pain, shock registers on his face as he sees bright red blood on his hands.

Trying to duck and pull away from Alton's strong hold around my waist. Throwing a big right at Thomas Jones—can't extend, missed. Covering up as he swings in again, catching his punch on my right arm, letting it slide off, getting my feet, pushing forward with Alton on me. Connecting with a good upper cut to Thomas Jones' stomach—he's gasping for air. Grabbing his big Afro, pulling his head back, hard right to the side of his face, cut opening up along his eyebrow. Alton's got me off balance, tripping over his foot. Falling down in a jumble of bodies—striking with my fists and elbows.

Getting to my feet, ducking under a wild right from Leroy. Going low and grabbing the bottom of his jeans above his shell toe Adidas and pulling his legs up as I go forward. His fist connecting with my left ear as we start to fall. Ear ringing—body landing sprawled on top of Leroy in the dirt. He tries to knee at me, hits my lower stomach.

I'm screaming something, but I don't know what. Looking through a haze, willing to take the hits and kicks to get close, get close and hurt him, hurt him bad, blind rage filling my vision.

"Get this crazy motherfucker off me!" Feeling my hands around his throat. Feeling no pain from the blows registering on my body. Positioning my body up his chest, "heeee… arghhh, ah," dimly aware of the croaking from his throat, "aaaaahhhh!" smothering his struggling with my weight.

Alton trying to pull me off, taking my hands off Leroy—looking at Alton from a distance down a long tube, watching as I get my full body behind a hard blow to his face. Stunned, he backs off in surprise, rage flaring in his face.

Nothing matters now but my hands around Leroy's throat. Registering kicks to my side and punches to my back. Leroy's nails digging into the back of my hands. Squeezing, thumbs right in his Adam's apple, his eyes getting big, fluttering side-to-side. He kicks at me, tries to scratch my face, using my arms and shoulders to shirk them off, ignoring his punches to my body. Shaking my head to keep his hands away from my eyes, body pumping with one desire.

"He's killing him!" a voice in the distance yells.

"Oh my God, Police! Police, help Police!"

Noises, voices near me. Can't hear them.

Shaking with animal power—kill him, kill him.

Feeling distant kicks contacting my side and shoulders.

White light at the side of my head.

Chapter 2

Slowly floating up from a deep blackness.

Seeing shadows of people peering at me in the distance. Looking up at them like I'm standing at the bottom of a deep well. I see them talking, but I can't hear anything. Starting to feel the pain in my body—face, ribs. My back feels the hard, rough cobblestones of the park path. Head throbbing.

Blinking my eyes, left feels swollen. Jaw hurts. Feels like there's a huge mound on the side of my face. Starting to recognize where I am. Tasting blood in my mouth. Trying to move my arms, my legs.

People murmuring in the background, muted voices.

"Call…" voices coming in and then fading out, "…police."

"Maybe we… Medical Center… there."

"He's moving," people touching me, trying to help me up.

Closing my eyes, opening them for a second. World spinning.

Slowly sitting up—head throbbing, sides ache, face in pain, loose teeth on the side of my jaw. Punch to the ear stinging still, pushing away the hands that try to help me. Hurts to breathe. Breathing deep to keep the dizziness at bay. Pulling my knees up, putting my arms around them—head resting on my arms.

Time moving slowly, hearing people talk, but only catching a few words here and there. Taking a look around, all three of them are gone. Stomach feeling sick—Alton's gone. Thoughts racing by and swirling around—he joined them. Rage spreading out inside me. They couldn't have stopped me, Thomas Jones is strong and crazy but I could have taken him and Leroy—Alton joined them. He let them beat me… Pulling my hair as hard as I can to deal with the hurt inside. He joined them!

Slowly becoming aware of pain shooting through my body. This was a good beating—must have laid into me when I was out. Had to be Alton who knocked me out. Feeling sick to my stomach, imagining him kicking and hitting me while I was down. Oh am I going to get those bastards—especially you Alton. Traitor, bastard!

Rage swirling through me—sick feeling sweeping though me as I try to move. Taking a deep breath, sinking feeling creeping into my stomach, recognition that I've fucked up again. Oh God. Oh no, I've got to face Coach, got to face Mom and Dad. This wasn't my fault. I shouldn't take the blame for this. It's not fair.

Anger boiling up, throat tight, having trouble breathing. Fighting off the tears that want to come to my face. Putting my head back down on my knees, people still standing there. I'm gonna get you motherfuckers, I'm gonna get you motherfuckers. Body sobbing.

I lost. I lost to Leroy—bastards. I lost to that prick.

How could Alton stand with them?

No one helps, people walking away, new people walking by forming up in the spectator circle. Feeling like I'm falling down, don't care what happens now.

Traffic still jammed, taxi horns blurting angrily into the air.
"Are you okay?" some lady in the gathering crowd asks me.
"Thhhink, soo," tongue feels swollen, trouble keeping her in focus.
"You want me to call the police? I saw those three boys."
"Nn noo, sssokayy. Just nnneed to get over to schhhoooll. Llate."
"You need to be careful, you probably hurt your head."
Wave of fatigue pulling me down, feels like the force of gravity is increasing. Putting my head back on my knees. "Bee, be okkkaayyy," closing my eyes to stop the dizziness, "Fffanks."

Stopping and propping my body up on a car as a wave of dizziness hits me. Vision collapsing into a long tunnel for a second, head feels fuzzy, ears buzzing. Blinking my eyes, vision returning. People looking at me then hurriedly walking away. Face the shame—get my stuff at school and go home, get some ice on my face. Get them back.

Taking a deep breath. Feeling empty other than the slow burning ember of what I'm going to do when I catch those three. Leroy doesn't stand a chance by himself. Thomas Jones is fast. Got to spring on him, use my height and weight advantage. Alton—up well of emotion surging through my chest, my fucking friend betrayed me!

I'm gonna get you last no matter what.

Staggering up the street, body burning with shame. I lost. I don't lose!

All these years we've been friends—basketball, working out for Golden Gloves together, arguing about which one of us was going to ask out Emily in seventh grade. Thinking back to when I met him in elementary school at PS 87. Sick laugh coming up inside me imagining those stupid try-to-be-cool, karate demonstrations we used to put on for the rest of the kids after seeing too many Bruce Lee movies together. Sitting around basketball courts talking about our favorite players, Knicks games, boxers, sharing lunch at the track meets we'd go to down in Riverside Park cause his moms was late for work and couldn't make him lunch that day. Hours and hours on the courts, practicing, traveling the city, looking to play with the best, challenging each other, competing with each other.

Cold anger running through me—how could he choose to stand with that shit Leroy? Feeling sick, kneeling down, trying to hold back the acidic vomit rushing up from my stomach. Retching again and again. Burning shame. What if my fucking father has been right? All the times I'd told him he didn't understand. Can't be real friends with niggers he'd say—too different, working is one thing, respect for ability another, just two sides of the coin… No, you're wrong Dad. You're wrong!

Bastards, I'm going to get you. I'm going to make you pay.

Walking up 15th Street, opposite side of the street from school. Woozy. Trying to shut out the noise. Spitting some of the awful taste out of my mouth. Catching a glimpse of Alton running out of the building with Mr. Elliot following behind him. Stepping back into the alleyway. Gritting my sore teeth together, that bastard wants them to come see me like this now, throw me out of school.

Resting my head against the rough grain of the brick wall in the alley, breathing, trying to work the fog out of my brain.

Hector and Julio at the school steps, they shouldn't be here.

"Man, Frankie, we heard what happened, those three maricon motherfuckers," Hector looks at my face, "you look fucked up man. Come in, we get you to the bathroom so you can wash up."

"Leroy's out telling people you a mad dog. Like you tried to strangle him 'n shit. Principal's out looking for you man," said Julio.

Shaking my head, trying to work my way through the fog that's settling in again, "Mmm fffucked, not mmy fault."

"You got that right," seeing Hector look at Julio out of the side of his eyes, other kids in the school walking over, whispering to each other and pointing at us. Fuzzy shapes—making out a couple of people. Richard coming over, Mary, Leslie.

"Are you okay?" asked Richard, his eyes moving side to side.

"Let him breathe," said Hector.

"My God, Frank, what happened?" asked Mary, can't see her, hearing the genuine concern in her voice.

"Those three putos Leroy, TJ and Alton all ganged up on Frank."

"That's not right," said Richard, "Alton's his friend!"

"Want to get my stuff and go. Get some ice on my face."

"Come on man, we got you."

Hands on my elbows helping me along.

"Man, Frankie, I told you that puto was out to try and get you kicked out of school. I love you man, but goddamn man, you stubborn. Why don't you let your friends help you man?" Julio holding my arm as we walk through the school, Mary walking in front, shooing people away. Seeing Cedar walk to the side.

"What happened here?" he looks concerned.

"Got into it with Leroy, Thomas Jones and Alton."

He takes a deep breath, resigned, shaking his head, "Man, Coach is gonna have to…" he looks away and then looks back at me, "right at the playoffs. Can't you keep it cool man? Right when we need you," he makes a fist and hits his thigh. "You stupid…"

He looks at me for a moment, "You gonna go fight everything you don't

14

get along with in life man?" he shakes his head. "You gonna find one long motherfuckin line." He walks away shaking his head.

Fog clearing a little as I walk up to my locker, kids around me. Mary trying to talk to me, Cat's friend Marta coming in with rapid questions. Mumbling answers, can't keep up. Third time trying to open the combination lock. Resting my head on the cold, steel locker.

"Man," hearing Hector talk to Julio. "We get that crazy mother Jorge and we go get those fuckers!" they slap hands.

"Hector," shaking my head. "Gotta talk to Coach, Richert. They've got to know what went down. They'll just suspend you. I'm gonna fuck all three of them up."

"We help you man, don't be no fucking lone ranger."

"Yeah, what are you, fucking Tonto?"

"Fuck you maricon!" his voice hurt.

Feeling people clear away from me.

"Oh shit…" said Julio.

"You need to come with me," a deep voice behind me, "Principal Richert wants to see you. Now!" Turning around as best I can. Blinking, seeing my Calculus II teacher Mr. Sturm. Disapproving look set on his thick Germanic face, hands on his waist. I open my mouth. He holds up his hand. "I don't want to hear excuses anymore," he turns and beckons.

"Yo Julio, let Cat know what's going on."

"Be cool, Frankie, we got your back," said Julio. Mary looking at me, her face set, her lips closed tight, Marta giving her a nasty look.

Embarrassment burning inside as I walk behind Mr. Sturm, kids lining the school hall looking at me, whispering.

Sitting alone in the Principal's cold, precise office. Holding the cold, bloody, ice-filled towel on my face. His office wall filled with pictures of famous scientists and engineers who had graduated from Stuyvesant High School, men looking out into the future.

Waiting, he's going to make me wait.

There he is, Mr. Cold Blooded, right outside the large office window. He's giving me a disgusted look now and then while talking to teachers like nothing's happened. Hearing Coach Valerio's loud voice as well as Mr. Sturm, Mr. Summers, Mrs. Marquez. Well, at least there are two out there who like me.

No eye contact from Richert as he sits down and looks at the clean green desk blotter then takes a few moments to line it up precisely in the center of his desk. He clears his throat, folds his hands together.

"So much for your promise."

"I didn't start it, it's not my fault."

He holds up his hands. "I don't want to hear it, I have had enough," he moves like he's agitated and then takes a moment to return to his calm know-it-all state. He sits back in his chair, his eyes sweeping over my face then looking at the glass door to his office, "You have got to be one of the most..." he looks down and takes a deep breath, "you are expelled. I will be talking to your parents."

"Principal Richert, I didn't start it. Doesn't that matter? I've done..." He's holding up his hand, looking down at his desk.

"Yes, I'm sure you have a very convincing story about how this all happened. I have two seniors who saw you on top of a fellow student screaming incoherently, two other students trying to pull you off while your hands were around his neck," he leans forward, "tell me then, this was your last chance... You promised to work with Coach Valerio or Mr. Sturm if you needed guidance and here you are in another altercation!" He slams his hand down on the desk and then sits back, taking a few moments to regain his academic composure.

"And you've thrown it away, haven't you?" he looks at me, his cold blue eyes directly looking at me. "Some of the best SAT scores we've ever seen here. A's in math and science, excellent grades when you're motivated in your other classes," his face turns stern and he looks at me. "Consistently arguing with your teachers. Arrogance, impatience..." He slams his open hand on his desk again, "Arguing with me... how dare you!" He takes a couple of breaths. "Well, I'm done with you," he shakes his head. "What a waste," he leans forward. "What most of those kids out there wouldn't give... and you just throw it all away. Damn you and damn your talent! It's time for you to realize your potential is not enough," he points out his window. "Go out there and let the world knock some sense into that thick skull of yours!"

"So, that's it?"

"That's quite enough. You are expelled. Go see the nurse, then go home."

Holding my swollen lips together, pain shooting through my jaw as I clench my teeth together. Standing up.

"I'll show you, I'll show all of you."

He stands up, making direct eye contact. "Get out of my office you wretch. Go get some medical attention. I won't have you and your bad attitude here for one more moment. You can come clean out your things after the expulsion has gone through."

Standing there staring at him as my body catches up to my mind. I've been kicked out of school. Feeling like I'm falling through the floor.

"GET OUT!"

The long, slow walk out of school is tougher than the walk in. Shame coursing through my body as a few students look at me then look away quickly, most going on about their daily schedule. I don't matter to them— I'm not one of them anymore.

Chapter 3

People staring at my face and then looking quickly away on the IRT Express uptown. Dirty, tagged subway car rocking back and forth as we pass the 23rd Street local station. Wishing I could sink back into my seat and disappear, fall through the earth, transition through each layer of strata down to the molten core and then melt away into molecules, atoms. Feeling like I'm becoming smaller and smaller. Fighting off a wave of fatigue. It can't be gone like that, Richert is just mad at me again.

There's got to be a way back.

Subway pulls slowly into the 34th Street Station, most of the passengers getting off the train, leaning forward and covering my face with my hands.

Two stops to go.

Sick feeling in my stomach thinking about what's coming next—time to face Mom and Dad, time for another big fight, hell, I should be used to it by now.

Feeling empty and alone in the sound of the subway, body moving with the motion of the empty car. Sinking deeper into the hard fiberglass seat. It's not fair what they did to me. It's not fair.

Burning acid coming up from my stomach.

I lost.

Using the handrail to walk up the worn dirty steps to the street. Letting a dizzy spell pass, catching a whiff of urine as I reach the busy street. I've had worse beatings and those three ain't shit. Standing on the corner of 8th Avenue and 59th Street. It's always crowded here. People, cars, busses. Looking west toward the Hudson River.

The worst beating I took… Looking up at the sky, trying to fight the emotion rising in my chest. The worst beating I took was for you Alton. I stood up for you and this is how you pay me back? Was it okay because they were a bunch of white guys that wanted to beat our asses? I didn't try to make peace—I was there for you.

Hitting my hand with my sore fist. You stood with fucking Leroy! You stood with the man who'd throw his mother under a bus to get the spotlight!

Feeling my feet move, brain feels miles away, people yelling at me when I bump into them. Moving like I've been immersed in cold water for a long time, life passing by in slow motion—people glancing at me, but not wanting to make eye contact.

Two days ago I'd had the best game of my life. I was in the bubble. Things moved so well, my shot was on, body calm, jumping well, rebounding well, defending… Thin smile hurts when the images and sounds of Cedar and the guys coming up to me after the game, hugging me, telling me I played like a professional. Body shivers remembering the feeling of

Cat's arms around me after the game, laughing and joking with Alton. His mom giving us both hugs cause we played so well.

I've been kicked off the team, kicked out of school.

Shame welling up inside me—Leroy knew what he was doing.

You fool Frank, you fucking chump fool. He played you.

Sick feeling in my stomach. That bastard won—he got rid of me. Sick laughter welling up inside, chest hurts as I laugh. Everyone says I'm so smart and I lost it. I was out of control and I got played for a chump. You fool!

Letting the feeling burn inside me—feed the fire of revenge.

Stepping into the quiet world of our apartment building from the noisy street. Long walk up creaky wooden stairs covered with well-worn carpet. Second floor hallway is empty. Dreading the walk up, my feet moving slowly, the third floor landing squeaking underneath my feet. Standing at the door to our apartment.

How am I going to face them now?

Quietly unlocking the door—listening.

Passing the perfectly preserved living room—expensive furniture not meant to be used, just admired for how much it cost. Stopping and listening—body relaxing, it doesn't sound like anyone is home. Filling an ice bag, smacking it against the sink to break up the cubes. Hungry, don't feel like eating. Walking into my room—keeping the light off, closing the venetian blinds. Ice on my face in the dark feels good.

Lying in my bed trying to shut out the images and voices, conversations, people, moving back and forth in my brain. Feeling like shit remembering the look on Coach Valerio's face, his words; what a shame, to let myself down, to let the team down like this.

Flash scenes from fight running through my head again. Pulse starting to quicken, breathing working, body reliving it as images play through my mind, anger stirring up. Alton must have knocked me out, he's the only one of them that's strong enough and knows where to hit. Disturbing image flashing in—closing it off quickly.

Image flashing back again and bringing a cold chill up my spine; an image of something wild with its hands around another boy's throat, the look on the creatures face telling me the truth.

Cold shiver running down my body—I wasn't going to stop.

Sitting up in bed, my hands on my face. Oh my God, what am I becoming? I can't get along with anybody at home. I can't get along in school. There are days I want to walk down the street and just punch people. What's wrong with me?

Lying back down on the bed, hands coming up to my sore, swollen face. Mind searching through situations where I feel good: playing a hard game of basketball, in the ring, my mind lost in the match, in the ocean free diving deep for striped bass, sometimes in math class.

Shaking my head, looking around the dark room. Everyone made such a big deal over my SAT scores, what if I was just lucky? My overall grades are good but inconsistent. The teachers' pets were pissed as usual because I beat them. Imagining their conversations about how that jock could get such good test scores when he doesn't even study. None of that matters now. My father thinking he's going to have some Ivy League or Division One kid— some fucking joke.

Looking around my dark room, street noise filtering in through the open window—cars, horns, people, radios; constant New York City background noise. Time ticking by, feeling of desolation growing. Lying back down slowly, my body complaining at each move.

What am I going to do now? This can't be that bad?

Coach will step up.

Changing the ice bag from my jaw, closing my eyes and putting the bag over my upper face. Cold feels good on my eyebrows.

Drifting off—to devoid of hope to dream.

"Frank?" She's knocking on my door, "Frank, come out. Your father and I need to talk to you." She waits. Body remembering the hurt as I wake up; hollow, empty feeling inside my stomach.

"Frankie, are you all right in there?" I hear her whispering, "I wonder if he's okay?" Stomach starting to tighten up, fucking old man won't even talk to me directly; he's got to send the Ambassador.

"I'll be right out, Ma," dread setting in.

"You okay?"

"I said I'd be right out!" What's the matter with that stupid woman?

Breathing out slowly—I can see her standing at the door taking a second to get her face and clothes all prim and proper before she walks away with that certain look she has, the "how dare I speak to her like that" look. Sitting up, head starting to pound, blinking to clear the crud from my eyes. Body starting to get amped up with pre-fight adrenaline, I know what's coming next. Fuck it.

Out into the hall and into the bathroom my sister and I used to share. It's so quiet since she's been away at the University of Chicago. Man did we have some knock down drag out fights when we were young. Next year she'll be starting grad school—first lawyer in the family. I'm proud even though she hates my ass.

Feeling my chest deflate as I look at the mess in the mirror. Left eye is a nice shiner, forehead and nose bruised, some crusted blood still around my nose and mouth—most has flaked off after it dried. Feeling my skull, egg shaped bumps starting to rise up. Rugby shirt stained with blood.

Washing my face with soap and water slowly. Jaw hurts when I open and close my mouth, chewing is going to be fun for a while. Slapping cold water on my face, drying slowly. Hands gripping and crushing the towel, pulling on it hard as a wave of rage rolls up through my body.

Moments lost looking at myself in the mirror. New school next year, I'll be starting over with a new team, new people. Cat, Hector, Julio, Richard, Mary, Alan, Jeff, Marta, Maria—names and faces moving by, they'll all be gone and I'll be in a different school. Is the team there going to be any good? How will Cat and I see each other?

Time to face the music.

"Took your time, didn't you?" Dad sitting at the kitchen table getting all worked up, Mom puttering around behind him listening, but not listening. She's done the summoning, now I'm before the Executioner. Sitting down, feeling my breathing start to come more rapidly.

"What do you have to say for yourself?"

Looking at him, catching the quiet shadow of lurking anger in his eyes. Our eyes locked, strands of our last argument fomenting inside me, feeling familiar anger build in my stomach. Looking over at Mom for a second, she's blithely staying out of the middle, but contributing a disapproving look now and then.

"Nothing, huh?" he leans forward a little, his stocky six-foot body shifting in his chair, thick shoulder muscles shifting underneath his shirt.

"You make me sick, all the things we've given you," heavy breath in. "This is how you pay us back? Getting thrown out of one of the best schools in the city? Disgraceful." He shakes his head, "What the hell is wrong with you?" He slams his hand down on the table and takes a deep breath looking over at my mom for a second. "Well if you think..." he looks back at me, his facial muscles starting to tense, "Mister Know-It-All, Mister I've-got-things-in-control."

I've seen this movie—first, he'll start with the taunting.

"What'cha gonna do now, Mister Big Man. Huh?"

"I'm gonna go get a job."

"Ha!" he exclaims, "drop out? Like hell! You're a damn disgrace to the family. If you think I'm going back to your school and beg them to let you back in, you've got another thing coming. After all we've done for you. Your cousin Bobby going to Fordham next year, your other cousin Joey going to medical school." He tilts his head forward.

"Listen to your father, Frankie," Mom looks at us for a second.

"And what does that make them, huh? Joey's a little worm. He'll be a worm who shoplifts and steals everything he can even after he finishes medical school. He's a little shit."

"Don't use language like that in MY HOUSE!"

Getting hot, "Is that all you care about? That for some reason I end up working with my hands and I don't turn out to be a fucking college boy?"

20

"Damn you disgraciato, don't use language like that in front of your mother!"

Breathing hard, looking at him. "It's always been how things look. You don't like my friends. Nothing is good enough for you. I go to some bullshit college and then I'm what? I'm different cause I got a fucking piece of paper?"

"You'll have respect, you'll have accomplished something."

"What?" slamming the table. "Like you've done nothing? My God Dad, you run a good business, that's nothing?"

"That's different, things were different then. You kids have no idea what it was like. The war, what it was like coming back after… It makes me sick to see how you disrespect the things your mother and I want for you and have worked so hard for. It's like some switch got thrown and you became a Frankenstein monster. These last years have made me wonder how the hell I didn't see any of this coming." Spittle coming out of his mouth, "You ingrate!" He's shaking his fists, Mom looking scared, "Look at what you're doing to us… from so much promise," he's looking around at the ceiling then at me as his fist hits the table, "to what? Some bum carrying around a tool bag or sweeping streets while other kids, kids with education get ahead, sneer at you. Is that what you want, second rate…"

"Listen to your father, Frankie," she sits down, her lips drawn tight. "Why can't you behave? Look at what you're doing to him."

Sitting back, looking at these two assholes who say they are my parents. "You don't even care that I didn't start it," leaning back looking at them both. "That's it, huh? Just like that, I'm the bad guy here." Face getting flushed, scar inside being painfully pulled apart again. "What would they have to have done to get some damn feeling out of you two other than I'm not good enough? Lose a hand? What, lose an arm? Get beat to death…"

"Oh yeah, the world's unfair," he's looking at me, mocking. "Poor baby got his ass beat. Do you want to cry? Huh? Want to cry about it? Think that will make it better? Want me to burp you, you big baby? Where was your best friend, huh?"

Gripping the edge of the table hard, feeling like bending it in.

"Oh, that bothers you. Mister Tough Guy, can't take a few shots? What, like a little embarrassment is too much for you? Couldn't walk away from trouble? Had to be the big man and take on a couple of other kids?" He puts on a pouting face, "What did they do, they talk bad about you? Oooh."

Jaw hurting from clenching my teeth together.

"Oooooo, and now he's getting mad, look at that, what are you going to do, take a swing at me? Big man, tough man! Is that how you gonna solve all your problems in life?"

Snapping, slamming the table and stepping back, "You want it, come get it!" Mom aghast. "You've been beating me since I was a kid. Come on, I'm not scared of you. Come on goddammit!" Standing, fists up, body fired up, energy coursing through my chest—memories of pain blotted out. "Stand up and I'll fucking kill you. Come on!" screaming.

"Get out of my house, you disgrace," his face livid. "You want to get a job, go out on the street and see how tough it is. Go see for yourself. I wash my hands of you, you, you," stammering for breath over his anger. "Break my heart, break your mother's heart," hurt looking coming over his face. "Go see how much your nigger and spic friends care about you. Go live on the streets for all I care. Go live in some rotten jail. Get out!"

Head starting to calm down, looking around at the kitchen. Table cracked, Mom's hands up by her face. She's looking at me, crying. Dad standing there, his shoulders sagging like something's been pulled out of him.

"Don't come back and don't call when you get into trouble."

"I want my bank book."

"That's your college money, you can't have it."

"That's my money, I earned it!"

"Tough shit, Mr. Big Maaan who doesn't need anybody. You go see how hard it is to find a job out there. Throw away all we've done for you…"

"Bastard, you thief," vision clouding up, red and black weaving in front of me, throwing the table aside, dimly aware of it crashing into the wall. Stepping toward him as he backpedals. Mom picking up the phone, screaming into it, "Police, help us, please, our son is like a mad man, he's threatening his father!"

Shocked looking at them. Stepping back like I've been hit.

Tears of rage and hurt starting to flow down my face.

"I hate you! I hate both of you! You, you…"

Running to my room. Standing in the middle of the room—gripping my head, ignoring the pain and pulling my hair hard till it hurts more than the pain inside. Looking over at the shelves over my desk. Feeling my insides twist as I look at pictures of me, Dad and Uncle Vin, big smiles on our faces, each of us holding up the big striped bass we'd taken spear fishing that day. Another picture after winning my weight class in a Golden Gloves tournament last year, Alton and I smiling like fools holding our trophies in the team picture when we won the City championship last year.

Glancing at the other pictures, feeling like I'm going to burst. Picking up my basketball, throwing it at my trophy shelf, smashing it. Watching marble bottoms and pieces of gilt metal flying around, picture frames smashing onto the floor, pool of broken glass.

Grabbing what money I have in my desk drawer. The Seiko dive watch I'd saved up for. Socks, underwear, spare red and white striped rugby shirt, hooded grey sweatshirt and work boots into my backpack. Denim jacket in, no room for anything else, this will have to do. Walking into the perfect living room picking up one of the fine hand carved upholstered Italian chairs and smashing it against the wall.

Slamming the door behind me as hard as I can.

"I hate you! I fucking hate you!"

Taking the stairs, two at a time. Tripping, grabbing the thick wooden rail, almost falling.

Out on the street. People walking by, cars driving fast to beat the red light, moving to get faster than all of them. Outrun the pain.

Sitting down on the stoop of a Brownstone, body shaking, fighting off the deep silent sobs coming up. Wiping my nose on my jacket sleeve. Fists balled up, clenched tightly, body shaking.

Damn you, damn all of you.

I hate you.

Chapter 4

Tired.

Aimless walk.

Watching my feet moving slowly along the pavement from a distance, my body feels heavier and heavier with each step, dimly aware of other people as they move around in their daily lives.

Late afternoon traffic picking up on 10th Ave.

Tired of the noise, tired of the people.

I'll die before I go back home.

Cool green of Riverside Park opening up in front of me, my eyes following the tall trees along the entrance to the Henry Hudson Parkway on 72nd St.

Taking a moment to look uptown toward the basketball courts at 76th St. Long rows of park benches stretching along the asphalt walkways, old people sitting here and there sunning themselves. White babies being taken care of by black nannies.

Sitting down.

Elbows on my knees, head in my hands.

Emptiness gnawing at my inside—world disjoint.

Head feels like it's spinning, body feels like I'm slowly falling.

Slight wind coming up from the Hudson River.

Is there a sickness spreading through me?

My best friend wouldn't stand with me—my parents hate me…

Too tired to even rage at betrayal and loss.

Dying embers of the flame heavy inside.

Feet encased in concrete.

I need to go some place dark. I can't stand being here, I can't stand knowing my best friend made a choice and it wasn't me.

I can't stand hearing my father's words in my head again and again.

Is blood the only way to free myself from this pain? Let the bad and the little good leak out upon the soil. Would that stop the hate? Would malformed weeds sprout from the ground I die upon? Is that it, just open up and let my red hate soak into the dark soil?

Insides wrenching at how much I miss Catherine, she'll never know how I feel. She's miles away at school. Her parents won't let me talk to her on the phone. Reliving the shame I felt at the low voices of the kids in the halls looking at me whispering to each other while I was led to Richert's office. And to that ass Leroy no less! Dammit! I lost!

Walking slowly downhill toward the great, gray, green, greasy Hudson River, through the short tunnel underneath the Henry Hudson Expressway at 72nd Street. Cool in here, echoes of the cars speeding across rough pavement and potholes above.

Stopping in the middle of the tunnel and looking back at the cracked asphalt path back up the hill toward Riverside Drive. Sad remembrance of how that hill once looked so big to me when the world was full of promise.

Six years old, standing there looking down the long asphalt path, gathering my courage to tackle the big mountain. My mother's words to be careful quickly forgotten. Hands cold, breathing rapid, excited, afraid. I just had to do it—I had to know that I could do it.

Getting on my skateboard, Mom yelling, "No, stop!" from the distance. Reliving the moments of delicious freedom, speed building up, transitioning to being out of control. The slow motion movie as I career down the hill squatting down low, the metal wheels roaring as speed built up quickly, the cracks in the asphalt throwing me off balance, body falling forward slowly, seeing my feet, then the ground coming up at me, skidding along the pavement.

Seconds felt like they lasted for minutes.

Sensation of heat on my knees elbows and forearms, pain in the distance, my mom grabbing me by the ear and shaking me, cussing away in Italian. Then the pain set in. Remembering the feel of those long scabs on my arms and legs for weeks.

There's no going back. Those days died a long time ago.

Finishing the slow walk through the rest of the tunnel. Looking down at my feet as I walk across the pitted walkway back to daylight. Slight queasy feeling in my stomach won't go away.

Looking out across the Hudson River. Leaning my elbows then my body weight on the two-foot thick, waist high, rough, cream/gray colored granite retaining wall. Running my hands across the rough textured surface of the cool stone. Barely noticing the people passing behind me now and then. Body feels so tired, closing my eyes for a few moments. Feeling like I'm falling—opening my eyes and catching myself.

Breeze coming up from the river brings the Hudson's wet, chemical, tar, rotting smell along with it. Looking over across the river at the granite cliffs of the Palisades of New Jersey, apartment houses teetering at the edge of the cliffs. Drifting along with a lone freighter steaming out toward the open ocean. Tilting my head down, looking down at the sixty-foot drop to the weed strewn softball field and the broken concrete of the handball courts below. Mesmerized by the depth.

How fast would that rush up at me? The distance is too short to reach terminal velocity. Turning to the distant squeal and rush of a train passing through the subterranean tunnels underneath Riverside Park. That's where I need to go—it's dark down there, dark and cool.

They lied to me.

Walking uneasily down the steep asphalt path to the lower park by the Hudson River. They lied to me, all of them.

Be brave, stand up for yourself—think for yourself. Don't be afraid to stick your head above the crowd even though someone might take a poke at you. Sick anger gripping my stomach—you liar, you bastard, all that talk about quality work, and how who you are shows up when the chips are down. Fuck you Dad, all you do is try and beat me down when things aren't going your way.

I won't go back there. I'll die out here first.

Weathered gray docks of the boat basin at 79th Street. Boats tied to the docks moving with the undulating motion of the Hudson River. Old rotting pilings standing up out of the water here and there, a section of a dock half underwater, a couple of houseboats, some large Chris-Craft motor yachts sandwiched between shitty looking sailboats. Hungry, stopping at a rough concrete water fountain, taking a long drink of water to fill the void. Stopping to see how much money I have—eight dollars and seventy-three cents. Reality smacking me in the face, that's two slices of pizza a day for the next week and then what... Where the hell am I going to find work, where the hell am I going to stay? Anger welling up that they won't let me have the eight hundred or so I've earned working construction the last few years.

Hitting me, of course—they want me to come crawling back to them. They want to drive in the shame, drive in the guilt. I'll die first. I'll eat the hate I feel growing inside me. I'll let the blackness consume my worthless flesh before I go crawling home.

Ramming in the black, rusty iron door that leads down to the train tunnels with my shoulder. It screeches open slowly. A cold metallic smell comes up at me as I shove the heavy iron inward and step into the cool blackness of the train tunnels. Road noise of cars coming off the Henry Hudson freeway and driving through the 79th St. exit fades away as I slam the heavy door shut and walk out on the iron walkway above the dark tracks thirty feet below.

Soft light of the exit to the train yards underneath the elevated freeway in the distance. Making a careful decent down along the cold iron stairs into the enveloping darkness. Calm in the fading light. Feeling the cavernous space of the tunnels open up around me. The tunnel roof must be easily fifty feet above me, four tracks wide plus who knows what kind of side platforms and structures are down here.

Dim red and green signal lights running uptown and then curving away in the distance. Stepping off the last rung of the ladder into the rock gravel bed running between the train tracks. Remembering Uncle Vin saying that it takes twenty minutes for your eyes to get fully accustomed to the darkness.

Deep black, pierced here and there by thin beams of light streaming down from the steel grated vents in the park above me. Listening for an approaching train, nothing but the distant sound of dripping water. Shivering at the slow, cold wind coming from deep underneath the city. Smell of cold steel and rust.

Eyes closed. Scramble of little feet—must be rats.

Deep, quiet wind.

Slight shapes slowly appearing out of the darkness—thick concrete support beams reaching up to the roof of the tunnel, silvery outline of train tracks polished by years of use.

Would I move if a train came right now?

Imagining a bright light coming toward me—then nothing.

Would that be any worse than this? Imagining that I'm a translucent jellyfish melting down into the dark earth, gravity pulling me down. Imagining that I'm slowly sinking past what I could have been—here I am, the wretch come from the proud.

How could I fail when people told me I had so much?

And it's right here—dark distance stretching away, sinking deeper into the imaginary earth. Blinking, my eyes continuing to adjust to the darkness. Stepping out carefully. Inching toward the distant train yard. Idea popping in, image forming of the abandoned warehouse piers across from the switching yard, I can sleep there.

Hunger clawing up at me, relieved to be feeling something different than weak nausea. Breathing deeply to take my mind off my stomach. Stumble, getting my feet back. Moving carefully along the train tracks. Rats scurrying along now and then. Staying in the middle of the tunnel—dark areas to the side are where people sleep and wait. Picking up a section of unused pipe, it feels cold in my hand. I'm not going down without a fight.

Staring up into the blackness of the immense train tunnel, wondering how far these go back under the City. They must switch into the tracks to the train bridge that runs over the East River. Dim lights of distant train signals stretching out into the distance. Rich red lights calling me into the welcome blackness, what if I turned and kept walking that way?

Losing track of time while I walk.

Dim, distant, light of the end of the tunnel up ahead.

Chills running up my back—something shuffling in the darkness to my left. Crouching down for a few moments, waiting, nothing—just the sound of dripping water. Someone there waiting for me to move?

Staying still in the deep, empty quiet—I'm not running away.

Waiting. Nothing.

Walking slowly to the waning daylight.

Tracks starting to become more than dim outlines, light beginning to illuminate steel polished by years of heavy wheels running over them.

Hustling up as I hear a train coming in the distance, body sore, head starting to throb again, another wave of exhaustion setting in.

Rough gravel under my feet, walking to a well travelled crushed granite path. Staring at the miles of abandoned train cars that stretch across the half-mile deep parallel tracks in the switching yards—hulks of rusted metal, rotting wood covered in spray-painted nonsense. The metal arches of the Henry Hudson Freeway soaring above me, pigeons fluttering around for no apparent reason.

No trainmen around. Looking at my watch, six-thirty. Hunger running up my body again. Walking fast toward the old piers—no light in there, need to get to a semi-safe place before darkness falls.

Hudson gurgling and lapping at the old tarred wooden pilings.

Stepping carefully to avoid rotten wood where I might fall through into the cold river below. Old cargo blanket coming apart in my hands, rats running out of the pile. Broken wooden crates, shattered windows. Nothing left unbroken in here, idiot kids like me have been here busting up what was abandoned a long time ago. Stopping, looking around the old warehouse—people once worked here, someone built this, someone was proud of this place. The voices of those people are long gone.

Pushing aside layers of old boards. Picking up a nice long section of an old lever. This will make a good heavy club. Worn cargo blankets, old, moldy, probably filled with rat shit and rat piss. Section pulls off easily, carefully pulling it with me toward the end of the pier—there's a good place hidden from the wind that looks out into the river. Shaking the wasted blanket carefully. Carefully climbing down.

Not much room here, putting my pack down—evening air starting to cool down, chill wind coming up the river.

Damn it's cold. Face feels oily, dirty. Teeth feel coated.

Lying back against one of the old wooden pilings, knees up, arms round my legs, looking across the river at the setting sun. Tensing and breathing hard to squash the wave of sorrow that wants to rise up. I'm never going back. I'm never going back. You can rot in hell, Dad.

Familiar burn of righteous anger returning, tomorrow, I start tomorrow. First, I take that prick Leroy, then Thomas Jones. Day after that it's time for Alton. He's got to pay for betraying me like this. Sequence of the fight running through my mind; awful realization that I'd been so filled with hate that I didn't protect myself. I could have gotten in some good licks on all of them had I kept moving, kept smart. I might have been able to take all three. I lost it in my blind rage.

Breathing deep to keep the emotion of losing away.

Losing isn't the worst though, is it? The worst feeling is that it's not the worst beating I've ever taken; the worst one I took was for you Alton, that day in Coney Island. Body going rigid—I could have walked away that day. I could have just stood back and called for help, yelled and screamed. You were my friend—there was no way I was going to leave you.

Smacking my head back into the thick wood piling.

He chose Leroy over me. Bastard.

Dark night—sound of the river slipping by.

Shivering, putting on as many layers as I have. Still cold. Need to go to the bathroom—no choice but to wait till morning. Bobbing lights moving by out in the river. Looking out at the distant homes and apartments across the river.

Terrible aloneness.

Closing my eyes, hunger and cold keeping me from the sense of losing my place in the world. Feeling like I'm slightly off balance and can't right myself. Putting on my work boots and an extra pair of socks to deal with the cold.

Snapping awake. Two o'clock in the morning.

Looking around—nothing, hollow, empty inside.

Pulling the musty blanket around me as tightly as I can, closing my eyes, shivering, trying to stop my teeth from chattering.

Chapter 5

People talking to me in the distance, I can't see them, faces just out of reach, shifting gray amorphous shapes slowly coming in and out of soft focus.

Sitting at the base of an ancient stone amphitheater at a ramshackle desk. Unseen people in the audience talking to me, others walking by with large framed pictures that I can't make out, but feel that I know. All of the people talking at once—words coming at me in a combined jabber of nonsense. Struggling to rip my way out of the thin chords tying me down. Pulled by a face I know in a picture passing by. The white teeth, flashing black eyes, rich black hair, stones beneath my feet feeling thinner and thinner, cracking, falling...

Snapping awake with a deep breath, blinking my eyes.

Cold river front air hits my face—immediate punch of hunger deep in the pit of my stomach. Face feels wet, opening my eyes to the light. Bladder so full it's uncomfortable—morning piss hard-on in my jeans. Cargo blanket all wet, the old black painted and rusting iron bollards on the dock are wet. Checking the time, it's almost six. Tired, face hurts, body and back sore. Need to get up and go take a shit.

Hands dirty, clothes full of the dust of disintegration.

Standing up stretching, dusting myself off.

Laying out the old smelly cargo blanket to dry.

Walking through the disarray of the rotting warehouse. Taking a look across the train yard. Nothing moving. Slipping on my backpack, trotting across the tracks toward the old train crew rest area on 60th Street that backs up to 12th Ave. There's a nasty bathroom in there, the park bathrooms won't be open for a while. Moving carefully past each string of railroad cars. Don't want to get caught in here. The train yard workers don't like kids fucking around with their stuff.

Up the old concrete stairs to where I'd found a bathroom a few years ago during a cold winter day with Alton when we were out trying to steal railroad warning flares from the trains. What idiots we were. A group of older kids dared us to do it and there we were. Laughing for a moment remembering how his mom whipped our butts good when she caught us lying about where we were.

Looking at the long desolate concrete walls and the overhanging second story. This place looks like someone who watched too many World War II movies designed it. Cracks running down the cold concrete walls, gang tags in magic marker and spray paint plied randomly on top of each other. Piles of trash gathered into disgusting rotting masses here and there.

Hiding by the bathroom entrance, cold wind coming up from the river. Doesn't sound like anyone is up here. Bare ceiling bulb throws a stark light on the broken floor tiles. Horrible stench. Peering into one of the toilet stalls. Almost throwing up the little left in my stomach looking at the layers of shit and toilet paper waving to and fro—the surface is full of maggots.

Closing the door. Next stall—at least there's water in the brown stained bowl. Checking the single sheet toilet paper dispenser—a few inches of those little pieces of sand paper left. Wiping down the toilet lid. This place reeks of piss. God knows what's on the floor here. Feeling the pressure on my bladder reducing with the long stream of urine, squeezing to work out a large, hard turd. Relief, wiping with the little rough paper squares. Who the hell invented these nasty things?

Taking my pack off while I wash my hands. The sinks have the "press once" for a few seconds of water faucets. No paper towels—a few drops of oily green soap. Teeth feel slimy and coated. Should have taken a toothbrush and toothpaste.

Looking at myself in the dirty mirror, peering at something I don't like looking back through the thin film of brown slime. Hair's a mess, face a mess, body stinks.

Stepping back, feeling something wrong.

"What'cha you doin in here?"

Large burly man walking into the bathroom—jeans, flannel shirt, unlaced black boots. He's standing there looking at me, looking at me up and down.

"Just needed to use the toilet you know. I'm leaving now."

"You one of those kids who comes looking for trouble round here?" Smirking, he rubs his ugly unshaven face with a big hand.

"No way," uneasy, "call the police if you think I'm up to no good."

"We don't call the police here."

"I don't want any trouble."

He starts walking toward me, something's wrong.

Weird look—that's it, predator.

Moving my hands to warm them up—breathe.

"You one of them boys who runs away and puts out in men's room to make some scratch? Sell your sweet little ass to make a little money? Is that right? You get roughed up a bit when you couldn't take a big man like me?"

Circling to get some room.

Breathing slowly to keep my head.

"Lucky I'm here now, I'll teach you how to deal with a real man," breathing starting to ramp up, side-glance at the window—too small to get out. Trapped in here. Nasty smile as he moves forward. He lunges a little, and then steps back to see what I'll do. Moving in a small circle with him. I back down and I'm dead meat.

Hands feeling warm, anger starting to burn my stomach, fuck this; this is going to be to the death.

"That's right, no way out for your sweet little ass. Nice looking big boy like you'd make good money in the joint after I break you in and pass you around here," he starts to crouch down a little, breathing to manage the adrenaline rush.

Putting up my fists, getting my body set for a charge.

He starts to laugh a cruel, low laugh. My vision narrowing, adrenaline charge coming in. "Oooh, he's gonna make me work for my nut," he puts his arms out like he's gonna come scoop me up, "I'm gonna fuck that rosy little ass of yours…"

Stepping back like I'm scared.

"I got money, take it, please don't hurt me," holding up my backpack, letting my arms shake like I'm scared. "Take it."

Pitching it to him in a light toss, slight surprise on his face. Making a rock fist and quickly stepping forward with my left foot, putting all my two hundred forty pounds into a big overhand right.

Adjusting my swing as he tries to come in low on me. Hard contact with the side of his head near his temple, he stumbles trying to grab me to get his balance back. Slamming into him, letting his body take my weight to tire him out. Taking his punches easily on my arms—hard blow careening off my head. Red swirls starting to move at the edge of my vision. Getting to the place where I'll take whatever punishment needed to win.

Uppercut to his gut, his grip loosens.

He's gassed already. And this fat fuck was coming at me like he had some shit? Deep mean coming up from my stomach. I'm going to hurt this motherfucker, bad.

Easily taking the weak punches and knees coming at me. Turning a hard elbow into the side of his head, stunning him. Grabbing his hair with both hands as he tries to grab me around the waist, pulling his head down as my left knee comes up and smashes into his ugly pig face with all my strength. Striking him again and again. Contact jolts through my body. Driving his jaw up—teeth crunching, his warm blood on my jeans.

Pitching the fat fuck back on the dirty tile floor. Breathing hard—raising my foot up to stomp down on his head. Shaking my head, looking around. Burning anger filling my body. "You FUCK!" yelling at him breathing hard, taking deep breathes to pull oxygen in. The place, the situation starting to filter in, bringing my foot down away from his bloody, mashed in face—I need to get out of here. I was lucky he wasn't expecting an all-out attack, if he's got some other ex-con buddies close by I'm dead, no two ways about it. I need to get the fuck out of here, NOW!

Running up the trash strewn fifteen-foot concrete slope toward 12th Ave.—climbing over the chain link fence and running hard up to 63rd and then east toward 11th Ave. There won't be many people there, but it will be better than down here.

Shifting my pace to a slow jog—body slowing back down, feeling calmer as the adrenaline rush starts to work its way out of my system. Coming up to 10th Ave. and heading uptown. Passing brownstones, small businesses and workers unloading the day's deliveries into basement storerooms from double-parked trucks. Dodging hand carts, thick voices yelling at me about why the fuck I'm running around here at this time of day asshole. Flipping them off as I weave my way through the maze.

Looking back at the empty street behind me.

Crossing 10th Ave. and walking the long block up to 9th Ave., then heading north, my knee starting to swell up from impact with his pig face. Walking with a slight limp—there will be lots of people around Columbus Circle, good place to get lost in the crowds.

Thirst, hunger setting in; dim recollection of no food since breakfast yesterday. Thinking about Gray's Papaya on 72nd, I can buy a couple of hot dogs and a papaya drink for a dollar. Hunger gnawing at me as I walk up 59th to Broadway. People dressed for work, looking at my watch, it's a little before seven. My breathing slowing now, body starting to shake. Realization running through my mind—if there had been two of them... Shiver running through my body—I'd be dead. Fuck that motherfucker; there was no way I was going down without a fight!

The people walking by me have no idea what was going on just a few blocks away from here. This is just another nice and normal Wednesday morning to them. Fucking city.

"Two dogs with sauerkraut and small papaya to go," as I move my way through the crowd.

"One dollar," said the Hispanic man behind the counter. Passing my money, my hands shaking. Looking at the crowd for a second, the lady next to me looking me over with a funny look on her face. Taking my brown paper bag and paper cup of juice outside. Need to get my breath back, rush of panic coming up my chest. What if that guy sends the cops after me? Walking up 72nd Street to Central Park. I can get lost in there. Passing delicatessens, bakeries, stores full of all kinds of goods. Salivating as the reality of how little money I have weighs on me. Hungry, resisting the desire to stop and eat—this is it for today. I need to make it last.

Crossing Columbus Ave. in between the coursing, jostling wave of yellow taxis heading downtown honking at each other for no apparent reason. Union rules, honk every thirty seconds or you're fired! Jerk wads.

Cool green of Central Park feels calming and soothing till the burn of hunger sets in again. Taking my mind off my stomach by jogging across

West Drive and walking to the Lake, the hot dog juice starting to soil the bag, the smell making me salivate.

Taking a sip of the papaya juice. Oh, that's good. Sick to think that normally I'd go buy a quart after a hard workout in the gym and drink it on the walk home.

Heading to the Bethesda Terrace, the fountain—that's a good place to go hang out for a while. Walking down the long stairs to the dry fountain, the Central Park Lake spreading out in front of me. Few people here, an old man walking a small white poodle slowly across the red brick paved terrace.

"Hey buddy," looking around. "Hey, here," following the source. "Help me out, okay? I'm a man in need. One of God's angels come among men and now lost after helping many find their way."

Turning to the voice coming from the corner of the stone stairs, almost an alcove. Old frail man dressed in tattered clothes from military surplus, white beard streaked with spit and what must be vomit. Recoiling from the horrible smell.

"Can you spare some change? I need to eat something... please?"

Looking at his blue eyes, the whites all yellow and bloodshot. Turmoil—hunger gnawing at me—so little money.

"I don't have much. I'm outdoors." Taking a deep breath. Stop being a big pussy, Frank. Decision made. "Here," passing him one of the dogs, "it's half of what I'm going to eat today."

He looks at me, bemused "Thanks," his hands trembling as he takes the brown paper wrapped dog and opens it slowly. Turning and walking to the edge of the Lake and sitting on the weathered stone wall speckled here and there with white rings of pigeon shit. Brown shallow water in the lake offset by the green trees around the shore. Tired gaze drifting toward the 5th Ave. apartment buildings rising up and surrounding the park. There's so much money over there. Rich fucks living there don't have a clue people like that old man or I exist, and it's not that they are rich and have money that pisses me off. I'm so far away from making any.

Bastard Father stealing my money. I'll show all of you.

Tired sting in my body, sitting here like a jerk seeing how long I can chew each bite. Body energy returning. Chewing and slowly turning each bite into a thin soup in my mouth. Hearing footsteps sliding toward me. Turning around and getting to a position I can protect myself. It's the little old man, he's starting to puff up—looks bigger.

"Mind if I sit?"

"Free park," shrugging my shoulders, washing down the last of my dog with my last sip of papaya juice. Looking across the small lake, trees coming back from a cold winter.

"You really outdoors?"

"No, I make up bullshit stories to start really interesting conversations."

He laughs, "Not used to it yet, eh?" tilting his head, moving like he's having two conversations—one out here, another some place else.

"Where you sleeping?"

"Old pier by the train yards on the Hudson under the highway."

His body shudders a little, he looks around and spits in the water. Most of his teeth are gone.

"Bad place there, people disappear. Big strong boy," he breaks off, his head moving, his mouth forming words but none come out. After a few moments, "Don't get fooled, pack of dogs can take down the biggest tiger."

Images flashing in my mind of fighting for what could have been my life a few hours ago.

"Runaway?"

"Got thrown out."

"Police'll be looking for you."

Looking at him, shrugging my shoulders.

"Happens all the time, big fight. Mom starts wearing down the Dad, calls the police," some of his teeth are colored black, his hands are calm, the beard stains look like they've been made with some type of marker. Shaking my head, laughing at myself. He's got a good con working—man, am I a sucker or what.

"Hell," spitting in the water, "my uncle's a cop. They will never call, they are too ashamed, too mad," fists clenching together and then relaxing, surge of impatience. Thinking about wandering over to Sheep Meadow and finding a nice place in the sun to sleep.

Getting up. "You might want to sit a spell 'n listen then you can make up your mind."

"What the fuck do you want?"

"Geez, you like this with all folks, no wonder..."

"Gonna teach me how to look shittier than I really am? I dig the tooth coloring. No one wants to get close enough to figure it out."

Sitting down as he laughs to himself, laughing at myself too—like I've got someplace important to go to. This is my life now.

"You got any friends?"

"A few."

"You better learn to let 'em help you. Tough out here on your own," he's looking out. "You're too big, too good lookin to play the helpless one like me," he winks. "People see what they want to see kid. Maybe you could work the bus stations, handle people with a story about a lost ticket," he looks around. "Yeah, that's probably your best bet. You stick out too much..." more mumbling, he starts to fiddle with his hands. "Transit cops'll peg you quick though, you got any street skills?"

"Construction stuff, framing, finish work, plaster, painting."

He's looking around, mumbling again.

"Let some woman take you in, take good care of you. Treat her nice, help you get back on your feet. Pawn that watch, you'll get a few bucks you'll need. Blood donations at most hospitals will net you ten bucks," he gets lost in another conversation inside his head, waiting for him to come back, "you any good with your fists? Your face doesn't say so."

"There were three, I lost my head. I'm going to get 'em," looking at him. "Busted up a big fucker over at the train yards this morning, bastard starting talking about how he was going to bust my cherry. Motherfucker..."

Old fart is giving me an "I don't believe you" look.

"I told him I had money in my back pack and chucked it over to him, clocked him when he caught my bag." Ben's eyes starting to gleam a little at the violence, "Grabbed a hold of his hair, pulled him down and kneed him in the face till he was a blubbering bloody mess and got the hell out. Is that what you want to know? This isn't my blood," pointing to my pants.

Different look from him now, his head nodding with me, then he breaks off. "Well, maybe you got some skills people like me find valuable. You get lost, come around here and ask the others for Ben."

Shaking my head as he gets up and walks off.

"Where are you going, Ben?"

"Off to work the tourists, play the old drunk," he winks as he walks away, his gait slows, his body looks like he starts to shrink as he heads back into the shadows.

Chapter 6

Taking a slow, solitary walk back up the wide, weathered stone steps through the esplanade to the large open grass field of Sheep's Meadow. Searching out a place in the grass where there's no mud or dog shit. Laying out my denim jacket on a clean section of grass, deep smell of damp earth greeting me. Looking up at the sky, watching the clouds go by. Eyes opening and closing, trying to stay awake, don't want to fall off into the blackness, wishing the hunger would die down and go away.

Daydreaming about what life would be like if I were the only person alive in New York City. All the things I could do and have. No boundaries. Imagining empty streets, no taxis. Image of the times I've been up riding my bike early in the morning when no one's around flooding in. It's so quiet in the city.

Warmer now, last night's deep cold working its way out of my body. Thirsty. Sitting up and taking off my sweatshirt. Rolling it up, lying back down on the grass. Turning on my side looking at people starting to mill around the park—a couple playing Frisbee, a game of touch football starting up, people walking their dogs. Old people sitting along the footpath watching the other people at the park, waiting. Watching an elderly woman staring off into the distance, immune to passing people walking their dogs or jogging in the park. I will never know the mystery of her life, what she's lost, what she's loved.

Wave of tiredness washing over me, feeling lethargic, can't think of any good music to play in my head, can't even dream of Cat's body. All the things I care about are out of reach and moving further away. A moment of guilt washing over me remembering Mom's horrified face when I told Dad I would kill him. How he shrunk back. He'll never talk to me again, he's got to prove his mastery over me now with the silent art of showing me how much I've hurt and disappointed him by proving that I don't exist. I've been annihilated in his world—bastard.

Waking up to the smell of warm grass. Trying to get back to the dream where I was running up and down rich, green, grassy hills. I could jump long distances—body exhilarated in the freedom of flight. Closing my eyes to try and recapture the feeling—nothing.

Sitting up, hunger clawing at my stomach. Looking at my watch, it's two o'clock. Good time to walk downtown over to Chelsea and wait for my good friend Leroy to come home from school. He likes to hang around at the basketball courts at 28th between 9th and 10th Ave.

Changing into my sneakers, easier to walk and run in to chase down prey. Guilt running through me, I haven't even thought about Cat.

No time for her now. I'll call her later after she's home from school. Her parents will just have to tell me I can't speak to her again. At least she'll know I called. I can have Julio or Hector call to let her know what's going down.

Ambling down Broadway.

Passing a long line of car dealer windows on 57th and Broadway. Stopping to look at the little silver-blue Fiat X9 convertible. Man, I'm so far from owning one of those... Imagining what it would like to be able to get out of the humid, smelly city during the summer and head out to the beach. Fixated on an image of Cat in the car next to me, her long black hair tossed by the wind. Thinking about her in a tight swimsuit, her body starting to come back to life to me, remembering the fire spreading through me when we are alone. Shaking my head—focus on Leroy.

Movie theaters on Broadway shifting from first run movies to XXX-rated as I walk downtown, streets dirtier as I get closer to 42nd Street. Disheveled white man, long hair greasy, worn Army jacket walking by saying, "Weed, Acapulco Gold, Thai Stick," watching him weave through people.

Looking down 42nd to the Hudson, theater after theater of adult movies, porno stores, peep shows. Rafts of people walking around here—nasty looking man watching people pass by, stringy hair looks like it hasn't been washed for days. Hmm, my future fashion look? Middle aged men, all colors and shapes looking side-to-side, furtive looks as they go in and out of the X-rated movie theaters. Laughing at the obvious professional woman escorting a middle-aged man into a dark movie theatre.

Fewer people walking about the deeper I head into the garment district. Twelve-foot tall clothes racks pushed down side streets, guys calling out to people they know, fat people drinking to-go coffees standing at the doorways checking cargo in and out.

Past 34th now, thirsty, need to find a bathroom.

Walking to 25th took less time than anticipated. Walk by Chelsea Park on 9th Ave. and go down a few blocks then circle around to see if I can find a place to hang out that will hide me from sight—then it will be too late for my friend, my teammate.

Hearing Mom's voice in my head asking me if this is going to accomplish anything—not that you'd understand. He deliberately set me up. He used that stooge Thomas Jones. My jaw still hurts from the blows I took. My friend Alton, that fucker sided with them and then helped beat me when I was down. "You dirty fuck," can't keep the words inside. People looking at me, snarling back at them, "What?" body amped up, they shy away.

Keep walking. Shaking my head, yeah, old Ben and me will be good friends in a few years. We'll have conversations going on in our heads with two or three people while we're talking to each other.

Checking out the pick-up games going on at Chelsea Park. Feeling warm in my rugby shirt, pulling up the sleeves to get a little more air over my body. Taking off my watch and putting it in my pocket, I don't want that breaking off when we're going at it. Stomach getting slight pre-fight flutters. Breathing, moving my shoulders and arms to keep my blood flowing—stay relaxed.

Circling back around the park, if he's coming, he'll be here soon.

Passing behind some trees, watching a good three-on-three pick-up game. Getting into the rhythm of the game, damn, wish I could go over and put up for the next game. Sweeping the people hanging around the park as the fault in my plan starts to become apparent. How many of Leroy's friends, or at least people who won't take kindly to me beating his ass, are here? I have to catch him before he gets to the courts.

Searching the small groups hanging out. No Leroy.

Thinking through where he'll likely come from. Let's see, he'll play ball and hang out. Then he'll see if one of those skank girls he's always bragging about is around and try and get something off them before going home. His mom works late at Key Foods, she won't care if he's out till eight or so.

Walking up toward 9th Ave, if I can catch him before he gets here and get in some good licks before people start to notice... It's likely he'll take the L train over to the IRT then down to 23rd. I think he lives over in one of the projects on 25th—I have no idea which one. Taking a last look before I go. This is harder than I thought.

Walking quickly to 25th and 9th Ave. Cursing myself for not getting here earlier and figuring this out. Looking down 25th, row of several twenty story projects on the right, small deli at the corner across the street. Lots of people starting to walk the streets at the start of rush hour.

Lazily watching people walking down the street. Nothing. Getting antsy, starting to tap away with my feet. A little rhythm coming back, music my parents hate, a little Kool and the Gang coming up to set the mood. Scanning the people walking by.

Nothing.

Go look in the building directories—Levanda Williams. If I can find which building he lives in, that'll help me figure out where to jump his ass. Stepping across the street as a wave of taxis, cars and delivery vans stream past. Walking past the small playground again, getting an itchy feeling at the back of my neck. Turning slowly, he's right there bogarting with a Puerto Rican honey. She must be all of fifteen, if anything. Slowing down, he's not paying attention to anything other than trying to put his arm around her waist while she's playfully slapping at him.

Paralleling them, matching their pace, keeping loose. Walking with them as they turn into a large tree-lined courtyard in the middle of the project, cutting an easy diagonal toward them. Five feet away, skin tingling, carefully laying down my backpack. Moving quickly, feeling like I'm on a fast break and I'm open for the perfect pass.

"My man, Leroy." Sprinting toward him.

He does a double take and starts running. He's not Thomas Jones. Kicking at his planted left foot, he goes sprawling across the concrete and tries to get up. Jumping on top of him and getting right on top of his chest, his hands moving wildly, swinging at my face. Hard right to his face smacking his head back against the pavement.

"How are you doin, my man?" hitting him with a circular left to get around his flailing hands. "How about that?" connecting, swinging again, fist grazing off his head. His face bloody, timing my next right hand as his head moves side to side and he tries to rock me off his body. I'm too heavy. Catching his head coming back to my right. Smack right in the nose—deep crunching sound.

"Aaaaa!" he starts coughing, crying out, his hands go to his face as he tries to protect himself. His elbows coming together, his back arching up to try and throw me off. High pitched female voice behind me. "Get the fuck off him, what the fuck are you doing? Help police, help!"

She's yelling and hitting my back. More voices, people starting to mill around and watch. Waiting for a good opening, good shot right to his teeth. Time to feel some pain, Leroy. He's moaning, tears running down his face, spitting blood.

"You motherfucker," spitting at him. Someone grabbing at my jacket, hands grabbing for my face, rotating toward them, punching out, connecting with something and then seeing the young bitch's feet flying up in the air.

"It's all about you. You couldn't just let me be! I asked you to let me be. You had to do it, had to! What you got now, motherfucker?" hitting him again and waiting for another clean shot. "You thought you'd play me and nothing would happen?" Crack as my left stuns him. Tears running down his cheeks.

"You don't give a fuck about Thomas Jones or anyone. It's what you want, no matter how many people get fucked up." My fist connecting with another good blow to his face, the skin above and below his lips opening up in a bright red gouge, his lips are the only skin holding it together. "What you got now, motherfucker? What'cha you got now?" one last good one.

Seeing people coming around to watch the fight in my peripheral vision. Leaning down, "I tell you, I see you again, Leroy, and I'm gonna fuck you up bad man, real bad and I ain't gonna stop, ain't gonna be no Alton to stop me. It's gonna be me and you and I'll fucking kill you," spitting in his face, heart racing, body throbbing.

Standing up, turning around, looking at the crowd, the girl who was punching at me is laying down, rubbing her jaw, and crying. A few people staring at me horrified, a couple of the kids amped up watching the fight start to box with each other. Old black man in a security guard uniform coming at me, "What the hell is this?"

"Rrrrrraaaa!" snarling and running at him, waving my arms, he backs off. Keep moving, breath coming in gulps. Picking up my backpack then making my way over 26th and up to 9th Ave. Time to get lost in the crowds, hands stinging from the blows to his face.

Images of his face starting to fill in as I run through crowded streets dodging people. Looking at my hand, deep cut between the knuckle of my index and middle finger, another across the top of my little finger. I split his mouth open from underneath his nose down perpendicular to his lips, with only a thin line of skin from his lips holding things together, cuts above his eyebrows, he'll remember me now. You took my team away, my school— you carry a scar from me.

Walking fast as I come up to 34th and 8th Ave., passing Madison Square Garden. Elation from the fight fading as I walk through the beginnings of the rush hour crowd. Looking at busy people walking with some place to go. A few like me with no place important to go, just hanging out. Work the bus station old Ben said. Shaking my head. How the fuck would I do that? Hunger coming back with a vengeance mixing with the slight queasy feeling in my stomach, almost like I'm seasick. Skin feels clammy.

I need to call Cat, call my friends. I smell like hell.

Public bathrooms at Penn Station are crowded. Men walking by, staring at me as I wash dried blood off my hand. "I hate to see the other guy," a man in a cheap grey gabardine suit talking from the next sink, he gives me a come on look.

Looking straight ahead, "Yeah well, he's not gonna eat well for a while."

Taking a thick roll of paper towels and wrapping my hands.

Long drink from a public fountain. Cold water immediately hits the bottom of my stomach. Stopping because my teeth are starting to hurt from the cold. Taking another long drink. Walking away from the fountain as the announcer starting to call out trains to Long Island. Swarms of business people in suits carrying folded newspapers and briefcases heading home to the burbs. Hundreds of feet passing in front of the man sitting at the shoe shine booth.

The tins of wax and leather cleaner trigger a long lost memory of the time Alton and I went into business together. We were in fourth grade, trying to setup our own shoeshine business. Remembering the hours passing by while we were sitting with our little shoeshine kits at the corner of 72nd and Broadway. Some guy feeling sorry for me let me not mess up his shoes. I think we each made a whole 50 cents each that day. It felt good though—we bought ice-cold quart bottles of Coke and walked up 10th Ave. talking about how we would come out next weekend and do this again; my friend.

Back on the street, dusk starting to settle into the city.

Waiting for a large woman to finish in the phone booth.

Guys hanging around the Garden—maybe there's some event here tonight, or maybe they are like me; no place to go, lost, looking for an opportunity to make some money.

"Hello," her mom, thank goodness it's not her dad.

"Hello Mrs. Sanchez, may I speak to Catherine please? Please?"

Silence on the line for a moment, she puts the phone down with a bang hard enough to register her displeasure. Miracle she didn't hang up on me again. Background traffic noise on 34th Street fills in the icy silence.

"Frankie, is that you? Oh, baby," she sounds upset. "Why'd you take so long to call? I'm mad at you," teasing anger, hurt coming through her voice.

"Easy, Cat, easy. It's been bad, baby. Big fight at home..."

Hearing her inhale deeply. "Frankie," her voice taking on a high pitch, "I've been worried sick about you, I can't hardly sleep. My parents, you know what they think, but they don't know you like I do. They've been on me to never see you again," feeling my eyes and face tense up. All these old pricks, they just need to squeeze the life out of everything they touch. Flavorless oatmeal eating things, passionless prunes, creeps.

"It's gonna be okay, Cat, I just need to get things worked out."

"Where are you, Frankie? Why didn't you call me, why didn't you stay around?"

Breathing, crowds of people walking by the phone booth, the nasty, dirty smell of the phone booth rising up, a slight smell of human piss.

"Cat," taking a deep breath, "I got kicked out of my house, things are tough now."

"Oh no," she goes quiet. "They can't do that, you know. I mean how could they do that?" her voice getting loud, "no Mama, it's okay."

Letting her have a moment—frigging operator coming on, asking for another ten cents for the next five minutes. Frantically searching through my pockets—relief at the sound of the coin dropping.

"So what are you doing, are you okay?"

"My damn old man wouldn't even let me have the money I earned working construction. I can't lie to you; I'm really hungry, and this just... This... this just hurts so bad inside, I'm so angry, they didn't even want to listen."

Her voice calls out. "Where are you? Come this way, I'll meet you. Oh baby, this is so bad."

"Your moms gonna let you out? I get the feeling their already low view of me has sunk down a couple of notches."

She's laughing, "Yeah, you really know how to make people like you, Frankie." I hear her start to cry. "That damn Leroy, Hector told me what happened. I'm so mad at him, he's just so jealous of you. He was beaming the whole day rubbing it in Hector's face."

"I got his ass good today."

She's silent. "I know you, Frankie, tell me you didn't do something crazy. You got that crazy in you sometimes. Tell me you're okay?"

"It's okay, Cat."

"You keep saying that, but it's not okay. They're saying at school that you," moments of silence on the line. Someone is knocking on the phone booth, holding up my hand without turning around.

"Cat, I messed him up good that's all."

"Well, good," she says and starts to laugh. Following along with her, first ray of warmth I've felt inside myself.

"I take that as an honor coming from the toughest girl in school."

"Yeah, I'm gonna mess you up, making me worry like this," her accent coming out when she's excited. Relaxing in a few warm moments of silence imagining her face.

Fire engine screaming down 34th St.

"Where are you, Frankie?"

"I'm down by the Garden."

"Come up by me, there's our place. We can sit and talk okay?"

"Sure, Cat, sure. What about meeting at seven?"

"Okay. Frankie, I love you baby, you remember that."

"I do, Cat, you're the only thing holding me together. I love you."

Hanging up, waiting for a moment, the ember of warmth kindled when I was talking to her is dying quickly, replaced by a feeling of dread. Got to figure out a place to stay, figure out how to get a job for the rest of this year and summer. What the fuck am I going to do?

Dropping another coin in—the man starts beating on the door. Giving him the finger. "Fuck you too," he yells and kicks the door.

Breathing deep to stop the bad from boiling over.

"Julio, what's happening man?"

"Frankie? Man!" his voice picking up. "Damn man, how you feelin?"

"Crazy man. I got that fucker Leroy good today. But let me tell you what's going on, I got thrown out, my pops and I got into another big fight and he told me to get out, didn't want to hear shit about what happened."

"Man, that's fucked up. What you doing?"

"Slept down by the train yard under the highway last night, that's a dangerous place man. Some guy tried to jump my ass there, talkin all kinds of shit about what he was gonna do to me. I busted his ass good though... Julio man, my dad wouldn't let me get any of my money."

"You know Frank what I have is yours, but you know us, there's not much."

"I know, Julio, I know. That's not what I was gonna ask. Can I get in and take a shower, maybe get something to eat?"

"Sure man, sure, come on over. Mom made a nice big pot of soup for us before she went out to work. My sister's here, she'll be cool."

Taking a couple of moments as relief spreads through my body.

"Julio, thanks man."

"Hey man, you know I owe my boy."

Hanging up, opening the door, the fat fuck looking at me all like he's all mad, "You gonna talk all night in there? Jesus!"

Bad coming out, hungry, mean. Getting in his face, walking him backwards, he tries to push around me, pushing him back. "What are you going to do you fat fuck?" Looking at him, he starts to back up and I shove him back into the crowd. Laughing as I see his feet flying up in the air.

47th and 8th Ave. Walking toward 9th Ave. on crowded streets.

Darkness in the city masked by thousands of lights.

Passing a dry cleaner shop on the corner, looking at the long conveyer belt of pressed clothes covered in thin translucent plastic. Julio's place is a couple of brownstones down.

Walking through a doorway thick with years of layer upon layer of paint—patches of paint falling off here and there. Walking into the small lobby—cracks in the ceiling paint, large paint flakes hanging by an edge waiting to fall. Walking up the creaking stairs with their familiar rusty mildew smell. Fourth floor. Knocking at their door, Julio opens up the door holding his little sister Carmella.

"Frankie, man come in," he steps back and then closes the door behind me. TV on in the living room, a couple of strings with laundry drying set around the room.

His aged aunt watching the evening news, "She any better, man?"

"No man, no," he shakes his head, looks down for a second.

Following him down the dark hallway, can't keep the smile off my face, as Carmella plays peek-a-boo with me. Passing old yellowing tropical travel posters on the wall—walls that are in desperate need of scraping, plaster and painting. Deep breath in brings my stomach to a cramp—nose alive with the smells of the place, salivating heavily. His mom sure can cook.

"Here man," following him into the long kitchen, his study books on the table. "Let me put the little one down for a bit. Soups on the stove, you know where what we have is, ain't much."

"Man this is perfect, it's been crazy," his warm brown eyes looking at me then he turns and walks out with his little sister. She looks so tiny in his strong six-foot frame.

Washing my hands with the thick bar of brown soap by the sink, then rinsing my face. Looking at my pants, dirty, grass stains. I smell pretty bad. Feeling like I'm sinking inside. Taking a bowl from above the sink and a clean tablespoon from their sparsely populated flatware drawer. Ladle in the big pot of soup—just one scoop, this is for all of them. Closing my eyes, basking in the warm fragrance of the soup for a moment—heaven.

Sitting down at the old Formica table, edges chipping off around the steel band circle. Slowly stirring my soup, big chunks of chicken, rice, vegetables, rich broth, hard to wait.

"Hey go ahead, man," he's laughing. Taking a large spoonful, letting it sit in my mouth, closing my eyes and savoring the flavor.

"Man that's good, oh man," body starting to relax a little—didn't realize how tight I was.

"What are you gonna do, Frank?"

Taking another spoonful of soup, eating slowly. My body feels like it's sucking in the goodness of the food, energy starting to return, the burning feeling in my eyes starting to ease. "I guess get a job, find a place to stay? Man, I don't know. Figure out what I'm gonna do for school next year."

Eating slowly—reaching the bottom of the bowl. Feeling like I could eat three or four more of these. His face full of concern, "Take some more, man."

"You eat? Your sister's still got to eat right? No man, this was good. It took some of the burn off. I'm going to see Cat later. I'll figure out something."

"You said you busted up Leroy?" he's shaking his head.

"What's up, Julio?"

"Man, I don't know…"

Looking at him.

"When you gonna let your friends help you, man? You did me right helping me out with Calculus," he leans his head toward me, "That motherfucking Hermano and his boys, you beat their asses but good when they ganged up on me and Hector…" Holding up my hand.

"Julio…" putting my hand on his shoulder, "I'm here, man," holding back the emotions rising up in my chest. "Man," taking a deep breath, "I got nowhere to go, this is good…"

He looks at me, a small smile breaking out, his head nodding.

"I was thinking, you could sleep here, shower when Mom isn't here. You know, till you get a place."

Thinking it through, "How would I get in and out?"

"Fire escape up the back, you can get in and out of my room. The lower level gets out to an alley that will take you back to 46th. Got to be quiet there, or you could leave early. My moms is asleep when I leave for school and you could come in late after she goes to work at the restaurant."

Nodding, "That could work for a few days, safer than where I was last night," looking at him. "I'll kick in for food, you know as soon as I get a job. Got to be a way to get at my savings," getting up and washing my dish and spoon. Putting them in the drain-board. Plan formulating in my mind—just go home and take what is mine.

"I owe you man, this is…"

"Sheeit," he gets up, "come on, get cleaned up, go see Cat. My moms gets back around midnight, so you got to be back here before that."

"Okay man, that's easy, they keep her on a tight leash."

"Hey," he turns as we're walking down the long hall. "Let me and Hector help you with those two putos, I never really trusted Alton," he puts up his fists and starts to dance and shadow box around.

"Okay man, okay," smiling at him holding my hands up surrender.

His room is good-sized—neat, empty. Books, posters of Carlos Santana, soccer players, hot women on the wall, good-sized desk with his Calculus homework carefully laid out. Walking up to the desk, he's working volumes using integration. That's what I'd be working tonight if... Lips getting tight, shit, what if they make me repeat junior year? Well, tough shit, Frank—you are the asshole that lost it.

"Man, you need any help?"

"Put you to work, home boy," he's smiling getting blankets laid out on the floor putting together a makeshift bed. Warm in here. "Like a big camp out."

"Man, we got to talk to your moms about me staying here."

"Sure man, sure. I'll talk to her tomorrow after school. You know, you should talk to Hector; his dad likes you, all that boxing bullshit. I bet that pussy Richard would let you crash at his place too."

Nodding, taking a final look at his desk—the neat writing, pages of paper crumpled up till he's got it right.

"Yo man, I hate seeing you like this but, you need to get your stinky ass in the shower," he's holding his nose, laughing.

"Julio, man," laughing with him, "suck my dick."

Chapter 7

Rough edge taken off by hot water and a good bristle brush, skin feels clean, fresh shirt feels good, refreshing cool night air on my face. Licking my teeth, the thick coating I'd felt on my tongue and teeth gone—Julio was laughing when I used his sister's toothbrush. She's a piece of work, always talking like she's going to make a pass at me. Julio embarrassed when she does. Looking at my watch—shit, got to hustle up. Fastest way to get to Cat is take the Express at 42nd to 96th.

Crowded subway, people pushing into the car without making any eye contact. Holding onto one of the poles, not that it matters it's so packed—sardine time, baby. My music starting to come back to me, Stevie Wonder's *Golden Lady* playing in my head, thinking of seeing Cat, shiver running up and down my stomach.

Can't help the smile that's breaking out on my face. She's standing outside the white glass façade of the Aegean Coffee Shop on Broadway. Her arms crossing across her light blue V-neck sweater, her face serious, worried as she sees me.

Walking quickly to her, holding my arms open. She looks around and then comes in for a quick hug, her arms up behind my back. She smells good, fresh. Moving my head back, brushing her long black hair from her face. Luscious lips slightly parted, kissing her lightly. She pushes me back a little, smiling, mix of playful mad. Right now I don't care if she doesn't like public displays of affection. Arm around her, walking the few steps to the coffee shop, body regaining a sense of normal.

Quiet with her, ignoring the loud background noise of people, plates being stacked, orders called out, people talking. Looking at the lustrous black sheen of her hair, her long fingers.

"Cat, I can't tell you how good it is to see you," looking down at my hands. "What a couple of days… I'm sorry I didn't call," looking away for a moment, "I was so… I don't know. That motherf… was my friend."

She looks at me, kind of sad look taking in my face and looks away.

"He's not your friend, you never listen to me on stuff like that…" her lips tight, "anyway, I can't stay long, maybe have a soda or something. I have to be home for dinner at seven-thirty, you know how they are," as she looks down at her watch. Catching myself about to make a comment about the Commandant—both of us with dickhead fathers, what a world.

"How'd you get out?"

"I told them I needed to pick up the keys for my new babysitting job," she dangles a key chain and puts it back in her jean pocket. Waiter hovering—looking at her, feeling ashamed at having so little money and not being able to buy something.

"I have money, silly," she says touching my hand.

Walking down Broadway, full stomach, feeling guilty at not paying, her hand in my back pocket. The feeling of her near me bringing a sense that there's some hope after all. Body memory of her warm skin, quick passionate kisses, the few times we've been able to find a place for ourselves, slight shiver thinking about my fingers feeling her warm wet pussy—her body shuddering, the smell of her, the sense of what the passion feels like with her filling me. Remembering her giggling at how hard I'd come as she cupped her hand over my cock, then needing her to stop moving because I was so sensitive. Pressing against the warm skin of her stomach, the wet feeling of me against her skin. It's like she can feel that memory too—her arm pulling me closer.

"What's bugging you, baby?"

She looks at me for a moment, then down at her feet.

"My parents," she looks at me, "they don't want me to see you anymore."

"So what's new with that?" uncomfortable laugh.

"It's serious, Frankie, they're really checking up on me..." she looks away. Rush of cold rising up in my chest; is this going to get ripped away from me too? How much of this can I take? Feeling my face tighten up. Jaw still sore from one of the shots I took. Looking out at the swarm of speeding yellow taxis moving around a city bus going uptown on Broadway. Sidewalks crowded with people.

Life would be better without asshole parents, damn them all.

Slowly pulling my arm away from her, frustration boiling up inside, breathing to try and keep my cool. They never liked me anyway, but at least at school we could see each other, get in as much as we could. Sitting on a parked car, looking at her as she stands in front of me, her arms crossed.

Feeling like something is pulling at all the things I care for, elastic bands glued to my body slowly pulled off, pulling the hairs out of my skin. Crossing my arms and squeezing my body to feel something other than despair.

"Don't take it like that, Frankie," she looks over at me. "I'm not..."

"What, Cat?" as she comes closer, she puts her hands on my arms. She touches my discolored eye and gives me a sad smile.

"You're not afraid of anything are you, Frankie?"

"Is this goodbye?"

"No Frankie, no," she turns and leans on my side, her shoulder near mine. "I just worry so much about you out here. I know how you get," she shivers a little. "You get that bad crazy sometimes and I feel so frustrated that I can't do anything to help you," she puts her head on my chest for a few moments.

"What, Cat?" Walking with her.

"Frankie, didn't you think about us? You talk about how much you love me, all the things we want to do. What if there's more than us at some point and you go off like this?"

Looking down at my feet as we walk slowly.

"Cat, I... I know baby. I just get so bad inside sometimes."

"Oh, Frankie," she puts her arms tightly around mine and pulls herself in.

"I don't want to lose you, Cat," moving the hair back from the side of her face, "I can't lose you." Touching the rich, warm, coffee skin of her cheek with the back of my right hand. She takes my hand in hers and brings it into her soft chest, "Knowing you're here, seeing your eyes, feeling how much this means to you," taking a deep breath. "I know if you believe in me that we can make it through this. I just need to take care of a couple of things. People make it through this, Cat. I can get a job, get back in school, get back on track." Holding her eyes, feeling a welcome intensity coming from my body. "I know I can do this, Cat. I know we can make it. I want this so bad—I know it's tough, but I know I love you, I know what I can build for us. It's there, Cat, it is there for us, I know it."

She smiles a little, "You better want this, you make me love you crazy like this and then you go off on these crazy things," she's kissing my hand lightly.

"What happened here?" looking at the cuts Leroy's teeth left.

"The little visit to Leroy today," feels good watching her smile.

"I bet he wasn't so big when he couldn't cry to the principal."

"He was crying like a little bitch."

Light in her eyes as she looks at me.

"Cat, if he messes with you at school, he's fucking dead," she cuts me off, her body starts to move side to side, she stands in front of me the Cat fire starting to come out of her eyes, her head and body moving in an S pattern. "He messes with me," she takes a deep breath, "me and my girls will mess him up good. Celia, Lupe and Maria hate his little black ass, Celia will cut his cheeches off."

Smiling at her.

"What?" she's looking at me, her hands on her hips.

"Toughest girl in school."

"Yeah, you better not forget that," she's smiling back and tucks herself back into me, her arm around my waist. Closing my eyes and holding her, leaning back against a parked car, feeling the welcome weight and warmth of her body.

"Most beautiful girl at school, too."

Hearing her purr a little, incredible heat coming off her body.

"I got to go, Frank," she turns and moves in between my legs, putting her arms around my neck then looks both ways up and down the street. She kisses me. Pulling her close—kissing deeply, tongues touching, lips feel surrounded by her. Raging hard on. She moves her head back a couple of inches and shakes her head to move her hair back over her shoulders. Her left hand comes down to my crotch and smiles at me.

"I wish we had time," sly look from her, "I think he's missed me."

"Oh, ya," getting up, adjusting my penis, working it up behind my zipper—full mast, less obvious. She's looking at me and giving me that little look she has when she's ready. The sense of how warm her body would feel now, what her pussy would feel like, smell like, taste like as my fingers move into her underwear, the sense of her naked breasts on my chest alive, rippling across my skin. She backs off. This is going to hurt in a little while.

"I got to go, baby," she comes close, puts her lips near my ear, "I'm not going to let them do it, you know, keep us apart. Okay? I love you Frankie, you better not forget that."

"I won't, Cat. I won't let us down."

"Here," she gives me a small blue envelope and starts to walk back to 90th, she turns and looks at me for a second, blows me a kiss and then holds up her hands—don't follow.

Sitting back down on the car for a moment, watching her walk away, her narrow hips and small, curvy butt walking away in tight jeans. Seeing other guys checking her out too, she's really blossomed the last two years, my five-foot-six Latin beauty, my mind's eye seeing her nice sized breasts—such wonderful shapes, her thin hips and nice curved butt. Remembering how she smells, what her skin feels like... Heart going out to her as she looks back at me, gives me a little smile and then turns round the corner.

Walking downtown, body has calmed down enough for me to walk. What's it going to be like when we go all the way? We've been messing around a lot, but we both said we would wait. Seems so long ago that we were at Maria's place for a party—time alone, we were on fire. Her lips touching and kissing my cock, the explosion, how that made me feel, what I wanted to make her feel, every moment electric. Body responding—uncomfortable position, stopping and leaning back against the mailbox.

Lights from Lowe's 83rd St. Theatre illuminate her letter. Sitting against a blue Chevy Nova, one tire parked up on the curb. Two ten-dollar bills inside—rush of shame hitting me. She knows me though; I'd never have taken it. Smiling at an image of her inside my head, putting the bills inside my pocket. Luxurious thoughts bouncing around in my head about where to eat, where I can get the most food for my money.

Baby,

I'm so angry, how dare they expel you? You're so smart. That Leroy is so jealous of you. My honey, I feel so much for you. Want to comfort you, take care of you. Please, for me, don't let that crazy I won't back down side get you into more trouble. It makes me proud and scared at the same time to see how you won't be afraid of your parents or nothing. Think of all the things we've talked about, College and after, you know. I believe you when you tell me it will work out. I love you so much baby. Just the way you make me feel sometimes, it's like my whole body is going to burst and I have to clam up so I don't show it cause it's too much. But when you touch my neck, oh, I just can't wait till this is all behind us.

Love, your Catherine

P.S. This new babysitting job, well, it looks pretty easy. They have a nice big place on 90th near Riverside and they want to stay out late. If it's safe, maybe, you know, we could be together. Call me at Maria's tomorrow after school.

Reading through her letter again and again. Body relaxing, weight falling off. They can't keep us apart. They can't do it.

People, colors, faces, coming into focus around me. Spending a few moments in the first rays of hope I'd felt for days. Closing my eyes, remembering her face—the look in her eyes right after we first kissed in tenth grade. Remembering how she looked the day in language lab when Hector brought in Cheech and Chong's *Big Bamboo* album and we played it instead of the conversational Spanish record. All of us laughing till we cried, trying to keep straight faces when the teachers would come by to see what was going on in there. Her face was almost beet red.

Looking at my watch, seven-thirty. Imagining what Cat's doing now—the Commandant sitting at the head of their wax shined dinner table in their neat apartment. The walls adorned with his degrees, honors and photographs of him with other professors at Columbia. He's always so precise, so formal. Visualizing her brother Charles sitting there too—I like that kid, funny in a quiet way and man, people think I'm smart, geez.

I must look like old Ben sitting laughing to myself at the real reason her father doesn't like me. How dare I hold my ground in a debate against the great professor? What an ass he must be like as a teacher—like there's only one way to solve a problem. The last time they invited me over for dinner, Charles was laughing as I held my ground when we were arguing about who was a greater success Edison or Tesla.

He was fuming when I told the story how Edison gave a college grad a problem to solve—find the volume of a complex shape. The poor guy was working and working away at all these formulas. Edison walked up to the shape, filled it with water, then poured the contents into a measuring cup and walked away.

He called Edison a dilettante, an experimenter and didn't like my line about breakthroughs in science coming from outside the mainstream—sometimes from self-taught men, passionate about their ideas and learning: Faraday, Leibniz, Edison and Ben Franklin. Like they sat around in gloomy dark classrooms listening to some old fart professor who's never done a bit of original thinking in his life. What lifeless, juiceless people they are. How that prick could ever have such a passionate daughter and not squash the life out of her is beyond me.

Laughing as I imagine her parents doing the hole-in-the-sheet thing to have sex. Cat's not like that—passion, skin touching, kissing, loving, letting the fire go. Someday our kids will rule the world.

Stomach grumbling, bringing me back to the street—where's the best place? Carnegie Deli, expensive, five bucks for a sandwich, but it's two meals worth of food. Mouth salivating as I think of that big six-inch high hot pastrami on rye sandwich. Go eat, then walk back over to Julio's place and get there about nine, after his moms has gone to work.

Stopping at an empty phone booth on 59th and Broadway. Checking out the people across the street hanging around the entrance to Central Park. Hustlers—men and women looking to make some money getting other guys off in the park. Recognizing the looks of some of the other kids there—predators, desperation, looking for some weak chump to come their way.

Making up my mind, I'm going in tomorrow, I'm going to take it. Mom will be out playing bridge from noon to four, time to go get my bankbook and a few more clothes. Pack up my duffle—get my shit and get out. Bad feeling inside having to steal my things, money I'd worked so hard for to save for college.

Surge of anger welling up inside—Thomas Jones, seeing his face running away and laughing at me. Shaking my head. Calling Richard—no one picks up. Walking up Amsterdam, hang out by the transient hotel on 73rd between Amsterdam and Columbus where Thomas Jones lives. Hide out in a nice dark alleyway, if I get lucky he'll never see me coming, it's worth a shot.

Laughing as I get off the phone with Hector—I love that guy. He laughed his ass off when I told him how I tripped up Thomas Jones by skidding a garbage can lid across the sidewalk then jumped him before he could run away. Beat his ass good till people starting calling for the police. Felt good when he said he'd talk to his dad about letting me crash there a few days and find some day construction work. Would Alton and his mom have put me up? She was always so good to me, so patient, tough, but kind.

Making fast time down 57th—walking past Carnegie Hall, coming up to the Russian Tea room. The disparity of my situation so easily exposed watching the elegantly dressed people getting out of big Cadillac and Mercedes ready for a big night out at the Tea Room. A night out here probably costs them more than a month's rent. Mom likes this place, wondering how the hell we can afford it—Dad always going on-and-on about how little money we have. Assholes, they've never given me shit, all Dad talks about is how much things cost, how much his business sucks out of him. Uncle Michael says Dad is rich as Croesus, just cheap—it doesn't make sense. He must spend it all on clothes for Mom and furniture no one in the family is allowed to sit on. Fucking dead museum at home, I'm never going back.

Passing expensive stores, a few still open. Tall beautiful woman working a jewelry store looks out the window at me. She's wearing a long black dress, low V-neck over her perfect white skin, thin long arms, dark brown hair and light blue eyes. She looks down and up my street clothes—turns away, no reaction—I'm invisible.

Line outside the Carnegie Deli on 7th Ave. Street guys trying to bum money off the chumps who've come from Long Island or Jersey all dressed up for their night in Manhattan. Waiting in line, the moochers look at me and don't even ask.

Inside, pictures of celebrities cover the wall—most signed with some bullshit about what a great place this is. Stomach growling, assailed by all the sights and smells—meats, cheeses, the rotating cake trays of ten inch tall New York cheesecakes stacked six high. Men working behind the glass counter filled with all kinds of cold meats and fish—slicing up meat for sandwiches, shoving plates in and out of the large stainless ovens.

Loud in here, long tables all crowded. Some of the people look uncomfortable sitting elbow-to-elbow with someone they don't know. People who come here often are digging into the bowls of pickles on the tables, joshing with the cranky waiters and waitresses. This is not a place for the meek when it's busy.

"How many?" asks the heavily made up lady working the line. She must be fifty, eyebrows penciled in, big glasses.

"One," she looks at me and then waves a single menu at a young guy acting as her runner. Following him, he points to an open seat in the middle of a long table crowded with people. Taking the menu and working my way in past people packed in together eating and talking, I don't need to look at the menu—I know what I want.

The family group to my right looks annoyed that I'm sitting here, they are all dressed up, jackets, ties, sitting stiff, not talking to each other—must be from Jersey. Picking up the thick distinct accent from the group to my right, a bunch of loud and crazy Jewish ladies laughing, having a good time.

Crusty old waitress comes by, "You know what you want?"

"Pastrami on rye with Swiss cheese, extra slices of bread."

"Anything to drink?"

"Water," she gives me a "why bother, you cheap bastard" look.

Ladies on my left talking about the Broadway show the *Wiz* they are going to see later. The name striking me—Dad's company built the sets and did all the engineering for that show. Bitter feeling in my stomach thinking back to all my happy memories in his shop learning to work hand tools, how to work with different types and grades of wood, basic welding.

Reaching for one of the dill pickles in the bowl—heaven. God that's good, nothing like a cool, crisp kosher dill pickle.

Laughing silently to myself thinking about how I used to have this little tool belt and walk around like one of the guys. The lady sitting next to me on my right gives me the total cold-shoulder. She's rotating her body over so she doesn't have to look at me. Table across from us filled with a raucous group—I don't even think they know each other, talking, eating away. The New Jersey contingent is amazed at how much food is on their plates, the kids in the group look miserable all prim and proper.

Six-inch tall stack of pastrami and an almost an inch of Swiss cheese sandwich gets slammed in front of me and the waitress walks off. Sitting looking at my sandwich for a few moments—I never knew how much food this was before. Breaking the beast of a sandwich into two using the extra slices of bread, slathering with some good dark mustard.

Warm pastrami feels like heaven in my mouth.

"He's been here before," one of the crazy ladies to my left says to her friend. Smiling at her as I chew slowly.

"Knife and fork or break it into two... You'd have to be a meshugenah to try and pick it up and eat it."

She starts laughing and they go back to talking about friends, kids, and husbands, going to Fort Lauderdale for vacation. Eating in silence, surrounded by noise.

Deep sense of dread absent, feeling relaxed. Putting the last of the second sandwich in my mouth and chewing slowly—feeling full. Leaning back as the New Jersey contingent gets up, they are all huffy at being crowded. Eating one more pickle, relishing the crisp, salty, slightly acidic taste. Wishing Cat could be here with me. So much to tell her, the river at sunset last night, the deep warm black of the tunnels, facing down that criminal fuck.

Leaving a dollar on the table and walking through the crowd of people waiting to be seated. Some lady complaining to the manager cause they don't accept credit cards. Paying with the ten Cat gave, lent me. Four dollars and forty-seven cents change. Back out on the street, enjoying the lights of the cars moving by, the people walking uptown, smiling for once. Looking in shop windows, passing by a one of the rip-off electronics stores on 7th Ave. the salesman working a couple of kids my age with tales of the great deal they can only get right now, just for them.

Lazy walk across town, business sections of Broadway and Eighth Ave. empty. Missing my room, my books and my music.

Stomach feeling bad—ate too much.

Folded blankets on the hardwood floor in Julio's room are heaven compared to sleeping on the pier under that rat shit blanket. No bone chilling cold here—relishing the warmth, both of us lying out in our underwear. Daydreaming while Julio's talking away about Celia, Leslie and Marta, he's all jazzed up about taking Celia to a party this weekend. Thinking back to Cat's letter, can't get over the idea of being some place other than a stairwell, secluded spots in the park, movie theatre, the nurses office at school to be alone and go at it with abandon.

Rolling over on my stomach to hide my hardening cock.

"Man, Frankie, it's late, I'll catch you in the morning."

Laughing to myself as he rolls over and goes to sleep, he talked for an hour straight. Rolling over and onto my back. It's quieter than my room at home, less street noise. The echo of the small courtyard amplifies noises from the apartment buildings. Toilets flushing, radio playing good salsa music, a couple arguing.

Looking at the dark ceiling, breathing slowly, flexing my leg muscles and holding my feet up off the ground for a count of fifty. Mind drifting to the Gramercy Gym on 14th St. imagining the sounds of people working the speed bags, heavy bags, skipping ropes, working the cable machines, the smell of sweat, feet, people farting, cursing, bodies smacked with leather. I've got to figure out how to get some work out time in when I find a job— missing the feeling of hard running for hours, playing basketball or getting in the gym and sparring till I can't move.

Still can't sleep, waiting for Julio's mom to go to sleep before I get up and use the bathroom in the hall. Quiet in the apartment.

Slipping on a pair of jeans still damp from running them through the washing machine and an hour in the little electric dryer they have. Walking in my bare feet carefully down the hall. TV in the front room is finally off— his aunt asleep on the couch. Julio's mom has a lot on her hands, three kids and her disabled older sister. His dad is back in Puerto Rico looking after his sick father.

Closing the door, the tile floor feels cool on my feet. Turning the light on, looking at my upper body in the full-length mirror on the door— discolorations on my ribs, face looks a little better. No wonder those New Jersey folks didn't want to have anything to do with me. Peeing, what a relief—aiming for the side of the bowl to not make too much noise. Long, long piss. Cleaning up the rim of the bowl with a little TP, flushing. Washing up.

Walking to the kitchen, need to drink some water, all the salt in the pickles and pastrami making me thirsty. Taking down an empty jelly jar from the collection of odds and ends they use for glasses and downing a couple of big glasses of cool tap water. Big stretch, yawning. Washing my glass, putting it on the drain board.

Nervous jolt as I hear a door opening, shit. Feeling the hair standing up at the back of my neck. Waiting—If it's his mom? I'll just tell her the truth.

Nothing, maybe I'm hearing things, could be another apartment.

Walking quietly back to Julio's room.

"Pssst," moving away from the sound and turning.

His sister, whew—feeling my body calm down.

"Geez, thanks for the heart attack, girl," quietly to her, she's standing with her door about a foot open, soft light coming from her desk lamp.

"Don't gimme that girl stuff. I want to talk to you," she shh's me.

Coming closer to the door. Jesus, she's wearing a thin nightgown over her short curvy body. Snapping my eyes back to her face as she gives me a little smile.

"What's up, girl?" needle her a little bit.

She looks at me, looks at my body for a few seconds.

"My brother, he idolizes you, you know."

"I thought you didn't like me."

"I don't," she laughs a little, "but I love Julio and I don't want him to get into trouble…"

Holding up my hands. "Easy, I love Julio. What did he tell you?"

"About you getting kicked out of school and all that."

"Look, Julio and Hector are pissed that I won't let them be involved. It's not their beef and I don't want them to get kicked out too. I'm not going to let them get hurt or get in trouble okay?"

She looks at me directly.

"You better keep it that way, you don't want to see me mad."

"Avenging angel?"

She laughs a little, can't help it now looking down at the top of her full breasts showing in the deep V of her nightgown. She leans a little more to the door—she knows I'm looking.

Feeling chemical electricity building up between us.

"You're bad, you know," her face softening a little.

"Don't be playing with me, girl."

"Why, you see something you like?"

Looking at her cute face, she's biting her lip a little bit. Thinking about Cat, she'd never know. I'd know though. Hands want to reach up and touch her body, feel her warm breasts through that nightshirt, smell and taste the warm salty skin. Face flushing as I get a huge boner. She's looking down at my pants. "Somebody's excited."

Stranded at the edge, paralyzed.

She looks at me again, "Come back when you're not so scared," and she closes the door to her room.

Damn. All I have to do is go in. Reaching for the knob, heart pounding. Backing off. My first night here—shaking my head; what am I doing? Hey Julio, hey Mrs. Salamanca, thanks for letting me stay here and have dinner and by the way I fucked your daughter all night long—idiot, moron, dumbass. Backing off. Looking at her door for a moment.

Lying back on the folded blankets, Julio snoring away.

Trouble sleeping. Dropping in and out of a light sleep. Lower body tingling—rolling over on my stomach and pressing my pelvis into the blankets, moving side to side as images of his sister flash up in my mind. Fuck, at least if I was home I could go take care of business; here, that'd be pretty funny for Julio to wake up and see me whacking off. Laughing to myself. Finally relaxing.

Thinking of Cat, her long hair...

Hearing Julio up getting dressed. Rolling over to hide my morning flagpole, the pressure on my bladder hurts.

"Hey man, we got to go."

"Hmm, yeah." Stretching, sitting up cross-legged with my back toward Julio. Putting on a slightly damp rugby shirt that was hanging over one of his chairs. Jeans on. Walking to the bathroom.

Julio in the kitchen—everyone else is still asleep. Feeling tired, big yawn, wishing I could go back and lie down. Time for a long day outdoors—library, museum or something then it's time to visit my house for the last time.

He's making hot cereal, Cream of Wheat and coffee.

"Yo, you want some?"

"Sure," morning hunger starting to kick in.

"You drink coffee, Julio?"

"Sure," he's busy. "You?"

"No way. Love the smell, hate the taste."

Walking down the stairs after my friend, feels good to start out the day with a hot breakfast. First thing I'm gonna do when I get my money is to buy something for these guys. Remembering the solitary condiment jars and a few vegetables in their fridge.

"Yo Frankie, I'll talk to my moms, come back around five man."

"Okay Julio," looking at him. "Hey... Thanks man, even if she says no, this was good man. I feel recharged. Go easy at school okay? Don't talk to

Alton; don't let him know that I'm coming for him. When he sees Leroy and Thomas Jones he'll know there's going to be a time to pay. Just tell him I'm on the streets and you haven't seen me."

"Okay, we'll make him sweat. Later, fool," he says walking up to catch the subway and on to school.

Chapter 8

Running my fingers over the cool-to-the-touch carefully polished black granite of the thirty foot wide circular Revson Fountain in Lincoln Center. Sections of stone perfectly aligned, tons of granite hewed from a mountain, formed, finished and brought here by truck. The work it took to build this. The time and care to finish. What it must have felt like to step back and look at the finished plaza when it was all done. What an accomplishment.

A few people walking around Philharmonic Hall looking at the concert schedules, others stopping looking at the large Chagall paintings in the glass facade of the Metropolitan Opera, their fingers tracing shapes in the air. Turning sideways to watch the shifting patterns of the fountain, the small outer rings go on for a few minutes pushing water up a few feet, then the large center spout shoots up fifteen feet, then the inner ring at six feet, then all three on at once. Light cool mist falling on my face.

Fighting off the feeling of loneliness creeping in.

This would be time for home room with Mr. Brown, then social studies, then Calculus II with Mr. Sturm—always so formal, his face showing emotion every once in a while when someone finally gets what he was teaching. His stories from the days he was doing naval engineering were the most fun, him drifting off into differential equations and heat transfer, Fourier... That was the coolest, how you really use the theory, the history behind the equations.

Instant of time opening—the noise in the halls between classes, joking around, girls flirting with me, Cat swatting at me, talking to my boys on the team. Last year Leroy and I got along like champs, this year, man we're like dogs growling at each other, the guy's a good ball player and all, but...

Wrapping my arms around my legs and putting my chin into my knees, feeling the cool dark granite stone on the top of the five-foot wide fountain edge through my jeans. Eyes moving over the lines of the light stone buildings, Philharmonic Hall, City Opera. What it was like to design these, to build these magnificent buildings, to watch them come to life and then stand here proud?

Do any of the men and women that designed and built this place come here and wander about? Ghosts of the creator back to remember what it was like to realize a dream. What if this place was the one great thing any of them ever did and now they wander between mediocre building projects?

Shutting down the uncomfortable thought—what if I've shut myself out of ever being able to do anything great because I lost control.

Long strips of the bronze sculptures suspended from the three-story ceiling in Philharmonic Hall glittering in the morning sun.

Busses, taxis running down Broadway belching exhaust.

Outdoor cafes across from Lincoln Center getting a little morning business, people reading newspapers looking up now and then to check out people as they walk by.

People around me getting fuzzy—feeling relaxed, tired.

Sound of water, closing my eyes.

"Excuse me," looking up, blinking my eyes to work out the daze. Thin white woman looking at me, dressed weird for a street handler. Almost business dress, sweater, flat soles, no make-up. Making brief eye contact.

"Hi," she looks at me and tries to give me a little smile, "would you like to come chant Nam Myoho Renge Kyo with us, it will change your life?"

"What's that?" not sure I heard her right.

"It's an ancient Japanese chant that helps us reach harmony with nature and live our lives in peace. We have a place nearby where new people can come chant and focus on the things in life they want," her face looked pasty white before, now some color coming in. "Help them discover what's in harmony with their inner light, learn how to find that peace, that belonging we yearn for."

Looking at her, "I have no idea what you're talking about lady, why are you telling me this?" feeling annoyed. "What? I have a sign on me that says I'm an idiot, come over and tell me things that don't make any sense?"

"Oh," she steps back a little, "you looked so sad over here."

"You don't know me, leave me alone."

"Your pain, you can fill that emptiness and replace it with love."

Words coming out slowly, "What do you know about my pain? Why are you bothering me?"

"You can be free of your pain."

Standing up, looking at the thin, frail looking woman closely, dark circles under her tired eyes. "When's the last time you ate?"

She's seems a little shocked, she moves back.

"I'm learning to live on less, my teacher tells me to learn to let my body energy be fed by the light I find inside. The more attuned I am to the universe, the more I can live off the life giving energy around us all, the less I need to live off the lives of other living beings."

Looking at her, she's starting to look wan, lifeless again.

"Look lady..."

"I'm Renee, not laaady!" she says.

"Okay, Renee, I don't have a lot of money, but if you're hungry I'll buy you breakfast, come. Come on. After that, you can go harvest the pained and the lonely, I don't want to be saved, I want to go out and do violence upon the world and a few of the people in it," anger starting to grow.

Her face recoils. "I'll chant for you."

"I don't want you to chant for me, chant for a hamburger, you need to eat some food, you look anemic. Here," taking out a five dollar bill, "you need to eat."

"You just don't understand."

"I may not understand about light and all that, but I know what people look like when they are hungry. That's not healthy and I don't give a fuck about what your teacher tells you," looking at her, "Renee, listen."

"You are a brute, you are filled with darkness, oh!" she turns shaking her hands like she's trying to rid herself of something, throw it off her body while she walks away.

That was great—what weirdo am I going to meet next? Let's have the nut job of the day contest. Hey, who knows, maybe I'm in her top ten. Fuck me, fuck her and fuck all of this shit.

Thinking back to last year when I was cooling down after a long run along the East River and this guy started telling me some shit about how he was into massage and lubrication. I was the fuck out of there. Should I have smacked that pervert? I was sixteen, like he cared. What a jerk.

Shaking that whole scene with Renee out of my head.

Sitting back down on the black granite fountain.

It's been a long time since I've seen my sister Vicky—memories of us playing at the beach in Rockaway floating in. Standing on our Styrofoam surfboards acting like we were surfing. My God she was fearless and full of life. What's she up to? How does she meet people, partners I mean? So much I don't know about her, what her life is like outside the house now, college, friends. Like she'd help me now anyway—my prick father is right about one thing, she hates both of us. Another charter member of the Frank Caruso fan club—hmm, maybe I could sell tickets. Imagining crowd noise in the background, Howard Cosell's voice coming in on the radio inside my head, "So Frank Caruso, tell us, tell us how you made your way to fame and fortune?"

"Well, it wasn't easy, Howard. I found out I had so many people who hated my guts, I created a live show and sold tickets to people who wanted to see me humiliated live and in color. The TV rights alone netted me a fortune. I got rave reviews for the last one…"

Enough of this, this is stupid.

Flexing my leg muscles, stretching, I need to walk. Heading uptown—idea filtering in, there's the small branch library on Amsterdam and 81st., walk there, go hang out. Body shivering, I'll need to walk by my old elementary and intermediate schools, PS 87 and IS 44, there'll be kids all over the place.

No one will know me there.

Walking up Broadway, crossing over to Amsterdam at 72nd, stomach wants to go into Gray's Papaya and stuff myself with hot dogs and sauerkraut. Body memory of going out to Nathan's on Coney Island when I was a kid with Richard and his parents, well while they still lived in the

States anyway. Man, did we stuff ourselves with those good dogs, the pistachio soft serve custard afterwards, walking along a weekend crowded Neptune Blvd, sunburned people coming up from the beaches smelling of suntan lotion—fat people.

Looking inside the shop, stomach growling.

No money to spare, move on.

Older men sitting by shoeboxes offering shines, they ignore me in my black high top cons. Heading up Amsterdam Ave.

Stopping by Tony's Pizzeria between 73rd and 74th, letting the mix of aromas of fresh dough, pizza's baking in the long stainless steel ovens, and sausages on the grill fill my body for a moment. Standing there as a few people go in and out of the place. Young kid walking out eating a big slice of sausage pizza—ignoring the temptation to go smack him in the face and take his food. Shaking my head and walking uptown.

Walking up Amsterdam Ave. past the mortuary between 75th and 76th, the Hispanic stores selling religious icons—stopping for a moment and looking at the paintings of Jesus, his body bloody with a crown of thorns, another painting of St. Sebastian pierced by arrows, blood running down his body while he's tied to a tree, his face peaceful, calm, no sign of pain.

Shaking off the spiral down, fighting off the urge to go get in someone's face and scream at him or her—stopping for a second as the pavement gets soft and my vision starts to swim. Momentary lapse passing, walking to 77th, can't resist the pull of the place. Walking past the large empty playground of PS 87, walking past brownstones toward Columbus, the large tall green trees along the avenue waving in the breeze. The playground at IS 44 is empty—kids are all in class, a couple of punks hanging around on cars by the front of the building.

On Columbus Ave, passing the Hispanic markets and record store with Salsa music blaring out.

Why the hell didn't I think of that? Looking over at the Natural History Museum. It's free and I've got plenty of time to kill. Thought running through my head about the library; I have two books in my school locker that I need to return, the *Sea Wolf* by Jack London and the *History of the Ancient World*.

Walking alone in the dark, cool hall of the Pacific Northwest American Indians. Looking around to see if any guards are around—alone in here. Touching the rich dark wood of one of the aged totems. People made this. Trying to feel what it was like back then. Stepping back looking at the different animals; eagle on top, badger, bear, antelope or deer. Wandering around the small dioramas depicting life in Indian villages—people making fish traps in the river, tanning hides, building the long huts they lived in.

Wishing I could be out there, living a life so different than being stuck in the middle of New York City, a forest of big-ass buildings, garbage, pollution. Mind drifting back to hunting with my uncle in the deep woods of upstate New York and Pennsylvania, learning to track, learning to set up a blind to ambush White Tail deer as they passed from their feeding plots to areas where they bed down, the rush of adrenaline seeing a big buck come within range... My knees were knocking together that first time.

Remembering the cold morning air, getting up at 4:30 in the dark and moving quietly, slowly into place. Waiting in the dark while the sun slowly crept up in the sky. Keeping calm, learning to breathe deeply to keep my heart from pounding, as the shape of a deer would start to emerge from the deep green.

Was I born in the wrong time?

Thinking back to when I used to be in Boy Scouts hiking at the Alpine Scout Camp in New Jersey, up early, the Rascal's *It's a Beautiful Morning* running through my head as I walked out into the cold quiet of the deep woods—all the other kids wimping out and complaining about how their feet were sore or it was too cold out.

How cool would that be to be out there with a bow and arrow, hunting for food—using all parts of the animal skin, sinew, bones. The things I wear are what I've got the skill and strength to take as well as the strength to give back. Respecting each part of the animal and the way of their lives. Damn I miss my uncle, the times we've been out in the woods or out on the ocean. He must hate me now. Taking a deep breath to force down the emotion. I can't miss him, I can't miss my father—they hate me.

Coming back to the dark, quiet museum, the ancient way of life represented behind these glass cases—the work of ancient hands that went into fashioning the clothing, the tools, the weapons, the instruments quiet in the dark hall. The stories they must have told, the lives these things made better. They are just bits of wood now, lonely, lifeless, meaningless things without the people, the stories, who made them.

Hall of dead things—am I dead and don't know it? I'm invisible to my family and most of my friends. If I disappeared right now a few people would know, not many would care. Why not leave? Go find places like this to live, to be free, take Cat and together carve out a new life from the raw earth.

Walking on down the long hall, looking up at the sparse line of tall totems. Without the intelligence and culture of the people who fashioned them, they are meaningless. I wonder what a native from one of these tribes would think seeing all this here—spirits kept prisoner?

I'll never know while I live like this.

What if I left the City?

Stopping dead in my tracks—looking at the tall totems lined up and down the long hall—what's out there waiting for me? This is up in the Pacific Northwest. Why not go? I'll have my bankbook; my money will get me a lot of miles on a Greyhound bus. I can live someplace where I can work and breathe clean air, fish and hunt.

Letting my imagination go, thinking about all the things I could be doing as I walk along the quiet halls of the museum. Would she come with me? We always talk about how stifling our parents are. Why not leave?

Starting to feel tired looking at all the dead, stuffed animals. Wouldn't it be magnificent to see these in real life?

Looking at my watch—getting close to noon, I can start back to my old house around 1:00, that will give me enough margin, time for Mom to be on her way to bridge club.

Finding a quiet area of the dark hall to kill time, sitting down, resting my head on my hand like I'm looking into the big diorama—lions in the tall grass hunting antelope. The Masai run the plains, tall, strong, brave warriors. Where are people like that here? Are we all dead? Would I be brave enough to face down a lion with a spear?

Story of how the bravest Apache warriors would jump into a pit with a Grizzly bear with only a spear coming to life in my mind. Body shivering. What if that were true? Imagining standing at the lip of the pit, only one or neither of us coming up out of that place alive. Feeling the drum beat, I will not stop, I will be the one, red tooth, blood coursing through my body, eyes that can see in the dark.

Closing my eyes in the cool museum, imagining running with tall strong men through the tall grass of the African plain, our long spears at the ready, tracking the lions that prey on our cattle.

The bravest lead.

Running with men who know no fear.

Singing songs of our families, our family spirits that guide us.

Ignoring the anger rising up my throat thinking about my father.

Going back to the deep golden plains opening up before me.

Running with men who know no fear.

Feeling like I'm slowly sinking below the surface.

Down into deep quiet.

Nudge, looking over—museum guard nudging me with the butt of his flashlight, "Hey, no sleeping in here," hushed authoritarian voice.

Blinking my eyes, standing up, old fellow, big gut.

"Okay, sorry, drifted off."

"Shouldn't you be in school?"

"Yes," walking away.

Out on Central Park West, mid-day sun overhead. I can follow this down till it turns into 8th Ave, then west on 56th. Walking, running through the list of things I need to bring out in my mind; underwear, socks, couple of pairs of pants, short sleeve shirts, basketball, my boxing gear—put that in my athletic bag. Some good shorts to go play ball, work gloves too. My tools are mostly at Dad's shop—damn all the money I spent on those and my bastard father probably won't let me have them either.

Hanging around the middle of the block, looking for anyone I know; waiting for a sign or something stupid telling me it's okay to go in there, to sneak in there to take what's mine. Sense of dread starting to creep in realizing I have to cross this line. I have to do it.

Can't shake this bad feeling.

City back to looking dark to me, wishing all these damn people, all this damn noise would disappear.

Hands icy cold as I put my key in the door lock. What if they changed the lock? Relief as it turns and clicks, nervous as I creep into their apartment. Stepping quietly into the hall, no music, no sounds from inside, just street sounds filtering up from traffic heading west on 54th.

Most important thing—get my money. My money!

Creeping past my sister's old room, then mine.

Slowly stepping into my parent's room, uncomfortable coming in here like this—thief. It's in her closet; I have to go in there. I have to take what's mine. Brain feels like it's separated from my body—body feels like it's moving through some kind of thick liquid as I open her closet door. Smell of my mother surrounding me, all the things she keeps secret from the rest of us. Forcing my hand to flip on the light.

Deep narrow closet, strings of scarves, shelves with lots of small cabinets, small drawers, belts, perfume, dresses. Weird sensation going through my body—when my parents do it, this is where she changes. Shuddering as I think of how beautiful she is, how formal, how stiff she's always been with me. A few cracks of warmth here and there, feeling everything in the world is okay though when she smiles or laughs.

Slowly opening a drawer, underwear, this is next to her body. Cold shiver running down my spine, staring at it, feeling the smooth silk, mix of her perfumes, her scent. Closing the drawer quickly.

Freezing—someone's coming in the house.

Turning off the light, oh shit, oh shit. Closing the door quietly. Idiot, idiot, idiot, the cleaning ladies come today. Things running through my mind quickly; run now, get my bankbook, grab as much as I can. Wait, chill man, they aren't my parents. They can call the police though. They'll start in the kitchen and the dining room. Flipping the closet light back on, quietly opening and then closing a drawer, nothing, opening others, looking at the contents. Having to push my body to move, every fiber rebelling having to touch her things.

Holding her history in my hands, jewelry, pictures from the old country—trinkets from her family, closing that one slowly. Feeling a

65

stabbing pain in my chest, feeling like my Grandpa T is looking down at me with disappointment in his eyes. I have to do this. The lid on one of her jewelry boxes open, old style silver jewel encrusted broaches, ornate necklaces I've never seen her wear.

Keep looking.

Finally, there it is—opening up my bankbook, feeling the thick cover, thick paper. Sense of relief spreading through me, I have money, freedom. Looking at the thick envelope of cash she's got in the drawer too. No, it's not mine. Stealing won't make it right.

Turning off the light.

Standing in their room, their bed always perfectly made, light green walls, some family photos of Mom's family. Dad's desk is always so formal, neat, a lot of pens in decorative mugs from the Broadway shows he's worked on, the shelves filled with years of the organizers he jots down notes into every day. Listening for Miriam and her sister. They are still busy in the kitchen.

Sneaking into my room quietly and quickly closing the door.

Making fast work of packing my duffle. This is good enough.

Walking quickly out the door, seeing them out of the corner of my eye. Why not? Waving to Miriam and giving her a big smile, she gives me a curious look and waves back. Mom's probably so embarrassed about this she wouldn't have told anyone outside the family. Miriam smiles and waves back as I leave this place for the last time.

Relief spreading as I take the stairs two at a time. Out in the street, walking down 10th Ave. Hoisting the duffle on my back, carrying the gym bag with my gloves, head gear, jump rope, wrappings, shorts, leg weights. Hitting me—what the hell will I do with all this stuff all day? Carry it around, not. Good thinking Frank.

Well, thinking through my options, I can go up the fire escape and put these in Julio's room, then hit the bank. Hunger driving my decision. I'm going to eat, big meal—stuff my face. I'll head down to Chinatown and go to the basement restaurant Yu Wen showed me where they serve a lot of cheap food and hot tea. The thought of that spicy King Pao chicken dish with all the red chili peppers making me salivate. Stay calm, walk calm and get the fuck out of here.

Making my way back to 46th, walking east—going slowly and checking out the neighborhood folks hanging out of windows talking to, laughing with others on the street or in the next apartments. Ducking into an alleyway, its cool and dark here. Trash alley, damn rats running around as I kick a bag out of the way, not quite the way I need to go—hang around in here so people on the street don't see me back out too quickly. Next alley is what I want.

Looking up, now all I have to do is figure out how to pull the retractable ladder down. Too high to jump for, it's at least eleven feet up, no room to get a running start. Taking out one of my hand wrappings, tying a leg weight on it. Over the bottom step, not long enough to let the weight all the way back down. Tying off the second—probably ruining these. Pulling down the stairs slowly, creaking as it comes down.

Clamber up quickly, pulling the ladder back up behind me.

Nervous walking past other people's apartment windows, some of the sections of the fire escape feeling loose. Stepping into Julio's room, quickly putting down my stuff and changing into a lighter weight knit polo shirt. The TV is on in the front room, volume set high for his aunt. Marta hopefully out at class—sense of the wet dream I had with her last night, how luscious it felt being inside her, how she groaned, how she looked at me. She'll be here tonight.

Walking carefully down the fire escape.

Looking up at the dirty brick walls, the network of fire escapes running along the building walls up toward the light blue-sky overhead.

Pushing the fire escape ladder back up.

Out on the street. Breathing easier, shaking my hands.

Up to 8th Ave., heading over to 42nd, walking quickly.

Subway uptown to the Central Savings Bank on 73rd and Broadway. No idea why Dad made me open my savings account there. The subway station is pretty empty, solitary bum sleeping on one of the benches covered up with newspapers. Transit policeman walking by too apathetic to even do anything.

Train driving through the dark tunnel, moving out to lights of the station as the Express rolls toward 72nd. Heading up the narrow stairs to the street. Pedestrian traffic still pretty light. Looking down Broadway at Odyssey Records—thinking about all the music I left behind. My music! Quincy Jones, Stevie Wonder, Temptations, Black Sabbath, Steve Miller, Traffic, O'Jay's, Harold Melvin, Kool and the Gang, West Side Story, Mandrill, J Geils Band, Kinks…

Breathing out. Julio's got nothing in his room, why the fuck am I complaining? Taking a deep breath, I earned enough to buy it all once, I'll do it again.

Walking uptown on Broadway toward the Central Savings Bank.

Looking up at the three stories tall, vaulted ceiling as I step into the cool quiet bank. Finding a short line at one of the teller windows, the marble inlaid island surrounded with decorative wrought iron shapes. Dope, you need to fill out a withdrawal slip. Walking out of line over to one of the marble tables where the banking slips are stacked neatly. How much to take out? Fifty dollars is a lot of money, but that will let me contribute to Julio's mom. Once I get a job, I'll start to look for a place, probably rent a room from someone. Richard's brother's apartment is so damn big and he's there by himself most of the time. Wonder if he'd rent me a room? If I go to the YMCA, at least I can put down a deposit.

Lady teller stiffly takes my bankbook, my withdrawal slip and compares my signature to a card in one of the filing cabinets behind her. "How would you like this?" she asks.

Looking at her, "Oh," looking up at the tall carved ceiling, amazing what was built here, "two twenties and a ten is fine."

Taking out my wallet and pushing the eleven one-dollar bills to the front and tucking in the rest behind them. Welcome thickness in my wallet feels good. Looking at my watch—an hour to kill before I need to get back to Julio's place. I'll stop at the A&P Market and come in with a bag of food. Like Dad always says, got to pay your way in life, don't expect something for nothing.

Ambling up Broadway, checking out the array of fresh fish arranged on a thick bed of crushed ice at Citarella's. All this good-looking seafood is giving me an idea; maybe later this week I'll whip up some killer spicy seafood pasta for Mrs. Salamanca. Passing the clothing store Pandemonium, laughing to myself at how frustrated I was last time I went shopping in there—they had little that would fit. None of the thirty-eight pants could get up over my thighs, arms too long, my chest was too big for most of the shirts. Picture of style, my size forty uncool Levi's boot cut jeans taken in to my thirty-seven inch waist.

Stopping for a treat at the Carvel shop, good frozen custard. Eating slowly—cold, creamy, sweet. Letting the custard melt so the inside of the waffle cone gets nice and soggy. Hanging out on the corner at 79th, finishing off the spongy custard-soaked cone before getting into the rush hour subway.

Feels good to buy two dollars' worth of tokens—eight rides. Realizing how precarious my existence is now, I lose my bankbook and what the hell would I do?

I need to square things with Alton and then it's time to get to work. Figure out school next year, or not. What if I left the City? Images of Jack London's early life out on San Francisco Bay running through my mind. Wild, uncharted, sailing into areas you don't know but just need to explore. What's right around the corner?

Standing up at the door facing the express stops, subway car is not crowded, but I don't like sitting down. Makes you an easy mark for someone looking to smack you upside the head and take your shit. Tag signs in thick magic marker in the subway, dirty cars, and cracked windows. Letting my body rock back and forth to the rhythm of the subway as it trundles along. Moving aside to let people in at 72nd.

Switching over to the A train at 59th Street.

Taking the local to the 50th street Station. My face must be less of a mess—what does it matter anyway, I'm just another subway rider, nothing to attract attention, just some asshole six foot five teenager in jeans and short sleeve shirt.

Store getting crowded—mixed here, feels good; white people, black people, Hispanic people moving, dodging, cutting each other off. Must be a lot of taxi drivers shopping here the way people are flinging their shopping carts around. Two big black women that must be related to the Budd sisters going at it arguing about what to get for supper. What the hell am I going to get? I know they like to make a lot of stews, grilled meats and love chicken. Okay—two nice plump fryer chickens with all the natural parts, thinking back to the good chicken heart stew my grandfather used to make. Breathing deep to deal with the rush of hunger.

Chapter 9

Lugging my paper shopping bag down 10th Ave., feeling good about the money I spent for their family—feeling rich for a moment. Stopping and looking at wave of people returning from work, if I don't go back to school, this would be my world. I have my union apprentice card, I can get good work and I'd have money. Shivering to think what it would be like to come home to Cat.

Heading up the creaky wooden stairs to Julio's place and knocking on the door. Mrs. Salamanca opening the door, stern look on her face changing to surprise as she looks down at my shopping bags.

"Hello, Frank," her arms crossed.

"Hello, Mrs. Salamanca." Waiting, standing in the hall like an idiot.

"Come in, I think it will be good to talk," she looks on as I go through the intricate process of getting the bag loops off my hand. "And what is all this?"

"I bought this for you. Julio let me have some of his dinner last night and breakfast. You know," feeling awkward under her glare, "I wanted to contribute."

She's shaking her head slowly, "Come in. Let's get this put away."

Unpacking, stacking items in the refrigerator under her direction.

"You have a good eye for shopping."

"My grandfather owned a restaurant, he loved teaching me and my sister all about food, how to cook, how to choose, how to prep... I have a lot of fun memories hanging out there." Feeling good for a moment remembering those times helping prepare for the huge family feasts out in Brooklyn when he was still with us. Folding up the paper bag, Julio nodding as he comes in for a glass of water.

He's hanging around, uncomfortable silence.

"Julio, I need to talk to Frank alone."

"Mom, please?"

She gets that stern as iron look on her face, he knows better. Starting to get a bad feeling about this. Well, there's always the frigging YMCA, probably too late to get to Hector's place. Feeling my face tighten up as she motions for me to sit down. This must the universal parent I-have-bad-news-to-give-you ritual.

"So, Julio's told me a little, I want to hear it from you."

Taking a deep breath, seeing her daughter's face in hers.

"I've been expelled from school. I... I blew it," looking at her dark coffee brown skin, a few streaks of gray in her black hair, her dark eyes steady. She's looking to see if I'm bullshitting her. "My parents threw me out of the house."

"That's illegal till you are eighteen."

Shrugging my shoulders. "My father told me to get out so I'm out. I've got money saved from working summer construction. I can contribute here. I'll get a job. I can do all kinds of things with my hands. I don't think I'll need to be here long, just got to find a place to rent a room, figure out what to do about school next year."

"Shhh, slow down. You can't stay here. I have too much to take care of already. Your gesture is touching, but it's too much."

Feeling my body deflate.

"I talked to your mother, they want you to come home."

Recoiling in my chair. Reeling a little bit.

"I'm not going back, no way, not after…"

She softens a little, "Trying so hard to be a man," more to herself, "look Frank, I can't afford any trouble with your uncle. You don't understand… Look I can't afford any trouble."

"Why would my uncle care? He's on Dad's side and that bas…" Catching myself, "He threw me out. Told me I was worthless, a disgrace to the family, a loser. I'm tired of it, I don't need them."

"Such big passions," she looks down at her folded hands. "You can stay here tonight, but you have to leave tomorrow. Where did you get the money to pay for all this?" she gestures at the refrigerator.

Taking out my bankbook and putting it on the table, "This is mine. I earned it. It's not in my father's name, not in my mother's, it's mine, my account, my hard work." She opens it up, looks at it, then looks at me, nods and slides the bankbook back to me.

"You have to go home, I'm sorry."

"I'm not going home, I'll go rent a room at a hotel, the YMCA. Hector or Richard can put me up, I'm not going home. I'll live on the street if I have to."

She looks at me, a deep sadness coming over her face.

"Frank, don't throw your life away. You drop out now and the road back is so tough. You've got to get an education. Don't throw all the things you have away cause you're so upset. Go home tomorrow; make amends with your family. If you don't, it will be a bad thing you'll carry. Sometimes you never get these things back."

Heart sinking down to my feet.

"I can leave now," sitting back, body getting set, feeling hard.

"No, no," she looks sad. "Let's make a nice dinner, I'll call your mother later, tell her you are going home. Okay?"

Nodding to her, lying, no way I'm going home.

Gloom broken by chopping, slicing—Mrs. Salamanca running her kitchen with an iron hand while trying to make light of the situation by talking a lot.

"Your grandfather taught you well," she looks at all the prep work, "we could use you down at the restaurant. Don't get any ideas though," she's smiling.

Marta hanging around laughing at all the work we are doing. Snatching a look at me now and then, that girl is playing with fire.

"That smells good, Mama," the sauce she's put together does smell delicious—convict's last meal.

Lying on the folded blankets in Julio's room.

Feeling like a fool for spending money on food for these assholes, well anyway, I'm back outdoors tomorrow. Breathing in, easy man, easy. Running through my head why Julio's mom would be worried about my uncle? He's over in Brooklyn, doesn't deal with things over in Manhattan. Julio quiet. Looking at the ceiling—letting the dim cracks in the ceiling form into different shapes.

Restless. Running through stories in my head about why I'm out looking for a hotel room. Construction story, here on a job, I can show my union apprentice card if need be. What if I come back all fucked up from my fight with Alton? That'll be tough to explain and as good as he is, it is a definite possibility. I'm going to have to get in close where I can use my weight, height and strength advantage. I'll take some good shots from him—he's very good.

Visiting family, hmm, how would that one work? Why would I be staying at a hotel?

Seeing trees, mountains in the ceiling—a map of the world. It's going to be back to the lonely world come tomorrow.

Daydreaming of a world with no one in it except Cat and me. Quiet city streets, just her lovely eyes, going where we want to, when we want to, doing what we want to with the whole city at our feet. No parents, no bounds, my body shivering with the idea of her all to myself—Julio talking to himself in his sleep.

Restless, time moving slowly.

Germ of an idea drifting in—I've got my gloves and training equipment, give the guy a line about coming to Manhattan to train with Gus down at the 14th St. Gym for a couple of weeks to see if I've got what it takes to turn pro. Where do I live? Hmm, how about way out on the Island, Upton or something. I came into the city to train to work with the best and I'll be here for two weeks. I should call before I go, just showing up could look funny.

Damn, how much is this going to cost?

Running through the story in my mind. What do I say if they ask why I'm not in school—time off for good behavior? Would I need some kind of permission? Maybe two weeks is too much, stay there for a week? Long enough to get set. So many things to take care of. Stupid, I easily pass for eighteen—just go there and play it.

Frustration welling up, feeling the burn in my stomach, I can't let Cat slip through my fingers, dammit!

Quiet morning. Julio won't make eye contact.

Walking down the creaky stairs to the street. Busy morning.

"Yo, man," he looks down at the pavement, makes eye contact for a moment. His thin gold necklace with a cross moving over his athletic t-shirt under his unbuttoned blue shirt, "I'm sorry man, you know, I thought..."

"I'll figure it out, Julio, thanks for getting me a little rest, man."

He looks at me, "You're not going home are you?"

"No way."

Feeling set, anxious to get going.

Need to find a quiet place with a phone.

"Man," he shakes his head, "when you get your mind set, man..."

Shrugging my shoulders, "I'm not going back, Julio," looking at him. "Hey I'll call you when I figure out what I'm gonna do. Tell Hector and Richard what's going on when you see them at school, okay?"

"We'll track down Alton man. Leroy's all messed up, people laughing at him 'n shit. TJ didn't come to school."

"Julio, look, forget about it, I'm out man. I fucked this up. It would kill me if you went down too. I'm going to get it on with Alton, whatever comes of that," feeling the burning rise in my chest. "Then I'll find work, find a place, all that bullshit. You want to help me, look out for Cat."

"Man, don't do something crazy on him."

"He's a good fighter Julio, he might beat my ass."

Julio shaking his head like I'm stupid, "Yo Frankie, man," he shuffles, "I don't know how to tell you this, but maybe you should stop this. Alton's good, we seen him fight right? But man, you get to a scary place. You got a whole different side to you, man." He looks at me, quietly, "What if you go too far again, man? I seen you, man. We heard about what happened with Leroy. You and Alton were friends, man. What if he was trying to help you and just messed up, getting caught up in the heat of the moment, you know?"

Street noise around us, feeling pissed that Julio is starting to wimp out. "Julio, man..." looking at him—thoughts, emotions tangled up, balled together all trying to come out at the same time, "I can't let this lie. All he had to do was to turn around to Leroy and Thomas Jones, it would have been two-on-two and they wouldn't have escalated shit. He chose to be a bystander, he got in the way when things got hot, he's the only one that could have put me out." Fists clenching, getting hot, can't stop my voice from rising. "Is that what your friends do?" he shrinks back a little.

"Easy, man, easy. I know how much heart you have, it ain't easy."

He looks at the stream of cars passing by, looking away down 47th toward the river. "Let me an Hector be there, you know, make sure you guys don't go too far, man. Let us help you."

Looking at him, "Julio, you'll be an accomplice, don't you understand? You got to get to school," taking a deep breath, "I'm in a different place now, man. I don't understand it, but it's different. I'll call you later."

"Man, Frankie, don't be that way."

"Julio, I'll call you later."

"Okay, man, don't do anything crazy."

Smiling—like the fucking hash of my life isn't crazy.

Hitting me, he doesn't know, he's still in his zone: school, sports, family, I'm in the fucking twilight zone—everything's been torn apart and thrown up in the air.

"Later, Julio," as I turn and walk toward 8th Ave.

"Later, Frank," hearing him call out from behind me.

Chapter 10

Broadway snarled with angry traffic, four lanes snaking down into two with the construction project at the corner of Broadway and 63rd spilling out into two lanes. Trucks rolling slowly, people moving across the street on the red light. Taxis stuck behind cement mixers, busses and trucks honking their horns—another cheery New York City morning. Image of what the forest near Uncle Michael's place would look like now; cool green, light fog rolling in, clean air.

Stepping over a deep pothole filled with thick, oily brown water. Trash strewn around the street, guys in hard hats hanging around drinking coffee and cat-calling women as they pass.

Looking up at the fortress like YMCA building as it looms up above me, the tall, green trees of Central Park surrounded by the dark, gray granite stonewall in the distance. It's been a long time since I'd been around here. Running my story through my mind—relax man, it doesn't need to be perfect, it can't sound rehearsed, man. Fuck if I was really here for this, I'd want a room and no bullshit from the clerk. Go play it like it's real.

Lobby surprisingly vacant, older man working the big desk in the center of the lobby. Man, he's one of the darkest men I've ever seen. He's calmly looking through papers, turning as I hear the elevator open, a couple of kids with long hair and small back packs coming out. They are looking at a city map, orienting it different ways pointing to areas and talking to each other in animated, colorful Italian. Feels good to hear my native tongue spoken well. They are heading to the front desk too.

"What can I do for you boys?" calm, like he deals with this every day.

"We ah want a to," the first kid searching for words, his hands moving in space, "Metro-polita Museao," he's looking at his friend. "Ah, directione?" he shrugs his shoulders and holds out the map.

"What?" the man behind the counter says as they bring up another map and start talking together quickly.

Stepping in, "*I can help you. Where are you trying to go?*"

They turn, big smiles lighting up on their faces. One of them pats the other on the shoulder. "*Hey, you speak Italian?*"

"*Hey, you guys are pretty fucking smart.*" They start laughing, pointing at me like I'm the funniest man on the planet... I'm surrounded by morons.

"*My name's Frank, where are you trying to get to?*"

"*This is Marcello, and I am Flavio. We are from a little town near Florence. We want to visit the Metropolitan Museum of Art, there's a special Rafael exhibit. What is the best way to get there?*"

"*Easy, easy, let me show you on the map,*" to the man behind the desk. "May I?"

"Go right ahead, Guido," a fat middle-aged white man with a comb over coming out from the back, hanging around listening.

Spreading out the map.

"*So Flavio, you are here now, yes?*" he nods, and I orient the map to the street outside. "*Central Park is that way,*" pointing down 63rd. "*You want to go here,*" showing them the museum on the other side of the park. "*It's not a long walk, the easiest way is to walk up to 72nd Street and then follow this drive,*" tracing out Terrace Drive through Central Park, "*when you get to Fifth Avenue, go North and the museum is right here. You understand?*"

"*Very good, very good,*" they look at each other. "*Hey you're from Southern Italy?*"

"*My family is from Sicily, but I grew up here.*"

"*Hey, we meet later, have some wine, talk, go talk to beautiful women, eh?*" he claps me on the shoulder. "*We are in room 872, okay?*"

"*Sure, I'll check in with you later, have fun. Get going now.*"

Looking at the guy behind the counter, shrugging my shoulders.

"I called earlier for a room, Caruso."

"Oh," the guy working the counter says and starts looking through a stack of papers. Checking out his nametag, Dexter, the other fellow meanders off apathetically.

"Here you go, one week, fill this out and pay a twenty-five dollar deposit."

Filling out the form, putting in my bullshit Long Island address and phone number that I copied out of a phone book at the library. Passing the form over and counting out the deposit money.

"What brings you in from the Island?"

"Got a chance to work out for a trainer, see if I've got what it takes to turn pro."

"You a boxer?" his face registering surprise.

"Amateur, I've done well in Golden Gloves."

He looks at me for a few moments, "Tough, tough sport man. Can be a dirty sport too, nasty people. Why you want to do that?"

"If you're good you can make big money. If not," looking at him, "well, that's what I'm here to find out."

"Other ways a doin' that than trying to be the second Marciano."

Shrugging my shoulders, "Plenty of guys telling me to go pro cause folks will pay to see a big white boy box, but that's bullshit. You either got what it takes or you don't and I want to hear it from the best."

"Well," he takes a key hanging in front of one of the small mailboxes organized into rows and columns along the wall behind the desk, he looks at me. "You might want to come here," he slides over a program of religious talks for the week. "Lots of ways to get through life, sometimes the most direct way isn't what you think." He looks at me, "These are the rules here," pushing forward another pamphlet, "read them, make sure you know them.

You break them, you're on a train back out to Long Island, you hear?"

"Yes, Sir."

"Seven-twenty-four. Elevator will take you up. Good luck now."

Long hall filled with doors, brown carpet is threadbare in places. Many of the bulbs burned out. Standing in front of my new room—feeling out of place, tired.

My God, no wonder the doors are so close to each other, the room is like a deep closet. Stepping in, closing the door and taking in my temporary home, at least I'm facing the street. Looking around at my room—desk with a lamp on it, double bed, small closet, bare tile floor and small bathroom. Smells of industrial disinfectant with a tinge of roach spray in the air. Black and white photo of old Central Park looking towards the Plaza Hotel at night over the desk. Dead quiet in here. Sitting on the bed, looking at the bare walls, empty desk, empty closet and a radiator with peeling white paint underneath the window.

Taking off my sneakers—lying down.

Sinking into a deep loneliness.

Fucking Alton. He fucking did this to me.

Blinking my eyes, mouth feels coated, feeling my shirt—damp, must have been drooling while I slept. Feels like I've been out for a day—sitting up, panic setting in—did I sleep through the night? I was supposed to be at Cat's babysitting apartment at seven-thirty. Watch reads six-oh-two, relief spreading through my body. Voices in the hall passing by my door, well, at least someone is laughing today.

Lethargic, yawning, body wants to go back to sleep. Forcing myself to get up, standing, feeling a little lightheaded. Starting to feel the effect of not eating all day. Dark gray walls of the room rising up, lights from the cars heading west on 63rd playing on the ceiling. Looking down at the street below—people walking, cars passing by, thin reflection of the sunset over the Hudson River.

Taking out my few belongings.

World moving in slow motion—shaking my head, I need to break out of this. Running in place, hitting the floor to knock out push-ups and sit-ups. Slight nervousness settling in my stomach again, we'll be all alone tonight.

Tiny bathroom, thank goodness there are towels here. Need to stop by the drug store on the way back here tonight: toothbrush, toothpaste, floss, deodorant and a nail clipper. Shiver hitting my body again—what was Cat thinking about private time? We said we'd wait, but should I get some condoms just in case? Just buying them, is that breaking what we promised?

Stepping into the shallow shower, lathering up with plain soap. Letting the water run down my body, down the drain at the bottom of the old fiberglass shower. Water, soap bubbles swirling around the drain. Laughing at how different this is from my daydreams about being alone in New York—no one knows I'm here, no one cares that I'm here. I am alone.

Drying off quickly. Room feels small, far away from home, like I've stepped into a different time.

Unpacking my duffle, changing into a little dressier shirt. Two days before I see my old friend Alton. Get some good boxing in tomorrow, rest on Sunday—be at his place when he gets home from school on Monday. Then what? Got to get a hold of Hector, see about work, start hitting the streets. Running through the numbers in my mind: if I lived here at fifty dollars a week, that's two hundred a month. I can find a cheaper place to live. Say I get a room for one fifty a month—likely won't be around here. What fifty a week for food? Got to buy clothes, figure out how to get some music. Bottom level construction should pay about eight bucks an hour: forty-hour week, two hundred forty before tax, figure I'll see one fifty in my pocket, six hundred a month. A little left to save.

How the hell am I going to have enough time to go to school?

What the hell am I going to do about college? Fucking Alton.

A creeping meanness forming as the numbers start to settle in.

Maybe restaurant work isn't a bad way to go—work at night, go to school during the day. Pay is shit, but I bet I could live cheap for a few years. What kind of life is that for Cat though? Looking at myself in the mirror, wave of frustration tightening my chest, fucking Alton.

Ducking quickly through the lobby. Out on the street, walking down Broadway in the cool night. Passing a brightly lit Lincoln Center. Wondering if that weirdo Renee is out chanting for people. What if I hadn't gotten so angry with her and just gotten her to eat a little bit?

Thirty minutes to kill before I call Cat. Give Hector a try.

Hustling up to get something to eat—wolfing down a couple of juicy slices of pizza at Ray's on Amsterdam and 74th. Walking up Broadway, the lights of the Beacon Theater illuminating the sidewalks, slight acid burn in my stomach. Looking up at the billboard, *Tommy* playing at seven-thirty. Looking back across Verdi Square, *Monty Python and the Holy Grail* playing at the Embassy Theatre. I'll go see that tomorrow—I need something to make me laugh.

"Hello, can I speak to Hector?"

"Hang on," it's his little brother, yelling for Hector in the background. Lots of sounds going on in the background, TV, people talking, music.

"Yo."

"Yo this, Fool."

A moment, "Frankie! Hey man, damn. Hold on," he covers the phone, but I hear him yelling for his little brother. "Hang it up when I tell you."

"Man, I ain't your secretary," in the distance.

"I'm a smack you good, Junior."

Background noise, Junior smacking the phone on the table to annoy us. Laughing to myself, that kid is going to be trouble.

"Hang it up," Hector yelling, click, the background noise drops.

"Man, I saw Leroy today, you fucked him up good, people calling Leroy fish lips 'n shit. That puto Thomas Jones, I chased him around a little to scare his ass some more. Fucking coach is mad as hell at you, man-oh-man. Leroy talking shit about how he's gonna get the police to get your ass. We started calling him fish lips at practice, he was so mad. People be tired of his shit, he started it and is whining now about getting his ass beat..."

"Hector, Hector, I got to make this quick. You know Julio's mom wouldn't let me crash there. I got a place, but I can't afford to stay here long. Can your pops find me a job?"

"Yo man, you came to the right place," his voice going up. "Anyway, my pops he likes you. I'll talk to him," he goes silent for a moment. "Yo man, don't be mad at Julio, he's taking it bad."

"I'm not mad, just disappointed."

"Yo man, Coach Valiero sat me and Julio down today and told us we go after Leroy or start up some shit then we are off the team and out of school."

"You guys need to keep it cool, it ain't going to help me if all three of our asses are out on the street," picture of my barren hotel room flashing in. "Man, I got to go. I'm gonna go play some ball down at the Riverside court in the afternoon. You guys come down."

"Okay, man," his voice drops off, "yo man, what's it like 'n all?"

"Hector, man," breathing slowly, to collect my thoughts. "It's weird not being connected, not being at home, I didn't think it would hit me this hard, but..."

"Come hang out over here, my pops, he likes you, man."

"Hector," taking a moment, "I really appreciate that, that's solid. Cat's got a babysitting gig you know, gonna go hang there for a while tonight, I'll catch you tomorrow, we'll talk... If your pops is good with it, staying there would be a life saver."

"Yo, Frankie," his voice rising, "you know I'm a stand-up guy for my boy. You can stay here anytime, fool."

"I really appreciate that, Hector, hey got to run, be cool fool."

"Later, Chump."

Dialing Richard's number. Ringing, counting to ten, nothing.

Checking my watch—time to walk some before calling Cat, need to work off some of this nervous energy, get lost in the streets for a while. Shallow breathing, thinking about her, about us alone. Shiver runs up my spine.

Chapter 11

Waiting for the light to change or a break in the traffic as dusk settles in on the busy corner of 79th and Broadway. Waves of people coming up from the subway, crossing the streets and going in and out of the shops along Broadway. The Woolworth at the corner bursting with people coming out of the store with shopping bags while others are pushing their way in. Why can't I shake this dogged feeling? What the hell is the matter with me? Walking slowly uptown, passing the Nut Shop—looking in at all the rows and rows of candies, dried fruit and nuts lining the walls.

Buying a couple of chunks of white chocolate that Cat likes. Looking at my face in the mirror of the store, some slight yellow left from my bruises, my dark southern Italian skin probably helps hide the reality underneath. Paying the nice little lady who runs the store. Back out in the street, coming up to 83rd Street, the theatre lights blinking and forming patterns. Poster for the movie *Shampoo* playing at seven, eight forty-five and ten-thirty.

Phone booth has a distinct odor of aged piss.

Coin dropping down in the phone, nothing. Working the coin release, smacking the side of the phone, nothing, Son of a bitch ate my dime. Crossing over to the west side of Broadway, give the open-air phones at the corner of 86th a try. Dialing the number she gave me.

"Hello," little thrill going through my body to hear her voice.

"*Hello my dark eyed beauty,*" in my best Spanish.

"*Oh you know if you talk to me like that you'll get into trouble.*"

"*I can use trouble like that,*" smiling at hearing her voice, she sounds more herself, "*is it safe to come over?*"

"*Make it thirty minutes so I can get this cute little boy to sleep, okay?*"

"*Sure my dear Catherine, thirty minutes.*"

Feeling lighter, the city looks less gray to me as I walk uptown along Broadway. Another thirty minutes to kill. Head down to 96th and stop in at the Rite Aid there, pick up things I need—quick smell of my arm pits, oh yeah, time for a pit stop. Walking downhill along Broadway toward 96th, checking out the Thalia Theater at 93rd between Broadway and West End. They always play cool old movies there, check it out, *Chinatown*, damn; I want to see that movie, if Cat can get out tomorrow or Sunday, we can go see it together. Thought of being with her in a dark movie theater—oh yeah.

Stepping into the brightly lit Rite Aid—aisles of more hair products than I can imagine exist stretching out into the distance. What do I need here besides, toothbrush, floss, toothpaste and some nasty Listerine? Old Spice deodorant—wow, they sell condoms right out in the open. Most places you still have to ask the guy at the counter and go through all the embarrassment of some old dude checking you out. Last time I bought some, what, it was for Richard cause he was too shy to go pick some up. Man, look at all these, brands; Ramses, Trojans, Four X... taking a couple of three packs of Trojans. Elderly lady walking by looking at me funny, feeling a little color come to my face. Walking quickly away from her watchful eyes. Waiting in line, looking around the store. Slowly rotating case of Timex watches, long counter stuffed with all kinds of lipstick and makeup compacts, an entire shelf of different types of film and batteries.

Unpacking my basket, the middle-aged Hispanic lady behind the counter looking at my purchases and ringing them up. Giving me a little smile when she rings up my condoms.

"You have a license for these?" not sure I heard her. You dope, Frank, she's playing with you. Giving her a little grin.

"If I didn't, would they get me for a moving violation?"

"Well, that depends on how well you move, Sugar," batting her long eyelashes at me. Ouch, paying, getting my change and getting the hell out. Feeling a little flushed, slight layer of sweat breaking out on my skin. Walking downtown.

Stopping dead in my tracks, held by the bright lights of the 96th Street Theater across the street, the *Man Who Would be King* playing there—I can see all these movies. Well, as long as I have money, I can go and do just about whatever I want. No school, no one to tell me when to get to bed or get up, what to eat, what I can or can't sit on. I'm free. I can read as many books as I want. Here I've been moping around, I'm free! Nagging feeling still inside me, mixed with a sense of how blind I'd been to my situation. All this freedom, if it weren't for that money thing.

Looking at the people walking toward me—seeing couples walking together, noticing their smiles, men and women in a hurry, wino at the corner asking for money; they've been shapes, shadows, seeing people for the first time in a couple of days.

Turning down 92nd, heading toward West End Ave. Lights of Broadway dropping off quickly, broken streetlights along here make this darker than normal. No way I'm letting Cat walk home by herself through this later. Feeling edgy in the dark street. Walking toward the lights of West End, traffic there, a few people out, a couple walking their dog, night air starting to cool down.

Stopping for a moment, unbuttoning my shirt and applying a couple of swipes of much needed deodorant—that smells a little better. Brush my teeth when I get there so she doesn't complain about my bad breath again.

Well cared for, clean three story brownstones line the street. Small planters surround the tree box cut outs in the pavement, fenced, flowers planted around them. Standing in front of the dark brownstone building at the address she gave me. She said to come down on the lower entrance—three steps down to the lower landing, thick wrought iron outer door. Bicycles locked up inside.

Ringing the doorbell. Waiting in the dark alcove, no foot traffic out on the street. So much quieter than my neighborhood, there would be music, people talking, yelling, cars honking away. The heavy door opening slowly, her pretty face coming around the side, her finger to her lips. Smiling at her. Thrill of the moment running up my body.

Following her down the hallway, surprised as I come into a room that's two stories tall. They've knocked out the middle of the first floor, left a walkway around the doors, but the middle is wide open. How cool.

Nicely furnished place, not sterile like our living room; it looks comfortable, lived in, a place for a family. Cat motioning me to come near her, "Let me check on little Daniel, wait here okay?" she puts her hand on my cheek, still carries the same worried look from the other day. Catching her hand, giving it a little kiss. She touches my lips with her fingers, gives me a momentary sad look and walks away.

Looking around the large living room—hallway to the right, walking over, there it is, bathroom down the hall.

Clean, bright bathroom, old style small octagonal tiles, large bathtub, mirrors on the wall and full-length mirror on the door. Walls painted a Café Bustello yellow.

Quickly breaking out my new kit—flossing, damn my gums are bleeding, spitting out. Dr. Stringer told me I needed to watch my gums and floss daily. Brushing slowly, going through the motions he showed me. Rinsing, foam with a little blood still in it. Moving my jaw around, its mostly recovered from the ass kicking I received.

Mixed emotions coming up thinking about Leroy; glad I beat his ass good, feeling I'd gone too far making him cry and humiliating him, wishing I'd beaten him harder. Looking at my dark eyes in the mirror, knowing that I'm still in the shit no matter how much I beat his ass. I'm the drop out and he's not. He's the big gun on the team and my ass is walking the street. Gripping the side of the sink and squeezing as hard as I can. I beat him, but I lost.

Stomach sick—I lost!

Tearing open the circular cardboard tube of the Listerine package.

Gargle for thirty seconds, oh man, is this stuff nasty.

Rinsing. Rinsing again, gargling, ah yuck.

Looking at my face in the mirror, only slight discoloration around my eye now as I lean closer in. Don't want to make any more eye contact with myself—I don't like the person I see.

Packing up my things, trash and all, I can throw that away on the way back to the hotel. Wave of anger, thanks Mom, thanks Dad. You know I fucked up, thanks for helping me through this you Fucks!

Breathing, washing my face, mad at myself now, cause here I've got time alone with my beautiful girl and all I can do is get mad.

Making my way back to the plush living room.

"Where have you been, silly?" she comes up to me, speaking quietly, hugging me, her face away from me though, nuzzled into my chest. Her touch, her smell penetrating me—the last few days drawing to a small point out in space, nothing here now, but her. Closing my eyes. Can't help my body reaction as my cock starts to swell up. Feels weird after having so little alive down below the last few days, so different from Frank the human tripod.

She moves her head back a little, her body still connected to mine at the waist. Reaching toward her with my right hand, moving her lustrous black hair from her face and sweeping it behind her ear. Lovely skin. Looking at her soft neck. Top button of her short collared white shirt closed, light pink cardigan sweater showing off the wonderful light coffee color of her skin. Body alive remembering what's underneath those prim and proper clothes— the line of her neck, her full breasts. Putting my hands on her hips, our bodies moving in an unconscious slow dance, her hands on my shoulders.

She stops for a moment, tilts her head in the direction she went before, her body stops moving with me. Leaning in, drawing her to me, kissing her neck, "You are going to be a good mom for our kids one of these days."

She draws back and looks at me. Finger to her lips again, takes my hand and walks to the large dark brown leather couch. Sitting down she gathers my hand into her chest, kicks off her loafers, carefully arranges her skirt over her knees and puts her head on my shoulders, her hair covering her face. She's quiet. My body going crazy, breathing in slowly and out slowly, dealing with the rush.

"What's going to happen to us, Frankie?" she asks in a low voice.

Her question cutting through me. Why now? Why bring all this up now?

The reality of the fight, Principal Riechert kicking me out of school, Dad kicking me out of the house rushing back. Feeling a gulf open up between us, image of me sitting alone in that small, dark hotel room with the bare walls flashing up. Urge to get up and go cause I know I can't go back to what I was just a few days ago. Skin feels cold.

Pulling my hand away, she doesn't let go.

"Talk to me, Frankie. You always have such good things to tell me. Talk to me," she's holding my hand a little tighter against her chest. Looking down at my thighs, her left hand on my jeans, her skirt covered knees resting against mine. Two weeks ago this would have been such a different scene, we'd both be out of out of most of our clothes by now.

Antsy feeling coming over me, like I need to get out into the night and run away from all this, run till I can't remember what it was like to be with her before all this. Maybe I should leave the city, get out where there's outdoor work, clean air, some place I can build a new life.

"Why won't you talk to me, baby? Is it something I've done?"

Images of Jack London's Alaska flooding in, hard living, hard work, clean living. What a man can do they can do, what they can't, they die for. Could I take it?

Noise coming from the other room, she sits up quickly, listens and gets up, walking quickly to the little sounds of sniffling that sound like they are breaking into crying.

Stretching back on the couch.

God, this is stupid. How do I end this? Should I end this? Head over to Julio's place and give his sister what for. Shivering at the thought of having sex with someone other than Cat after all the talk about what it would be like, why we should wait.

Clenching my fists hard, squeezing till my arms shake. Getting up, walking to the bathroom, taking a long drink of cold water—stomach feels empty. Drying my face in the mirror and not making eye contact with the person on the other side.

Quiet apartment. Hearing a door opening and closing, panic for a second. What if that's the front door? Seeing her come out of the little boy's room in her socks. She gathers her hair behind her head and puts an elastic band in her hair.

Sitting back next to me, sinking down in the couch, her feet out resting on the lightwood and glass coffee table, arms crossed against her chest.

"Do you want me to go?"

"You go and I'll scratch your eyes out," her fire coming back.

"What then, it's like waiting for someone to pass sentence on us."

"You," she gives me an elbow in the side.

"Hey," feeling a little lighter, she comes in for another and I grab it, pulling her across my lap. She's smiling but puts her hand over her mouth so I can't kiss her.

"I want to know if you still love me, Frankie. This is tearing me up so badly, I can't see you at school, after school. My dad and mom are giving me such a hard time, I have to lie to them."

"Like you never did before?"

"Hey shut-up, it's different now. They find out and it's curtains."

Looking at her as she sits up and moves next to me.

"Cat, Cat, Cat," brushing a strand of hair off her face, her full red lips and beautiful dark eyes. Lost in the millions of things I want to say. "I…" forcing it out, "it has been so, I don't know… Like something's been ripped out, torn up and thrown up in their air and it's just so hard to pick up the pieces and make sense of this all. Sometimes I'm so consumed by anger at my parents, then I feel free of all their bullshit and then I get so anxious about what's going to happen to us. It's hard to keep my head on straight sometimes, Cat. It's like this weird roller coaster ride."

"Oh, Frankie, I want to be there for you." Feeling her move closer to me on the couch, her arms wrapping around mine.

"I keep thinking I should wake up from this, but I know it's not a dream. Just can't believe how... Like a big pair of scissors came and started cutting all the things tying me to what I knew. It's like I'm floating, trying to hold onto things. Like I'm so far away from you and I can't do anything about it and it makes me so mad. I'm fighting against something dark and oppressive around me, thick, suffocating. I get so mad at people sometimes walking along in their stupid, safe little worlds. And to think I'm losing you, it's worse than any pain I could feel, Cat. To know you are out here and I can't see you, that I can't tell you how I feel."

Taking a deep breath, "You know sometimes it's the little things I miss, Cat. Sitting next to you in homeroom, watching you study, hearing you laugh when you mess with boys trying to get sweet with you. Sneaking in a kiss here and there," mind drifting back to images of us together at school. Smiling for a moment at a past I didn't know I could lose. Giving voice to the growing anguish in my chest, "I can't shake the feeling like I'm losing you."

"You're not losing me, Frankie!" she throws her arms around my neck, "I'm so worried about you out there by yourself. How could they do this to you? It's not right," her arms tight squeezing me. Holding her to me. Losing track of time.

Talking to her with my eyes closed, enveloped in the feeling of her, "Cat, just knowing you care keeps me together. I don't know what's coming next. All the things we talked about, college, being together away from our parents are like a big blur and I don't want that," seeing her face look at me. "Like they are on the other side of a deep canyon and I don't know how to reach them. I'm searching for a way to get across."

"Hold them, Frankie, feel me, they aren't far away. They are right here." Holding her, body feeling electric.

"I was so mad, still boiling from the big fight with my dad the night before. It was like all the hate I felt for him couldn't be bottled up. Leroy showed up and played his hand, I exploded. But it's like all this," can't bring myself to say the words; this has been coming for a long time. "And then there are moments like all this is just nothing but you, Cat. Times when I break through for a moment and it's like coming up from the deep, cold ocean and break out into the clear, open sea. I can see you, this wonderful, smart, beautiful vision and I feel ashamed that I can't do more, frustrated because there's so much that I know we can do together. But you're there and that's just... Like if it got knocked away, the rest of me would come crashing down."

Mind searching, free for a moment to tell her.

"Sometimes it's you calling me back from the darkness, baby, telling me a promise that things are better ahead. Like remember in class when we studied the Greek myths that the Gods would speak to people from different places. No matter how dark or how depressed I feel, there's this presence of you that helps keep me from falling deeper."

"I'm right here, baby," she takes my hand and puts it over her heart. "I love you so much, can you feel this?"

"I do, Cat," touching her face with the back of my hand, her eyes luminous. "I feel it when I'm away from you, lounging underneath those prim and proper clothes you wear," she swats at me. "Is it wrong to want to be nothing but that feeling? I can remember it, I can wish for it, but it's only alive when I'm with you and I'd do anything to hold it, to make it last, to cherish it," her eyes relaxing, "yes, I feel you my lovely Catherine, I love you with all my heart."

Lips coming together in frenzy, tongues, teeth, playful biting, both of us starting to laugh a little bit, moving my head back from her. She's starting to unbutton her shirt, three top buttons off, the thin gold chain with her cross dangling on her chest, the barest outline of her bra showing. She leans forward and takes off her sweater then looks at me, takes my hands and puts them on her breasts. Electricity racing through my skin, my body shivering in a deep recognition of what I feel when we're together. Arm around her, pulling her close, her hand on my thigh.

Just want to move with her body, unconscious rhythm, body feels like it's swelling as she moves against me, her breathing starts to quicken. Kissing her neck, the upper part of her chest. Unbuttoning the rest of her shirt, feeling her shiver when I reach my hand into her shirt to touch her stomach. Loving her reaction to my touch, like there's sweet rich nectar coming from her that I can taste. Her fingers working open the buttons on my shirt. Pulling her to me—closing my eyes and bathing myself in the feeling our bodies together.

Kissing her deeply, slowly moving down her neck, her body moving with mine. Kissing the tops of her full breasts, hands moving behind her back, trying to spread my fingers as far apart as I can, feel as much of her skin as I can.

She's pulling my shirt off my shoulders, taking her time to knead my muscles and look at my chest, moving back to get my arms out. She takes off her shirt and unhooks her bra, her eyes holding mine all the time. Body throbbing, cock so hard in my pants it hurts in the position it's stuck in. Trying to move my legs to ease the position, don't want to be digging around in there.

Reaching in with my finger tips to touch her nipples underneath her bra as she raises her arm above her head while she takes off her bra. Looking at my love, her eyes warm, seeing the fire I'd missed so much, entire body resonating with the moment. Pulling her to me so I can feel the full length of her against my skin. Her arms tight around my neck, her knee coming over my lap, her touch sends another wave of electricity down my spine.

Pulling her hair lightly, tiling her head back to kiss her neck, working my way down to run my tongue between her breasts, tasting her fresh salty skin, her nails running along my back. Taking my time to kiss, hold, taste every inch of her delicious body—stomach, back to her breasts, taking her nipples in my mouth knowing how excited she gets when I do this. It's such a turn on knowing I can make her come like this—amazing. Her body starting to move faster as I kiss, lick and suck harder, biting a little bit to play with her.

Her hand coming around to rest on my lap, slowly moving along the length of my penis through my pants, letting out a low moan. Letting my right hand move down her waist, across her thighs, her legs parting, reaching up underneath her wool skirt, touching, and caressing the soft skin of her legs. Taking the time to move my fingers slowly along each part of her legs. Giving her a firm, intense finger massage on the outside of her thigh, moving to a soft, gentle massage with my fingertips on the inside of her thigh where I know she's so sensitive.

Brushing against her panties with the back of my fingers. Feeling her delicious moist warmth radiating from her little rosebud. Imagining how wet and luscious her pussy will feel underneath those thin panties. Wave of need moving through me, pulling her to me, hands behind her back, can't think, can't distinguish anything other than the need to pull her close to me—deeply conscious of the force driving me to her. Bodies writhing on the couch together, moving my fingers up beneath her underwear, feeling her soft curly pubic hair, the outside lips of her pussy so warm, the wonderful smell of her coming up to me, her hand grasping my penis harder through my pants.

Reaching behind her to unfasten her skirt and then unzipping carefully. She's always a little resistant round this part. Taking her underwear down slowly, a discrete shyness comes in as I know she wants to turn down the lights—loving the moments I have to look at her body in wonder. Her eyes meeting mine then she looks at my body, her lips slightly parted, her quivering breasts, beautiful dark patch of pubic hair between her legs—she's so shy about this but loves it when I do it. Sitting her upright on the couch, kissing her breasts, her stomach, working my way down the thin downy line of hair that starts below her belly button. Feeling her body stiffen as I get near her pussy. Kissing the tops of her thighs, working my way in between her legs and she slowly surrenders and opens her legs a little at a time as I kiss and lick the soft inside of her thighs. Her legs opening up, the musky smell of her body filling me, doing everything I can to not rip my pants off and feel what must be wonderful—my cock going deep inside her.

We said we'd wait.

Licking the area where her thighs meet her pelvis, running my fingers over the outside of her wonderful little flower, using my thumb to come up to the area she likes me to circle around. Coming forward with my face, her hands on my shoulders resisting. I know she'll like this, moving forward.

Running my tongue along the full length of her, feeling and tasting the full wetness of her, my body excited, feeling the wetness of fluid leaking from my erect penis. Moving my tongue faster, deeper into her, moving past the thin outer layer of soft curly hair, loving the taste of her, loving how her body responds to this, her hips moving with me. No holding back, she's guiding me, moving me with her rhythm. Pushing my tongue deeper inside her now, then licking up the length to the secret spot she showed me, circling faster—running across the top with the tip of my tongue holding it as hard as I can for a moment then moving quickly again. Staying with her as she moves with me, the heat of her body radiating through me.

Her fingers gripping my hair and pulling as she starts to shiver.

"Oooooo," she's trying so hard to be quiet as her hips and thighs quiver and shake, "toooo, muuccchh, oooo," slowing down, moving my tongue ever so lightly across the top, moving down to reach up deep inside. Using my thumbs to caress the outside of her delicious pussy lips, spreading them so I can sink my tongue inside.

"That's so good, Frankie," she's pulling my head up, kissing me unashamed. "You make me want to cry sometimes, Frankie," as I slowly move my index finger inside, she feels so soft, so wet, so open. Gently kneading the soft flesh of her inner thigh with my left hand, bringing my index finger out and putting my middle finger and index finger inside, feeling her body arch up as I do that, her body taking a deep breath in. Furthest I've ever felt inside her. Moving my fingers in and out slowly. My other hand on her breast, circling the nipple, the area where they contact her chest. Feeling her body starting to shake and shiver as I move my fingers deeper, faster.

Feeling a slight pop as I sink my fingers deep inside, her body winces a little. Slowing down, bringing my head forward to lick her secret spot. Her body regaining the rhythm again, moving with me—brain feeling a wave of insane desire, pubic area moving along with the rhythm of her, needing to rip off my jeans and feel her skin on my lower body, feel my penis on the warm skin of her legs.

She's coming again, snapping my mind back to the present.

Her legs tightening around my hand as I use my thumb to massage her swollen secret spot, moving my head up to her chest kissing and sucking her breasts hard as she holds my head in her chest, slightly sweaty now.

"Oooooo, Frankie, oooooo", her body rock hard for a moment, breathing quickly, sweat is glistening between her breasts. Then she relaxes, her head falling back on the couch, breathing hard. Her hand on mine, "Oh, go slow. Oh you take such good care of me, baby," her body still quivering. Looking at her, bringing my hand slowly out of her.

She looks at me through the slits of her eyes; "Poppy's going to have to get that shotgun if this is how good it feels."

"You taste so good, baby."

"Ewww, don't talk too much like that. Hmm, it makes me feel so good though, too good, but I kinda feel like I'm being bad."

Smelling my fingers, the deep musky smell of her. Seeing that uptight prick of her father officiating and pontificating at their dinner table. Laughing at the thought of shaking his hand with his daughter's warm pussy smell still on my fingers. Moving up on the couch, pulling her near me, feeling her nakedness through my jean clad pubic. Kissing her shoulder.

"I think that was my virginity," she says with a mixed look of happiness, concern, something new on her face.

Sitting back surprised, concerned, "Did it hurt, are you okay?"

She slaps at me a little, "That felt so good, the way you take care of me. You're like so many different people. When you play basketball, you're so focused on the game, so aggressive taking it to the other team. The intensity on your face when you take down a big rebound or block a shot, it's thrilling, like I can feel how good that feels to you. When I've seen you box, you get that, I don't know, a naked look in your eyes and you push it. It's hard for me to watch sometimes; you know when you take the shots but keep going. I love that you don't give up. Then you're like this and you talk to me so beautiful," she closes her eyes and holds me to her. My testicles starting to feel so full they hurt. Moments locked in our embrace. Feeling the room slip away for a few moments.

"I wonder if we should do a little, you know, to feel what it's like," she says softly in my ear. The words traveling up and down my spine, head spinning a little.

"I thought you wanted to wait?" looking at her, hungry for her, hungry not to trash another thing in my life. Looking at the genuine feeling in her eyes.

"Frank, I know, but it's how I feel."

"Cat," looking at her, "I am so completely in love with you there's nothing more I want right now than to do it, but..."

"What, Frankie?"

"I can wait, Cat."

"I want you to be the first, Frank. I've always known that you'd be first. I don't care what happens after this. Maybe we have to grow up faster, do the things we want. I'll be eighteen next year."

Moving to talk "shh," from her, as she puts my fingers on her lips, she takes my hand and starts to kiss the palm, turns the outside and starts to kiss alongside the outside of my hand. Feeling her soft warm wet lips on my skin starts to make my head spin again. Leaning back on the couch, putting her hand on my pants moving it so she can feel how hard I am.

"Oooooo," she says slowly, "it's been a long time since I've seen him. I think we need to let him out." Moving her body to my side so she can unbuckle my belt, my breathing quickening as she pops the top rivet button and unzips my jeans, lifting my butt off the couch as she slides my jeans and underwear down. A little embarrassed at first, standing tall there.

She smiles at me, moves her leg across mine.

"I bet it would feel so good."

"I can't control myself, Cat. I'm ready to explode baby, we should use some protection," she shifts her body, wraps her leg around my thigh, puts her head into the area between my shoulder and neck, both her hands come up and surround my tall hard penis, my body shivering.

"Oh, you like that?"

"Yes, baby, the feeling of your skin on my body, your wet flower against my leg," she brings up one of her hands to her face, I can hear her quietly putting a big dollop of saliva in her hand, moving it slowly down to where she's holding me at the base of my rigid penis. The warm wetness of her, she starts to move both her hands up and down, moving to get them wet.

"Oh my God, Cat."

"Yeah, let me take care of you like you take care of me."

Feeling the soft skin of her breasts on my chest, her hot pussy working back and forth on my thigh, flexing my leg muscles with her. I can feel her start to get into the rhythm. Electric current running up and down my body, colors starting to appear in my vision. Violent spasms as I feel a deep orgasm coming out, she rotates across my thigh, pulls her body close to mine as I erupt in a volume of hot come, feeling her naked body next to mine, wet, warm as my body continues to throb and pulse, my penis against her flat stomach, wanting to slide deep inside her as she moves rapidly up and down my leg. Leg muscles starting to hurt a little at being tight for so long, feeling her nails start to dig in my chest. Her back arches.

"Oooooo, God, oh God, Cat."

"Yes," she's moving furiously against my thigh muscles, "oh yes, just a little, oooooo," her body rigid, her legs gripping mine for a few intense moments, then a wonderful peace descending on us.

She collapses on me.

"This is crazy, Frankie, why do we have to wait for all this?"

"After next year, we'll be in college somewhere, away from our parents. We could have this every night, just the thought of that, being with you. The freedom."

"Being with me how?"

"Together, but not like our parents. I don't know how they can live like they do, Cat. No laughter, everything has to be so controlled, you never talk about real things. I guess," looking at her, "living without shame about how we feel. Everything is so secret, so compartmentalized with Mom. Imagine what it would be like to live how we feel. I mean if we argue," she rolls her eyes and swats at me, "so what, to not be bound by all their bullshit guilt? I mean can you imagine being able to be like this when we want and not have to be ashamed of our bodies. To be able to have you, look at you. You're so beautiful, Cat, so rich," she looks at me, questioning. "It's like there's a huge well of care, generosity and passion in you coupled with a fierceness, a fire I see in your eyes. I can't tell you how much I love just watching you at times, all the faces of my little kitty Cat. And yes, some drive me crazy." She pinches me.

"What?"

"Oh, when you're in Queen Bee mode and the world's wrapped around your fingers, it's all you baby, the rest of us don't exist or when your mile-wide stubborn streak comes out."

"I'm stubborn? Look who's talking?"

She sits back and folds her arms.

"Yes, but I know there's this wonderful heart underneath all that. So pure, so kind, so crazy at times, I guess it's the genuineness, I mean, how do I say this?"

"Talk to me, Frankie, I love how you talk to me, how you make me feel. It's like I need your words to be there when you're away. I get this vision of you in my head sometimes and it's more than words or how you look, like all of them come together for this moment and my little body just tingles. I feel so warm, so loved."

"Oh Cat, there's nothing I can do but love you. Everything you are is the antithesis of the smallness and meanness I see in my family, in so many people and it just makes me see different things, inspires me to dream big about what we could do with our lives. And it's not like you're some ice princess, like Marcie, blonde and perfect. I think you are prettier than her, but there's so much more here, your fire, your poise..."

"What, Frankie?"

"Knowing that you need this too, Cat. Knowing that you are hungry for being with me. I can't tell you how crazy that makes me, how much I know I'd suffer if I didn't have these moments with you."

The leather couch feels sticky on my sweaty back. She's gently fondling my stiff penis, her leg rubbing against mine, her breasts on my shoulder, her eyes holding mine, living in the fire from her body.

She looks at me, "I love you for thinking of me and thinking about us, I love you for talking from your heart." She kisses my ear, my cheek. "I could feel how much you wanted to be near me, how much you wanted to take care of me," she feels down on her stomach. "Feels weird," touching herself with her finger tips, "babies from this," she brings her fingers up to her nose tentatively. "Smells different than I thought, good," my cock hard as ever. "We've always been so rushed, Frankie..."

"I got..." she looks over, "I got some... You know... Just in case."

She looks at me, "Let's get cleaned up, then show me."

Giggling as we walk into the bathroom, my cock wagging side to side.

"How much time do we have?" as she's washing off her stomach and chest with a wet washcloth, I'm rinsing my still erect penis, rinsing my stomach and then drying off.

"At least an hour, we shouldn't risk it more than that."

She's turned down the lights in the living room.

"So small," she looks at one of the oval packages. "Do you know what to do with these?"

"Not really," looking at the condom, "no instructions on the box."

She's laughing, her voice light—she's so much more comfortable when it's dark.

"I wish you weren't shy of the light, you have such a beautiful body, Catherine, my Latin beauty."

"Oh shh."

Ripping open the container, looking at the condom, small bubble on the end, slight oily feel, putting it on the top of my penis, looking at Cat, she's watching me intently.

"Doesn't seem to work this way," can't unroll down, flipping it over, new sensation as the close fitting latex unrolls over the length of me, the end coming an inch or so from the base of my penis.

"Feels weird," she reaches out and touches it.

"Softer and thinner than I thought. How does it feel now?" she tucks her hair back, slowly bends over and takes me lightly into her mouth.

"That feels so good, Cat, oh yes."

"Let's try it, Frank, I want to."

"You sure?"

"Yes," a distinct thrill running down my spine. This is the full commitment for my life, commitment for us all the things we've talked about. Hope bubbling up in my chest—the dark ravine, the voices that have been calling to me from the depths to come down and revel in the blackness receding in the light. The black gorge separating me from the things I hold dear filled with wide bridges and pathways rising up from the depths.

Her fingers surrounding me, trying to guide me, giggling after a few minutes of trying to find a good position and figure out how to make this work, pushing but things just not working.

Lifting her knees up, she's breathing hard. "Relax, baby, relax."

Minutes passing relaxing, exploring her body, circling and feeling her warmth, her wetness with the tip of my fingers, then the tip of my erection. Sliding my hand underneath her butt to position her body differently. Contact at the tip—shiver runs down my body, powerful currents stirring inside me. Moving the tip of my penis around the outside of her pussy.

"You feel so warm, it feels softer than I thought, Frankie."

Moving the head of my penis slowly in—a new world opening up for me. Heaven, absolute heaven, looking at her as I move inside, her eyes opening up wide in surprise, in wonder. Moving out so this isn't too much all at once and then slowly back in.

"Oh, oh," she's starting to pant a little, "oh, Frank."

"Do you want me to stop?"

"Oh no, no, no," she's shaking her head, her hands on my butt, pulling me. Moving with her, powerful forces gathering inside my body, feeling my lower body tighten. "I can't believe how sweet this is, how sweet you feel, how open, oh, Cat."

"Yes, baby, this feels so right, so right to be here with you," pushing in deeper, deep inrush of air into her lungs, "Oh my God."

Moving faster now, body stiffening, rush from deep down inside my body, body pulsing, penis engorging, pressure building, intense pleasure, almost too much, her hips moving with me, looking at her, eyes closed, biting her lower lip, her hands pushing down on the couch, pushing up into me.

"Oh, Cat. Oh, Cat," my body becoming centered on my cock, the exploding pleasure as I come in the condom, pushing deeply into her, holding her, putting my arms around her, deep kisses as she puts her arms around my neck.

"I'm so close, Frankie, so close."

So sensitive it hurts to keep moving, staying with her as best as I can, "Right there, little to the right." Moving faster now as the sensory overload lessens, "Yes, yes," she bites my shoulder, "oooooo," my body muffling her cry, feeling her pussy, her body tense up, shaking. Moments lost in time, ears sensitive to any noise.

Cat quivering underneath me, sweat of our bodies mixing, melding, can't get enough of her, still moving inside her—a switch has been thrown in me, insane energy that has to be with her. Kissing her deeply, then her neck and breasts. Tasting the sweat of her skin.

"Frank," coming back from a long ways away, "Frank," her voice sounding more urgent, blinking my eyes looking at her, "It might not be good to stay in too long."

"Okay," slipping out, still hard, condom filled with my come feels weird. Sitting up, have to touch her. "That was, I don't know how to say it, fantastic, so wonderful, so close to you, Cat."

"I know, baby," she kisses me, her arms around me. Sitting back, she's watching me as I slip off the used condom, then she reaches out and pokes it a little.

"Strange," she stands up, bringing her stomach close to my face, kissing her pubic hair. She moans as I move my head down to slip my tongue between her legs.

"We got to stop, this is crazy," feeling her pull back a little.

"Something went off in me, Cat."

"Me too, Frank, but I'm scared if we get caught like this, so good."

Taking a long deep breath, coming out of the haze, feeling her moving around. Following her to the bathroom, she's gathered all our clothes.

"I need to take a quick shower, my mom will know right away," she sounds nervous, "I feel so good, it's scary."

"Second thoughts?"

"No, no, no," kissing me, "I want to make sure we can do this again and again. I don't want to get caught and ruin this feeling."

Water running in the shower, wanting to go in and there and do it again. Not a total hard on now, feeling like another orgasm is just below the surface and wishing we could go right again.

"I feel like something's changed, different. So good," hearing her moving about in the shower. "You looked so, beautiful isn't even a word I could use to describe it. Like something new came in, something we didn't know about and it was wonderful. Your face, your body is just glowing with life, radiant. All the crap I heard in church about how this is the devil's work. My God, no wonder those jerks who've never had sex talk about love like that."

Opening the shower curtain to see her.

"Shh, what are you doing?"

"I want to see you every moment I can."

"Close that silly, I need a few minutes. Come on, Frankie," her face pleading. Closing the curtain.

"I'm so happy, baby. I feel like I want to hold all this inside and not let anyone know, just our little secret. No one to make fun of me, tell me I'm stupid for loving you, tell me this is wrong."

Ideas percolating inside, "Hey call your mom and ask if you can go over to Maria's to study, tell you've got a big report due next week. That will give you time to unwind, we could talk on the phone."

"That's a good idea," she says, hearing the wheels turning, "but you know you couldn't come over."

"I know, I know," putting on my clothes, not wanting to wash anything off my body. Smelling her on my fingers, closing my eyes. Looking at my watch. Crap. Picking up my brown paper bag, flushing the used rubber down the toilet.

"I'll go straighten out the living room."

It does smell like sex in here—opening the front windows set behind the heavy wrought iron bars, feeling like we pulled something over on the world. Folding the thin cloth blankets that were setup on the couch, putting the pillows back in place. Walking around, putting magazines back in place on the coffee table. The casualness of this place is harder to reconstruct than the perfection of our, well my parents, living room.

Getting Cat's books out, setting papers around the coffee table like she's been studying, she'll have a reason for gathering things up.

Cat coming out brushing her hair, she must have put on shower cap. A little make-up back on, all buttoned up, nice and fresh. Her face still has a wonderful glow, walking over, taking her hand and bringing it up to my lips, holding it for a few moments.

"I set your things up there so you could move around and collect them when the Hendy's get back."

"Okay," she looks shy, her eyes starting to tear up.

"What's the matter, Cat?"

"Oh, that was so good. To have to run away and be ashamed like this."

"No, we don't have to be ashamed of anything, this was for us."

She nods and takes a deep breath.

"I'm going to call my mom."

"I'll go, okay?"

"Okay, let me follow," bringing her into my arms, holding her like this was the last moment of our lives, striving to relive the open moments of rapture, timelessness I felt.

"Movies on Sunday? *Chinatown* is playing at the Thalia, you might get Maria and someone else from the neighborhood to go."

"Let me try, I'll call Maria. I'll let you know," she reaches out and touches my lips, her deep black eyes bringing a depth of sadness. "Go now, this is cutting it close, I'll see when they'll need me to baby sit again," weak smile on her face.

Touching her hand, letting go.

"Frank, call me at Maria's a little after ten, okay?"

"Sure," smiling at her, "I love you, Cat."

Turning and walking up the stone steps to the street, watching her nervously close the door. Heading toward Riverside Park away from their likely route home. Breaking into a run, wishing I had super powers so I could grab the world and shake it—shake away all the walls between us. Shake stupid old people out of the way, smash all the phony bullshit, smash the racist fucks who think they really know who people are, break through to where we can have each other when and where we want.

Running hard, carrying my pathetic things like a football.

Moments of heaven—falling back to a dark and lonely earth.

Bunch of drunk kids in their private school jackets trying to pick up a Volkswagen and put it on the curb yelling at me to come help them. Bums sprawled out by the Soldiers and Sailors monument at 89th Street asking me for money as I jog by. Following Riverside Drive downtown. Sprinting, trying to outrun the bad feelings trying to creep back inside. Missing her, missing her so much. Stopping, closing my eyes—furiously putting every thought I have into a picture I have of her, the look on her face the moment I first entered her—the amazement, the wonder. Hold it. Hold it.

Past 79th, past the basketball courts at 75th, up 72nd, Broadway starting to teem with swarms of people and traffic in constant motion. Breathing hard, slowing down to a walk and trying to ignore a wave of deep loneliness setting in. I'm a castaway bottle bobbing on top waves of people walking up and down 72nd Street. Stopping in Gray's Papaya—pushing through the crowd, people complaining, douche bag in a suit asking me what hell I think I'm doing.

"Large papaya to go."

"You mean the yellow container?" Longhaired, stoner white dude behind the counter points toward a stack of quart size containers.

Nodding, "Sure thing."

Paying and leaving as people are yelling at me, telling me how rude I am, animal and on... Fuck all of you.

Walking downtown, shoulders and feet feeling heavier, sweating. Not caring what's in the distance, moving so people stay away from me, thought of going to that empty room after being with her is disgusting. How different it would be if we were up there together. Wave of despair washes over imagining her beautiful face in a dirty dilapidated apartment, sorry Julio, like Julio's; wash hanging in the hallways, little food for the kids, my chest tightening, having trouble breathing at the thought that this is that the best I can do.

I have to change this. I have to break out of this somehow.

Sitting down in the thin slice of Dante Park across from Lincoln Center. Ironic, this is the right place for me after living for a few moments in heaven. Drinking my juice slowly, another good dinner.

People in evening clothes walking from the Metropolitan Opera, talking outside in the square near the fountain, swarms of taxis converging on the place looking to pick up fares.

Throwing the yellow plastic container in the trash, walking toward the fountain in Lincoln Center, ignoring the few "are you going to mug me" looks. Weaklings.

Lights from all the white marble buildings shining out into the emptying square, a few couples talking, busy sounds of the city fading into the night, sound of the fountain and light traffic along Broadway starting to dominate the soundscape. Resting my head in my hands. Looking at my watch, too early to call her if she got over to Maria's.

Boy has Maria got it rough.

Two families, two girls—one doesn't give a shit what she does as long as she doesn't rock the boat at home, the other has to control each and every thing she does. They need to have the perfect daughter. Stupid, stupid, stupid, everything Cat does isn't good enough? Can't they see what a gem she is? Brave, caring, smart, alive, then there's pretty little Maria who tries so hard to be like Cat and her drunken mom who doesn't give a shit.

Wishing we could put all these old farts on an island where they can sit in perfect little apartments and just live the dead lives they want. Let us young people have room to live what they've forgotten. I hate dead old people like Cat's dad. Creaky old fart. Laughing to myself at the Italian curse for a fart jockey—that's her dreary dad. Can guys like that even get a hard-on? Are their dicks so soft and flaccid that her uptight mom puts on rubber gloves and jerks him off for an hour or two? Bet he doesn't even have enough energy to shoot a good wad. Probably dribbles a little and then mumbles some banal bullshit to his fat little wife. How could those two desiccated cretins have such a vivacious, beautiful daughter?

"Well, Frankie boy, I think you've stumbled upon a living example of the word irony," getting up off the cold stone, walking toward Columbus where it turns into 9th Ave. Phone booths there, don't want to go back to that dreary hotel.

Body amped up. How the hell am I going to sleep?

Thoughts spilling over, I could drink beer and stay up all night. I could go watch porno movies. I could go beat the shit out of some weakling and take their money—make them scared. Shaking my head. I could go down to Washington Square Park and hang out till late. Next! How about finish off my business with Alton and get a fucking job!

Wondering if I can test out of the rest of my junior year? Phone booths open across the street, waiting for a break in the traffic and sprinting across.

"Hello Maria, hey did Cat make it over?"

"Not even a hello, geez..."

"Sorry, Maria. Hi how are you?"

She tsk's me over the phone, "Frank, is that you?" from the background. Maria saying something in the background as Cat takes the phone.

"Hey Cat, you made it."

"Oh gee, this was a good suggestion. It was so hard to look at the Hendy's in the face when they came home. They asked if I was okay, said my face looked flushed and all. Said I was feeling hot and opened the windows. They're all worried I'm coming down with something from the baby. I told them not to worry."

"It's good to hear your voice," in the background I hear Maria's little sister chanting, "Catherine's got a boyfriend, Catherine's got a boyfriend," Maria yelling at her. That should get their drunk of a mother all pissed off. Hearing a smack in the background, sound of crying.

"That little Louisa?"

"Oh the little angel, Maria just smacked her a good one, what's that? Wait a minute, Frankie," her hand goes over the phone. Cars, people passing me, need to get to a bathroom soon. I have all the freedom I want and I get to spend so little of it with her. Signal to drop in another nickel—dime goes down, the phone chimes out the little audio tones. Not much change in my pocket left.

"Sorry baby, Maria's mom is all pissed off, but she's kinda, well you know how she gets…"

"Cat, you want me to bring over a pizza or something? I know how her mom is. There's never any food there."

"No baby, that's sweet, but let's meet on Sunday at noon. Maria's going to invite Hector over, she still has the thing for him," smiling at the thought of that.

"That will be fun, we'll get to referee."

She's laughing.

"It's just a little while and I miss you so much, Cat."

"We'll be together soon. You be good okay? We're getting the evil eye, meet me," she hesitates, "no, they might see us there. Maybe we should go to a different place, downtown or go to the East Side you know."

"Good thinking, I'll see what's around. Talk to Maria, ask her what she wants to see."

"Okay," she's quiet, "I feel good, Frankie. I feel warm inside."

"Bout earlier, making love for the first time?"

"I freaked a little. The thought of them coming in on us like that, feeling so much, feeling so vulnerable. I didn't want anyone around us. I'm sorry I didn't even say good night…"

"Easy Cat, easy," taking a moment, "it's been tough for me too. Like we'd been some wonderful place that's far away from all the noise and confusion our parents serve up because they don't understand what it's like to be young anymore, those dried prunes. I feel like we found a clearing, a place that was clean, fresh and filled with wonder. And then here we are thrust right back into their bullshit," chest tightening up. "You're okay with what we did?"

She's quiet, I can hear her thinking, "I am, Frank I really am. I wish I wasn't so scared," heart rushing to my mouth, "I kind of," her voice trailing off.

"What's that, Cat?"

She's quiet. I can hear her softly breathing. Closing my eyes and letting the moment of my world opening up with her surround me, hold her there for a moment before we diffuse back into the jangled noisy city.

"I can come there right now. I won't let anyone hurt you!"

"Shh, I'll be okay and I know. I feel so safe with you, listen, I'm sorry."

Shaking my head, "I don't understand Cat, talk to me."

"I just panicked a little bit, I didn't think it would be like," abrupt, "Maria, get out!" sounds like a hand over the phone, rapid Spanish exchange, can't make out the words. "I'm back, you know how nosey Maria is. She wants to know everything."

"You told her?"

"Sure, I mean I need to talk to my friends."

"You were saying you didn't think it would be like this."

"Oh," she pauses, "I didn't think it would affect me, so much... So important you know and it hit me, and I'm not saying it was bad. No, something," buzzing of the phone line is the only sound, "like I found something there that's scared me for so long. I was scared I would like it too much and be, you know, bad. Like I want to fight it but it was welling up with so much feeling and there you were, so alive, so fresh. I felt carried away, like there was this magic fire coming out of you that was licking at me, painful, cause I wanted to cry but I didn't want you to think I was weak, but I was mad. I wanted to throw everything away and stay like that and... I was like losing my head and all so many crazy feelings hitting me. Dizzy almost in the freedom, but scared cause I was near the edge. Like it was so good, so much that I wanted to feel with you for so long."

She's quiet for a few moments.

"I felt torn, a little guilty for going crazy and giving myself to you, guilty for having this feel so good and then having to hide it from my parents. But something's changed in me, Frankie, and I'm not sure what it means. It's like I've crossed over something. I feel exposed, that if this didn't mean as much to you that it would cut me so deep. Tell me, Frankie. Tell me that you love me. Tell me we did the right thing. Tell me that you're thinking about me. Tell me that you need me."

Body passions raging, timbre of her voice changed, deeper, richer. Mind swirling in the deep memory of the moment when she had to let go and let our being together overwhelm all reason and ignite something inside of us.

"Catherine, Catherine, what I thought I knew about love changed today," closing my eyes, searching out the place I was in just a little while ago where I'm not afraid to let out my words unfiltered, uncolored by anger. "It changed from what a boy knows and what a young man learns entering in a sacred place with his love when he becomes lost in a completeness of being. A completeness that spoke to me, told me things I didn't know how to speak, but I was yearning for."

"What did it tell you, Frankie?" in a hushed voice.

"It told me about what it means to know death after finding such rapture, where every fiber in my body was reaching out to you in a storm of pain, passion, care, strength and reverence. Not that I long to test our love, but to know this feeling and then to know what could be lost. It would be like all the color and music were drained out of the world and we had to exist in a silent purgatory of easy virtue wasting our time living lies. Raising our hands to answer questions about dead people that won't make a difference in our lives... My God, we get graded on how well we understand Shakespeare, but know nothing about the passion he wrote from, we're asked to recite his words like some idiotic magical formula."

"Oh, Cat, I'm just lifted, inspired. These days have been," taking a deep breath, "confusing. I mean I've been raging about like a wounded bull. Tonight there was a moment that changed me, it was like I was released from the cold bonds of the deep and it was like being able to run my hands over the surface of a stormy ocean and it became calm. And in those calm moments you were there, your face in the glassy clear water. Your eyes were speaking to me through the depths, calm, not the siren song of death calling me back from the easy path of righteous anger. You told about a place of reverence, a place of birth, a place of deep searing need for love, a place I think I knew about, but had no idea how to get to. And there it was, out of the blue, it opened and we were there. Cat, there was an electric jolt that went through me. I still don't know how to talk about it, but it was like this is it, this is what I want, this is where we belong. I'm sorry if I'm going on like a drunken idiot."

"No, Frankie, oh baby, I wish you were here now so I could show you how I feel. You talking to me like this, it makes it so much easier to realize we did the right thing, being together like that."

Loud people yelling inanities about the Rangers game behind me. Ignoring the drunken assholes.

"To say I love you is easy, Cat, to say I need you, yes to all those. I don't know how to say it's more, but I can feel you trembling there on the phone. I can feel that deep well of passion inside you. I can feel how much you care about me. I'll always have that moment of love in your eyes when you looked at me when I was in you the first time and we moved together. And I know tomorrow I'll be raging on again because we just can't drop all this crap around us and go find some place that's ours alone. I'll be in a shitty little room at the Y and you'll be surrounded by people who want to tell you how to think and all, but there's a place that I can go now inside me where I can see you, where I can hold you that's all ours and God forgive the person who tries to come in and ruin that."

"Oh you make me feel this way and then," hearing her breathing in deeply, "I don't want to be afraid, Frankie, I don't want to be afraid that I'll lose this. Hearing you talk like this to me, it's like so many things. Like I'm a silly little girl bubbling with joy. Like when I was a young girl dreaming about you and waking up in the middle of a passionate dream realizing it's not a dream any more. Feeling you pulse through me, pull me, push me to a place where I'm not afraid to give myself to you." She's quiet now.

Imagining I'm holding her.

"It's like something has broken inside me too, Frankie, and I try to hold it back because I want to be swept away, but I know that if I am my people won't understand and they'll try to take it away from me. I want to be swept away, I want this so bad, Frankie," her voice changing tenor, charged. "Please, I know you, I know how you get sometimes. Like in school, I'd see the frustration building up when the teachers won't step down off their podium and really talk about things, how you go off in your mind. So much always turning around in your head and how it busts out by being bad or poking at people, playing with their arguments till they get enraged. You know, you scare people sometimes, you," her voice getting small, "you scare me, how you make me feel and all that I want for us, for us and then I don't know what you'll do."

Silence on the line, "I understand, Cat. Sometimes I don't know how to get the bad out of me. Maybe finding a different school is good. It's not like I can't figure out most of the shit they throw at us and then go memorize the rest, like that has anything to do with being smart," feeling awkward, feeling like I'm losing that place I was speaking from. "But that's not going where I want to go, Cat. I knew what I wanted before but I didn't have a clear vision of what it was and how to get there and what it was like when I was there. I see that now, Cat, and that vision surrounds you. I want to create that place for us, carve it out of rock, build it from the earth... shape it with our hands, our sweat. Something new rising from the turgid slime of all these dead people we have around us. Something just for us."

Nagging feeling—got to talk it out, "Cat?"

"Yes, my baby."

"I got to tell you something, it's not about us, its just been bothering me. We can talk about it later though or tomorrow. I don't want to ruin the moment."

"No, Frankie, you talk to me. There's nothing you can't say to me."

"Even how good your body tastes, hmm, I'm holding my fingers."

"You watch it, talking like that."

Laughing with her.

"Talk to me, Frankie."

"I still feel so betrayed by Alton. It's just burning me up inside."

"He didn't stand by you. I told you he was weak. He worships you, but he doesn't love you like Hector or Julio."

"I know, I know, Cat, but we were tight for so long and I stood up for the man. How can you do that to a friend? I mean, it makes me sick, I want to just," breathing in, pissed that I'm losing the mood we had. "I didn't want to bring this up, but I can't lie to you, Cat. I need you to know that I'll tell you how I feel."

"He's betrayed you, Frankie. He's been drafting you for so long and you're so loyal you didn't see it. I mean, he's your friend and all, but there's only so far he'll go. He's not like Hector who'd stand through anything, Julio wants to be like that, but he's still so young."

"I can't let this lie."

"I know he stabbed you in the back and for what? For that little becho Leroy who doesn't care who he has to step on as long as he's the star. So many people at school hate him for what he did, they are mad at you too for not..."

"I know, Cat. I let a lot of people down cause I was out of control," looking down at the dirty pavement. "This is a twelve round fight, baby. I lost the first round. I couldn't keep my cool. Many more to go, believe in me, Cat. I'm not going to give up."

"You give up and I'll, I'll…" passion ringing in her voice giving way to quiet, "listen I've got to go, Frankie. I'll figure out a way to see you Sunday and have to figure out how to get through my aunt's party tomorrow. Maybe there's a way I can, you know."

"What?"

"Your new place…"

"Oh God, I didn't think of that! Yes, it would be all ours."

"Sunday? We meet uptown and then…"

"Yes, yes, yes. I can't wait, baby."

"Me too. It's going be tough to sleep tonight remembering how hot and strong your love is, how you made me feel. You can be so tender sometimes and take me away like you're on fire. Oh…"

Smiling into the phone.

"I got to go, Frankie, I love you so much, baby."

"I love you, Cat."

Hanging up, feeling lighter—taking a deep clean breath that even the noxious exhaust of the bus driving down the street can't stain. Walking slowly, drifting along Broadway, looking through one of the square holes cut in the wooden fence so people can watch the construction project at 63rd. Smelling dirt, wet wood—walking across the damp, foot thick, square timber logs covering the excavation going on underneath the sidewalk. Deep foundation hole dug into the earth. Passing underneath a covered section of walkway and turning toward the old YMCA hotel, the block ahead is dark and empty, but I am filled with her light.

Window open in my room, thin curtains waving, then still.

Waking up thirsty, looking at the dimly glowing face of my dive watch, 3:30. Stretching, body feels empty, hungry and thirsty. Hunger will have to wait till morning: no food, no kitchen to wander into and open up the fridge stuffed with the good food Mom buys. Turning on the small light near the narrow bed, looking at the floor as roaches scurry to hide from the light, lovely.

The blank white walls of the room look old and gray under the light. A few lights on in the tall apartment building across the street. Eight blocks from home but miles away, right? I can never go back there. No, that's not true—I could go back, surrender and walk in like a puppy that's been beaten. I will not go back.

Walking into the bathroom, letting the water run for a few moments—making sure it's clear, turning it on hard to drive water down into my empty stomach. Washing up and catching a distant smell of her on my body and lingering in the images of her eyes and the remembered sensation of her fingers on my face.

Taking another deep drink of cool water and trying to quench the deep, deep hunger.

Light off in the bathroom, turning off the small light near the bed and laying sideways since the bed is not long enough for me, uncomfortable having my heels on the wooden foot board. Closing my eyes trying to recapture what it felt like earlier; what she smelled like, her words—that look of wonder in her eyes, the raw rapture in her body.

Drifting in and out of light sleep.

Waking to people banging around in the hall.

Someone's knocking at the door.

Ignoring them. If it were someone I knew, they'd be calling my name.

Chapter 12

Blinking my eyes, stretching in my tiny bed. Still tired, looking out my single window as the sun illuminates the cream-colored brick building across the street. Sitting up, noticing for the first time that someone had come in here and tossed through my stuff. Fuckers—lucky there's just my clothes and smelly boxing gear here, hope you took a big sniff of my jock strap you pricks. Getting up, looking at the door—no sign of forced entry, probably some asshole with a passkey. Remembering that senior Paul Deacon at school who used to steal keys to any place he could—elevators, janitor's room, supply rooms and classrooms. He used to brag how he would do it with his sophomore girlfriend in different places at school—loser, having to get it on young girls.

Gear together—there are good lockers down at the 14th St. Gym. Shaking my head at the thought that nasty, smelly place is safer than here. Finish packing my backpack—double check that I'm not leaving anything I don't want stolen. They've stolen my basketball—bastards.

Out on the cool street, sweats and sneakers, people passing by, construction crews busy—taxis honking, people yelling as trucks double park and then pull into the site, yup, what would morning be like in New York City without some choice tirades launched in reference to mothers, assholes and cocksuckers?

Taking off toward the tall trees of Central Park, the flowering trees, apple, cherry and magnolia just starting to bloom. Moving at a slow jog, stretching out my pace—heading downtown toward 59th Street. I'll take the subway to 22nd and head over to Johnny's Diner for breakfast. Nice big plates of food for the money there.

Walking down long, grimy, white tiled halls to the train station. Cool down here, a few people hanging around, loose sheets of newspaper floating around the tracks, looking off in the distance for the train.

Subway car is unusually empty, couple of young white guys on the train look like they're getting home from a helluva party. Standing up by the far door on the local.

Crowded at Johnny's this morning. Mostly working people.

Wedging into a seat at the counter.

"You want coffee, honey?"

"Sure," I'll have to learn to like this crap if I'm going to be a workingman.

"You know what you want?" She's giving me the aged to perfection I'm wasting her time look.

"Three eggs scrambled, sausage, potatoes, whole wheat toast."

"The Special."

"Me or the breakfast?"

"Like I need humor, you see me laughing?" shrugging my shoulders as she slaps the counter and trundles off. Looking over at the guy next to me who's eating runny, sunny side up eggs. He's dipping toast into the nasty yellow centers, streaks of yellow in his bushy mustache, body does a slight shiver—runny eggs are disgusting. Remembering how my sister Vicky would chase me around the kitchen with her horrid concoction of toast strips dipped in soft-boiled egg yolk, nasty, nasty, nasty.

Waitress slams my cup down and does a quick fill.

"Anything else wise to say?"

"Thank you, Ma'am," she harrumphs like a fat sea lion burping after a meal of raw fish before she goes off to spread her love to the other customers crowding around the noisy counter. Time for coffee medium, two sugars and some cream, only way this stuff is drinkable. Stirring, drifting off for a moment, body aching to be with Catherine again.

Mind filled with the images of last night.

Warm coffee feels good in my stomach, noise of Johnny's starting to come back to the present, people talking loudly, waitresses yelling to the kitchen behind the well-worn counter, trays of dishes being slammed around. Looking down the counter, mostly men here—guys with ConEd uniforms, sanitation workers, a couple others from the Port Authority.

Stomach twisted in hunger. Salivating at the thought of food.

Breakfast arriving with a slam on the counter—a big oblong white ceramic plate sitting before me, no sign of aftershocks. The waitress is on to her next bombing run before I can say thank you. Shrugging my shoulder, putting some pepper and Tabasco sauce on my eggs. Fighting the urge to eat quickly—this is going to have to last for most of the day, make it count, Frank.

Chewing slowly, deliberately.

Mind drifting back to the food Mom keeps stocked at home; refrigerator is always full, tons of pasta, sauces, herbs, good fresh mozzarella, olives. There's the fresh bread—I could eat and eat...

Walking cross-town through the morning rush of noise. Still morning air filled with car exhaust, people in a hurry. Full belly—a good long shit at the diner, life is good. Laughing to myself at the guy in the stall next to me calling out about a courtesy flush, like all of us shit roses—moron.

Easy pace up 14th Street, walking by a newsstand—headline in the New York Times is all about an investigation into high oil prices. Need to head to the library later after a good workout, find some good stuff to read.

Sitting in the open space of Union Square Park, time to let breakfast digest before getting into the Gym and throw it back up. Eyes moving along the night shift of drunks, bums, hookers and street kids who've been out looking for easy prey as the shift changes over to a different set of bums, drunks, hookers and street kids. I wonder if they had a time clock down here? How would the union shop steward manage overtime and infractions?

Laughing to myself, envisioning some big fat guy working the time clock, yelling at the crowd. "Hey, Missey, you only did three johns last night, you're behind schedule. Larry, snap-too, you're falling down on the freakin job, you only drank two bottles of MD 20-20 last night and puked once, you only annoyed the hell out of two groups of teenagers. Hello in there, get with it, you're under quota! And you—new girl Milley, hey you, what's this about you not wanting to give bennies in the park? It's a free country, some asswipe from Jersey wants a blowjob you give him a blowjob, that's your job. Jesus, I got a business to run here..."

Ah, the life of genius at leisure.

Walking up the creaky wooden stairs to the gym—sounds of guys working out filtering down toward the street. Should be a light crowd this morning, Gus won't be here for a while, that give me some time to get loose. Got to come clean with him, he won't stand guys who aren't straight up—doesn't matter who you are. Most of the pros will be here later today. Guys who are fighting tonight will be resting. Nodding, stacking fists with some of the older guys I know in here as I pass through to the locker room.

Welcome sounds of speed bags slapping against the drum, guys skipping rope, working the heavy bags, grunting and talking trash. The gym hangers-on checking out the fighters, bullshitting about upcoming matches and settling in for a long day in the thick humid smell of men working hard and sweating.

"Yo, Alex," as he takes a break from working a heavy bag, he nods back. Man that guy is in shape—he goes pro soon. He's always working it. Gus says that he's gonna be a great lightweight.

Into the locker room, familiar smell of years of gallons upon gallons of sweat built up in a place that never dries, pine cleaner and mildew. Stripping off my sweats, a couple of guys I don't know suiting up. Changing into my thin over ankle height training shoes, plain gray sweatshirt, bag gloves on, leather jump rope. Energy level picking up—feels good to be here. Time to lose myself.

Finding an open place to train in the main gym.

Couple of guys in the main ring I don't know going at it.

Start slowly with my rope, single skips—work up a good sweat, work into double skips, cross rope, cross back, work my left leg, work my right leg then switch. Getting my head into a place where I can train for hours.

Blood moving, guys laughing, talking about women, more of the old guys who hang around the gym starting to show up and taking their usual places in the high chairs surrounding the sparring rings. Ex-boxers, bookies, people with nothing else to do who love the game. Well that's what Gus says, they just a bunch of faces to me. Every once in a while some of the slimy ones try to get conversations going—Gus always shuts them down or has his boys chuck them out.

Walking over to an open heavy bag, pictures on the walls of different fighters; white, black, Hispanic, Filipino, Korean… Gus doesn't care. If you can fight or you love the sport, you've got a place here.

Moving my body, shadow boxing to get loose.
Got to be warm before going full power.
Maybe this is where I belong, a place I feel at home.

Punches have good pop this morning. Getting into the groove, letting the last week out on the bag. The fights with Dad giving me extra energy—Leroy, Alton, seeing their faces and letting it burn. Vague sensation of guys I know talking as I hit the bag.

Mind blank. Getting to that serious place—connecting to frustration, hate, joy, freedom. Power punches flowing, punching Leroy's ugly face. Chest energy picking up, connected, power coming up from my legs, my back. Big body blows. Smacking my father's angry face for each, "You're a loser!" "You're a disgrace, a bum," hard punch. Each, "Big man hanging around with his nigger and spic friends, loser that's what you all are," gets a round house with intent to do damage.

I'm alone now. Energy welling up, big right hand makes good contact, leaving the heavy bag shivering. Stepping back, feeling good, body pulsing, timing feels good, muscle burn.

"Damn BUB," said Bowtee. "You gonna have to buy Gus a new bag," he's laughing and pointing at me.

New guy next to him, "What's BUB?"

Bowtee looks at him, Hernando and him slap five "Big Ugly White Boy, fool," he shrugs his shoulders and walks back to his speed bag. Few people fuck with Bowtee, including me. He's got some serious shit.

"Hernando, what's happening man?"

"Not too much, Frankie, how you feeling?"

"I'm good man, how are you feeling?"

"Hey kid, you wanna make a little money sparring with my heavyweight over there?" coming from behind me. Turning to the voice. Muscular brother in the ring working with a partner I don't know, looking at the guy—dark skin, Spanish accent. Gus won't like this, but hell, he's not here now. If I get in a few rounds, no one will care.

"How much?"

"Ten bucks."

"Sheeiit, ten bucks a round is the going rate for anybody good."

"Young buck like you, you got to learn, got to pay your dues."

"What's your name, man?"

"Panama."

"Okay then, Panama, no thanks."

Warming up getting ready to go back at the heavy bag.

"Twenty-five, you got to go three rounds."

Turning around, that's food for a few days.

Looking at him, guy seems slimy trying to work me. His eyelids thin like he's checking me out. "Show me."

He fishes out a twenty and a five, hands it over.

Putting it into my jock.

"Yo Nando, can you tape my hands man?"

He looks at me and the guy in the ring, "Gus ain't gonna like this, Frankie."

"I need the money, Nando, things ain't good." He gives me a slow understanding nod. He must recognize the desperation. Giving him a five for the tape job. He brightens up. Guys gathering by the ring, people starting to talk, point. Fuckers are betting already. Nando starting to work my hands, feeling my body energy change, focus changing, flip the switch.

Nando looks at me, "Hey there, easy now. Sparring, right?"

"Yo, Panama," calls out Bowtee, "best have your boy be careful in there, the kids got some shit!" He shrugs his shoulders when Panama waves him off like he's talking crazy. Letting the people in the gym over talking to Panama and his man fade into the background.

I've got two inches on the guy, but he looks strong, good muscle definition, looks fast. Energy in my chest rising, loving the feeling, slipping on the fourteen ounce gloves that Nando holds out. My opponents smiling, laughing—no mistaking his eyes, he's looking to beat the shit out of the chump white boy—fuck him!

"Yo, Baby White Boy, you ready," he yells, his corner man slapping his gloves like this is some big joke. Anger starting to burn inside watching him prance around like some wanna be Ali who ain't even close to Ali.

Guys over by the side talking, Terry walking away yelling at Panama, "Well I told you, man," getting waved away like he's an idiot. Terry walking off shrugging his shoulders and slapping five with Bowtee as they settle in around the ring to watch. Bowtee giving me a nod and a hard look, letting my eyes tell the story—time to let this motherfucker have it. I may not win, but I'm going to show up. Bowtee nods back, he knows what it's like to be in the zone. This motherfucker's gonna feel some bad intent.

"Watch this puto's elbows, man," as Nando puts on my headgear, checks the fit, "I'll be right here," as he checks my gloves and puts my mouth guard in. Nando walks over to the other guy—he's got a serious set to his body. Nando is a lightweight, but he's got a nobody's-gonna-fuck-with-me vibe. Mr. Wanna-be-Ali looks pissed when Nando checks his gloves.

Nando winks at me as he leaves the ring.

Moving to stay warm, dead calm inside, looking at my man, feeling the rhythm, keeping the power waves in my chest, waiting for the release. Breathing steady.

"Let's move it, come on," yells Panama. Bell ringing.

Coming into the center, guy trying to start with some bullshit dancing, looking at me like I'm a monkey. Moving, circling, keeping my feet, feeling him out. Snapping off a couple of quick jabs, fake coming in and stepping back when he tries to throw some weak shit, counter punch with good left to his head.

"Shit, Panama," the guy says over his mouth guard, "we got a white boy who thinks he can box," he gets down, flurry of quick jabs and combinations coming my way. Taking most with my gloves and arms, staying inside the circle, not backing up, coming in with hard shots to his body—he pushes me off after a hard right to his body and starts some more dancing baiting.

"Yeah, we got some spirit here!" he comes in fast, right connects, he dances back from counter, then comes in, quick combo, hard shots, shrugging off most of it. Moving left, two good hard jabs snap his head back. Moving left then right, he's starting to crouch a little and come up with big punches, stiff jabs snap him back. Sliding my head in as a big right comes steaming in, fucker's head hunting.

"What's the matter, Baby White Boy, thought you like to mix it up?" he's moving his head and body side to side, looking to set me up. Jab, big right to his head, he pushes off and back pedals jabbing away, laughing as he throws a flurry of quick punches trying to get me off balance so he can head hunt, working to measure his rhythm, get the timing.

Power punch just misses as he slips to the side.

"That's right, that's what I'm talking about," he waves—come on.

Chest, body throbbing with energy, the bad inner things starting to bleed out, my father's fists, the taunts, the arguments, the beatings. Fake a jab, slip left, massive left hook to the side of his head as I eat a strong left jab. He steps back a little stunned, his eyes narrow—coming in fast, body punches, tying him up. Trading rabbit punches, anger welling up as he tries to head butt—shoving him back.

Watching his head move, getting the timing down.

"Got him mad now, Pana..." connecting with a big left hook to his liver, his body stiffens and he stands straight up his eyes wide open, getting all my body power behind a big right to his head, timing his movement, connecting, his body crumbling back against the ropes, his eyes fluttering. Left, right combinations to his body, his arm caught on the rope, hearing guys yelling off in the distance, big right causes his body to slump and fall to the floor, people pulling me back, turning on them, Nando getting right in my face—yelling. Shoving me back. Pushing to get to that fucking clown.

"Enough, Jesus Christ, Frank."

Shaking my head, stepping back, looking around, conscious of breathing again. Bowtee yelling at Panama while he takes his man's head gear off, their trainer coming in, looking evil at me, "I told your dumb ass, I told you that boy had some shit! Do that bullshit try to be Ali shit in here, sheeiit."

"WHAT THE FUCK IS GOING ON IN MY GYM!" Stomach falling, Gus's voice ringing through the whole gym. Guys on the tall chairs exchanging money, one of the regulars who have seen me work is laughing while he collects money from another man.

Gus climbs in the ring followed by his guys; Tony and Maurice, furious look on his face. He's the only man I've seen take on my Uncle Vin and not back down.

"I know you," he looks at Panama getting his guy onto the stool, smelling salts bringing him back. "I don't like you," he points to Maurice, all six-four, solid muscle of Maurice. "Get that piece of shit out of my gym."

"Yo, Nando," said Maurice, "give me a hand."

Hernando's dark eyes clouding over, nasty smile on his face. Maurice may be past his prime, nobody but nobody fucks with him. He knocks motherfuckers out. Imagine even Bowtee would think twice before fucking with Maurice.

"You heard the man," said Nando. Panama and his trainer are looking worried and hustle to get their man out of the ring, one arm around each of their shoulders.

"You!" Gus pointing at me, his baldhead turning red with anger, "I want to see you in my office. Now!" he goes storming out of the ring.

Alone—catching my breath, feeling sweat drip down my body. Tony coming over, "I get that off ya, you get ya ass to Gus, ya hear," his Louisiana accent coming through. Nodding my head, no escaping now.

Knocking on Gus' office door.

"Get the fuck in here!"

His desk is a total mess, papers, flyers, stat sheets all over the place. Walls covered with photographs of him with hundreds of boxers, some he's trained and some he's mentored. Champions, contenders, some of the best, and there's Gus smiling, intense.

"What the fuck do you think you're doing, getting in there with a bum like that? Take the chance that idiot would cut you bad? For someone who's supposed to be a smart kid," he takes a deep breath, takes the smoldering cigar in the ashtray, sticks it in the side of his mouth and takes a couple of puffs. "Out with it, you know my rules."

"Gus..."

"What the fuck is wrong with you? I'm getting aggravated here!"

"I fucked up. Got kicked out of school, got kicked out of the house, I needed..."

His big bloodshot eyes getting big, "What?"

"I fucked up Gus, I got nothing… I messed up bad."

He sits back in his creaky wooden chair, hands behind his head.

"How long?"

"Three days now."

"And you waited this long to get here!" he's getting really mad. "What the fuck is wrong inside that thick guinea head of yours? You wait this long to tell me?" he chomps on his cigar. "You sleeping on the street, tell me you're not stupid enough to sleep on the street, tell me you're not that fucking stupid?"

"No, Gus… I was ashamed," looking down at my taped hands, sweat running down my body. "I got some money saved, I got a room a the Y till I can figure out what to do, I know, I've got to come clean here."

"Your uncle knows about this?"

"I don't know Gus, I don't know," taking a moment to try and get my act together under his glare, "he'll side with my pops no matter what. I couldn't take what he was saying anymore. I'm not going back, I can work and I can…" Gus holds up his hand, takes a deep breath, swivels in his chair for a moment.

"Don't get a big head. You're lucky that guy took you lightly, you would've tagged him eventually, but had he been more careful, he would 'a worked you hard. You got that mean explosiveness in you though, can't teach that."

"He let me time him, Gus, like you said, it wasn't where he was, it was where he was going to be," bemused look on Gus' face, "he was trying to head hunt."

"That's why he's a shit boxer who fights for a shit manager who makes him throw shit fights and be a bum. He's a bum because he doesn't put in the time to learn the craft. You want to be like that?" Shaking my head. "You got a long way to go, you got the raw talent. Don't know if you've got the heart to be a Champ, or the brain. You remember why you lost your tournament fight?"

Face coloring up, "Couldn't keep my cool, got points taken away."

"That kids going to the Olympics, he'll be a force to be reckoned with. A year older than you kid, but years ahead as a boxer. Now I don't know if you would have won even without the penalties, it was damn close, but I guarantee you, you work to channel that rage you got, work your skills, learn to keep cool under pressure and you got a chance to be in there with the best!" he looks at me. "You hear what I'm saying kid?"

"I do, Gus, I do, its. It's just…"

"Hey dumbass, of course it's hard. That's why only a few become champions. Ali may talk a lot of trash, but that's to promote, he's bigger than life. The man has phenomenal tools and he works it, he trains hard, he's always learning," he sits back, more to himself as he looks at a picture of him and others with a young Cassius Clay. "I hope he doesn't start to believe his own bullshit, with his style," shaking his head, "he'll get hurt bad, real bad."

"Anyway, back to this hard headed idiot sitting across from me," swinging around and looking at me. "If you don't have the heart to make it I'll tell you, you hear? You look like you gonna get long term hurt, I stop managing you. I told you, you could make easy money, promoters looking for a quick buck, get a big good looking white kid, Italian at that. Get you punched out in a few years, might have a few bucks in the bank, damaged noggin and all. You go the easy way and we are done, you hear? That's not how I run things."

Nodding, "Yes, Gus. I know that's not what I want."

Sounds of the gym coming back to life in the background—speed bag, ropes, guys talking loud, laughing, cursing, talking trash. Looking at the pictures on his wall.

"So, what are you gonna do?"

"I don't know. I got money saved from summer construction. Not gonna last long though. I had no idea how expensive things are..." shame filling me, "I'll get a job though, get back to school and all."

He's silent.

"You got two years, two years at least before you're ready to go pro with me, maybe longer. You got to dedicate yourself to the sport, to the art, put any fast money out of your mind. You go around me, we are done."

"I know, Gus, I'm sorry. Just twenty-five bucks for a few rounds of sparring, that's three or four days of food."

"Hmm," he's tapping his fingers on this desk.

"Summer's coming up, probably find you a place to work up in Catskills, get you training full time with Morty and his guys. Probably three or four quality amateur fights up there, make sure you don't take anyone's head off. Your uncle's gonna be the tough one, he says no," he looks at me hard, pointing at my chest, "we are done, you hear?"

"They don't give a damn about me," emotion rising up in my chest.

"Don't kid yourself. Your dad's a hard man, but I seen this before... Both of you damn eyetalians!" He takes a puff of his cigar.

"How you thinking of making money?"

"Get a job doing what I know, work construction."

"That's no good for you if you're gonna be a pro in a couple of years. I'll find something for you. How far you pay for the Y?"

"Through next Friday."

"Get your ass down here, I got a lady who can put you up over in Brooklyn Heights. Keep your ass in the gym regularly and we'll see what we can make out of you. You want that?" he rolls his eyes, looks up at the ceiling, "here I am running a fucking social service for thick headed guineas," he stops for a moment. "Next year you finish your high school, you got me? You study, you train harder than any opponent you face," he looks mad again.

"Well?"

"How will I pay my way, Gus?"

"You work hard here, you learn your skill, you mature, and you show me you got what it takes to develop into a champion. When, and if, you go pro, you go under my contract. You can't sign it now, next year," his hard eyes boring into me, "you want that?"

"Yes, Gus, yes!" relief, anticipation, anxiety gripping me, what's Dad gonna do? Mind flashing back—him and all my uncles cheering me on in the ring. Uncle Vin still does, what the fuck happened to my dad? Calls these guys bums and crooks. Not Gus, he puts me up, takes care of me, he should get a cut. Right? But what does it mean? It means fighting with my hands. It means freedom from those bastards—good fights, good money and time with Cat.

"Get the hell out of here, finish your work out," getting up. "I catch you sparring with a bum again and you are out. I invest my time, you go by my rules, now get the hell out of here, I got a business to run."

"Thanks. Thanks, Gus. I mean…"

"Awww," he picks up the phone and waves me out, "get the fuck out of here!" loud so people in the gym can hear him.

Drinking a large Orange Julius at the corner of 14th.

Body feels good, calm settling in after my long work out.

Looking at my hands—make money with these? Feels good to have a few extra bucks in my pocket. Dwelling on the fight business. There's a big drop off between the guys that make real money and the rest. Even the guys that make any good money, there's an even bigger drop off between the top three or four.

Can I be one of them? Defense, quickness, willing to take the pain, willing to take the punishment for as long as I have to—power is not enough. Mind drifting along the greats; Sugar Ray's numbers are mind-boggling, one hundred and seventy-four fights, Marciano going undefeated.

Would Cat be with me if I were a pro? My face isn't gonna look too pretty at times. Taking a slow sip of my drink, people looking at me in the shop in my sweat soaked sweatshirt and pants. Imagine earning five to ten thousand a fight after a few years. Starting to run the numbers in my head— how many fights can you really do and not get punched out? Five or six short rounders a year? That works out to sixty grand tops, before all the fees. Say I get half that, at two thousand work hours a year that's fifteen bucks an hour. Not much, but not bad. Imagine getting up to the next level… Imagine earning a hundred grand a year in the ring.

Gus has a stable of fighters, one or two of us make it big he wins, the rest average or better probably cover his costs. Letting my imagination dwell on being in mountains, clean air, fishing, hunting again, time to train with good people. Cat would be so far away, but I could take a bus back to see her. Hell, she'll be away at summer camp anyway. Then when she's in college, we'll be free, I'll have money.

Shiver thinking of her far away, reality of what we did last night. Determined to figure out how I could take care of her in college. Maybe we trade off, I box for a few years, get my butt back in school. Uncomfortable image flashing up in my mind—shut it out; image of some of the old guys at the gym, cauliflower ears, massive scar tissue around their eyebrows, slow thinking, they've been hit too many times and couldn't afford not to fight. Rocking back and forth as the Express drives along underground, sweat drying, stink rising, people staying away from me on the crowded train.

Lying down in my bed after a long shower.

Naked, looking at my toes, the curly pubic hair down by my groin, flat hard stomach muscles from hundreds and hundreds of sit ups. Strong core muscles to take the hard body shots.

Lonely in the quiet of the hotel, mind drifting—no matter how much I can take in the ring, I couldn't take Leroy's shots though could I? I couldn't walk away, and nothing's going to change the fact that he won. Alton you fucking bastard, you really helped me out. Cat's words about Alton running through my mind and it doesn't matter that Cat and Alton never really got along. We were tight, we were a team—you can't be friends for five years and then sit on the sideline.

Drifting off into a light sleep.

Hunger taking over. Carnegie Deli, then the big bookstore on 57th and Broadway. I get to see her tomorrow. Monday Alton, Tuesday, get my stuff from school, go check in with Gus, get setup in Brooklyn Heights—easy run from there across the bridge to the gym. Good places to eat. Away from Mom and Dad—which is good, closer to my uncle—bad. Hell, he's got bigger things to worry about than me. Fuck if he cares anyway.

Long afternoon stretching into night.

Tired, but not tired.

Don't want to read.

Looking out the window of my tiny room.

Frustration burning in my stomach; how am I going to take care of her?

Chapter 13

Hanging out in front of the Great Eastern Chinese Restaurant at 103rd and Broadway—Cat, Maria, Louisa and Hector will be here soon. Light traffic on Broadway, calmer weekend people moving at only 90 miles an hour. Feels good to have a little money in my pocket, to be able to take care of them. Drunk passing by starting to talk some shit about helping him get back on his feet—right, all the way to the liquor store at the corner.

"I got nothing for you."

"Come on man, help me."

"No. You want me to bullshit you, or you want me to tell you the truth?"

He gives me the finger through a finger-less gloved hand. Ignoring him as I see the girls coming up Broadway. Big hug from Cat, she looks both ways and then gives me a kiss. Maria looking on, her arms crossed, her little sister Louisa pouting.

Quietly to her, "How'd your mom let you out of the house like that?"

"I snuck out," she's laughing, in her tight T-shirt, sweater around her waist, "and I can wear this later."

"I'm hungry," says Maria's little sister.

"Hey, let's go upstairs and eat."

"I don't like Chinese food," as Louisa stamps her foot.

Kneeling down in front of the little pistol.

"What don't you like? This place is good, there's all kinds of stuff."

"Sick of just rice, blah!" she sticks out her tongue at me.

"Oh, there's more than that here. You like sweet? They make a nice sweet and sour dish, lots of chicken, pineapple all kinds of stuff. How about that?"

She crosses her arms, wary.

"Hmm, okay. I'm not staying if I don't like it."

"Deal," reaching forward to shake hands with her.

"Come on shake," her little hand comes near mine, I start moving my body back and forth, "come on, shake," she starts shaking too, smiling and giggling a little.

"That's right," reaching forward and tickling her. Cat's smiling—Maria's rolling her eyes like I'm a total ass. Man, Louisa's going to be some piece of work when she grows up.

Huge main restaurant room is almost half a block long, twenty-foot high ceiling and filled with large round tables with white tablecloths. Feeling free from what Mom and Dad always order—Mom and her Shrimp with Lobster Sauce, Dad and his Beef and Beansprouts.

Nice big bowl of War Wonton Soup showing up.

Little Louisa looks at the soup and stuffed wontons with big eyes. She's digging in as well as Maria. Cat eating slowly, looking at Maria and Louisa then giving me a sad look, understanding the dark rings under Maria's eyes—she's probably hungry most of the time. Cat told me about the beatings they get from their psycho mother, even the little one. Cat must see the cloud of anger rising on my face, calming down as I feel her touch my leg under the table. Looking at her, our kids will never go hungry, never.

More dishes starting to show up, spicy Kung Pao Chicken, Szechuan Squid, Broccoli Beef, Sweet and Sour Pork, Egg Rolls for Maria and Louisa—some good thick Black Bean and Chow Fun noodles for the table.

Louisa and Maria cleaning their plates.

"This okay, Your Majesty?" to Louisa, she sticks out her tongue at me. Laughing with her. Maria getting up to go make another phone call.

Enjoying the spicy food, Cat waving me off when I offer her one of the hot red chili peppers. She'll eat most of what I'll eat, but… Hmm, good chili burn going on in my mouth, nice drink of hot tea and some rice helps cut the heat.

"How long can you stay out today?" looking at Cat.

"Oh, gee. If I get home before eight or so… How about you mi Maria?"

As she shits down from another call, "Like it matters anyway."

Looking at my watch, "I wonder where Hector is?" more to myself.

"He's not coming. We got into a big fight last night, I hate him," Maria looking sad for a moment, then getting back her in her proud I-don't-need-anybody posture. Mirror of someone I know?

It feels good paying for lunch.

Maria and Cat talking quietly, little Louisa sitting by herself on one of the worn metal chairs with red vinyl seat and back cushions lined up along the long restaurant lobby. She's kicking her feet back-and-forth while she looks at a black and white poster of a sampan motoring along in front of a four-story floating restaurant in a harbor. She looks at me for a moment, smiles and then goes back to looking at the different posters along the wall.

"Frank?" turning to Cat.

"Hey."

"If you say no, well, it's okay."

"What's up Cat?"

"Well," she looks over at little Louisa and Maria talking together. Louisa crossing her arms on her chest and sitting back against the red cushion, her chin set in her chest. "I know we wanted to spend the day together, but Maria and Hector… you know. Can we watch the little one for a bit? It's really tearing Maria up inside. Please?"

Shrugging off a tinge of disappointment, "Okay Cat, but what should we do with her? Movie?"

She shrugs her shoulders, smiles.

"I don't want to see a movie," Louisa standing with her feet apart, her arms crossed, "I want to go home. I'm going to tell."

"How about an ice cream?" Cat looking at her then me, nodding her head like she's trying to convince me it's a good idea.

"No! Where's is my sister? Why did she leave me? I'm going to tell."

"She just needs to take care of a couple of things and we'll bring you home in a couple of hours. Let's have some fun. Okay?"

She stamps her feet on the sidewalk, "I don't want to go to the movies, or museum, or park. This stinks. I'm going to tell Mommy."

Cat looks exasperated. An M104 bus roars past us on its way uptown.

"Louisa?" getting down on one knee in front of her.

"What?" her arms crossed again.

"I have an idea. It's a beautiful day out, how about going to Central Park? We can rent a rowboat. There might be little fish you can see."

Her eyes narrow, she's thinking. Her lips are still pursed.

"There's a great view of the Belvedere Castle from the lake. We can row across the whole lake and we might even try to catch a fish."

"Hmm," she's tapping her foot. Catching Cat shaking her head side-to-side with a slight smile on her face.

"We can go down to the Woolworth's on 79th and pick up some line and a hook, some bread and we can have a little adventure. What do you say?"

"Maybe," she's looking at me trying not to get too excited.

"Do you know how to fish?"

She shakes her head and I reach out my hand.

"Well, maybe I'll go," she takes my hand and holds on while we walk downtown along Broadway.

"You want a shoulder ride?"

"Yeah, okay," she says shyly—still trying to look disinterested. I'll fix her.

Lifting the Little Pill up, spinning her around a few times while she gives out a big "Whee!" and putting her on my shoulders.

"That's more like it."

"More."

"Nope."

"Meany," she tugs at my hair as I start to tickle her. Laughing with her as she giggles away. Cat walks close to me, takes my left hand. Holding onto Louisa's right foot to keep her balance as she turns quickly to watch a fire truck heading uptown.

"This is really nice, Frankie."

Smiling at my love.

"Maria's going to kill us you know," snapping out my haze. Noticing we are next in line at the boat rental. The Boat House restaurant is busy, people chatting away, waiters moving about, people launching rowboats and clunking away at the dock with their oars.

"What's that?"

"She's going to be climbing the walls with all the Cracker Jacks and soda pop you've bought her."

Shrugging my shoulders, taking a few minutes to look into her beautiful brown eyes. Taking her hand, bringing it to my lips and cherishing the moment where she's relaxed and not worried about what other people might say. Feeling like there's so much room in the world.

Louisa dressed up in her little lifejacket standing at the dock looking at the boat bobbing calmly. Helping Cat into the aft thwart.

"You better not sink us, Frankie," her voice is high pitched, she looks a little worried, her eyes moving rapidly side-to-side.

Rolling my eyes—we really have to watch out for severe storms on the lake here. "It's okay Cat, the lake is calm. I've spent years out on the ocean."

She still looks a little unsettled as the boat rocks side to side.

"Now for you, your Majesty."

Louisa looks at me, then the boat.

"It will be okay, I promise."

"Let's get a move on Mister, I got a crowd here."

Stifling the fuck you. "Louisa, take my hand, we will be fine."

She gingerly reaches out, her hand feels cold, her skin clammy and follows my guide into the rear. Cat looks unsure as well, her eyes darting around boat, she's got a killer grip on one of the gunwales.

"Relax, enjoy the day."

A few strong strokes pull us away from the dock, the blade of my oars just a few inches below the surface. Cross stroking to keep away from an oblivious boater as I make my way out of the crowd milling around in the cove near the docks.

Cat looks more nervous the further we get away from shore. Looking over my shoulder to get a quick fix on the Bethesda Fountain. Wondering if Ben is over there working the weekend tourists. Keeping the silhouette of the Metropolitan Museum behind me to keep my bearing and taking easy strokes along the shoreline.

Cat starting to relax, Louisa turns around, puts her elbows on the transom and rests her chest on the thwart. Catching Cat looking at me, a few moments of her beautiful face framed by the green trees of Central Park.

"You should see what it's like out on the ocean at times, Cat. Some days it's like a smooth lake there… miles and miles of calm blue. The colors of the morning, the seagulls crying about when we'd set out to sea from Montauk Harbor," shaking my head, "it's miles away from here, but…"

"What, Frankie?"

"It's so close, it's painful."

She cocks her head at me, her way of asking what's going on in that crazy head of yours.

"All the trouble lately and all this wonder out in the world that's so close to us… Rockaway Beach is right out there, about an hour by subway. Just to be out there with you, be away from all this, just us."

Sculling slowly, turning to head along the shore toward the Bow Bridge.

"You would look so beautiful there. A slight wind coming in from shore, blowing your hair back, our skin salty from the ocean..."

She waves at me, "Shh," and points to Louisa.

Feeling my chest fill her as an image of her when we made love flashes by. Cat's lips distinctly, slowly speaking, "I love you."

Feeling my eyes tear up for a second.

"Oh, look," little Louisa almost launches herself out of the boat. Cat quickly grabs her by the lifejacket collar.

"Don't scare me like that."

"There's a little fish!"

Laughing, Cat splashes me with some lake water.

"We'll go to a place I used to go when I was your size, Louisa. I bet we can catch one."

She turns around, her face bright, her body wiggling in her seat.

"Drop the hook down slowly."

"Oh, look at them all... Wow!" she's pointing toward the group of Golden Shiner and Brown Shiner minnows swimming up to the ball of bread on the hook I fashioned from a safety pin and nibbling away at the bait.

Cat smiles, shakes her head as she looks at me, and then looks off toward the Dakota building on West 72nd Street.

"Hey," Louisa cries out as the small ball of bread falls off the hook and a small Perch swims away with her bait. Kneeling carefully in the boat and helping her put another compressed ball of bread on the small hook.

"Shall we try another?"

"Sure, oh yes," she's looking over the side, then waves to another boat rowing close by, her little body trying so hard to stay still.

"Now carefully, when one of the larger ones comes in and takes the bait, pull up."

She's nodding, not really paying attention.

Fish swarming in, "Wait, wait now."

"Shh," Louisa waves me away. Laughing at her, Cat shaking her head, blowing me a kiss. Feeling a slow, warm current passing through my body as our fingers touch for a moment.

"Darn, he stole my bread!"

"You were a little too quick on that one, let them take the bait in their mouth."

Leaning back and looking around the lake as Louisa fishes quietly. Cat brushes her hair back off her face and leans back against the transom on her elbows—finally relaxing. Letting my eyes slowly capture each languid moment of her closing her eyes and tilting her face up to the sun. Tracing the outline of her breasts in her tight t-shirt, the wonderful curves of her hips. Eduardo starting to rise remembering how smooth her coffee skin feels along mine.

Flapping in the water. Louisa shrieks as she pulls the line up quickly and a thrashing perch lands in the boat with a splat. Cat shrieks and looks worried as the boat rocks side-to-side. Quickly picking up the small struggling fish by the gills.

"Do you want to touch it? Just keep your fingers away from the spines. See? They are really pokey," as I brush the dorsal spines down.

"It's cold and squishy. Ewww," she says as her thumb and forefinger gently pinch the fish's belly.

"Let's put him back so he can grow into a really big fish."

"Oh, this is the best day of my life," Louisa calls out to the Universe and starts putting another ball of bait on her hook as Cat leans over and kisses me on the cheek.

Louisa sleeping on my lap, her head nestled into my right shoulder on the crowded crosstown bus. Feeling Cat wrap her arms around my left arm and pull herself closer. Shiver running down my body—this could be our child on my shoulder in a few years. A perfect moment, the people on the crowded bus disappearing into a glorious vision of what our lives could be like, punctuated by what I know is waiting for Louisa at home.

Father who is never home, drunken mother that beats both girls in fits of rage and then cries with them for hours. Burn of anger in my stomach. How can this be, God? This little person so full of life, so full of joy... Is she just another innocent crushed under the oppressive weight of indifference, and there's nothing I can do? Eyes tearing up for a moment, could this be our child? What if I can't control myself? What if I'm not there to see them? That can't be me. How can that be me when I feel like this?

No, it will be okay. I can make this work, just one more thing to do.

Catching sight of Maria on Broadway and 90th. Cat and Maria hug each other quickly—little Louisa rushes in and gives me a big, long hug.

"See you, Your Highness."

"I think you should be my boyfriend," pointing to her chest with her thumb, getting a little huffy with Catherine before she marches off. Cat laughing.

Looking at the crowds of people walking up and down Broadway. Our eyes meeting, her eyes alive, her arms coming around my neck, "You're such a good man, Frankie, I had such a good day," kissing me, her hand folding around mine, the world receding until there's only her. No crowd, no street noise, no subways running under the street, just her.

"We've got the rest of the day," she squeezes my hand, and starts walking taking big strides, turning around and looking at me.

"We could go to the movies," image of her beautiful skin flashing in my mind, "or go anywhere you like."

She smiles at me, puts my arm around her shoulders.

Surprised, usually she doesn't do this in public.

"You could show me your little room like we talked about," she says in a low voice. Feeling a wave of electricity running up and down my body. My God, almost four hours together, shuddering at the thought.

"It's not the worst, but it's... small, kind of..."

"I don't care right now... I'm sure it's better than some of the places we've been together. It's just after today... I want to be with you."

Nodding at that, images of the stairwells at her apartment. Quick, listening for any sounds, fingers, hands moving with abandon—Cat with her tissues cleaning up afterwards.

She's laughing, her hand fitting in my back pocket on my butt.

"God you feel good, Cat."

"Of course I do, silly," she looks at me. "You love me, right?"

"Yes I do my beautiful, Catherina, I love you deeply."

Sad look from her for a second, then I feel her walking faster.

"So what was that movie about, my moms will ask?"

"Oh, we'd better pick up a New York magazine, there's a synopsis of the movies playing around town."

Crowded lobby at the Y, lots of people coming and going. Catching a glimpse of the elevator door closing behind her. Trying to look calm walking through the lobby—no one I know working the desk.

Tapping my feet waiting for the other elevator.

Giddy as I unlock the door to my room.

"This is small," she says quietly as I turn on the lights. "It's cozy," she swats at me, "I thought this was going to be really nasty."

"Well it's..." she turns, giving me the hairy eyeball.

"You should see poor Maria's place, oh," she shudders, "you'd think living right across the street from us in that nice building. They have almost no furniture in their rooms, their mattresses are right on the floor. Clothes in piles... Tell me that will never be us."

"That will never be us, I'll go into the ring, I'll tear down the heavens first and fight my heart out for us. Gus wants to train me to go pro, I can make good money for a few years, get you through school and all."

She looks at me, "Shh, turn off the lights," close to my ear, "I just want to hide away for a while, okay? Make the world disappear for me, Frankie."

"Yes, my Love," my hand on her waist, the world disappearing, body excited, the past days swept away in the deep need for her.

"I hope you've got enough, of you know..."

121

Following the narrow beam of light coming into the room through the closed cheap curtains to her naked hips on mine. Coming back from drifting off. Fantasizing, replaying the images from being out of our minds for the last four hours. Time to go slow, freedom to go fast with abandon. Out of condoms, the thought of more sex making my sore penis start to rise. Smell of our sex is overpowering, wonderful, swallowing the small room. This place seems so much more alive now, so much brighter. Warm white versus the dull gray I'd seen last night.

Walking slowly up Broadway our arms around our waists.

"I knew it would be like this," she looks at me, "we can tell you know."

Giving her a "you're kidding me" look.

"That's why a lot of the girls at school are jealous of me."

Holding her closely, walking in wonder that the Cat who's so loving in the dark, so shy about her body. I look down at my pants so she can follow my eyes. Mister Happy reacting to her being close.

"You're too much," she reaches across with her right arm, takes my hand and bites it a little.

"Hey, it's not me," wishing we could walk slower, wishing Zeno's paradox were really true—wishing we could keep walking half way there and never really get to a point where I have to walk back alone.

"It's going to be so hard to be at school tomorrow without you."

Alton's face swimming up, moving it to a different corner in my mind and staying focused on her.

She stops at 89th, gently moves away and puts on her bulky turtleneck, her little purse around her neck and pulls her hair back into a bun, the studious, the proper Cat coming back. Letting the image of her face in rapture fill me for a moment.

"It will be so nice when we don't have to hide like this," she says.

"Cat, we'll make it work. I know it."

"I know, Frankie, I know," she puts her fingers on my lips, looks at her watch. "Walk with me around the block again? Then I've got to go. I want to make this last."

"Sure, Cat, sure," happy for each moment of grace.

Watching her walk away slowly, she stops, turns and looks at me this time. Eyes meeting, people around us disappearing, my world filled with her wonderful eyes, breathing in, feeling of her running through my entire body. The people, colors and sounds of Broadway coming back in focus as I head back downtown alone.

Chapter 14

Hating this morning.

Get it done and over with.

Sitting up in my little room, wiggling my toes, stretching—eyes sore from tossing and turning most of the night.

Looking back at the bed, closing my eyes, a moment back with Cat, her lips, her warm skin, moving with her, kissing till our face muscles were sore, laughing when we were walking home about how we'd go for the world record next weekend. Envisioning her on top of me again her breasts swaying and moving, laughing as we tried to figure out different positions.

Deep breath—get going, get this done.

Dirty, nasty, noisy streets, city turning grey—flat people, flat feet, sidewalks, cars and taxis fighting for position like rats running in a maze when the light changes. Asshole jumping in cab after it stopped for an old lady. Seconds too slow to grab his scrawny pencil neck and pull him out of the cab. Waving down another for her in a pathetic attempt to pay back my debt for tripping an old lady in Riverside Park on purpose when I was a kid. They dared me to—what a chicken-shit move that was, I didn't have the courage to say no. She smiles at me as she gets in the cab, closing the door and continuing my walk up Broadway.

What if no matter what you do, you have to answer for all the things you've done, the good and the bad? No dispensations, no praying it away, no bullshit confession. Blind justice. What if you just have to live with it? What about Leroy, what about what I want to do to Alton? Do all these make me evil? Isn't what they did wrong? It was intentional with Leroy, I may have gone overboard, but that fucker deserves some of this too. Leroy and I will both go down.

But my friend…

Can't let go of the sting of betrayal. Was I just a convenient person for him to hang around with? Some easy mark white boy that when push came to shove, he sided with Leroy 'cause he's black? I took a bad beating for him. I could have run away when we were out in Coney Island fishing for crabs and those punks wanted to kick his ass. Remembering his face, his eyes—the feeling of no escape coming over me, no backing down. Five of them, older than us, taunting us, call me a nigger lover, calling me a faggot asking me if liked black dick. Body tensing remembering the fight, kicking, punching—getting to that crazy red rage place where they'd have to kill me to stop me. I got two of them really good though, one was all spitting mad cause I knocked out a couple of his teeth. Man, did we take a good beating when more of their boys showed up. We were lucky some men came on the pier broke things up, we could have been hurt real bad. Real bad.

But I didn't run! You don't let your friend take a beating without going down with him. You don't do that!

If I have to pay for what I'm about to do, I have to pay.

Time inching by no matter how many times I look at my watch.

No appetite for reading. Looking at my watch with anxious dread.

This will be over soon, then I can focus on a job, training, Cat, school.

Eating a good lunch then walking slowly toward 44th Street. I'm not going to jump him—we have to have it out straight up. He runs away, he backs down, then that's his choice.

Blocks moving by, people invisible as I clench and unclench my fists. That motherfucker, he stood with Leroy. He stood with fucking Leroy of all people! Anyone else and at least I could have a story about why he didn't want them to get what was coming.

Fighting back hot tears, realizing it's not Leroy that's bugging me.

He stayed on the sidelines when I was there, when I needed help.

Stinging. All the things my father said about Alton. Was he right?

Grabbing my hair, pulling and shaking my head.

Man in a suit looking at me like I'm a fucking weirdo, condescending look on his smug face. Getting close to him, his eyes widen, "Rrrrraaaaaaa," yelling at him, chasing him down the street and laughing as he runs away. Laugh turning to a sick grunt—got to stop this, how far back is it to you, Cat? How do I stop this creeping meanness?

Sitting on the stoop across from his house.

Hour or more to wait, flexing my hands and moving my shoulder muscles to stay loose. What if I walk away now? What will it matter? Counting cars as they pass by. Old rusted Honda motorcycle chained to a streetlight.

Coming down the street, there he is, jolt going through my body.

His strong face, short 'fro, easy swinging walk.

Getting up, walking across the street to intercept him.

He stops and stands there staring at me.

"So this is the way it's gonna be?"

"That's right, Buddy," with emphasis on the buddy.

He stares at me, his fists clenching and relaxing.

"You know what it is, Alton, you stood with that motherfucker Leroy. You let me take a beating. Time to face me now man. You can't do that and then walk away clean. Not after all that we've done, not after we been tight so long."

His jaw clenched, his eyes looking at me, stiff.

"Man, you talk about Leroy being a one way motherfucker. What's this? Huh? Got to be your way, got to be how you think it should be without even taking the time to find out, without thinking what would 'a gone down. You talk about what can and can't be like you know some shit, like you own the world!"

"Don't play that, Alton, I stuck by you in everything we did."

"So what, now you got the right to tell me how I should be when you won't even take a look at what went down? Man you pig-headed, selfish mother... What were you gonna do, Frank? You gonna kill Leroy cause you don't like him talking shit to you? I'm talking shit to you, you gonna kill me too? Come back trying to help your ass," his body shaking in anger. "Man, fuck you! You gonna take everyone down with you cause you so proud you can't see anything. I ain't gonna go down with yo crazy ass," he's choking up for a second. "I worked too hard to get someplace to throw it away."

"You're a fucking coward, Alton."

"Man don't talk to me that way, I tried to save your dumb ass. Where would you be if you kill't that boy?" his arm pointing back someplace. "What about that huh, you'd be in jail. I seen that crazy in you."

"It was okay when I stood with you in Coney Island. All the time in school, all the time practicing together working our shooting, setting it up so you could train with Gus," can't help the yelling. "It was okay then, just not when it got tough? You fucking..." my eyes blurring up, "you chose that piece of shit over me!"

"Fuck you, Mister Too-Proud-To-Listen, Mister Too-Proud-To-Walk-Away sometimes. What the fuck kind of friend are you? You don't give a shit about me now, you just acting from wounded pride. Pride before the fall. That you? That you, the favorite angel, the golden boy, can't get your way now and that just burns you?"

"You can spew all that bullshit, but you fucking backed down when it was time to stand up. All you had to do was stand with me, fucking Leroy and Thomas Jones would have never messed with us two-on-two. You know that," body shaking as that morning comes back in, "you fucking know that! You tried to be the peacemaker, not choose sides and be the big man. Not choose sides with me! ME!!" putting my hands up. "It's time to go, man. You can't stand on the sidelines now!"

"Man, I got a future. They are looking at me for college man! Don't you know what that means? Fuck if I'm gonna throw it all away like you just cause you'll burn the world down cause 'n you mad 'n shit. I can't do that," he's looking at me. "If I fucked up, I fucked up," his body shaking now. "You got nothing else, nothing to lose, that's it? Whose fault is that? What kind of friend are you? Cause I ain't you and take on the world at the drop of hat, that's it? I'm done? I'm Leroy? I got moms to take care of, what you gonna help her too, save all us poor stupid black folk?"

"Man, fuck you, that's never played with me, that's a cop out."

"Okay, Mr. Big Man, what if," his body rigid, eyes moving around in his head, "what if I was wrong? I see you there, I know you, ain't no matter is it? You been wronged. Who the fuck are you to be so important you can't take some shit!"

"Me take shit?" wave of rage flowing up, "I been taking shit every motherfucking day at home, taking the baiting from Leroy every day for the team, keeping it... What, was it too tough for you to have to stand there and man up? You could have put ten Leroy's in front of us, all the schools, all the trappings and I wouldn't back down if they were after you. They'd have to kill me first. My best friend," body shaking, people starting to gather behind him.

"I ain't motherfucking like you, don't you understand! You lose some shit you go on. You get a job, big white boy, go carry shit at some motherfucking construction site and make eight bucks an hour. Like they gonna hire me. You talk shit about knowing the streets, you don't know shit."

"I know if we was out there and I'm making that eight motherfucking bucks an hour, half of it would be yours. You can piss about the world but all that don't mean shit if you're word ain't shit, if you're not ready to man up."

"So, that's the way it's got to be. What I say as a man don't mean shit."

"That's the way it's got to be."

Seeing his body tense up, decision made, "Well fuck you man, you have to get what you want no matter what, fuck you."

Alton charging, he's going for a desperate knockout blow. Covering up moving to the side, then pushing forward, taking hard shots to my head, arms shoulders. Quick punches up to his body, world around me collapsing from a hard fist, mind drawing out, body in slow motion for a split second. Moving, creating some space with a hard flurry, a few making good contact. Feeling my power move. Getting my weight on him.

Stepping back. Alton faking, dodging, quick jabs coming in. Circling, moving with him, taking the hits cause I know if I'm willing to take more than him I'll get hard shots in. Getting him circling, get his back to a car. Hard shot to the side of my head, goddamn strong. Feeling warm blood start to run down my face. Springing forward, he tries to dance back like we're in the ring—bumps into the car. Hard shots to his body, full power behind them, he tries to grab me, tie me up, slipping back, big right to the side of his head. He stumbles, left to his gut, his muscles not ready for it, hearing the wind rush out, his head coming down.

Rock fist coming up with all my body weight behind it, connecting to the side of his face. He crumbles to the sidewalk, his face hitting a metal car bumper on the way down.

"That's what it's got to be, that's what it's got to BE! Telling me what's going to be. This is what it is!" looking at him on the ground. Breathing hard, body shaking, chest torn apart—anger, sorrow at seeing him crumpled up, helpless. Hot tears starting to stream down my face, his words in my head. Just about pride?

"WHY," standing there, body shaking, "it's not about pride," yelling at him as my heart feels like it's being pulled in two. Sick understanding settling in. That's all it was ever about, body reeling from an awful wave of nausea sweeping up. Standing there, body shaking from the adrenaline.

He's too still, oh God no.

"Oh God, what have I done?" looking at him, rolling him over, sickness rushing up my throat—hot acid, sick. The left side of his face caved in—his cheek bone, blood leaking from his mouth, "Oh no, oh no. God no," he's breathing badly.

Standing there, panic rising in my stomach, people crowding in, others yelling behind me. Sinking down to my knees, swelling knuckles feeling the rough concrete pavement. My world spinning out of control, mind looking for reasons to justify—but it's all bullshit.

Snapping out of it. Well of sorrow in my chest—I've got to own it no matter what. Seeing Cat slip away, seeing Gus joining Dad, Coach all the others standing there, arms crossed, staring, disapproving.

Heart up in my throat, horrible sweet music of death walking next to me as I head up the stairs to his apartment—got to get his mom. No matter how much hurt I feel I will not leave him like this. Feeling like a fucking weakling, all that shit about how I felt betrayed—you poor stupid man Frank, you impoverished animal, she'll never forgive me; he's her world.

Knocking, loud, "Mrs. Brown!" knocking again.

"What's going on there?" opening the door, seeing her smile for a second when she sees me, her face turning to concern as she holds onto my eyes, "what's the matter?" Stuck, stammering, can't say anything, her eyes open she sees the blood on my face, "What have you done?"

"Alton," breathing hard, "call an ambulance."

"Call what?" her voice rising.

Yelling at her, "CALL A DAMN AMBULANCE!" crying, pleading, "he's hurt," she runs past me, the door to their apartment wide open. Standing there—own it man, eat the pain, eat the death that's growing inside, the leavings of what I've killed. Stepping inside.

Picking up their phone, "Operator, I need the police, it's an emergency."

"Connecting."

"Emergency."

"44th between 11th and 12th, young man down hurt bad, bleeding, we need an ambulance here quickly."

"Slow down now. Who are you? What's happening?"

"Frank Caruso, my friend Alton Brown, he's bleeding, his face is crushed in, he's hurt bad, you've got to get there, 44th between 11th and 12th Ave. It's an emergency."

Turning and walking down the stairs slowly, coldness creeping up inside me, time stretching out. Going down to the street. People are crowding around Alton and his mom.

"That's the man!" someone yelling, moving to Alton, feeling like I'm moving through something thick, have to push my body forward. Moving through people, ignoring their angry faces, hands pulling at me, trying to keep me away. Pushing back, rage flaring at someone yelling at me, hitting him in the gut. Sinking down to my knees, something pushing behind me.

"Oh my God, my baby," Alton's mom taking his hand, holding it to her chest. "What did you do?" crying, looking at me, "oh, what did you boys do?"

Rumbling siren in the distance.

"We called the cops Etta, throw the book at him. Hold him, get him."

Hands coming over me, feeble fists striking me, feeling nothing through the daze.

"Oh my boy, oh my good boy," holding his hand to her face, her body rocking back and forth, another wave of sickness coming over me.

She looks at me—her eyes stabbing steel of anger, her hands that could be so soft at times even with the practiced hardness of toiling for people like my father and mother. Hard slap to my face, incoherent words coming from her as a faceless person pulls her back. Surge of hurt, rage, shame, loss washing over me, ripping my arm back from one man, punching the next one in the face. Screaming at the top of my lungs, people shrinking back in fear, can't hear what I'm saying, sounds of the world disappearing—the beast loosed on mankind crying for the humanity it's lost.

Looking at him, looking at her.

"RAAAAAA!" pulling my hair, giving voice to the loss crying out inside me, people shrinking away in horror. Stumbling up the street, image of an older man holding her trying to keep her from falling over her son flashing in. Sirens closer. Walking, bouncing into cars. Shaking my head to get my balance. Hard to breath, stopping by a trash can and retching out all the acid, all the sickness in me. Retching again and again till there's nothing left. Walking, feeling numb, 10th Avenue vaguely passing, no idea where I'm walking—fixated at the vision of my friend lying there.

I am a bum, a thug, a loser—I am a fucking loser.

Crying cause my father is right, bastard, bastard. Not about Alton, Cat, Hector—about me, he was right about me.

People shrinking away from me, realized I've been yelling out loud.

"Get him to the hospital, look at his face," someone saying to me. Looking at them, not understanding, someone taking my arm trying to lead me uptown.

"Are you okay? Did you get mugged?"

Laughing, walking with them.

Is that it, body without a Soul, some kind of monster? Tears forming again, stumbling along, people looking at me and shrinking away.

Up the steps, starting to realize where I am.

Emergency room at Roosevelt Hospital taking shape as I watch a man walking away, people asking if he's my father, he's holding his hands up so they leave him alone as he walks out.

"Can you hear me?" looking at nurse, putting a pen flashlight in my eyes. Nodding my head, ducking away from the light, "Mild concussion."

Empty hollow dead clay.

"What is your name?" repeating things back to her. How do I face Cat now? Is this how I treat people I love when things go bad, am I a time bomb? What if I hurt her? Hands balling up and hitting the table—need to feel enough pain to take away the vision of what I am.

"Hey, something's wrong here," she backs away from me.

Two male orderlies come in.

"Are you okay, kid?" then to the other, "maybe we need to get him over to Bellvue…"

"Hit my head hard," they look at me, "basket… basketball, took an elbow."

They look at each other. Blinking, looking at them. Got to get my shit together, no escaping what I've done. What if he's okay? What if it's just a bad bruise—the angle he was lying at. Feeling coming over me that no hope can mask, you know it wasn't. You know it wasn't. He's hurt bad and I did it. All for my fucking pride.

People moving me, talking to me, not paying them any attention.

"Follow the light, Son," moving my eyes, seeing a man in a white coat.

"You take a hard hit?"

"Yes, Sir," he looks at me and nods.

"Headache?"

"No, Sir," blinking, brown eyes, brown hair streaked with gray.

"Not a bad cut, a few stitches, too close to the eye for pain killer. You're just going to have suck it up."

"Yes, Sir," nurse running gauze pads over my face with some kind of liquid. Cut stinging, pain feels good, only feeling inside me. Even if Alton is okay, I know I went over the edge and I don't know how to get back. Here I was with all the love and light in the world and in a moment transform into a fucking beast. How could that happen? Is what I want to believe I am just a thin veneer on top of some dark thing I don't have the courage to look at?

"This is going to sting," feeling the needle piercing my skin. Breathing in with the sting, the thread moving through my vision. Another pierce and then two more—he looks at my head, cuts and ties off the thread. Head throbbing.

"Hurt?" he looks at me.

"A little," he looks at me for a minute.

"You had us scared there for a moment."

"I apologize, Sir."

"How'd you get that?"

Shrugging my shoulders.

"You be careful."

"Sir, is this bad? I mean I'm training, boxing."

"No, let it heal for a few days, get a good trainer to get the stitches out. Wait another two weeks before hard sparring." He looks at me, "Anything else you need to say?"

"No, Sir."

Filling out forms, might as well put my real address, name, parents. Asking if I should pay now? Laughing on the inside when they ask if my dad has insurance. Telling them he runs a full Union shop. He's got insurance up the wazoo.

Back out on the street.

Looking down West 58th Street to the Hudson River. Got to go to there. Not paying attention to anyone. Body not working well, missing easy steps, stumbling here and there, taking a fall as I climb over the fence to the train yard and slide through garbage.

No one looking that I can see. Crossing the train yard, uptown to the old pier, my hiding place. The old rat gnawed, moldy blankets still there. No other squatters today. My kingdom.

Lying back, looking out across the river, tired, so tired.

Letting the world fall away.

Trying to run away from the stories in my Sunday school Bible classes— God's favorite angel. He couldn't admit that he was wrong. Sinking into my little hell of rat shit, rotting blankets, rotting wood over the stinking gray Hudson River water.

Time not registering—welcoming the darkness.

Drifting in the sound of the river moving by the dock toward the open sea. Body struggling in silent pain—aching at what I'd lost.

Waking up cold, head pounding, neck sore as hell. Dark shadows reaching across the river. Body going on alert—sound of people moving in the old warehouse, hushed voices.

"Man, I tell you Marty said he saw something crossing the yards."

"That asshole's seeing things."

"Yeah but if it's the same shithole that broke Cheech's jaw, we gonna beat him till he's dead and throw him in the fucking river," another voice said.

"We keep looking," said another deep decisive voice.

"How we know if it's him?"

"What the fuck are you, Sherlock Holmes? Cheech said it was a big kid, curly hair. We find one of them, we club him to death, tie some of these old carrier weights to him and throw him in the river."

"Shit," said the first man, "I say we turn him in."

"Pussy, we take care of our own here," silence, breathing painful—controlling my breath, heart pumping, fingers searching for the club I'd set here days ago. A familiar mean current coming up inside me, these guys are hunting me. Body shivering, deep understanding settling in—this is who I am. Tears in my eyes for Cat, for the people that believed in me that I've let down. Time to show these fools the beast.

Moving slowly in the shadows, my fingers wrapped around the heavy club, they think they are hunting me.

Boards moving, refuse being thrown around. Circling toward them, moving in the deep darkness. Lights moving in the distance, edging my way toward them in the shadows—slow drumbeat inside my chest, death-chant, gripping the heavy wooden club.

Closer, closer, get the first one quickly. "Yessss," low voice speaking to me in my head, "kill them," serpent song, death song. "After you kill the first one, move into the others before they know what's happening, then kill them as they run."

He's a few feet away. Slowly raising the club.

"Shit, ain't a motherfucking thing here. Check the next dock over... Hey you, you two fucks," yelled the man with the deep voice, "quit dicking around and get over to the next pier and find that piece of shit."

"Alright, alright man, keep your damn pants on."

They need to come a few more steps more, skin itching.

Footsteps walking away—body breaking out in shakes.

Dampness of the river air reaching my face.

Stink of the place rising—sewage, chemicals in the water, rat shit, rat piss, rat farts. Quietly looking at my watch, close to five o'clock. Bladder bursting. Dusk setting in. Careful walk north along the packed gravel road, good traction, voices way behind me. People playing on the handball courts not paying any attention to me as I throw the heavy club over the rusting railing into the Hudson River.

Cleaning up in a public bathroom at the playground at 74th Street. Using the tiny hard squares of toilet paper to dry my face. Back out into the fading sun, looking around. Groups of kids are playing, laughing, running around the park in blissful ignorance. A couple of mothers looking at me suspiciously, most of the other women must be nannies—deep African faces, foreign accents taking care of lily white babies.

Looking at the kids on the swings and seesaw.

They're free, playing, laughing in joy.

Sitting down on empty park bench in the dusk, fingers reaching up into my hair and pulling. Body muscles rigid. Eyes clenched shut. What the hell is happening to me? Looking down at my hands—are they a lie? How can they hold her, touch her and then be ready to do... What was that talking to me? What if I'm fucking insane?

Body shivering, the one who's fallen from grace that is talking to another in the chosen darkness—is that it now? Am I worthy only of the company of Lucifer? Was I always the fallen one and I didn't know it? Was it only when my Father started to glimpse who and what I am that my real life started? Clothed in gilded trophies, people overlooking the beast beneath the surface because of the bright shiny things they'd given me for the things they wished I would become.

The good son, the good athlete, the smart one—and most importantly the proud one standing there on my proud tower not seeing the cracks that were working their way through the foundation. Time, pressure, water— enemies of stone, the little I'd built laying around me in ruins, piles of rubbish. Truth was my enemy, the first silent crack. I am where I am now because of who I am. Quickly shutting down that thought.

Silent tears running down my face for my lost friend, my lost humanity and the people that used to believe in me.

Chapter 15

Head throbbing. Blinking in the late morning light, grimacing at the pain shooting through my head like a white-hot dagger.

Slip of paper under my hotel room door telling me to come see the director. Yeah well fuck him, I'm going to pick up my library books at school, pack up here and head to Gus' gym. Time to recognize who I am. Where else should I be but in the ring? Empty eye sockets staring back at me from the mirror.

Maybe it's not too late to change? Maybe Alton's okay?

Starting to come out of it, working different stories in my head about what happened on the way down to school. Trying to tell myself that it wasn't really my fault, my inner voice sounding shallow against the deep drumming of knowing—I had a choice.

Thankful for empty halls at school.

Nodding to Simone as she walks to the bathroom. She mouths, "What are you doing here?" Pointing to my locker. More footsteps, Mr. Crabbe raises his eyebrows and hurries away. Looking through the useless stuff in my locker—packing my two library books in my backpack. Textbooks, those stay. Papers, tests, looking over them as images of the classrooms, teachers and other kids come flooding in—that's gone now Frank. Putting the things that stay here in the bottom of my locker. Putting my good Adidas and library books going in my backpack. Feeling kids looking at me, then going away.

Lost for a few moments in the team basketball picture I hadn't brought home cause my father would have just gone off on his bullshit. Alton, Leroy, Hector, Cedar, me—the starting five kneeling down in front of the other kids in the second row, Julio, Brian, Kenny, Thomas Jones.

"You Frank Caruso?"

Startled at the unfamiliar, deep voice behind me. Turning.

Large man in a tweed jacket, white shirt and tie way too short for his stocky frame. He's looking at me, direct, calm. One look and I know— police officer. Bucking up against the sinking feeling inside.

"Yes I am, Officer."

Why are they here, why are they bothering me?

He looks at another man in a dark blue jacket, white shirt with a red tie.

"I'm Detective Malan, this is Detective O'Neal, turn around, put your hands against the wall, spread your legs."

Looking at them, shaking my head.

"But, it's... Why?" skin feeling cold and clammy, short, shallow breaths.

"Make it easy on yourself, kid."

"It was a fair fight," looking at them, "why?"

The taller man puts a heavy hand on my arm, "Turn around, put your hands against the wall and spread your legs."

Kids coming into the halls as the class bell rings, forming a circle and staring at us, Julio pushes his way to the front out of the corner of my eye.

Turning slowly toward the lockers, O'Neal kicking my feet back as my hands go against the wall. Hands searching me, taking my wallet, bankbook and thoroughly going over my body, "Nothing on him."

"Where's the sap?" asked Malan.

"What?"

"Turn around, put your hands behind you."

Doing as he says, "You don't have to cuff me, I'll come quietly. My..." cold metal snapping around my wrists, shame spreading through my body. Looking at the kids that are gathering around. Teachers trying to herd them back to class. Heart ripping out of my chest, pain running through me—Cat standing down the hall, shocked, calling out to me and pushing her way through a group gawking students. Mrs. Brooks pushing her back. People asking what is happening, teachers motioning them back to class.

"Come with us, son," strong hands on my arms, leading me away to the auditorium. Standing outside, kids being kept back by the teachers. Seeing the window shades moving in front of the small safety glass windows in the auditorium doors.

Standing there, the two detectives with me.

"What's, what's happening?"

"You'll find out soon enough."

"Why are we standing here, who's in there?" looking to the auditorium.

Moments passing, breathing harder. Mind rushing, but can't hold the thoughts, numbness starting to spread through my body. Looking up and down the halls.

"Come with us."

Leading me back to the main entrance, most of the kids out of the halls—a couple dodging teachers to see what is going on. Outside, two black and white cars, one plain—lights on. People gathering.

"That's the motherfucker!" someone yelling, people running over.

"You big white ape," a man I don't know yelling at me.

"Think you bad, wait till we get you inside!"

"Back off," said Malan, waving one of the policemen over.

"Keep back!" O'Neal shoving at the gathering crowd.

Curses, people pushing. Looking back at the school, Cat looking horrified at me—my feet stopping dead, O'Neal getting pissed, yanking me. Black hands grabbing me, "We're gonna make you pay Whitey, think you fuck up my cousin Leroy and get away with it?"

Something snapping inside—lunging at the man yelling at me, hitting him in the face with my forehead, stunning him, driving my body into him, slamming him into a car. Hitting him with my face, my knees, sinking my teeth deeply into his arm as he yells for help.

Fists hitting me, people screaming and yelling.

Body lifted up and slammed into a car. Dazed, getting pulled back from the car again and my face slammed into the side of the car then thrown in the backseat—door slamming shut. Blinking my eyes to clear my head. Feeling blood from my cut start to trickle down my face.

Batons swinging outside the car, Julio and Hector jumping one of the guys who was yelling at me, Hector incensed, kicking him in the face. They run away when more police show up. Turning and watching the brawl as the police car drives away, feeling relief as I see Julio and Hector ducking back into school as a couple of big brothers are being cuffed by uniformed officers.

"That big fucking mooley," one of the detectives is laughing, "he'll think twice next time, huh?" He's laughing while he pulls out onto 1st Ave. The other officer looking at me for a few seconds, then at his partner, hard look ahead as we drive through traffic.

People are looking at me in the back seat while we stop for a red light. Hollow feeling gone, replaced with burning shame; all the people I know seeing me taken away like a criminal. Mind stopping for a moment, body has to violently shake against the cuffs.

"Hey, you fucking stop that!"

Car stopping in front a police station—not paying attention, dazed. Taken forcibly up the steps.

"Book this asshole, assault and battery with a deadly weapon. Get him in a holding cell for questioning," passing me to a uniformed officer. "He resisted, watch him."

"Oh," the cop looks at me, puts me in a painful wristlock. "Coming with me, Big Boy? You like to dance? Huh?" following him, trying to relax through the pain.

Fingers rolling along the cool black inkpad; ink on my fingers, being pushed in front of a camera—lights going off, moved forward and processed in a line of people, filthy rag wiping away a little of the ink.

Numb, feeling numb.

Downstairs along a tiled stairway into dimly lit cell rows.

Thrown into a cell, cuffs taken off, door slammed and locked.

Body shivering.

Becoming aware of the sounds in this dark limbo of holding cells—male voices talking, complaining and yelling at the guards as they pass by. Smell of piss, vomit, fear and industrial pine cleaner. Holding onto the bars like they'll keep me upright in a heavy wind and then sinking down on the ceramic tile bench. Dimly aware of the completely tiled cell—nothing here but the hard ceramic tiles and the rusting drain in the middle of floor.

Sitting down slowly—forcing myself to breathe. Don't be a bitch. If this is what it's going to be, then don't be a whiny bitch. First guys that get picked on my uncle said are always the ones who start complaining. Fighting back the rush of emotions, breathing hard, wishing I could erase all this and step back to Cat like we were yesterday.

Throat choking—I failed you baby, I'm so sorry, I'm so sorry. I failed you. Twisting the bars with all my strength. I failed you, Cat.

Head down on my cold hands, no idea how long I've been here. Dimly realizing they'd taken everything from me and put it in a big brown envelope and signed something.

People pacing in their cells—doors opening and closing, someone howling and banging on the cell with something. Men yelling at him to shut the fuck up, "I'm sick, I'm sick, I need a doctor," sounds of a body hitting something, "Oooowww, man I'm sick!"

"You tell them, you get me one too. Get me one motherfucking doctor!"

"What you looking at, hommes?" Hispanic voice rising up, "Don't be eyeballing me."

"Fuck you poncho, yo ugly ass don't own this place."

Sound of something hard hitting the cell bars. "Shut the fuck up for I turn the hose on your nigger ass."

"Bronco, watch that nigger shit, you hear."

"Hey now, Henry, we're all blue here," he sounds like that should make a difference.

"Just the same."

"What you got to say, Big Mouth?" from the man they called Bronco.

"I tell you what Mister Whitey, Mister Cracker Motherfucker, you come suck my dick, how about that?"

"Take that troublemaker out of here," door opening, sounds of fighting. "Your ass is going over to Rikers now," sounds of meat being hit with something hard.

"Man, ow, fuck you, ow, mother..."

Things quieting down, someone struggling, getting hauled up the stairs.

Closing my eyes, minutes passing, hours passing? Day's events running again and again through my mind, like if I think about it enough, things will change. Skin clammy, feeling cold. Footsteps approaching my cell,

"Geez Lieutenant, if we had only known."

"Get me the arrest report," a moment later, "NOW!"

Oh no, oh no, I know that deep voice, blood rushing to my face, shame, first fear I've felt in days. Wishing I could fade to black and sink into the walls. You'd all be better off without me—Cat and everyone would be so much better off without me. God how I miss you, baby. Tamping down the visions of my mom, my dad during happier times. Did they know somehow that I was this, what, this thing, this beast? Were they just pretending to be nice to me all these years? Standing up slowly.

My uncle's stern face set in deep anger, his thick neck, large shoulders fill the cell door. Looking at him, another shape coming in from the shadows, Shrinking back at my father's angry face.

Staring at them, trying to hold the beast in.

"Disgrace, you fucking disgrace," my father so mad he's spitting, "you not only have to shame me and your mother, you have to shame your uncle's good name. Cretino, mad dog, if your grandfather could see you now, oh the shame... I wash my hands of you. You have what you deserve. You rot in there, discratciato."

Feeling the steel door slam down inside me. Locked in a room with my enemy—this is it, we'll always be at each other's throat.

"You tell him," yells a voice in the background, "ha, ha, ha."

"I wash my hands of you! You rot in jail, you disgrace! I have nothing to do with you. You're dead to us all. Disgraciato!" he flicks his hands apart.

"John," Uncle Vin moving from his stupor, touching my father's sleeve.

Looking at Uncle Vin, his dark brown eyes cold, drilling through me—deep disgust registering on his face. Feeling like I'm fighting for air, the ruins of any hope I had left with Dad or Uncle Vin crumbling before my eyes. Can't hold the tears back, but I won't make a sound now. Grabbing the bars, gripping, twisting the unmoving steel. Squeezing my stomach, swallowing the acid so I don't throw up. Uncle Vin looks at me, looks at my father for a moment, instant of remorse showing—then he's a cop again.

Lines set in stone, unmoved and unmoving.

Slow venom-filled words, "There's no weapon..." Struggling to talk, "I beat those three bastards with these," holding up my fists, "you understand that you fucking little man!" reaching out, stopped by the bars. "Next time we see each other there's no father and son, only hate. I hope you die alone choking on how much your children hate you!" making a fist and shaking at him.

"Enough," Uncle Vin booming, "you watch what you say to your father!"

Dad shrinking away, defeated. Pained look on Uncle Vin's face. He looks at my dad, who looks away.

Standing there in the sounds of their footsteps walking away, smothered by the noise of people yelling and screaming. Stepping back into the shadows away from them. Head down in my hands, hot tears running down my face. Convicted—abandoned, deathly silence coming over me.

This is my world now, I have to learn take it. The words searing inside closing a door on the pain—my father left me here. My father left me here—the words twisting like a dull dagger turning slowly inside me.

My father left me here.

Chapter 16

Cuffed, shackled. Following a line of people into a set of dark blue busses—steel covers over the windows, thin slots cut out, impossible to see inside the bus.

"Name."

"Caruso."

"Bus two, move your ass."

"Name."

"Henry."

"Bus one."

"Name."

Voices droning on behind me as my eyes start to adjust to the interior. White kids, brown kids, black kids, Chinese kids. No way this many got on here—must be a pick up stop. Couple in the back poking at each other, can't make out their faces, they look up at me in the gloom. Moving to the back, white street kid sitting sprawled along the back seat, knees wide apart, long hair, just making out a scrawny mustache, trying to claim the whole back row.

"You gonna move, or am I gonna move you?"

He tries to give me some attitude then moves over along the bench to the side. Looking over at him, see if he'll make eye contact. He looks straight ahead. Sitting down, thinking about what my uncle told me about how guys are supposed to act in prison—don't make eye contact, don't start fights, don't stop if you get into it, hang with your own color, don't whine or act effeminate, show the guards respect, don't be a punk.

Dark bus roaring to life—transport to the underworld.

Other kids looking through the slats as we move through the city— looking over at my bench mate, he's trying to catch a look at things too. Sitting back in the darkness, leaning my head back against the torn seat. Closing my eyes for a few moments—fuck the city, this is my world now. God I'll miss you Cat.

Skin feels cold and clammy, nervous quiet settling in on the bus, nobody making eye contact. Afraid—they're afraid. Breathing out the nervousness, it doesn't matter what I want or what I don't want, there's nothing to be afraid of because this is what I'm in and I'm going to deal with it.

Looking at the kid in front of me, he looks pretty calm.

"Yo, man," low voice to him. "What's up? First time?"

He shakes his head side to side and motions back toward the guard walking down the aisle. Nodding to him.

Assholes Malan and O'Neal going on for hours trying to get me to confess that I'd hit Alton with a blackjack or a pipe. Short laugh to myself, those jerks thinking leaving me handcuffed for hours and not letting me pee, drink or eat would make a difference. Malan yelling at me, kicking my chair so the cuffs yanked my wrists, telling me I was a lying piece of shit. Oh did he get hot when I told him he had a lot to learn from my dad about how to make people feel guilty. Telling me there were witnesses and that I'm going away for three years. Man, what the fuck did these other kids have to go through? Well, maybe some of their parents actually give a damn.

"Prisoners stand in line and get your asses off my bus," tall uniformed guard yelling, others walking around outside with sunglasses, smacking their hands with their batons. "You'll be given numbers, you will be addressed by your number, you are nothing now, you are fucking criminals. You will address me and all my fellow officers as Mr. Corrections Officer, do you hear ME?" fighting the feeling of being small and being out of control by picking a spot on the wall behind them and focusing on it. Do what they say. Don't give them a reason to bust your ass.

"Yes, Mr. Corrections Officer," yelling out.

"I didn't hear you."

"Yes, Mr. Corrections Officer!"

"You will march in line after Guard Hanley. You will be getting a prison uniform and all the things you need, you will have your photo taken in it, your number will be assigned to you. Your clothes will go into a cardboard box, which will be given back to you when you leave, should you leave. You will then carry your stack and be given a delousing shower after which you will put on your prison clothes and follow Guard Hanley into the main hall. Conditions are crowded here—many of you'll be living in open-air bunks. Any infraction of the rules and you will be punished, do you understand me?"

"Yes, Mr. Corrections Officer!"

"Hey man, I have a question?" keeping my eyes forward, it's the longhaired asshole from the bus. The big guard walking over to him getting in his face, "Did I say you could talk, you maggot?"

"Hey, I know my rights…" air coming out of his stomach as the big guard hits him in the stomach with the end of his baton. He's gasping for air on all fours.

"Do any other maggots here have anything to say?'

"No, Mr. Corrections Officer!"

"After you are in your new uniform, you will be taken to a training session where you will learn the prison rules and regulations. Are there any questions?"

"No, Mr. Corrections Officer."

He walks up the line, stops in front of me, looking me in the face— keeping my eyes off in the distance over his head"

"How old are you, boy?"

"Seventeen, Mr. Corrections Officer," say it loud.

"You a big faggot? You in here cause you like to suck dick?"

"No, Mr. Corrections Officer."

"You telling me I'm a liar?" looking at him for a second, he's gonna fuck with me no matter what I say—show the others he can make the biggest of us powerless.

"No, Mr. Corrections Officer!"

"What are you saying, you maggot? Are you gonna stand here and lie in my face like that?" spittle flying out of his mouth.

"No, Mr. Corrections Officer, this prisoner does not suck dick."

He looks at me long and hard, keeping my eyes calm. Tensing my abdominal muscles to take the blow that's coming. Doubling over fast, don't want another one, tensing, breathing in and out hard out to deal with the pain. Standing up as he's walking up to one of the black kids.

That bastard is starting in on him now.

Back in line, the long hair walking doubled up from the blow—pussy.

Walking into the large, dirty, dark gray brick building, barbed wire spun on the fences around the top of the building, sun setting behind us in Flushing Bay, jet engine sounds in the distance from LaGuardia Airport, the whole area taking on an unreal sense. Adolescent Reception and Detention Center, ARDC, home sweet home.

Feels good to get the shackles and cuffs off. Guards yelling at us to move our asses, get our clothes off, get our stuff in boxes, write our name down on it in legible block letters. Helping the black kid in front of me write his name on his box—he's got the shakes from something. About to get my ass chewed for talking when the guard sees what I'm doing.

"Stand at attention!" we all stand to whatever we think is attention, naked, holding our folded stack of clothes in front of us. Guards walking by, poking kids in their balls, laughing at some kid saying he's got a tiny dick.

"Move your fucking asses, Maggots."

Number 10789.

One-piece light blue dungaree overall, sleeves too short for my ape arms. Sitting in the most decrepit desk I've ever seen, a man in a short sleeve shirt, black slacks, shiny tie and comb-over telling us to memorize the twenty prison rules.

"10789."

Snapping out of my daydream.

"Yes, Mr. Corrections Officer."

"What is rule 11?"

"Prisoners must only eat at meal times. No food is allowed out of the mess hall."

"Rule seventeen, Ass."

"Prisoners must obey the guards at all times."

"Man, why we have to do this shit? I want to do my time and get out," said one of the Hispanic kids.

"Mr. Reeve. You call me Mr. Reeve, dickhead."

The other uniformed guard grabs the kid, takes him out into the hall, and has him start doing pushups while he yells at him.

Walking with all the new fish as the guards shepherd us through walkways between buildings. All the weak ones have already been pulled out—they must put them in a different area. Kids lining up to check us out as we come into a cellblock, this must be where they put the strong ones.

Two levels—looking up into the second floor. Open cells with what looks like four kids packed into a tiny area. Two by two guards patrolling the second floor, large open area at the bottom setup with rows and columns of bunk beds. Standing there, looking things over, breathing to stay relaxed, calm as I can be, not catching any eyes and giving attitude—someone brings it though…

Looks like a section of the bunks in the middle are some kind of neutral area—a few kids hanging out there. They look scared, mixed up, just trying to stay out of the way. Other areas looked organized into groups; white, Hispanic, black. Some tough looking kids here, others look like they are nervous waiting for the more dominant kids in the group to do something so they can follow along. Recognizing a kid I'd fought hard and beaten on points in Golden Gloves a last year, man that was a tough fight.

"Hey, man," quietly. He turns, gives me a why-the-fuck-are-you-even-talking-to-me look. "We were in the ring together last year, you're Derek Brown right?" he looks hard, a moment of acknowledgement, then concern.

"Talk over there," he points to the open area near the stairs up to the second floor. Long tables with flat benches bolted to the floor, kids hanging around—reading, jockeying for position, kids on the stairs checking out who's going up or coming down.

Walking around bunk city.

"Got to respect boundaries here."

"Okay."

He won't make eye contact, won't acknowledge he knows me.

"What you in for?" he asks quietly.

"Assault and battery with a deadly weapon. You?"

"Stealin a car," nodding at him.

"How'd you do in the last tournament?"

"Man too much shit, too little time, didn't even enter."

"You were good."

He shrugs his shoulders. "I'll catch you later. Frank, right?" Nodding. "I'll pass the word to my bros that you're all right. Watch out for Artone," about to ask him what's going on, he's gone.

Checking out the common area, a few bookshelves, books and comics strewn around. No paper, no pens. Nothing sharp, music coming from a couple of the cells on the second floor—pure R&B.

Walking to the white end of bunk city.

"This taken?" to a strong blonde kid standing next to the bunk.

"Suit yourself," he doesn't look up.

"I'm Frank."

"I don't give a fuck," his eyes coming down hard. He's scared.

Looking away, nodding. He's not a power guy here. Looking around, there's a group of Italian looking kids hanging closer together a few bunk rows away.

Walking over to check them out.

"Can I help you, Big Boy?" one stepping forward, deep Brooklyn accent, he's not particularly big, just got the attitude. Bust their balls a little.

"I don't know, I was thinking maybe I should order a pizza or something. What do you think? You deliver?"

He's doing the "I'll laugh as I get mad enough to fight" laugh. Other guys starting to look over, "Hey, we got a comedian heeere."

"Yeah, well what we really have here is a bunch of pussy boys who don't even know what the fuck I'm saying in their own mother tongue."

They look at me like I'm from another planet.

"What? You mama luca's don't even know how to speak Italian?" holding my hands out at my side.

"Hey, who the fuck are you, the great Italian Moses come to let his people go? If so, part them bars over there, if not, get the fuck outta here."

"No man, no parting here, I'm a regular fucking Jerry Lewis, and you're my retard kids. Now where's a spare bunk or do I get the full show of you douche bags walking around drooling looking like morons so the TV audience sends in money. What?" holding my hands wide apart.

They look at me hard for a moment and start laughing, "Fucking guy coming over here and talking shit to us like this, you got some fucking balls, Big Boy," smacking each other on the arms. The other kids are clustered together—this is still on the line.

"We might let you bunk here, you can add some muscle to my crew if you can do more than talk. I'm Tommy, this is Silvio, Tony, Eddy, Mikey, Jimmy, Eddy and Fucking Louie over there."

"Hey," nodding at them, "I'm Frankie C."

"Frankie C, that's funny. What you in for, oh wait, another honest man?" he slaps one of his sidekicks on the arm.

"Assault and battery with a deadly weapon."

"You do it?"

"I beat all three of those motherfuckers, two are in the hospital."

"Holy shit, an honest man. First one I seen," said the kid they referred to as Jimmy. Tommy, Tony and Mikey look pretty tough, well muscled, calm—the other kids watch them to take a clue on what to do. These guys stay as a pack.

"So what's the layout of this place?"

"Baddest kid in here is Artone on the second floor, black kid, he works for that fucking mooley Mister Willie. Next down the chain is Elonzado, a spic fuck who runs a rival gang. He's right over there with his boys, tattoos and all, not that tough, just a lot of them here. Both of those guys run a lot of merchandise in and out of the joint."

"What are you, fucking Switzerland? Guards make a little on the side for looking the other way?"

"Hey, you're a smart one."

"Where do you fit in?" looking at Tommy.

"We setup connections."

"Be careful of that Artone, he always tries out the new big kids," said Tony.

Looking at him, nodding.

"Lights out in ten, Scumbags," the guards yell as they walk by.

"Where do I bunk?"

"You like that one?" smart-ass kid Eddy starting in.

"Sure."

"Well tough shit," said Eddy, laughing looking at his boys. They're looking at him and then at me to see what I'll do.

Looking at him, nodding and laughing, acting like this is funny. He's trying to see where I fit in the pecking order. Stepping over and laying back on his bunk, looking at him, my hands behind my head, "Ah, this will do just fine." The guys look at me then the skinny kid, wise-ass Eddie.

"You best get the hell off my bunk!" he's starting to get nervous, his body swaying, he can't give up the act this easily.

"You tell me, Eddy? I'm going away for a few years," deadly serious holding his eyes, "who's gonna give a shit if I cave in your fucking rib cage, you little shit. What's another three months?" looking at him, waiting for him to make a move. He looks at the other guys.

The tough kid Tommy looks at me, nods, "Looks like it's your bunk."

Looking directly at Eddie. His eyes get small—the rest of the guys start laughing at him.

"Hey settle in, here comes Marion and that prick Letterman," said Silvio. Eddie muttering and straightening out another bunk, then pushing one of the kids at the outside of our area who backs off.

Lights out.

A couple of kids sobbing in the night.

Scared at how fast I'm fitting in.

Welcoming the black emptiness—fighting off the scream inside me at how much I miss her, how much I fucked it all up. Tensing my body, holding the awfulness in. Days ago I was as close to heaven as I dreamed, now, I'm surrounded by snoring, farting kids, some quietly talking about the girls they are fantasizing about as they beat off. Other kids are having quiet sex a few bunks away—must be some of the boys who were too ashamed to be seen talking with the two who were walking arm-in-arm flirting here and there earlier. They found their way in the darkness.

Breathing deeply to fight off the nastiness settling in.

Someone moving in the darkness—they are slowly coming toward me. Rolling off my bunk on the opposite side quietly. Stepping around between the bunks—it's darker here. It's that little sneaky fuck Eddy and he's got something he's trying to hide by his waist.

I know they are watching me—nobody's making a move. He looks back, he's trying to walk close to the bunks so I won't see him coming. Cocking my arm back, getting my weight set.

Dark outline of his face at the top of my bunk, violent snap, full body behind my rock fist—connecting with a short strong right to the side of his head. He drops like a rock.

"Holy shit," said Tony quietly. Guards stop walking for a moment, listening for anything else. Tony taps Tommy on the arm. I pick up Eddy, sharpened end of spoon in his hand, taking it, passing it to Tony who tucks it quickly under his blanket.

"He's out cold," to Tony. He looks at me and nods.

Lifting Eddy up and putting him in the bunk by the grouchy blonde kid, then quietly moving back to my bunk. Mikey, Tony and Tommy checking me out.

Chapter 17

Another monotonous morning counting off in line, reciting rules when called on by the guards. Waiting in line for breakfast, muscular, light skinned black guy up ahead, turning, trying to dog me, get me to lock eyes.

Fifth straight day with a breakfast of colorless, tasteless powdered eggs, tasteless oatmeal and tasteless white bread.

Tommy coming over, concerned look on his face.

"Yo, Frankie C.," He sits down, nodding to him, taking another bite of my tasteless food. Tony sitting down alongside, "I got word that Elonzado wants to talk to us."

"No disrespect, Tommy, but what the fuck am I, the social director here, we having a party for that maricon motherfucker?"

"Now's no time to be a comedian," serious look on his face.

"He heard how you handled Edgar, he was the only guy Artone had to think twice about in here. You took him apart," said Tony snapping his fingers.

"So what, doesn't make sense," looking at Tommy, "unless…"

"Yeah," said Mikey joining in, "like what, that stupid fuck Edgar's gonna be drinking from a straw for a long time."

"Mikey, sometimes you need to shut the fuck up," said Tony.

"What's the angle? He gonna make a move against Mr. Willie?" looking at him, "he wants us to back his play."

"That's what I'm thinking," said Tommy.

"Guards ain't gonna like someone fucking up the system."

"No shit," said Tony, "there better be a big pay-off for putting a target on our backs."

"So how we play this? Got to be a price for saying yes and a price for saying no."

"That's what I like about you Frankie C, you think about the what if's." Both of them nodding slowly, the other guys in the crew trying to get into the conversation, but are quiet when Tommy and Tony are thinking.

"I think we need to hear the man," said Mikey.

"It means that Mr. Willie's gonna come calling," looking at them, "you know if he sees we are not neutral. You're connected, Tommy, so they both got to be careful."

"Yeah, but Mr. Willie's connected to a guy who pulls a lot of weight."

Looking at them.

"Sounds like it's time someone put Artone in the hospital with Edgar, people might have more numbers than us, but they'll think twice about trying to push us into a corner right? Leave the bear in the cave alone."

"I get it, but we got to be careful, you take him, it fucks up the power structure here. Some of these pig guards make good money from that prick, Mr. Willie."

Nodding, eating.

"We talk what's gonna happen on the outside Tommy? We got to get clearance or this won't stick," said Tony, looking at his friend.

"I know, I'll call Big C. tonight. Be nice to have some breathing room," he looks at me. "If you take him, it's got to look personal, like he's going off his leash. Mr. Willie hates when Artone gets out of control."

Nodding.

"You be careful with Artone, he's a dirty motherfucker."

Rolling my eyes, another day in paradise.

Chapter 18

The sum of quiet conversations in the hall during another shitty lunch produces a low steady background rumble. Shoveling in my food, tired of listening to the same old stories from these guys. The worst part of this place is the same-old-same-old stories every damn day.

"I'll catch you guys later," need to get away from these assholes, go find a place and work out some of this energy. Go setup a basketball game in the yard. Only place I can jive with some of the brothers. Taking my tray to the long conveyor belt. Feeling someone coming near me—side stepping and turning before he can get close. Artone with a cocked smile on his face, his boys hanging back—moron.

"Yo man, you stepped on my foot."

Looking at him calm, shrugging my shoulders, moving to get loose. Let him play this bullshit. Let him go off leash.

"Excuse me then, no disrespect, my man," relaxed, looking at him, move to his right, get him used too moving with me. Set him for a big shot if he wants to play this hard.

His boys coming up behind him.

"Yo, you stupid too, White Boy?" he says to his boys who start laughing, smiling at them. He shifts over to block me, while he's moving I move easily to his left—guys don't expect someone to lead with their left the way I'm standing. He looks at me not sure why I'm looking at him now. He steps left, his body a little off balance trying cut me off again; dropping my tray and launching a big left hook, surprise on his face as he moves into my rock fist. His legs buckle, eyes wide for a second—only stunned him—fuck, he stumbles back. People rushing over, noise breaking out. Fucker can take a punch.

Catching him with a good hard right to the side of his head as he tries to get some room, taking his weak wild punches on my arms, kicking his feet out from under him, he falls down face first, his head bouncing off the floor. Moving in for the kill as he tries to roll away.

Kick to his stomach flips him. Hands grabbing at me, punches coming in, wave of body weight pushing me forward—too close to punch, coming down on his face with massive elbows, his nose splitting, huge gash opening over his left eye—again, again.

About to come down with another big elbow, his eyes fluttering, his body going limp, turning to try and get away from the mass of arms and legs whacking at me.

Stronger hands on me; nightstick around my throat pulls me up, cutting off my air. Struggling—unconsciously grabbing the stick pulling it down with all my strength, spinning my body like a shark caught on long line fighting for its life.

Slipping down, getting away. Another kid kicking at me, hard contact on my back, yelling out in red hot anger, grabbing the kid's foot, tripping over a wiggling body—shouts, curses, people breathing hard.

Arm coming up in my face, biting down on it hard, the owner screaming as I sink my teeth in, punches to my face, kicks. Punching, kicking, blind energy—standing on some kid's face and grabbing the rest of the body that came with the arm—punching him repeatedly in the face. He's crying out for me to stop, his voice is too far away from me. More big hands on me, pain breaking out on my legs—shots from nightsticks, sinking down as another stick comes around my neck, barely getting any air, struggling as the guards haul me back, feeling my face getting red, colors starting to circle in my vision.

Slammed down on the floor, hard shot to my head bringing my arms up to protect my face—sound of wood smacking meat registering a long way off in the distance, pain following. Dazed, dragged, watching the ceiling lights moving past me like I'm watching a movie, hands putting me into something with rough texture.

Feeling warm.

Can't move my arms, thrown into a room.

Door slamming, pitch black darkness, stifling silence.

Drifting in and out of total darkness. Don't know if my eyes are open or closed, pain starting to register and spread throughout my body.

Shaking in my bonds—can't move my arms, fighting off the panic that tries to constrict my throat. Rolling, can't free myself. Breathing starting to get tough, can't keep the panic from rising. Fighting whatever it is that's holding me, struggling, trying to unwrap myself. Hard to breathe, yelling, screaming out in the darkness. Throat constricting, rolling—something taking me deeper, pulling me down.

Barely able to get to my feet, pulling with all my body, yelling, running fast—face crashing into something cold and hard. Sinking down stunned—can't breathe, black tentacles reaching up to my throat, pulling me down, panic rising. Struggling beyond exhaustion.

Blackness. Surrendering to the pull of the deep blackness.

Not afraid of the cold hands pulling me down.

Waking up exhausted—no idea how many days I've been here.

Sleeping, sobbing, hating myself for being weak.

Hands on me, lights on, blinded.

"Sit up you fucking animal, you lie down again we going to beat you bloody." Lights off, door slamming.

Colors swirling in my mind, I think my eyes are open.

Deep pain trying to sit up like this cuffed as I am.

How long have I been sitting here?

Hours, minutes—mind blank, so tired I can't think.

Body shaking from the slow, long pain.

Feeling steel on my wrists and ankles.

Can't move my arms, can't shift my body weight.

Hurts like hell swallowing, throat dry and sore.

Tongue feels like sand paper, lips cracked, sitting in my own stink.

Slowly rolling over as fatigue-filled tendrils pull me down to the cold floor. Moments of peace, watching a movie on the wall of the room but the words are out of reach.

Jolt, someone kicking me, deep guttural growl coming up from my throat as people beat me and sit me up again.

"Stay up, you fucking maggot," taking another blow to my back.

"Fuck you," spitting where I think they are, hard fist to my face.

Feels so real here. Seeing the early morning woods in Pennsylvania by Uncle Michael's hunting lodge. Looking down at the small stream running in front of the house. Clear, clean water running over rocks. Deep green grass on the banks of the stream, gravel and sand path down to where I used to skinny dip.

Must be dreaming, there's no pain here.

Blinking my eyes in the darkness, someone's in here with me.

Usually it's those two bastard guards at night.

"It safe?"

"You're a joke." I know that voice. Staying calm, he comes close...

Face coming close to me, feeling the warmth, "You cost me, you owe me."

Staying still. I don't know this one.

"This motherfucker sleeping?"

"He hears you. He's a dangerous one, lull you in by being quiet, then lash out."

"Sheeiit."

"We got ways of taming him." There he is, following his footsteps as he walks behind me. Feeling a face coming near me again. Can't tell if I'm hallucinating.

Throat feels raspy. Placing things.

I know who this motherfucker is now.

"Your boy wasn't too smart, Mr. Willie, I offered respect..."

"You might be too smart fo yo own good."

Voice I know coming in softly, "Yessss, talk to him, let him be close. You know what do to..." Image of his bald head coming into view in my mind—his eyes fluttering, his hands coming at me as I slowly push my thumbs down into his throat, my body weight keeping his fluttering death throes from making any noise.

"Adversity is the motherfucker of learning. Ain't that right, Mr. Willie?"

"Still got some spunk in ya? I like that, you come out, you work for me.

You don't, you end up back here. I own yo ass now. You nod show me you understand."

Nodding slowly. Footsteps moving back out of the door.

Swallowed back up by the blackness.

Coming to, can't tell if I'm still dreaming. Blinking my eyes, can't distinguish the difference. Hunger blending with pain, raw animal meanness growing inside at each beating. Bastards know I can't sit like this for a long time and when I can't take the pain of sitting like this... Soft comforting voice, "No one can, they just bring you closer to me."

Gnashing my teeth. I'm going fucking going nuts here.

Bastards are going to have to kill me.

I got nothing out there, nothing in here.

Staying up as long as I can, then rolling over for a few seconds of relief. Throat raw, doesn't even sound like my voice, "Come on!" Yelling into the warm blackness, "do it!"

"Shut the fuck up in there. Don't you learn?"

"Hey Harry, looks like it's our favorite pass time, guinea pool."

Door opening—body shaking, "Bring it, motherfuckers!"

Chapter 19

Voices around me, feeling like I should say something, but they are too far away to hear my words. Sitting some place too deep to make out what they are saying.

Hands on my body again, moving me.

Cold water—feeling the cold from a long way away, like I'm watching things while sitting up on the ceiling of my cell. Awful sensation under my nose, head snapping up, taking in big gulps of air, pulling my hands to my face—both wrists handcuffed to the side of a bed. Splitting headache pounding in my head, eyes hurt opening them just a crack to the light. Teeth that were cracked from the beatings throbbing and hurt like hell. Blinking, dull shapes around me. Lifting my knees—they'll only move so far, steel on my ankles too. Painful to move my arms, elbows on my knees, putting my face in my hands.

Drifting away again.

People talking in the distance.

Barely able to pick out every third or fourth word, "Jacket," "Concussion," "Trouble," "Judge," "Recognizance."

"Frank," surprised to hear my name, not 10789. Blinking, trying to make out the hazy face, frustrated because it should look familiar but I can't see.

"Take him," mumbles blending together, "come on."

Hearing someone getting mad—probably some fuck joking about putting me in with the adults again. Muscles straining against steel remembering the bullshit those pricks that beat me every night would ramble on about. "You think you're a badass, you're gonna get fucked and be some mean brother's bitch in there, Tough Guy." Then they'd laugh cause I'd laugh with them, maybe they knew that I might get raped, but someone's going to die.

Awful sensation under my nose.

Able to mumble out, "thh-headed," mouth won't make the words to help stop the pounding in my head "th-head poppping." Falling down a dark hole again. Distant voices.

"You get him fixed up NOW, I'm going to have your fucking asses on a plate," voice familiar, too tired to place it, trying to lie back down to ease the pounding in my head. Just want to move back to the welcome blackness, following the song, following it back down.

People taking my arms, lifting me up, making me walk.

PAIN—pain shooting through me.

Head feels like it's going to explode.

"Keep him," mumbles, wanting to let my head flop, pain shooting up my legs, "more." Blinking my eyes, fuzzy gray shapes in the room offset from the light.

Can't make anything out. Oh no—anything but this.

"Eyes, eyes, d-don't work," panic rising against, arms starting to grab hold of me. Weakly pushing back, trying to get away. Loud voice, different hands on me, sitting me down. Trying to blink, force myself to see—no God, no. Tears running down my cheeks. Is this my penance? Oh please no, blind. I'm blind!

Chin in my chest, body sobbing uncontrollably.

Shuddering, calming down, people leaving me alone.

This is it—I'm blind. Feeling something pricking my arm.

"Don't go to sleep," someone saying, trying to blink and see them, outline only. Trying to take in the room, breathing coming more regularly now.

"Smacked himself against the wall in lock down like an animal."

"Yeah well where the fuck those marks come from, you think I'm a fucking idiot? Are you that stupid? You don't think I know how it's played here?"

"Hey, it was like taking down a raging mad man, we'll teach him manners."

"The hell you are!"

"You don't have jurisdiction here, this is my house!"

"You think so?" seeing more of the outlines—guards, man in a long coat, man in some kind of suit, "I'll have a judge's order here in thirty minutes, and I'm going to have your ass on a plate in front of the Commissioner. You cross the line with me, you never get back, you unnerstand ME!"

"Easy, easy Lieutenant," another voice chipping in, outline of a man in a smooth suit, "we're all on the same team."

"You want me to calm down, you get your boss here now or I call the judge."

Grey soft light starting to appear—hurts to shake my head.

Blinking looking around, two guards starting to emerge from the fog. No, it can't be. Uncle Vin? Tilting my head forward trying to make him out, things moving in slow motion, outline of the other man emerging from the haze—he gave me the orientation... Deputy Warden Harding? Why's he here?

"You monkeys, out of the fucking room."

"Hey, you can't talk to me like that," sounds like one of the guards.

"You wanna dance with me, is that it? You want to dance with someone not in a straitjacket or cuffed. Are you that stupid?"

People shuffling around, door opening. Can't make them out now, sitting back, moving to lie down. Hands on my body.

"Don't lie down," different voice.

"H-head splitting."

"You have a concussion, looks like some of your teeth are badly damaged. You're going to feel like shit for a while."

"Oh you mm-meean, feel nn-normal."

Shape shaking his head.

"Always a wise ass."

"Unn, Unncle Vin?" fighting back any chance of hope so it can't be dashed, they left me here.

"Shh, we'll get you fixed up."

Quiet—fighting to keep the ray of hope walled up inside. He'll be gone soon and I'll be back in the hole. Breathing quietly, tensing my chest and abdominal muscles to force down the feelings trying to work their way out. He's quiet.

"Quite a mess you've made here."

"Pprison bull, bully... Works for the g-guy who runs trade inside," head pounding, "he made th, the f first move."

Silence. His face set in stone. Choking up knowing he's gonna leave me here again. "Wwhat ddo you want from me?" can't keep it in. "Tell Ddad how f fucked up I am? What?"

"Easy."

"L'liars, hypocrites!"

"Watch your mouth," he's pointing a finger at me.

"Yyou all, always telling me to s-stand up for what I believe, not, back down from bullies, think for myss, myself, take the hit if you need to..." Tears starting to run down again, flood opening, can't help it, "b-be honest, say wha, what I think the tru truth is, stand up ffor what I believe, nn... Never quit!"

Fighting to catch my breath. "Nothing but sma, smacks, yelling from my ffucking old man. Ttelling me I'm shit, no gg... no good."

Trying to get up, dizzy sinking back down. Hollow inside.

"Just leave me here!" fighting back the tears running down my face. "All you told me what a man should be, all I trriedd." Dad's face when they left me, "Leave me in jail. I did it, I fucked up, I got nothing! NOTHING. Just leave me here, leave me alone."

Holding my arms to my side, squeezing my body.

"SO, WHAT DO YOU WANT FROM ME!" yelling with all I have left, quieter now. "What dd-do you want from me?" looking at him, his face impassive his eyes locked on mine. "What, you got to gloat now? I'm never going back, never."

Body sobbing, pain shooting up and down my arms, legs, head. Breathing to get control of myself, the waves subsiding, gray fog setting in.

Holding out my palm, punching down hard. "I'm no fucking good, leave me alone." Doubling over but not from the physical pain. Fool, thinking there was some hope left. He's here to gloat.

Deep breath, this is what I need, the pain, just the pain.

Feel it, take it, own it—then I'm going to make people pay.

"I'm not gonna quit," breathing deep, I have to say it for myself, "I'm not gonna quit, you can't make me. I'm not gonna quit no matter what... They put me back in that hole and I'm not going to give in. Those fuckers can keep beating me." Quiet roar like the wounded animal I am getting ready to get in and keep fighting—this is to the death. "I won't do it!" looking at him defiant in the pain, "I won't give up, all of you will just have to beat me to death."

My uncle taking a deep breath, his eyes watery, he looks away around the room. Fuck you voice. I'm not going to give in to you either.

Door opening and closing, the absence of sound cutting through me. Good, they are leaving me alone. Tell yourself that, Frank.

Breathing slowly.

Don't fight the pain that's here, Frank, adopt it, adapt to it—surrender to the pain. My face hurts at the smile forming on my damaged face. I'm going to take Mr. Willie's head in my hands when I meet him. I'm slowly going twist his neck in my hands. That smug motherfucker, I'm going to hurt him bad, real bad. Maybe he has an accident—then we run this place.

The pain feels good. That's all that I have now.

Breathing out slowly.

Someone lifting my arm, another prick.

Looking around, room closing down.

Coming back to the light again. Lying down. Muscles sore.

Hands on my arms, helping me up. Making me stand.

Feeling faint—forcing myself to stand, Mr. Willie wants me to be his boy. Hurts to laugh. Need to get my head together. Holding onto the side of the bed, vision getting better. Head still splitting—hurts to even breathe. Closing my eyes, deep breath.

Realizing the cuffs and shackles are gone.

Mr. Willie, wait till it's dark, wait till we're alone.

Shifting my body, trying to get a picture of how damaged I am. Moving my fingers and toes, I can feel all of them—knuckles feel raw, elbow sore. Forearms badly damaged, deep bruises to my bone where I covered up from the nightsticks. Knees okay just sore as hell, skin on my thighs still stinging, deep muscle bruises on my legs and calf muscles. Lower back hurts like hell. Mouth and jaw hurt like hell.

Trying to move, making a fist painful.

Chest hurts to take a deep breath.

People coming in the room, guards—shrinking back, ready.

Body gripped in anger. Here to beat me again? Shaking.

"Easy, kid," Doctor coming over, "sit down, no one's going to hurt you."

Looking at him uneasily, sitting facing the guards—I don't want my back to them.

"Take these," he gives me a handful of pills and small paper cup of water.

"Help that king-sized headache. You're going to need to get those teeth looked at."

Hard to swallow, almost gagging, throat dry—giving me a larger glass of water. Stomach feeling sick, "Don't vomit, breathe, good, good," as I keep it down. "Keep it down, breathe," Doc leaving. Looking at the guards. One of them walking up to me, he doesn't work the hole.

"Kid," shocked at his tone of voice, "put the good word in for us, huh? We didn't know, we'll fix the bad apples, okay?" Looking at him, not understanding, "Your uncle's raising a shit storm."

"Ssure, ssure."

"That fucking Artone, you tuned his ass up good. Some of us feel you did this place a favor."

"Happened to him?" chin sinking down to my chest.

"Broken nose, broken jaw, broken ribs, broken collar bone, lost a lot of teeth, he's gonna have a new face, ain't that right, Charley?" he says to the other guard, recognizing the tall guy who smacked me in the stomach the first day. He's putting on an act—it will be, Mr. Corrections Officer, when they get me back inside. "Uncle said you were 28 and 1 in Golden Gloves, hate to see the kid that beat you," the Charley guy trying to be friendly.

"He's going to the Olympics next year, strong, fast, he'll be a real pro."

Phone ringing—head starting to clear a little while one of the assholes talks in the background.

"Let's go, kid."

"Yes, Mr. Corrections Officer."

"You don't need to do that now," looking at him, cocking my head—not sure I heard that right. "No hard feelings, kid?"

The Charley guy looking at me hard, "No, Sir."

He looks at me, not flinching from his look. He nods, "Okay."

Following them through long administrative halls—rooms filled with filing cabinets, women and men typing, reading through forms, men and guards walking the hall. A couple of kids from the bunk are looking at me as I walk by, talking to each other.

Large room, looking around not understanding what is happening as the guard plants me by a desk—no cuffs. Woman with an elaborate beehive hair-do working there, she's acting like I'm invisible, sitting there chewing her gum, giving it a nice pop every few minutes. Guard puts a folder on her desk. Uncle Vin out in the hall talking to people in suits, a couple of his guys come up and joke around with him.

Soft voice, "Yo, Frankie C." Snapping out of my daze, Tommy is standing by the door, broom in hand. Turning to the Bride of Frankenstein, "Do I have permission to talk to my friend, ma'am?"

She rolls her eyes, "Be quick about it," and goes back to typing.

"Hey Tommy, what's going on?"

"Man, oh man," he looks at me and ducks his head a little closer, "I ain't seen nothin like that. Man did you fuck that guy up, two of his boys too. Everybody's talking about it."

"10633, get back to work," a passing guard shouts.

"Yes, Mr. Corrections Officer."

"When you're out on the street, you come look me up, you and me could make a fortune with those brass balls. I got connections. Canarsie, ask at Benny's Meats for me. Man, a lot of people were cheering you on, man. What they doin?"

"Could be sending me to one the adult corrections houses, I don't know. That fuck, Mr. Willie," looking at him, "they brought him down to my cell. Told me I'm going to work for him."

"No shit," he looks worried. Leaning in close to him.

"Don't worry, man. I stay here and I get Mr. Willie alone, he's gonna wish he never saw me, I'm gonna cripple that prick and I'm going to do it slowly," he's looking at me with wide eyes, nodding, digging the vibe, "then we take over this place."

"You got some brass balls, Frankie C," he's running angles through his head. "I'm in, with Elonzido weak and Artone out, this place is ripe for the picking. Don't worry, you go to the adult side, I get you connected, some rough fucking moolies in here, but our guys will love a tough fuck like you," he looks around, "full blooded Siciliano, brass balls... When we outta here, we gonna make a fucking fortune."

"Hey, what the fuck did I tell you 10633?" the guard coming over.

"Got to go," he rolls his eyes. Fucking Tommy.

"Later."

Sitting back down, Uncle Vin's gone off now.

Catching myself before I start letting go and getting all wishy-washy. You know the rules. Steeling myself to deal with a whole different kind of animal if I go into the men's joint. Artone was big and tough, but he was stupid—couldn't see not to fuck with me and then couldn't see I was setting him up. No way big time guys would fall for that chickenshit. They'll have weapons there too; they deal with men not boys. Deep breath, I may not win, but if I have to fight, all me is going to show up.

"Sign here," she says in a whiny voice, her heavily made up face coming into focus. Looking over the form, my name and prison number, starting to read. "Look, I ain't got all day," signing, pushing the form back to her.

"Now this one, both places," signing away like it matters.

"He's all done," she waves over the guard, my new best friend.

Following him out. Searching the halls for any sign of my uncle.

Steeling myself—he's gone again. Fuck it, I've been in for three weeks now, I'll learn the rules on the other side and deal with it.

Following, walking down the long cold halls.

Long sections of fluorescent bulbs flickering on and off.

Cardboard box with my name shoved in front of me.

"Why am I getting this?" looking at the guard, "are there different uniforms in HDM?"

The guard looking at me like I'm a complete idiot, "You're being released on your uncle's recognizance, dumbass."

"What?"

"Get moving fore he changes his mind and throws your ass back in."

"Yes," opening the box, "yes, Sir," moving as quickly as the pain will let me.

Putting my clothes on—weird mothball smell.

Folding up my prison uniform, putting it back on the stainless steel table. Guard pointing at the same door I came in a couple of weeks ago. Stepping outside, blinking in the late afternoon light. Head pounding from walking.

Seagulls chattering away out in the bay, the smell of the ocean replacing the industrial pine cleaner, fear, piss and shit I sat in for days and days in the hole. Passing through the chain link fence. Dark blue Dodge parked in the gravel parking lot, driver's seat empty.

I guess I'll walk back to the city and the way I feel, it's going to be a very slow walk.

Looking across the long bridge back across the bay.

Chapter 20

Seagulls crying out in the bay.

Walking slowly along the edge of the bridge.

"You want a lift," turning around as a car slows down next to me.

Taking in the big stern face, thick neck and broad shoulders.

Airplane taking off at nearby La Guardia.

Staring at him. "I..." stuck, there's nothing to say to these pricks.

He gives a big humph, motions to the car.

About to get in the back seat, "What am I, a fucking chauffeur? Get your ass in here," he points to the front seat. Sitting in the car—smells of coffee, cigar smoke, old vinyl, radio chatter in the background.

"This is 121, I'm code 7."

"Roger that, 121," comes a female voice over the radio.

He drives off slowly, looking back at the Rikers buildings. I had no idea how large that complex was. Driving across the long two-lane bridge over the Bowery Bay, the prison disappearing behind. Looking back, trying to sear all the memories of that shithole in my memory so I never forget the place, the smells, the people, the guards—I see Artone or Mr. Willie again and I'll be back in solitary again.

Shifting on the car seat. Feeling weird, like I shouldn't be here. Relieved, confused, replaying things that happened too quickly to catch everything—people, action, faces, words. Background chatter on his radio stills for a moment, my uncle's frame filling the large, unmarked car.

Watching him from the corner of my eye, watching people walking the streets. Passing streets I should know, rows and rows of stores, people of all sizes colors. People talking, kids out causing trouble, teenage boys checking out teenage girls, old people sitting around folding chairs in front of small social clubs playing dominos.

Weird. Head hurts. Hungry. Feeling empty inside. I don't want to be here—rather be on the streets alone. Uncle impassive, watching the streets, wonder what he sees here as we're driving around.

Right, now it looks like it is time for the famous Caruso family silent treatment.

Light shining in my left eye and then my right.

Answering questions, following the light.

Poked, prodded, stretched and pulled.

Room is clean and spacious, medical diplomas on the wall, posters of the human body—muscle structure, organs, nervous systems. Speaking only when spoken too, Uncle Vin's disappointment with me so clear.

No reaction from my uncle or the doctor till I take off my shirt. Pained look on his face for a moment, then he looks away. Soreness and stiffness in my arm, leg and back muscles growing as the days goes on.

"You're going to feel very stiff for the next week," he walks around my back while motioning for my uncle to come over.

"A couple of cracked ribs, I'll wrap him up," as he breaks out the widest Ace Bandage I've ever seen, and starts wrapping it around my chest. "Other than that, he needs time to rest and recuperate. I'm worried about the blows to his kidneys, must have hurt like hell. He'll keep pissing blood for a few days; if it's longer, get him in quickly, blood clot there could be bad news. Lucky he's in such good shape, his muscles took a lot of the blunt force trauma."

"Thanks Doc, I owe you for getting us in so quickly."

"Not a problem, Vincent, any time for you," they shake, "you know that."

The doctor turns to me, "You can get dressed, take three Tylenol every four hours for the next couple of days. Get a couple of days rest in bed, get in a hot bath every day to work the muscle soreness, stay away from any strenuous activity for a week, you took a lot of hard shots," to my uncle, "any sign of fainting or dizziness, you get him to the emergency room, pronto."

"Will do, Doc."

"You gonna go after the people that did this?"

"Oh yeah," seeing the anger in his eyes for the first time.

They leave the patient room, doctor speaking back over his shoulder, "Come on out when you're ready," slowly getting my clothes back on, hurts bending over to tie my shoelaces.

Feeling like an old man.

Going in and out under the light in the dentist's chair.
Face feels numb as he's working in my mouth.
At least the gold teeth will be in the back of my mouth.
Fuck, four broken teeth, three others need to be repaired.

Sun setting. Face feels the Novocain slowly receding.

Wondering how long the silent treatment from Uncle Vin is going to last, with Dad, let's see, I have to calibrate given what's gone on in the past; guessing this would be worth at least a month with time off if there were really good groveling and signs of penance involved. Ha, like that's going to happen. I get my bankbook then I'm gone. They steal my money again, I'll go find that guy Ben, or go find Tommy, work strong arm for someone then get the hell out of New York, Uncle Vin will never let me work the streets for long.

Go visit my mom's uncle in California, figure out how to live there. Vision of the beach, sun, Cat—fighting back a wave of aching sadness.

Streets starting to look familiar, this is my aunt and uncle's neighborhood. Uncle Vin shaking his head, his body starting to move uncomfortably in his seat, feeling my eyes open wider—surprised to see him getting ready to talk.

How much more shame do these guys need to make me feel, this isn't enough? Looking off to the outline of the Williamsburg Bridge to Manhattan. East River, then the Hudson—maybe it's time for me to go. He takes me home and I'm leaving. Time to go west. What about Cat? I thought I'd never see her again.

Like she'll have anything to do with me now.

"I never," he takes a deep breath in, "in almost twenty years, you hear me!" deep voice, laced with emotions. "YOU HEAR ME!"

"Uncle Vin, what? What did I do?"

"Your aunt and I have not had a fight," his mouth working, quiet for a couple of moments, police radio chatter fills the car. "Must be almost ten years since we had a big fight. She has been at me the last few weeks like a Harpy." He looks over at me, "Cause of your ass, you stunad," he takes a big breath and lets it out slowly. "She's the only reason I checked to see what was happening over there."

Shaking my head. Fucking Italian families, everything we do has to have some goddamn drama—some huge emotion behind it. What now?

"I ought to wring your neck," he laughs to himself, "I know how little good it would do." Deathly silent car filled with radio background chatter as we drive around—he's circling the neighborhood.

Checking out the neighborhood to keep from looking at him, old growth trees, two and tree story houses packed in close together, very different than the brownstones I know. Some brick, most have different types of vinyl or aluminum siding in different colors. Stores reflect the mix of people and religions here—more folks from the Middle East starting to move in.

"My brother's a good man, don't you forget that!" He lapses into thought for a moment and then almost absent minded, "Both of you got that "stubborn as a bulldog that sets his teeth and you got to kill it" them streak in you a mile wide."

Turning to a different route now.

"How long was I out?"

"Two days, you had us worried."

Driving along the streets of Queens and into Brooklyn, passing under the elevated train. Big Hispanic neighborhood—Salsa music blaring from a record store, markets overflowing with fresh produce on the street, clothing stores, and religious art stores.

Waiting for him, he's got something that's hard to say.

"You know I've never pulled any punches with you, Frank," nodding, looking at him, "your father doesn't want you back home."

Hurts even though I know it. Taking a deep breath, holding it, ribs and muscles hurt. Nodding to acknowledge my uncle.

Breathe the pain out slowly.

"I can make it on my own, Hector's dad can get me job doing construction, and Gus offered to train me, see if I got what it takes to turn pro. I can do it. I know I can make something of this on my own. You all told me you were done with me."

"Like hell you WILL!" he yells, his face getting red, he punches the dashboard.

Enveloped by the suffocating silence in the car.

Streets moving by.

Men and women coming home from work, walking the streets. Searching through the tired faces, desperate faces, satisfied faces—I'm not special. I need to get my ass out there and work, make some money. Fuck school, I'm tired of doing what a bunch dead of people want me to do.

"You're going to live with us while we sort through the legal proceedings, then we'll figure out what happens next."

Shock running through my body.

"What?"

"She was right," his big hands gripping the steering wheel hard, he looks at me, "you tell her and I'll…"

Another block, slowing down as a delivery van blocks the street. Cars start honking. Uncle Vin gives his siren a tweak—guy comes running out of the building, pulls up and over. When we are next to him, "Hey, you block these fucking streets again, I'm gonna impound your truck, you savvy?"

"Sorry, Officer, sorry."

"Asshole," as we drive off, he rolls up the window.

Blocks moving by slowly in stop and go traffic.

"Broke my heart to hear you back at Rikers, Frank, just broke my heart. Doesn't mean you don't have to own up to what you did, you hear?" his voice rising again. "My brother thinks he was doing the right thing by riding you so hard, Kitty saw it though, frustrated that she couldn't do anything about it. Your mom… well you know how she is and how those two got along—oil and water."

"She told me that John and I were wrong about you and that I needed to be man enough to admit it and get involved," he takes a deep breath. "I hate it when she's right like that," he waits a minute, his hands relaxing on the steering wheel, "and she was," he won't look at me, "she was right, seeing you like that, all the things you could 'a been. Just pierced my heart."

Shaking his head.

"Look, gonna be rules you need to live by. Gonna have to earn my trust."

Looking at him—yeah, like I trust you.

Wishing I could be any place but here.

"Legally your father's in a bind, him chucking you out and all underage. Next year, he'd been free and clear. He doesn't know what I'm doing and I'm sure it will piss him off to no end, but I don't think he sees how things like this end up. I do."

"Tomorrow I'm gonna start showing you what you got to look forward to if you don't get your shit in one sock, cause I won't put up with criminals in my house no matter how you impressed those little shits in juvie. You go over the line again and I will come down on you harder that you can believe, family or no family. You hear? You savvy?"

"Yes, Sir," my flat tone looks like it pisses him off as we pull into the driveway.

"I'm hungry, you got someone who wants to see you. Why, I have no idea?"

"Oh, Frankie," my aunt Kitty giving me a big, big, long hug. "Oh, Frankie, let me look at you." Must be a mess judging from the look on her face as she looks at my arms, she's starting to get angry. "What did they do to you in there, you look awful! Oh come in, come in. You must be hungry," she looks at my uncle, gives him a kiss on the cheek then a stern look, "you, I'm gonna talk to you later," she's shaking her open hand at him giving him what for.

"I'm so glad you're here, come on in to the kitchen," her Brooklyn accent coming through. "Sit down, sit down." Her kitchen smells wonderful, big pot of sauce slowly simmering on the stove, fresh basil in the washboard, something sautéing on the stove, big salad. Wonderful smell of fresh bread drawing out the hunger from not eating for what must be a few days. Bread sticks on the table.

"Here," she pushes a plate of olives, some good Ricotta Salata and fresh bread toward, me, "eat, eat." Sitting there, looking at them and then looking at the food, my aunt looking at me, "You're home now, Frankie, eat something," tears starting to roll down my face, doing everything I can to force them back, throat choking up. Waves of memories coming back of what it was like to be with the whole family out in Rockaway during the summers or at big family gatherings when Grandpa and Grandma were still alive—smiles, food, kids playing, getting into trouble, out in the streets when we got too rambunctious. Grandpa T playing the mandolin after dinner, Uncle Vin telling me stories about growing up in Brooklyn when they'd come over from Sicily.

Got to shake this off, don't be weak. I don't want to feel this. I want to leave.

"Bedo Figio," she says holding my arm, and giving my uncle an evil look, "it's okay now, it's okay. Eat something, you'll feel better."

Ashamed that I'm crying in front of them, can't look at my uncle. Taking some deep breaths to get ahold of myself, mad that I'm blubbering away.

Reaching for a bread stick, hard crunchy crust covered with sesame seeds hurts my teeth but tastes so good.

"Good, that's right. It's okay now, you're home," she gives Vin a hard look—catching him out of the side of my eyes looking down at his strong hands as he rubs his left hand around a shaking fist.

She gets up and is working away at the stove. Uncle Vin sipping at a glass of red wine, he jumps when my aunt slams the stove with her wooden spatula. She's standing still there, her body rigid for a few moments, turns a little and then goes back to what she was doing.

Absurd—the most feared policemen in the city, no match for Aunt Kitty. Wishing my mom had her testadudo. He looks at me, smiles a little, points a finger, whispers, "Don't you say a fucking word." Tension I didn't even realize I was carrying starting to drain off.

Big bowl of pasta with fresh sliced spicy sausage on the table, my uncle getting up to grate some fresh Parmesan cheese. Aunt Kitty filling his wine glass, setting his place, serving him and then me. Warm tomato sauce, rich with garlic, fresh basil, chunks of onion, oregano—she always makes it with a nice kick too, some red peppers. Heaven over the good thick Bruno's cheese ravioli. Trying to eat slowly. Stomach feels hungry, rejecting the food. Oh God, putting my food down as a wave of nausea rolls over me. Mouth feels full of saliva. They go quiet watching me.

Running into the hall bathroom.

Aunt and Uncle talking quietly about family gossip to fill in the growing silence while we eat. Starting to take in her whole kitchen, uncomfortable in the familiarity of so much time spent out here and all the memories—this could have been another hallucination on the black wall in the hole.

"Hey, he's alive after all," says Uncle Vin.

Small smile, food is so good versus that shit at Rikers.

"So," she says looking at him.

"So" he's shrugging his shoulders, hands up by his chest palms up.

"So!" she looks at him.

"Oh, okay," he turns to me. "I'm gonna talk to my brother John tomorrow let him know what's going on. Let him know you'll be staying with us for a while. You can stay down in the basement, it needs cleaning, lots of junk down there, but there's a sofa bed, a bathroom, plenty of room. Give you something to do to fix it up. Your Aunt and I need you to follow rules while you're here, capisce?"

Nodding. Here we go again.

"Nobody, but nobody comes in the house without our permission," getting my body set to memorize them, "you will not drink any alcohol here unless your aunt or I offer it. You will not be under the influence here or in any of your doings, you unnerstand?"

"Yes, Uncle Vin," biting back the smart-ass comments.

"You will either be here by the time we say at night, or you will call to let us know what is up. When I'm on duty, I'll give you a number where they will find me no matter what. You will help your aunt with all the chores she needs. She works and is not running a hotel for problem kids. Unnerstand?"

"Yes, Sir," working to keep calm while feeling the good being sucked out again—they're going to treat me like a frigging child.

"What you do on your time is your business, you keep your nose clean. I've taken legal custody of you," he holds out the thumb and forefinger of each hand making a circle. "This is my circle of trust. You earn your way in you earn the right to stay there. The longer you're there, the more freedom you get. You fuck up, it's back to zero. We monitor everything you do. Capisce?"

"Yo capito."

They are quiet. He's looking at me right in the eyes to see if I'm bullshitting him, nothing to hide from either of them—couldn't do it anyway. Doesn't mean I have to put a bullshit smile on my face.

"Help your aunt with the dishes then come downstairs and we'll get you setup. I want you to get some rest for the next two days then I got an appointment with the two guys that took you in, time to go through stories, get everything straight. You go in front of the judge in three weeks," he sits back and looks at my aunt. "No matter how much I feel for you, Frankie, I won't interfere here. If you're guilty, you're going back in."

"I understand, Uncle Vin."

"I'll make sure you have a good lawyer, I'll make sure the truth comes out, but I will not lie, I will not use my influence to get you off or get a lighter sentence." He's starting to get worked up, the hard face I saw when he came to the holding cell in Manhattan with Dad.

"Easy, Vincent. Easy, he knows," Aunt Kitty's hand on his shoulder.

He takes a breath and calms down some. He's looking directly at my eyes—hard look, burning in. "Good, that's the first step. You got a long way to go to get back, it's gonna take time, it's gonna be painful at times. You get impatient, you want the fast payoff you get what you got now and how's that working out?"

"Not so good."

"No shit."

"It's not how you think it is, Frankie," my aunt looking at me, looking at my uncle and putting her hand on his, putting her fingers down between his fingers and holding his hand. "You're not alone, you have people who care for you, people who'll fight for you on your side. Okay?"

"Oh and you don't want to see her pissed," my uncle starts laughing a little. She gives in and laughs a little too. Big smile on her face, "Very true, very true," she's laughing. Trying to laugh with them too, weak smile is the best I can do.

Walking into their basement, old familiar smells coming back—cool, musty, oil, all the equipment, tools and trophies down here. Some of the big fish my uncle caught on the wall. No room for them upstairs. Expertly stuffed and mounted, his spear guns on a big peg board, the work area where he takes care of dive gear.

"When's the last time you were in the water?" he asks.

"Must be five months."

"We got to fix that," passes me a box, "take these out to the garage, your aunt is clearing an area up there as a temporary space."

"Okay, Uncle Vin." Don't know if it's the food, or being out of Rikers, "Hey, Uncle Vin," holding the box, muscles sore as hell, "what if I start feeling dizzy or something?" trying to hide my smile while busting his chops.

"I'll give you dizzy you won't forget. Get your ass up the stairs."

He's looking around the large finished basement.

Heading up the old creaky wooden stairs through the house and out to the garage. Stopping for a second as I feel light-headed.

Only one car in the garage, the rest used for my aunt's gardening supplies, tools and workbenches for building furniture. Seeing so much of my grandfather here. Some of the old pieces he built when he first came over from Sicily and worked as a cabinetmaker resting under covers. I miss you Grandpa—standing in a well of shame thinking how proud he was of me when he was alive.

Back down to the basement, the light work feels good, head pounding slowing down to a low roar. Tiring quickly. Uncle Vin taking a break for a moment.

"You wouldn't happen to know anything about a guy in the West Side train yard who says some big curly haired kid jumped him, broke his jaw and stole his money would you?"

Meeting his gaze, nothing to hide on this one.

"You mean a guy who likes to corner runaways in the men's room and try to rape them?" Feeling the anger of that moment coming in, "The guy whose good buddies walk around with clubs talking about how they are going to beat the curly haired kids brains out and throw him in the river?"

"That's probably the one."

"Never heard of him."

He looks at me, "I didn't think so, but don't get too smart for yourself. Next couple of days you're gonna learn a lot."

Looking up the stairs—Aunt Kitty is out of hearing distance.

"He said he was going to fuck me and pass me around to his friends. He made the first move, Uncle Vin. I swear... I know I went after Leroy, Thomas Jones and Alton and all, but this guy came after me, there wasn't any choice."

He looks at me.

"Well," his face getting hard, "then he fucked with the wrong kid!"

"I got lucky, he thought I'd be afraid, didn't expect…"

He's looking at me.

"Whole lot you need to learn about how to diffuse situations like that, kid. Maybe you could, maybe you couldn't. That ex-con had a rap sheet longer than my arm," he moves another box my way, then stops and looks at me. "Bullies like to interview people, see how they'll react, they see you're afraid, then they'll continue to bully and make it worse. Getting angry or too aggressive doesn't give them a way to back down either. Sometimes being calm, showing respect but letting them know they fuck with you there's no turning back will help the smarter ones—give them an opportunity to back off. My guess is you didn't have a choice, other than being there in the first place you stunadude. You've got that white knight in you, you see evil, you want to attack and kill it. Not that there's anything wrong with that, you just can't lead with your fists all the time, you throw the sin of pride on top of that and look at where that's gotten you."

Nodding at him, part of me fighting his words, part of me hungry to talk about what went wrong, what happened in solitary.

"My gut was telling me I was fu…" he holds up his hand, "sorry, messing up, but I just didn't know what to do. Other than…"

He moves another couple of boxes.

"Takes skill Frank, kid, courage, strong stable emotions, brains, ability to stay cool under pressure. All that needs to be conditioned just like your body when you train for a fight. Real world, people fight with a lot more than fists, sticks and guns, more deadly than you can know at your age. You've got your fathers passion and ability to focus on a single thing you want, you've got that ability to commit yourself, like when you're in the ring, you've pulled out a lot of fights cause you wouldn't give in, you went deep." He stands up. "You need to develop the life experience and wisdom to go with that, Frank. Learn some flexibility, learn how to talk to people and read them. You got the tools, we'll have to see if you got the will and the patience to develop them." He looks at me for a few seconds. "Talent and raw ability are not enough in this world kiddo. I think my brother… Well, we'll talk more later."

"Uncle Vin?"

He turns, "What, Frank?"

Looking down, don't know how to say this. "I…"

"Easy kid, relax and say what you need to say."

"You won't like it."

"I don't like a lot of what I've seen, but that doesn't mean I won't listen to someone who talks to me like a man."

Looking up at him for a second to see if he's bullshitting me.

"After the fight with Alton," taking a deep breath, "I wanted to be by the river. I just couldn't be around people, and," taking a deep breath, "I wasn't kidding about them searching for me."

His strong eyes drill into me.

"You got something you need to say? What did you do?"

"I," closing my eyes, cold shiver running down my body remembering the voice that spoke to me, "I wasn't going to run, Uncle Vin," looking at his eyes, "it was dark in there, I started circling them like... like when we hunt. I had a club." His face intense, eyes drilling into me, "They were impatient and left, but..."

"But what, Frank?" his body relaxes a little.

"I was so," looking up at the rough ceiling, "I was torn apart by what I'd done, I'd seen something terrible in myself. When they had me cornered, there was," he's looking at me, "I was steps away, I wasn't going to run, I wasn't afraid."

He's looking at me for a long time, seeing a glimmer of something I recognize—Dad doesn't have this, he doesn't understand this.

"Your dad doesn't know how to talk about this."

"I tried to a couple of times, he got mad and..." feeling awkward.

"You're growing up fast, Frank. Things like this take a lot to understand. Superb steel takes fire, it takes patience, it takes lots of work to mold, form, fold, hammer fold again and then sharpen. It takes work to maintain its edge."

He's looking at me.

"I never want you to forget the extreme that you can go. It's in all of us, some are able to admit it, hold it and use it without becoming entranced by it. Few people ever scratch the surface—they only look at one side of life. In my world I see it all. Think about this, Frank. You have a choice about who you are and what to do with all the things you've been given."

Nodding more to the depth of his voice, the power there.

"Get some sleep, we've got a lot to talk about the next few weeks."

"But," blurting it out, "if I go back in, what if I can't control this?"

"Only one person can make that choice and I'm looking at him."

He turns and starts to walks upstairs.

"Uncle Vin?"

"What's that, kid?"

"When I was in solitary," looking down at my feet. "There were two of them. At first I thought they just didn't like me cause I'd caused trouble. They used to laugh about teaching me manners."

He's looking at me.

"One night, I don't know, I was so out of it. The kid I took on, he was the enforcer for the guy running merchandise in and out. They let that prick in my cell. I go back in, I see this guy... Those guards they were dirty."

He's nodding at me, his hands flexing into fists.

Sitting on the old bed. Tired, anxious about being here.

Lying down. Street noise filtering in mixed with the familiar smell of their basement brings back memories of when Vicky and I would play down here making believe we were diving in the ocean, looking at the fish and gear my uncle had down here.

Shifting sideways so my feet don't hang off, head feels a little better. Duffle and things from my locker at school here—he must have gathered all of this up after he heard I was taken in. Got to thank Hector, man I thought all this was lost.

Glimmer of light, I get to call Cat tomorrow. Light turning to gray—what the hell do I tell her? How do I talk about any of this fucking shit? Wishing I was still in there. At least there was some finality. Now—how do I face her?

Fighting to keep my eyes open, giving in, drifting deeper.

Images flashing in my mind of how at home I feel in the ocean.

Chapter 21

In and out of deep sleep.
Tossing and turning in the new bed.
Eyes sore, dull throb in my head, teeth sore from dental work.
Noises upstairs in the kitchen.
Soft morning sunlight filtering in through the basement windows.
Back, arms, legs—one big mass of soreness.
Hard to get up.

Washing up in the tiny bathroom, blood still in my urine. Jesus, it's been two days now—bastards. Looking at the stacks of clean clothes my aunt must have done and brought down here.

Putting on a clean sweatshirt. Sitting down, head feeling light.

Choice of what to wear feels weird. Imagine being locked up for years—my God, the monotony of that place! That would be the hardest thing to deal with.

Walking the creaky narrow stairs up to the kitchen, body fighting every step still feeling the deep bruises from those bastard's nightsticks.

"Well, look at what the cat dragged in," said Aunt Kitty as I look around for Uncle Vin, "he went out to pick up some pastries for breakfast. You drink coffee now?" She's wearing slacks, a black and white checkered blouse and big puffy slippers.

Making a yucky face. She laughs, "Well, try this before you make up your mind," putting out a mug for me, pouring in about half a cup and then puts in a little half and half; no sugar, oh, this is going to be bad.

"Okay, Aunt Kitty," taking a sip of the coffee, eyes lighting up looking at her—no bitter burnt flavor, "hey, this is good."

"Real coffee, not that garbage they serve in most places."

Taking another sip, feeling warm inside.

"Aunt Kitty," she looks at me, "Uncle Vin told me you were the only one fighting for me and," slowing down under her direct look, "I wanted to say, you know, I was getting close to the edge…"

Getting a little anxious—she's not saying anything.

"Frank," serious look on her face, "I do not condone what you've been doing. To be perfectly honest with you, I think you've been acting like a big baby." Feeling her words slap me in the face.

"But Aunt Kitty, it's not my fault. I didn't start the fight. Leroy did it on purpose to get me kicked off the team and I showed him," feeling rising anger, seeing his face.

"You showed him and now look at where that got you," she goes back to stirring something on the stove. "Your pride was hurt, you lost and what did you do? Strike back even harder? Just what your father would do." That cuts deep. I'm not anything like that bastard.

"That's not fair, Aunt Kitty."

"Yes it is and you need to hear it from somebody. Your family and your uncle, God love him, will beat around the bush. What about all the little things that led up that day? Hmm?" She turns off the burner and faces me again, her hands at her waist. "All the little things you've probably done to compete and put down these other kids. I've seen you, Frankie, and sometimes you don't have a sense of grace in you, you compete in everything and I imagine you let people know about it when you win."

"But that's what's supposed to happen, we're supposed to win!"

"Winning is good, how you win is important. You know you're much more gracious in your boxing matches, maybe cause it's one-on-one, I don't know. But in other sports, you expect people to follow you and do what you think is the right thing, no matter what they want."

"But if you're the best, shouldn't it work that way?"

"Are you the Team Captain?"

"No, Cedar is?"

"And who is the best player on the team?"

"I am."

"Any reason you think why he was elected and not you?"

Uncomfortable feeling creeping up inside.

What does she know about sports and all this anyway?

This is such bullshit.

"Frank, don't try and duck out of this, I deal with kids your age all the time." Quiet breaking out in the kitchen. "I'm not going to force you to talk or reflect either. I want you to start thinking about what your part in creating this whole thing has been... think about it, Frankie. I know you've got a good memory, think about last week, last month and last year. Takes two sides to create tension, Frank, where were you a threat, where were you a friend, where were you really concerned with them other than what you needed?"

"Me, a threat? Leroy's always been an ass..." feeling shame as she gives me her don't-bullshit-me look. Not wanting to listen to this. What the hell does she know about sports anyway?

She looks at me, "You have so much to learn. Just think about it okay? I think you're a great kid, but look, sometimes you got to run into a wall and look right here," pointing to my chest.

Uncomfortable, getting frustrated—she doesn't understand me.

She's watching me squirm over here.

"You want to win some points with me, be honest with me."

Oh, I hate this.

Minutes passing. Looking down at the bowl of oatmeal she's put in front of me. It smells good, nice thick cut oats, raisins and brown sugar with a little butter melting on top.

"I hate this," my hands feeling sweaty.

Her arms crossed.

"I don't know what you're getting at, I mean," putting my hands on my head, elbows on the table, "I know I screwed up, why is everyone always picking at all the things I do, it's never good enough. Why am I the one that's wrong?"

"Frank, Frank…"

She sits down across the table, shaking her head.

"It's normal you know, this age, wanting to be responsible, wanting to be a man but not being able to connect all the things you need together yet. I see so many teenagers get into trouble because they start to break away and form their own identities that either their parents, school or society doesn't want to or know how to deal with. Sometimes they end up in gangs some end up on the streets working… Well you're not a naive kid, some end up in jail doing time for doing dumb emotional things," she looks at me for a long time.

"Some skip through life and don't get touched, they're probably the most unlucky because when things pop up later in life, they haven't developed the strength to deal with it and it always happens some way or another."

Taking a spoonful of oatmeal. I hate this place.

"You need to stop feeling sorry for yourself," looking at her as she hits another raw nerve. "That's right, Frank, your father's hard on you and that's no excuse. Your teachers are hard on you too, that is no excuse either. You have to learn to deal with these things, people won't tolerate having you around if you are always trying to beat the world into submission," she sits back a little. "Sometimes really smart kids like you aren't challenged hard enough, and you, unfortunately, have the worst combination," she leans forward again looking at me. "High energy, high intelligence, creative," feeling the blood rush to my face, "competitive."

"I've been watching you and your father for all these years now. He was so proud of you, seeing you do so well in sports and most of your subjects in school. My feeling is that John started to get worried about how you'd be able to deal with life if you're always the golden boy and he started in on you the only way he knew, maybe the competition at home got a little too much and then," she puts her hands together and then moves them apart quickly, "boom."

"You don't have to say anything, Frankie. Just think about what I've said, okay?"

"Okay, Aunt Kitty," overwhelmed, mind racing—staying here, how long, that means I can see Cat, will she want to see me, I can see my guys at school, what's going to happen in court? "I don't even know…"

"What's that?" says Aunt Kitty.

"Oh," looking up, "I didn't even know I was talking, sorry."

"What were you thinking about, Frank?"

"Oh," sitting back in my chair turning my spoon over on one side looking at it and then turning it over again. "I didn't even know how long I was in there," tensing up remembering the feeling of panic that clawed up inside when I realized I was bound and couldn't move... "In there, in solitary."

Sneaking a look at her, seeing her face darken.

She lets the silence of her kitchen fill the void in our conversation.

"What was it like?"

Shifting side-to-side in discomfort having to summon memories about skirting at the edge of the darkness. Involuntary shaking of my head, she's waiting.

"You don't have to talk about it if you don't want to."

"It's not that, Aunt Kitty, it's just," taking a deep breath, "I don't know," looking out her kitchen window, the neighbor's house a few yards away. "It changed me, like I saw a deep meanness coming on. They made me sit in a really uncomfortable position in a straitjacket, and then put me cuffs and shackles. I couldn't even go to the bathroom... just sit there and stink in my own mess till they hosed me down. When I got too tired to sit up and rolled over to sleep they'd come in and beat me. I was starting to growl and try and bite them, fuckers would just laugh." Realizing I'd cursed in front of her, "oh, I'm sorry, I..."

"Shh, easy," her face filled with emotion, "let it out."

"I never understood you know, stories about men coming out of prison and how they'd be more violent. If you and Uncle Vin hadn't stood up for me," eyes watering up again. "When they tried to hunt me down by the pier, I felt it then, like I wasn't going to hide, just this intense concentration, I knew it was them or me and all I could think about, it wasn't even thinking, it was, putting everything I had into attack them, get in close, hurt them, surprise them so they run and then..." looking at her, "get the slow one or two and if I go down, then so be it. They were just a few steps away and I got lucky I guess. They went someplace else to look for me. But in solitary..."

She's holding herself well, listening.

"I think what changed me... I didn't really know about evil till I was in that dark cell and they'd come in and beat me. I'd hear them talking to each other, laughing about it. Their words didn't register at the time, it was like there were people talking a long ways away from me," realizing I'm crushing my hands together, my forearms shaking from the tension, deep breath breaking the hold. "I was helpless, exhausted. And it was always these same two bastards at night. I'm sorry, Aunt Kitty, I shouldn't be talking about this. I know I'm bad."

"No," she slams her hand down on the table. "You are not bad, you are immature, you made mistakes, you need to atone for them, but you listen to me, Frank Caruso, you are not bad. Those people are evil and they'll get theirs and I'm so glad you are out of there and back with family."

Body relaxing a little at her words—I love you for doing what you've done, Aunt Kitty, I love you, but I don't believe you.

Looking at her, feeling someone else there, looking around seeing my uncle holding a couple of white wax paper bags from the bakery. He looks at me his hands shaking, looking at my aunt, his face set in silent rage.

"You were in solitary for ten days," his words coming out slowly.

Embarrassment flooding over me—how much did he hear?

"And yes, I'm gonna see those pricks get theirs."

Intense look from my aunt to my uncle.

Chapter 22

Constant background chatter of my uncle's radio, road noise, cars and trucks honking their horns, the steel grating of the bridge generating a growling sound as we drive over the Williamsburg Bridge into Manhattan.

"She's a very wise woman, kiddo."

Not wanting to admit so much of what she said struck home.

"This afternoon I'm going to show you some things that will give you some perspective."

"Okay, Uncle Vin," chest feels tense, emotions pulling me in multiple ways, thoughts jumping around. Thinking about all the good times I had with Dad at the beach, out diving when I was young. Something snapped between us when I was in that holding cell—there's no going back.

Eerie feeling as I walk toward the double door entrance of the imposing 14th Precinct Police Station on West 30th Street. Lots of squad cars parked out front, uniformed police officers going in and out—a few here and there saying hi to my uncle, stopping by to chat and shake his hand. He stops me before we go in.

"Remember, you will apologize for your bad behavior and then you will speak only when you are spoken to, you unnerstand? You will address me as Lieutenant Caruso while we are here, you will address all active duty officers as Sir, you unnerstand?"

Having to work up my voice, "Yes, Uncle... Yes... yes, Sir."

"Good, let's get going."

He flashes is badge at the desk, "How's it going, Sergeant?"

"Outside of the hemorrhoid on my ass named Dinkins, things are good. What can I do for ya?" my uncle chuckles at that—no idea what they are talking about.

"I'm here to see Malan."

"Second floor, Lieutenant," he turns back to his paper work.

All sorts of people walking up and down the wide wooden staircase, a few in hand cuffs—policemen and a few policewomen moving about in the same hurry. Plain-clothes officers with their jackets off, snub nose .38 revolvers in shoulder or waist holsters, cuffs. Files moving, handed about, launched here and there, people yelling at each other. Bleeding black man being brought in yelling at the cops to take their motherfucking hands off him. String of hookers being brought down the stairs—must be from the latest round up over on 14th Street.

Walking into a big room, desks setup in rows and piled high with papers, folders, old coffee cups, trash cans filled with to-go coffee cups, white cardboard boxes open here and there. Walls covered with pictures of groups of detectives—parties, baseball games, fishing trips, headlines of past famous captures.

Many of the men gathered up in groups, a couple of them coming over to shake hands with my uncle.

"How you been, Georgie?" he asks one of them.

"Mullaney's an SOB, but he's a good commander. What brings you down here?"

"Need to see Malan."

"Let's go find him," and he yells out, "Yo Malady, where the fuck are you?"

Malan and O'Neal come out of an office, they wave my uncle over. Shaking hands, hard time making eye contact with either of these pricks.

"Come in, Lieutenant," a voice from the office.

"How are you, Mullaney?" he comes in and shakes the hand of a tall thin man behind a large desk—the sides stacked high with folders papers and whatnot. The center of the desk is clean and organized.

"What did you need from these two?"

My uncle looks at the two detectives. "Brought the kid up," thumb over his shoulder at me, "he wants to apologize for his behavior during the arrest and I want to make sure we're on the same page with getting all the stories in front of the judge."

"Is this on the record?" Mullaney asks.

"Any way you want to play it, this is your sandbox."

"Let's go in my conference room, coffee?" as the other two detectives head out of the room and open a glass door next to Mullaney's office.

"Sure," my uncle says as we walk in the hall. Mullaney waving to a woman at desk across from his office, "Margie, four coffees and some of those good crullers from the corner."

"Yes, Lieutenant," she rolls her eyes.

Door closing behind us.

"So," Mullaney says sitting at the head of the table. "Let's start off the record and we'll see, you good with that?" he says looking at Malan and O'Neal. They nod. My uncle nods, he briefly looks at me, then my uncle looks at me, "You're up, kid."

Standing up, body nervous, breathing quickly, skin feels cold.

What baloney—apologize to these people. Like they happened to forget about leaving me handcuffed to the table and accidently kicking the chair out from underneath me. Take a deep breath, just get it done, apologize and get away from these creeps.

"Lieutenant, Detectives," all the words running out of my head that I'd been thinking through, "I apologize for my behavior. I made some bad mistakes; I know I have to take the consequences. I'm sorry I caused more trouble, I didn't," losing my way, skin cold and clammy, "I didn't think about what I was doing, I didn't think about how it would reflect on anyone else. I was selfish and stupid. I'm sorry."

Malan looking at O'Neal, they nod.

"You good with that?" Mullaney asks Malan.

"Yup," he says as my uncle motions me down.

"Now down to brass tacks, there are not going to be any complaints from him or his lawyer on Miranda or anything else, we want the full story of what went down in front of the judge—no punches pulled."

"I'm good with that, I've already reamed their asses on the sequence," said Mullaney.

"Lieutenant," said Malan, annoyed, but looking at my uncle, "we got statements from all the witnesses that saw the original three on one fight where he took a beating. O'Neal has been working the three follow-on incidents. It's conclusive that there was no weapon involved. The kid Alton Brown, even though he can't talk, confirmed it was a fist fight." Body shivering, "Worst case, he'll be charged with aggravated assault. With the father offering to pay all medical costs, my guess is the Judge and DA will accept the lesser charge."

My uncle nodding, "Good work getting through all the conflicting stories. The guy he jumped during the arrest going to press charges?"

O'Neal starts laughing, "That piece of work?" he smacks his partner lightly on the arm with the back of his hand, "he nearly shit his pants when Sonny over there threw him like a rag doll and told him he was going to rip his heart out. Nah, he's a big guy who likes to talk. Besides, he grabbed the kid."

Raising my hand.

"Yes, son," said Mullaney.

"Lieutenant sir, Detectives, what happened to Alton?"

Silence in the room and the detectives look at my uncle then me.

"Hospital," said Malan, "operated on twice over the last few weeks. Cheekbone and jaw shattered, they saved his sight. Probably in Roosevelt for another two or three weeks to recuperate," said Malan. A cold clamminess coming over my body, his words drilling deep, looking down at my hands clasped together, gripping my hands nervously. "Lucky you owned up and got his mother right away, another hour, the doctor's said the pressure from internal swelling might have pushed a shard of bone into his optic nerve. Would have been blind in one eye for life," said Malan.

"That's why we thought you hit him with something," said O'Neill.

Stomach feeling sick, empty, skin cold and clammy.

Looking down at my hands, "Thank you, Sir."

"You called the ambulance didn't you?" O'Neal looking at me.

Nodding, feeling like I'm shrinking, getting smaller in front of them, my uncle looking at me for a few seconds and then at the other detectives.

Uncle Vin and Mullaney stand up, "Thanks Mullaney, Malan, O'Neal, owe you one." They nod, stepping out of the room. Malan walking next to my uncle, "We'd a gone any way you wanted on this, but thanks for playing it straight."

My uncle looks at him, "Only way I know, Detective. You get bored here and want some real action, come look me up."

"Thanks, Lieutenant, I'll keep that in mind."

Not paying much attention to the people around me. I can't believe it—Dad stepped up. Why? I can't believe it. Got to be a mistake. Walking through the police station—all the noise of the place fading into the background. Alton in the hospital for another two or three weeks, my God, he almost lost the sight in one eye.

Shaking my head.

Yeah, like that will get the vision of him crumpled up on the sidewalk out of my mind. Fucking pride. Deep breath—fight down the anguish gripping my throat. Goddamn you, Frank.

Uncle Vin talking and joking with a group of uniformed officers—they're trading stories.

Alton's words before we fought swirling through my head. Fighting them, fighting off the sheet that I want to throw over the uncomfortable truths showing their dark faces from the deep—am I evil? Am I like those two bastards in jail?

Knees feel week, leaning back against the wall.

"You okay, sugar?" woman stops, looks closely at my face.

Nodding weakly.

Out on the street, opening my collar, breathing deep.

"Uncle Vin?"

"What, kid?"

"I got to go visit Alton." Looking down at my feet, shoulders hanging down. Moving out of the way at the wave of people coming and going from the station. I don't see him, but I can feel him looking at me.

"I'll pick you up in front of the hospital in three hours. Remember my circle of trust, you be there on time, you start earning your way in, you're late, you stay out."

"I understand, Uncle Vin," turning to go, stopping, looking at him, words of thanks, of wanting to talk to him about what happened, what I felt like frozen in my mouth.

"Get out of here, we'll catch up later."

"Uncle Vin," he turns, his trench coat flapping, "why'd my father do it?"

He shrugs his shoulders, looks at me. "My brother's a lot of things, one of them is that he does what's right by folks," he looks at me for a second, "even if it galls the hell out of him. You're underage, parents need to step up."

"How that going to work, I mean, we never have money at home?"

Uncle Vin walks away shaking his head.

Chapter 23

Subway station's not very crowded at mid-day. Reality hitting me that I'm alone without someone telling me what to do or behind bars; body shivers thinking back to Rikers, dwelling on the reality of going back to something like that when I'm found guilty—and I am guilty.

Sitting down in the subway car, watching the stations pass by on the express. There's going to be a whole new set of things I need to learn to get by in there so I don't, so I don't become an animal. But if I do...

Up on 59th Street, lunch hour crowd starting to hit the street. Stopping at a newsstand and buying every sports magazine I can get my hands on.

Slow walk toward the Hudson River, it's only a few blocks to the hospital but it feels like I've walked miles. What the hell am I going to say to him? My aunt's words this morning, Alton's words about pride.

Don't want to acknowledge the burning feeling in my chest—that I wasn't a big enough man to accept an apology; that I couldn't get over my wounded pride. What if his whole athletic career is over? What if he never boxes again? He'd be okay with that, but to not play basketball! Awful feeling rising up from my stomach, acidic, rank—look at what I've reaped, from promise to a steaming pile of shit.

Stopping outside Roosevelt Hospital, the dirty old red brick building looming up before me. Wave of uncertainty coming over me; what if he doesn't want to see me? Why should he even? Fuck it—get in there and put yourself in the game. He'll never know how I... He'll never know that I understand if I don't go in. Maybe it doesn't matter to him, but it matters to me—don't wimp out cause you have to admit you were wrong. My life may be shit, but I don't have to act like a shit.

Bored people working the hospital front desk.

"Hello, I'd like to see Alton Brown."

Woman in a white uniform looks through a large Rolodex—people walking in and out of the hospital. Smells of medicine, industrial cleaning products and warm bodies packed together fills the waiting area.

"He's on 379, but he may not be able to see anyone. You'll have to go ask at the nursing station."

"Okay, thanks" looking around, "oh, which way?"

"Big elevator straight ahead, follow the numbers on three. Can I help you?" as she turns to a well-dressed old lady waiting behind me.

Stone still people in rooms watching television.

Eyes following me as I walk down the hall.

Elderly in wheelchairs, bags attached to metal poles sticking up off the back. Heavy smell of medicine, ointment and unwashed bodies emanating from dimly lit rooms, lonely eyes looking at me, seeing if I've come to visit them.

Old Hispanic woman standing by a wheel char, talking away, frustrated with one of the nurses who is speaking louder in English to see if she can make her understand. Her words coming in as I walk closer.

"*My family, when is my family going to come? The doctor told me it's okay now.*"

"Go back to your room, Mrs. Rivera, your medicine isn't till 3:00 o'clock," now I see the old lady is holding onto the railing along the side of the wall for dear life.

Looking at them, "She's asking when her family can come visit."

Nurse looks at me, purses her lips and gives me a why-the-fuck-are-you-bothering-me look. "Well I can't call them, it's not my problem. I want her to go back to her room."

"I can call them."

"Knock yourself out, just get her out of my hair," and she huffs off.

"Where does she need to go?" What is the nutty nurse doing?

"322 and don't bother me anymore, I have a lot to do."

"Bitch," taking a deep breath.

"*Mrs. Rivera, may I speak with you?*"

She looks at me, her eyes getting a little brighter; her face looks a little less anxious. "*Oh please, I need someone to call my Felix, no one will listen to me here. I'm so worried about them.*"

"*The nurse asked me to tell you that you need to go back to your room, I could call them if you like?*"

"*Oh thank you,*" she reaches out, her old gnarled hands on mine, "*thank you,*" as she pats my hand. Pushing her wheelchair down the hall while I look at the different room numbers. These are big rooms with six patients in each room, their beds segregated by curtains. There's her room.

"*How will I contact your Felix?*"

"*Oh,*" and she rattles off a number, "*tell him to please come visit me, take me home. This is a bad place. They want to kill me here. I can't stay here.*" Her eyes getting a terrified look as she points to some of the sleeping elderly people in her room. Young girl in one of the beds must be twelve or thirteen, big cast on her leg.

"*I'll call him, okay?*"

"*Thank you, thank you,*" she's fishing through her night stand bringing out a little coin purse and pushes a dime in my hand. Trying to refuse, but she pushes it back. Writing down the number I remembered and showing it to her to make sure I've got it right. Waving to her as I walk out of the room, another harried nurse and an orderly coming, at least this lady speaks some Spanish.

Wandering around looking at the room numbers.

There's Alton's room.

Looking through the small square safety glass door. Single room.

Feeling my vision collapse around me, grabbing the door handle to steady myself—his face heavily bandaged, tubes going into his mouth and face. Forcing myself to look at him, looking at my hands, looking back at him.

"Can I help you, honey?"

Turning around to a tall, strong, striking looking black nurse.

"I was hoping I could see Alton."

"Not today, honey, come back tomorrow. He's still in a lot of pain and can't talk. He needs to rest."

Feeling my lips get tight, looking at her and nodding my head.

Walking away slowly, stopping and coming back for another look.

She's still there, "Can I leave these with you?"

"Sure honey, that's nice, I'll make sure he gets these, he's been lonely here. What's your name, honey?"

"Oh, ah, Frank."

Outside the hospital, traffic rushing up 10th Avenue.

Hour to kill before my uncle comes to pick me up, no need to call him earlier. Small burst of energy—hustling over to a phone booth and dialing the number Mrs. Rivera gave me. Letting it ring—ten times, fifteen then twenty and hang up. Finding an out of the way place to go sit down on the hospital steps.

Letting the cars and people moving by form a blur, a moving collage. Replaying the conversation with my aunt. "You're acting like a big baby," running through my head. "Feeling sorry for yourself," no, no, no, no—I did what was right. They started this. Her words, my uncle's words, Alton's words—pride, NO! Shaking my head. What's wrong with winning, standing up for myself?

She's wrong.

Car pulling up, seeing Uncle Vin. Getting up and walking to the window, "Uncle Vin a lady asked me to call her husband, tell him it's okay if he comes and visits. I tried earlier, can I give him another ring?"

"Make it snappy."

Running over to the phone, nagging voice telling me that my aunt was spot on, putting that aside as the sound of the dime drops in the phone—same as before—nothing.

Car smells of coffee as my uncle drives with one hand, to-go cup of coffee in the other. Working his way across town, it looks like he's heading for the mid-town tunnel at 34th. Flashing his badge at the tollgate—grimy white tile walls in the tunnel go flashing by, lights on the ceiling showing up in random patterns with sections of bulbs burned out. Windows rolled up.

"Your aunt loves you, Frank," he's looking out of the car, "she doesn't pull any punches," he smiles to himself.

Don't know what to say. Question popping up, struggling not to ask it, embarrassed to ask my uncle.

"Uncle Vin?"

"What's up, kid?"

"Ah, nothing," Frank you are a big fucking chicken.

Driving cross-town through the morass of taxis, busses, and crazy bike messengers driving against the flow of traffic weaving in and out of cars. Masses of pedestrians on 5th Avenue keep coming past the green light, cars behind us honking.

"You sure?" looking at him out of the side of my eyes.

Feeling like I'm shrinking in the seat.

"You were there? All she said?" relieved not having to look him.

"Yup, and I tell you, it's good for you to hear, good for you to talk about what you went through. You said some hard things," nodding looking at him.

"Is she, you know, right about..." hard to mouth the words.

"Acting like a big baby?"

Silence. Guy running a hot dog cart getting into an argument with a truck driver on 3rd Ave, my uncle looks at them for a couple of seconds, guns his siren for a second and motions for the hot dog vendor to move from the loading zone. Shaking my head as the guy flips off Uncle Vin as he prepares to move. Uncle Vin muttering, "Dumb fuck."

Long block over to 2nd Ave is packed.

"Well, in her world people don't get anywhere solving problems with their fists. In my world, well... She has high ideals and I think it's good for people to reach high," he looks over. "You'll never reach higher than what you think about, kiddo. So I give her credit for aiming high."

He's focused on driving as we head downtown on 2nd Ave.

"I see a kid who's at the age where he's struggling to be a man, nothing wrong with that in my book. Your dad and I were hell on Pops. Uncle Michael was the little angel and we used to beat the crap out of him, God did we get in trouble all the time."

"No kidding? The way Dad carries on..."

"Well, maybe he's trying to pass on what he's learned over the years and help you bypass some of the dumb mistakes we made."

"Look Frank, the hardest steels can take a wicked edge, but they have a low breaking point. Best swords have softer more flexible steels that have been layered to get the flexibility and the hard stuff at the edge to last through tough use. No one can doubt your heart, but you've got to figure out how to get more flexibility into you. You're too rigid, too committed to a certain way of approaching situations, you keep going like this and you'll break and none of us want that."

Silence in the car.

"Sometimes it's right to fight like hell, but you've got to have more moves in your game. In the gym you do foot work, heavy bag for power right? You work the speed bag for hand-eye coordination and timing to go for the head, all kinds of different moves, right? You're going after life like you only know how to throw a big right hand and getting pissed when things aren't working so you start throwing more and more of them. And we know that ain't working too well."

Breathing out slowly. Damn it, it's hard to listen to all this shit, too much hitting too close. He starts laughing.

"Hey, you think I was born yesterday and lived a day for nothing? Where you think you get those genes from, kid? You don't think I see a lot of myself and my brother in you?"

Arms crossed against my chest. Looking out the window.

What a pain in the ass this is.

"Living a life of valor is more than just being a fighter, you need to start asking yourself some tough questions. You ask a lot of others, your dad, your teachers, but what do you ask of yourself? What does being of service to others mean? What is the purpose of all the things you do?"

Agitated, wishing I was someplace else.

Better to be hungry and free than this.

"What's up with the Brown kid?"

What's the minimum I can say and not get another lecture?

"Couldn't see him."

He nods. "You realize he may not even want to see you?"

"I do, Uncle Vin, but I got to," searching for words, "if I don't make the move, he'll never know what I need to say."

My uncle smiles and nods his head.

"Your heart's in the right place, Frankie," he's thinking for a moment. "I needed to hear that for myself, it's not that I don't trust you, but in my world trust is earned. I know my brother; it breaks my heart to see how you two have gotten to this point. Maybe you'll mend the fences, maybe not. If it's going to happen, it's gonna take time."

Thought of apologizing to Dad burning me up inside.

No fucking way.

Questions swirling in my mind.

"Uncle Vin, do I go back home? What about school next year? What about training with Gus? If I stay with you and Aunt Kitty..." he raises his hand.

"Slow down, slow down. Look, you going to stay with us for a while, at least till we see the judge and if there's a trial, see what's up," he's looking uncomfortable. "You know your father doesn't want you back." Even though I know this, the words are still hard to hear. "Well anyway, worst case, you're with us till you go off to college or wherever."

"And Mom's done nothing," more to myself.

"You need to take that up with her," hearing a different tone in his voice.

"What do," his hand coming up again.

"That, I don't want to talk about, capisce?"

"Yes," body feeling the weight of her unwillingness to stand up for me or at least fight for me—ice, beautiful ice. "Yes, Uncle Vin," so different than Aunt Kitty.

Colors and shapes of Brooklyn passing by in a blur.

Turning away from my uncle so he can't see my face.

"Hey," he turns onto Flatbush Avenue, "I'm going out to Montauk in a couple of weeks and get wet, you coming?"

"You bet," brightening up at the thought of being back into water. "Gee that's, that's great Uncle Vin. Is Uncle Michael still getting in the water?"

Shaking his head, "No, it's been years now."

Turning down Bushwick Avenue, neighborhoods getting progressively worse as we drive. Dawning on me—he's taking me through some of the areas he works in the 79th, 81st and 88th Precincts, Bed Stuy and Crown Heights.

Liquor stores every couple of blocks now, piles of garbage strewn here and there on broken sidewalks, potholes in the streets. Passing an invisible gradient where people give less and less of a shit about their surroundings. A few blocks here and there are kept up, usually around a church, the others decaying quickly the further we drive—people looking at my uncle's car warily. All ages, all colors here though it's mostly black and Hispanic.

This section of Crown Heights snapping to a different look and vibe— got it, Orthodox Hasidic Jews in beards and black hats. Cleaner, vibrant shops, then the slow transition back to decay.

My uncle stopping to talk to police officers in patrol cars now and then, people passing by look at me trying to figure out what a kid is doing in the police car. Areas new to me as we drive—played ball out here in a few tournaments, but didn't hang out here much. It's not the dirt or the trash strewn around the street that's starting to register—it's the eyes. Wary, looking, sizing things up, watchful. I've seen this look before—Rikers Island. All those kids back in there. Those two evil fucking guards—what else are those bastards doing to kids out there in the dark?

Driving down a block with a number of buildings demolished that look like big gaps in someone's mouth where teeth were knocked out—a few kids playing in the bricks and garbage of the empty lot. Group of serious looking kids and young men hanging around in front of one of the still standing brownstones, hate in their eyes coming at us. Following prison rules—don't lock eyes, stay calm, don't be a bitch, but don't look away. They puff up and drift off yelling at my uncle as he pulls up in front of the small building and stares them down.

"That's a nice bunch of characters."

"Bunch of pussies, the real bad ones don't pose."

He's watching the group of men walk down the street and then starts to follow. Sirens wailing in the distance, the direction of the sound is going away from us.

Uncle Vin talking back and forth with dispatch, pace of their conversation picks up. Looking at a frail looking black woman walking down the steps of one of the more dilapidated brownstones, boards in most of the windows, rags and garbage strewn around the streets. Old man pushing a shopping cart down the street filled with shoes, and what looks like junk stopping every once in a while and mumbling something.

"You stay put in the car," as he puts a magnetic emergency light on his hood and guns the engine, car rocketing forward.

"What's up?"

He holds up his hand as police codes start coming over the radio. Cars moving out of his way, as he guns the siren, massive slide around a corner. Holding on for dear life.

Uncle Vin with a group of other plain clothes policemen and uniformed officers, one of them is pointing up at the five story run down brownstone, wash hung out to dry on the fire escapes facing the street.

Emergency Services Team pulling in—men in dark jump suits, body armor, automatic weapons getting out of the large van. Crowd of people forming, people asking me what's going on or what did I do? Fire trucks and ambulances starting to show up. Cordons being setup to keep the crowd back. Background noise level keeps going up with more and more people arriving—talking, asking questions. All kinds of wild shit being talked about; bank robber hold up with lots of money, must be a white family in that building for all these pigs to be here, police are here to murder a Black Panther leader.

News vans arriving, cameras being setup.

Man being brought out of the decayed brownstone in handcuffs, crowd surging, yelling. Guy looks a little deranged, an average guy dressed in a Parks Department uniform. EMT carry stretchers out of the building. People yelling that the police were in there assassinating the black man. Crowd surging against the line of uniformed policemen, bullhorns going off warning people to keep back.

Man from the building being taken away in a black and white—lights flashing, passing a few feet away from my uncle's car, working through the crowd as people pound on the side of the car. People starting to yell and point at me.

"What's the man doing here?"

"He a stoolie?"

"Look at that cracker motherfucker," people trying to push to the car.

Man getting through, moving away from the window boxing his arms away as he tries to reach in for me. Grabbing his fingers and twisting them back. He cries out in pain. Feeling warm saliva running down the side of my face. Wiping his spit off my face with my sleeve, hot anger burning in my stomach.

"That's what you deserve, Whitey," the man says being dragged back by a police officer, they start to go at it. The man who spit in my face is being egged on by the crowd, he's yelling at the police officer to take off his badge, show him how much of a man he is. Fighting urge to get out of the car. Now he's looking at me.

"What you gonna do, White Boy?"

Looking back at him hard—don't say anything Frank, don't say anything. You come near me and I'm going to fuck you up, but I'm not starting shit.

"That's it, you just gonna look bad at me?" taunting me.

Loud moan goes through the crowd, turning around, kids being brought out on stretchers. "Oh my God," collective gasps going off, "Just keiiids."

"Oh my sweet Jesus."

Bodies in the crowd shift toward the ambulances as the tenor of the crowd changes from anger to concern. Lots of uniformed and plain clothes detectives going in and out of the building now.

Can't see my uncle, crowd dying down.

Uncle getting in the car and taking a deep breath.

Driving, Uncle Vin solemn—I know not talk to him now.

Circling the neighborhood, radio chatter in the background.

"You got some fucking nerve," surprised at the angry tone in his voice.

"Uncle Vin, what'd I do?" thinking through the car, the guy spitting at me. He shakes his head and keeps driving.

"Think you have life so fucking bad, I seen bad. You don't know shit!" he's shifting around in his seat. Looking at him, he won't turn toward me. Feeling like I'm shrinking on the inside. It's going to start all over again.

It was too good to last with my uncle and aunt.

If I go this time I'm leaving the City—get as far away from all these fucked up people as I can. Go where there's green, where there's clean, open ocean.

Chapter 24

His car stopping in front of a row of crumbling brownstones—boards in the windows, garbage mounds around the broken sidewalks. A few hulking burned out cars setup on milk crates lining the street. Baby carriage filled with junk—bottles, rags, broken radio. Quiet here, siren breaking out in the distance.

"Get out of the fucking car."

Doing as I'm told, walking to the sidewalk. Anxious, Uncle Vin is a whole different animal than Dad—bucking the rising fear in my stomach. If this is what it is, then this is what it is.

"You think you've had a tough life, think it was tough at Rikers?" pointing his strong index finger at me and jabbing me in the chest, "I'm gonna show you what's really out here."

"Uncle Vin…"

"Shut the fuck up!" he draws back, his dark eyes taking on a whole different look. I know that look. He looks at me for a couple of seconds like I'm some piece of shit he's dealing with on the street. Into his car for a second, taking out a long stainless steel flashlight. "Follow me, do what I tell you and keep your trap shut," he takes his coat off, clips his badge to his shirt, adjusts his revolver so it's right over his front pant pocket.

Down trash covered steps to a basement apartment. Area strewn with baby formula cans, welfare food cans, beer cans, wine bottles, old newspapers, filthy bits of clothing, used baby diapers and all kinds of empty food wrappers and chip bags. Having to fight through the urge to recoil from the smell of shit, urine and wet decay as he pushes open a door into a dimly lit deep, dark room. Looks like most of the walls were knocked down long ago—just the support columns have been left. Rubble and refuse all over the place, a couple of dim lights deep inside the cavernous space.

Pushing myself through the hesitation, stepping in after him. Shapes around the large room coming into focus—people sleeping in random piles. Dirty people, clothes torn, the light from Uncle Vin's flashlight showing hollow faces, eyes barely registering the light. Woman walking, stumbling around, heading to a corner of the basement, oh God—piles of shit, bits of wadded up newspaper lodged in places over there. She drops her raggedy pants, squats and pees next to a support wall.

"Bitch, what the fuck you doing?" comes from a couple of people, as she tracks shit out on her shoes, she starts screeching unintelligibly back at the voices. Trying to make out the voices in the darkness. They are almost all black folk here—a couple of nasty looking white women as well, stringy hair, dirty beyond belief. Faces distorted from missing teeth.

Fighting to keep my head from spinning, thick air filled with the stench of dirty bodies, shit, piss and vomit molding and decaying where it's left. Oh

Jesus, there are maggots growing here. Fighting the rush of bile. Turning quickly, pictures of the piles of trash organized into little areas for groups of people to sit starting to filter in. Group of people in the far end of the room sitting around a dim light bulb hanging from a single wire from what's left of the ceiling. They're slowly playing cards—one of the men smacking a corn rowed woman's hand as she tries to reach inside a bag of chips. He unzips his pants, whips out his cock, gestures it at her. His mates laughing as she tries to give him a blowjob—she keeps losing her balance.

"Bitch, don't bite my dick," he starts yelling pushing her back and away from him. She starts to laugh hysterically. Uncle Vin moving toward them out of the shadows. Passing a mother breast-feeding a baby, the skin on her face a shade of gray brown, deep black circles under her eyes—people lying on cardboard boxes staring out into space. Skin crawling.

"Yo, Carleton, we gots company," the group looks over at us.

Fighting the urge to run out of this place, retch my guts out then breathe clean, cool air. Pushing down at the panic that's rising up inside. Mind numb at the unreality of the place. This is real, don't look away, don't be a punk. Seeing my uncle looking at me in my peripheral vision. Forcing myself to look. People starting to whisper at us, asking for help, food or money, weak hands reaching up, body shrinking back as someone touches my legs—old man trying to figure out what I am.

"What you po-police motherfuckers want in my house?" one of the men sitting around the light said.

"Your house?" said my uncle in a dangerous tone. They look at him for a couple of minutes—letting my eyes take in the area around the card players; table made out of old fruit crates, tablespoons, short lengths of surgical rubber tubes strewn around, small plastic bag of brownish white looking powder partially underneath a cartoon page. The first guy slowly pulling the page over the bag—starting to become aware of what is going on.

Heroin—addicts coming in here to shoot up, lie around in a daze.

The card players go back and try to act nonchalant.

"I didn't think so," said my uncle, one of the guys starts to say something, the guy who must be the leader putting his hand on his arm. My uncle starts to look over the people in the room. Mind can't deal with the sensory input coming in—starting to get tunnel vision. Emotions wavering erratically between horror, disgust, pity, and anger that places like this exist. Powerlessness, disgusted mixed with morbid fascination. Some of these people have been where I've been and didn't come back.

Uncle Vin taking notes now, looking at an old man.

Bending down he feels for a pulse—shaking his head, standing next to the neatly organized piles of belongings; a few books, I can only make out the title at the top, *Fire Next Time*, worn picture of a family, healthy, strong black people smiling in front a nicely kept house, small crucifix sitting on a shoebox.

"What'cha looking at, Whitey," said a voice from the blackness.

"Shut the fuck up!" snapped my uncle.

A couple of voices muttering, "What's happening with Herb?"

Brown gray shapes shrinking back from my uncle's powerful flashlight beam as he turns it on and shines it around the room. Feeling like the walls are closing in on me. Forcing the fetid air down my lungs to keep my head from going.

He's sleeping in a strange position, must be uncomfortable as hell his body twisted like that. Uncle Vin's light sweeps over his face—flies going in and out of his nose. Shocked, stumbling back—hoarse voice yelling up at me, can't make out what they've said, stepping in something squishy. Uncle catching my arm to help me get my balance, his strong hand leading me back to what remains of the front door.

Taking deep breaths out on the street as my uncle talks with the dispatcher. Hands on my knees, can't stop the feeling of my mouth starting to water—retching into the gutter till nothing but acidic bile comes up, mouth stinging from the taste of stomach acids, spitting out as much as I can. A few moving shapes on the street, looking down at my sneaker—smell making its way up to my nose. I stepped in human shit, oh God!

Stomach makes a move to heave again. Deep breath to get my head back—scraping my sneaks against the curb, looking at the bottom of my sneaker, shit deep in the grooves. Uncle still on the radio, walking over and sitting on one of the decrepit steps of the brownstone, images of that horrible room flashing back.

Head in my hands, the smell of death and dying still in my nose.

Ambulance pulling up, driver getting out and walking up to Uncle Vin. Squad coming in next, guys putting on rubber gloves, police officers getting out pump-action shot guns.

"Wait here," from my uncle as he leads them back in the room. Watching dark shapes running out the back into the yards of fallen bricks and trash.

Watching the ambulance driving off in the gloomy night. Uncle Vin talking to the two policemen, he pats one of them on the back.

"What?" he's looking at me. Feeling stupid and pointing at my shoe.

His lips purse together, he shakes his head.

"Take 'em off, and put 'em in the trunk dumb shit."

Unlacing my shoes, "Here," he says throwing me an old newspaper. Feeling the cool concrete of the pavement through my sock. Thirsty, hungry, body fatigued. Wrapping my soiled sneaker in the newspaper and putting it in the trunk next to all the gear my uncle has in there—shot gun, first aid kit, bull horn, flares and bullet proof vest.

Silent drive. He looks at his watch, silently cursing, puts his flashing light on the roof, and knives through traffic.

Feeling stupid walking into the church with one shoe. Doing my stations of the cross before sitting in a pew in the rear. Well-dressed people gathering here—mostly black and Hispanic, most of the conversations being rattled off in rapid Spanish. Recognizing the conversations, they work with my uncle.

He's shaking hands with a couple of men. Letting my gaze follow around the church, the place smells of years of incense, old wood and cool stone. Not a huge place, but overflowing with ornate fixtures in gold leaf, vivid paintings of Saints and all the horror they dealt with, large stained glass windows showing a rose colored cast in the late afternoon sunlight. A couple of young girls look at my stocking foot and start laughing.

Baptism today. Baby crying away—husband and wife dressed in their Sunday best, Godparents surrounding them in the church. Body not adjusting with the transition from a netherworld to being surrounded by proud families and smiling children. Same skin colors as down in that hellhole and here's a totally different universe just a few miles away. How can they let places like that exist? Why? That man hated me without even knowing who I am.

Following along with the ceremony by heart.

Why God? Why do your people live like that? The beautiful thing you've created between men and women—for a potato chip. Why? Why would people beat helpless people for fun?

Trying to find some sense of calm, watching the little girls in their pink dresses as they talk to each other and are shh'ed by a stern parent—one of them makes a face at me, sticks out her tongue and then looks away.

Laughing quietly, trying to mask the hollow pain inside.

Does the knowledge of evil beget evil Lord? What would these little girl's lives be like if they were to see that hell hole my uncle took me to? Image of that woman dropping her raggedy pants and peeing on the floor flashing in—she was someone's little girl once. Where is their choice? Where is their free will? Is that all bullshit? Image of the dead children being carried out in stretcher flashing in; that was their father for God's sake!

Fists clenching and unclenching, acid burn rising up in my chest from my stomach; is that it, Lord? I stand when I'm supposed to, I kneel when I'm supposed to, I speak when I'm supposed, I say my rosary, I go to confession and I'm okay? What about the evil I felt? Shouldn't my fingers have burned when I dipped them in the holy water?

Walking out into the cool evening air.

Uncle Vin smiling and talking with men and women. Shaking hands with people, meeting new people he didn't know, people showing him a lot of respect. Thinking back to Julio's mother talking about how she didn't want trouble with him. What could he have done? Why's he so damn mad at me? I want to go sit back in the dark basement. I just want to go sleep.

Uncle Vin silent as we drive through the City.

Stopping at a busy Chock Full o'Nuts coffee shop, the car door slamming as my uncle walks off without a word.

Staring blankly out onto the opposite side of the street.

Door opening, Uncle Vin pushing a white cardboard box across the bench seat and folding his big body in the car. He's taller than Dad, at least six-two, but he's got to go at least two hundred sixty pounds—thick neck, big muscular shoulders and arms; he's got a little bit of a beer belly, but he's a big man.

"Eat," he grunts as he takes a bite into a nutted cheese sandwich and drinks some coffee. He's got three of the cream cheese filled with nuts on raisin bread sandwiches and some the thick powdered sugar cake donuts. Making quick work of one of the sandwiches and a couple of donuts. Stomach settling down for a second before an acid burp burns my throat.

Pulling up to a hospital.

"I tell you Frankie, kid like you," he shakes his head, "so many breaks in your life, so many advantages, so much potential... makes me mad as hell thinking about you in this situation with all the," angry glare breaking through. "Lot of kids would give their arm to be you and you're fucking it all up!" he yells, looks at me in the dark light and slams his fist into the dashboard.

Jaw tightening. You fucking think I don't know that, Uncle Vin?

Silent wall growing thicker, wishing I were someplace else; what the hell do these people want from me?

"Piece of shit we pulled in earlier, Jamaican family, father lost his job with the city," he takes another sandwich, unwraps the white waxed paper and takes a bite, drinking some more coffee. He's looking out the window as cars pull in and out of the parking lot. "He took a butcher's knife and killed his wife in front of his five kids. Neighbors reported the screaming and fighting going on," he turns and looks at me, "he was going after one of the kids and the mother fought like hell to stop him. Can you imagine what that must have been like? He stabbed her fifteen times, she wouldn't stop," he shakes his head. "After he killed her, he killed the youngest and severely wounded another before we showed up," his lips tightening up. "Little girl bled to death," more to himself. "Dammit!" he takes a couple of moments.

"He was threatening to kill the others, EMS guys took him down before he could get another. Kids were scared shitless, now they'll become wards of the state split up and put in foster homes. And who knows what a mixed bag that is, some of them are good, some of them, what they do to the kids..." He looks at me, "Their lives changed just like that," he snaps his fingers, "and here you are complaining about how tough your father is on you, how mad you are at your friends cause of a stupid fight," he takes a deep breath. Looking down at my lap, losing the taste for the rest of my donut. Uncle

Vin gets out of the car and walks toward the hospital.

Following him, lopsided jogging to catch up.

Wishing I could disappear.

Stocking foot feels the cold, waxed linoleum floor of the hospital as we walk in. Uncle Vin talking to a lady working the desk. Taking a long drink from a water fountain—water almost too cold, need to stop and let my mouth warm up for a second, drinking more. Stomach still feels sour, another smelly burp coming up.

Nun in a hospital uniform walking briskly to my uncle and shakes his hand. Watching them talking, sitting down in one of the chairs and tucking my left foot behind my right. Can't make out their conversation, seeing him pointing at me every once in a while. She looks like someone who's used to being listened to—very calm, very still when she's listening to my uncle.

Reluctant to move as he waves me over.

Uncle Vin looks annoyed as I get up slowly and walk.

"Frank, come over here," he's waving his hand, "Mother Mary Joseph, this is the nephew I've been talking about, Frank Caruso," she holds her hand out to me, looking very composed. Smooth skin, thin, intense look— she must be in her fifties. Extending my hand to meet Sister Mary's firm handshake.

"Good to meet you, young Mr. Caruso."

"Good to meet you, Sis... I mean, Mother Mary Joseph."

"Frank," turning to Uncle Vin as a group of nuns dresses in hospital nursing uniforms pass by, one of younger ones giggling at something and getting a stern eye from the Mother—she's judge and executioner here, "I'll be back in a couple of hours," getting that shrinking feeling in my stomach.

"What?"

"Listen and follow," he turns and walks away. Gritting my teeth. Can't stop feeling angry and stupid, even with her stern eyes on me.

God does this suck!

Image of a long wide beach running through my mind, wishing I were any place but here, any place but here.

"Shall we?" she says still looking at me, nodding and following.

Eyes feeling tired walking under the fluorescent lights and light green walls. This place is much cleaner than Roosevelt Hospital.

"What happened to your other shoe," she asks as we are standing uncomfortably in the elevator.

"I lost it crossing a river."

"Ah? Are you going on a journey, young Jason?"

"I think I'm in the middle of one."

"Well then, there's no time like the present," she walks into the opening doors.

Elevator hums as we go up.

Walking out on the sixth floor, she goes up to a nurse's station and speaks to one of the nuns for a moment. Busy floor here—doctors, nurses all moving around, what must be concerned parents in a hushed conversation with a doctor, carts wheeled through the hall.

Long line of windows on either side of the hall receding from the nurse's station, "Here, put these on," she hands me a set of green fabric shoe covers. Doing as she says and taking a couple of long steps to catch up, feet making a funny sound in my little slippers.

"You know your uncle's talked a lot about you. This is tough for him."

Shaking my head at that, "I don't understand."

She stops and looks at me, "He was very proud of the things you were accomplishing in school, in sports. So proud," she looks right into me. Icy shrinking feeling coming on again—why the hell can't all these people leave me alone. She turns and starts walking, "Well, it's good that he's dealing with this."

Does she even know I'm here? Have I turned invisible now that I'm the family black sheep? What the fuck is going on here? I want to get out of here—go sit in the basement, go to sleep. Figure out how I get out.

"Well, I'm sure it's hard on him," venom inside me coming out.

She stops and looks at me, "Yes it is, to see someone you love throwing their life away and not knowing how to help," she holds her gaze, "but you're too young to know that yet, the bliss and blindness of youth."

"Yeah well, my father tried to beat help into me, so my uncle's got to beat help into me in a different way, Mother," sour taste from my stomach coming up again.

Her gaze patient, looking into me.

"Come with me, young Mr. Caruso."

Following her to the long windows, maternity ward starting to appear—row upon row of babies, little bodies, some sleeping, others crying for something, others looking around at their little world. Who knows that they comprehend any of all this shit.

"A number of these babies are orphans," she looks at me, "they were left here by parents who have the dignity to at least try to take care of the child, others are brought in by the police, fire or welfare services when they are found on the street and left to die," her eyes boring into me. "Others are here because they are premature and need the advanced care we can provide thanks to people like your uncle, by the way. He's one of the best fund raisers for our hospital." She's looking at me, "Ah, but how would you know that? Did you ever think to ask or find out why your uncle and aunt never had children, young Mr. Caruso? Did you ever think about what it's like to not be able to have a child of your own?"

Her eyes still on me—uneasy feeling descending.

"He tells me you're making adult decisions now, young Mr. Caruso, it's time for you to start hearing about adult situations, even if they are uncomfortable. When you have time, you should think about all the people that were invested in you. People that took the time to help you, people that took the time to lavish their affection on you, enable you to do things. Think about what they might be feeling seeing the direction you've been going."

Right, like they really give a fuck. I'm sure they have a great story of how much they suffered for me. Italians are great at being wronged, for suffering from how much they love someone; gee, was that before or after all the beatings Mother Mary?

She turns and walks to another section of the ward behind the long glass window. Babies in what look like incubators, tubes in their little bodies, some of them are smaller than a football.

"Your life, your situation may well be hard. I have only a passing knowledge," and the intensity of her look increases, "you have different choices, you've had a head start. You've been blessed with intelligence and strength. What are you going to make with it, what are you going to do in life? What about these poor little ones who've been given a cross to bear in this world? Ah, you say it's not fair. How could the good and loving God let the sins of the fathers be visited upon the sons or the daughters? Is it even possible to the mind of man to comprehend what God is or what is the will of God? Those are things to ponder, young Mr. Caruso. Little people like Lucile; they come into this world with what they have. Some leave without even having the opportunity to learn to ask that question."

She's quiet.

"Her mother was a heroin addict who died giving birth. The little girl was born addicted. What do we do now, young Mr. Caruso? What is the responsibility of the strong to help the weak? What is the responsibility of the weak to improve themselves, to accept where they are in life and do what they can to make of it what they will?"

She beckons me to follow her—having trouble looking at the rows of little babies, brown, black and white in the incubators. Guilt and shame in a tug of war with the desire to push this all this crap away and go be alone. Feeling stupid in these damn slippers. Looking down at my light green feet walking along the waxed linoleum tile floors of the hospital.

Uncomfortable silence as we drive through the City.

Tough time keeping my eyes open, heart feels sick thinking about those poor little babies. Not a word for the last hour as we drive. Can't wait to get out of this car.

"There are my boys," my aunt opening the door with a big smile and then standing back and looking at us. "Dinner's ready for you," she looks at us, "what's wrong, what happened?"

"I'm not feeling good, Aunt Kitty. Can I just go to sleep?"

"What?" she looks at me. Uncle Vin taking off his overcoat.

"I," wanting to run out the door so bad I can taste it, hating being here. Another damn jail, "I'm really tired, can I just go to bed," clenching and unclenching my hands, "please?" hate sounding weak like this.

She looks at me, looks at Uncle Vin behind me.

"You can go," deep voice from behind me.

Walking down the steep flight of stairs into the musty, cool smelling, dark basement. Hungry, too bad, anything is better than having to be around those two old people.

Washing my face, I can't look at myself in the mirror. Turning off the lights, closing the blinds—I want it dark. Images of Cat, trying to regain the feeling of those moments, grasping for something where I felt wonder, a sense there was promise.

Would she come with me to California if I left? Frustration boiling up thinking about how her mom wouldn't even let me talk to her last time I called.

Hearing them upstairs.

Light off, lying back on the bed in my underwear. I hate this. I hate this. Voices rising upstairs—nervous feeling going through my body, Mom and Dad never, I mean I never heard them yell at each other. I can't remember—it was always deadly silent combat.

"You took him where?"

Making out a few words of Uncle Vin's.

"Is that all you and your brother know how to do? Beat him?"

His low voice not carrying through the floor.

"If that's what he needs then why isn't it working, you and your brother just not hitting hard enough? Is that it? Madonna!" her voice fading, laughing a little at the stream of Italian curses it sounds like she's letting out.

"I won't stand for this in my house," my uncle near the door, body tensing—if he comes after me; heart rate picking up.

"Vincenzo, I love you so much, listen, he's still a teenager."

"That doesn't matter if he keeps goin' bad, he's gonna get tried as a man."

"I know, I know that's what you and your brother are worried about, but you've got to, I don't know," sounds of items moving around on the table, "he's so big, he's so mature in so many ways you keep forgetting that he's seventeen. A year makes a big difference at this age."

"But what if he doesn't unnerstand what the world can do?"

"Honey, I know how much he means to you, to both of us. The will to change has to come from him. You know that. I know you know that, if you want him to start acting like a man, you need to treat him like a man. You've got to trust him, if he doesn't have the will to change, to become what he can, you can't put it in."

"Another goddamn tragedy!"

"If need be Vincenzo, that may be the only way he can learn. He's got to swim or drown," muted voices now, sounds of a chair moving. "I know how hard it is to watch him make mistakes, but he's a smart kid, you can't live it for him."

Quiet in the kitchen upstairs now—refrigerator opening and closing, plates moving on the table, chairs moving. Voices lower.

Staring up into the dark open frame ceiling.
Frustration building, I'm living in just another damn cell.
Breathing getting short, rapid, got to break out of this.
Holding my muscles rigid through the pain and soreness.
What do these people want from me?
Why can't they leave me alone?

Chapter 25

Door opening above, "Frank, come up from the dungeon."

"Okay, Uncle Vin," blinking my eyes, my jaw feels sore—teeth clenched most of the night. Brushing my teeth to get the stale taste out of my mouth, running a brush though my curly hair. Doesn't help. Deliberately looking away from the image in the mirror, I don't care the bruises have cleared out. Looking at the small toilet, less blood in there today. It still hurts to take a deep breath.

Walking slowly up the stairs.

I just want to sit down here in the dark.

"Come in, Frankie," said my aunt, "hungry for breakfast?"

Nodding, looking down at the floor.

"You missed a good meal last night," Uncle Vin dressed for work, his shoulder holster in place over a dark blue long sleeve shirt, red and blue striped tie, jacket back over his chair. Sitting down carefully looking at both of them. Wondering how long this will take—body craving to go back down to the dark, quiet basement.

"I think we might have gotten started on the wrong foot," looking at Uncle Vin as he sits forward with his hands folded on the table. "Your aunt and I are worried about you, Frank. Lemme ask you, you think you're headed in a good direction?"

Looking at him warily, looking at Aunt Kitty sitting next to him, she's ready for work too. Seconds ticking away, thoughts swirling in my head, tough to grasp, filtering out the impulses to ask them what the hell they are doing, that they don't know anything, that I want to leave, that this sucks.

"No" looking down at the feet, shuffling—what the fuck does he want from me now? "Can I say something?"

"Okay," he looks wary.

"You keep asking me that question, I keep telling you no. What are you looking for?" Aunt Kitty puts her hand on his arm as he starts to get impatient.

"Okay, fair enough. What are you prepared to do about it, Frank?" She's relaxed, whereas my uncle's energy is simmering and churning underneath the surface.

"I don't know," looking down, following the outlines in the tile floor. Aunt Kitty getting up and plating up food at the stove—putting a hot plate of scrambled eggs with sliced sausage, cheese and green onions in front of me. My mouth watering at the smell, good thick toast, potatoes, the hint of garlic and hot red pepper.

"I mean... I need to finish school right? Work this summer, but I mean," picking up my fork and then putting it back down, "I could be going away too."

"We see the judge next week for an arraignment. I've asked to speed things up. My brother wanted to hire a lawyer, but after thinking about it, I said no, cause that'll show we presume you're guilty. I'll be there as your guardian," not knowing what to say, looking at him. Not a word of this last night.

"I figured you didn't want me around," looking at my uncle. "Why don't you just let me go to live with Uncle Robert in California? I'd be better off out of everybody's hair."

Jumping a little as he slams his hand down on the table. "NO!" he sits back, pissed off. Looking down at my feet. I hate this.

He moves uncomfortably in his seat, looks at Aunt Kitty. Following his eyes, she's standing there, her eyes locked onto his. Looks like he wants to get out of here.

"We want you to stay with us, Frank," he takes a deep breath. "I'm sure your head's spinning which way and all, but this is... Well, it will take some time to figure out, for all of us," he looks at me, looks at my aunt. Trying to break the scowl on his face, "We're family, right?"

Those words searing into me. Can't help the rush of anger and hurt—images of Dad and Uncle Vin coming to see me in jail and then leaving me in that fucking place with nothing, Nothing!

"What?" he's looking at me, about to say something—Aunt Kitty puts her hand on his arm. Breathing deep to keep things in check, fighting to keep level. Can't look at them need to look away.

"You don't have to talk, Frank," her voice coming in.

Can't stop the rush in my chest.

"Kid," my uncle, his voice different now, "look, it's gonna take time for things to work out. You put yourself in a difficult situation. Maybe I jumped to a conclusion, maybe I was wrong, maybe, I was right. Look," relaxing so I can look at them, chest loosening up a little. I can't wait to get this over with. "What's done is done. You can move forward and get your shit together." Kitty taking a sharp breath. "You can look back at all the bad stuff that's happened and make yourself miserable. Our family is good at developing bad situations into mortal wounds," he laughs at his all too accurate joke.

"Frank, I'm sorry if we got off on the wrong foot. I want you to live up to your potential, Frankie, I don't know how that's going to turn out, but I'll back you till you show me I can't trust you. Okay?"

Trying to fight back another wave of mixed emotion, looking at them. Images of the hospital flashing through my mind—the little baby in intensive care already damaged for life. Them leaving me in jail, the other kids there... Fucking shit!

"What do you want to do with your life, Frank? Where do you want to go?" my aunt's soft voice coming in. "You don't need to answer right now, but take this time to start thinking about that, okay?"

Uncle Vin checking his watch.

"You want me out of the house when you're not here?"

"Heavens no," said Aunt Kitty. "Keep your room clean, this isn't a hotel. We'll figure out how you can help out around the house later today when I get home from work. Take this time to read, think, talk to people."

"You probably got some fences to mend," Uncle Vin looking at me, giving me a half hairy eyeball.

"Yeah, one or two, something like the Great Wall of China," feeling a slight ray of humor cracking through the darkness. Looking at them, "What do you want me to do while you're out?"

"You can come and go as you want," he said. "Back by five, Hon?"

"Sure."

"Curfew at night is ten, unless you call and talk to us. I'm guess you'll be helping out with the wash, shopping. Your aunt has a bunch of work for you in the garden that I was supposed to do," she playfully smacks him in the arm, "but hey, one man's loss is another's gain," he shrugs his shoulders and laughs a little.

"My God, he still can smile," she says.

"I'm off," he bends over and gives her a kiss, musses my hair a little. "Be good, we'll figure this out."

My aunt looking at me, "I have to go too, Frankie. Take advantage of this time to read. Think about what you did. Use this time wisely. You know how to get in touch with your uncle. Here's my contact information at school if there's an emergency. You need some pocket change?"

"No. I mean, thanks Aunt Kitty, just need to take some out of the bank, but I can pay you back."

"Easy," she pushes a ten-dollar bill. "You'll pay it back in trade. Don't worry."

"Okay," smiling a little bit.

"That's more like it, no union rules here. Well I'm off, eat your breakfast and lock up when you leave. Oh, here's a set of keys."

"Can I bring some of my things here?"

"Sure," she waves as she puts a sweater on and walks out the back door, car starting up in the garage then pulling away.

Slow motion. Cleaning up the dishes, washing, suds building up, rinsing and stacking. Water running down the drain. Cleaning out their sink. Wringing the water from the sponge, setting the dishtowel over the drain board to dry. House quiet, mechanical clock in their living room is the only sound.

Comfortable living room, warm, lived in. No museum pieces here protected with plastic covers and invisible "keep off" signs. Sitting on the large couch for a moment, pictures of my aunt and uncle's wedding on the wall, Mom and Dad there. My other uncles and aunts—memories of my

Grandpa T coming alive as I look at Grandma and Grandpa in the picture, he'd be so disappointed in me.

Clock ticking.

Eyes shifting across different framed photographs in the room.

The three brothers together in military uniforms—Dad and Uncle Vin in their Army uniforms, Uncle Michael in his Marine uniform, big smiles, must have been shot right when they joined up.

Clock ticking in the quiet house.

Twenty minutes on the subway, another five to the hospital.

What if he won't see me?

Chapter 26

Subway car lurching back and forth as the train hurtles through the long tunnel under the East River, only a few people on the train in the late morning. A little old lady sitting across from me holds one of her feet out every few minutes to look at her shoes. Drunk passed out lying across a section of seats. MTA policeman walks by without doing anything.

59th St. Station crowded, people moving between train lines, walking through the station with a purpose. Not all of them anyway. Up on the street walking toward the Hudson River. Stopping, taking a moment to call the number Mrs. Rivera gave me. No one answers.

Remembering my way through the hospital wards, the familiar smell of bodies, ointment and medication greeting me on my way.

Standing in front of his door—no one inside but Alton. Forcing my hand toward the handle. Fighting with the force holding me back, making my body move slowly; pushing forward like I'm moving through deep, thick, cold mud, door opening inward—seeing him sitting up in the bed. Skin feeling cold, stomach hollow; his face is heavily bandaged with draining tubes protruding from his cheek.

Stopping. His eyes looking at me, his body shifting—agitated, he looks away, won't make eye contact. Voice frozen. Rooted there unable to speak. Images flooding through my mind of places we'd been together, sounds of us joking and laughing during good times. Trying to pull a dark shade over the ugly things I'd done.

Taking the cold metal chair by his bed.

Sitting down, goose flesh on my bare forearms. Why can't I talk? Trying to pull back all the lines I'd rehearsed. Feeling the pressure in my chest growing, fighting the desire to walk out—be a man Frank, own up to what you did. Trying to open my mouth and let the gusher of remorse, sorrow and shame out.

Nothing—dammit, why can't I speak?

Magazines lying where I'd left them, hell he doesn't even want… Oh no. Hitting me—they've got his elbows strapped to the side of the bed. He seems so uncomfortable. His skin looks like it has a grayish tone.

Heaviness settling into my chest—how could I have done this? How could this have happened? He must be so uncomfortable; they're keeping his hands away from his face. Remembering what it felt to be like bound when I was in solitary. There's no way he'll know. His head turned as far away from me as he can.

Picking up the March *Sports Illustrated*, Kentucky basketball player on the cover. Flipping past the Toyota and Datsun car ads, cigarette ads and whiskey ads—here's the cover article, "It Will Be A Horse Race" starting to read out loud, anything to fill the awful silence of the room.

"The NCAA is throwing a California Easter party this weekend and there is no guest of honor. For the first time since Helen Gurley Brown was a cheerleader, the final round of the national championship shapes up as a basketball tournament instead of a UCLA prom. Any one of the four finalists—Kentucky, Louisville, Syracuse or UCLA—could end up as King of the Hoop…"

Letting my voice carry as I read through the article.

Stopping for a moment as I flip the page and stare at the photograph of Jim Evans in a facemask running up the court. Will this be him? Alton's still looking away.

Reading on, not looking at him, sound of my voice calming me down. Flipping over to page 28. Baseball, let's see what else is here. More ads for cars, cigarettes and booze—some sports magazine.

"You want to hear about hockey or baseball?"

He's quiet. Flipping to an article on fishing for bonefish. Better than nothing. Scanning the story and then on to the pro basketball section. Article on Randy Smith, this is better. Clearing my throat to read.

Putting the magazine down. Room taking on a hollow interior silence. Sounds from the hall filtering in, must have left the door open when I came in. Looking down at my hands, rubbing them together.

"Alton, I," dammit why is this so hard, "I had to come."

Breathing to get my head back.

Closing my eyes, leaning forward, putting my head in my hands.

"I don't know where to start, I mean, we," taking another deep breath, "no that's wrong, I know I crossed the line and we can never go back. I didn't come here to ask you to forgive me, I came here to apologize, to say I'm sorry."

Lost in my mind for a few moments. Sorrow welling up inside.

"You know, there was part of me that knew I was wrong all along. I was," searching for words, "I was out of control, like some… I don't know," not wanting to say the word monster. "Just that little bit, one move and things could have been so different now, but I couldn't take it, couldn't get by my pride," feeling my eyes well up.

"And I hurt you. I wanted to hurt you cause I was hurting so bad inside." His muscles look like they've shrunken the last few weeks in here. "Alton," shaking my head, "I wasn't man enough, but I had to come tell you now that you were right. I'm so sorry that I chose my pride over you, but that's no excuse, what I did was wrong."

Crash out in the hall, people rushing to deal with whatever is going on.

"I'll do everything I can to help your moms. All the money I saved up, I'll work, help pay this off whatever it takes," silent crying, "Jesus man, I'm so sorry."

Deep hum of the hospital ventilators.

"It's all gone away too, man. My father threw me out of the house, I lived on the streets for a few days," emotions of those days running through my head, "man, that was crazy. I was in jail at Rikers, more of that to look forward to. My dad washed his hands of me, told me I was a disgrace, told me I'm not his son anymore."

Images of our last basketball game together—things went so well. Top of the world for a day; we both played well, scored a ton of points. Hurts to remember how happy we were in that moment.

"And it's likely I'll be going back to jail," those words bringing a curtain over the fleeting bright images of a few weeks ago, "cause I'm guilty."

"All the things we worked so hard for, just gone," looking up at him, his eyes on me, but looking away quickly. "For what it's worth, man. I pray you come out of this okay. Come through the pain, at least one of us can get ahead and not get pulled down into this shit," choking up, "making their mark. Man if both of us..." tears rolling down again. "If I fucked up both of us, man, I don't know how I'll live with that. How does a person come back from this? From being some kind of crazy?"

He's still looking away.

"You're right to hate me and be angry," closing my eyes, wishing I could take that few minutes back, eat the anger I had. Have him look at me as a friend again. Sitting in the deep loss I feel.

"I hope someday you find it in your heart of hearts to forgive me for what I've done... No forgive is too strong a word," looking down at the sports magazines, "maybe there'll be someplace where you look at the stupidity of a boy and put it in place. Some place I'll never see. I'm going to miss you. I'm sorry, Alton."

Standing up, putting the magazine on the stand near his bed.

Alton's eyes catching mine for a second, his eyes tearing up too—pain, anger, frustration. Taking his hand for a second, he tries to pull it away.

"Get better. Get strong! You can do it, I know. I don't know how, but I know you can. You're too strong, too good and too smart to let this stop you. Do it!"

Letting go, feeling like he's holding it for a second or not sure if he's still trying to pull away. Blinking, wiping the tears away from my eyes. Looking at him for a moment, another memory to sear into place—turning toward the door.

Oh God, Mrs. Brown standing right there.

Wave of shame coming over me, looking down at my feet, mumbling, "Sorry, shouldn't be here. Just had to say," looking at her, stepping by her, embarrassed.

Can't make eye contact as I walk by her.

"You wait now," firm voice from behind me. Stopping, wanting to keep walking—go to the park, go see Cat and... Maybe it's time to go back to the river again and stare down in that blackness. Maybe that's the only place for me, end all the turmoil, put an end to the pain inside. "Mrs. Brown, I..." she's holding up a calloused hand.

"You come with me now," she turns and motions to a small waiting room down the hall. Following her slowly as people pass us in the hall. Dreading what's coming next. Sitting down slowly across from her. TV in the room on, volume turned off, magazines strewn over the table, *Outdoor Life, Life Magazine, Time*, well-worn copies of *National Geographic*.

"I heard what you said to my son," looking at her, looking down at my hands, listening to her as she takes a deep breath—feeling her looking at me. Forcing my body to look at her, "I can only hope you meant it, I can only hope you truly understand what you took away from him."

Her face twisting in anger, hurt, frustration, her lips pulled hard together. Feeling my eyes tearing up. She's shaking her head slightly.

"He used to talk about you, Frank this and Frank that all the time. He looked up to you so much. In some ways you were like a big brother." Intense level gaze right at me, "an look what you've done to yo self, look what you've done to my son." She's shaking her head, "Oh lord, oh lord forgive me," as she shakes her hand.

Remembering the slap she gave me.

"It's taken me some time now."

Ticking of the wall clock is the only sound.

"I had to pray not to hate you after what you done. I had to tell myself that something good will come of all this, that the Lord works in ways we can never see, that my hate for what you done was just as much of a test."

Folding her hands in her lap, regaining her composure.

"I think what's hurting him the most, all the time you boys put in together. And then when you was both getting ready to really shine, the promise of our peoples living deeper than the color of our skin no matter what. All the things you boys could have done is shattered now," direct look at me, "he'll never be able to box again you know, that's gone."

Closing my eyes, shaking my head.

"If he plays basketball he'll have to wear a protective mask for six months or so and thank the lord his teachers are being understanding, it will be weeks before he's back in school."

Feeling like I'm sinking slowly.

"Mrs. Brown, I know I messed up bad, but I can help out, I got money saved, it's all yours. I can help with his studies and all."

Listening to her breathe for a few moments.

"It's too late for that, Frank."

Feeling like I'm shrinking.

"You know, I know your father never thought much of black folk, Alton told me about how he used to ride you about hanging around with him. I was always glad you didn't knuckle under, but I tell you, he surprised me when he offered to take care of all this, the surgery and then any follow on."

"But how, he's always saying how little money," she cocks her head at me incredulously.

"So much to learn," she looks at me, takes another deep breath.

Sounds of the busy hospital fill the room as she goes quiet. Feeling cold inside. Saying goodbye to Cat, my aunt. Feeling like the river is the only place for me.

"I don't know if anyone else is gonna tell you this, but you gonna have to face the evil side you got in you. You got a good side, I seen it in you. Both cut deep. As high as heaven, as deep as hell, an if 'n you ain't careful, you could become a tool for evil in this world," her words, her look making my skin crawl.

"Lucifer was God's favorite angel, pride was his downfall and now he goads us all into following his path, pride, anger, greed…" her eyes looking through me.

"You always had a hard place inside you where you won't bend, that's a gift and a curse 'n you gonna have to figure out what it is 'n make some hard choices. That place is scary to most people, they close their eyes, but you're not afraid to look there, not afraid to look at the place where the angels wrestle. You know that, don't you?"

"Yes," remembering the pier.

"Takes a lot to look at all of life and not become a brute or a paper saint. God willing you'll be scourged by the darkness and learn to accept that side of you. Do your penance for the evil deeds you've done and look for the salvation on the other side of the darkness through our Lord Jesus Christ."

Difficult to breathe, speaking in only the whisper I can squeeze out, "It's ugly, it's also terrible because it's… it's freeing."

"The face of God ain't like you see in them lily white churches ya'll go to, it's terrible, its beauty. It's power and majesty. It's terrible in its power, in its love for all his children. It's terrible in its vengeance."

"I don't understand. I want to be good, just sometimes I can't control myself. Like something just takes over, like some beast."

"Yes," she's rocking back and forth. "The beast is close to the surface in you. I've known you for almost seven years now, part 'o me was always wondering when you were going to start breaking out of that cage, like one of them tigers in the zoo," she's looking at me with strange far off look, "pacing, looking outside, waiting, can't tame the beast."

She's quiet for a few minutes.

"I always wondered how your daddy was going to deal with you when you got older. Seemed like he thought it was funny when you were young, he was so puffed up and all. He didn't have the eye you see. I didn't think he'd like it when you started to grow your claws, when that wild thing started to look out of the dark 'n sees that it was strong, real strong. I don't think my boy understood when I used to tell him to be careful. Not in a bad way, but wild things sometimes need to go their way 'n if you ain't ready to follow…"

Painful memories of fights with Dad flooding in.

Head bent over, words coming slowly, "It started with his hands, I don't know years ago," pain of my mother never doing anything rising up in my throat, "then when I got too strong and fought back he started using a cut down bat. I took it from him and told him if he hit me again with it, I'd…"

"What you got to say?"

"You know," deep breath, "the beatings and fighting wasn't that bad you know, what came next, the invisibility, the silent digs, the constant belittling of what I did, my friends, the things he used to call us…" closing my eyes, "and she didn't do anything," fighting to keep from being weak again.

"Now, now," she's patting my arm, "I had a feeling something had gone wrong. I'm so sorry, so sorry it boiled out and took my boy down with it too. So sad when love can turn to hate…"

Sounds of the busy hospital starting to come in, not sure if I was talking out loud or in my head, wave of shame running through me talking like this after what I'd done. Something's clearing up through the confusion.

"So what are you going to do now? Give in to hate and self-pity? Or are you gonna go wrestle with them angels and find out how to put that strong nature of yours to good? Protect not destroy? Takes strength not to give into hate, Frank, as much as I hate to say this, I can see your daddy thinking he was doing the right thing trying to get you into line, his heart was in the right place, but he went about it wrong. You need to be inspired, you need room."

Lost in her words.

Looking up, her dark eyes crackling full of energy.

"It's not a short road you know, maybe this is a calling to something," she's pausing to let it sink in. "What's probably going to make it tough is that it's off the road most of your school friends will have and it will be a lonely place, Frank," her face changes, like she's coming back. "Pity my Alton had to be part of this," her eyes tearing again, "but maybe it will be the spark that sets him on fire. In his own way, he's been coasting on your coat tails for too long," she goes quiet, "the Lord works in strange ways."

She's quiet, sitting in her blue print dress with white flowers.

"For better or worse now, you can't go back" she's shaking her head, "you can never go back, remember that."

Sitting there, looking at her.

"You seen something didn't you?" she's rocking back and forth. "Yes, tell me now," her voice rising.

"Yes," looking down at my hands.

"Hmm, ah ha."

"They were chasing me down by the docks when I was out on the street. It was after Alton," my hands feel sweaty, gripping them and then relaxing, "I was so torn up inside, I was looking down at the river thinking about how I could have done what I did, wishing there was a way to end the pain, wishing there was a way I could stop from doing all these things. It was dark in that place, these men they wanted to…" Looking at her, she's rocking back and forth slowly eyes closed listening to me. "I wasn't afraid."

Shudder running through my body.

"A voice spoke to me in the darkness, it was like a hissing sound. I wasn't afraid, but it spoke to me, told me to wait till they got close in the darkness, to…"

"Hmm, yes. Ah ha. Devil's a strong angel, Frank, come to you when you're weak. Come tell you things you want to hear. Did you do what he wanted?"

"No."

"Other angels will talk to you too, you got to learn how to find them, got to learn that good will talk to you too 'n that sometimes it's just easy to listen to what you want to hear. Remember, as high as heaven, as deep as hell. You remember that voice now. You remember what you did to put yo 'self in the path of the devil. Ain't no salvation you walk on that path."

Chapter 27

Walking through busy streets, people passing, pushing.

Empty steps have just enough energy to carry me along with the current of people. What if Alton's mom is right? If it's all changed? Stopping for a moment as people just walk by me on the street.

Realization hitting me—she is right, I am different, I can't go back. None of the people I know will understand what happened in the dark. Shiver running down my spine—my uncle would understand though.

How the hell do I talk to him now?

Drifting with the crowd of people walking downtown.

Impervious to the noise.

Am I more than darkness? If I'm evil, can I love? Was what I felt with Cat just an illusion, a joke to make the monster I am feel human, like some pitiable Frankenstein searching for his misshapen other?

I won't argue there is evil in me, but I am more than that? I made the move to help that poor old lady when all the people's whose job it is to care didn't do shit. I've helped Julio, Alton and lots of other kids with schoolwork when nobody was looking. What about standing up for my friend? That time I got ejected from the game sophomore year when that jerk almost tackled Cedar and he hurt his knee—Coach wasn't too pissed that I punched that big ass six-foot-ten freak so hard he fell on his ass and was dazed for minutes... Was that just the veneer on top of the beast? The easy things I can do to cover the monster below, to hide from the thing I really am.

Easy, calm down Frank. Here I am getting all wound up again.

If I am capable of both extremes—what do I do with myself?

How do I control the monster inside?

Feeling my body bubbling with ideas, places coming into focus.

Maybe this was inevitable, to be standing here like this, adrift in a sea of humanity with my humanity just out of reach... I don't belong here.

Walking without noticing where I am.

Stopping when the crowd stops, starting when the crowd starts.

What options do I have? Quit school and work, imagining what it must have been like for Jack London growing up on the waters of San Francisco Bay fishing, poaching oysters, journeying to Alaska. Wow, I would be free.

I could go with Gus and train to be a professional fighter if he'll have me now. I could go back to some other school for a year or whatever. I could go someplace else, travel, stay with my cousins in California.

She talked about a calling? Would Cat come with me?

Shiver running through me. How much time in jail would I be looking at? Where would I go? Brain and body feel like they are being pulled in two different directions—my uncle could get me off, but he never will. Hard lesson isn't it Frankie baby; he won't surrender his values for me or anyone else no matter how tough it is—strength, conviction, principle. That's why people fear him and respect him. They know who they are dealing with. Me, I'm all over the damn map.

I'll have a criminal record...

Good luck getting into law school like sis or medical school like Mom and Dad wanted me to. I'll be a convicted felon.

Stopping on the street, flow of people passing by me again. Hands rubbing on my face, taking a deep breath. And I can't blame anyone else—as mad as I was at that manipulative prick Leroy, I didn't have to do the dance. I had a choice and I made it.

It was a matter of time. I was always out of place at school.

Street coming into context, 5th Ave. and 22nd—the arch at Washington Square Park in the distance. Looking up at the tall buildings, people, taxis, trucks, noise of the City starting to register again. Where have I been walking all this time? What time is it? Checking out my watch—three thirty-five. It's been almost two hours.

Setting out with a long stride.

Do my time. Deal with what I have to deal with.

I'm not letting anything stop me.

Dad's a rat bastard, but look at what he was able to do; started his own company building the things he's passionate about, doing something he loves. In college, his draft deferment pulled when they needed men for the invasion of Europe, goodbye to Fordham. Then after the war meeting Mom, getting married, making his business a success and making a home for us all.

Uncle Michael didn't go to college and he owns car dealerships in Queens and on the Island. Even if I do go away, there are lots of ways to slice it—go to CCNY, learn, figure things out. Get good grades and use them to vault into a good graduate program. I'll be older than most of the other kids, but that's just tough shit, I'm going to have to do it the hard way.

I can make a place for us Cat.

Wind picking up from the east. Walking toward 2nd Ave.

Will she come with me? Should she come with me? Her board scores were good but not great, her grades are good, but not great... Her dad went to Yale and teaches at Columbia though, so she's wired for Ivy League and she should be—smart, competitive, intense; they'll never know what hits them when she's in college.

Not many people hanging around Stuyvesant Park, a couple of people walking dogs, resident winos lying back on the park benches deep asleep in grimy clothes. A couple of people in white lab coats standing in front of Beth Israel Medical Center smoking and talking.

Sitting down, letting my eyes follow the patterns of the hexagonal paving stones across the park. Lethargy setting in, a deep weariness engulfing my body—as much as I've been fighting it, as much as I'd like to blame Leroy for all this, Alton's mom is right, Aunt Kitty is right; this has been a long time in the making.

Shiver running through my body thinking back to the times I've taunted Leroy and some of the other seniors, how much I got away with cause they were afraid of my fists—what a fucking fool I was. It was competition. It was my boys, Alton, Julio, Hector and I against the rest of the team. Competition between Leroy and me on who was gonna be top dog. Yeah, I played hard and did my best out on the court, worked the offense, put up big numbers, worked the boards, shut down the good forwards we played against.

I remember Coach telling me to think about why I wasn't voted team captain and all I could do was just be pissed and put it off to jealousy—people getting back at me cause I was turning out to be the best player on the team. I couldn't hear him. It didn't make sense when he told me people elect their leaders.

I was out for what I wanted to do.

Taking a deep breath, eyes up to the sky.

What a great fucking time to learn this.

Can't do a damn thing now.

Standing up, angry.

Why the hell didn't they tell me?

They'll be getting out of school soon.

Walking slowly up 16th Street. Last time I was here, people saw me getting arrested, now I'm the outsider. The high school dropout, no way I'm going to become some parasite hanging around here trying to relive my glory days.

Laughing to myself, glory days my ass. Memorizing the street, the red brick building and the steel fire escapes on the facade. This is it for this place. Cause I was a stupid motherfucker. People making such a big deal about my board scores, how smart I am—going to MIT or some good school and here I am out on the street with a good chance of going to jail. Sounds like a weather report; today's forecast for dumb shit Frank Caruso is a continued dark cloud following him around with a chance of time behind bars. Yeah I'm smart, a real genius.

People part as they walk around me, a couple of wary hellos here and there. Cedar sees me, he's with Anthony, nodding to them in greeting—cold feeling inside as they turn and walk away.

"Yo, Frankie," Julio hurrying toward me.

"Hey Julio, how you feelin man?" Doing a brother handshake he's gripping me on the shoulder. More people coming over, big smile from Mary, "My God, Frank, are you okay? I mean, what happened?" more people gathering around. "We heard you'd gone to jail."

"Hey, look at this loser," turning my back to Leroy, his face still healing from the scars. Julio trying to keep a straight face as he cups his hands in front of his mouth and starts repeating "Fish lips," to annoy Leroy.

"How are you Mary? Things good?"

"Oh I mean, who wants to hear about all this," as she waves her hand back at the school, "What happened to you?"

"Yeah," Richard jumping in. "What happened, what was it like?"

"Fool," said Hector, looking at him, "you think this is like some TV bullshit?"

Nina, Marta, Lewis and some other kids coming over too, others just looking at us for a moment and walking away talking amongst themselves.

"Man, I tell you," looking at their fresh faces, my words just heightening the gap between where I've been and who knows were I'm going and the place they are all living in. Looking at them, feeling the gulf.

"Anybody mess with you?" Richard again. He's the most fearful of the lot. Cat coming in, harder to focus on their bullshit—she's angry, standing there with her arms crossed.

"I hope that place is something you never have to know," mind snapping back to the deep panic of being bound by the straight jacket in the blackness for a moment.

"You must have showed them though, man," said Hector, his eyes searching for something to hang onto. Eyes sweeping their faces—they have no clue. Breathe to keep the frustration down.

"Yeah well, I took out the baddest kid there, but you upset things, they try and break you, they put you in the dark," words stuck in my throat, no way to bring the reality of the place to them. "It sucks," taking a deep breath, "and there's a good chance I'll be going back after the trial…"

Feeling their eyes on me. Face feels set in hard mask.

"I saw Alton today, he's," hard to say it, Cat's eyes softening a little bit, but not her body, "he's messed up. They did a bunch of work on his face, it must hurt like hell and itch like hell cause they've got his arms secured so he can't reach his face," catching my breath. "Tubes, bandages 'n shit all on the left side of his face. You want to do him a favor, go there and say hi. He'll be there for another week or so before they allow him to go home. He can't read, can't talk yet, eats through a tube," not much coming back from my adoring public now, my lips pushing together, "all because…" Hard look at Leroy, he starts to back up a little. Hector putting his hand on my shoulder. Fighting down the wave of hate inside. What did my Alton's Mom say? Takes strength not to hate? Eyes on Leroy, hearing the voices whisper how good it will feel. No.

"All because of me…" deep breath, no, enough of this shit, "well anyway, my uncle got me released till the trial."

"Yo man, Coach is pissed," said Hector. His voice starts to quiet down, must be seeing that I don't give a shit about this anymore. "Losing two top players 'n all."

Nodding, shrugging my shoulders.

I can't do anything about this anymore.

"He's not the only one," Cat starting to work herself up. "You know they have this great invention called a telephone," her hands on her hips as her head and body start to sway, "your ass needs to learn how to use one," as she points at me and is making and "s" motion with her body. "You can't just be showing up here, talking about all this like we're some soap opera audience and shit. Uh, uh, no sympathy here, Mister."

Julio, Hector and the rest giving out the obligatory, "Ooooo."

Bone deep tiredness penetrating my body.

Nothing else to say to them, is there?

What if I just walk now? Whatever ties are here, just cut them. Looking at her, feeling my eyes start to well up at the rush of jangled swirling emotions—joy at seeing her, distance, shame for being so far away, rage at not being able be near her for the last weeks; and at the same time, I'm not the same.

Fuck it.

"Well, I'll see you around then," deep breath, turning and walking away.

"Hey, don't go," hearing Hector. "Cool it, Cat, the man's been through some serious shit."

"And what do you know?" hearing that edge in her voice, imagining him backing down. "Don't you go walking off there, I ain't finished with you."

Not stopping, hoping they'll all just disappear back into the school, make it just one big painful pop and have all this over.

Done, I'm done with this.

Hand grabbing the sleeve on my short sleeve shirt.

"What you think you're doing?" angry tears in her eyes.

"I can't do this, Cat. I can't play this."

"You can't do what. You owe me an explanation about all this!"

"No."

"Fuck you!" cheek stinging from another slap.

Shaking my head, feeling my lips tighten up, my gut churning at Mrs. Brown's words, my aunt's words, my uncle's words all hit me, vision of Alton laying in the dirty street, blood from his mouth—body erupting. "Don't you know when to stop? What the fuck is wrong with you?" loud voice, people looking over, nervous looks on their faces, "I'm trying to give you an out, I fucked up," looking at her, not able to control the timbre of my voice, "don't you get it, I fucked up. I blew it!" clenching and unclenching my fists, "it was stupid of me to come back here…"

"That's all you've got to say?"

"What? You want to hear that it's tearing my heart out to see you, see my friends and that my fucking life is going to be dealing with assholes like Tommy, Johnny, Tony..." Shaking my head.

Stop it Frank. It's not their fault. "Look, it's not your fault, this..." looking at her, she's stepped back a little. Her lips tight, she looks confused, hurt. "It was too painful to miss you, Cat. To have to remember the wonder, the joy of being with you," looking at her trying to believe it again. "Trying to remember what it was like to be near you, smell your hair, remember your laugh. And then to be powerless to do anything about it and stuck in the most damn monotonous routine. Asshole guards, scared kids, bullies... Look, Cat, I'm sorry. This isn't what I wanted to say. I messed up," looking at her, "maybe we really had a chance there for a while. I couldn't see where I was going. I couldn't see the cost of what I did. That's no excuse though. I'm really going to miss you, Cat. Maybe I just needed to come here and say goodbye," shaking my head, trying to deal with the rush of emotions. "You know, Cat, I really know how much this meant to you. I can only imagine what it's been like. I'm sorry, I'm so sorry..." Looking down at my feet, turning and walking toward the park.

"You walk away, Frank Caruso, and I'll scratch your eyes out," feeling her running up and putting her arm through mine, falling in with me. Feeling a weight falling off my body, the seething cauldron cooling down.

Closing my eyes to just feel her, smell her. Tightening my arm so she's pressed into my body, her head on my shoulder—feeling like time is suspended.

"I missed you so much, Frankie. This hurts so bad."

Stopping, turning to her, "I'm so sorry, Cat, I'm so ashamed that I've caused so much damage. To be with you like we were and then to have it just ripped away from both of us... If it was anything like what I've been going through..." catching her eyes for a moment. "I'm so sorry I've let you down and then to not be able to call, and then lately, your mom's just hanging up on me."

She stops walking, busy traffic on 1st Ave. fading to the distance. Her arms crossed again, she turns away but backs into me, her head down.

"I've been so miserable, not knowing if you're okay, if you're in some horrible place, hurt, in pain... Missing you so much and there's nothing I could do," she looks over at me for a second. "That's the worst part, feeling so helpless. Like sometimes I just want to take you in my arms and let you know everything is okay, like I can make everything good."

Leaning back against a parked car, her body moving with me.

"It was scary, Frankie," she looks at me. "For a few moments when we did it you know," her voice becoming hushed, "afterwards, it was like I could see you so clearly, so strong, so clear and I just had this like electricity go through me, through my whole body from well, you know... Up to my heart and it was for you. I was so hungry for more, to just let that feeling take me over, but I couldn't... I didn't want... I mean is it supposed to be like that? And then I got all panicked about being there like that. They weren't coming home for a couple of hours but I felt so bad, so guilty, like I wanted to do it, but shocked..."

Letting her talk. Body reacting to her voice, her words—the remembrance of what her body felt like when I entered her, the look on her eyes. Aroused, the colors of the city coming back from the dull gray I'd been seeing, her sweater, her skin.

"And then after what we did at the hotel, I was just so overwhelmed that it could be like that and then I couldn't see you or talk to you," putting my arms around her waist, my face coming near her neck so I can inhale the scent of her body, her hair. Bask in the closeness of her. "I missed you so much, baby, I was so scared for you, so frustrated that you were just taken," she's turning slowly, spreading my legs so she can come closer as she wraps her arms around my neck. "Don't do this again? Okay? You've got to find a way to let me know what's going on, how I can be there. Don't do this to me, Frankie."

"Yes, Cat, I promise," she puts her books on the hood of the car.

Bringing her closer, slightly embarrassed by the raging erection growing in my jeans, doing my best to focus on her. Oh man, are my balls going to ache later. Kissing her, looking at her face, her eyes closed, memorizing the details of how she looks now, how she feels now—her body in full contact with mine.

"Looks like somebody else is missing me," she whispers in my ear and then looks at me with a little sly grin.

"Oh yes and you'd better watch out," laughing with her, "he's a mad man."

Time passing, just holding each other.

"Why don't you come over to the pizza place, we can hang out, I'm sure all your little friends will want to come over too. See," she looks back over her shoulder, "they are still there."

"I don't know, Cat. I feel different now with all that went down."

"What does that mean for us, Frankie?"

"It means that I just want to hold you for a few minutes."

Her arms around me.

"Sometimes I wanted to believe this was all dream. Anything to keep out the pain of knowing how far away I was from you and at times... It seemed like I was... There was nothing but pain, blackness. I..."

"Don't talk like that, Frankie. I'm real. I love you so much. Oh my, baby," the strength of her body hitting me.

Moving my head back, looking at her as she brushes a tear back.

"Making me get like this and all," she swats at me. "Let's not be sad okay? Let's go talk and laugh. We all missed you, Frankie."

"Okay, okay Cat, you guys can get your juvenile delinquent quota for the day," just hugging her to me, feeling her strong shoulders and breasts in my chest, laughing softly.

In her ear, "I'm either going to have to carry your books or pull my shirt tails out." Stepping back she holds up her books and beckons me on—holding her books in front of me—she's looking at me and laughing.

Warm food, teenagers yacking away about meaningless shit. Finishing up another slice of mediocre pizza—listening to them go on about classes, teachers and all the high school things that are becoming meaningless to me.

Rock bands, concerts, gossip about who has a thing for whom, complaints about tests and homework. Keeping quiet—I'm not a part of this anymore. Who knows what I'm part of?

We have the big table by the front window. Julio and Marta arguing about something, Hector rolling his eyes, Cat giving Mary the stink eye, Richard totally eyeing Cat, cause he thinks I'm not looking, Billy sitting down trying to mooch a slice—his fucking dad's a rich psychiatrist and he's always trying to get over.

"Billy, put a buck on the table."

He puts his hand on his heart like he's been wounded and playing around so he's not embarrassed. He always pulls this shit.

"Come on," giving him the hairy eyeball as the other kids starting to bust his balls too. Cat's hand on my thigh, wanting to do nothing but move her hand to my crotch, stroke up and down. Billy wanders off after letting the moth out of his wallet and putting a dollar on the table. Kids stopping by and talking, trading insults, girls flirting with some of the other boys at the table.

What's the worst that can happen to me? What, go do six months to a year—keep myself out of trouble, I'll have a record, but that's not the end of the world, finish up high school a year late, get into a good school, good basketball program. Maybe not what I'd have had before, but tough shit—make the best out of what I have now and stop dreading the future. You have an idea of what juvenile jail will be like—so why the awful feeling?

Mind drifting around the room, taking in the talk about movies, more bullshit about who's dating whom, argument about how tall Sean Connery really is—one kid claiming they cast short people in the movies to make him look taller. New kid this year in school who transferred in from the Fashion Institute of Technology talking about hair with a couple of the prissy fashionable girls who come in from Forest Hills. The boys who don't understand he plays for the other team are giving him disgusted looks.

"Frank," blinking my eyes and looking at Cat, "you're ignoring me," playing like she's hurt and slapping at me, "Walter's having a big party this weekend, and I was, you know?"

"Absolutely," shaking my head a little, coming back to the room full of noise. Taking a deep breath, feeling some of my old energy back. Whatever is coming, if I meet it weakly, it's gonna suck. Just make it work, figure it out, work it and keep working it. Don't give up, don't be a big baby.

"You've been quiet, you get this distant look in your eyes sometimes," she's coming close to me, feeling the soft wool of her sweater and then the fullness of her breasts on my bare arm. "What's going on in that big cabeza of yours?"

Looking at her, putting my hand over her arm.

"Just thinking about what could happen and what I can do about it," looking at her, then out to the people passing by on 1st Avenue. "Got to be a way to make this turn out. It's like I'm letting all the negative stuff turn into the only things I see." She's trying to figure this out—laughing to myself.

"What's so funny?" she looks annoyed.

"Oh," as Uncle Michael's face comes into focus for a second, "my uncle Michael's always is talking about making chicken salad out of chicken shit, looks like it's that time, right?"

She rolls her eyes, "That's silly," she squeezes my arm, "but I'm glad you're getting your head back on straight."

She pushes her chest a little harder into me, people starting to wander off to other tables now that the food is gone and the couples are starting to join up. People giving each other bullshit hugs—like their fucking lives are not going to turn out if they go off without the big emotional send off. Just giving a couple of nods.

Just want to be left alone with her.

"Now," tilting my head, playing with her, "you wouldn't just happen to be the instigator behind this party would you?"

"You mean, little me?" she puts her right hand on her chest, leans over and gives me a kiss on the cheek. Smiling at her.

"You know, Richard's got a nice big place too and his brother goes out of town often, I'll work that angle."

"Oh, you're making me into such a bad girl!" she tosses her hair.

"I know, I'm just despicable," the world returning to bright colors for a few moments seeing her happy in her element as Queen Bee.

"Something like that," she starts gathering up her stuff. "So," giving me a hurry-up look, "are you going to walk me home?"

Outside on 1st Ave., cool wind blowing down the wide avenue as we head over to 14th to catch the L Train across town. People walking hurriedly—heavy traffic heading uptown. Corner crowded, looking down at her, leaning in to smell her hair, capture all these things, hold them just in case. Looking through the crowd—checking people out, sizing them up, who's strong, who's weak, who's not paying attention and who is paying too much attention.

Dropping a token in the slot for her, letting her go first.

"A real freaking gentleman," some cranky lady behind me going off cause I'm blocking the turnstile. Flipping her off with a smile on my face as I pass through, heading down the two flights of dirty, badly maintained stairs—always a mix of damp decay, smell of piss and various other rotting trash. Walking down the long subway platform, get to the front, makes the walk at 8th Ave. shorter.

Looking down the long tunnel—trains come here from under the river, they bring a rush of cool air from the deep tunnel with them. Checking out the people on the platform. Drunks walking up to people and bumming money, I love the bullshit excuses people give him.

"Hey man, spare some change?" stepping between him and Cat.

"No," just looking at him, staying relaxed shaking my head. He's unused to people just telling him like it is—he keeps walking.

"You're so quiet today, where's your head, baby?" she says from behind me. Looking at her. Trying to cover the gulf.

"A lots going on in my head, Cat."

"What do you mean?" her warrior queen starting to come up.

"Seeing you, seeing the kids from school… The things you all are doing," looking at her looking down at the dirty subway tracks, the channel in between the black tar coated railway ties filled with dirty water.

"I'm fighting like… like a sense of unreality. Just a couple of days ago I was in hell. I mean my uncle and aunt, they are trying to be nice and all. I don't know where I fit in now, Cat. I don't know what's going to happen to us."

She's fighting that off—getting a determined look on her face.

"Don't you trust me? I love you, Frankie, why can't you just count on that?" her arms across her chest. "Why all this up and down now? It's hard enough you know…" train coming into the station. "Why can't you just be happy sometimes?"

Sitting down next to her on the two-seat bench near the car-to-car subway door—taking the seat toward the rest of the car, between her and the crowd. Train rumbling off, she's sitting away from me on the bench, looking away too.

"Look, Cat, it's not like that," uncomfortable, turning to her, speaking loud over the train as it starts to leave the station, "you're keeping me steady. If I lost you…" she hears me, but is not looking back. Keep telling yourself the lie Frank, maybe you'll believe it.

Watching the tunnel lights fly by.

Stopping—people getting on, a few getting off at 3rd Avenue.

Long quiet walk up 86th Street from Central Park West.

What if I am evil? How would I know? What if it's more complicated than that and there are no easy answers and I have to learn to put all this to

216

work? Feeling like I'm fighting off one of the times when I just want to walk up to people and punch them or yell at them. They make me sick, so smug, they think they are so secure.

Why don't you do that?

Here you are Mr. Motherfucking attitude and you say you hate bullies don't you? What's the point in beating a weakling? Thinking back to the last fight I lost in the ring—goddamn that was a good fight; I gave everything I had. That kid was just too good, too fast, too skilled on defense, it would have had to be ten round fight—enough time to work his body, slow him down. Two judges had it his way, one my way. My dad was pissed—how they could judge that nigger winning that fight after all the heart I'd shown. His words leaving me cold inside, cause I knew how good my opponent was—he beat me straight up. After the fight, he told me I was the toughest kid he'd faced and hoped he didn't have to fight me again. I got some good power shots in though. Gus said in a longer fight there was a good chance I'd have beaten him cause there was not way he could have stood up to the punishment, but in Gus' fashion, he asked me how I liked to lose. It fucking sucked and I couldn't wait to fight him again win or lose, you have to go after the best to be the best. Right?

"Talk to me, Cat," looking at her, "you say you love me, then talk to me, even if you don't like what you're gonna say."

She gives a brief look, "It's not that..." she won't make eye contact, sinking feeling inside, "it's just after what we did, what I entrusted to you," she's looking down, "why do you keep doubting me?"

Her words cutting into me, "Baby, I don't doubt you..." she waves her hand.

"And now you talk about going away. This is just tearing me up," her books dropping on the side walk, her fists coming at my arm. "Damn you," and she turns toward the building. People looking at us, man looking hard at me, anger rising inside, body shifting over. He walks away. Looking at Cat, her body shuddering, back toward me. Hands on her shoulders bringing her to me, she's not fighting.

Feeling the sobs wrack her body.

"I feel like I'm fighting for you, fighting for so much and you..."

"Say it, Cat."

"I feel like you're quitting on me."

Shaking my head, "No, no."

"Then fight! Damn you! Fight for us. You do what you have to do to not go to jail, you do everything you have to be to... to not to be a loser," cold ice spear going into my stomach.

Turning her around, her eyes puffy. "You think I'm a loser? Is that it? Jesus, I'm trying to figure all this out, I'm trying to get my head on straight..." looking up to the sky trying to keep the hurt from boiling out.

"What's it gonna be next, Frankie?" her voice cracking a little. "After what we did, after what I trusted you with and then you were just, gone!" she shakes her head, slams her fists into her thigh then bends down to pick up her books. She stops and looks at me, "How am I supposed to trust you," her head moving side to side, "when you get that stubborn thing all up? What if there are other people you need to think about, not just yourself?"

Feeling blood drain from my face—staring at her like I've been hit.

"Are you pregnant?"

She hits me in the chest, "No you asshole, but what if I was?"

"Is this boy bothering you," man in a suit coming over looking concerned.

"No, he's just... He's just a jerk," she turns keeps walking toward Broadway. Pushing the man's hand away from my shoulder, he's saying something, but I can't make out the words. Taking off after her.

"Seems like you used to like that side of me."

"That was before..." she stops, "oh you asshole, I didn't know what it would be like to lose you. After we... the hotel," she stops then starts like she's pissed she even has to say this. "And then you were gone for like four weeks... And now you just want to talk about how bad things can get for you," her body starting to shake a little. "Don't you care about what this is doing to me?"

"Cat, don't get like this."

"Stop telling me how I should get!"

A block away from her apartment, wishing I could rewind the conversation. Traffic on Broadway is moving slowly. Dusk settling in, busy people walking quickly to get home from work.

Frustration building.

"Cat," as she starts to walk into her apartment building.

She doesn't look back, "Dammit."

Chapter 28

Rush hour crowds, people tired, impatient.

Jammed tight up against a middle-aged lady reeking of perfume and carrying multiple shopping bags. Subway car is hot with all the bodies packed in together—no air circulation. Letting my eyes wander around the crowded car, quite a mix tonight—brother with his hair done back in a stocking cap, men in suits, old man wearing a building super's uniform, guys in overalls, women in business suits; all of them trying not to meet any of the eyes checking them out.

Long subway ride back to Brooklyn in the crowded car.

Stomach feeling cold and empty.

Is it going to be a slow death spiral with her now? We've fought and argued like hell in the past, this is just... Why is she doing this now? Got to talk to her. How do I get around her asshole parents? Call Marta, deal with her bullshit—she'll be playing with me. If Cat only knew what her little friends were trying to pull... It's not going to be me. Have her give Cat the number at my aunt and uncle's place. Dummy, you should have given her all this earlier. What are they gonna be like—yelling at me to get off the phone or not?

Frustration rising up, looking at the people near me—tired faces. Torn between wanting someone to come fuck with me and knowing that would be giving in to what got me in this damn mess in the first place.

Tired, drained.

Slow walk to my aunt and uncle's house; Alton's face running through my mind while I reflect on his mother's words. Pissed I couldn't talk to Cat about any of this—she didn't give a shit. Icy cold feeling in the pit of my stomach as I replay her words, "Loser."

I'm not a fucking loser! Dammit.

"You don't look so hot," my aunt giving me the once over.

Shrugging my shoulders. Flopping down at the kitchen table.

She's waiting, looking at me—voice blocked, pushing harder makes it settle deeper into place. Fiddling with the edges of the tablecloth.

"Well," she stretches a little, "at least you're home when you said you would be, your uncle will like that."

"What time does Uncle Vin usually get home?"

"Depends, he called earlier... Late night tonight."

Nodding, brief eye contact. Like she's waiting for me to spill over.

Eyes back down to the red and white-checkered tablecloth.

"You know, you can talk to me about anything you like, Frank." I can't see her, but I can feel her looking at me. "You don't need to say anything though if you don't want to. Okay?"

"Okay, Aunt Kitty."

Pissed at myself cause there's so much I want to talk about, but she said I was acting like a big baby—is this just more of that? Do I just suck it up and be a man about all this? Not complain, just... How the hell do people figure this shit out? Maybe I'm not as smart as people think I am. Cat, school...

"Those gears sure are turning," watching her out of the corner of my eye—she smiles a little.

Throat choking up, feeling like a big weakling.

"Shall we make dinner?" nodding at her, trying to not smile. "Good, I'd like to see if anything your grandfather taught you is still in that thick skull of yours."

Feeling my anger and frustration ebb in the concentration of chopping and prepping—garlic, mushrooms, shallots, salt and a little black pepper. Listening to Aunt Kitty pounding out the chicken breasts for the Marsala. Getting the artichokes and asparagus ready for a quick steaming. Cutting the tops of the artichokes off to make a flat plane and stuffing some of the chopped garlic down into the leaves. Images of my grandpa in his restaurant laughing, looking—giving people some a good Italian cussing out when they didn't do things up to his standards.

Artichokes stuffed with garlic go into the pressure cooker to steam.

"Chicken's ready."

Lightly coating the pounded out breasts in flour, good olive oil, butter and a teeny bit of garlic into the hot pan, quick sauté. Chicken out—mushrooms, chicken stock, sliced shallots, Marsala wine and a little more garlic in—letting it reduce slowly.

Chicken back in to finish cooking.

"Hmm," she comes over, "I'm going to call up your uncle and let him know what he's missing. This smells really good."

Looking at her for a second, thought of how I'd be in prison running through my head.

"I can't believe it."

"What?"

"You actually smiled for a second," as she looks up at the ceiling and spreads her hands apart like Moses parting the Red Sea, "the darkness parted for a second."

Blood rush to my face, turning away—checking the progress of my reduction.

"You don't have to say anything, it's okay."

Plating up for my aunt—I think Grandpa T would be okay with dinner, as I look things over. Sitting down at the table, Aunt Kitty with a small smile on her face—taking in a deep breath.

"Hmm," she smiles at me, "a little wine?" She looks over.

Nodding, putting my napkin on my lap. She pours a couple of inches of wine in my glass from the straw wrapped Chianti bottle.

"Buon Appetito," she says holding up her glass, saluting her.

Eating in silence—this turned out okay. Relief.

"I was," finishing my food—taking a small sip of the nice dry Italian red. "I was laughing at myself. I'd make a good little prison wife if I get put in with the adults."

She looks at me for a few moments.

"I can make you a cute little apron?" she says and smiles.

Smiling back, some of the tension melting.

"Do you feel cooking like you do makes you any less of a man?"

"No," knowing that I'm about to lie. "Well, I know it was Grandpa T's business, but," cutting another slice of chicken, "I mean, none of the other kids do anything like this," looking back at my plate—embarrassed, feeling like I've disrespected Grandpa T's memory.

"Frank, Frank… you have so much to learn," she shakes her head for a moment and looks at me. "You know, something's been bothering me… Can I ask you a question?"

Oh no, not from her now.

"No," looking at her, she starts laughing.

"Okay, Frankie, it's okay. You talk when you're ready. Eat now."

In a small voice, "Yeah, well, I guess."

Moving my food around my plate, not making eye contact.

"Are you disappointed in your uncle's refusal to intercede?"

Taking in a deep, thin breath, elbows on the table, rubbing my face. Yeah like that's going to make all this shit go away. Cat falling away—laughing at myself saying I'm not going to meet her at school when I know damn well that I am. Better to fight it out than die a slow death, right?

"This will stay between you and me Frank, but you don't need to answer that if you don't want to."

Peeping through my fingers at her, she's calmly looking at her folded hands on the edge of the table. Images of Uncle Vin and Dad at the holding cell—the look of disgust on their faces. I could always talk to Aunt Kitty in the past—why's this so damn hard now?

Yelling in my head, what the fuck is wrong with me?

"Let's clean up here okay, I have to go to the market after dinner."

"I can do that for you," something to make up for disappointing her.

"Well," she's looking at me as I sit back in my chair and finish off my dinner, "I've been meaning to drive over to Coluccio's in Borough Park, you could help me out and then we could go over to Saravesse, get some good sfogliatella and canole."

"Sure, Aunt Kitty, sure," getting up to start cleaning up.

Sitting on the long bench of her big Buick Skylark.

She drives differently than Uncle Vin—he prowls like a tiger shark.

Evening lights of the neighborhood passing as we drive.

Checking out people on the street walking, taking care of their evening shopping. Looking around at the inside of her car—so clean. Thinking of Dad's prized 1972 Oldsmobile Toronado—fucking things more important to him than... Breathing deep, clenching my fists—stop the poison from filling my core. Mind's eye drifting out to the deep country, trying to recall the clean smell of the deep forest, something far away from all this. Moment of elation sitting in the thought of being out in a clean environment—sun shining in through the thick trees, far away from prison, school, the children's hospital, the dark drug room my uncle took me to.

"They just left me there..." surprised I'm talking now.

"Where was that, Frank?"

"When I was arrested... You know, going after the three kids who beat my ass in the park near school. When they thought I'd hit Alton with some kind of weapon..." quick look at her, she's driving carefully.

Deep breath, "My father told me I was a disgrace to the family, to him, to my uncle. That I was nothing but an animal that deserves the streets after what I'd done to him and Mom. He said I was dead in his eyes," sorrow and tears welling up now instead of the anger I felt then—embarrassed to be feeling like this.

Sound of the heavy car going over cobblestones.

"You know, he told me about that. It really tore him up seeing you and your father like that."

"Yeah, Happy Days right there at the 30th Precinct."

Quiet as she turns onto a busy 5th Avenue.

Letting the people, the street scenes become a blur as we drive by—time passing, cloud of anger at Dad passing, empty.

"But no, Aunt Kitty, I'm not disappointed. I'm guilty."

"What do you mean, Frank?"

"You asked me if I was disappointed that Uncle Vin hasn't interceded. He got me out of jail and released here. I'll get what I deserve when I get in front of the judge... Mom and Dad can go to hell for all I care."

"Oh don't say that, you must be mad, hurt. But don't say that. The bond between you and your father's been badly damaged, but..." she stops at a red light. "It may never heal, but I hope someday you'll both be able to get over that "stubborn you'll have to kill me before I admit that I'm wrong" attitude."

"What do you mean both of us?"

"Frank," she looks over and gives me the hairy eyeball.

"What?"

"Come on, I've known you since you were a baby. You and your father are like two big bulls locking horns pushing and shoving. Like it or not, you're cut from the same cloth."

Shiver going through me—no way, I'm not like that fucking asshole.

"I'm not like him," between my teeth.

Market alive with people, food, wonderful mix of scents—aged cheeses, salamis, prosciutto hanging from the ceiling, sawdust on the floor—barrels of olives, rows of sauces and olive oils lining the walls. Dried herbs, pastas, imported canned goods. Following my aunt as she walks through the market talking to people, working the counters, laughing with them. Embarrassed at being introduced. The old farts like that I can talk to them in good Italian. Smiles all around.

Silent drive back to their house, the lingering odors of the markets taking me back to the neighborhood markets near Grandpa T's old restaurant. Nice that Aunt Kitty isn't pushing me to talk.

Looking up at the unfinished basement ceiling in the darkness.

Tough to go to sleep—agitated.

Watching the random lights reflected in from passing cars moving over some of my uncle's hunting and fishing trophies. The varnish of the fish reflecting a soft light punctuated by the shadows of the deer and elk antlers.

Another temporary place, a couple of bags worth of clothes, a couple of books and that's it. Other than that I don't exist. I get why they care, but why do they care? Maybe it's best for everyone if I go away.

Imagining the deep, dark river.

Visualizing the end of *Martin Eden* where the main character is diving deeper and deeper into the ocean, pushing himself down into the blackness. Chest twisting up for a moment, Cat's slipping away—what next?

Quiet house. Fewer cars, fewer people moving outside than Manhattan.

Missing the street noise of my old room, the street scene.

Do they even think about me? Sis is away—thank goodness she got out.

She hates me now.

She never lied though. She could have acted like all the other girls, but she stood up to him. She told him who she was; she stood up to all the abuse, the derision, the talk about what a loser she was, that it was all a cop out because she didn't want to deal with men. God was she brave.

Did I quit on her too? Was it easy to have been so busy with sports and school or was it welcome relief to have anything to talk about to break the deathly silence at the dinner table.

Does sis ever think back to summer days in Rockaway? She was fearless. She was always the first person to jump off the highest rung on the boardwalk railing into the sand. I was her little brother then and heaven help anyone who messed with me. What hell is wrong with our family? What hell is wrong with me? How can you not love someone like that?

Chapter 29

Tired, nothing to wake up for.

Letting the drowsiness carry me back to a restless sleep.

Stretching in the tiny bed, don't want to get up, need to pee.

Walking across the thin area rug to the hard, concrete linoleum floor—cold on my feet. Underwear pushed out in front like some stupid flagpole. Need to bend over and aim so I don't make a mess. Relief.

Washing up, looking at my face in the small mirror, distant eyes looking back at me. Eleven o'clock—nothing to do till three when I go into the City. Shit. Funny how my aunt and uncle want me home in the evening when I could do just about what I want during the day. All I need to do is find the army of women to invite over. Yeah right.

Moving in slow motion around the quiet basement.

Need to get out of here—library, run, go play some street ball or go hang out. Where the hell would I hang out? Go find a bunch of losers like me—up in Queens where that kid from jail said I could find work. Oh, Uncle Vin would love that—staying here, collecting debts for some small time fucking bookie in Queens.

Lethargy creeping back in as I sit back on the sofa bed and stare at the unfinished ceiling.

Feeling calm—no rage, no anger. Am I one of these people that can't be around others? That can't get along with people? Laughing at the idea of me as some wop mountain man—there you go, Grizzly Caruso slinging meatballs along the Rocky Mountains, the first Italian to bring pizza to the Indians. Well, I guess a career in comedy is out-of-the-question.

Where have I been happy?

Images of hard street basketball games drifting in, brothers talking smack, the crowd going wild when someone makes a crazy move, hot summer days on the court. My body moving with the game for a few moments, shutting it down as images of summer league with Alton bring up what could have been. Next year would have been our year—Leroy on to St. Johns, we would have ruled, and now... that's all gone. Pushing down the lump forming in my throat.

Maybe school and the opportunities I thought I had in my life were all a dream I've woken up from and I'm the loser my father proclaimed me to be. Here I am, sitting alone in a dark basement with nothing to do. Oh yeah, I get to go be the drop-out later today and pathetically wait for Cat after school. Fighting off a wave of revulsion—I need to get out the hell out of here.

Slow walk up the unfinished wooden stairs—still feels strange stepping out of the confines of the basement in their home.

Listening for a moment to make sure no one is home.

Feeling the cool air of the open refrigerator on my skin. Staring in at milk containers, left over lasagna in a pan covered with food wrap, eggs lined up on the door, varieties of hot mustards, one of the crisper drawers filled with fresh vegetables and herbs, the other with waxed paper covered cold cuts. I don't know what I'm looking for here—not hungry. Kitchen clock ticking in the background as the emptiness of the room grows louder.

Passing by the wall of family photographs in the long hallway. Stopping by a photo of Grandpa T when he'd just come over from Sicily, his face set, eyes intense even as a teenager. His dad looking off to the left, into the future—he was the engineer. Grandpa T worked as a carpenter for many years while he learned English... Image of the pieces Uncle Vin saved sitting in the garage in need of refinishing. Remembering Dad telling me stories about how Grandpa T would write out the words he was learning on the unfinished under sections of the pieces he'd work on with his carpenter's pencil and how the other workers in the shop would make fun of him, but he kept working away. Grandpa T's older brother, Lorenzo, the mathematician, the doors opening for him at Fordham because he spoke the language so well... Thank God my family came over here with skills, so many of our people from Sicily and Italy came here as unskilled laborers. I wonder if that's why so many of us took the path of least resistance and drifted into a life of crime? Is that why Uncle Vin hates them with such a passion?

Some of Grandpa T's work is right outside in the garage, it's just sitting there under dusty old sheets and blankets. Shiver running down my spine— am I worthy of even touching the work he did so long ago? Would the wood recoil from my touch? Shaking my head, that's stupid. What the hell is happening to me?

Why can't I shake off this sense of dread?

Living room clock ticks quietly away in the background.

What did his handwriting look like back then though, what words where hard for him to learn? Hours working calmly with a dovetail saw, miter box, hand drills, chisels and dowels—from a set of unfinished boards to a finely crafted cabinet or table. No whining about how tough it was to come to a new country and have to start again, to have to work with his hands to help support the family.

His pieces are sitting right outside.

Pushing through the thin viscous film of lethargy encasing my body.

Quickly outside, ignoring the weeds starting to infest their backyard. Another job I'm supposed to do when I'm granted leave from the basement.

Stepping into the quiet coolness of their garage and letting my eyes sweep across the sparsely populated pegboard laid out for Uncle Vin's tools on the back wall, the stack of boxes, furniture covered with sheets, and gardening tools stacked by the front. Chuckling, that's the only section that's neat and organized—Aunt Kitty's domain.

Time lost in gathering up tools, organizing, discovering, dusting, creating a work area, sorting through the different strata of wood finishes, stains, varnish, white and orange four pound cut shellac in cans showing various levels of decay on the shelves beneath the peg board. Projects my uncle started but never had time to finish?

Taking off the outer layer of sheets over Grandpa T's work.

Can't stop the smile from breaking out on my face as I uncover one of the tables from the old summerhouse in Rockaway. Stepping into an instant of time as the place comes flooding in—the smell of hot summer by the ocean, kids running, yelling. I need to get out there soon. That was such a happy place. How do places like that disappear from us? Did I just get busy with school, girls and sports?

This was an end table by the couch in their living room. Lifting it off the blanket cushioning the next layer down, the deep dark stain of my grand parents living room credenza starting to show. Wow, image of their home in Brooklyn popping in; the large lace runners my grandmother would carefully arrange on all the furniture, the cut glass bowls always filled with Golden Delicious apples or deep purple grapes, the narrow shelf that ran all the way around the dining room six inches or so below the ceiling that was filled with tchotchkes from Sicily—I can almost look out the window to St. Anthony's across the street.

Blinking my eyes. Dust slowly settling in the stream of light shining in through the small window of the garage door. Shaking off a pang of loneliness.

The credenza looks like it is in good shape.

Carefully moving through the puzzle of stacked furniture. There's no way Aunt Kitty is going to be able to get her car in here—oh, well.

Working slowly, buzzing of the fluorescent lights in the background.

There—the card table from the beach house. Smile on my face remembering watching Grandpa T in pinochle death matches with Dad, Uncle Vin, Uncle Michael and Aunt Nancy. Oh how they'd get pissed when Vicki and I would start up on one of our running arguments about whose turn it was to do one of the interminable chores while they were playing.

Wrapping and carefully restacking old memories under sheets and blankets to bring some sense of order back to their garage.

Squatting down to look across at the surface of the table for signs of warping—hmm, looks pretty good for all the use this experienced. I need more light in here. Lifting the garage door where Aunt Kitty parks her car and taking a brief look out into the neighborhood street, quiet day here as a car passes down the street, the long branches of the willow oak across the street waving slowly for a moment, then settling down.

Laying down a drop cloth to cover the smooth, clean concrete floor.

Flipping over the table, sunlight on areas underneath that have not seen the light for many years now. Carefully looking at the dovetail joints on the supporting frame he'd fashioned by hand. Not a gap, no filler—even on the bottom where no one would looks, no sloppy work. Heart ticking up a notch, *especial, expect,* written out in a neat, compact flowing style. Even his handwriting is precise. On my hands and knees moving slowly clockwise around the table—*forte, fort, percolate*... And here I am feeling sorry for myself. Yeah I've worked hard, but hell, he didn't have anything near what I have, what I've been given. Feeling my throat constrict—and then I've gone off and destroyed all the... Fuck!

Sitting on the cool concrete floor cross-legged.

Moments lost staring out into the empty street, a slight wind passing through the willow oak on the other side of the street.

Setting the table back on its legs.

My guess is he'd have finished this with the orange shellac for the darker wood. Easy to tell, take a clean cloth and a little denatured alcohol, rub a spot on the under lip of the tabletop and see if it softens.

Searching back through the array of old quart and gallon cans underneath the tool bench. Success—not much, but it will be a start, I'll need to cut it with denatured alcohol anyway. Now all I need are some rough rags. Minutes of searching through old boxes, nothing clean enough here, looks like it is time to sacrifice a pair of my old worn corduroy pants.

Laughing to myself, well, I must look like an idiot as I've discovered yet another use for garden shears. Folding over a few layers of pants legs cut into mostly square rags, liberal application of alcohol on a small section of the table top, letting it sit then rubbing in small circles as years of worn finish start to dissolve.

Losing time track of time in slow, careful work.

Stepping back to stretch my back after working bent over so long.

"Hey, what do we have here?"

Feeling my face blush a little, hearing the door to Aunt Kitty's car close as the engine runs. Shrugging my shoulders. Well I should have asked anyway.

"Your uncle will like that you are working on these."

Turning sheepishly.

"You are not mad?"

"Heaven's no. It's nice to see you come up from the cave and get into something I know you used to really like."

"I saw this and remembered summers out at Rockaway."

She nods looking at the table and then in the garage.

"Vincent and I really miss that place. You all had so much promise..." her eyes distant, she probably doesn't see the insult, but feeling the dagger anyway.

"Well, there's promise," crossing my arms. I need to head into Manhattan soon. I can finish stripping down the finish tomorrow, build a sanding block and clean up, then prep the surface.

"I didn't mean it like that, Frank."

"Well, it's true. Anyway, I promised my friends I'd go see them after school."

"Don't get like that, Frankie."

Shrugging my shoulders "Let me clean this up for you. Is it okay if I keep a little work area on your side of the garage?"

"Sure, Frankie, sure," sad smile from her, "like I said, your uncle will really like seeing these again."

Time for a shower, then a run—I need to get out of here.

Light sweat forming under my shirt waiting for the train at Lorimer Station. Not many people here at this time of day. Looking down the dark tunnel. Hating that I'm drawn back to her like this, hanging around school like some lost dog. Pissed that the calm I felt starting the refinishing process is fading quickly.

Cool air pushed forward by the train. Standing close to the edge, feeling the cars fly by me then slow down. How else should I play this? Tell her it's over—ignoring the gut feeling that tells me it is over. Can't be, can't end like this, just whimpering out after all we've done over the last two years. I should have written her a letter yesterday.

Crowds out at Union Square—hanging around to kill some time.

Drunks, thieves, hookers; people streaming in and out of the S. Klein store, guys putting up signs on the Union Square Theater—some band I'd never heard of. Walking through the park, side stepping bottles, beer cans and assorted shit. What a mess this place is.

Passing by two drunken brothers arguing.

"Hey man, Mister Big Ass White Boy," one of them looking over at me, "give me some motherfuckin money." Keeping the smile off my face, looking around like he's talking to someone else.

"Who?" pointing to myself, pointing behind him, "who's that?"

The chump looks away, he's pretty fucked up. Walking my way.

"Man fuck you, you ain't shit," from behind me.

Checking my watch—another twenty minutes to kill before they get out. Don't want to be waiting there, but what if I miss her. I'll have to bribe Marta to get her to come out with Cat. Sneaky little Marta. Walking to the East River slowly.

"You looking for a date there, honey?"

Shaking my head and walking by a nasty woman—holes in her fishnet stockings, overweight, patchwork chinchilla or something fur jacket. What do they do, take you back and give you a blowjob for five bucks? Body shivering at the thought—with so much pussy in the city, why do people do that kind of shit? Better to go beat off.

Here early. Skulking around like a pathetic asshole, loser. Feeling some of the meanness start to creep in as school kids walk down the metal stairs. What did Mrs. Brown say—got to choose? Get your head back.

Leaning back on a parked car, arms crossed. Take a deep breath—don't be a jerk. Well any more than normal I guess.

Kids I used to know calling out my name as they walk by.

"Yo, Frankie," Julio's voice, he's surrounded by gaggle of giggly sophomore girls.

"Ha," from a loud voice to my left.

"My man," smiling as I stand up, Leroy—you motherfucker. Body energy rising, people gathering around—dogs looking to pounce in on a fight.

"Mr. Criminal, hanging on cause he's got no place else to go... isn't that choice?" he looks up at the sky. "Oh Lord, how the mighty have fallen."

"Oh Lord, how the mighty might make you cry for your mama again in front of all these people," calm down, calm down. Fuck, why can't I get a hold of myself?

"Oooooo," he looks at me, hands on his hips. "You can talk all the shit you want convict, cause look at this," he holds up a letter with St. John's letterhead. "Full boat to St. John's, baby."

Bastard—wave of jealousy storming through my body.

"What? Nothing to say, huh?"

"Yo, man," hearing Julio's voice, "don't do it," voices from the gathering starting to egg us on to a fight.

Hard to say it, deep breath, "You won the prize, Leroy."

"What," he puts his hand behind his ear like he couldn't hear.

"You've got the full boat. Congratulations. You're still a piece of shit," taking a fast step toward him, feeling Julio reach for my arm. Leroy's eyes getting big as he looks at me, "YAAAA," in his face.

Kids laughing as he backpedals quickly and almost falls over.

"Funny, say what you want Mr. Great White Dope, you can come sit in the convicts section, watch me play next year. I'll send you season tickets."

"Fish lips," Hector hand in front of his mouth, coming up behind Leroy. The other kids starting to join in the taunting, "Fish lips."

"Man, fuck all you losers!" said Leroy stomping off folding up his scholarship letter, the crowd laughing at him as he storms away. Quietness settling over me, kids milling around, talking to me, nodding back at them like I'm listening while I look for Cat. Recognition of how far my chances of getting to play basketball in a top ten college have slipped—pretty much down to zero. Goddamn Leroy.

"We could have used you," turning around to Cedar's deep voice.

Nodding at him, "Rice beat us without you and Alton there," he looks at me and sighs. "No guarantee we would have won anyway, but you know..." he's with his girl Linda, all five-foot-four of her and all lean strong six-foot-eight of him.

"I checked in on Alton at the hospital, he'll have to wear a face guard, but he'll get to play again."

He nods, his strong features calmer than last time.

"What did you hear from Michigan and Notre Dame?"

"Scholarship offers from Michigan, Cincinnati, UNLV and Iowa. My Pops wants me to go to Michigan, so I guess that's where I'll go."

Reaching out my hand, "Congratulations."

"Thanks," he looks at my hand, turns and leaves me hanging.

"Yo Frankie, man it was a good game with Rice," said Hector—waving at Cedar as he walks off, shaking off Cedar's diss. What do you expect, you messed up his chance at a city championship.

"Wish I could have been here, man," people starting to drift off.

"You guys seen Cat?" Feeling like a punk for even having to ask.

"She had to leave early today," said Marta piping in as she snuggles into Julio's side. Frank, you are such an asshole.

"Yo man, come hang out at Tony's and tell us what crazy shit you've been up to," said Hector, "I can break down the game for you."

"You guys gonna be at Walter's tomorrow?"

"You know it," said Julio.

"Alright, I'll catch you guys tomorrow."

"Man don't be that way, Frank man," Hector looking disappointed. "Things ain't the same old same old without you pulling crazy shit at school."

Laughing with him.

"Come on, Frankaaaay," said Julio jumping. "Fuck Cedar, whitest black man you've ever seen."

"Man, fuck you," coming from that punk senior Rodney, trying to look bad at Julio in front of his girl.

"Oiya, Rodney," Julio walking toward him, "what's happening? You come to dance, baby?"

"Man, fuck you, Julio," as he walks off quickly with his girl in tow.

Hanging back, not my place to keep all these dogs from going at each other. Laughing to myself as an evil thought goes through my mind; as much as the teachers and school staff hate my guts, now that I'm out, there'll be more trouble like this as guys try to figure out who's got the stuff and who doesn't. Julio, Hector, Jesus and Roberto will form up—they've probably got the most power. None of the white kids will fuck with them— with Alton gone, there's no real threat, the kids from rich black families look down on the poorer black kids from uptown or over where I grew up and won't stick with them. What a fucking world.

Swallowing to keep the feeling of not belonging here down. Keep your cool Frank, "Yo Hector, Julio, we'll hang out tomorrow night man. I'll have to tell you about what my uncle showed me. It was some heavy, heavy shit man. Like, think of the worst place you could imagine and this was worse man, like a nightmare."

"Oh, man," said Hector, some of the girls looking at me. "What, Frankie?"

"I'll catch you tomorrow, fool," turning and walking quickly toward 1st Avenue, hearing kids I knew saying, "Later," as I walk away, weaving through school kids, feeling like an asshole. I can't come here again.

Walking quickly, fighting off the sinking feeling in my stomach.

Faces a blur, keep a bop in my walk, don't show what a chump I feel like.

"That was different," girl's voice coming from my right.

Looking over. "Oh," bemused look on her face, "hey Mary, how are you?" stopping and hanging for a second.

"I'm pretty good," she looks down at her feet. Awkward moments as a gaggle of sophomore girls walk behind us giggling. Looking back toward the group I'd left, slight smile—it's like I wasn't even there now, Marta playing with Julio chasing him around.

"Well," she says, "nice seeing you."

Nodding to her. Damn it.

"Hey, what did you mean?" as she's turned away and walking to 1st Avenue. Walking with her, if Cat gets pissed off, then too bad. She's giving me a long look with her bright hazel green eyes as we walk. Always does that with people—like she's trying to look in and see what's there.

"Well, maybe you should get kicked out of school more often."

Double take. "What?" feeling my face go flush, "is this funny?"

"Don't get all sensitive on me."

"Yeah, that's something I'm accused of all the time," walking away.

Out on a busy 1st Avenue walking toward 14th Street.

Mary walking with me, nice of her to land some shots. Man, I'm such an asshole for hanging around here.

"Well, this was great," giving her a sarcastic grin, "we'll have to get together and do this again sometime, nice seeing you, Mary." She stops and takes a deep breath, direct look.

"Listen Mr. Big Shot, I thought you showed a minuscule portion of poise with someone you don't like and even offer them congratulations when they don't treat you well," gathering herself up. "Do you always have to act like such a jerk?"

"Jerk? Look Mary, we've always been friends... You come and tell me I should get kicked out of school more often as some kind of offhand comment. Jesus!" Stepping closer to her, "This has been just..." looking at her, feeling stupid now. Stepping back. "Look I'm sorry, I'll see you sometime." Turning to go.

"And you're going to skulk off now?"

"Mary, what do you want from me? I feel like my whole world's been turned upside down, I've lived on the streets, I've been in jail, I got the shit beat out of me by the guards there, I've been thrown out of school, most of those dumb fucks think this is really cool… Well it's not," battling to keep my head on straight here, looking at her, looking at my hands, relaxing them, crossing my arms, down at our feet—my black cons, her black pumps, black stockings. Damn, forgetting what nice legs she has. "I'm trying to pick up the pieces," intense look from her, "and anyway, maybe I can be a professional skulker."

"Yeah right," she looks pissed, "you need a lot more practice."

"Mary, what the fuck have I done to you?"

She crosses her arms, quiet intensity in her green eyes.

People moving around us like we are rocks in a fast moving stream.

"Like you said, Frank, we've been friends for a long time."

"And?"

"And?" she rolls her eyes. "Guys are so stupid!" and she starts to walk away.

"What?" following her. Oh, no.

She turns, "Maybe I don't want to be friends, Frank Caruso," big accent on the F as she sways her head side-to-side on the last word, leaving it hanging out there.

"What do you mean?"

"Rrrrr," she smacks at me. "You thick headed creep… If you don't know." She storms off toward the subway station.

Catching up, "Hey Mary, don't do that. Let's just go talk okay? I mean if you've got time and all being a week night."

She's looking at me from the side of her eyes, her lids slightly closed. "I might have time," and now with a sly look, "how about asking me nicely?"

Shaking my head, played by another one.

"Mary, I know a great little Italian place a few blocks from here, we could get something warm to drink and just talk for a while," looking down feeling embarrassed now. "It would feel good to get some of this off my chest… There's been no one to talk to."

She's nodding her head a little.

"Okay, I'm listening," looking at her watch, "I can hang for an hour or so, then I need to get home. Deal?"

"Deal."

Stepping into Veniero's Pasticceria, the aroma of all the baked goods— the cookies and pastries bursting into being as we step in the place. Long line at the counter, men and women working behind the tall glass display cases filled with cannoli, sfogliatelle, assorted cookies, tarts and cakes.

"Oooooo, this smells wonderful," her face breaking into a big smile. "I've never been here before," her eyes darting around to take everything in.

"It's one of the few real Italian pasticcerias left in the City," motioning her to follow me as I move around the crowd. A couple of old ladies waiting in line positioning to cut me off if I try to cut in. Smiling at them as we walk by. Walking around the counters to the other side where there's table service.

"*How are you today Madam? Seating for two please, by the window if possible? Okay?*"

"*Hey,*" the elderly lady managing the seating area smiles. "*It's nice to hear someone young speak Italian so well. What's your name? You speak with a southern accent.*"

"*Ah, very good, thank you. My family name is Caruso, we're all from Sicily.*"

"*Can you sing too or are you just good looking?*" as she pinches my cheek and starts laughing, Mary laughing with us.

"*No, we're not related to the tenor.*"

She gives Mary the once over and then, as if she approves, walks us through the crowded cafe to the front tables near the glass doors that open during the hot summers.

"*Enjoy, enjoy,*" she says waving over her shoulder.

The place is filled with people older than us—a bunch must be from out of town judging by the way they dress.

"I didn't realize you speak Italian too, your voice sounds so sexy. Do you speak Italian at home?"

"Was that before of after I was kicked out of the house?"

"Oh," she looks down at her hands. Shit, another great mood management moment from the master.

"Sorry. When I was young, Italian was all that my mother and father would speak at home. They wanted to make sure I didn't forget where we came from. Picking up Spanish was more just learning from some of the guys at Dad's shop over the years and out on the streets… I've got an ear for language."

She smiles politely, looking down at the menu, her hand on her chin, her loose, long brown hair hanging over part of her face as she concentrates on figuring out all the goodies.

"Shall I order?"

"Sure, there is a lot here, wow."

"Are you a coffee drinker?"

"Sure."

Man in his twenties coming over.

"What do you like, eh?" heavy accent, acting like taking our order is a feat of unimaginable drudgery.

"*A small plate of Pignoli cookies, two sfogliatelle and two cappuccinos.*"

He jots some notes down on a small spiral pad and walks off.

"He's charming."

I shrug my shoulders looking around the room.

"What did you order?"

"A couple of my favorites, not killer sweet, but something you won't find in most places in New York, well, unless you're out with a wop who knows places like this."

"Which I am."

Smiling at her, warming up to the situation. Staying charming to keep away from any topic related to her not wanting to be friends. I want things to work with Cat. Or do I? Do I know anything about what the fuck I want? The ever-present feeling of being slightly sick has faded into the background.

Quick side-glance at Mary, she's looking at the ornate decorative stained glass ceiling and all the people here.

"All these little worlds here in New York and you could be a few feet away and not even know," she shakes her head. "I love coming to new places," she gives me a little smile. "Thank you," her face is bright checking things out. She looks at me, big smile on her face, "Hey, get a menu, I want you to tell me everything that's on it and then tell me what it is."

"Yeah, I can tell you some things in Italian all right."

"I'll bet you could," she's smiling, getting a little coy here.

Time passing, looking at people, catching glances at her.

She pushes her brown hair back over her ears, seems a little unsure.

"So what was it like?" almost at a whisper. "If you want to talk, you know," her eyes probing, looking, watching.

Moving uneasily in my chair—looking at her.

Feeling a slight shiver in my body. Feels good to have her interested in what happened, but I haven't told anyone about this. Cat didn't want to hear it—is it right to talk about this?

"Are you sure you want to hear about this?"

She nods, holding my eyes.

"Why, Mary?"

"Hmm, well," her turn to squirm a little, "I think there's so much to life that's not on the surface. You know, not a lot of people talk about it though. Like it's some taboo to talk about what you really think or feel." She's watching me now.

"But why? I mean, what difference does it make?" catching my impatience. "Sorry, I mean are you being a tourist here?"

Shaking her head, "That's not fair Frank. Look, if you don't want to talk about it."

"It's not that, Mary," looking at her, the deadly silence creeping in as she looks around the room, "it's just," looking around at the room now, using the space to put my careening thoughts together, "it's not pretty, and this sucks…" swirling emotions in my chest, "bastard Father," looking down at the dark varnished tabletop and rubbing my hands together to release the frustration building up.

Jumping back a little at the light touch on my arm.

"Oh, sorry," she jerks her hand back.

"So, why Mary?" feeling like a pussy for letting her pull this out of me.

"I guess I want to know what people are really thinking and feeling. You've always got so much going on, at school it's like watching molten lava move around inside you shifting, moving, thinking, talking, joking, serious sometimes and then so off the wall at others. I mean, we used to talk a lot and then, well you know," she looks down at her hands.

"Don't you ever feel like a burning desire to really know what someone is thinking? Maybe it's being around my parents too much and all the things they talk about now and then… their patients, the conferences they go to and the like. People are so complex," looking at me. "The things that are off limits because they are uncomfortable to talk about. I don't understand that and I thought it might be good for you to talk."

"Junior psych job on me?"

She tilts her head, her face growing cold.

"Look, I guess this…" looking away, "we can talk about something else," she's looking at the thin watch on her wrist.

"Mary, look… I don't know what I think and feel sometimes. It doesn't make sense, like why doesn't my mom or pop want to know anything about this. Can someone just die like this and there's nothing? People just give up on you? Man!"

Her eyes starting to come back to me.

"You can tell me anything you want to, I'm not afraid."

Leaning forward a little, elbows on the table, folding my hands, resting my chin on top of them. She sits forward, her hair falling over part of her face.

"Which part? Homeless, getting arrested, my father telling me I'm a disgrace and throwing me out, being in jail and dealing with the other fucking criminals? What, solitary confinement and being bound in a straitjacket, getting out of Rikers and having my uncle totally distrust me, seeing how bad I fucked up…" Breathe man, easy, easy.

She looks at me her eyes quiet now, open listening.

"The worst was confinement," looking down at the table. "It was dark, they bound me in a straitjacket. I couldn't move." Mind pulled back to that dark place for a moment. "You don't know what that's like," well of frustration in my body boiling up, "not being able to move, not being able to do anything about it, fighting and fighting till you lay there like a pitiful mass of sobbing shit… And there's no one. Well that's not entirely true," stopping as some of our order is placed brusquely on the small table.

"There were two guards would come put me in a really uncomfortable sitting position and then come in and beat me, tell me I was big faggot, a big pussy when I couldn't stand it and I moved to try and get comfortable or fall over when I was too tired. I'd pass out and the two would come in and either smack me around or set me right back up," looking at her eyes, letting some of the hurt out.

"I lost sense of time, could have been minutes, hours in the darkness. These same two guys, night shift, I knew them from hearing them talk. When they took the jacket off and had me in cuffs, they'd laugh while they came in, they called it guinea pool... Seeing if they could smack the eight ball."

"Oh, Frank."

"I could feel something inside me getting mean," looking at her, one of the people I've always been able to talk to, she's not shying away from the intensity growing inside. "Mean like a dog chained and beaten. I could feel it inside me, asking me to give in to it, telling me how good it would be to go hurt people," looking at her for a moment. "If my uncle hadn't gotten me out of there... I understand why people come out are filled with hate. They're supposed to be rehabilitated. And I was only in confinement for what, ten days... Can you imagine having to deal with that for months and years?" shaking my head.

"No, I can't."

"And I may have to go back you know," she's sadly nodding her head. "So much that I took for granted, people, situations." Taking a deep breath and looking at her, her pretty green eyes looking right at me, "things to look forward to."

"Why didn't your uncle try and get you out earlier?"

"It was my aunt Kitty," smiling to myself, feeling my throat choke up. "She didn't give up on me, she kept fighting. I guess where my dad and uncle come from, if you want to break a young stallion, you beat it till it obeys or you kill it. Plus who's he gonna side with right? His brother or me?"

"I don't understand, don't they talk to you?"

"Sure Dad talks to me," images of him giving me the silent treatment and then the insult treatment. "He tells me what a fuck up I am, how much damage I've done to the family, about how such a big man..." emphasizing the way he used to drone on to me, "a big man should be able to make his own way in the world, why would I need him and Mom?" Rubbing my hands together again, cold sweat breaking out on my palms, stomach feeling warm as the remembrance of anger rises up, "Yeah, well," looking at her for a moment, "it got to the point where they were going to have to kill me to get me to do what they wanted."

"Who Frank, the people in prison?"

Shaking my head, "No, my dad, but I guess it's the same. I tried to bite one of them when they put me in the straitjacket, guess that didn't go over too well," looking at her as she's just staring at me, "Hey, let's eat some. Okay?"

"Okay, Frank," her voice lower, softer.

Feeling a moment of relief from my bullshit watching her try new things. Smiling at her, watching her face react to the new tastes.

"Oh my, these are really good. Wow."

Smiling at her.

"I don't understand it you know."

"What, Frank?"

"How people can hate each other so much, how they can be so satisfied with their little bullshit worlds and the things they have. So fucking smug. Part of me really hates people you know. Like school, all the bullshit about teaching us to think and then getting in trouble all the time because I question and probe and... Ah, sorry to get all wound up in this."

"No, that's one of the things that I always liked about you, you weren't just a big jock. I always think about you as someone who's not satisfied with repeating back the litany of facts like the others would," she puts her small coffee cup down and licks a little foam off her lips. "It takes a lot to stand up like you do, believe it or not, all the kids think you are scary smart." she starts laughing. "Evan, Marcy and all the little teachers pets were so pissed off when they found out about your board scores."

"Hmm, I'll make sure I put that on my application for juvi prison. Wonder if I'll get accepted? That would be funny, the Ivy League penal system... Only the best and brightest behind these bars."

She gives me a polite laugh and a shy look.

"This feels good you know," looking at her, warmth spreading through my body when our eyes meet, "thanks for not being too put off earlier."

Draining the last of her coffee, "This is nice, Frank."

Standing close to her and blocking off the surge of bodies getting on the subway at 42nd Street. Looking through the doors on the opposite side of the car and over to the downtown station—crowded there too. Glance at Mary's thin frame, her preppy jacket and skirt—her angular pretty face, prettier than I remembered, those fine chiseled Irish features. Slight shake of my head as Mary's eyes come up to meet mine. Holding her gaze, body stirring uncomfortably.

"Were people afraid there?" her lips almost touching my ears, her hand on my arm for balance.

"Lots of posturing. Most of them were scared or too stupid to be scared," looking at her. "They put the weak ones in a different area. The place I was in was overcrowded, people jammed together, bunch of the guys who were there who had connections to smuggle cigarettes, drugs and whatnot ganged together, gave the guards kickbacks."

"Sweet Jesus," she looks out at the window, seeing our reflection in the window as the tunnel lights pass by quickly.

"I knew I needed to deal with it, be respectful, don't cause trouble, but if shit goes down, be ready to go to the max. Kid who's probably a year older than me tried me out. He was the enforcer of the group that smuggled in drugs and all sorts of contraband." looking at her.

"What happened?"

"I tried to give him an out, he wouldn't take it and I beat his ass. That's why I was thrown in solitary. They were pissed because I'd upset the structure, right? The head guy lost his most powerful player, someone's gonna challenge him now and that could mess up the flow of money in and out. Asshole wanted me to come work for him."

"I can't believe that," shaking her head, "could people be that corrupt?"

"Oh, you bet," looking at her.

A New York cross section in the subway car—blue collar guys, a bunch of suits, housewives, students coming home from school, bums and probably a few thieves. In a low voice as the trains pulls into 72nd Street to change over to the local, "I hope you don't have to go back, Frank," touching my arm. Looking at her hand, then her.

"Me too, Mary, me too," looking away, thinking about Cat. Why can't I write her a letter? Why didn't I call her house—even if they won't let me talk to her, she'll know I'm trying, "I don't know what I'd be like."

Walking next to her toward Riverside Drive.

Confused, I need to get out of here before I do something stupid. How did I miss this? Stopping in front of her building on West End Avenue.

"You want to come in for a bit and, you know... talk?"

Time slowing down as I look at her, "Uh, thanks Mary, my uncle's keeping me on a tight leash, need to get back to Brooklyn for dinner and report in. Wouldn't your parents mind though?"

"They won't be back till late and I come and go as I want," she's looking right at me. Looking up and down the street.

Fidgeting a little.

"Must be nice," taking a deep breath. "You'll be at Walter's tomorrow?"

"Sure, it's turned into a big thing, quite the scene."

Looking at her, feeling warm inside, blinking, her eyes seem to sparkle a little.

"Hey then, I'll see you tomorrow."

"Okay, Frank."

"Thanks Mary, for talking an' all."

She's putting down her backpack and writing on a notebook page. Tearing it out and giving it to me, "You can call me anytime, I have a line in my room. Okay?"

"Sure, sure." Wow, so different than my parents.

My God, if Cat had this freedom.

"You want the number at my uncles?" why the hell am I doing this—digging my grave one shovel full at a time.

"Sure," writing it down in her book.

"See ya, Mary," turning—time to get the hell out of here.

Got to get some air in my lungs, clear out my head. Walking quickly up to Broadway. Moving through the crowded street, long strides. Two hours to kill before I need to be back at my uncles. Maybe I misread that? Bullshit, if I'd gone up to her place—no mistake. No idea how far we'd go, but man oh man.

Stop Frank. Go find a phone booth and call Cat.

Call her. Maybe her pops won't be there—her mom's not so strict.

Standing at the phone.

"You going to call or not buddy?"

Ignoring the moron, dime dropping in, dialing, nervous.

"Hello," her mother. Don't try and bullshit.

"Hello Mrs. Sanchez, this is Frank. I heard that Catherine had to leave school early and I wanted to see if she was okay. Can I speak with her for a few minutes please?"

Silence.

"You know we don't like you calling here," stiff, formal voice.

"I know, Mrs. Sanchez. Please, please just a couple of minutes, or just let me know that she's okay... That's all I ask."

Silence, she puts the phone down a little softer than last time.

"Hello?"

"Hey Cat, it's me."

"Frank?" surprise in her voice, "Mmm, okay, wow..."

"I missed you at school," nothing back from her, dull hiss of the phone line. "I was thinking about what you said the other day and I needed to call you, let you know that I want this so bad, not being able to see you is like a part of me is torn out. I got so much to say to you... Hard to get out, but I'm sorry that I've let all this get in our way."

"This..." noise in the background, "Dad just got home. Frankie, I've got to go. We can talk tomorrow okay?"

That's it? Not even an acknowledgement? What do I say now?

"Okay, Cat."

"Bye, baby," phone hanging up on her end. Slamming mine down. Cold feeling growing inside my chest—God does this suck.

Doing the dishes after a quiet dinner—glad Uncle Vin was in a talkative mood. Could sit and listen to the details of his day. At least they are starting to cut me some slack cause I've come and gone by the rules. Court next week. Taking a deep breath, that's when I'll find out.

Stacking the clean and dry dishes.

"You okay, Frank, you're quieter than usual?"

"I'm okay, Aunt Kitty."

"Sure?"

"Sure."

"Okay then," she looks at me, "it's the start of two days off for your uncle, so please be extra quiet in the mornings."

"Okay, Aunt Kitty, I'll be quiet, probably get out and go run or do something." Shit, I need to ask permission to go out now. "Oh, um, can I go to a party tomorrow night in the City?"

"I think that's okay, you need to be home by eleven."

Biting my lip, "Can I come home at twelve, that's when my parents would let me stay out to?"

"I'll talk to your uncle, you've been doing a good job."

Feels like hours spent looking up at the unfinished ceiling in the dark basement. Feeling tired but can't sleep—vision of making love to Cat and what that meant, or what I thought that meant. I wonder if you can ever know the last time you'll be with someone? Just going along, fat dumb and happy—like all this shit is going to work out. And then "poof."

Thinking about Mary and how good it felt talking. Mind drifting to Cat—so different—we never talk like that. Wait, that's not true—we laugh, we joke with each other, tease each other, talk about school, people and all.

So what, I don't go diving with Cat either and when's the last time she tried to dribble a basketball. Laughing to myself thinking about the time we were playing around on the basketball courts by school, her face lighting up doing that terrible I-can-only-go-right dribble pushing me off with her left hand. Seeing her face in flashes—the places we've been; falling on each other like idiots trying to ice skate at Rockefeller Plaza at the small ice ring underneath the statue of Apollo; the few concerts we've been to together; baseball games we've gone to out at Yankee Stadium with the tickets my Uncle Michael gets. Heart racing thinking about her beauty, her long slim hands, how her eyes look when she's concentrating on something she's interested in. Then too—she's so popular at school. School, like that matters.

But does it? I know it means so much to her, where she's going next and what people think and all. Uneasy feeling moving through me—I thought about her at Rikers, but not often. When I was on the street, but not often. Then when things were clear again.

Maybe I'm full of shit.

Turning in the small bed, staring at the blank screen of my closed eyes. Worried that I don't feel as bad as I think I should.

I don't feel much of anything.

Mind drifting lazily to those poor orphaned babies I saw at St. Anthony's. Horrible, stomach churning at how sick it must be to be left helpless in a garbage can. How the hell could the Roman's leave unwanted babies exposed to die if no one wanted them or how tough was life like then or how different are we now? Hell, I don't know.

Up early, quick breakfast—out in my sweats and sneakers.

Pacing the empty basketball courts, street cleaners out early spraying dirty water on dirty streets, gray water with floating bits of garbage running down clogged drains. Delivery trucks driving down the street.

Stopping at the foul line, going through the motion of shooting like the thousands of times I've been on the court after practice shooting, working that small muscle memory, working that feeling, remembering that feeling of what it's like to be in the bubble—everything going well in the game. Enjoying the freedom of running, jumping—not having to think about the game, playing hard.

Off the court, running slowly, whole day to kill.

Getting into a good mile-eating pace.

I'm going to run till my body hurts so bad that I leave all this behind.

Chapter 30

Hallway in Walter's apartment building on Broadway and 99th Street smells like roach spray, old age and musty plaster with years of dampness saved up in the walls. Walking up to the third floor. Sounds like the party's going strong already—Rolling Stones seeping out from behind the door. Stretching, body sore from putting out so much today. Buzzer going off, if she's going to play this at a distance, then I'm hanging with my guys and whatever.

"Hey, Frank! What took you so long?" Walter's pockmarked face and curly hair poking out from the door—looks like he's had a few already. "Can you make a run to the liquor store, man? People have kicked in money, but no one's got the nuts to make a run."

"Sure, Walter, let me make a sweep and then I'll head down."

"Come in, come in, that's what I wanted to hear!" he's patting me on the shoulder like I'm his best friend. Right. The long hallway to the kitchen and the living room are full of people standing around, sitting around, moving and trying to be cool smoking cigarettes. Most are from my old school.

"Yo, Frankie," Julio calling from down the hall—passing a bedroom that's been turned into a black light room, Peter Max posters on the wall, kids sitting on the floor smoking weed. How Walter's brother lets him get away with this, I have no idea.

"What's going on, man?" doing a brother handshake.

"Just hanging. Cat's here with Marta and Sandra," looking over at the couch near the two large windows, the three girls on the couch talking, looking around. Other kids are sitting around the perimeter of the room— formed into little groups, a few people mixing. She's gonna have to come to me. Hector, Bradley, Richard coming over. Some kids I don't know giggling, drinking beers like it's the first time.

"Go slow, man," looking at them, "it will kick in fast."

"What are you, the play-by-play guy," the smart ass looking at me.

"Yeah, I'll be in the bathroom standing behind your dumb ass when you're throwing up giving out the details about the first time you had a beer."

"Man, what do you know?" he shrugs and turns away, his attitude pissing me off.

"I know you're a dumb shit, maybe I should save all the people here a headache and throw your ass out?"

"Yo, Frankie, take it easy man," Julio coming closer. Hector looking concerned.

"Walter, who is this weirdo?" the smart-ass asks Walter.

"Oh man," Walter looks at me, "what's up, Frank?"

Poking at the smartasses chest, "You got anything to back up your mouth, douchebag?"

The two start to look at little scared as Hector comes over and looks mean, Julio a little nervous, but standing tall.

"Walter, these guys put any money in the kitty?"

"Nope."

Grabbing the first smartass by the ear and twisting. He buckles, looks scared and flails a little 'til I twist harder. Hector and Julio taking the other kid by the arms and they are out the door.

"Man, Frank, why'd you do that? They're harmless kids from down the hall?"

"Walter, fucking idiots drinking away like it's their first beer, just being friendly telling them to slow down. They give me attitude; I got no time for attitude! I can invite them back in and you can go buy your own fucking booze while me and my boys take our girls and go find someplace else to party. It's your call?"

"Oh man, don't be like that," he looks hurt. Hector's laughing and slapping me five. Walter sulks away.

"Man, Frank, we miss you at school," he's laughing talking to Julio, then loud, "YOU SO CRAZY!"

People coming over, wondering what we did, some of them laughing, others looking at us like we are retards—which we are. Mixing back into the living room, checking out Cat, she sees me but goes right on gabbing away with her two friends. Turning and exchanging a nod with Kenny who takes a momentary break from another of a long series of important arguments with Anea.

Who knows, maybe the world will change tonight?

"How can you say animals are more important than people?" his face intense, his white guy afro bobbing around as his head jerks side to side.

"I didn't, Kenneth. Why are you so angry because I want the school charity to select Animal Rescue? There are so many groups, charities, and organizations for... Look at all that was presented in the auditorium yesterday. And it's a vote anyway. Why do you keep attacking me about this?"

"Oh, the whole slide show you put on during your presentation, sad kitty pictures, sad puppy pictures," as he makes a sad droopy face. "All you girls getting all mushy, oooh, poor kitty, poor little kitty. We need to save the kitties... Let 'em out in the woods, they are animals, they can take care of themselves. I didn't show pictures of sick kids in wheelchairs all emaciated to get folks all gooey inside!"

"Maybe you should."

"What? People shouldn't be able to think? We all have to be emotional wrecks like you and put on the big sob story?"

"Kenny, why are you so mad at me?"

"I hate all the lack of talk about real problems, people walking around like big emotional bowls of mush. What, were you happy with Nixon because he had a cute dog? Is that your criteria for good people?"

"You're telling me abused animals don't have rights?"

"Sure, right after abused people. People should come first, Anea!"

Bored, walked away—they are always going at it.

Checking out this really tall girl, must be at least six feet—looks like she comes from a mixed family—light skin, nice full, rich lips, thick wavy black hair, nice, very nice.

Edging away from the bozos as the next record starts to play, Traffic, *John Barleycorn Must Die*. She's ignoring Mike, who's trying to talk to her—looking right back at me. He's probably on some political rant.

"Hey, what's your name girl?"

"Cherlyn," she bats her eyelashes a little. Mike is getting pissed.

"I'm Frank, how you feelin?"

"Pretty good," she looks at me, brings a cigarette up to her lips, long, well-formed fingers.

"I don't know you from Stuyvesant."

"I'm at Trinity, Nina invited me."

"Ah," looking over at Nina and her little clique of girls, "I'm going to make a supply run, anything special you like? From the store anyway?"

"Hmm," she gives me a little eyebrow, "some nice sweet wine maybe?"

"Don't go away now."

"Alright," a little smile, "I'll be right here." Smiling at her.

This is going to be trouble.

"Yo, Walter, let's get this going," he's collecting money from kids.

"I'm hanging with you, man," said Hector.

"That's cool."

"So, get a fifth of Gin, Sloe Gin, Vodka and some six packs," as he counts out money. Place on 103rd Street and Broadway I've bought from before. "I've got plenty of juice and mixers."

"How much in the kitty?"

"Let's see," he's clumsily counting out money.

"Just give it to me. I'll cover what's needed, if it's too much, I'll take it out of peoples hides."

"Okay, thanks Frank."

"Sure," looking at him, "I see the idiots, you want me to invite them in?"

"Nah," he shrugs his shoulders, "they are losers."

"Let's go Hector, where's that maricon Julio?"

"Man he's sniffing around Marta like a dog, man."

Heading down the stairs.

"Man, that Cherlyn girl is hot," he says.

"You know it."

"What's on your mind, Hector?"

"Nothin' man."

"The action is in there, man."

"Hey you know, I miss hanging out with my man."

Out on the street, cool out now—buttoning up my jean jacket.

"Yo, at the store, go hang out down the block right? If they see us together we're gonna reek of underage party."

"Sure, sure," he's walking fast to keep up. "So what's up with Cat, man? She was giving you evil looks when you were talking to that fine black girl, Cherlyn."

"You know, Hector," looking at my friend, "I'm not playing her bullshit game. Trying to put all this shit back on me. If she wants to break it off, then fuck it. I'm not going to be some punk. I love her like crazy man, but…"

"Whoa man, what's going on? You two were tight?"

Back on Broadway, now walking uptown.

"She's telling me that I'm not serious you know, that after we did it, I should be making better moves. Like I really wanted all this bullshit to come down. I tried to tell her what it was like and she doesn't want to hear it, wants to hear about how we'll do the college thing, then being together after that. If you can't talk to your woman, then what man? I mean, I can understand her being upset about all this stuff coming between us, but it's like…" Stopping for a red light and letting a stream of cars pass before jay walking. "Man, I don't know, like she's supposed to be on my side right? I get the feeling that she doesn't like how this effects the things she wants and we're not on the same team."

"Yo man, you guys did it?"

Looking at Hector. That's all he heard. What a dickhead.

"Yes, Hector, we fucked like crazy for almost a whole day before I got busted."

"Damn," he's inside his head.

"Wait down the block," walking purposefully into the store. Leaving the dipshit outside.

Walking out of the store with my arms full.

Laughing with the guy in the store as I walk out—he's just glad to hear the cash register ring. Nodding to him as the door closes and the little bell rings. Walking back toward Walter's and stopping for that dipshit Hector to catch up and let him carry some of this crap.

People flocking to the kitchen for the goodies.

Walter's happy now that there's more booze—his favorite subject, how much he drank and how much he's going to drink, he pops a cold one, starts setting up mixers and what not. Volume of noise in the apartment has picked up—animated conversation about music, school, politics; how could Ford pardon Nixon, how fucked up their parents are, sports, movies.

Bored with all this mental masturbation. Stopping for a moment and looking at all these kids—what spoiled kids, they have no idea what's going on a few blocks from here. I don't know how much of this bullshit I can stand. Images of the drug warren my uncle took me to filtering in.

"Who's up for one of my famous Sloe Gin Fizz?" yells out Walter.

"Oh me, I like that," spouts off Suzanna.

"How about a beer?"

"Let's order some pizzas."

Rolling my eyes as Walter mixes up a strong drink for his little sophomore chickita. Walking by her, "Hey kiddo, take it easy on that, it tastes sweet, but it will kick your ass." She gives me a shrug. Pouring out a glass of Spumonti for Cherlyn and making myself a Screwdriver. This should piss Cat off nicely.

Out in the hall—Cherlyn standing back against the wall looking good in her tight jeans, black turtle neck with her sleeves pushed up and a scarf around her neck, talking to Kenny now, listening to him politely. He must be going off on another rant about how to make the world a better place, trying to look smart—her body looks like she wants to ditch him. My eyes consciously following every curve and nuance of her body—she doesn't have a lot upstairs, but man, oh man. She's watching me look at her.

"You see anything you like?"

"Oh yeah," nodding to her, little smile from her. "See if you like this," handing her the glass. Kenny's annoyed. He's wary though—he knows he can't bowl me over in a debate. I'll give it right back.

"Hmm, that's tasty, I like the bubbles."

"Kenny, there's beer and all kinds of stuff in the kitchen."

She looks at him, then to me. I look at her and then him.

He shrugs his shoulders as he walks off. Cherlyn laughs a little.

"I'll catch you later, Kenny," to Mr. Try to be Cool here. "I think we need to get something to dance to on, you coming?" nodding my head towards the other room. She gives me a sly little look, sipping her wine and follows me into the living room.

Gotten hot in here, she's near my side, "God, he's boring."

"No shit."

"I bet he's…"

Looking at her, holding up my little pinky.

"No," she swats at me, "that's not what I mean."

"But it's true."

"Oh you're bad, you're bad."

"So, what do you like?"

"Oh, you mean like music, fashion? I like to dance and have fun you know. I don't like guys like this," and she holds up her little pinky. Laughing with her.

"Oh well, you'll hate hanging out with me then."

"Yeah right," she gives me a little shove. Flipping through albums, setting them out so she can check them out.

"There's some good rock here, but you can't move to much of this." Squatting down by another piles of records, Cherlyn close to my ear.

"So who's the pretty Latin lady on the couch with the crowd?"

"Why do you ask?"

"She was giving off some nasty looks, I may have to talk to her…"

Flipping through records—Joanie Mitchell, Elton John, Eagles, Aerosmith and James Taylor. On and on with the white music, well at least I'm getting to some Santana, O'Jays, War, Otis Redding. Keep looking.

"That's Cat, we are an item or used to be an item, who knows anyway and besides I don't really give a shit about high school games anymore," shaking my head, "most of this music sucks."

"I brought some of those buster and what do you mean high school games?"

Looking at her—time to bust some chops.

"Oh no," holding my fingers to my mouth in feigned surprise, "were you expecting one of those turn down the lights parties, where all the virgins lay on the couches, listen to Elton John and moan about the boyfriends they wish they had?"

"Oh you're bad, and besides, I wouldn't qualify."

"So what do you suggest?"

"About music?"

Smiling at her, "Well?"

"Oh, you are bad."

Looking over at the couch for a second, Julio behind it talking to Cat and Marta. Twinge in my chest as I see how he's being with her. He wouldn't. Catching a glimpse of Cat eyeing me and then turning back to her circle.

"I still think she still wants to be an item."

Giving her a funny look, "What makes you say that?"

"She keeps looking at you."

"Yeah well," looking at Cherlyn's broad face, dark eyes, "How about you?"

"I see different guys you know."

Checking her out. Getting the feeling that she goes where she wants and gets what she wants. Probably likes that I'm moving her around—doesn't like boys who are followers. Thought hitting me—maybe that's what I lost with Cat, she doesn't believe in me. I can make the opening, but she's got to want to follow.

"How about this?" holding up War's *The World is a Ghetto*.

"I like that."

"You pick the next one."

She hands me the Temptations *Cloud Nine*.

"Nice."

"You're not like these other kids."

Removing the current stack of albums and replacing them.

People complaining when I take off the current record, holding up my hands, "Guys, just shut the fuck up and dance," a couple of nervous laughs then they go back to their little worlds. Taking a sip of my drink—got to take it easy on this. Adding Santana *Abraxis*, and the *Sound of Philadelphia* by Mother Father Sister Brother to the stack. Should shake things up. Distinctive beat of *Cisco Kid* comes on, cranking up the volume. Standing up starting to move, she moves along with me. Nice body on this girl, and man, she moves well. This is heating up faster than I thought—shit, Mary is here too. Well, maybe I get to blow it all tonight.

"What did you mean about high school games anymore?" she flicks her hair back.

"Oh, that's a long story... Suffice it to say I got kicked out for being a trouble maker."

Her eyes open at that, "One of the bad ones?"

"One of the dumb ones," laughing to myself as I make a move and look around the room. Catching Cat dragging Julio up to dance. Marta looking at them with daggers in her eyes, Julio nervous.

"What bullshit," mumbling to myself.

"What's that, Frank?"

"Oh, just thinking out loud," giving Julio a hard look. He wisely backs off, tells her something and heads over to the kitchen.

Cat all in a huff—damn she looks good though.

"Used to be an item? Right." Cherlyn gives me a wry smile.

"Yeah well, I bet you have broken hearts all over Manhattan."

"Maybe," batting her eyelashes, "I'm sure I'm not the only one."

"I guess we are doomed to be desired," using my thigh muscles to slowly sink and dance with the music, body moving back and forth. She starts moving down with me.

Music moving. Temptations playing.

Not talking much with Cherlyn. Looks like this is losing its momentum, not that it's a bad thing.

"Hey you want a refill?" looking at my empty glass.

Damn she does look good. All I have to do is make the move.

"Sure, Frank, I'll hang here. Nina looks like she wants to talk."

Waving her in, she comes close, "Nina doesn't like me."

"I can see why," she puts her finger on my nose, holds my eyes for a second. Holding her eyes for a moment, moving off through the crowd, stepping over little knots of kids talking, things starting to loosen up, Walter and his child bride making out in the corner.

"Yo, Frankie, I didn't mean anything by that."

Turning to Julio, "You know if Cat and I are over, that's one thing. But that would be fucked up if you moved in."

"I know, I know. She's pissed that you're ignoring her, man."

Shaking my head.

"Well you better get back to minding the store, looks like they want someone to boss around."

"Frank, don't play that, that's cold."

Walking to the kitchen, it's a little after ten. Nodding, smiling at people talking to me in the hall. Hell that's great, my sophomore fan club is here now, I need to ditch and ignore Katrina. Kids are drinking fast. Wonder what my uncle would do if I came back blitzed. Well, I'm not going to find out—make the next one really, really light, it's called orange juice.

Cherlyn in the hall with Nina and her posse of mod girls who worship the 60's, "Nina wants to go to another party downtown. I wrote out the address if you want to come." She looks at me, "I'd like that."

"Okay, I'll catch you later," her number's on this too.

Looking at her number and then looking at her.

"Call me," long look from her.

"I will," as she gives me a smile that looks like there's more here than talking on the phone. She brushes my lips with her long fingers and smiles as she leaves. The rest of the Mod Squad strolls off as Nina gives me a nice fuck-you-smile. Giving her a nice fuck-you-smile back. We'll never get along, her with her phony British rock groupie bullshit. Time to find Mary.

"So are you going to ignore me all night?"

Turning, looking at Cat, my face feels tight. Feels like standing on one side of a deep canyon with her on the other.

"You know, Cat, I get it, I get how all this has made a mess of the things we've talked about, I get how I've been," anger coming out in my words, looking down, back at her. "I don't know, not putting us first. But this is bullshit, if you want out, say it, don't play games."

Play of emotions running across her face.

"I love you. I love you so much, Cat, but I won't be a punk."

Her lips come together hard. Blinking, looking at her closely. Can't believe that her eyes are watering up. Did I misread this too?

"Why do you do this to me, Frankie? I love so much, Frankie, this hurts so much sometimes and I don't know what to do about it. I don't know who to talk to... I mean, my friends, they don't understand," her arms crossed. She turns and walks to the back of the apartment, abruptly turns to me where it's less crowded. Explosion of arms round bodies, lips in contact, her leg hooking around mine.

No reserved Cat here, full on.

She's saying, "I'm sorry" in my ear. Her body electric, her breasts pushing into my chest, her hips pushing into mine. People looking at us and then looking away. Swaying a little with her. She pushes me into one of the bedrooms where people have been stacking their coats. I lock the door behind us. Fumbling wildly with belts, zippers, laughing as our clothes are strewn across the top layer of coats. Moving them back to create a space, she pulls my underwear down and sits down on the bed, leaning in to lightly kiss the tip of my penis, my body shivering as she runs her fingers along the side.

Kneeling down in front of her and slowly moving her nice pink panties across her curvy hips as she rises up off the bed and moves side-to-side. Each breath is filled with delicious, musty electricity. She's looking right into my eyes as I move her panties over her feet and she slightly parts her legs.

Running my fingers across her wonderful smooth coffee-colored skin. Body so excited. I'll come in two seconds, time to nestle in and taste that wonderful pussy, bring her along too. Her eyes close as I stroke her thighs and the inside of her legs. She reaches behind and removes her bra as I slowly kiss inside her legs. She takes in a shallow breath as I reach out with my tongue and lick across the top of her pussy. Oh man is she moist, her rich, thick pubic hair already starting to glisten with a wonderful rich wetness.

Moving her thighs apart, moving my tongue up and down and then side to side across the top of her pussy, pushing in a little further and licking around the sides of her clitoris. Her hands running through my wavy hair, her breathing picking up as I move my head down and push my tongue into her vagina and circle around the outside lips. Body on fire, penis quivering with excitement, skin sensitive to her touch.

"Yes," she says as I move faster across the top and sides of her clitoris. "Yes, Frank."

Her hips in motion with me as she lifts and pushes them forward into me. More pressure on her as I randomly move around, side to side, up and down.

"Oh yes, yes," her grip tightening on my hair.

Her body shudders and she wraps her legs around my head, holding me in one place with one hand, the other in her mouth.

"Oh my goodness, oh Frank," holding me, breathing hard, a slight trickle of warm sweat beading up between her breasts, her skin, her pussy smells so good. Slowly tasting her, moving her where I want.

"I want to feel you, baby."

Moving back and searching to find my pants and wallet to put on a condom.

"Do a little without that so I can feel you."

"I'm going to explode baby, I don't think it's safe."

"I just had my, you know last week, so it's a safe time. I can't... I just want us to be together," she pulls my hips to her, her fingers guiding me in.

Incredible sensations of warm, soft, wet, connected pleasure running up and down my body as my penis slides slowly into her. She moves her legs wide apart.

"Ohhhhh, yes, it's you. I can feel you. You feel so good, baby," kissing her deeply, tongues moving. Putting my hands underneath her bottom, and pulling her slowly to me.

She starts moving faster. "God that feels good, Cat."

"I want you so bad, baby, it's been so hard to be away from you, to be like we were. I want this all to disappear and be lost in this."

Sensations building into frenzy of passion as my body moves faster.

"Yes, oh yes. I can feel how excited you are, don't stop, Frankie."

From the tip of my penis up through my spine a switch going on, can't hold back. Pushing hard up inside of her as deep as I can.

"Cat, oh baby, ooooh," coming hard, penis, body pulsating. Her breathing short, rapid, "Don't stop, Frankie, I'm close."

Moving as fast as I can, my body feels so alive. Penis so overwhelmed with sensation it's painful to move. Pushing deep into her, holding her so my pubic bone makes contact with her clitoris, big circles and then moving side to side as I feel her nails digging into my back. She's biting my neck to keep from making too much noise.

Feeling her body relax, suffused in a warm glow with her, our sweat intermingling, my penis still heavy with blood and pleasure. Moving slowly in and out, feeling another orgasm close to the surface. Can't stop.

"This is so good, baby," she puts her head back. "I still may have to slap you for messing with that Cherlyn girl."

"Cherlyn who?"

"That's right."

The feeling inside her changing to a thicker consistency as my come mixes with her rich warm pussy juices and sweat. I keep moving in and out slowly.

"I'll fix you, my little Kitty Cat," as my sensitivity drops from painful to feeling good and I can move in and out further and faster.

"Oh yesss," as she lies back into a small pile of coats and just gives in, moving slowly, feeling another orgasm building deep in the distance, her hands on my lower back pulling me in.

Bodies entwined. Warm flood of wonder breaking through the gloom, "I can't imagine not having this, Cat."

"I'm sorry I was so bad on the phone," she moves her hair back behind her head. "My mom told me what you said, that was nice to do. I hate that all this is between us."

"It really bothered me that you didn't want to hear what I was trying to say."

She laughs, "Guess we are just destined to be locked in combat or a lover's embrace."

"Hmm," putting my hand down on her rich moist pussy and moving slowly across the top, "I think I could live with that."

"Oh, I think I could live with this," as she puts her wrist on her forehead as I start to massage her breast and begin to massage her pussy with my warm penis, "Wow, that feels so warm. Hmm, I like it that you're not afraid of my body or touching me how you want to."

"Isn't that what people do when they love each other?"

"Like that Cherlyn?" She opens her eyes, "You know I heard about you and Mary going off the other day."

"Just friends, baby."

"Hmm, better be," as she closes her eyes as I roll her over, pull her up to her knees. Her back muscles tense, her body pushing back into me as I enter her.

Back in the fray of the party, ignoring the crappy music. Graduating to the couch as she sits close to me. Holding my left hand on the tall back of the couch so I can turn and inhale the wonderful rich smell of her on my fingers. She sees me doing that and smiles while slapping at my leg. Surreptitious looks from Mary. She heads out of the room. Next record dropping down—crap. Another round of white boys with little dicks trying to sing like black men—fucking Rolling Stones. Marta and Julio dancing uneasily.

"What time did the Commandant tell you you'd turn into a pumpkin?"

"I need to be home by twelve," checking my watch, it's after eleven.

"Me too."

"You want me to walk you home? Ditch these bozos?"

"Sure," getting up. "Wait," she puts her arms around me and gives me a long kiss. The little beast, making sure all the other girls know this is hers.

Walter panicked cause he needs another booze run.

"Got to go, man."

Walking downstairs—she's got on her little bomber jacket. Looking at her I can't tell that we were going crazy earlier—make up roughly the same, her skin glowing.

"When you told me you wanted to make this work, there was so much I wanted to say, my mom was right there."

"Oh," feeling stupid, "I thought you were blowing me off, Cat. I'm sorry, baby."

She stops. "Frank," her dark brown eyes a mixture of soft and intense. "Never doubt me, baby. You know it's tough sometimes and I have to hide this all from my parents and all, and it makes me feel like I'm out of control, but I love you, Frank. I love you so much it scares me. Put your hand here," as she takes my right hand and puts it on her chest, feeling the warmth that's pulsing out of her body.

"I feel that, Cat."

"It's only you, Frank. Be easy with me at times."

"I will, Cat," walking down slowly, arms around each other, hands in our back pockets. Bright colors in Broadway—neon signs flashing, people in shop windows. Feeling like I've been let out of a little room, feeling like there's so much room in the world that anything can happen. Cool breeze coming up into our faces. Laughing with her for no reason. She gives me a playful elbow as I brush my hand across her delicious ass.

Closing my eyes. Hold this memory man—savor the moment.

Chapter 31

Sitting back on the hard fiberglass subway seat, oblivious to the noise, relaxed, letting the memory of being with her surround me. A rosy barrier between the trash, the dirty seats, the tagged walls of the car, the empty eye sockets of people sitting like they've been on this train for all their lives and the high I feel now.

Subway pulls out of the last station before the long tunnel underneath the East River.

Imagine having her every night. Oh man—freedom to be and do what we like. That's something to work for. Shutting out the stories I'd heard about how my father was like a man possessed when he met Mom after coming back from the War; starting a business, accepting nothing but success. This is different—Cat's no ice princess. Heart pounding in my chest—she'd fight for her kids. She'd fight for them and so would I.

Uneasy twinge, why did Mom give up on me? Why didn't she fight for me? Am I such a huge disappointment to them?

Drifting off the rhythm of the train.

Commotion to my right down at the other end of the car snapping me out of my daydream, young girls, must be fourteen or so pushing something away, blinking my eyes to get the situation in focus.

Man in an open long, dirty green raincoat standing near the girls. Other people in the car sitting stone faced looking away. What's he doing? Dirty face, scraggly bearded white man, wild leering look in his eyes.

Oh Jesus, he's got his dick out of his pants, is playing with it and trying to stick it in their faces. Motherfucker! Jolt of energy running up my spine, toes tingling. Hesitating for a moment, I'm already in trouble. Girls trapped on the seat he keeps moving in front of them. One of the girls looking out to the people in the car pleading for help and the rest of the people in the car just looking away, acting like they don't see it. If they don't see it, it doesn't exist.

"HEY," getting up, body surging with adrenaline—trying to keep the mean from making me jump in and start hitting him. Breathe, get relaxed, can't punch with power if I'm tight. Shrugging my shoulders, moving my arms to loosen up.

"Stop that. Leave them alone!"

He turns and looks at me, starts waving his dirty cock at me, starting to prance around like a crazed animal in front of the girls, saying something I can't make out. Feeling the warm drum beat in my chest. "Leave them alone, you sick fuck!"

"Oooooo," he's shaking back and forth like he's mocking me. He grabs at one of the girls hands and tries to pull it to his dick.

Focus narrowing—click, body relaxing, keeping my eyes relaxed and stepping forward. I know what's coming next. Switch it on!

He's not paying attention. Another step forward, his eyes catch me closing in—too late. Rock fist connecting to his jaw, full body weight behind it. He goes tumbling backwards, his shirttails flapping around. Looking at the girls. Motioning for them to get behind me. They are slow, in shock.

"Move!" they jolt, looking at me then stumble away. A middle-aged lady who was looking away gets involved and takes them by the arm and pulls them away. Stepping forward as the guy sits on the floor fumbling in his pockets.

Shit, that blow should have put that rat out.

He puts his hand on the floor to get up.

Fuck, rat man's got a knife! Surge hitting me—remembering the shadows at the river, absolute focus, whipping off my belt and stepping forward. There's going to be blood. I'm not backing down.

Hispanic man in green maintenance uniform sitting near him stands up and steps on his knife hand. Speed—two big steps, hard kick connects with his scraggly face. He goes flopping back over, the knife skids away, his head bounces off the floor.

Crazy fucker is laughing, feeling a cold feeling in my stomach. Focus spreading through me, time slowing down. Looking at him differently. Energy moving to a different level—I'm going to stop him, period. He's not going to get up this time. He's not going to get that knife—my body knows what that means.

Man in green kicks him in the side as he tries to get up and go for the knife. Rat man tries to roll around me—grabbing a strong hold on his ratty hair and bringing his head violently down into the left knee I'm thrusting up and connecting as hard as I can, his body going limp, turning his head, getting my full body into it—rock fist to his temple, his body crumpling to the floor.

Breathing hard, stepping back, if he's dead—then, I understand.

Taking the ends of his raincoat and wrapping it over his head, tying him up with my belt. His chest moving slowly, he's breathing, weird. His eyes moving like crazy underneath his eyelids. I've seen guys get put out—nothing like this. Like a rabid dog—he's starting to struggle again. Ready to step in and stomp on his scrawny neck. If he can't breathe, he can't move.

"Easy, Amigo," hand on my shoulder, looking over at the man who stepped on the knife and then tripped him up. "He's not going anywhere," he takes out a strong cord from pocket.

"Here, help me tie him up."

Holding rat man while my friend hog-ties him. My breathing starting to slow down, *"Thank you, my friend that could have been bad."*

"No problem. Let's throw him off the train at the next stop, he's crazy in the head."

"*No, my uncle's a policeman, I'll call him. Get his ass off the street. You do that with me, talk to my uncle?*"

"*Sure, no problem,*" he shrugs.

The girls coming over, people starting to come over and crowd around now that they are safe. The bullshit stories about what happened already taking root in their weak little minds.

"My God," said a lady. "Why didn't he stop? Is he dead?"

"Look at him," as the little prick starts to struggle.

Big black man coming over, "Let's get his ass off here. Call the po-lice."

The girls approach us warily, "Thank you. Oh, thank you. That was so disgusting, I couldn't believe it. So gross..."

Looking at them, "My uncle's a cop, he'll get some guys over here quickly. They can take you home if you want... Tell them your story; get this guy off the street. Okay?"

They look at each other, subway stopping at Bedford Avenue.

Picking up the struggling man—not too much strength in him. The big black man taking his legs, "Man you sure came down on hard on this motherfucker, he's got to be on something to take shots like that."

"Yo, you right, Hommes, man must be on something," the maintenance man coming along too, talking to the girls. Other people clamoring around asking if they are okay, if they can help. People shouting out that they'd be witnesses for the girls if they wanted to press charges. Out of the subway door.

"Hey, man," to the Hispanic man, "get the knife if you can." Then to the guy helping me, "Let's get him to that phone."

People following us, conductor asking what's going on. Middle-aged white man giving him a run down and coming back saying the MTA police will be here soon. The big black guy laughing as he sits down on top of the struggling pervert.

"Yo man, what's your name?" as I dial my uncle's number.

"Maurice, you crazy white boy, taking on this fool like that. You got a name or you gonna ride some shit off into the sunset," laughing with him while I'm waiting for someone to pick up.

"I'm Frank, Maurice, thanks man."

"What's your name, my friend?"

"Jorge."

"Thanks guys. That could have been ugly."

"Someone took an ugly stick to this motherfucker," said Maurice holding out his hand for five. Smiling giving his open hand a slap. Phone ringing as more people gather around. The girls are sitting down at the other end of the long wooden bench, women gathering around, talking, comforting.

"Lieutenant Caruso's direct line," gruff voice, "this better be important."

"This is his nephew, Frank, I've got an emergency. Man tried to molest a couple of teenagers on the L train just now," breathing hard, trying to slow down, "Need to get someone here to help."

"Slow down kid. Where are you?"

"Bedford Station, we've got the perv tied up, he tried to pull a knife. We got him though."

"Okay, wait one," his hand cupping the phone, dim background noise. Looking at the people around me, train doors closing—people losing interest in the situation and ducking back on the train, looking out of the windows as it pulls away.

"Would you have jumped in if they were sisters?" Maurice asks.

"Hell yes!" He gives me a long look and then nods.

Smiling, "Yo Maurice, if they were sisters though, we'd a had to pull them off his ass after they busted him up."

Maurice starts laughing. "Damn right," him and Jorge slap five.

Hum of people talking, Maurice and Jorge talking.

"Go ahead, Frank," Uncle Vin's deep voice.

"I'm here at Bedford Station on the Canarsie line, guy on a train tried to molest two teenage girls. Told him to stop, he wouldn't. It wasn't just talk. He had his willie right out trying to make them touch it. Shoving it at them. I had to bust him up. He tried to pull a knife. A couple of people on the train helped out we have him here, but the little bastard is still struggling. I've got him tied up in his jacket," Maurice whacking the guy in the head and laughing as he struggles to get what's probably three hundred pounds off him.

"I need help, can you get someone over?"

"Sit tight, I'll have a car over ASAP. I'm on my way. Out."

He hangs up. Putting the phone down, turning looking at Maurice and Jorge's expectant faces. "My uncle's sending some guys over."

Jorge looks at me a little differently, crossing his arms nodding his head. The girls are crying on the bench, situation finally catching up with them, one of the elderly ladies from the car with her arm around one of them.

"You saved my ass Jorge, as crazed as this guy is he'd have probably cut me bad and I'd have had to kill him."

"Knife would have made me run," said Maurice giving the weirdo a hard whack.

"Stop hitting him," someone from the crowd calls out as Maurice hands out another big whack.

"Man, fuck you. Your honky ass was sitting and shaking while this kid here made the move."

"That doesn't make it right."

"You hold this fool then," he looks over, "nothin' to say now, go back to watching TV, Motherfucker."

Commotion on the stairs, uniformed officers racing in.

"Easy now people, NYPD, make a hole, let's go," people moving aside slowly not wanting to give up their view of the scene.

"Which one of you'se is Caruso?"

"Here, Sergeant," stepping forward.

Maurice calling out "This dudes on something, he took three big shots and all they did was startle him, you be careful, you hear," as the policemen come over. People starting to yell about what the pervert was doing in the car as more officers come down the stairs. Plainclothes police.

"This is the Police," the first officer yelling at the hog-tied perv. "Calm down, do not move. We are going to get you some help."

"Aaaaaaaaaaa!" comes out of the coat as they untie and unwrap the coat and try to get a grip on his arms. The guy struggling in a mad frenzy, kicking, biting, spit flying out of his mouth.

Three policemen taking him on, "Fuck," one of the uniformed officers grunts, steps back and smacks him with his club. The guy claws at his face and scratches him. The plainclothes guy jumps on and puts hard wristlock on the perv. He keeps struggling.

People shouting.

More men in dark blue rushing in.

Maurice standing back, chuckling to himself in a low voice, "Nice to see the man get it now and then," he looks at me satisfied, shrugs, "no offense my man," then he's looking back at the action, smiling.

"None taken."

Four cops take him down hard, cuffs on his hands and legs.

"Motherfucker," the man who was scratched yells and kicks the sick fuck, their combined weight finally getting him under control.

Two police officers start talking to the girls, the other two keep the man restrained, a plain-clothes officer talking to Jorge. Two more uniformed officers show up. MTA officers and the new policemen start arguing about who has jurisdiction. Big voice telling people to back the fuck off, unmistakable, my uncle's big frame and his energy dominating the scene.

"I'm Detective Lieutenant Caruso, this is my scene, now get the fuck out of here. Unnerstand!" The MTA guys look at each other and wisely step back.

"Give me a rundown, Matt," he holds up his hand to me as I'm about to start.

"Well, Lieutenant, it looks like the perp there was taking out his privates and trying to assault the two teenagers there on the train. The big kid there stepped in and told him to stop, the guy didn't. He popped him. The guy tried to pull a knife, which I have secured. This man," pointing to Jorge, "stepped on the guy's knife while the kid took the guy down hard and ended up wrapping him up in his coat. They hog tied him, got him off the train and called it in." My uncle nodding, looking at the plainclothes guy he called Matt, looking at the girls, the crowd.

"The guy must be hopped up out of his mind on Angel Dust, Big V. It took four of us to get him cuffed," my uncle nodding. Another plainclothes man coming up to my uncle, not big but with the most incredibly muscled jaw and chiseled face I've ever seen, red hair, thick neck and blue eyes taking the situation in. Cops struggling to get the perv up and get control of him. The officer with the square jaw comes over, picks the perv up off the ground like he's a baby, shakes him a few times, screams in his face, smacks him violently into the wall face first a few times and hands him dazed to two of the blues.

"Fucking, Kelly," they laugh and take rat man up the stairs.

"Good, get the witnesses down to the station for statements."

"Hey, Lieutenant," called the first sergeant on the scene.

"What's up, Casey?"

"I think that's the prick that cut Franklin last week."

"Good, " he says, turning to the officer who was scratched, "you okay Mikey?"

"More surprised than anything, Lieutenant."

"Go see a doc and get a rabies shot or something," he's laughing.

"Fucking dozen, who knows what that sick fuck's got," the guy says laughing.

"People, PEOPLE!" Uncle Vin holding up his hands. "You can help us by coming down to the station and tell us what you saw. We think this guy here has been behind an assault on a police officer as well as multiple reported sexual assaults... The more we can get from you, the more help you'll be at getting him off the street. Okay?"

"Give the girl's parents a run down," he said to one of the officers.

Stepping back so the girls can pass by with two police officers.

"Thank you," one of them reaching out to me and touching my arm. Nodding to her as I watch Uncle Vin handing his card to Jorge, words passed between them and a handshake.

"Get in," following Uncle Vin.

"I was gonna get to a phone to let you know that I'll be home late."

"Wiseass," as he closes the door.

Hands starting to shake from the adrenaline bleed off.

Sitting down.

"You okay, kid? No fucking around now."

"I think so, Uncle Vin. Am I in trouble?"

"Hell no, although you're lucky that guy didn't get his knife into your sorry ass the way he did Franklin. Nasty wound, you see that again, don't be stupid. You're lucky that man helped you or we'd be mopping up... You unnerstand?"

Nodding to him.

"You hungry?"

"Yeah."

"We'll get some food at the station, I'll call your aunt so she doesn't take a rolling pin to you when you get your sorry ass home."

Driving quickly through dark streets to the 88th Precinct.

Busy front desk—people crowded around the desk trying to talk at once to the sergeant, others sitting on the beaten up long benches, some with a faraway look in their eyes. Sergeant nods at my uncle and waves us through, two big uniformed men come and help transport the struggling pervert.

"Get him into a solitary holding cell, we're gonna need to let whatever he's on bleed off and then get him to a doc," said the first Sergeant on site. As I pass by he looks at me, "Hey kid, good fucking job," he punches me in the shoulder. "Just don't get too smart and put us out of a job."

Rubbing my shoulder, "Thank you, Sir."

He winks at my uncle who shoves me along. "Let's go, Hero." Walking upstairs on the old creaky wooden stairs, officers walking past us talking to my uncle, a man in cuffs yelling about how the police were the devil's henchmen on earth.

"Another fun night," mutters my uncle. Walking to a big room with desks set front-to-front. Men talking on the phone, carrying big fat folders and loose leaf binders, a couple coming over to my uncle.

"What'cha got, Big V?"

"Need a statement from the kid. I'll get Schmitty up to speed."

"You've got it," he says to my uncle.

"This is Detective Arnold. He's a good man, tell him everything from the beginning to end."

"Yes, Sir," to my uncle as he walks off.

"Sit down over here," he breaks out a notebook and pen like it's business as usual and sits down at the desk.

"Yes, Sir."

He looks at me, "Don't hear that much these days."

"Is that bad?"

"No, no, just a nicety. Okay, let's take it from the top."

Blinking my eyes, sugar high wearing off, the adrenaline rush long gone. Stretching and looking at my watch, it's after two in the morning. Strong hard man coming in to the office, flat top haircut, not as tall as my uncle, rock hard.

"This the kid?"

"Sure is, Captain."

Standing up.

"Frank, this is Captain Schmidt. Captain, my nephew, Frank."

Schmidt holds out his hand, strong, strong handshake.

"Good job," giving me a hard look. "Chip off the old block, huh?"

"Jury is still out on that on, but generally non c'e male."

"Fucking A," he smacks me with the back of his hand on the chest. "Looks better than not too bad to me. That prick you took out was handful. He carved up one of my guys last week. You realize how lucky you are?"

"Yes, Sir."

"He's busted up good, broken jaw, broken teeth, vicious cut over his eyes. Looks like you gave him some good shots," he's smiling at my uncle and me. "He could try and come after you for civil damages, but we've got an airtight case on him. Warrant for his arrest for assaulting an officer with a deadly weapon, tons of witnesses tonight, prior counts of assault, prior counts of lewd public behavior, likely blood testing will show heavy presence of PCP."

He's looking at me, his growing serious.

"So, you couldn't sit there and watch."

"No, Sir. I mean, those girls, they were terrified. I..." looking at Captain Schmidt and my uncle, "it wasn't right, no one else was going to do a damn thing... I just couldn't sit there. When he pulled the knife," he's looking straight at me.

"You can say it," said Uncle Vin.

"There was no way he would get through me, no matter the price."

"Good," he looks at me hard and gives me another hard smack in the chest. "You'll make a damn good Marine one of these days. We need more people like you out there."

"That crazy bastard, who knows what he might have done, carve up those girls or what. You did good, Frank," from my uncle.

"Thanks, Uncle Vin," looking at him, haven't seen him smile in a while. "Did the two kids get home okay?"

"Yup and speaking of that, time to get your ass home. Your aunt is worried about you."

Policemen patting me on the back as we walk back out of the station, guys trading barbs with my uncle, other guys asking me to take the subway more often.

Breathing in the cool air.

Feels good being out in the night.

Chapter 32

Nervous energy—can't stop fidgeting. Hands feel cold, clammy.

"All rise for the Honorable Judge Heiman," called a uniformed bailiff.

Standing up in the small courtroom. A small, well-groomed man comes in wearing a black robe, his sharp eyes looking across the room and then sitting down.

"You may be seated."

Sitting down next to my uncle—tucking my tie into my jacket. Still uncomfortable wearing a suit, shirt neck feels a size too small.

"Good morning," the judge clears his throat. "Who is representing the minor?"

"I am, Your Honor. Vincent Caruso, the boy's uncle."

"You have not retained counsel?"

"No, Your Honor, not at this time."

The judge nods and reads through the paper.

"Is the State complete with its preparation?"

"Yes, Your Honor," said a thin man in a grey suit at the table to our right.

The judge spends time looking through his folder. Taking a deep breath to fight the nerves. Stomach fluttering.

"I've read through the reports, as well as the actions taken by the accused and the immediate parents. I've also spoken to Mrs. Brown at length about this situation and read through the recommendations and concerns from your teachers, principal and coaches."

He looks directly at me.

"Were this an isolated situation, Mr. Caruso, I might be inclined to not move this to trial. Your father has made reparation to Mrs. Brown and her son. We understand that Mr. Alton Brown will not lose his sight and is recuperating well given the quality medical care your father has taken responsibility for."

Relief spreading through my body.

"However," cold chill spreading as he looks down at another set of papers and clears his voice, "I am disturbed by a pattern here that I see emerging. Given the nature of the other confrontations you've had with schoolmates, the difficulties you exhibit with authority figures at home and school and the consistent admonitions from your principal, as well as your recent stay with the City, even with the extenuating circumstances, which I understand we are investigating, isn't that right Mr. Battaglio?" to the man in the gray suit.

"Yes, Your Honor."

"I am concerned that unless you take significant measures to change your behavior and channel your intelligence and energy in a more productive way, we will be seeing you before us for a graver situation. As such, I am unwilling to outright dismiss this matter."

"What do you have to say for yourself, Mr. Caruso?"

Uncle Vin nudges me to stand up. Sinking feeling inside—the weekend with Cat. Relationship starting to thaw with my uncle, it was too good to be true.

"Your Honor. I know how I handled things was wrong. I couldn't see the impact of my behavior to my parents and people that cared about me. I didn't understand the price that other people would have to pay for what I did. I let a lot of people down and almost cost my friend his eyesight for life. My actions were selfish and I was wrong. I am thankful that Alton will recover, I have a high price to pay for my action and I don't know how to repay my debt to his family and my family. What I did was wrong and I bear the full responsibility for my poor choices, Your Honor."

His eyes on me for a few moments.

"That sentiment does you well," the judge looks at me and takes a slow breath. "Were you to decide to serve your country in some manner where you have the opportunity to mature, I think the court would gladly see fit to dismiss this matter. Otherwise I will move this to trial. You might look at this as a big step off the road you were on, which unfortunately your actions proceeded to close. You also might look at this as an opportunity to learn from your mistakes and become skilled at thinking about others and developing into a man that other people can trust and respect. In the long run, that might turn out to be more important," he looks directly at me, "that is my decision in this matter. Does either side have any questions? No?"

He looks at us all.

"Then this hearing is complete," he slowly gathers his materials and stands. "Any changes to the current situation must be submitted to me within thirty days or I will move this to trial."

"All rise," from the stiff bailiff.

Standing up, my head swimming. No jail! Well not unless I join the service—Peace Corps, military, what else is there? Free! Sinking feeling, what's this going to do to Cat? Stomach sour—remembering Alton's face when I saw him in the hospital, nodding to myself, knowing that this is square on me.

Got to pay the price.

As the judge walks out, he takes a circuitous route near my uncle.

"Nice to see you, Lieutenant."

"Good to see you too, Your Honor."

Chapter 33

Driving back to Brooklyn. Sitting uncomfortably in a new future.

"What'cha thinking about, kid?"

"Geez, Uncle Vin, I don't know, I thought this was likely to turn out that I do time with a slight chance of getting off. The service. Wow, I mean I never thought about it for real. I mean I've read and heard from you and all, but…"

"Could be a good thing for you."

"But it puts so much on hold."

"No shit, and oh and all the kids serving their country? You deserve better?"

"No, wait," I can see his face taking on that disgusted cast, "it's just so unexpected. How long do you think I'd have to be away?"

"Three to four, kiddo."

"Oh," heart sinking.

"And who put you here?"

"I did, Uncle Vin."

"For my money, you getting off might have been the worst that could have happened. I know you think you know how much you messed up and I believe what you said to the judge. I see all kinds of people in my world. Frank, you got a lot to learn about yourself. Bumping around in high school and college, in my opinion, won't stretch you hard enough, you'd a breezed through." Driving in silence for a few minutes.

"Look, I seen you since you were a little kid. You've been this bigger than life thing that your father was so proud of. He didn't think you respected your gifts, respected others. You got real good at looking at the world from your perspective, not that you don't care about others. You do care, I seen it. It's just that a lot of what people deal with is invisible to you cause you think you can figure it all out. It's the curse of the extremely talented or strong… They think everyone is like them."

"You got something to think about, Frank. You saw yourself, how you acted on the subway. You told me how you acted when those guys were hunting you. I seen this in you too and you need to think about it. What if your friend Alton hadn't taken you out? You and I both know you would have killed that Leroy kid. Right? And don't bullshit me, I know you. That fellow Jorge on the train, I talked to him, he told me he was scared when he saw the change in you when the guy had the knife, you wasn't gonna stop. You gotta take control of that part of you, learn when to switch it on and switch it off. You don't, a guy like me is gonna put you away for a long time."

He takes a deep breath.

"People that care about you don't want to see that," feeling his intense look. "YOU UNNERSTAND!" he yells across the car and smacks the dashboard with his fist.

Cold feeling moving up my spine, feeling a little dizzy, most my uncle's talked to me in my whole life. How does he know all this?

Sitting there looking down at my hands.

"Yes, Uncle Vin, I understand."

"I love you like a son, Frankie, and I have a different view than my brother cause of what I've seen and done. I've seen the evil that men do in war and in life. I seen the good that men do in war and life, the sorrow, cowardice, sacrifice, honor, bravery and death. I've seen good people die cause they were unlucky, I seen evil people get away with things that shouldn't be. I seen what fear, outrage, jealousy, greed can do. I've seen what happens when good kids, smart kids turn bad. What you got made you good in the ring... Out here you got to learn to handle yourself. You're like a drawn sword."

He's quiet as we drive.

"Part of me is sorry that you have to go this way, that you have to go the hard way. Kitty told me about your girlfriend and all that. This is going to be tough. I think in ten years you'll look back at this and, if you get a clue and make every minute of your life count, you'll see this as a turning point for things you never could have imagined. They may not be the things that Madison Avenue tells us are important, but hard men, men who are warriors will look at you and recognize you for the man you are."

He stretches for a moment.

"Don't kid yourself, you kids see these stupid movies, read these asinine books, warriors can be priests, doctors, teachers... Don't need to carry a gun to serve and make the world a better place. It takes commitment and it takes skill and years of discipline. You got the capability to be a good man, Frank, you take the step to make this meaningful and I'll be with you every step of the way. You try and shirk your responsibility, well then..." he's quiet driving, radio chatter on in the background as we drive over the Williamsburg Bridge, "well then, that's where I get off."

Looking back at the skyline of Manhattan falling away.

"The people that stick with you now are the real people. The people that are here for some other notion, well, they'll fall away. This is a catalyst for what's coming, a quickening. You unnerstand?"

Breathing in deeply. Letting my breath out slowly.

Things sinking in, "My friends will be getting out of college before I'm even starting. I'll be four years behind, plus I won't even have finished high school," what fucking top tier school is going to look at me after this? Forget about a top basketball program. I'll be second rate, a loser. Awful feeling descending over me.

"Could be that, could be something else, you don't know."

"Could be better to do the time, at least I'd only be a year or so behind."

"Yup, that might give you a different perspective on life. You'll have a criminal record, but you'll lose less time."

"Uncle Vin, can we just drive around? This is really heavy."

"Heavy, huh?" he winds his way down from the bridge, "I got a better idea."

Close to home he turns onto Flushing Ave. Stopping in front of the Sportsman Bar. "Come on," as he gets out of the car.

Looking down at my hands for a moment, wishing I could just shrink down to something small and stay hidden for a while. Stepping out into the cool night, another weird day with my uncle.

Stepping into the dark, stale smell of beer and cigarettes hitting me. A couple of guys in the bar greeting my uncle, he waves me over to a booth. Checking out the walls—a mixture of sports trivia, Dodgers, Giants, Yankees and Mets. A mish-mash of old signed photos, bats, balls, dust, bad lighting and depressed people hanging around.

"Here's a Coke," he slides a glass toward me and sits down with what looks like a scotch with a couple of ice cubes in it and a bottle of Miller beer. Big band music playing, TV with the vertical sync going out every few minutes at the bar, old, tired people watching the TV, talking to each other now and then.

Flat, tastes different than Coke in a bottle or can. More like syrup.

"You might feel sorry for yourself for a while," he takes a drink.

"It's just… I mean, I figured I could work hard and get back on track you know," shaking my head "man oh man, four years."

"Look, genius," his hands cutting through the air like he's chopping down a tree. "One of my guys had a kid who fiddle fucked around in high school, dropped out, worked as a carpenter for a few years and then got his GED. That kid went to CCNY, kicked ass there and then got an advanced degree from MIT, so don't fucking tell me you're off the track. You might have to work harder than you would have before, it might take some more time and the only place to put the blame is right there," pointing at my chest.

Nodding at him, but not really listening—rubbing my face with my hands.

"You're right."

"Fucking A I'm right!" he takes a drink and looks around the bar.

"Well, you could do Peace Corps for two years or so. I think there are deals where you can do three years active service and then three years active reserve. Plus, I think there's still a program for people who serve active duty to get money toward college when they get out."

"I've thought about being in the Army, but that's been, you know, cause of a war or something." He looks at his drink. I've seen that look—like he's talking to a moron.

"If, and I hope it never does, a war broke out tomorrow, who are the guys who are going to be on the front line taking the hit while guys like you get trained up and ready? Look what happened last time. Draft a bunch of lower class kids, train them for a few months and stick them in the jungle and get 'em shot to shit," he swears under his breath. "Not that I don't think we shouldn't have beaten those commie fucks, but we fought that war like a bunch of damn idiots. Made a hash of so many things in our country and in our military. A lot of guys serving in blue now were overseas in the Army or Marines, some of the shit they talk about..."

"Frank, the stuff you seen on TV is bullshit," he looks at me. "From what I hear, the Army today is not the Army I served in. Looking at me funny, huh? Different time, different culture... When I wore my uniform, there was respect. Today you walk around in military uniform and a lot of people think you're a loser, a thug. That's it, isn't it? Torn by what your friends say and what your dad, Uncle Michael and I have talked about?"

"It's," looking at the TV for a moment, "I don't know. Like people think it's cool to laugh and make fun of the military as just a bunch of stooges running around with guns. I don't think like this Uncle Vin, but I hear... Like it's the older generations that got us into this mess and wants to keep bumbling along. They laugh when you talk about patriotism or what a huge leap forward this country was. The things we have now."

"Got to be honest, that makes my blood boil. Everyone now is too special, has too much to live for to sacrifice anything."

"Sometimes I..."

"What's that, Frank?"

"Sometimes I just hate people, Uncle Vin. I want to hurt them... So smug, thinking cause they've got some expensive suit or a nice car they are safe. Fat, lazy, living off the work of others."

He laughs. "I can understand part of that, it's the hurt part you need to mediate. Look, people can piss you off all you want, but you gotta learn to choose where you spend your time, kiddo. Each moment you spend hating, angry, thinking about how you want to hurt the world is wasted time. Think about what you want out of life and learn to let the assholes roll off like water off a duck's back. Spend your time getting what you want instead of being pissed off at what you don't have."

He takes a drink and looks at me for a few moments.

"You know why I'm so good at what I do, kid?"

Shaking my head.

"I pay attention," he laughs, takes another drink. "Everybody thinks differently, I sit back and try to put together what makes them tick, how they think, what's important to them. We all swim in the same soup, but people are pulled by competing thoughts, ideas. In our family, we've always talked about service to our country, standing up for democracy, standing up against bullies... Maybe different than the kids you go to school with and hang out with. For most people, stuff like this is as you say, it's somebody else's problem. They think, hey, go draft some poor fuck without an education, I'm too smart, too talented, too special."

"I tell you, I have a lot of respect for the guys that dropped out of college to go over and serve in Vietnam. Too bad so many people were put into a tough situation and our leaders weren't committed to winning, they were committed to not losing. Big difference Frank, I see it all the time in the Department."

"But, Uncle Vin... Dad hated the Army."

"Jesus did he ever, but he was the first of us to sign up."

Looking at my uncle, itchy feeling, so much about Dad I don't know. Sitting back and looking at all the photos on the wall.

Uneasy thoughts settling in.

"You got something to say?"

"No, Uncle Vin."

"Bullshit, you want me to trust you, you say what you think."

"What if you don't like it?"

"Well, that's my tough shit then isn't it? My brother and I are different that way. I think it's a waste of time to pussy foot around with important things."

"Did you set this up with the judge?"

He looks at me, his face stone cold. He laughs a little to himself.

"Smart ass. No, I could have gotten you off, but like I said, I think that's the worst thing for you. Judge Heiman is a good man, a good judge. I personally think he made the right call."

"Am I that much of an asshole?"

He laughs.

"Fucking Frankie, you're pretty thick sometimes you know," he rolls his eyes. "Look, come here," and I lean into the table. "You've already done things and seen things that few kids your age has seen or done. You've been out with men in the open ocean spear fishing since you were a little kid, hunting and getting damn good for your age, you won your division in Golden Gloves... Like it or not, you've not led an ordinary life and now you're pissed that you're not going to go do the same old shit that everybody else does. Jesus Christ, Frank! Go fucking explore the Amazon or go walk across the country! My God, do something stupendous and, don't live a mediocre life. You've made some outstanding fuck ups, now go out and do some outstanding things in life."

He's watching me.

"Yes, there are kids that will go onto good schools, Ivy League whatever. Are you smarter than most? Probably. Your principal is pissed at you because he thinks you're in that top 1% and you don't give a shit," he looks at me, "not that you don't give a shit and not that I blame you, but hey, who'd want to be some fucking walking brain with no balls swinging between your legs like that fart jockey?"

Laughing with Uncle Vin.

"Your father and I disagree on this, he wants you to be successful like people think successful is. He didn't want you to stray from the best high school, best athlete, best college and best job track. He wanted what he wanted for himself, for you. I think the fear got him."

"Me, I think it's what's inside the man that makes them a man. What he's able to do when the shit hits the fan. You can't lie about what you can do. Right? You get to the foul line, you can either make it or not. You hit ten out of ten, you're a good shooter right? You miss five out of ten you're mediocre. I mean, I see assholes all the time that puff up the things they've done, but in my world, those guys get found out quickly. Life won't let them hide. Isn't that why you stay after practice and take hundreds of practice shots, foul shots, work your moves? You hate mediocrity, Frank."

He takes a sip of scotch.

"Isn't that some a what you and my brother fight about?"

Sitting back, like another crystal particle was dropped into a solution and a shape begins to form out of the cloud, forms coming from nothingness. Looking into his deep dark eyes, nodding.

"It is," then shaking my head.

"In my opinion, you need to be out in the world exploring, learning, doing things, kid. Sure you could figure out a nine to five gig at some point, I think you'd slowly kill yourself. I think you'd waste a great talent, exactly for what, I have no idea," rolling his eyes. Laughing with him, sipping my soda. Slurping sound as the last of the liquid is pulled up through my straw.

Chapter 34

"You getting hungry?"

"Sure am."

"Let me call Kitty, tell her we'll be going out."

He gets up and walks off toward the bathrooms.

Watching people in the bar for a few moments, strange vibe here. Like time was left at the door. Staring into their drinks or out into space, random comments spoken here or there. Awful place.

"Let's go," looking at my uncle.

Following him out the door, the bartender waving as we leave.

"Uncle Vin, why do you go there? It's like a morgue."

"Quiet, out of the way." He gets in his car, sitting down into the familiar smell. "Sometimes after this shit I deal with, it's good to go cool down."

Pulling out into early evening traffic, squad radio chatter disappearing in the lights and movement of the city. People in cars looking at me and then look away.

Short drive to McManus Bar and Grill.

"They have a good Corn Beef and Cabbage here."

Policemen all over the place, "Watch out for the badge bunnies in here," he smacks me on the shoulder.

"What?" scanning across the women in the bar—young and middle aged women trying to look young, more than a few in business dress.

"Most of these chicks are looking for a good time with cops."

"No!"

He shrugs his shoulders and rolls his eyes.

Taking a booth by the back, he waves a waiter over.

"Hey, Lieutenant, how are ya?" middle-aged man with a comb over coming to the table, big smile on his face.

"I'm good, Freddy, how's the family?"

"Real good, what can I do you for, Lieutenant?"

"Couple of specials, Cutty on the rocks, Coke for the kid."

"Coming riiiight up," he wanders off, stops by the back and starts yelling into the kitchen. Looking around at the place, must be sixties rock and roll from juke box, pool tables, darts, walls filled with beer advertisements, pictures of what must be Ireland.

"Fucking Italians in an Irish bar," a big voice comes up from behind me, "someone ought to call the cops."

"Sit your butt down, Schmitty."

"That anyway to talk to your boss?" he sits down looking at me like I should help, then Uncle Vin looks like he needs to think about that for a second, "Yup." Captain Schmidt comes over, looks like he's pissed for a second, then they both start laughing.

"How's the criminal as a young man here?"

Face flushing, no way my uncle's talked to these guys about me.

"Judge Heiman gave him an out," and then looking at me. "That's if he's smart enough to take it."

"Service?"

"Yup."

Schmidt gives me a hard look—gray blue eyes, grizzled grey hair.

"What'd the genius think about that?"

"Typical."

"Whining about how unfair things are," Uncle Vin laughing as he goes into a high whiney voice, "Oh why me, why can't I keep playing with my tiny pecker in the shower in the morning imagining what it must be like to have a pair? Why can't I have all my little shiny things?"

"Pretty much," they both look at me. Stone faces looking at me.

"Can someone shoot me now? I don't know how much more of this bull... baloney I can handle." They start chuckling.

"Ah if we didn't love you, we wouldn't rib you kid," says Schmidt.

"Yeah, like they say, I can feel the love."

"I got your love right here," and Schmidt grabs his crotch under the table. Freddy hovering.

"Bushmills straight up, water on the side."

"You've got it, Captain."

"Fucking sycophant," as Freddy wanders away.

Uncle Vin chuckling, "He knows you need it, Schmitty," and my uncle imitates someone bowing.

"Yeah, well fuck you too," he's laughing, looking at me now.

"So what'cha gonna do, kid?"

Tongue tied, "I don't know sir, I hadn't thought much... I really don't know," thoughts streaking through—childhood games in the park, Dad and Uncle's admonitions on guns and gun safety, the first time my uncle let me fire a revolver—the weight, the explosion, the recoil, some of the stories Dad told me about the war and life in the Army.

Schmidt gives a silent, derisive snort. Freddy puts his drink down and backs off as Schmidt ignores him.

"Well, let me tell you something, kid, there's only one service that's worth a shit and that's the Marine Corps. God's gift to this planet is the Marine. You know what Semper Fi means, kid?'

"No, Sir."

"Well there's the simple Latin for always faithful, but it means hell of a lot more than that, it's always faithful to a brotherhood, a warrior culture, a tradition of excellence, of service to our great country that goes back to the revolutionary war," intense look from Schmidt. "Honor, bravery under the most trying conditions, commitment to make the ultimate sacrifice in the name of our freedom. That's some of what it's about. Civilians have no concept of what it means to belong to that brotherhood, no concept of what people like us have done for this country. You can't read about it, you can't listen to someone else talk about, you have to DO IT, you have to LIVE IT!"

He takes a drink, smacks his lips in enjoyment.

"Best thing for you, kid, get to see a slice of life most people will only know second or third hand, get to learn things about yourself you'll never get anywhere else. The depth of human strength and character is fucking beyond what most people understand. Courage, cowardice, sacrifice, leadership... How will you act when your team needs you and you might have to make the ultimate sacrifice and you're alone? You're wet, you're tired, you could likely die and no one will ever know. How will you act? Will you be like Leonidas and face down thousands of enemy warriors with a few hundred because it is your honor, your duty to lead, to set the uncompromising standard of not yielding in the face of the enemy?"

Body resonating with the passion in his words, looking at my uncle, he's uncharacteristically quiet nursing his drink.

"I guess the second best for form of life is the Army Ranger, way above that pond scum which passes for the Navy who's real job is to pick up and drop off Marines," Schmidt taking a dig at my uncle who rolls his eyes.

"Another word of wisdom from the high diddle-diddle, straight up the middle and eat machine gun bullets for breakfast Marines," he looks at me. "Now you want to talk toughness and brains, you need to think about going Ranger."

"Oh, now it's coming out thick," says Schmidt, "I guess the weaker sex needs to hear about you panty waist fucking dog faces, blah, blah, blah, this is how great we are compared to Marines," they start laughing.

"We should get the kid in touch with Williams and Hermosa, they'd be good for him to talk to," said Schmidt to Uncle Vin, "that crazy fucker Kelly too."

"Good idea, I'll set it up," Uncle Vin nodding.

"Kelly was a Lurrrp, did two tours in Nam, Hermosa was in the 3rd Marine Division, served in Korea and Nam as a sniper, cold blooded killer. Williams was a pilot."

Uncle Vin nodding, "There are a bunch of other guys too."

Taking a sip of my coke, Schmidt looks at my uncle, "Think we should let the panty waist have beer?"

"I guess if he can't handle it, we can always shoot him," says Uncle Vin. Schmidt whacks him on the arm with the back of his hand.

"Probably do him good, or from what I hear, it might just piss him off."

He waves Freddy over, "Draught, not too much foam."

"What's a Lurrrp?" trying to keep up.

"Long Range Recon Patrol, these were the guys that were way out in the deep jungle doing reconnaissance work, ambush operations and the like all on their own. They lived or died by their ability to be good in the woods," then to my uncle. "You know, if, Andrews didn't drink so damn much, he'd be good to yak with too." Schmidt looks at me, "Navy Seal, damn good man," and then to my uncle, "with all the diving you crazy wops do, going Seal or UDT might be a good choice, but then he'd have to be a fucking squid."

"Squid?"

"Large animal which lives off Marine life," and he starts chuckling.

"Yeah, let's wait on Andrews, he's been hit or miss lately."

Looking around at the people in the bar, Righteous Brothers song coming on. Lady at the bar checking me out, looking away, Uncle laughing at me.

"Yeah 'ol Brenda there will eat him alive," and Schmidt smacks my uncle on the shoulder with the back of his hand.

"Captain Schmidt," catching his eye. "When did you join the Marines? What did you do?"

"Oh my sweet Jesus H. Christ, here goes the fucking evening" my uncle smacking Schmidt back on the arm and rolling his eyes. "Wait, wait while I roll my pants up cause it's gonna get awfully deep here."

"Is this the respect I deserve? Fucking treacherous Italians, e tu Brute and all that bullshit."

"Only the best for you, Boss."

Freddy waiting with three plates of food.

"Put them down, man!" yelled Schmidt, "and bring that fucking beer!" Freddy almost drops one plate. "Dipshit," says Schmidt under his breath.

Schmidt and Uncle Vin dig into the big plates of corned beef and steamed cabbage. At least they have some good strong mustard here—cranking open the top and putting a big dollop on my plate.

"Why the Marines?" he looks at me. "Well, first cause I'm a romantic son of a bitch, foreign shores, being with the toughest outfit, especially being such a goddamn good looking and virile man." Uncle Vin rolling his eyes. "Hey, there wasn't much choice," he smiles at me, "you believe that?"

"About half," smiling at him as Freddy puts the beer down in front of him. He motions for me to slide over toward the wall, and pushes the beer over. Cool suds going down feels good.

"About half too much!" from Uncle Vin.

"You know, I may have to shoot both of you, rid the world of two more smart ass wops," he takes another big bite of corned beef and finishes his drink, points to his glass and Freddy scurries to the bar.

"1930's in Pittsburgh," he stops for a second, "you probably hear this from lots of old farts like us, but you have no clue how fucked up things were back then. It's unfortunate that history has such a short life expectancy on the young."

"What do you mean by that, Sir?"

"Call me Schmitty when we're in a social situations, around the stations it's Captain. You savvy?"

"Yes, Sir."

"Good."

"You can go read about it, watch movies about it, but you have no idea what it was like to have shit for opportunities. Living at a time where no matter how hard you worked, what you did might not make any difference. Today your generation can't understand that. You've been born into a much richer world, not that we don't have a shit load of problems, but you immediately think the natural progression of things as college and careers, then cars, houses, clothes, all kinds of crapola. Or at least where you can, with hard work, make a good life for your family."

The next round of drinks shows up. Freddy looks suspicious at the beer and me. "Fuck off, Freddy," says Schmidt waving him away.

"My family were steelworkers, God bless them. Many are still at it. All through high school we suffered and struggled to make ends meet, parents wouldn't let me quit school to find work." He's quiet for a second, like he's looking at something inside his head. "Damn they were tough," he looks at me. "Well there needed to be one less mouth to feed and I needed to get money home, so I enlisted. Worked my ass off to be the best damn Marine I could be... Boy there were some crazy sons of bitches in there," smile cracks on his strong face. "Went to night school, made selection for officers training and when the bombs fell on Pearl, I was a 1st Lieutenant leading a rifle squad. Damn they were good men, they had their shit squared away."

He stops for a second.

"We were one of the first elements landing on Guadalcanal, and we were there for some fucking pay-back!" he's quiet for a second, about to ask him a question when I see Uncle Vin moving his hand for me to be quiet and wait. "Jesus, that was tough," he looks at me hard. "When you've trained with men, you know their strengths, you've kicked their asses, led them and learned to love them," he takes a deep breath, "and when you need to send them into a situation where most will die... well that's the toughest thing I've ever done. But there was a job to get done or more will die..."

"No place for candy-asses, we had to go up and into hell's teeth and we did. We advanced; we moved; we overcame! They were tough bastards, but we kicked some Japanese ass. Had to live off the land and what we could scrounge up cause our supply was so fucked up. Battlefield promotions and I was running what was left of a rifle company. At the end, we were so shot to shit we were rotated out to train and rebuild, missed Tarawa and were in the second wave at Pelileu."

He takes a long drink of water,

"My God that was a brutal battle, we paid a hell of price, but we goddamn won!" he slams his hand on the table. "My men had to endure weeks in mud with rotting Jap bodies strewn around, constant night attacks, vicious hand-to-hand fighting. Hell, one guy killed a Jap who stabbed him with a bayonet in the gut by driving his thumb into his brain through the bastard's eye socket. That tough son-of-a-bitch died of infection."

He takes another drink. "Savage fighting for every inch. Some guys went kill crazy, some broke under the strain. You saw the full range of human nature. Stupid bastard..." he's looking inside his head again. "Saw a marine prying out a gold tooth from a Jap that was still half alive," he looks at me with a hard piercing stare, the look of a killer. "I shot that damn Jap in the head with my pistol and gave that idiot an ass chewing. Get out of here, go kill the bastards that are still out there fighting you dumb son of a bitch!" his voice heating up, people in the bar staring. He looks back at us like he just came back.

"Few medical supplies, exhaustion, little food," his voice calmer now, he shakes his head. "How men could go through that... And I tell you we hated those bastards. Brought a real meanness out of us, some of the things they'd do to boys they captured or ambushed. Barbaric. They didn't take prisoners."

He takes a deep breath, noticing I'm not breathing either.

"But there was no turning back, it was win or die for all of us."

"Nothing incremental about it," said Uncle Vin.

"Absolutely fucking not, we went in to kill, to win. It makes me sick to my stomach to think people go into war to pussy foot around and don't go all out to win. Sherman understood this. If life is precious, then you do everything in your power to waste as little of it as possible. You want to win, you go all out—you fucking destroy the enemy," his voice raising, people in the bar looking over again. "Tell that all those fucking anti-war pussies who can't let go of their tiny little dicks long enough to think about anything other than jerking themselves off with their thumb and index finger." Intense look from him, "They think you're a fucking monster when you say that getting the damn thing over as fast as you can is the only way to go to war." He shrugs his shoulders and moves around—sweat beading up on his brow.

"Like any of those pieces of shit would have had the balls to get up and take out that pervert on the train the other day like you did. Oh," and he starts talking like some hippy asshole, "you're a bad man, you need to stop invading that persons space, you need to respect them. Stop," and he slaps in the air, "Stop."

Uncle Vin laughing, "You know, Schmitty, you do that almost too well."

"Go pound sand," he looks at me. "Shot twice, lost a kidney, still carry a load of shrapnel around in this body, but goddamn I can say I lived. I've seen worse things than you can imagine, I've seen actions on the battlefield that still bring tears to my eyes. You'll never get that in a classroom or a book."

He takes a drink.

"The problem with doing it is that there's no instant replay, no do over. You might be killed, maimed or blinded. War is horrible, it is horror and anybody who says different is a fucking liar. To me the question is, when the next one happens, who is going to be ready to stand up and say No! Where will the men be who know what a sacrifice it is to leave their loved ones, their homes and take up steel and stand together. Is it someone else? Some poor fuck that can barely read or joined up cause they can't do anything else? Some of those kids will be okay, most will continue to be fuck ups."

Uncle Vin nodding.

"From what I hear, the entrance standards are constantly being lowered, my beloved Corps still has the highest standards for entry thank you. But what about you, is this someone else's job? Why shouldn't the be best and brightest spend time raising the bar in all parts of our service?"

He laughs to himself and leans into the table.

"Fucking peaceniks tell me about Gandhi and look at what he did," his eyes glare again, "I tell you what he did only worked because the Brits had that school boy morality beaten into them about how precious life is. If the Japanese had conquered India and Gandhi had tried the peaceful demonstration crap, standing in front of trains and the like, the Japs would have massacred them without mercy just like they did in China and the Philippines. Bastards, and now I'm supposed to buy a fucking Sony radio. Kiss my ass!" Uncle Vin laughing along with him.

"Well anyway, enough of the sermon," he looks at me. "I'm not saying it's your job to right all the world wrongs or nothing. Just something for you to ponder, kid. Hell, you may be better off doing something else. It's not for everyone, that's for sure."

He's looking at me.

"He's got the look though," looks at my uncle and then back at me. Uncle Vin nodding. Finishing my beer, head swimming more from what he said.

"Hey, Vinny, got to get going. I like him, let me know what I can do to help," he slips on his jacket, "O'Reilly and Melrose going to be ready for the DA tomorrow?"

"You bet your ass, Schmitty, and we got Inspector Gillette at 11:00 right?" Schmidt nods, "Hey you better get your ass home. We know if push comes to shove who the baddest Marine in Bensonhurst is!"

"Oh, don't we ever" and he rolls his eyes and turns to leave.

"Captain Schmidt," he turns, "thank you, thank you, Sir."

He gives me a wink and tussles my hair. Off duty cops either drawn to him or staying away from him as he heads toward the door. Uncle Vin looking at me. The noise of the place filtering back in—people talking, arguing, laughing—balls on the pools tables banging together on a break, Country Western music playing on the jukebox.

"You got some good stuff to think about there, don't cha?"

Nodding to my uncle, head swimming.

"I want you to think about something else," he stretches for a second.

"What the Captain told you is important. If you get to spend more time and he's in the mood, you'll hear stories that make your blood curdle. It's amazing how tough and how much him and his men went through on those island battles."

Not knowing where he's going on this. Eating, body craving food.

"I tell you, there's another side to all this," he stretches and plays with the last of his food. "The military or come to think of it, any large organization, geez, I deal with it almost every day," he looks right at me. "You'll meet some of the thickest, stupidest, laziest people on the planet and unfortunately sometimes you'll be working for a complete fucking idiot that got where they are cause they were riding someone's coat tails and got lucky. I seen it in Sicily, in Normandy, fuck," he looks around the room agitated, "fucking glory hounds from West Point... Well anyway," he moves to loosen his tie, grimace on this face, "people serve for all reasons kid. Family history, honor, patriotism, adventure, for some it's the only opportunity available and on and on. There are all the slogans, the posters and the uniform to make it important. Remember, all the mix of idiots and fuck-wad bureaucrats you see out here exist, and may even flourish, in the military. That's why your father hated it so much. He couldn't tolerate lazy, stupid people."

Laughing as he says that.

"How'd you..."

"Let's go," as he counts out some bills, waves Freddy over.

Lady at the bar giving me the once over again as Freddy gushes over the tip.

"Uncle Vin," as we walk outside into the cool evening, policemen coming nodding to my uncle, saying hi.

"What's up?"

"I just," throat choking up as I try to get it out.

Getting into his car.

"Hmm?" as he starts up the car. He looks over at me as the big hemi engine roars to life.

"I wanted to thank you, I mean, I still don't know how to talk about it," his big head still, "this... I don't know. I feel like you and Aunt Kitty believe in me, you're giving me a chance." Dammit, my eyes are watering up. "It's nice to have someone on my side," balling up my fists, breathing to try and keep some semblance of cool.

He smiles, "You have one beer and you're getting all sentimental on me, huh?" Laughing with him, "Oh man," wiping my face with my hand. "With all due respect, Uncle Vin, kiss my grits."

He's laughing hard now.

"Hey," he reaches over, a little unsure. He tussles my hair, "You're a good kid, Frankie. You had us worried for a while, but I think you'll get through this and be a better man for it. I'm on your side. I'm tough on you cause I

277

think you need to start looking at life and thinking as a man," he holds up his thumb and forefinger close together, "just don't forget this, you were this close to manslaughter when your friend Alton put you out."

Shiver going through my body, shame spreading through my chest at how I treated Alton.

"Frank, people don't make up Judge Heiman's mind. I was honest about what I saw in you and made sure all the data got in the reports. You have to learn to control the situations you are in, you can whine all you want about how unfair it is the Leroy kid got your goat and three of them kicked your ass. You need to own up to what you did to be in that situation."

Thoughts boiling and jumping around in my brain competing for my attention—chorus of it's not fair matched by the remembrance of the feeling in my gut that I ignored and couldn't get over, the indignity, the false pride.

"And, thanks for saying what you said. Your aunt and I love you. We want to see you grow up to be the man that you can be. Gonna be tough, but you can do it, Frank. Reach for excellence, put that competitive side of yours, that stubborn side of yours to good use versus listening to your pride. Capice?"

Chapter 35

Driving back to their neighborhood.

Mind bombarded with the stories Captain Schmidt told me.

"So how'd you do it, Uncle Vin? Deal with all the things you said made your brother crazy? You went up the cliffs at Omaha. That was tough too, right?" He chortles to himself. Driving on.

"Easy there, kid," he stretches out in his seat for a second, "my brother John's got a short fuse, always looking at things and seeing what he can make out of them. You ever seen some of the early drawings and paintings he did? Who do you think does all the designs and sketches for his shop?"

Shocked—how could that hateful man be any semblance of an artist? Shaking my head, this doesn't make any sense.

"You don't know shit, do you? Well anyway, things there made him crazy and he went out and made other people crazy... sound familiar?" he gives me the hairy eyeball.

"I'm a different kind of man, your dad likes to go out in the forest and hike around, think about things, hunt—maybe make a kill. I go out, I'm going out to kill. In the service, I got away with so much... It used to drive him crazy when we'd talk." Uncle Vin's quiet for a moment.

"You know, I made sure I was the best at everything I did. Whatever the standard was, I figured out what I needed to do to meet and exceed it," he smiles at me for a second. "When you're the best and you've got your shit squared away, when you jump in and lead, you know, be the guy that's helping the sergeant or officer in charge get their mission done," he chortles to himself, "they fucking need you and you can get away with things that other guys can't. You get that?" he pushes me. "You got to make yourself so valuable to the command chain, they'll do everything they can to promote and take care of you. That doesn't mean brown nosing. I mean you get shit done! You kick ass and make the big boys look good. Then you're golden, you make the rules."

Chuckling with him as we pull up to the house.

"That works in the NYPD too?" looking at him out of the side of my eyes.

"Fuck you, Wise Ass," as he opens the front door smiling at me and cracking up as I start laughing. We're both laughing as we walk in the house.

"It's nice to see you smiling, Frankie. What's so funny you two?" putting her hands on her hips.

"Uncle Vin told me to..."

"Hey, watch your mouth," he acts like he's going to pull out his revolver.

"Oh, he told you to fuck off."

"Kitty!" he looks slightly annoyed and she shrugs her shoulders.

"You guys want a late night snack?"

"Sure do," still hungry.

279

"Well, go wash up and come in the kitchen. I've got some nice fresh Mozzarella, some nice Ricotta Salata, good olives and some fresh bread sticks from the market."

Uncle Vin jumping in front of me like he's boxing me out, going for a rebound.

"Too slow! After me, Sucker, ha!"

Quiet sounds of the house, car lights from the street arcing across the unfinished basement ceiling, letting the conversations of the day run through my head. Fighting off the sense of dread growing inside at talking to Cat about this—anticipating the reaction of my guys. Most will probably think it's cool. Shuddering at the images Schmidt talked about—sitting in and around dead rotting corpses, images of movies I'd seen from documentary films on Dachau, Auschwitz, Buchenwald and others—guards shooting hundreds of people at a time, the gas chambers, the images of bodies being put into ovens then the ash and bone being removed at the other end, the live medical experiments on prisoners.

Stories Uncle Vin had told me about how horrible Dachau was—how horrible it smelled, the deep look of going beyond starvation on their faces—emaciated to skin and bone, piles of dead and dying left to rot. How they had to burn down buildings to stop the spread of disease.

Body shivering.

A few moments of dark silence caught up in a web of disquieting thoughts. Could I do it? Could I kill a man in combat?

Could I point a rifle and pull the trigger at someone I don't know, some face? Could I use a bayonet to kill someone in hand-to-hand combat?

Images of my fight with Leroy, Alton and Thomas Jones rearing up—in a fit of rage, I had almost done that, hadn't I?

What about the pier?

Realization I'm asking myself a stupid question.

Is that the evil Mrs. Brown talked about?

Can I be a good man and kill in the name of my country or anything else? What if I'd had to throw that pervert off the moving train or something to stop him? Would I still be good or are you tainted and can never go home? The ending to one of my favorite movies coming to mind, John Ford's *The Searchers*—at the end of the movie, the Ethan character doesn't go into the house with the rest of the characters. He stays outside the house—he can't go back home.

Time ticking away.

Is this a stupid conversation? Look at my uncle. He went to war, he faced hardship came home, my Uncle Michael, my dad…

Basement layout becoming familiar—knowing how to walk around so I don't whack my head on the low hanging pipes on my way to the bathroom.

Lying back down on the narrow bed.

Black and white image of a film shot in World War I that I'd seen running through my head. It was shot in Belgium where the Germans had rounded up civilians in response to a German soldier being killed. They'd shot the film right before the condemned men and women were to be hanged. One man, strong, bearded, enraged, a rope around his neck yelling at the camera, defiant—others were terrified, crying out, looking for some way to stave off the next moment, others apathetic and withdrawn. Then the cart was pulled away—bodies fighting for breath, kicking and writhing, then still.

God, what have we done with thy gifts?

Body tense, cold sweat beading up.

What could have made those men kill civilians like that?

Wave of cold coming in, shutting my eyes to try and escape from the thought—can't run away from it though. What if that same capability for the full range of good and evil is inside of all of us? What if I have the same capability and I can tranquilize myself that I was just following orders? How horrible.

Rolling over on the thin mattress. Letting my mind drift.

Imagining being a Roman soldier—walking forward slowly with sword and shield in a line, advancing toward a hoard of men with long swords and spears, shouting, waving their arms and then charging at us. Just having to walk into that and fight face-to-face. No quarter. Retreat and you and your comrades die. The fear and adrenaline that must have reeked through bodies at first, the ability to get over that and stand and fight.

Drums beating, trumpets calling out signals, Centurions keeping the men at the front line fresh by rotating through with your line. Shields locked, the striking with the shield, cutting with the short sword, taking blows on my armor, the mail and cloth layers underneath taking some of the impact. Sweat running in my eyes, feet slick with sweat, blood. Tired, hot. Standing while men fell around me, standing on wounded and dying. Wounded, tired—I will not fall to defeat.

Need to talk to Uncle Vin. Need to be brave and ask him, ask him about how he was able to stand and fight, face the fear of what it must have been to go up those cliffs at Omaha Beach.

Forcing myself to think about the dive trip coming up next weekend. It will be just the two of us out on the boat—I'll talk to him there.

Blinking my eyes. Tired but not wanting to go to sleep.

Going in and out of light sleep.

Got to talk to Cat tomorrow.

Chapter 36

Rubbing my eyes at the breakfast table.

"When will he be back?" pissed that I didn't get up before Uncle Vin left for work.

"Oh," as Aunt Kitty puts down a plate of scrambled eggs with sautéed mushrooms, green onions, a little spicy Italian sausage, fresh basil and a touch of garlic, my mouth watering at the aroma.

"He's going be very busy the next few days, hopefully he'll still be able to go out to Montauk next weekend. I know he was really looking forward to that."

"Is everything okay?"

"Well," she sits down, "it's not hard to imagine your uncle as a very uncompromising man."

"I can see why people might think that," chewing slowly, savoring the flavor.

"He wants action taken on a couple of dirty cops, and well, he thinks they are dragging their feet to try and not risk embarrassing the department. Unfortunately, it's high enough profile that he said all the big brass are choosing sides... whoever loses," she picks at her food. "Well suffice it to say, I think your uncle will take early retirement if he loses."

"No!" jaw dropping, "how can they let that happen? That makes no sense?"

"He'd like to hear that from you," she smiles. "Sometimes that doesn't matter."

"Fuu... Farmers," looking at her.

She smiles, "I feel that way too. He's such a good man, such a good policeman, tough, smart, dedicated to making life safe and better here... His guys love him and heaven help the guy he finds on the take. He's routed out a lot, just so damn endemic..." she takes a deep breath. "If he goes, there are going to be a lot of happy mafioso."

Shaking my head.

"So that's what Captain Schmidt was talking about last night?"

"What's that?"

"When we left McManus last night, the Captain talked about meeting with the DA. Aunt Kitty, do you know Schmidt?"

She gives a little snort, "Oh yes. He's a character, maybe a little over his head on some things, but your uncle takes good care of him."

"Uncle Vin seems to really like him."

"Yes, he does," she eats a little bit more. "Eat, Frankie, eat before your breakfast gets cold," she says as a little bit of egg falls out of her mouth, she starts laughing.

"What's so funny?"

"Did you know you'd be living with a nice Jewish Italian mother?"

Smiling at her. Mom hardly ever joked around.

"So your uncle told me what happened with the judge. What are you thinking about?"

Using my bread to mop up the last of the egg and juices from the vegetables.

"Geez, I don't know, Aunt Kitty, so much going on in my head, I don't know where to start. I mean," waiting till I finish chewing and swallowing, "the thing that's hitting me hard is..." feeling embarrassed to say it.

"What, Frankie? This will be between me and you, okay?"

Looking at her cockeyed.

"I promise, okay?"

Trying to sort out the monkeys jumping around in my head.

"Part of me is excited to go do service, contribute back to our country but part of me is fighting this cause," taking a shallow breath and looking down at my hands, "well, all my friends are likely going off to college and whatever after. I'll be so far behind them and," my voice going softer, "I'll be so far away from Catherine for three or four years," looking at my aunt. "We had so many ideas of what we could do when we're away from the home, so many plans. That's all gone."

She's looking at me, letting this sink in.

"Can I ask you a personal question, Frank?"

"Uh, okay I guess."

"Is she pregnant?"

Feeling my face flush.

"No!"

"Frank I'm a High School Counselor, I doubt there's anything you could tell me that I haven't seen or heard. Okay?"

"Okay."

"Be careful Frank, this is a time when kids like the can feel backed into a corner and take risks they might not normally take."

Thinking back to Walter's party—shiver running down my spine.

"Okay, Aunt Kitty."

Sitting back, feeling my back slump back against the chair.

She's drumming her fingers on the table.

"Is everything okay?" looking at her.

"I don't want to get..." she looks at her hands, "well," now at me, "to be honest, the idea of you going into the military doesn't thrill me either. It's not that I believe serving our country isn't important," she takes a slow breath and folds her hands. "There are other ways to give back, Frank. Other choices."

Room quiet for a few moments.

"I don't understand, Aunt Kitty?"

She takes sip of her coffee.

"Young men like you going into the military at this age are very impressionable, which is one reason they'd rather have young men versus unwinding years of habits and culture. They get to mold kids like you into what is needed for war."

"Okay, I'm following along, isn't that what they're supposed to do though?"

She nods, "Look I don't want to sound wishy-washy, but there's so little attention to the human cost that you might pay when you are done with the service."

She takes a breath and folds her hands on the table.

"Look Frank, talk to your Uncle Vin, talk to your Uncle Michael, that's important, but talk to other people as well. Our priest at St. Anthony's, Father Fiero, he was an Army Chaplain in World War II, he can give you some different perspectives. The world needs all kinds of people, Frankie."

She looks at me. "What, you looked so sad for a second there?"

Feeling my face flush.

"Oh," breathing to not let my chest get tight, "I wished for a second... you know," looking at her, "when you talked, I wished my mother had fought for me, had tried to talk to me..." my last words coming out softly.

Breathing in to keep it together.

Aunt Kitty looking at me.

"She's a very beautiful woman, Frank. Sometimes the curse of great beauty is people make your life too easy and you don't have to fight. Things get taken care of for you. I've never had that problem," laughing to herself. "Matter of fact, I know your Uncle Michael used to give Vincent a hard time because he had the most plain wife of the three."

"No."

"I overheard the little creep one time when your uncle and I were first dating," she looks like she's reflecting back a long time ago.

"Your uncle and I used to fight like hell too. I think he's different than his two brothers. He's got a bit of the dreamer in him, but he likes putting his hands into the muck and clay of life and forming the things he wants. He's willing to get in and get dirty and I think your father and your Uncle Michael are more inclined to dream big, put out everything they can to get it, but then it's never good enough," she's nodding her head. "Like there's always something just shy of their ideal and that makes it not good enough. Maybe that's why they've made a lot of money, always looking toward the future. The present or the past isn't good enough. Where your uncle seems to have much more respect for his past and family, he wants a good life in the future, but not at the expense of ignoring things that are important to us."

Weird feeling coming over me.

"What, Frank?"

"That's good Aunt Kitty, I got a glimmer of something that's bothered me so much. That's been tearing me apart."

"You want to talk about it?"

"Well," fighting to not clam up, don't be such a big fucking pussy, Frank. "How things went so bad with my father? What changed? I was like, there's something wrong with me, there must be to all of a sudden be not good enough. It made me so mad," stopping before something in my mind. "Like that mean came out in other ways, at school. Uncle Vin talked about not settling for mediocrity, like it drove me crazy that I tried so hard and nothing was good enough."

She's nodding.

"I can understand that. You know, your uncle and I couldn't have children. I lost our first baby and had to have an operation to save my life, which…" tears start well up in her face, "well, it put something we both wanted out of reach. But your uncle was such a strong man, I could see it hurt him, but he's never wavered. Now he puts so much energy into the Children's Hospital and helping out with all kinds of kids programs. Who knows, maybe we'll adopt one of these days. We've fostered a couple of kids… it's so tough given his schedule."

She dries her eyes.

"I understand," nodding, body shivering a little, "he's staying with it, making the situation work out and not getting mad that things aren't good enough and going off to do something else."

She nods, smiles a little. "Sometimes you have to walk away from things that don't work, sometimes you have to stay in and fight. That's a big part of growing up, Frankie. I love your uncle so much for not giving up."

Looking at her, smiling, silence pervading the kitchen.

"Having you here has been nice. For a long time I couldn't understand how your father couldn't be satisfied with having great kids like you and your sister."

Looking at her for a second.

"She hates him you know."

Aunt Kitty nods. I wonder if she knows.

"Your sister has always been different. Most men of his generation think they have to admit that there was something wrong with them to have a kid that really isn't interested in the opposite sex. It's so stupid, to ignore all the wonderful things she is and get all screwy on what she's not. That's not unconditional love. You love someone; you love them! Kids need that like plants need the sun. Not to say they don't need some tough love too now and then…"

"How do you know all this stuff?"

She snorts and laughs a little.

"Frank, besides having studied the clinical side of all this for years and getting my Masters, I work with all kinds of kids from all backgrounds and most importantly," she leans in close, "I really listen to people. What they say, how they hold their bodies, how they say it, what they do."

Brain feels like it's going to burst, too much coming at me to organize.

"Aunt Kitty?"

"What, Frank?"

"I need to digest this... my brain feels like it's overloaded. I mean I don't want to be rude; I need to go run or do something. Okay? I mean..." taking a deep breath, "thank you for talking to me like I'm a grown up."

"Sure, sure," she smiles, "your uncle and I are here for you."

Looking down at my hands.

Words lost in my mind.

Sitting on the concrete stoop.

Basketball courts and playground is empty. Sweat pouring down my face, still breathing hard from my last set of full court suicide sprints. Standing up and stretching. Dribbling a well-worn basketball I'd found in the garage and pumped up. Feels so good moving up and down the court—moving like I'm in a game.

Damn stupid not getting out and playing.

Fast layup, yeah baby, good firm dunk.

Taking a few moments to stretch out.

Standing under the basket—holding the ball at my chest, jump up and touch the rim with the ball—ten times baby. Rest a few then do it again. Legs starting to feel a good muscle burn.

Dribble sprint to the other end of the court for a tomahawk dunk.

Freedom, Yes! Loving the feeling of the steel rim on my forearms.

Another ten times—ball on the rim.

Breathing hard.

Chapter 37

Home after a game with weak players—dipshits thinking they were going to have an easy time running the white boy off the court. The house sounds empty—Aunt Kitty must be out enjoying her day off.

Taking a hot shower in the tiny coffin shower.

Man, I called this home earlier. Stepping out of the coffin—drying off. I have more freedom here than I did back in my parent's place.

It's only been a few weeks—that feels so long ago now.

With both kids out of the house, it must be nice and quiet there like Mom liked it. We were the "out-of-sight out-of-mind" kids. Dress them up nicely for church and social functions. Like living in a fucking museum—the pretty little prison that Dad laid at Mom's feet.

Dressed for cool weather. Checking my watch—plenty of time to eat, get to the library at 42nd and start reading up on the different services and service options before I meet Cat at 4:00 at the Aegean Coffee Shop.

5th Ave. traffic behind me, hotdog and pretzel vendors setting up their stands. Looking at the stone lions and the facade of the public library at 42nd Street. Wonderful building. It must have been so cool to build this place. People walking in and out of the building, people sitting on the steps reading newspapers, books or just hanging around checking people out.

Quiet walk up to the third floor.

Sorting through trays of cards and filling out my book request form. Pity we can't wander the shelves of books they have here—if you are only searching for what you know exists, how will you find anything new?

Taking my time searching for books on statistics in World War II, the Pacific War, then move onto Europe. Maybe I can find a history of my uncle's 5th Ranger Regiment and then what was it, tapping my foot, hmm—29th Infantry and then special assignments with 42nd Infantry to supporting the breakthrough during the Battle of the Bulge?

Waiting in line. People in suits with the business sections of newspapers folded under their arms—must be looking for jobs—ratty student looking types too. Let's see, that would be me. All manner of disheveled people here—probably getting out of the cold morning.

Line moving slowly, ruminating on the things Dad told me he hated about the military—waiting in line was a big one. His theory is that it was all done on purpose to prove to the enlisted man that he was servile. Dad never looked at the math—how many men per second could be served by the mess line. If the number of people waiting is greater than that, you form a queue, how fast the queue is served…

Looking up at a pair of 1950's spectacled eyes.

Handing my request form to the grumpy lady in rubber soled shoes. Hey, where's the fishnet in your hair, Lady?

Annoyed at the number of people up here in the huge Rose Reading Room. Letting the craftsmanship and size of the ornate ceiling filter in and change my mood. Carrying my armload of books to a remote table. Quiet in here—periodically a cough or the sound of one of the heavy carved wooden chairs scratching on the floor rises above the low hum of the background library noise.

Alone at a table in the back. Huddling down by the table light.

Organizing my stack of books by subject—Pacific War Battles, D-Day, Omaha Beach, Concentration Camps. Note pad out. Reading slowly, trying to put faces to the statistics. First Marine Division, what regiment was Captain Schmidt in? Guadalcanal—six months of tough, tough fighting on Guadalcanal—little food, dysentery, fighting off wave after wave of attacks. Over a thousand US dead and almost three thousand wounded Marines—some of the survivors were so weak with fatigue and disease they had to be carried off the island, roughly twenty-five thousand Japanese casualties. My God.

Rubbing my face with my hands. Take roughly two times the number of people in my High School and that's how many Marines died. In my mind trying to look at all the faces in the Gym during a basketball game, and then they are all gone. Seven Japanese killed for every Marine.

Searching for sections on the next battle Schmidt talked about—Peleliu.

Hair rising on the back of my neck—almost one third of the first Marine Division were killed or wounded during the battle. Putting my book down and sitting back in my chair. Looking around the room—one in three people here. Stories of the landings, battles for the fortress on the Point, Bloody Nose Ridge—six days of fighting the 1st Battalion suffered 71% casualties—and they kept fighting. They kept fighting. My God, what men!

Putting my hands behind my head and leaning back.

Becoming aware of the quiet sounds of large reading room. People reading, flipping pages, coughing here and there.

What would have happened if we'd lost to the Japanese? Could they have invaded? Probably not enough of them to take over the US, but what if they'd gotten to Australia, India—the resources they would have controlled. After what those fuckers did in China.

Becoming aware of two other people sitting at my table.

Back to reading.

Iwo Jima, seventy thousand Marines attacking twenty seven thousand entrenched Japanese soldiers. Different tactics from the Japanese—dig in, no suicide counter attacks. Over six thousand Marines killed and over nineteen thousand wounded. Twenty thousand Japanese soldiers killed. Shaking my head. Write it down, Frank. Write it down so you don't forget. Okinawa, the Army and Marines had over twelve thousand killed and over thirty thousand wounded. The Japanese Army lost over one hundred thousand soldiers. Squirming in my chair reading through accounts of how flame throwers were deployed to attack Japanese bunkers. They wouldn't surrender. They wouldn't surrender. Reflecting on one story of how a group of men held grenades to their stomachs and detonated them so they couldn't be taken prisoner.

Taking a break.

Stretching, looking at the pages of notes.

Three hours—three more to go before I need to leave to meet Cat.

Hungry. Don't care—too much here to learn, too much to think about. Why the hell don't they teach any of this in school? Feeling pissed, learning all that shit about dead Greeks. Panning around for a second, checking out the new people at my table. Middle-aged lady and kind of disheveled looking guy a few years older than me. He's glancing at my books and the going back to reading his Mother Jones magazine.

Schmidt was there—he survived this, different view of the man emerging. Stretching again—adrenaline churning through my body mixed with a deep sorrow—fascination, horror hitting me.

Time to read about what Uncle Vin lived through.

Bloody Omaha they called it.

Two thousand two hundred casualties in one day, my uncle could have been one of them. Adrenaline causing my hands to tremble while I read the accounts of Rangers scaling the cliffs and fighting to maintain a toe hold, small arms against entrenched soldiers with machine guns in thick concrete pill boxes, field artillery, a few tanks, mortars and all kinds of barb wire. Some companies were entirely wiped out on the beach. Pictures of bodies floating in the surf, pictures of the cliffs the Rangers climbed under heavy fire. Trying to imagine the determination needed to slowly approach the beach under heavy fire, people around being hit, killed... And you had to just stand there.

On the beach, move under fire, people around you getting hit, crying out. Fear, adrenaline, confusion, noise.

But they did it. They stood to when then they had to.

Man, do I need to talk to Uncle Vin about this. Shiver goes through my body. The man I've been driving around with, the man I've known most of my life. Just Uncle Vin—he was in the middle of this. He won a Silver Star for bravery at Omaha. Dad won his Bronze Star during the breakout from Saint Lo. Shiver running down my body. Dad was wounded right before the Battle of the Bulge—I remember him saying that had he not been wounded, it was likely he would have been killed as his company was almost decimated during the initial German attack.

And these guys just walk around today and nobody knows. How many other people are in here now with stories like this or others that are locked away and we'll never know? Looking at the people in the library—guys older than me. Had they been there or something like it? Had they been in Korea or Vietnam?

Soft voice speaking, shaking my head, blinking my eyes to get back to the present not sure if I'm hearing something or I'm hearing things in my head.

Distinct whisper coming over, "You some kind of war freak, huh? You get off on this kind of stuff?"

Not sure what I'm hearing.

Looking carefully at the guy across from me.

"I see you reading through all this shit, taking notes," he says in a low voice barely covering the tone of present anger. "What are you some kind of sadist?"

"Shh," whisper—getting pissed at being interrupted again. Lady at our table giving us nasty looks for talking.

"Fuckin war monger."

"Why don't you mind your own business? You have no idea what I'm about or why I'm reading these books," shifting in my seat—keep cool, Frank.

"Oooooo, big man. All jacked up reading about the glory of war. What are you going to slap me down and make me give you twenty-five? What's next, gonna go put on some jack boots and burn some books, Big Man?"

"Can't you be nice to him," lady looking me from across the table.

"What?" trying to keep my voice down.

"Do you have to be so rude?"

"Are you talking to me or what?"

Taking a deep breath—ignore the pair of them. Change your focus from the rush of desire to slap his scrawny face. Asshole. He's squirming in his seat. Looking at my book but not reading, fighting the desire to go grab his long stringy hair and slam him a few times into the table. Quietness of the place starting to seep into me, the rat bastard looks bored.

Dachau—Uncle Vin told me about being there when the allies liberated the camp. Blinking my eyes, hard to get my mind off the douche bag across from me, focus, Frank, focus.

He's mumbling something to the lady at our table.

Body shivering at the uncomprehending horror spreading before me, good God, this was one of the work camps not even one of the death camps further east where millions were murdered. Photo's of what the allies found in Dachau—piles of emaciated bodies who died of starvation and disease, hollow eyes of men on the verge of death after working for years in the camp on starvation diets, train cars filled with decomposing corpses, human beings used in medical experiments. Those bastards were murdering people right up to the end—thousands of Jewish prisoners marched east to the death camps at the end of the war. Thank God many were liberated.

Millions of people murdered, they murdered over fourteen million people in the death camps alone—women and children—it didn't matter, bastards. Rubbing my face, cold shiver running through my body. The number is beyond comprehension—take everyone out of New York City and kill them, the young and weak killed quickly, then others worked to death by those Nazi bastards. Shot and thrown in mass graves, hung, starved to death or gassed in the showers and then burned. How they hell did they get away with that? Didn't anybody fight back? Feeling a deep rage growing inside.

Fourteen million people—bastards.

Meticulous records, photographs, inventories… Looking at the pictures, the faces of people as they are brought in off the trains at the death camps. Fucking children, old, women, families—terrified, the kids clinging to their parents for protection, guards laughing as they pull them apart, bastards.

Bodies stacked to be burned, bastards.

"You like that? You want to do that?"

Slamming the book down—on the edge.

Loud whisper, "What the fuck is wrong with you? Go away!"

"Oooooo, big military boy. I been in the real shit, what have you been in? Do you know who I am?"

"I don't give a shit," leaning forward. "Leave or I'm going to get someone from the library. Go find another table."

"No way, man, this is a free country. People need to stand up to the man, speak up about how we're being mind controlled. People like you who think that's all real," he's gesticulating at my books. People around us going "shh."

Keeping my voice down in controlled rage, leaning in.

"You're an idiot. My uncle was here when they liberated Dachau, he told me what it was like. Mind control… Are you stupid?"

"Ha," he sits back, "like you know anything."

"You served?"

"Who'd be stupid enough to do that?"

Asshole. Ignoring him.

"What," he looks at me, his eyes trying to zero in, "you're going to be one of them robots, ain't you?" The lady gets up and shuffles off to another table.

"What, serving your country is wrong?"

"Patriot, ha. What are you a big baby, believe all that John Wayne bull? I feel sorry for you man, another misguided animal," he leans in, "we need to put guys like you in there," he's pointing to a picture of the gas chamber.

"I'm going to say this once, you want something here, you have to make the first move, I'm telling you if you start something, I will fucking hurt you," letting my voice rise, pulling back the curtain, letting some of the intensity out, direct look into his eyes. He's a little startled.

"Oooh, like I'm scared, man," his body posture backing down.

I'm an idiot for getting all worked up here.

Waving him away, "Go bother someone else."

Turning back to my book. Flipping pages.

Reading a section on the experiments that Nazi doctors performed on prisoners. Horrible deaths—injecting people with gangrene to watch how the disease would progress through their bodies, injecting women prisoners with chemicals to try and glue their uterus shut, experiments to see how much pain they could take.

These men were doctors; they took an oath to do no harm, bastards.

Asshole across the table starts beating out a rhythm on the table.

Looking at him, I either beat his ass or I get someone from the library. That's the threat I made… follow through.

Approaching a security guard walking in the main lobby.

"Excuse me, Sir."

"What's up?" says the middle-aged man.

"There's a guy at my table who's talking and won't leave me alone. I've asked him to be quiet or move."

"Okay," he rolls his eyes, "let's see if it's one of the regulars."

"You're kidding, right?"

"Oh yeah, we got a regular crew who come here and hang around. Most are harmless. Let's see what you've got."

"Thank you, Sir."

"What, your dad a cop or something?"

"Uncle, why do you ask?"

"Not many people call me, Sir."

Walking back to the table, people watching us. I've got six inches on the guard. My tablemate is still sitting there, quietly working on the same rhythm.

"Hey there, Henry," the security guard says coming up to the table and speaking softly near the jerk.

"Guard Roberts," he looks a little leery, his body assuming a more harmless posture, "man, this guy, this Nazi dude, he's been messing with me man. Fucking military faggot or something, he wants to hurt me man, I can see it in his eyes."

"Let's keep it down, Henry. Now, you know I don't want to ask you to leave. Why don't you move over there and let these people read in peace."

"Man, it's a free country."

"Henry," the guard is stiffening up, "I've asked you once, I'm going to ask again, if that doesn't work, you're out of here for a week you dig?"

"Don't come down on me like that. It's all his fault, he's provoking me, man."

"Henry, that's twice," the guard staying calm.

"Oh man," he yells, people all around us looking, "I'm tired of being kicked around by the system." He looks at me, "I'm gonna get you."

"You'll be better off never seeing me again."

"Easy now," the guard looks at me hard, "don't exacerbate."

Taking a deep breath, backing off.

"Let's go, Henry, it's over there and quiet or out... choose."

Standing in line to return all my books. Hope that jerk follows me outside—we'll go someplace quiet...

"What's with all the books?"

Surprised to see the security guard next to me.

"Gonna join up and wanted to start reading up, learn some of the history, help me make a decision on which branch to join."

He nods, "I was on my way to twenty in the Army and busted up my knee, got a medical discharge at 18 years. I got a coffee break coming up and be glad to rap for a few."

"Okay, I got some time now."

"Meet me at the little Greek place over there on the corner of 42nd and 5th."

Chapter 38

Coffee shop crowded as hell—jumping in and sitting at a table as soon as a couple leaves. The guy I beat out for the table giving me attitude even though he came into the coffee shop after I did. Looking directly at him—make your move or go the fuck away.

He mumbles and turns away.

Thick smoke, loud conversations—the waitress is giving everyone a load of sarcasm. Waving to Roberts as he comes in. He nods, talks to a fat guy with the comb over and dirty white shirt working the register.

Sitting down he waves Mrs. Happy over.

"Rachel my dear, how are you?"

"I'm peachy, my kids are a bunch of drunks, my husband's a lazy bastard and I'm constipated. How the hell are you?"

"Ah, you need to leave them and come live a life of sin with me," he chides.

"Right, you stick it in and I wouldn't be able to walk for a week," she slaps at him laughing. "This one," she looks at me, "I could teach him a thing or two."

"Hey, hey, don't make me jealous now. Two coffee mediums, I'll have a cherry danish. You?"

"Just coffee."

"Well, that was my thrill of the day," she rolls her eyes and walks away yelling at the guy standing next to our table to move his fat ass or what.

"So," he looks at me, noticing his eyes are a little droopy, silver slivers starting to show in his fro. Waiting.

"What's a nice white boy like you joining up for?"

"Judge gave me a choice and I'm not all that nice."

"Yeah, you got that young buck feel about cha, can't help but try and rule the yard," he looks at me. "I been around all kinds of folks in my day, some of you young bucks get wise, some end up being kicked out by stronger, older bucks," he looks at me, "you know as in jail, dead, drunk and all that. Some motherfuckers don't learn no matter how many times they hit their head on the wall."

What, am I wearing a sign? Calm down, he's trying to be nice.

"What did you do in the service?"

"Eighteen years in the Military Police and I won't say I seen it all, but damn close. Did two tours in Saigon... that was some craaazy shit. Lived all over the world. Hurt my leg in a motherfuckin car accident of all things."

Coffees and his danish get slammed on the table with a smile.

"Man, she'd scare Godzilla's ass off if he ever came to NY."

Roberts starts laughing. Sipping my coffee—at least it's warm.

"When you gonna join up?"

"This week," taking another sip. Table behind us leaving, new group coming in—just as loud as the last, time for them to get their ration of shit from the waitress.

"Which branch you gonna join?"

"I'm thinking either Army or Marines," putting my cup down. "Leaning toward Army, my uncle was in the 5th Ranger, stormed the beach at Omaha."

"Army's changed a lot since then, what's your name kid?"

"Frank."

"I'm Clarence, I was a Master Sergeant. I had good setup down in Fort Bragg..." he looks into his coffee cup. "Damn. Well anyway, if you're going in today one of those specialized MOS is the way to go. Average infantryman quality has gone way down. Lack of standards, lack of leadership, lack of morals, just breaks my heart to see so many young kids drifting in and out of the service."

"What's an MOS, Sir?"

"Military Occupational Specialty, medic, radar operator, truck driver, military police, you know. When you sign up, make 'em set you a contract for your MOS, going into Boot without one you get pulled into wherever a warm body is needed."

He takes a couple of bites of his danish then wipes his mouth and hands with the thin paper napkin. He's a very neat man. His guard is uniform crisply pressed.

"You want to get you one of them technical specialties if you ask me. People stay out your way for the most part, take it easy."

"Do you miss it?"

"Oh yeah. It has its bad sides, but the Army is one of the better places for a black man to get ahead. Get yo twenty in, then get a cushy civil service job, double dipping baby," he takes a bite of his danish. "There's the elite folk from West Point, all the officers and stuff, but for the working man you can be black and run a company of white boys and your word is law. Whole lot of brothers going in cause there ain't shit out here."

"What brought you back to NY?"

"Grew up here, family here. Easy job at the library through my cousin."

"You waxing on about the life," fat guy in a greasy raincoat, tie tied way too short for his fat belly, collar open at his dirty neck, hands full of OTB racing forms.

"Hey there. Fat Mike. How's the life?"

"Lost big this morning," he looks at me. "Don't be listening to his baloney about how great the Army is. Bunch of crap if you ask me. Serve your country and all, what a joke... Just want to get the workin man to go fight for some fat cats. Pump you young un's all full of bullshit images of glory and for what?" he's shaking his head. Clarence looks like he's going to take this shit.

"Like a fat fuck like you even's got a clue," anger flaring.

"Got a firecracker here," he looks at me, his lazy eye looking at me.

"Easy now, Fat Mike," from Clarence as the fat toad trundles a little closer, standing up. Fat Mike backs off, people cursing at him as he steps on a group of working men drinking coffee. Clarence starts fishing for his wallet.

"Damn, you one full of piss and vinegar white boy, he's just talking, got nothing else to do. The talk of the lonely, you gonna have to learn about that," he looks at me, shakes his head when he sees I have no idea what he's talking about. "Probably would have loved to sit down and carry on. Anyway, I've got to go."

"Can I buy, Mr. Roberts?"

"Sure, kid. You not in jail, you come on back you want to talk."

"I will," he gets up and starts weaving through the crush.

Fishing out a five—leaving a dollar for the Bride of Frankenstein.

Walking uptown along 5th Ave.

Too bad my uncle's going to be so busy till the weekend.

Pushing down the rash impulse to walk across town to the military recruiting office at 42nd Street to sign up. Walking along the ritzy stores on 5th Ave., well-appointed ladies coming out of Saks 5th Avenue, Cartier a little ways up 5th. Then there's a guy like Clarence, nice guy and all who spent eighteen years in the service and has to work as security guard now probably making ten bucks an hour. Freaking strings of pearls in some of these window display cases are probably more than he makes in a year.

Feeling like the people and streets are pushing in on me.

Fighting the voice deep inside my head.

Loser.

"Frankie, there you are. I've been so worried about you," unlike her to hug me in public. She's holding my arm as we sit down at the coffee shop counter together, the little silver animals from her charm bracelet making little metallic sounds on the hard counter.

"Tell me..."

Looking at her. Trying to photograph how fresh she looks. Her light coffee colored skin so vibrant and healthy, rich dark hair, full lips. She's looking back, searching for something in my eyes.

"Come on, Frankie!" more pleading than anything.

"Just let me look at you, Cat," running my eyes down the curves of her face. She starts to get worried. Brushing her thick black hair away from her face.

"It's okay, Cat, there's good news and bad news," looking at the busy cooks working the grills, then down at her hand clasping my left arm. Putting my hand on hers to feel her skin. Closing my eyes for a moment and wishing that I could cut an opening, a door to someplace for us to step into

296

where all this shit would drop away. Just the two of us, no time, long sand beaches, cool places underneath the Boardwalk.

Noise of the place, the pressure of her hand on my arm brings me back.

"So, the judge won't take this to trial if I do at least two years of public service, military, peace corps, something like that," opening my eyes to look at her, "otherwise it will mean trial and likely prison time."

"Oh," feeling her body go a little slack. She looks away for a second, puts a smile on her face and looks at me. "But that's good, right? I was so worried that you'd have to go to. You know..." she's being really brave.

"It's good, but..." looking at her, "just puts a wrinkle in what we, you know. I mean, it means time apart."

She nods her head.

"Man, I just wish we could step into a different time, a different place, where we could travel, see things that were unspoiled." Looking at her, then away, "Wouldn't that be wonderful? Some place fresh with lots of room, no parents around to bug us about things that don't matter."

"Why are you telling me this, Frankie, this is good news isn't it? I mean, a couple of years, we can write. I'll be away from home next year. We'd be in college soon anyway."

"I'm sorry, Cat, just so much coming at me."

"My Frankie," she puts her arm around in mine, "what's so troubling?"

Looking at her.

"It might sound weird, but staying with Aunt and Uncle has been good... Some things about why Dad and I are at each other are coming clear. It's been nice having someone to talk to."

"And what is this?"

"No, no, my aunt, she's a high school counselor, sees lots of things kids our age go through. Although she asks a lot of uncomfortable questions."

"Like what?"

"Like, are you pregnant."

"You told her we're doing it?" she sits back shocked.

"Yes."

"How could you talk about that with anyone else?"

"Wait, wait, you're talking to your friends and all."

"But that's different."

"Why? It's a new world Cat, who knows where I'll be in a year. It's good to talk to my aunt, my uncle. They've done a lot of living. It's like calming. Times I want to walk down the street and hit people, others like I'm walking around feeling, I don't know," taking a deep breath, "horribly alone."

"Don't I count for anything?" She crosses her arms on her chest.

Taking a second, frustrated she's not listening to me.

Pushing down the frustration—breathe, breathe.

"Cat, look at how close I came to losing you cause I couldn't control myself. It's got me thinking about... Just got me trying to figure out how to make this work for us, how to stay in control? Remember?"

She's looking at me.

"You told me to promise that I'd think about us. I don't want to go off the deep end again, Cat. Sometimes when I was in jail and knew that no matter what I did, I couldn't see you. It's like here I can meet you after school, at parties, soon we'll have so much more freedom. But, it was like I had to sit there and…"

"What do you mean, I'm not getting this."

"Around all the kids at Rikers, at meals, or when I was in the dark and not being able to see you, talk to you, it was terrible, like something got ripped out of me. I could see you at times, your eyes the night we first did it. Like every fiber of my body wanted to break out."

"Why not do it, Frankie?" she looks at me, her face intense. "Break out. Why is this so complicated, so confusing? Why is it always what's wrong with what's going on around you, then you come so close to being that…" she shrugs her shoulders.

Feeling the sting of her rebuke. What's happening here? Why doesn't she want to listen to what I'm feeling?

Quiet settling in as the space extends between us.

Ordering tasteless food. Face feels flush.

"What if we broke out?" as she slurps the bottom of her Coke, "I've got money enough for train tickets to California. We could live near Mission Beach in San Diego. I've got family on my mother's side living out there that are always telling me about how great it is. You want to break out, let's do it."

Her eyes fastened on me.

Off limits, bodies out of control, raging fire between us on the bare roof. Surrounded by the heat of our skin, drowning out the cold world around us in a welcome oblivion. Nothing exists but the need for her.

Panting, laughing—our clothes are a mess.

"How would we do it, Frankie?"

Coming out of my haze standing, still holding her up, her legs surrounding me, body still throbbing from the fire. Putting my hand behind her head to press her lips to mine as hard as I can. Letting her down slowly. Pulling the condom off my still hard penis, filled with come—tempted to chuck it off into the street. That would be a funny load to drop on some prissy lady. Putting it down on the gravel roof. Smelling her on my fingers.

My lips throbbing from her biting me when she came.

Helping Cat get straightened up. Taking a breath.

"We leave. Now, I mean we'd have to just cut. I can make good money doing construction work. Put you through school. Good medical schools out there, when you're Doctor Caruso I'll switch over to part time and finish up my schooling. Cousin Robbie told me there's great diving out there. Lots of fish, great beaches." Wagging my eyebrows at her, "Great to see you in a bikini most of the time."

"That would be nice," she's holding me close, her body still trembling. "I wish it didn't have to be like this," she says looking toward the Hudson, lights in the tall buildings across the river starting to show up in the darkening sky.

"We can change it, Cat. It would be a big step, right?" Imagining the reaction of my aunt and uncle. "Our families would never forgive us…"

"No, they wouldn't," a wave of sadness washing over her face.

"It would be tough, I could do it, I would do it for you," looking at her.

Sad smile on her face, "I know you could."

Waiting for her to tell me that she could do it too.

"What about you, Cat? School is out soon. You'll be eighteen this summer…"

She starts to straighten her hair up. She looks at me for a moment.

"I need to get home. Wait up here for a bit, okay? Take the stairs down and you should be okay? Okay?" she stops, "I love you, Frankie, I love you so much," she hugs me, holding me hard and then turning quickly so I can't see her face.

Sound of her feet walking away on the loose gravel.

Can't explain it, don't know what I'm feeling. Like something's slipping away—first the cut earlier, then when I want her to leave with me she walks away. How do I fight this?

It's too important to give up. Right?

Deep breath.

Alone on the roof.

Looking down at the street below.

Cars going down 90th Street, people walking.

Looking at the building across the street.

No one noticing me.

Chapter 39

Cold morning at Montauk Harbor.

Swells in the harbor signal a rough passage out to our favorite spot for striped bass. Worried about my uncle—he looks beat. Doing as much as I can to get all the equipment stowed, checking the gear and getting the boat ready.

Working the deck lines as we cast off.

He's said just a couple of words. Not a thing about how his case is going. Hopping off the bow when we reach the refueling dock. Quick hitch on the bow then the stern as he slowly docks the Kitty Cat. Standing back in the cold, dark, gray morning light and looking out past the breakwater. Diesel fuel fumes mixed with brisk salt air.

Cranky sea gulls squawking at us—their way of saying, "Hey what are you bone heads doing up so early? Get your butts busy and feed us!" Turning around so Uncle Vin can't see the hard on in my pants as I think about last night's crazy roof top sex episode. What the hell is happening to us? Restraint falling away, but what's taking its place. Hopelessness? All the talk about what it would be like in California feels more and more like a weeklong childish fantasy we find refuge in without having to make the tough move.

Face grimacing at the cold ocean air.

Soft sunrise in the thin morning fog, ocean bouncing us around like a fleck of foam, Uncle Vin expertly piloting the boat, just fast enough to move us through the swells at the right angle. Standing next to him in the lightly protected deckhouse. His strong face focused on the sea.

"Visibility is going to suck today, lots of surge."

Nodding. "Uncle Vin, you want me to pour you coffee?"

"Sure, kid."

Balancing, timing my movements to coincide with the swells. Carefully unscrewing the stainless steel thermos full of hot coffee. Pouring about half into the cup top as we slosh around. Laughing as I let my arms float up and down as we drop off a swell, filling the cup back up to make up for what I spilled.

"You gonna wear that or what?"

Gingerly passing the cup to my uncle.

He's sipping his coffee while piloting the boat.

Time passing.

Swell after swell—looking toward the stern, land out of sight now.

"Gonna be too rough for us both to be in the water at the same time," looking over at me, "suit up and I'll circle around while you work. Take your time in the water, we'll switch out after a couple of hours."

"You sure, Uncle Vin? I'd be glad to work the boat for a while."

"You get in there first, scare up some big ones for me."

"Don't hold your breath, all the big ones are coming up on my stringer."

"All I hear is a lot of talk," he grins—gets back to watching the sea.

Carefully suiting up—squirting soapy water on my legs so I can get the thick bare neoprene wetsuit on relatively easily. Looking at my black wetsuit bottom—it's been repaired a bunch of times, but it keeps me warm. Working it over my legs slowly, slipping the farmer john style straps over my shoulders. Spraying my chest and arms—working on my hooded top. Neoprene smell mixed with the salt spray makes me feel good, body starting to warm up. Remembering good times out here on the boat with Dad, Uncle Vin, Uncle Michael and the occasional cousin. Slipping on my thick booties.

Water is going to be butt ass cold.

Getting on my weight belt—just enough to compensate for all the rubber. Clipping on my steel cable and sharpened gill spike, dive knife, bubble depth gauge, watch on the outside of my wetsuit. Suit feels good—glad I left it roomy in the chest. Three foot long Cressi Sub free diving fins ready, spitting in my low volume Scuba Pro mask, scrubbing around in there. Quick check of my long spear gun and attached reel.

"You ready already?"

Nodding to my uncle as I slip my fins and mask on, adrenaline picking up anticipating the drop into the cold Atlantic. Pumped to be back in the water. Wishing Cat could see this out here, just how different the world is a few hours away from Manhattan—she's such a City Kid.

Uncle Vin times the wave and throttles back as we coast down a nice three foot swell—he gives me the thumbs up and I do a simple back roll into the water, quick clear of my snorkel and hard kick back toward the boat. He passes me the long gun. Giving him an okay sign I kick away from the boat, my body rising and falling with the swells, breathing quickly at the shock of the ice-cold water—working to control my breathing. I'll get used to this, it just takes a few minutes.

Enjoying the freedom of being in the water. Bobbing with the waves for a few moments while I put the butt of my gun in my chest and pull back the three long thick surgical rubber tubes and lock the stainless steel wishbones into my heavy spear shaft. Everything looks good.

Taking a 360-degree look around the surface as a swell picks me up. Relaxing looking into the murky depths—I love this, I don't understand how folks get scared of blue water diving. Kicking easily to move along the surface, breathing deep to start working oxygen in my body.

Lots of junk suspending in the water, looks like about ten feet of visibility. We are sitting above sixty to eighty feet of water. Kicking down through calm quiet waters. Low clicking sounds in the background, wiggling my jaws to equalize as I slowly kick deeper. Calm, hovering for a few seconds, looking for the telltale shapes of the big stripers. As the water warms up, they'll be deeper.

Lungs starting to burn slightly as I head up slowly.

Easy surface break, looking for Uncle Vin, giving him a thumbs up. He returns the signal.

Down again, calm, let your body get used to the depth, Frank.

Each dive getting closer to what I know I can do. Relaxing, working my way to the point where I can dive sixty feet for a couple of minutes bottom time. Warm now, letting a little cold water into my chest to cool down. Mind clear. Deep breaths on the surface feel good as I slowly kick.

Smooth surface dive, time to head for sixty feet.

Clearing my ears by swallowing and wiggling my jaw. Nice and easy kicks with my long fins. Glancing at my depth gauge, passing forty. Feeling the pressure of the ocean slowly compressing the air in my lungs. Relaxing through the feeling of being short on air. I'm good for at least another couple of minutes.

Leveling off, moving slowly, coasting with the surge. Gun out in front of me, relaxed slow kicks with my fins—as little movement as possible. Catching the outline of a nice fish cruising along almost parallel to me. Slowly vectoring my body, lining up for a shot.

About a twenty pounder—passing it by. It catches my movement anyway and darts away. Body starting to tell me it will need air soon, relaxing looking around. Exhaling a little to get some of the CO_2 out of my body. Taking another look and heading slowly to the surface. Picture in my mind of the slope of the rocks I saw. Strong exhale to blow out my snorkel, kicking to swim on the surface to get back around what looked like the edge of pinnacle at sixty feet we like to hunt. Good stripers like to hang between sixty and eighty and feed on smaller rockfish.

Setting myself up on what I hope will be a good course in taking advantage of the slight current. Deep breaths, smooth surface dive down.

Little bubbles trapped on the surface of my facemask rushing past.

Following the current.

Nothing.

Working the two minutes anyway to keep my lungs and rhythm going. Slow easy kicks back to the surface. Relaxed breaths.

Pick another angle and go back down again.

Missed, too much of a lead on the fish.

Working my way easily to the surface to reel my spear in and reload. Looking at my watch, over two minutes at sixty-five feet. Yeah baby! Intoxicated by the freedom of moving and diving like this. Feeling good about my bottom time, plenty of oxygen to get to the surface.

Big dark shapes rising up in front of me at close to seventy feet.

On it this time, I'm just a big floating ball of seaweed. Making a calm adjustment to my approach, easy vector toward a possible big one. Coasting slowly now, spear gun extended, no abrupt movements. The big fish have gotten big by not getting caught by goobers like me—momentum slowly carrying me forward.

There! Three shapes moving calmly near the pinnacle. Visibility is about fifteen feet, better than anticipated. Adjusting my body ever so slightly to intercept. Slight kick with my fins is perfect.

Lining up my shot on the lead fish—staying calm. Don't care how big it is now, not enough air to come back around—focused on the area right behind and below the gill.

Squeeze the trigger gently. Lungs starting to cry out for air, shit, I pushed my bottom time. Spear shaft violently ripping through the water, staying on the fish to follow through. Looks like a good hit, letting the fish take the thick line out as I kick to the surface. Stay calm, Frank, relax—fear and panic just burn more air.

Lungs bursting as I pop up. Crappy surface exit, but I need air. Snorkel out of my mouth as I take in a couple of huge gulps of air. Head feels a little light, but don't want the fish to get away. Snorkel in, face in the water.

Working my long gun to my left—reeling in, working the fish up. Heavy bugger. Swimming away from where I think the pinnacle is—don't want this big bugger to hole up under a rock and have to go down and pull him out.

Slowly working him in, kicking back to the boat.

His large shape fighting the spear, it was a good hit, fish thrashing away making big circles. Deep breath, diving down—I want to end this before some other big predator comes in sensing the thrashing. Letting my gun float, good hold of the line, coming in with my gill spike. Elbow up protecting my body from the tail that's smacking around. The big striper goes ballistic when I grab the area underneath his gills. Kicking to get him to the surface, his tail smacking against me, driving the gill spike down through his eye socket toward his brain.

He's still thrashing, but its death throes now.

Waving to Uncle Vin, looping the gill spike and stainless steel wire through the fish's gills, kicking toward the boat, towing my spear gun.

"Hey, you catch a nice little goldfish for my aquarium?"

Smiling at him as I hoist up my catch. He reaches down, gets a good hold under the gill and pulls the big striper into the boat. Kicking away from the boat as I get my spear shaft loaded into the gun, bobbing up and down while I reel in the heavy line.

"You gonna be there all day? I'm gonna give you a fucking parking ticket."

Passing my gun up butt first and swimming up to the side, passing my long free diving fins in then grabbing the top of the transom on the way down and pulling myself up and into the boat.

"Damn," he holds the fish up as the boat rocks. "Nice fish, Frankie!" swells have calmed down a bit in the last hour. Nice rolling one to two foot swells now. He holds it up, "Feels like fifty or so pounds," he holds out his hand. Good firm shake. Feeling the smile on my face.

Taking the bungee cords off one of the big marine coolers laid out with a base of ice. Uncle Vin drops our first catch in. My body starting to catch on to how cold I really am. Lips trembling. Pulling my hood back. Shaking my hair.

"What's the layout?"

"About fifteen feet of visibility down there on the pinnacle," teeth chattering as I talk, "I used the current to come in really slowly and got on three nice stripers," holding my hand up where the first here and motioning where I thought the pinnacle is. Uncle Vin nodding, his face intense—stress of his work vanishing, subsumed by his passion and love for the ocean and big striped bass. He hands me a cup of hot coffee—it feels good going down.

"Good, get your ass up here and work the wheel," he smiles as I get my belt off and secure it. "All you're gonna see is assholes and elbows for a few moments and then I'm going to show you how to catch a real fish."

Making my hand move like a mouth and squawking like a parrot.

"Rrrrrraaaa, big fish. Rrrrrraaaa, big fish, close range, Rrrrrraaaa."

Uncle Vin smiling, flipping me off as he's getting into his gear. Shirt off as he pulls his wetsuit pants up, his back a swirling mass of burn scars left from when they tried to assassinate him by firebombing his car after the war—he must have caught too many big Nazi fish. Motoring slowly around so I can get him into a good approach point and then be on the other side of the pinnacle when he comes up. Body feeling so alive, everything looks brilliant out here. Body shivering, stomach warmed by the hot coffee.

Man—I haven't felt this happy in a long time now.

Passing his spear gun to him in the water. He calmly kicks away from the boat like he does this every day. Checking that he's okay. Revving the engine slightly and turning to starboard to give him room to maneuver. Go out and make a slow circle. Feels good piloting the boat. Feels good that he trusts me. Watching him work to get his breath—moving easily in the water. Relaxed surface dives, then staying down longer and longer.

Circling around as he starts working the pinnacle.

He's much more focused now—full hunting mode.

Scanning the ocean for sharks, boats or any signs that nasty weather is coming in.

Looking across the Sound, watching my heading on the compass. West, northwest—if I stayed on this course I'd hit New Haven. Cat's there with her Dad for a Yale Alumni function. Wishing I could pull her here with me for a few moments so she can see the wonder of all that's out here. Her eyes glaze over when I talk about this.

Staying close to the area Uncle Vin is working.

Mind drifting back and forth between managing the boat and Cat.

Laughing at the boner starting to pop up in my wet suit.

Uncle Vin surfacing after a deep dive.

Signaling: Okay?

He returns it and prepares for another dive. He's going against the current, must be on something. Watching the swells to see if I can safely slow down. Choosing to move to where he'd likely be carried if he were focused on fighting a fish he's speared. Pushing Cat out of the way for a few moments.

Timing his dive. At his max capacity he's a good three-minute free diver. Making a slow circle.

Getting a little concerned. Breathe Frank. Relax, watch for him surfacing. He might be behind a swell. Coming up on a swell—there he is. Looks like he's reloading. Shaking my body slowly to relax my shoulders, quick drink of water.

Swells picking back up.

Uncle Vin dives again.

Taking a deep breath of wonderful crisp ocean air.

What a great day!

Would she like it out here? Curious is one thing, but is she tough enough? She's talked about wanting to dive and do more outdoor activities.

Watching for Uncle Vin to surface.

She's such a City girl. Shiver moving down my spine. It's stupid to think she'll give up the whole Ivy league path for me, or is it easier to think that way and not have to deal with the her saying yes to my insane idea of running away together. I don't see her as being one of those stupid bitches that go to a good school to find a cute little hubby, stamp their ticket and never do a damn thing with their education.

Flapping sound at the surface. Turning to my left as I continue my slow circle. Skirting the lip of a big swell to turn and get close to Uncle Vin as he works to get control of a nice one. Holding my safe distance, letting a swell carry me slowly closer to him at an angle so the boats momentum won't carry me into him.

Ease off on the throttle.

Hauling his fish into the boat—still kicking as I drop him on the deck and focus on my uncle. Taking his spear gun, keeping my balance as the boat rolls with a good-sized swell. Things are picking up out here. He chucks his fins up and over the transom and then pulls himself up and in.

Grabbing his weight belt to keep him from rolling back out of the boat. "Where'd you get him?" moving to the fish. Looks like a real good one, nice and chunky—probably a fifty-five pounder, or bigger. Taking the fish firmly by the gills, giving it a quick coup de grace.

"Nailed him at sixty feet," he's looking around at the weather.

"Damn, I think yours is a little bigger," as I hold his striper up.

"Ha, there's a couple of things old farts like me can still teach ya!"

Good to see him smiling. "Yeah, like how to get lucky."

"Luck my ass," he's looking back at the gathering storm too.

"We should head in, Uncle Vin," pointing back over my shoulder.

He nods at me, "Shame, more good fish down there, but I don't like the look of that either. Probably hit us on the way in."

Nodding to him while I check his spear gun and stow it next to mine.

Getting the engines revved up and on course for Montauk Harbor. Setting an easy pace to stay with the swells, don't want to knock us around while Uncle Vin gets out of his gear.

A quick look over the horizon.

Missing her like crazy.

Uncle Vin back in his thick wool pants, pea jacket and knit cap. Breaking out the last of the coffee. He takes a sip and starts to eat one of the sandwiches Aunt Kitty made. He's still shaking a little from the cold water—looking at my watch—he was in for almost two hours.

He makes a motion to speed things up after he's checked that all our gear is secured and ready, nodding and kicking it up to a safe speed in these swells.

"Not the most productive day we've had," he's talking loud over the engines and wind, "but not too bad."

Smiling at him. "Yeah, I can already hear the stories about you getting the big one."

He punches me in the shoulder, "Rank has its privileges, kiddo."

Focused on the weather, speed, swells.

Thinking about a quote from George Washington I'd read in the library the other day. "It must be laid down as a primary position and the basis of our system, that every citizen who enjoys the protection of a free government owes not only a proportion of his property, but even his personal service to the defense of it."

What do we give back to our country? What do we give back to the land? What am I going to give?

Hosing down the boat.

Couple of elderly fisherman kibitzing with Uncle Vin about our fish, sea conditions and the like. A couple of gawkers asking about how we could get them with spear guns.

"Hey," a voice yelling down the dock, "you assholes leave any for me out there?"

"Oh look, it's the fair weather spear fisherman," from my uncle.

"Let me get a couple of pictures," says one of my uncle's friends Rick. "Oooh, those are nice. Let's get them on the scale. The kid take anything?"

Uncle Vin pointing at my fish. Rick starts laughing.

"Looks like he got a nice one today."

"He's a lucky bastard," Uncle Vin mumbles then goes into a boxing stance and messes with me.

"Let me get some pictures of youse guys."

Hanging our fish and standing next to my uncle. He puts his arm around my shoulders—Rick snapping off some shots with Uncle Vin's range finder camera.

"You want me to clean these out and filet them?"

"We got Kitty's cousins coming over tonight so filet mine out, take the guts out of yours and we'll stuff him and bake him. Yes, you can show off your fish. I'm sure your cousin Little Robbie and Roberta will be impressed."

"Eh," putting on a goombah accent, "Whatta we have heeah? We got little Bobby, we have Big Bobby, Bobby the Toes, Bobby the Nose, Bobby the Lip, Bobby Potatoes, Bobby I don't know who's on first, too many Bobbies" as I'm going on, Rick's looking at my uncle.

"What you give the kid to drink out there?"

"Ah, he's naturally an idiot," he looks at me, "you done yet?"

"Eh," shrugging my shoulders, I know this bugs my uncle doing the big dumb Italian routine, "I got more Bobbies than I know what to with wit."

"Get to work on the fish, Asswipe."

Seagulls chattering and cackling as I chuck skin and fish guts into the water for them. Uncle Vin and Rick over on Rick's boat talking and drinking beers. He's got a nice, closed cockpit, thirty-four foot deep V hull. I like Uncle Vin's twenty seven foot Boston Whaler—been lots of good times on this boat, lots of good weather, lots of bad weather, lots of fish taken. Wrapping up the two huge fillets along with the cheeks and getting them on ice, then washing down my big fish and putting him in the chest too. Hands smell of raw fish. Fish scales all over my hands and forearms. Rinsing off, washing up, the Door's *L.A. Woman* running through my head.

Hosing down the boat and packing up all our gear.

Light rain and fog starting to come in.

Getting all our gear in the car—letting Uncle Vin relax.

Checking the boat cover is completely cinched down over the boat.

"Got the Kitty Cat all set Uncle Vin," Rick's cabin smells of cigar smoke.

"Hey," he looks around, beer and cigar in hand. "All right!"

"Good work, kid," and Rick holds up a can of Schlitz, silently asking Uncle Vin if it's okay. He holds up one finger. Beer feels good going down.

Looking through Rick's nautical charts as he and Uncle Vin talk. There's New Haven. I won't see her till Tuesday. She's babysitting that night.

Chapter 40

"This was a good day, kid," light traffic on the Sunrise Highway.

"What'cha thinking about over there?"

"Oh," snapping out of my haze, "just thinking about what I've been reading about at the library. Books on World War II, World War I, Korea... lots of books on history before the wars, like how did they happen. I read a book by Barbara Tuchman *The Guns of August.* I had no idea of the complexities, the people, choices the leaders made thinking they didn't have choices and had to go to war and the millions of people that suffered because of those decisions." Checking out at a passing station wagon chuck full of kids coming home from school. "In the back of my mind, I'm thinking a lot about people I know, what kids would talk about at school, all the nonsense about which German tank was better, which American tank, planes," shaking my head remembering all the arguments with Richard and others when we were younger. "I also remember seeing the anti-war demonstrations on TV here, so much that doesn't make sense. Like how'd we turn to distrust and hate the military?"

"Uncle Vin, the anti-war protests and all," remembering how mad Dad was at times, cursing and throwing things at the TV when I was ten, "How'd that make you feel after all you did in the war. Geez, I remember Dad almost being almost apoplectic watching the TV news. One of the only times I heard him and Mom argue was when he and some of his guys were going out for the hard hat protest."

His body changing posture, he looks aggravated, gripping the steering wheel hard and rotating his hands up and down.

"Whew," he's looking straight out ahead breathing out slowly, "it's hard to talk about, Frankie. Especially since, as I was reminded often back then, I was a pig."

"What happened to us?" looking out at the road, feeling the adrenaline start going up in my body. "Are we becoming a nation of weaklings? Everybody wants the good stuff in life and what nobody wants to see what it takes to get that? Man, I wonder what it would have been like if we'd drafted all the protesters and shoved their ass in the jungle and let them see what it's like."

Getting the sense that he's not listening to me as we drive.

"We all want the world to be how we think it should be, Frank," he lets that sink in. Sitting there not following him.

"War is a terrible thing, Frank. Your dad, your Uncle Michael and I hate war movies, all the things that so many kids watch that trivialize and glorify war," he lets out his breath slowly.

"To ask someone to go off and fight and maybe die... Well, that's a big step. Hell there were people who thought we shouldn't get involved in Europe in 1940." He's shaking his head. "Not quite the same as all the anti-war long hairs who were jumping up and down in the 60's, but even then that wasn't everyone. A lot of good kids went off to do their duty. I've never been able to get my arms around what set so many people off. It was a kind of hysteria that swept the nation. TV know-it-alls, egghead academics... I don't know. People can whine about how we could have won the war, others about how we never could have won the war. My own feeling, we didn't have the will to fight, to go all out and win."

"It made a lot of crazy how people kept on thinking you could bargain with the North, idiots. How do you bargain with someone that's committed to win no matter how much it cost? They were willing to lose as many men as it took to win."

"I guess it's too much wealth now, maybe, too much easy living, too much easy pussy, oops," he's looking at me while I'm laughing, "forget I said that. Too many academics, too many people trying to figure out the cost of war like it's a business, like they can figure out some idiotic schedule, some win/loss statistic that says this war is going to turn out okay. Fucking idiots, people who don't unnerstand that there are always risks you can't foresee, things that you can't predict."

"The more I think about it, Frank, the more I think this trend to de-humanize war and make it a numbers game, the more wars we are going to get into. You remember what Schmitty told you when we were at McManus the other night? Think about that. I hope and pray you never see what I seen, that you never have to do what I done there. But I tell you kid, I also pray that if you get put in harm's way, that you do everything that needs to be done to win."

He's stretching. Turning and looking at the small islands of businesses along the highway and then stretches of homes surrounded by green trees flash by.

"You know, kid, change is the only constant thing in this world, and it's funny, well. Well, not really, pretty fucking sad if you ask me, all the people who think they can figure life all out and not have to deal with the uncertainty, the grit, the sweat of life. I'm starting to see it more and more in the department. Fucking suits think if mistakes happen it's because my guys weren't smart enough, didn't plan enough, didn't know enough. Whatever."

"People's common sense about how fast things should happen is getting all screwed up, they want things quick and easy like on TV. You have idiots being portrayed on TV like Archie Bunker; all these stupid shows where problems are solved in thirty minutes to an hour. Father Knows Best. That father don't know dick. One day you'll thank your father for not letting your brains rot by watching that goddamn box."

Evening settling in as he turns onto 97.

Passing groups of houses, then dark open fields and trees illuminated by the lights.

"This is going to sound strange, but I got to tell you, I hated the fucking anti-war movement more for the people that were involved with it than anything else. What a collection of self-involved little shits, too special to have to sacrifice anything for their country or people living in other countries. Why the hell should people look up to us or trust us in the world? When things get tough now, we talk big and turn tail and melt away."

The heat level in the car rising.

"Here's a fucking statistic for you, and this doesn't justify war one iota, but people yell and scream that we lost fifty thousand men in Vietnam in over ten years, which is horrible. Why don't all these bleeding heart do gooders stand up and scream about the fifty thousand people killed in traffic accidents each year, or the hundred and fifty thousand people that died of cancer last year, most from smoking no less, or the over one million violent assaults that happened last year which nobody gives a fuck about because most of the victims were black men," he smacks the dash board with his hand. "I guess it's the sheer laziness I see around me that infuriates me. I tell you I got more respect for someone who's a Quaker or Mennonite who stands up as a pacifist than fucking people who don't want to be bothered. I tell you, that's a cancer that's eating away at our society," he looks at me. "How many people stood up to help those teen girls in the subway the other day?"

"Nobody, till I did."

"You're a leader kid, you took a stand. The way I know you, I imagine you didn't wait and you didn't fuck around. You don't have the mental tools and maturity to go with your heart yet, but for my money, you got to go some place where you'll learn to lead."

He takes a deep breath, starts fiddling with the radio.

"Go some place new, different. Get the hell out of the States for a while... Go see the world. Go build roads, go carve out an empire, go help people." I can't see him, but I can feel the intensity of his look, "Gonna be lonely as hell at times, most people want what's in front of them. They can't handle stepping out into the unknown just like guys who can't deal with being out in the blue water with us. Your girl may not be there when you get back. Question you got to keep thinking about is what kind of man are you going to be? I tell you the answer to that will change, kid. The answer to that will change."

He snorts, laughs, something like that.

"People who think they got it figured out at your age are either stupid or lazy," he's nodding to himself now, "I got something I think we should do tomorrow."

"Back to another dungeon?"

He looks over at me giving me a little hairy eyeball, more to bust my chops than anything else.

"You liked that, huh? Places like that all over the City. Places like that have a smell to them, you'll never forget it will you?"

"No way. That place was heavy."

"Heavy? What kinda bullshit is that?"

He's mumbling to himself for a second, looks annoyed.

"Human body must give off a smell when it's close to death, sitting in despair, hopelessness, too tried to know that you're hungry or that you've shit yourself... waiting to die. The eyes..." He's quiet. "I'll never forget the eyes of the people on the edge dying in the camps, the smell of the place," he's focusing on the highway, as we turn onto 495 in light traffic.

"That's one of the reasons I became a cop you know," he glances over at me, "Army offered to send me to college, wanted me to stay in cause of a shortage of officers with my background, even with my battlefield commission. After Germany surrendered, I led my company in security operations in Weimar and then Jena through '47." He looks at me, "We specialized in ferreting out those Nazi SS fucks. That's where I fell in love with detective work."

Driving past Ronkonkoma—what a great name.

"After my second tour, I just, well, I couldn't stand to be away from Kitty any longer, wanted to get back into college. You know the rest. Finished up at St. Johns and then joined the force cause after what I'd seen and learned in Europe, no way I was going to let any of that happen here without putting a big ham fist in the middle of it."

Shiver going down my body imagining what it must have been like entering the death camps.

"What was it like, Uncle Vin? When you first found the camps?"

"We'd heard snippets here and there about them from some of the towns we'd over run. As we got close, the fucking idiots from Army Intelligence gave us a briefing on what we might find. Can you believe those assholes? They knew tons about what was really going on and they told us squat." He's shaking his head in anger.

"It was quiet, fog and light rain that day. A few of the healthier prisoners had managed to capture a few of the guards who were starting to sing their song about how they were just doing what they were told, how they were under orders. The people there were like rag dolls. Hollow eyes. People wandered around the camps in a daze, the ones who could still move where like there was some horrible weight was lifted and there was nothing but the gray emptiness of death around them tying them to the place. Some were looking for some shred of the people they'd come with and had been murdered. Some hugged each other and cried and cried."

"Names," he looks at me, his eyes animated, "people were trying to tell us the names of people they were looking for or who'd been murdered. They touched us to see if we were real. Some were happy, some dropped deeper into despair. Many tried to kill themselves. I wonder if it was like the horror had become normal and then once the ordeal was over, a person would have to recognize the horror they'd gone through. It must have been too much."

He shifts in his seat.

"People who hadn't been to the camps used to wonder why me and my guys went after those SS rat bastards with such a vengeance. They thought… Well anyway. I'll always remember how quiet the places were. What was horrible was the huts where people who were too exhausted and near death to move were housed. They were packed into these tiny wooden bunks, nothing but skin and bones."

He takes a deep breath.

"It took weeks to get things in some semblance of order, get food and aid into the place. We had to burn down a lot of the buildings for fear of disease and all. And then there were the piles of clothes, the belongings of the people that had been processed and sent on to the death camps…"

"The number of people murdered by those bastards doesn't come into play… I mean, when you see huge piles of personal affects. They were hurrying up to kill as many as they could till the end. It was the personal things, the kids shoes, the little suit cases, the little overcoats that got me."

Must be ten minutes passed before he says anything to me.

Watching the lights on the highway.

"When people tell me that it never happened, I want to slap their smug little faces and wish I could drag them into that time. Let them see and smell what it was like there."

Quiet in the car, only the road noise. Body upset—feeling like I need to move, punch, run. His words—what kind of man do I want to be? Need to fill the void.

"So, what's the surprise tomorrow?"

He's almost startled by my voice as we get close to home.

"VA hospital, talking about war and all is one thing. I want you to see a side of life that nobody wants to see. What happens after the fighting is over, Frank. You up for that?"

Deep breath—anxious, truck slowing down for merging traffic.

"You know, Uncle Vin, I read a book that had a story of a World War II VA hospital in Pasadena. I guess this was one of the places where people who were badly disfigured were sent for reconstructive surgery and rehabilitation. It made me sick when I read that some of the people in town complained to the hospital because some of the men were walking around outside where they could be seen. What the hell was wrong with these people, in the middle of war and all? Not a "thank you" to those people, no "what can I do to help you." Just get out of sight you ugly people."

"You know, Frank, there are a lot of ingrates in this country, people with short memories, white bread people, manicured lawns, all the special little things in their lives, their ceramic garden gnomes, assholes that name their houses. I see it all the time..."

Pulling off the freeway, driving in silence the last few blocks.

"Good day today, Frankie," as we pull into the driveway. "Hey, it's tough to talk about, but I'm glad you ask me about what it was like and all. Give you some context for your decision."

Nodding, looking back at my uncle, realizing how much I love him and my aunt, how much I'm going to miss them when I leave.

Sitting next to cousin Bobby—looking at him, shaking my head. Hey, who knows if he's Big Bobby, Little Bobby, Bobby the Nose, Bobby Big Toes, Bobby Quick, Bobby Slow. Laughing to myself as he looks back at me. Bobby, the fat little fuck is more like it. He gives me a nice fuck-you look back.

Keeping a smile on my face during the obligatory small talk with my Great Aunt Nancy.

Uncle Vin holding court at his end of the table. Wine flowing, huge table full of good food and surrounded by big eaters. Reminds me of holiday dinners at Grandpa T's.

Wonder what it was like for Grandpa T to send his three boys off to war. Imagine those last days when you don't know if you'll ever see them again. Wave of emotion hitting me—like this little fuck Bobby would ever get off his fat ass and do anything risky. Fat Bobby goes on about the Yankees and the player statistics. I think I hate baseball.

Aunt Nancy nodding like she has any idea what he's talking about. Cousin Penelope needling him. Patting him on the arm—it's my turn. "So big Bobby, what's going on with those first place Red Sox?"

Just keep that shit eating grin on your face, Frank.

Bypassing the after-dinner small talk by staying busy—cleaning up after Genghis Khan's horde.

"You don't have to do all that," says Aunt Kitty as I start to work on the pots and pans. Getting ready to transform myself into a dishwashing God.

"Oh yes I do, cousin Bobby is driving me nuts."

She smiles at me and waves me away.

"Your uncle had fun today. It's so good for him to get out on the water. It takes years off him. Nice to see him happy."

"It was a good day."

"He said you had some good talks."

Nodding as I transfer the big pasta pot into the rack.

"Talked a lot about what happened during the war."

She nods and starts to dry pots as I rinse and stack.

"I think he's starting to like having you here more than he thought he would."

Looking at her, head cocked slightly.

"Me, too."
She musses my hair.

House quieting down.
Uncle Vin snoring in front of the TV in the front room.
Taking the heavy table leaves out of the dining room table.
Aunt Kitty putting the lace table cloth back on the table.
Looking around. Is it weeks, days or months before I go off?
I'll miss this place.
Aunt Kitty stifles a big yawn.

Lying back in my bed. Body still amped up from all the oxygen pumped into my body. What a great day. Concentrating on her face, vision of her so clear, trying to reach through.

Chapter 41

Another dirty look from Aunt Anita.

Fidgeting—uncomfortable in my suit as I sit in the well-worn pew.

Plenty of us sinners in here today.

How did I get stuck next to this old biddy anyway, dammit!

Oh man, I'd better watch my language here.

Thinking about it... That's stupid, like God is what watching TV and only tunes in when we are in church? What about the rest of the time when I'm saying fuck, shit, piss, cock, cunt... that doesn't matter? Why is only now holy? Why is this place special and no other places? Who said this was the place that is special? The Pope? What if all this shit is made up by people who thought they understood what Jesus was talking about—amazing how they got to be put in charge after they were the accepted interpretation and killed off anyone who disagreed.

Snickering to myself, getting another evil eye from Aunt Anita.

Where was the big cheese during the on-going struggles, the competition, the killings and all between the different Christian sects in Byzantium that Robert Graves wrote about in *Count Belisarius,* the Blues and the Greens?

Still, feels weird to even think like this in here. Fuck.

What, no lightning coming down?

I want to have sex with Catherine all day long.

What, no earth ripped aside and Lucifer coming and pulling me down to the depths of hell?

I want to eat pussy.

Giving my aunt a shit-eating grin.

Time to stand up, kneel down. Turn to page seventy-six, blah, blah, blah...

This must have been how the early Christians attempted to show the Romans they weren't a threat—they'd just bore people to death. Marble carving of Jesus on the cross behind the altar. How would a man as weak as they depict him been a carpenter? He'd have strong forearms, strong hands, well developed back and shoulders.

Amazing how Uncle Vin has a lot of police business to deal with on Sunday mornings. He's a smart man.

"Frank," Aunt Kitty looking at me sternly as we walk to the rectory, "you need to snap out of this grouchy mood." Nodding, wishing there was some way I could speed up time and get his baloney with Father Fiero over, I'm joining up on Monday, enough is enough.

What will I tell Cat? When will I tell her? Maybe Wednesday.

Walking into the warm, three-story brownstone next to the ornate church. Am I being a big pussy by waiting for my girlfriend to give me permission? I'm going tomorrow and do it. I'm going to tell her why.

Walking slowly up the well-worn wooden stairs like I'm being summoned to the principal's office for being bad. Maybe Father Fiero got a message from God that I'd been cursing and thinking about all kinds of wonderful sins during the sermon.

Mind shifting back and forth between wanting to get the hell out of here and thinking about what I promised her—I promised to make this work. How does going off and enlisting live up to that promise? No, I have to talk to her first even if this is something that she won't like. Not living up to my word makes me an even bigger pussy.

"Father, so good of you to make time for us after service today," snapping out of my daydream at my aunt's voice. I hate this.

"Oh please, Mrs. Caruso, it's always such a pleasure to see you. Come in, sit down, sit down," he motions us to a couch across from a low, ornately carved dark wood coffee table. Looking around the room he uses for greeting parishioners while he and my aunt small talk—weather, Uncle Vin, her work at school. What a waste of time this is.

Black and white photographs of groups of men in uniform, looks like the place was very cold. Tired eyes, smiles on their faces though. Other pictures of a younger Father Fiero standing in front of mud brick buildings, dense jungle in the background, a group of short, dark-skinned natives with him, some smiling, some looking directly at the camera with blank looks.

Mind flitting through the freedom of being back underwater, the ecstasy of coming inside Cat. The calmness afterwards, the open spaces… Here they are talking away and I'm getting a boner. What did Jesus do when he was a teenager? The holy wrist exercises maybe or the holy cold shower or the holy scourging the sin out of the body—probably using sandpaper… What bullshit.

"He doesn't like to small talk, does he? It looks like he's amused at something."

"Frank."

Coming out of my daydream. Aunt Kitty and Father Fiero put down their thin ornate coffee cups. "So your aunt tells me you are considering joining the Army?"

"Yes, Father."

"How do you feel about that?"

Mostly gray hair now, severe haircut. What is it that bugs me so much about him? The voice, the I-know-it-all timbre, the deep eyes looking at me calmly while he waits to dispense wisdom—like he fucking knows it all. Crossing my arms, shrugging my shoulders, nasty look from Aunt Kitty.

He's looking at me, calm, his hands together in his lap, fingers interlaced. I wonder if they have to go through a "Here's How to Look Calm and Collected in all Things" course back in the seminary.

"Have you thought through the moral consequences of what you may be asked to do?"

Asshole. "Ah Father, the moral consequences. I'm curious, is that the same moral consequence advertising people who do their best to convince people to smoke or drink and live on Park Avenue will face? Why are the people who do their best to get people to do things which are bad for them, which lead to a slow painful death, looked upon as so much better than people who ensure that someone who's trying to hurt our country or our people have a quick nasty death?"

He sits back in his chair a little, face impassive but with a little glint in his eyes—he likes this, he likes combat.

"The soldiers at Kent State, were they doing their job? What if you were asked to do that? Fire on civilians?"

"How about the people that were rioting Father? There were multiple days of rioting and protests before the National Guard was called out. How about the leaders of those riots? Aren't they just as much to blame?"

"So you justify the shooting?"

"No, just that nobody is free of sin, Father. We have this thing called elections here, if those students had really been committed, I mean really committed to protest, they could have taken other avenues. But that would have taken time, effort, maybe even ruin their little college careers and they may have ended up working with their hands. It makes me sick to see how people want easy things. Like hunger, greed and injustice are new and they'll stop because they run around with a few signs? It's cool to be anti-this and anti-that, especially when you don't have to take a stand and pay a price. Oh, how dare they call out the National Guard when we are rioting and burning buildings? How dare those thug soldiers be human beings and be nervous and anxious about crowds of people yelling and hurling things at them?"

"Ah ha, we have a philosopher here."

"Is that wrong?" leaning forward, feeling agitated, patronized.

"No, no, no. On the contrary, it's good to learn, to think."

"No sin of pride, Father?"

"Maybe, but I'm not the judge of that, and anyway, moral atrocity, the quick and visible or the slow and unseen are equally wrong. God's time is not our time and peoples' actions have to stand for what they are when they are judged."

"What if we are not judged, Father?"

"Oh ho," he sits back, "do you doubt that God exists, my Son?"

"No, Father. But what if the God we know is an invention of what we can imagine. The story of God, the possibilities that are God have changed over time. Does that mean that God does not exist? No. Does that mean that you," pointing at him and all the bric-a-brac, "you have all the answers about God? I don't think so."

"Then why has each civilization held God and his children in such a sacred place?"

"If we are all biologically similar Father, maybe our common need for certainty in a hostile world led us to invent what we think of as God, or for that matter what we know about Jesus. The gospels were written years after his death."

"Oh," he looks at my aunt, "I see you have quite a handful here."

"Frank, you're being disrespectful."

"What, Aunt Kitty, I can think this and not say it? If God's everywhere, then why be a hypocrite?" she folds her hands, her lips taut. "Father, what if God does exist but not as we imagine? What if it's an impartial God, we have what we have, and we make what we make out of it."

"God in our own image?"

Nodding my head, "What would they say in France if we were dueling Father? Touché?"

"What makes you think we aren't?"

Aunt Kitty looking very uncomfortable, Father Fiero calm, having fun.

"So if God doesn't exist, Mr. Caruso, what is good and evil? Are they even important?"

"I didn't say God doesn't exist. Look if you brought someone from the Stone Age here today and they saw a car, what would they think it was, a beast, a monster? Just because we think God is a certain way, doesn't mean God is that."

Looking at him. Starting to warm up, at this point in school I'd have teachers yelling at me that I was too young to be debating with my wiser and more knowledgeable elders.

"Is that funny?" he looks annoyed.

"No, Father, I was thinking that back at school, before I was kicked out, I would have been sent to the principal about now and you're just as relaxed as can be."

"Is that why you question? To remove yourself from uncomfortable situations?"

Looking at him.

"Maybe," quick glance at Aunt Kitty—her hands are folded in her lap, she's looking down at her hands, "maybe it's a way of testing to see if people are serious about thinking or stuck in some set of theories they can teach but don't know why they were invented in the first place."

He laughs a little at that.

"That's very good," he nods at me, "I had a teacher once that said those who can, do—the rest teach. Your philosophical questions are appropriate for someone your age and I believe it is good to be thirsty for knowledge, good to be interested in how to think. If knowledge is power, then learning how to think with knowledge is even more powerful. But we get off track... I am curious. What is good and evil to you, young Mr. Caruso?"

Taking time to think.

"I don't know what good is, Father, but I believe evil is intentionally hurting someone who is innocent. That would be stealing, lying, hitting, killing and I guess verbally going after them. But then you have to ask what is innocence in a given situation? Did a person's actions put them in situation where they need to take some of the blame? My uncle Vin says you can't con an honest man. So if that's true, then if I'm looking for something on the sly, say someone wants to sell me something that I know can't be an honest sale that they've stolen, but I don't ask then I'm just as guilty in the act. If that's a good definition of evil, then good would be not hurting others intentionally, resisting the efforts of those who would do evil."

"Is it moral to kill to prevent evil?"

"I don't believe in morals, Father. Morals presuppose that someone got the word directly from God about what is right and what is wrong, wrote it down correctly without leaving out any commas or periods."

"So you don't believe in natural law?"

"I don't understand what you mean by natural law?"

"Law of nature. Natural law is a theory that certain rights or values, morals if you will, are universally known by virtue of human reason."

Can't stop laughing at that one, "Oh, so idiots or the insane wouldn't recognize natural law."

"Frank," Aunt Kitty getting uncomfortable again, Father Fiero makes a calming gesture to her.

"So shall we sacrifice a lamb and divine the future from its entrails like the Romans? Would we see natural law there? I'm sorry, Father, that's just stupid. I wonder what the sacrificial lamb's position would be on this anyway? What if this is just all some weak attempt to make sense out of a world we can never understand? I'm sure you have Marx's quip thrown at you often, Father, you know about religion being the opiate of the masses."

"What do you think about that?"

"I think ethics are more interesting, Father, at least they are invented by us humans to figure out how to live together, how to behave. They evolve as we evolve and figure out what works and what doesn't work. At its best, the Ten Commandments represent the wisdom of people living together for hundreds of years and figuring things out."

"Fair enough, so do you think it's ethical to kill to prevent evil?"

"Yes," he looks a little surprised that I don't hesitate.

"Why do you say that?"

"Whose responsibility is bad behavior, Father? What right do I have to kill you or steal your things? None. If I do these things then, who should bear the consequences? If a person makes the choice to cross the line Father, they were intent on doing evil to the innocent. They made the choice to transgress, why shouldn't they suffer the consequence that comes with that?"

"So you believe in Capital Punishment?" he looks at me calmly.

"Why should we have to pay to keep murderers in jail, it's a waste of money and resource. Either put them to work to help raise their keep or off with them."

"If it's immoral to kill…"

"You said that, Father, I didn't say it was immoral. I said it was wrong, I said it was evil. Look at the all the lost capability we suffer when people go about killing people. I saw…" taking a deep breath, "I watched a man being taken away who had killed his wife and one of his children with a butcher knife. What did we lose then? Who could that child have grown into? What would their contribution to society have been? We'll never know, that man took the choice from her."

"Is killing the killer another evil act?"

"Why shouldn't we get rid of bad apples?"

"Who makes that decision? What if they are wrong? What about all the people condemned to death by the Nazis? Their philosophy twisting and turning any rational system of laws into a machine of death."

"How can anyone ever be one hundred percent right? Are you telling me there are innocent people in jail? You're probably right. I was in jail, but I am guilty. I bet ninety-nine percent of the people in jail today are guilty. Of course then what's the definition of crime or crimes against society? Where does rightful disobedience come in to play, Father? The Founding Fathers took the path of armed revolution against the lawful government of the time. Unlawful to us in our logic and belief, lawful if you were a member of the British Parliament. Maybe the people at Kent State were doing the right thing by violent protest. Maybe one of those people in the National Guard was new, inexperienced and afraid. Maybe he shot because he was scared and human. Isn't that just the tragedy of life and the world we live in? Maybe he was a very religious man, Father? Maybe what he did was a sin."

"That's a very severe outlook, my Son."

Shrugging my shoulders.

"Yeah well, my dad yells at me at home because he thinks I'm a loser by hanging around with what he calls spics and niggers. The spittle flies out of his mouth sometimes when he says those words, Father. There's no disguising the hate, yet on Sunday, he puts on a suit, dips his hands in holy water, partakes of the body and the blood and then magically things are okay? What rank hypocrisy."

He's looking at me.

"So then, what is the heroic? Is there good in this severe world of yours?"

"Whew," looking at the ceiling for a moment, "I really don't know, Father."

"Think about it, you've come up with an interesting definition of evil, I have a slightly different view, but not quite that different if all be told. What is heroic?"

"I guess standing up to evil when it's tough to stand up."

"What do you mean?"

"Well, a man was exposing himself to a couple of young girls on the subway and I jumped in and stopped him. People said that was heroic, but it really wasn't. It was the right thing to do, but it was easy. There was not another choice for me. Right?"

He's looking at me, looking at Aunt Kitty—she's a little more relaxed now, watching the interplay. My voice lower now, "Now, when I beat up a kid once because I was egged on by a bunch of older kids, yeah he was wising off, but so was everyone. I didn't have the strength to look bad in front of the other kids. Saying no would have been heroic in my mind, but I didn't, I was a coward," looking at him now feeling my eyes water up, images of summer days playing two-on-two half court with Alton against all comers up at 110th, "I didn't act when I had a chance to not listen to my pride and accept a friend's apology. Instead I had to challenge him. Look at where that got me."

"God's favorite Angel."

Body jumping, looking at him. Cold rushing through my body.

"Yes, Father," nodding, my eyes clouding up. Am I evil? "Did Lucifer know it when he fell? Was he marked? Did he know what he was, like Jesus knew, before he was betrayed? Was it just that he needed to see what he had become? I wonder... Is the fall gradual, something we are blind to for years and years, but it eats away inexorably, or is it a grand event?"

"What do you think it is, my Son?"

"I think it's gradual till the day your realize it's too late, when you hear the sound of the doors slamming behind you," chest getting tight, "or the day your father tells you that you're not his son and he leaves you in jail."

They are both quiet—hard to breathe for a moment.

"Well, my aunt and uncle helped me look back and see a lot of the things that I'd done that put me in a position to where I'd do... All the little things, pride, arrogance, anger... Then the great crying out that things are not my fault," sick laugh coming up for a second, "but they were, and there's nothing I can do to change that."

"Have you thought about confession?"

"No, Father."

"And why is that?"

Feeling my lips purse.

"I just... It seems phony to me. I don't believe it," feeling agitated. "To be honest, Father, I think confession, absolutions are inventions created to keep the weak in the churches under control. What's a sin one week, is okay the next week," feeling my aunt start to get tense on the couch. "A decree comes down one week, the inquisition decides something the next. A King is rich enough to propose something to the Pope that warrants an absolution. I don't believe in the arbitrariness of man, Father."

He's looking at me.

"I think we have an agnostic in our midst."

Patronizing prick.

"Do the foul acts of men done in God's name prove or disprove the validity of God, Father? Or is this just proof that we are imperfect? God sent his Son to show us the way, not to rule us. That came afterwards, in his name."

Aunt Kitty jumping in, "Frank, I think you've…"

"Shh, it's okay," he looks at her holding up his hand, "and besides, we don't have any firewood left for a nice heretic burning," he starts to laugh. "We used it all last week."

Laughing with him.

"So is anything that man has created reflective of God?"

"Music."

He nods, "Good answer." Room becomes quiet, Father Fiero sipping from his dainty coffee cup with strong fingers that look scarred and calloused.

"So my son, I'm curious… On one hand I see you struggling with important questions. Who am I? What do I believe? What is right and wrong? What is Faith? These are good and I encourage you to keep going. You might read Thomas Merton, or Teilhard de Chardin amongst many others."

He takes another sip of coffee.

"May I make an observation?"

Uneasy, weak of me to back down now after putting out such a challenge.

"Okay, Father."

"You seem to have a good mind and I admire your striving to think through and understand ideas that many people ignore or accept as rote. I wonder how much of all this is to keep people away, keeping the world at bay?" and he moves his hands about. "At the same time, I sense a terrible aloneness in you, my son." Feeling the ice pick driving into my chest, "Coupled with a rigidity, an uncompromising side… Part of recognizing God's place in this world my son, is recognizing that through all this you are part of God and that you are worthy of God's blessing, as well as being responsible for your acts. Maybe one of our biggest sins is keeping ourselves out of God's grace. People make mistakes, Frank, they learn, they deal with the consequences, that's human. You are human."

Body fighting his words—room feels like it's collapsing.

His eyes holding me.

"You've thought about killing yourself, haven't you?"

Sitting back like I've been slapped. Hands cold, clammy—fingers jittering. "Yes," looking down at my lap.

Feeling my aunt's eyes on me, her body starting to move. Fiero is shushing Aunt Kitty, his hand motioning her to be calm.

"When was this, Frank?"

"After I got in trouble at school, my father and I had a big fight, he told me to get out," breathing out as the emotions from that night resurface, "I was on the streets," looking down at my hands—images of the abandoned rotting dock flood in, the deep, dark tunnel. "I'd found a place down by the old docks underneath the West Side Highway. Rotting cargo blankets, rotting wood" the feeling of the place coming back for a few moments, "it was there, I was looking at the black river…"

Looking back at that place in my mind.

"What pulled you back from the edge?"

Blinking, refocusing on the room.

"I still think about it now and then. The first time… couldn't give up, my dad and I thought everyone had all given up on me, but even if I was all alone dirty, hungry, little money, I wasn't going to give up and take the out. I mean I wanted to hurt my father and mother, but that seemed like the easy way out."

"That would have been the easy way out."

Nodding, "And besides, I had to get even first."

"So, you found justice?"

"No, Father, I found how much my pride blinded me to what I had. I found how much I'd squandered and then it was too late. It was gone," snapping my fingers, "chance at a top University basketball scholarship gone. My best friend is in the hospital. A shot at the Golden Gloves title in my age class this year, gone," taking a deep breath, "Father, Mother, gone… girlfriend, who knows…"

He takes a slow breath, "So where do we go from here?"

"I'm going to enlist in the military."

"There are other options. We have programs through the church where you can help people in other countries. Central America, China, India. I'm not saying military service is a bad thing mind you. There are options."

He looks at his hands for a moment.

"What skills do you have?"

"I can build, I'm good with languages. I'm good with math."

"Can you teach?"

"I don't know. But I can do," he gives a pleasant laugh at that.

Room growing quiet again.

"Were you in Europe during the War? My uncle told me what it was like storming the beach at Omaha, what the camps were like and what he did after the war helping round up war criminals."

"Was it glorious?"

"No, but it seems like a place where a person can't hide who they are."

"And what if that person is not someone you like? What if the time comes and you are found wanting?"

"Isn't that something I should know?"

He looks at the walls, photos of men in uniforms.

"When I think back now, I feel a great sorrow. So many young men… so many dead, so many horribly wounded, so many lives irrevocably changed and torn apart. There's a terrible but undeniable beauty that happens in an instant, an act of bravery, an act of mercy or the end of a horrible suffering. It's horrible to see men maimed and killed. It's horrible to see men destroy themselves because they are not capable of standing and killing another human being in combat and are branded as cowards by the military."

"Men who otherwise would be fathers, friends, contributors to society. It's horrible to see the things men do to give themselves false courage and have to face shelling, battle after battle, little food… And what's left at the end." He takes a moment, taking a last sip of coffee. "Singed casings, impassive faces, a great numbness settling in to protect what's left of the spirit. Then there are the few who do not feel and get their thrill in blood and death… Are they brave? I don't know…"

"Then there are the rare few who can look at all the glory, sorrow, horror, death and can lead men. The Greeks used to say these were one in ten thousand, the man another thousand warriors would follow."

He looks uncomfortable with saying that.

"That's all well and good, it's important, but I wonder if it's more important to think about what else those men could do? How much richer would our world be if all that focus and passion were dedicated to building, healing, thinking? Does one have to kill to be a warrior? Think of the dedication, the ability to spend long hours focused on an outcome, the skill to lead. The ability to overcome obstacles. Isn't this what we need in our teachers, our doctors, our scientists, our leaders?"

He looks at me—looks at his watch.

"I unfortunately have to wrap-up this conversation soon, but I want you to think about what we discussed here. What can you do in the next two years that helps the human race? What skills can you develop in your time of service that helps the greatest good? And that's not to say that standing up for our freedom and the freedom of others isn't helping the good. The arts, music, architecture, religion have flowered in stable countries where people had time to think, learn, and communicate with each other. But it's not the only way, Frank. It's not the only way to join the human race."

Nodding at him, looking at my aunt—she's more relaxed now.

"Thank you, Father, this has been good," taking his hand and returning the handshake.

"You are very welcome, please come back if you choose. I have some rich commentary on some of your ideas. We Jesuits are always looking for good people to think with and keep sharp."

"Thank you, Father," said Aunt Kitty getting up, straightening her dress.

"You are very welcome. Please give your husband my fondest and tell him I expect to see him next week."

"I will, Father."

Walking in the cool, clear Sunday afternoon air.

"Is there anything you don't want me to tell your uncle?"

"No, Aunt Kitty."

Throng of churchgoers melted away long ago, a few scraps of paper being tossed about by the breeze. Walking next to her. Annoyed, thinking about what Fiero talked about. He's right there are many choices. I could be the basketball missionary, teach people to do it fluid on the court all around the world. Riiiight. Learn to dribble and dunk for Jesus.

"What was it like, the days after you had the big fight with your father?"

"Bleak, I was so angry that they wouldn't let me have the money I'd earned... Pop's way of trying to make me crawl back and ask forgiveness, but it had gone too far, something broke. I was going to die first."

Kids playing stickball on the street stopping and jeering at passing cars that dare interrupt their game. Glancing over and watching some hot little chickitas out playing with fire.

"I learned what it is like to be hungry, though it was probably nothing like the hunger strike guys in Belfast, only a few days in my case."

Kids running, laughing. A car honking at them to get out of the street— bunch of choice Spanish curses hurled at the driver. Kids kicking at the car as it goes past.

"I think you're right, you and your father let this get past a breaking point. I'm glad you didn't get violent with each other."

"It was pretty close, I think it scared him how close we came, cause I wasn't backing down any more. Just tired," looking at her, "tired of being not good enough, tired of his putting down my friends, calling them... Well you know how he could go off on a rant."

Why do I find it so hard to say nigger or spic or Jew, how about Jew bastard? Let's see, whom else do I need to insult to be an equal opportunity ass? They are just words right? Is the hate behind them inside me too? Fuck, I grew up with all kinds of guys, Leroy, that sack of shit, Cedar strong, smart determined to go places. Alton... Man did I mess that up. Where does all the hate come from?

What if you say these words thousands of time? Do they lose their potency or does the fear or anger that lies underneath just stay there like a silent cancer?

"John and I don't see eye to eye on a lot of things, Frank."

She's quiet, car parked down the block.

"I didn't expect that you know, with Father Fiero."

She gives a little shrug, "He's a very perceptive man, Frank, who's been through a lot, his faith has been put to the test in more ways than we'll know."

Nodding to her as she opens the door.

"And besides, he's not a dogmatic person. He loves people, ideas, loves his role as a shepherd."

"Shepherds," sitting down, nodding, "they kill wolves don't they?"

Chapter 42

"Aunt Kitty tells me you had an interesting conversation with the good Father," said Uncle Vin, light traffic passing by in the early evening. "Wish I could have been a fly on the wall. Kitty said she started to get nervous, you went right after some sacred cows."

"You're not mad?"

"Hell no, awful lot of bullshit that goes parading around as religion. I'm a simple man, Frank, you do good, you live by your word, you work hard to live a good life, you take care of your family, you believe in God and if you don't," he smiles and pats his sidearm.

"Can I at least get a running start?"

"You ain't even fast enough, Big Boy."

He takes the Fort Hamilton exit off 278.

"So tonight, I just want you to relax, look the guys in the eye. Ask them if they need anything. Tell them what you're thinking about. There'll be other volunteers tonight. Some will be helping the guys with bingo games. Some distribute magazines and what not. Couple of my guys will be here. Both were in Southeast Asia, one I'd like you to talk to sometime. I told you about him, long-range recon patrol, damn good man, nobody fucks with him on the streets. He hated the Army, but he'll be good for you talk to. Questions?"

"None, Uncle Vin."

"Okay."

He pulls up to a tall building.

"Hey, kid," he looks at me, "I'm glad we didn't pull you out of the river."

"Well, for once you would have caught a bigger one than me."

Sly look at him.

"Oh sweet Jesus, save us! He thinks he's funny."

Big lobby, dark marble floor, pictures of various old white men on the wall, security guards stationed about, a couple of middle aged men in wheel chairs—one wearing a dark blue hat, must be Navy, CVS-12, USS Hornet in gold embroidery. The other guy a younger black man, no legs, big tape player belting out R&B, one of the guards giving him a hard time about the noise.

"You need something?" from the crusty guy working the desk.

"Sure, Smiley," said my uncle, "we're here to see Doc Guardino and help out tonight."

"Guardino, I don't think he's on," he goes back to reading a *Mad Magazine.*

"Call him," order from my uncle, his eyes narrowing on the twerp.

"Hey, watch it Mister!"

Uncle Vin getting pissed, taking out his ID wallet, "What'cha going to do, call the cops? Now call the Doc before I get pissed, capice, Sssmiley?"

"Okay, okay," the guy grunts along, "don't need to get so pushy."

More vets coming out of the elevator in various civilian and hospital garb, most walking. Guards getting loud about the music—the man in the chair going on about how he lost his motherfucking legs for our country—least thing he could do is get down to some Mandrill without this stateside motherfucker giving him shit. Uncle Vin rolling his eyes as more guys get into the conversation.

"Lots of energy, not enough to do. Let's get the hell upstairs."

Say it—his name is Artis Glendenon. Look him in the eyes.

Don't look away. His prosthetic jaw covered with dark brown plastic to try and match the color of his skin. His grip loose, his skin clammy. Left arm prosthetic too, looks like his legs may have been damaged as well. Another of the silent ones home from war, hidden here in plain sight.

Listening closely, nodding my head as the words come slowly out of his voice box. "Down the hall'mm, second roomm," the electronic voice, eerie at first.

Pushing him slowly down the hall.

"Do you like talking about home, Mr. Glendenon?"

"That's long way'mm away," he seems to tire easy.

His area of the room is neat, pictures of Jesus, Hank Aaron, a group of smiling black men in green fatigues, looks like some kind of mobile unit. "Truck Your Muffler Ho Chi Min," on the sign behind them over some dirty, green trucks, bulldozers and a backhoe. Wall covered with postcards from all over the South.

"Mem family sends 'em now 'n then."

"Can I help you get in bed?"

"No'm, nurse later, mmabye play some cards."

"Sure," reaching for a well-worn deck of Bicycle playing cards. "What would you like to play?"

"You'm play Pinochle?"

"Sure," switching to the other deck of playing cards.

Dealing the first hand quietly, noise down the hall where there's a big game of bingo filtering in. People transiting the hall now and then, the smells of the place starting to register—ointments, bodies that can't wash themselves, floor wax, plastic—the smell of aging, sick bodies.

Not a particularly strong hand—bidding conservative.

He wins and shows the meld. Trading tricks, not letting him win, but not playing for blood like Grandpa-T.

"Who'm taught you the game'm?"

"My Grandpa Tomasino, he loved to play Pinochle. Games with him, my uncle Vin and Uncle Michael were blood matches."

He slightly nods, focused on his cards. Tired looking nurse stops by the door and says hello to Artis.

Slow pace of the hospital moving past us.

"Why'd you'm come here?" as he plays a nice trick, "Nice to see'm young fellow, but don't get too many."

Dealing out the next hand.

"Joining the Army," as I look through my hand. "My uncle wanted me to come, to give thanks to people who've served before me, see how I can help," sounds stupid coming out of my mouth.

"Tourist?" he's holding himself tighter, his eyes moving about.

Taking a deep breath, "No, Sir."

"Why you'm signing up?"

"Judge gave me a choice, serve or go to jail."

"Why'm Army? Better education in Navy or Air Force'm."

"Uncle was a Ranger in World War II, figured if I was going in, I should follow what he did."

"He'm big fellow, long coat? See'm here sometimes'm."

"He's a policeman now."

"Didn't try'm to get you off?"

"No," laughing as I take a trick, I'll win this set. "He made sure all the facts were on the table but wouldn't interfere."

"Like'm already," he nods slightly, relaxing, "too many white boys'm skate by."

He takes the next hand. I should get the rest.

"Grandaddy'm taught you good," as I take the next two hands.

"Thank you. Were you drafted?"

Shuffling then jotting down our scores—pretty close so far.

"Yes'm. Pulled out of 'm good 'struction business, joined'm Navy to avoid being ground meat, needed'm guys who could run heavy machinery. Picture'm there of my guys'm in the 'struction battalion... Seabee's."

Nodding to him, looking at the faces in that picture—strong healthy men.

"Built'm forward airstrips, got'm shot to shit in NVA attack. Lot 'o good'm men died for nothin in that damn place'm. Lot of black'm men went in who didn't get no college'm pass, lot of em came back'm in bags."

He's quiet for a few moments.

"Navy'm better n Army, most kids like you just a name'm an number to officers'm... many killed cause o can't find'm ass with both'm hands. Got's to fill them quotas'm, get that count, get out there and get that count... Saw'm on bases we built'm." He must mean body count.

Feeling cold inside—am I going to be a name and a number? Idea hitting me, not paying attention to the game—that's like being in prison. Looking at Artis—served his country, disfigured, postcards on the wall from family and that's it for the rest of his life. Looking at the four walls where he'll likely die one day.

"Not pretty'm."

"No, Sir," looking at him, "you get angry about it?"

He puts his cards down on the table, turns his head slowly and looks at the wall behind me. Putting my cards down too.

"I'm sorry if that was out of place."

"No'm, just lots to think'm about. Been though'm many phases... first about'm pain 'n how bad was I hit," he stops for a moment, looks at his guys. "Pain'm in better control, how'm I get back to my men 'n all. Starts'm setting in, all damaged'm. Doc talking bout change'm and what they can do nowadays'm and all. Kept'm thinking something's gonna'm happen to make this okay, but after time'm no miracles coming my way'm."

He stops for a few moments.

Would Cat stick with me if this happened?

"More time'm angry with guys that came back okay, why'm me and all. Jokers ain't care for nuthin'm came back without a scratch. Others like me'm here, well," he looks at me. "I was twenty seven'm when this happened, nineteen sixty nine'm."

He's been here six years, he's thirty-three. He looks like fifty. "Long time to go'm," he nods his head. "Long time to go, hard time'm too. Get sad'm, but no way out'm. Hard to see'm what I used to'm look like."

"Now, there you go," big woman coming in, thin pencil like eyebrows. "You there talking up a storm? You got to save your strength Mr. Artis. Scoot you," as she waves me off.

"Thanks'm, kid. Be'm careful."

"You are welcome."

Nodding to him thinking of his words as the nurse hustles me out of the room. The "thank you," the welcome to come back and talk again—damn right I will. Sadness of the place leeching out some of the stories I'd pumped myself up with about being a soldier.

Imagine what life must have been like before hospitals like this? Ancient Greek, Roman soldiers—standing in line with swords facing the enemy. Walking toward each other, slowly at first—a charge, yelling, adrenaline pumping, rocks, arrows, dogs. And then the maimed and wounded, what happened back then? Dying of infection, arms and legs lopped off 'cause they couldn't do surgery to close off shattered arteries. World War I— remember section in a book talking about how wounded and maimed British soldiers were forced to beg for food after the war.

Shudder going through me—this is not something to take lightly.

It is a sacrifice. It is a risk.

What if this is my life in a few years?

Suspended in time in a place like this.

Forgotten to most.

What do you do when no one is watching? How many acts of bravery here are locked away? How many guys here who were just unlucky? Feeling like I'm walking along a trail that ends ahead at a vertical granite wall.

Go up, go down, go back.

River running deep below, deep vertical drop down. I can go back.

What's up top? What's waiting on the other side?

Quiet drive back home.

Sitting in the experience of the place, the people, the stories.

Mumbling good night to Aunt Kitty as she exchanges looks with Uncle Vin.

Sitting in the deep black of the basement. Faces of the people I'd seen and talked to coming back with their stories—the older disabled vets who'd retired and were proud of their service wanting to talk about it, the younger wounded and crippled from Southeast Asia—angry, depressed, a few proud of their service, disgruntled with the shitty VA care, lack of opportunities. More often pissed off about how little of what they gave was even acknowledged. Now they are neglected men, used men—they're waiting to die. No one gives a fuck.

Telling myself that they could have been hurt on the job or in a car accident too. How many countless people, old people, are ignored and forgotten when they are no longer the bright shiny things they were when they were young like me? Damaged, aging slowly, can't move.

Tossing in my little bed. Time ticking by.

Sitting up, agitated, can't sleep.

Quietly sneaking out of the house.

Empty streets, feet feel heavy, sweatshirt hood over my head, sitting on a well-worn wooden bench in the park.

It's not so much that it's gone, just... Are we just helpless wretches ground up by the gears of life and spit out? Inexorable death, walking toward it every day. No matter how many scholarships I'd get, how many matches I win, how many times Cat and I make love, there's going to be an end—a little room smelling of medicine with pictures on the wall of people from long ago, empty, meaningless.

Breathing in the cool night air. Car driving slowly down the street.

Imagining all the days this playground is full of kids screaming, laughing, playing, no idea where they are going, just they are having fun. What was I like back then? Remembering how all my aunts, uncles and cousins would laugh when my father brought out the old 8mm movies he shot of me running around like the Tasmanian Devil when I was a little kid. Mom had me on a frigging leash cause she couldn't keep up with me. Lost for moments, painful to think back about happy times with those two.

Ass starting to hurt from sitting so long.

Tired, but mind feels clean.

Death is inescapable. So what if all the baloney we're taught in church is true or not—I can't escape the fact that I will die. What will I have to show for the life I led? Am I going to go out quietly like a lamb being led to slaughter?

Remembering my uncle's words—live a big life.

Get out and do great things, make great fuck-ups.

I'm good at that. What does that mean—warriors as healers, teachers, scientists, builders?

Rats scampering out of a garbage can.

Big suckers, one of them looking at me, skimming a garbage can lid across the pavement at him. He scampers off.

Hearing the window opening up from the house behind me.

"What the fuck are you doooin at three in the morning you asshole? I'm gonna call the cops!"

"What was that Harry?"

"Fucking asshole vandal out there."

Time to get the hell out of here.

Chapter 43

Trying to shake off the gloom settling in after her distant hug at the door.

Fighting off the need to cut into her enthusiasm as she prattles on about her Yale weekend, all the great people, the history of the place, the opportunities, the excitement, blah, blah, blah. Feeling like she's not even paying mind that I'm in the room—she's filling time now.

"Oh and you'd just love the library, so many books, so much history there. They have these great big tables—all kinds of students studying away, piles of books. There's like this buzz there, people were so involved in their work," she's moving on the couch closer now, but she's just rattling on. Body feeling heavier—shrinking under the weight of creeping sadness.

"I met the Dean of the Biomedical Engineering School, he's such an impressive man. I didn't know that he and my father were friends in college. He showed me around all the labs, they are doing so much important work there—I saw this one lab where they are working on connecting nerves to artificial limbs. Imagine helping people who've lost an arm. Wow," her arms crossed across her black turtleneck, "I'd never thought of going into engineering, but it's so important."

"Cat, I thought you wanted to be a doctor?"

"Yes, but I could do biomedical engineering first and then go to medical school," she's not looking at me. "The Dean was talking about what a pleasure it would be to have such a bright young woman studying in his department. It was so different than I thought."

Nodding to her, keeping the smile on my face.

"Afterwards, my dad told me how impressed the Dean was. How I could really be such a model, a Hispanic woman going to Yale, getting her advanced degrees there and going on to do research. Wow." She's looking off in the distance.

"But Cat, you talked about being a pediatrician? All that gets chucked out the window 'cause of one weekend with another stuck up?" she almost jumps up from the couch, her slim hand making fists, hitting the couch.

"Does every professor have to be a jerk in your world? What about all the great things they've done there? Medicines, technology, computers?"

"What about all the great things that weren't done there?"

"Why can't you let me enjoy this, Frankie? Why do you have to pull me down?"

"It's not that, Cat, just... You had such a dream of what you wanted to do, how much you didn't want to be like a lot of the people you see your dad hang around with. And now..."

"But this was different than I thought. Can't I change my mind? Just because I have opportunities doesn't mean," she's quiet, sitting back, the sting of her words settling in. "I didn't mean it that way."

"Bullshit, Cat. You're just being a bitch."

"Screw you, Frankie. You think you know so much…"

She crosses her arms again, looks up at the two-story ceiling. Feeling like I've made a mess of yet another evening.

Looking at her looking away from me.

"Frankie, look at the opportunities that could open for us," she looks at me. "If you could have met some of the other kids there. It was so… I can see how free they are, so many smart people. You'd love it there."

Fighting the sinking feeling inside, the gulf between us opening up again. Shutting it out. It's just a bad day. I shouldn't be stealing her moment.

"I'm sorry I called you a bitch."

"You better be. I might have to hurt you."

"I think you'll scare the hell out of most the boys there."

"Silly," she bumps into me with her shoulder.

"It sounds like a great place for you, Cat, I'm happy. I really am."

If I keep saying it, maybe I'll start to believe it.

Noticing the space between our sentences is growing longer—never had to push things before like this. Clock ticking in the background, a few moments remembering how we were here a month or so ago, something so new, so fresh, so wonderful that was just for us.

"What are you thinking, Frankie?" her eyes down in her lap.

"I don't know, Cat, it's like you don't want to hear what's going on…"

"What?"

"We keep dancing around what's going on."

"Don't you think this is hard for me too, Frankie? I just can't turn on and turn off things like you do," looking at her, both of us still as some loud coughs come from the little boy's room.

Frustrated, feeling the tension underneath the surface we won't address.

"So tell me then, Frank, I really don't get it," her arms crossed on her chest. "I don't understand why you don't want to touch me."

"Cat," shaking my head, "look, there's nothing I want more than to be with you like we were here."

She looks agitated, "Then why, Frankie, why all the ups and downs?"

"Cat, isn't this important to figure out? I feel like we've been doing it to try and put off the inevitable."

"Damn you, now you try and make what we're doing wrong?"

"No, Cat," taking a deep breath, "why won't you listen to me?"

"Shhh," her hands waving down, wave of frustration passing on her face, her arms back across her chest. Her face and shoulder slightly turned away from me.

Silence in the apartment growing larger by the moment.

"You used to talk to me so nice, Frankie."

Feeling stuck, chest tight.

"Cat, where do you think that came from? Reaching out to you, words coming to life to express the love I felt inside, words to caress you, words to share our passion," it seemed so easy then. "Isn't reaching that place the result of stepping out before the one you love without pretense, without protection, without fear and being who you are. Being there with you makes me want to be that person with you, the person who talks from their heart. Maybe it's heavy at times, but isn't that what two people who are in love do? It's you when you're bubbling on about the new places that are opening up. It's you when your heart is brimming with love and passion for me, for our bodies to be lost in the blinding light of being without boundaries for a few moments of bliss, of what it must be like to be close to God."

Her posture softening a little.

"It's you when you're raging on about how your mom is always nitpicking you about your clothes, your room. How nothing's ever just right."

Dim light of our reflections in the large TV.

"Why can't all those be you, Cat? Why can't I love all of them? I don't know, Cat." Turning on the couch, laying my head back. "Maybe I'm just incapable of being happy? Here we are with precious time and we're at odds. I just thought..." taking a deep breath holding something, an idea I can't reach, a quick vision that passes but leaves a lasting impression, a synthesis of the ugly, the tragic, the wonderful that I've seen the last few months.

"They are so wrapped up together. My uncle took me to a horrible place. It was like a holding yard for people near death, people who'd given up. I saw a picture by a man who'd died in this dark trash filled basement, a picture of a smiling proud family. Strong faces, strong people... and here he was, all alone."

Looking at her.

"Did he have something like this once? Was there a woman who made the world a wonderful place to live, that made him want to bring the riches of love to her and maybe their children? He had a few books... that was it. How many lives like this are out there, Cat, how much tragedy?"

"But why you, Frankie? Who are you to carry the weight of the world on your shoulders? Are you going to change it all? What does this mean to us?"

"Cat, I think it means that there's a lot to life we don't know a damn thing about. We live and swim in this soup of humanity but we're separated from it, and maybe rightly so. For as much as your parents make me crazy, I understand why they want to protect you."

"As for why me. Why not? Why not see it all, figure out what I can do to help make the world a better place. It's not the easy way, but just look at so many kids at our school. They don't know shit and they'll be going on to be engineers, doctors, businessmen, lawyers and they don't know shit. It's all book learning. Doesn't that bother you deeply? It's like we are just copies of a copy of a copy with something lost in each copy."

"My uncle said that I needed to get out and really experience life, really live life and then go make something meaningful of college."

"I hate your uncle"

Sitting with that.

"He's a good man."

"Oh, like my dad's a bad man because you don't like him?"

"Well..." shrugging my shoulders. Where the hell do I go now?

Suffocating silence.

"So your mind is made up?"

Shrugging my shoulders, not looking at her.

"But why you, Frankie? You scored in what, in the top one percent of high school kids in the country on the SAT, look at all the things you could do, things you could build. You're smarter than a lot of the kids I met last weekend. Look, it may be book learning, but look at what you could do with that when you get done? You've so much more common sense than..."

"But why not me, Cat? Don't we need smart people in the military too? Why am I special? We only know statistics about the kids who take the SAT, how about the kids who don't have a good school to go to, or had to work to take care of their families? There may be kids way smarter than me out there who are just, I don't know... nobody tracks them."

"That doesn't invalidate who you are! If ten people can carry a gun and only one of those can design a new heart, why should that person get killed like everyone else? Look at what the world loses," she's kneading her thighs, "it's not fair, it's not right."

"But what do you give up by doing that, Cat, and how can you be so sure that test scores mean anything? Look at Evan, he got good math too and did really well on English right? He can't do shit unless someone maps out the problem and the solutions, once he's got that, then he's a monster."

"That's my point you thick headed, rrrrr," and she smacks my arm, "you got that crazy smart... When you don't have your head up some place, you can see things from different angles, figure things out... It's different than Evan or any of the other brainiac boys. Damn, sometimes it's so frustrating talking to you."

She starts slapping at me, poking her back a little.

Laughing with her.

Stepping in from the cold for a few moments of warmth.

"So what are you? What are you going to do?"

Ideas, stories running through my head.

Looking at her dark eyes—all I have to do is tell her about how I'll get a technical job in the Air Force or something, take lots of college courses, take advanced placement tests, do three year active, three year inactive reserve, see each other as often as we can and then we'll be back on track. She wants to hear how this is going to work even though there's no way we can know. All it takes is a story that just calms her fears, let's her stay connected with the fantasy we've been living in the last few weeks to stave off...

Then there's sex, there's warmth, there's keeping with her. But it's a fucking lie. Father Fiero's words, my uncle's words—what kind of man do I want to be?

Lie to make it easy now?

Wanting to swim in those deep brown eyes. But what does that mean about my love—when it's convenient I'll make up some bullshit story. Why am I even thinking about this? Am I that much of a big wimp?

"Frank, why won't you talk to me, baby?"

Deep breath.

"Cat, I can't lie to you, I want to try out for the Rangers. I want to join the Army. I could go into the Air Force or Navy, get all kinds of tech training, get a bunch of schooling, I could do volunteer work through a church group, but... I can't lie to you. I want to see if I could make it where my uncle did, to do something physically and mentally extreme, to see if I have what it takes," her face growing impassive, her body stiffening. "Cat," turning my body on the couch toward her, my right leg folded, left leg over my ankle, She's looking out across the room, her body tighter, "I'm going to sign up, Cat. I'm going in the military." She pushes me away.

"You didn't even talk to me about it!"

"You knew the choices I had, I told you what I was thinking. What's this we're doing then?"

"Damn you!" her body slackening. "How can you just drop that on me?"

"I love you, Cat, I can't... no, I take that back, I won't lie to you even if it means losing this. I'm just not going to be that kind of guy. I start cutting corners now, what's next? I'm away playing around, I lie about that, you know I'm bullshitting, you start to play around and what we have just erodes like a sand castle at high tide, the bottom washing away a little with each lie and it just collapses. That's not how I want us to be, Cat. You told me to fight for this, right?"

She's looking at me out of the side of her eyes.

"We can make this work. You'll be out from under the control of the Commandant. I'll be away from my asshole father. I'll have money coming in to save. There's still the ability to get under the GI bill, Army will pay toward my college education. It might not be MIT undergrad, but then again it might be. We can make it work, Cat. We have to believe," my hands balled into fists, body feeling energized.

Looking at her. Give her time to think.

"We have to believe... No, that's weak. We have to know we can make it work. I love you, part of me wants you to run away with me, maybe I'm just jealous 'cause I love being around you when your brain's in a whirl and you put things together. You'll run that place and at the bottom of my heart I don't want you to give up all the things you could be. Go to Yale or better. Get into medical school, I'll be out then, we can live together, we can make this. After school, I want to be married to you. I want our kids to have you as a mom, smart, funny, a fighter, ambitious… They'd be so lucky."

"This weekend my uncle and I were out on the ocean. I keep looking across the water toward New Haven. I wondered if you'd like it out there with me, out in the sea, fresh, untamed, dangerous, uncompromising and at the same time wonderful, beautiful… I can't wait to take you with me someday, show you what it's like under the water. Show you how calm, how quiet it is, like a sanctuary at times."

Smiling to myself, "Of course there's always the thought of seeing you in a nice little bikini, or maybe less," laughing to myself at the vision of some fisherman coming up to our boat with us going at it. No wonder they only sent men to sea, Cat and I wouldn't get anywhere, unless there was some kind of sex powered engine.

Hmm, what would history have been like if instead of enslaving and forcing people to row the ancient galleys they would have recruited teenage boys by saying they could have a much sex as they like every day as long as they row? Hump, row, hump, row… Would have given thar she blows a different meaning, Melville would have written about a different kind of dick. Oops, get back to this conversation.

Her face tense.

"So that's it, Frankie?"

"Yes," watching her become resigned, "I don't know, Cat. I mean I could have gone to prison, but… You don't know what it's like to be around that caged meanness, people looking to take… then to have a record."

"What about the Peace Corps? You know how to build."

"That's true," lapsing into thoughts about the photos at Father Fiero's.

"But it's not exciting." Wincing from that dart striking home.

"Is there nothing I can do to close the gap, Cat? What about people who went away to fight Hitler? Were they just a bunch of jerks?"

"But that was different."

"How, how do you know what will happen next week, next year? Shouldn't we care about that? Shouldn't we care about what's happening in the world?"

"Why does that have to trump everything else?"

"It doesn't. You talk about me being black and white, look people stay together through things like this."

"So what, you'd write to me, come see me?"

"Of course," feeling a moment of sunlight breaking through the clouds, laughing on the inside. "I'd write you an ode to your beautiful breasts, then the smell of your skin, then how much I like to lick your toes, then how good your," she's starting to smack at me as I think that the next thing the row-hump-a-lots would do is organize a union: hey got to have a coffee break between humps, I've been working here and sweating all day…

"Frank!"

"Gots to tell the truth," smiling at her.

She sits back on the couch; her body looks a little more relaxed.

"Well," shaking her head, mix of emotions crossing her face, "it's something anyway." Not the reaction I was looking for.

"We need to talk more okay, Frankie?"

"Okay."

She looks at her watch, "Tomorrow? Meet me down on 72nd and Broadway after school. You could walk me home and we could talk?"

"What, like at the Embassy Theatre?"

"Sure," then she smiles, "you know there's a nice party coming up this weekend. Richard, Bradley, Ivan, and Corky are going to throw a big bash," she looks at me. "Richard's brother's out at Fire Island for the weekend and as long as the place isn't left a mess."

"They've got a big place," nodding to her as she comes over close putting her arms around my waist, head on my shoulder. 5th Avenue, a couple of blocks away from Washington Square.

"Should be a gas, they're collecting money and all."

"Just Juniors?"

"I think it's gonna be a free for all," she starts perking up.

Looking straight ahead.

"What's wrong, Babe?"

"You think I should go? I mean, I don't go there anymore, school you know. Feel like I'm hanging around..."

"Are you kidding? People ask about you a lot at school. I told them about that weirdo guy you took on, Hector and Julio have been buzzing all about that peppering me with questions. They're bummed you don't come around."

"You're kidding, right?"

She shrugs her shoulders, "Maybe I'm lying, how would you know?"

"You little beast," grabbing her and starting to tickle her.

"Ow, easy, don't forget how strong you are and how tender I am."

"Tender little beast," tickling her as she laughs harder and harder.

"Shh" she puts her finger to my lips, starts to kiss me, "before you go."

Can't escape the look on her face when she closed the door.

The tone of her voice when she said "What, you'd write to me, come see me," coming back to me while I walk down the dark, quiet street. I didn't catch the sarcasm.

Grappling with a rush of anger, breathing to manage the need to punch someone. No Frank, this is what got you here in the first place.

This just sucks so badly.

I can't even go back there and make this right.

Chapter 44

Insane morning at Uncle Vin's station. Uniformed officers hustling a group of angry black folk into lock down. Another group yelling trying to push their way into the station, more scuffles breaking out. Big wave of frenzied bodies enveloping me as more officers run come down the stairs to restore order. Pushing my way back to the wall, need to get upstairs.

"Motherfucken racist pigs!"

"We know we got rights, man!"

"You can't treat us like this."

"Fuck the MAN!"

"Man, fuck you," an officer yells back, "keep back."

"Get these assholes in the tank," yells another police officer struggling with a wiry man with a big fro, his dashiki torn from the scuffle.

"I'm gonna get you, Whitey," strong looking black man kicking at another one of the white officers. Batons making hard contact to his legs, the man yelling out in pain. He kicks a baton-wielding officer in the nuts— he crumples. Two plainclothes guys grab a hold and run him full speed into one of the big cast iron radiators. Holy shit—that dude is out, blood seeping out from a deep cut, crowd going off, getting more violent.

"They've killed JT!"

"Kill me Motherfucker!" guy yelling right into the face of a policeman pushing people back with his stick. More cops jump in, people who were hanging around are trying to get the fuck out of the way or are joining in too. Crazed looking black man jumping on a cop's back and biting him.

"What you lookin at, White Boy," turning and stepping back. Angry eyes dogging me, he's stepping toward me.

"Easy man," hands up, palms toward him, "no harm, no foul."

"Fuck you," his eyes moving side-to-side, "you think you are funny?"

He moves toward me shifting to his left like he's gonna throw a big sucker punch at me. Fuck this. Closing the distance. Dropping him with a big overhand right hand as he draws back for a roundhouse.

"Oh shit," a man struggling being held by two cops looking at me, "oh shit. You gonna get it Mr. Motherfucking Policeman, you gonna get it," stepping back further from the edge of the fray. "This big freak done kilt Maurice." Yelling, things flying around the room. Guys being dragged back to the holding tank. Rush of blue uniforms coming in and breaking up the crowd. People backing away from the swinging sticks and go scrambling for the double doors.

Cops laughing at the guy I knocked out.

"Gee, you gonna press charges now?" the cop looks around then adds, "huh Mister Badass Nigger?" and kicks him.

"Yo Kevin, slow down," black cop he didn't see, "watch that nigger shit you mook motherfucker," as he gives the guy I put down a good boot too.

"Yes, your Blackness," the first cop salutes, laughing.

"Nice shot, kid," the black cop looks at me as two white cops pick up the guy I dropped.

"That's Big V's nephew," says one of the plainclothes guys securing a struggling big black lady who's cussing him all which way up and down.

"No shit," the black cop looks at me, differently. "Get 'ch ya ass upstairs while we clean this mess up."

"Yes, Sir."

Walking up the stairs—people coming in and starting to cry and yell pointing at the man they ran into the radiator. Plainclothes and uniforms running down the stairs, Uncle Vin with them.

"Great day for a fucking riot," he looks past me, "Hey!" his voice booming in the room, "you two, block the fucking door!" he stops a group of plain clothes guys. "Relieve the uniforms, get them out in front with riot guns, set up a barrier. Sergeant Finley!"

"Yes, Lieutenant."

"Get your ass out front and see if we need to bring in help."

"On it Big V," he's with the guys pushing people outside.

"You," he runs downstairs and picks up a man by the back of his neck who's going to hit one of the uniformed officers with something, Uncle Vin shakes him like a big lion killing an antelope, "You don't fucking hit my men, you fucking unnerstand!" He slams him into a wall and hands him dazed to another officer.

Schmidt and a couple of his guys enter the fray—him and my uncle driving order through the volume of their voices. The guy Uncle Vin shook makes the mistake of talking shit to Schmidt who rams his thumb up into his solar plexus—the guy is on the floor barfing, gasping for air. Crowd dominated, people thrown out yelling about fucking pigs. Sounds like rocks and bottles starting to hit on the front as another wave of people come storming in through the front doors.

"Time to charge those assholes and get them the fuck out of here," said my uncle, Schmidt nodding.

Officers in riot helmets, shotguns and big riot sticks lining up in front of the Sergeant's desk.

"Break that crowd up," yelled Schmidt, at the top of his voice, "push them back from the station. We got reinforcements coming in from the 90th and 79th, if they don't disburse, arrest the lot," he's ripping off the torn sleeve of his dress shirt. Massive forearms, Marine Corps tattoo on his upper arm.

"You got it, Captain, let's go!"

They head out the front door, crowd noise rising, sirens getting closer.

"Wait for me up in my office," my uncle looks back and heads outside with his men. Not waiting around, heading upstairs past the few secretaries standing up by the balcony watching the mad house down below.

"That was fun," Uncle Vin steaming, slamming his office door.

"You wanted to see me, Lieutenant?" the red haired detective with the fiery eyes and square jaw, from that night in the subway station. His shirtsleeves rolled up, ripped, showing thick wrists and forearms. They called him Kelly.

"Yeah, Tommy, get him the fuck out of here," he looks at Kelly. "Some shithead wants to press charges against the big white cop who knocked him out." Quickly pointing at me, "Detective Kelly here's gonna take you far the fuck away from here for a few hours, you weren't here, you unnerstand?" he looks at me.

"I've been out playing ball all day, Uncle Vin."

"Shag ass, Detective."

"You got it, Big V," brusque motion for me to follow.

Out the back door—sirens, people chanting, "Kill the police! Kill the police!"

He comes to an alley with a tall steel gate. About to speak—he puts up his finger, looks around and squats down low before peering around one of the corners. He motions me in close.

"We're gonna go out this gate low," speaking very quietly, "we cross DeKalb quickly through the parking lot and then over to Claussen, move calmly, stay with me. Nod if you understand." Nodding to him.

Moving quickly running through the stopped cars, people milling about trying to look at all the action in front of the station, folks coming over from the projects to see what's going on. Running down the first alley.

Kelly motions me to stop with his left coming back underneath his body. "Can you jump up and get that fire escape ladder?" motioning for me to look. Nodding.

"Good, get it, pull yourself up and lower it for me." He motions for me to calm down and breathe.

"Go," as he moves up carefully and opens the gate.

Breathing deep—like taking a big layup. Hands grasping the bottom rung easily, knees bumping into the rough bricks, pain registering, deadened by adrenaline. Pulling myself up the rungs, gym work paying off.

Lowering the ladder down.

He's up like a monkey. Damn this guy moves well—compact movements as he pulls the ladder up. His service revolver out as we move up the rickety fire escapes to the roof. He motions me low as we come near the edge. People being arrested and hauled into big police vans. Following him away from the street—mimicking his movement.

He lays a work ladder across to the next building.

"Can you make it across?"

Nodding—no idea if I can, but damn if I'm going to wimp out.

He moves over and easily crosses the gap.

Looking forward, focusing on the other side.

No time to be nervous.

Running now.

Jumping over to the next building.

Motions me down. Stay put.

Street starting to take on a different buzz—people talking, cars passing by slowly, barricades coming down, streets reclaiming their normal rhythm. Following Kelly down to the street, through dark staircases—smells of piss and mildew. He's walking with his hand cupped together at his waist, his service revolver concealed behind them.

"Walk easy, nice and calm."

Willoughby St. quiet, walking past a small market. People standing in groups talking and looking at the damage to the police station, lucky they are not paying any attention to us. He takes a left on Lewis Ave., his hand moving freely—must have put his weapon back in his holster. Down the stairs to the subway—he flashes his badge and we walk in through one of the exits.

"You having fun yet?" waiting for the subway.

"What happened back there?"

He won't look at me for long—his eyes always moving.

"Evictions, brownstones being torn down for a new development. People are pissed about being thrown out of their homes... this has been going back and forth for months now. Don't blame 'em."

Looking at him funny.

"How'd you feel about some rich bastard paying off just enough people to change the zoning laws so they can evict you from a place you've been living for years and got a valid rental agreement? Pretty pissed, huh? Some of those assholes were piling on cause they've got to have something to bitch about, too bad, real grievance there."

Subway coming in, background noise drowned out by the train noise.

"Where we heading?" speaking louder

"Figured we'd take the L into Manhattan and go disappear in the Village for a few hours," he turns and faces the train coming—stepping inches away from the train.

He doesn't say anything on ride into the City.

Walking at a fast pace down 6th Ave, stepping into another little micro world in New York. Tie-died clothes walking down the streets paraded in skinny bodies here and there, drunks, a couple of leather boys walking along arm in arm giving me the eye. Passing people, cars. Kelly doesn't say a damn thing—feeling like I'm an imposition.

Good games going on the 4th Street courts on 6th Ave—lots of brothers—oh man, good move and dunk. Looking around, Kelly walking past the park down West 4th. Stopping and looking at the game—damn, I wish I were out there.

Hustling up after him.

Passing the Purple Onion, old-fashioned 1960's style photo's outside—Uncle Vin told me once this was a big Mafia hangout. Moving faster to catch up to Detective Kelly—at the corner he turns into the little pizzeria.

"Two sausage sandwiches," he's ordering.

"You want something to drink?"

"7 UP."

"7 UP and a Coke."

The taciturn man behind the large flat grill working mounds of onions and sausages nods. "To go?" Kelly nods.

"Ain't seen ya for a while, Detective."

"Workin the 88th now."

"Gee, that's a rough place."

"You ain't fuckin kidding."

"On me," he passes me a bag with our food and drinks.

Kelly looks at him—shakes his head, takes out a ten, pushes it toward the man, points at me with his thumb, "Big V's nephew."

"No shit," he looks at me differently now. "Your uncle's sometin else. You come down here anytime, you ask for Johnny you got that?"

"You got it," nodding thanks as we head out.

Chapter 45

Sitting in Washington Square Park on a bench facing the dry central fountain—all kinds of folks out in the cool afternoon hanging around—guys playing congas, others with guitars sitting on the two foot high sculptured concrete fountain ledges, dirty kids with longer hair than me out trying to be cool, couple of dipshits in surplus Army jackets dealing drugs, teenagers moving around the fountain—look like they are in from Jersey or the Island, fresh meat for the guys trying to work them.

Good looking black guy dressed in a nice light brown, form fitting, leather jacket, silk shirt, bell bottoms rapping with one of the white girls. "You baby, I been to Jersey, you should let me show you the life here, got some good clubs we can go to check out some good music, get in a good groove. I bet you like some of that good Latin jazz baby the way you move, hmm, hmm, hmm. I know you like to party, baby, don't you?" Chubby girl looks happy with his attention.

Kelly rolls his eyes. Unwrapping my sandwich—not hungry, but feeling empty coming down from the adrenalin rush. Chewing the warm juicy Italian sausage and grilled onion sandwich—good firm Italian bread sopped up with lots of grease and onions.

"These are good, thank you, Detective Kelly," my man still rapping with the Jersey girl.

"Call me Tommy."

"Okay, Tommy."

He's eating his slowly too.

"You used to work this area?"

"Five years. First four were fucking fantastic, then I got on the wrong side of the wrong people and man did that suck. I thought I was out and all," he looks at me, "I got rescued by your uncle," he looks at me, direct intense blue-green eyes. "You better respect that man kid, he's a real warrior."

Shaking my head. "Why'd you say that?" sitting back surprised by the intensity.

He looks right at me—like he's probing me, taking his time—not getting mad, but not looking away either. After a few long moments, he leans toward me a little.

"Any of us would take a bullet for him, he's one of the few guys on the force these slimy fucks who think they are above the law are seriously scared of. He's smart, he can't be bought, he won't stop, he's ruthless and he's organized. Put up a legal wall of bullshit, buy off a judge and he'll just wait in the background like a big python, waiting... That's why they are scared. They know he's got a lot of patience, but when he hits, oh man, oh man." He laughs to himself.

"Fucking makes me sick that most of the guys gunning for him are in the department nowadays, they want the glory of pulling his unit in and then get rid of Big V cause he's so independent. When Schmidt retires, well, it's gonna be fucking ugly."

"I don't understand?"

Looking at me, less intensity, impatient, "Your uncle's pissed a lot of powerful people off and it's unlikely he'll make Captain or Inspector. It's not that he's not a smart political player... just so much mediocrity and guys you know, cops who find it convenient to look the other way for a favor, if you know what I mean."

Nodding, corrupt cops—my uncle hates them with a mean implacable hatred. "I'd hate to be one of them in his crosshairs."

He laughs, "Yeah, you're talkin about one sorry motherfucker!"

Looking at the range of people hanging around the fountain—laughing with him, but imagining my uncle's wrath and realizing he's not joking. The two dipshits in the army jackets walking our way—Kelly locks eyes with them. The smart one taps his friend on the arm and talks to him, the not so smart one trying to give some attitude. They walk off.

Kelly doesn't say a word to me as he slowly finishes his sandwich.

Tall pretty girl with beautiful long black hair, long rough-out sheepskin jacket hanging around with a short guy carrying a guitar case—leather bomber jacket, Frye boots, jeans, turtleneck, aviator sunglasses—little Joe Cool.

She looks at me for a second, looks through me as they move on, floating through the park. Must be well off village residents—they have the cool clothes, but they look too clean. The guys out playing and getting a good rhythm going are rougher around the edges.

But she was beautiful.

Watching her walk away.

Kelly laughing as he watches me, I shrug my shoulders.

"So," he takes a sip of his soda, holding the bottle easily, "you wanna be a Ranger, huh?"

"Yes, ah," looking at him. "Guess my uncle told you? Yeah, I'm gonna try."

He looks at me. "You don't try something like that kid, you do it. You fucking do it! Listen, there are guys that do it to see if they've got what it takes, there are guys that have so much crazy energy they're better off..." He takes a moment looking at the people in the park. "This is something I think about a lot, something your uncle understands too. There are young men with the body to be a Ranger but they don't have this," he points to his head, "they don't understand the purpose, what it means to be a warrior. You think about that?"

"You mean protecting people?"

"That's a part of it. What about standing up for what you believe when it's not easy, when it could be your last act. You stay behind so your buddies live. You stand up to the pack of wolves to protect your flock. You fight to the death because that's what you do!"

About to answer, but he puts up his hand.

"It's more than that. It means taking a hard look in the mirror. What are your strengths, what are your weaknesses? What are they? How do you address them, prepare? How do you train for the time when your skills are needed? NOW! You getting some of this?"

Nodding my head.

"You think about what that means." Intense look on his face, "If you're serious, you start now," he holds my eyes, "you ready?"

"Sure, what do you mean?"

"I mean NOW or are you full of shit? Let's go," as he throws his half full bottle and wadded up tin foil into the trash can and starts trotting off toward Thompson—following him, catching up. Noticing he's got some kind of soft leather shoe with a crepe sole.

"Get loose, move your arms, get your shoulders warmed up."

Feeling stupid, people looking at us like we are two nuts trying to take off—but hey, down here in the village... Turning east on 3rd Street jogging faster down to Mercer—playground in one of the newer building complexes down here.

"Two minutes, let's see how many pushups you can do."

"You're kidding?"

"You said you were serious, you bullshitting me?" mean, intense stare.

Getting down in pushup position, people starting to stare—mothers and nannies with small kids scurrying about.

"Go at a good pace, not too slow, but don't go nuts. You'll need to do at least fifty good ones to pass the test."

"Get set... I'll count 'em out, down till your triceps are parallel with the ground, then up. I'll only count the good ones."

Moving up and down as he counts out.

"Twenty-seven, twenty-eight, twenty-eight, keep your body straight," his voice raising. People in the park are all gone for me—focused on keeping my body straight, focused on fighting the pain.

"Forty-two," getting hard, really struggling. Staying on my toes like Gus showed me, taking a second to breathe—thighs and stomach throbbing.

"Don't hang out too long, you're fighting gravity."

"Forty-seven," arms burning and starting to shake. Getting mad.

Do it, do it, do it.

"Fifty-five," arms starting to give, "fifty..." Turning to stop from falling on my face.

Breathing hard, looking up at the sky.

"That's damn good, for a civilian anyway," he's giving me a funny look as I sit on my butt breathing hard. "Take a minute to get your breath. You're

348

about minimum Ranger qual—under stress, tired from all the other stuff you'll do… You get the idea?"

"Sure do," shaking my head, sweat dripping down my face.

"Okay, up, let's see how good your sit ups are. Knees up, hands behind your head, you come up to a vertical then go back till at least your shoulder blades touch. Again, don't go too slow."

"Get set," he's down holding my ankles.

"Go… one, two, three…" working these like I do in the gym—should ace this with as much core muscle work as Gus has us do.

"Thirty-five, thirty-six, thirty-seven, good pace, keep it up."

Eyes relaxed, breathing to help manage the burn.

"Fifty-six, fifty-seven, fifty," working hard to get this, "eight, good give me sixty," struggling, "good sixty-one, sixty-two, sixty… time!"

Laying down breathing hard.

"Where'd you work your core muscles like that?"

"Boxing," breathing hard, "Gus makes us work hard to take," trying to catch my breath, "to take body shots."

"That down at the 14th Street Gym?"

Breathing hard, "Yes, Sir." He nods and lets me take a short rest.

"Let's go see what you can do on the bar," walking over to one of the play structures. "Not great, but this will work," he looks at me. "Normally you'd have run five miles in under forty minutes, you can do that on your own. This is what gets a lot of the big guys. They don't have the body strength for pull-ups. See if you can knock off fifteen. Big guy like you should work this hard, you'll be going up and down ropes, buildings, hauling your ass in and out of helicopters and what not."

Putting my hands on the bar used to suspend the steel net of the structure. "Back of your hands facing you… get set, go."

Pulling up, hard, body moving slowly.

Pissed at how weak this feels.

"One, two, speed it up."

Focused on pulling up quickly.

"Five, six, seven, come on."

Struggling… can't make nineteen.

Lowering myself down, trying to pull up again—half way, muscles losing it, hanging down, kicking my feet to try pull up again.

"That's it, you're done, eighteen."

Down on the ground—mad, mumbling—fuck, fuck, fuck…

"Not bad, like I said, a big guy like you should work this hard, go find a place with a nice thick climbing rope, practice on that, get in lots of pull-ups," he looks at me, "I'm impressed. You're in better condition than most who showed up for Ranger selection."

Breathing pattern slowing down. "What was it like?"

He looks at me, points to my head, "Ninety percent is in there, you gotta be able to get past what you think you can't do. You got to learn to stay in something and not give up. You'll be tired, hungry, confused," intensity coming back to his eyes, his hard finger poking me in the chest. "Can you get through it? Do you have what it takes to win, to develop the edge? You'll face things that most people will never understand and if you make it all the way through selection it will take a couple of years off your life. I lost almost twenty-five pounds... sounds good, huh?"

He relaxes a little, "And it's not being a badass jock, you can get kicked out if your team doesn't like you or you can't work well with others. You can get kicked out if the trainers think you're cheating, you can get kicked out if they think you're a psycho."

Looking at him, no idea what to say.

People in the park are losing interest in us.

"My uncle said you... Well, he said I needed to talk to you."

He chortles to himself. "That's putting it mildly."

He starts walking toward the exit, following him, sweat coating the inside of my shirt. Thirsty, muscles feeling raw, face flushed, walking on Mercer St. toward 4th Street as the sun starts to settle in over the Hudson. Waiting for traffic to clear.

"You have any idea what you are in for?"

"No Det... Tommy. I've heard a lot from my Uncle Vin, I've heard a lot from my father, who hated the Army. Besides that, it's been reading and imagining what it's like."

He shakes his head. "What didn't your father like?"

Laughing, "Geez, where do I start." Walking across the street back to Washington Square Park as more people show up to hangout and rap. "He said he hated being told what to do by people he thought were dumber than he was, he hated waiting in line for everything, he did everything he could to get away with as much as he could. He never told me this," realizing I'm smiling when I talk about my dad, feels weird, "this came from Uncle Vin, but he was made a scout cause his platoon sergeant wanted him killed off. He won a Bronze Star by capturing a German patrol though," laughing, "that must have really burned the hell out of them."

Kelly cracking a smile for a moment.

"You know, I love your uncle and I think I'd like your dad... too bad you two didn't get along too well," he's looking around the park—he's always looking, watching people. "I have a ton of respect for what your uncle did in the war. Looking death right in the face and going up those cliffs cause you had to get the job done, Rangers Lead!" He's shaking his head in admiration, motions for us to sit—one of the concrete outer rings near the plaza round the fountain. "But I tell you..." he takes a deep breath and lets it out slowly, "I served my time honorably. So many incompetent assholes..." his thick jaw muscles working back and forth, "the good men they got killed," his fists tensing up, "you'll never know what that's like till it happens to you."

People forming up in groups around the fountain in a mass of hugs, embraces and laughter—stream of people trying to be cool walking about, guys checking out girls, girls checking out guys. Total underage kids drinking beer, like the paper bag around the can fools anyone. Getting chilly as the sweat cools underneath my rugby shirt.

"For me it was always about being able to win in the shit, making sure we did our job of finding those NVA fucks, making sure my guys were taken care of," he's nodding at me like I should get all this. "After that... fuck the rest of them. My guys..."

He laughs to himself.

"You know how to tell if someone is lying about Nam? Huh?" his eyes drift over the current of people swirling around in front of us. Some guys decked out in varieties of surplus clothes decorated with peace signs, various military insignias I don't understand. Others in various combinations of knit, leather, jeans, whatever they could throw together, knit hats, a couple of wide brim leather hats.

"Their lips are moving," he laughs at his own joke. "So I'm not going to say shit other than you are going to deal with some of the dumbest motherfuckers on this planet who are locked into doing things the same old, same old. Mental midgetosis, baby, and these fuckers get people killed," looking at me again. "Get you killed, Sonny. You'll deal with mind-numbing bureaucracy, people who hide behind it cause they want to protect their little asses more than get the job done, people who love it cause they don't have to think for themselves."

He stands up, "This is pissing me off just remembering this shit, let's walk," and he starts off straight through the crowd, checking people out—stopping and giving people a hard look now and then, challenging them.

"You'll deal with criminals, dumb fucks who are too stupid to do anything other than be in the Army, you'll deal with idealists, religious nuts and a few good people who really want to serve their country. If you're lucky and you're smart you can put up a pretty good barrier between yourself and most of the fucking bozos. No matter what though," he stops and looks at me, his index finger poking me in the chest again. "No matter how good you are, you're always at the whim of some General who's God in his own mind and can do mostly what the fuck he wants. Think about that kid, you'll be a fucking grunt, a little piece of a big machine with a bunch of fat cats at the top."

"You complain like those folks this morning," hard blow to my arm. "Their places getting torn down because of some back room city deal and guess what," his eyes boring into mine, "they are right. You do that shit in the Army and you get what? A nice trip to the stockade," his jabs getting harder, "they fucking own you. What do you think of that huh? Pretty fucking glamorous, pretty fucking John Wayne?"

Walking quickly with him.

"So why do we do it? I'll tell you why, because we are warriors, dammit! We don't quit because of incompetence. We don't let the idiots win."

"Geez Tommy…" shaking my head, confused.

"That didn't convince you did it?"

Laughing, "No, Sir."

"Figures, your uncle is a stubborn bastard too," he takes a deep breath, "I laid it on the line at least you'll go in with your eyes open. You make Ranger and things are a little better anyway. Here's a bit of wisdom, you want to get away with as much shit as you can? Now say, "yes Detective Kelly"."

"Yes, Detective Kelly."

"Then be the best at all the things they ask you to do. Be absolutely the best… when they tell you to be on time, be early. When they say show up with your pack at a forty-pound load, show up with forty-five pounds. Keep you shit squared away and make your boss look good. Plus, Rangers love guys who can box," he's laughing, "you'll probably have some asshole Major drooling over the prospect of getting a first class heavyweight," he's looking around, looking at his watch. "I'm going to cut you loose" he looks at me, "work your upper body, come see me anytime, kid. Good fucking shot on that asshole this morning," he waves and walks off, turns for a second. "Good luck… you make Ranger, I'll buy you a beer and you can tell me all about the Darby Queen, oh, yeah," he looks back, "remember, get it all in writing kid, your service contract, don't let the pretty boy recruiter bullshit you."

Looking at his back.

"Hey," he yells at me, "toughen up your feet, get some good boots that fit, walk, run, eat, sleep in 'em. Ask your uncle, or come see me. There were some guys who had blood pouring out of their boots in selection and had to drop out cause of their feet. Get a head start."

Nodding at him as he turns and walks away. What the fuck is Darby Queen? Dairy Queen—they even have those here in the City?

Cold chill running down my spine—oh no, I'm late to meet Cat. Oh shit. Breaking into a run up to 14th Street.

Shit, shit, shit.

Dodging people, cutting across people—they are yelling at me.

Token in the turnstile, running down the stairs to catch the L train. Body amped, snapping my thumb, willing the train to get here. Five minutes late now. Will she stay? Will she walk uptown? I could get off at 79th walk downtown and try and pick her out of the crowd as she walks uptown. Shit, shit, shit.

Finally a fucking subway!

Assholes, why can't these things run faster?

Amped up, standing at the subway car door, pulling people into the car in my mind, feet tapping the floor willing the doors closed. Wishing we'd get going. Frustrated at the time people taking sauntering in and out the car while some asshole starts to spout poetry looking for a handout—assholes. Frustrated, feeling stupid.

Running down the long tunnel from the L train to the IRT.

Jumping in as the doors close. Breathing hard—middle-aged lady on the bench giving me a major stink eye. Like my heavy breathing is going to fuck up her world. Part of me wants to get in her face and yell, spittle flying out of my mouth, face contorted like a berserker. Calm down Frank. Standing by the subway door. One stop. Eighteen minutes late.

Passing stations, tunnel lights, the car rocking back and forth.

Twenty minutes late.

Pushing my way to the door—brother asking me what the fuck is wrong. Don't have to answer. Running up the narrow stairs, long line at the single exit doors—running through the turnstile, out in the street. Heavy traffic going downtown on Broadway—running across the street—looking across the street at the theatre, she's not there. Fuck!!!!

Break in the traffic, running across—taxi honking his horn at me after narrowly missing me. Looking up Broadway—could she be late? No, she's never late.

What was that Kelly said? Be five minutes early. Starting up Broadway at a jog. Dodging people and delivery boys in front of D'Agostino.

There, she's looking in the store window of Pandemonium.

Relief flooding in, smile breaking out on my face, "Cat."

She turns around, sees me, her arms crossing—she looks pissed. Her head bobbing side-to-side, "Just where the hell have you been? I've been standing around like a stupid idiot. Pervert asking me if I wanted a date," she slaps at me.

"I'm sorry Cat, I messed up. I had to meet my uncle, there was a big mess…"

"Don't you go on with all that," her head bobbing side-to-side, her left hand and on her waist now her right hand extended to ward me off. "You have no idea what I've had to go through at home lately. I can't wait to get out of there," she starts walking uptown. Settling in next to her, breathing starting to settle down.

Looking at her, she won't make eye contact.

Blocks, people moving by, feeling like shit.

"So, we just gonna go on like this, Cat?"

Still not talking to me.

"How am I gonna trust you, Frankie? You're late, you do this, you do that? We talk about going away and then you never say anything about it. I talk about all this great stuff in college and then it's I-want-what's-best-for-you. What is all this?"

"Hey wait a minute, I asked you," feeling my shoulders bunch up, "you just passed on it."

"Listen, listen," she looks at me, finger pointing in my face while her head bops side-to-side, "you can't just say something like that and expect it all to snap into place just cause you want it to." Snapping her fingers in my face. "How do I know you're serious? You never brought it up again. I was waiting to hear more... How we'd live, what we'd do? You just can't put big things like that out there and leave them there? We're gonna talk about the future and here you are and late looking like a mess. How does that make me feel?"

Crossing 86th Street. Four blocks.

"Look, let's go someplace and talk"

"No, I got to get home."

Petrified silence. Watching her walk into her apartment building.

Looking at my watch—almost five.

I can make it down to Times Square in twenty minutes.

Fuck it.

Subway downtown jam-packed.

Looking at people—gray faces. Dirty walls.

Express train rocking back and forth.

Walking upstairs to Times Square—lights blaring from all the signs. Crowds, cars moving up and down Broadway. Crossing with a wave of faceless people to the Recruiting Center. Cold feeling in my stomach, determined to get this done. Ignoring the feeling that I'm rushing things once again.

Fellow in the Navy Office smiling asking if he can help me—moving to the Army office. Tall, light-skinned black man putting on a well-pressed dark green uniform jacket, all kinds of stripes on his sleeves, ribbons on his chest.

"Hello there," he looks over and turns on the charm. Must be how they pick these guys. My new fucking buddy, "I'm Master Sergeant Collins," he holds out his hand—good firm, warm handshake.

"I'm Frank Caruso and I'd like to enlist."

His eyebrows go up, "Okay, I was leaving, but we can talk a bit, get you started, you're lucky there's a test run tomorrow." He must be seeing the weird look on my face.

"Standard tests to help figure out where you'll be best, called the ASVAB," he raises an eyebrow, "Armed Services Vocational Aptitude Battery test."

He motions to the chair near his desk, "Take a seat."

Watching people outside as they walk by the long windows facing the sidewalk. Lights of the XXX movie theaters across the street flashing on the venetian blinds. Fighting off feeling like a loser sitting in here surrounded by all these recruiting posters—Kelly's words ringing in my ears.

"So how old are you, son?"

"I'm seventeen, Sir."

"Call me Master Sergeant or Sergeant Collins okay?"

"Sure, Master Sergeant."

"Parents know you're doing this? They'll have to sign a release."

"Yes they do, and I'm sure they will, they'll pay you to take me."

He gives me a polite smile.

"Why do you want to join the Army, son?" he folds his hands on the desk looking at me.

"Well," sitting up, ignoring the people outside. "To be honest, I hadn't thought about it much. I did something pretty stupid and the judge offered me a choice to serve or go to jail. After that, I started to read a lot. I talked a lot with my uncle, he was in the 5th Ranger Regiment, stormed the beaches at Omaha. I talked to lots of other folks as well who served in Korea and Southeast Asia, they were pretty honest about what I'd find."

"So you haven't finished high school yet?"

"No, Master Sergeant."

He nods, "I take it you can't defer for a year to finish school? That would open up a lot of opportunities for you, certain specialties require a high school diploma."

"But I have good grades and good College Board scores."

He looks at me patiently.

"Well, we'll see how you do on the standard tests."

"Is a high school diploma required to be a Ranger?"

"No, but if you want to go on into any of the technical fields…"

"No, Master Sergeant, I'm going to be a Ranger."

"Tough qualifications, seventy-five percent of the people that turn up for selection fail," he looks at me and takes his time to let that sink in.

"You an athlete, son?"

"Yes, basketball and boxing."

"Boxer, huh. How'd you do?"

"I'm twenty-eight and one in Golden Gloves, Master Sergeant."

He nods, folds his hands and rests the tip of his nose on his hands.

"A lot of history in the Ranger Regiments, kid, a lot of proud people serve in those, not easy to get into. Look I want to be honest with you; the Army isn't a place to run away to. Everything you find out here, you'll find in the service with lots of other responsibilities piled on" he looks at me, "you sure you want to do this?"

"Yes."

"Okay, Frank," he takes out sheets of paper from his desk, "take your time and fill all these out. You want something to drink, Coke or something?"

"No, thank you."

Forms; languages I can speak—wonder if jive counts. Well at least there's Italian, Spanish and English—skills, grades, blah, blah, blah. Time ticking by. Working through all the pages answering questions—no criminal record, no drugs...

Handing back the forms.

"Okay," he starts flipping through the forms. "Here's where you'll need to be at oh-eight-hundred tomorrow morning. Be prepared to spend the day, the morning there and then I'll be out there to check-in with you and the other candidates. Sign here and fill in your contact information. This is not your Army contract, we'll talk about that tomorrow."

Looking at the paper—Fort Hamilton, I was just out there.

"I've been there."

"What's that, son?"

"My uncle took me to do volunteer work at the VA right near Fort Hamilton,"

He nods. "Outstanding," he stands and offers me his hand, "I look forward to seeing you tomorrow. Make sure you have all the questions you want answered ready, okay?"

"Will do, Master Sergeant."

Insides feel unsettled—no going back.

Lonely subway ride back to Brooklyn.

Not looking at people.

I knew it was coming, but here is the final barrier to cross.

Remembering her look as she went into her apartment building.

Cold shudder.

Chapter 46

Busy morning subway station, waiting for the D train. People standing about reading their newspapers folded up into fourths—more NY Post readers here than the NY Times, convenient posters to hide behind so they don't have to make eye contact.

Train finally coming in. Looking at my watch—feeling like a fool going to the first day of school. Chest getting tight, fighting panic welling up—no matter how hard I hold on, how can I keep her? Body gripped by the feeling she's being pulled away from me and she's not fighting it. Dammit!

Walking on the train bumping into people coming off, not giving a fuck if they like it or not. Part of me hoping for someone to talk some shit so I can smack that motherfucker upside his head. Talk some shit now!

Hard look through the car, people's eyes down on the floor.

Moment passing as the subway accelerates into the dark tunnel.

Mind flashing back to Aunt Kitty.

She looked so worried this morning. I hate to let her down.

Feeling my eyes water up. If she hadn't believed in me…

What a fucking mess I am. Asshole.

Rocking with the train.

One moment I want to fight till I can't move or I'm beaten down like a mad dog and the next I'm whining away like some big fucking mama's boy. Yeah, I'm a real badass standing in here in a crowd of people who absolutely don't give a fuck about me. Why should they? I don't give a fuck about them.

Ignoring the flashing image in my mind that I can never hold her. Breathing in, sitting down in an empty seat, leaning back on the hard fiberglass seat. Of course you idiot, asshole, fart jockey, shit face… Stop being a big baby—she's got to want to stick with me through all this. If I keep acting like this, then it's proof that I've lost her.

Walking in through the Fort Hamilton main gate, guys with white hats waving us along. Verrazano Bridge in the distance framing the historic casements of the Fort. Kids from all kinds of backgrounds roughly my age converging on a shabby two-story building. Concrete walkway cracked from weather, small weeds growing up here and there.

"You here for the ASVAB?" a thin man in a green uniform asks.

Showing him my paper.

"Room 210," he turns his attention to the other kids streaming in. A few white kids, mostly black and Hispanic kids filing in. Different eyes than in prison—they look like me, confused, wanting to get this over with.

Stairwell up smells of mold, wall painted a light green, cracked in places.

Filing into an old classroom—old style chairs with a well-worn writing surface. What a dingy place. Is this what all the Army bases are like? Sitting next to a Hispanic kid who's looking around.

"Good morning," a man with a well-ironed, crisp green uniform enters the room. "I'm Sergeant Stanley, I'm going to manage the test procedure for you this morning. When I call out your name, answer present."

He starts droning on and on.

"Present," when my name is called. Surprised at how many names he calls out who are not here. Kid in the hall complaining about them not letting him in cause the bus was late—dumbass.

Jesus, this is easy.
Whipping through the tests.
Must be making mistakes—going back through all the answers.
Double-checking.
Shrugging my shoulders when the Sergeant calls time.

Outside during the lunch break—hungry, but don't want to follow the throng. Kids who came together talking about the test—going on about an easy math question they missed. The kid who was sitting next to me just hanging around too.

"*What's your name, man?*" he's surprised to hear me speak in Spanish.

"*Jorge, how about you?*"

"*Frank. What did you think of the test?*"

"*That's a lot of bullshit, man.*"

Laughing with him.

"What are you signing up for?"

"Going into the Air Force. I'm going to be an electrician, get trained and get a good job when I get out."

Nodding to him. "How about you?"

"Don't really know, going into the Army though."

He shakes his head. "My wife's nervous about where we'll get stationed, hopefully somewhere on the East Coast."

"Wife?"

"Hell yeah. Man, they give you extra pay if you're married. Don't you know anything about what you're getting into?"

Shaking my head as he takes a picture out of his wallet—cute, plump woman holding a baby. "Wow, how old is your baby?"

"Three months now," he's looking at the picture smiling, "jobs suck out here man. At least I'll get paid and learn a trade. I'm going to get something to eat, you coming?"

"No man, I'm not hungry."

"Check you later, Hommes" he's heading with the rest of the kids.

Jorge has got to be what, a year older than me—he's married and has a kid. Mama Mia—married. What about Cat? Stopping and taking a deep breath—what about that? So early, so young.

Waiting.

Kid's names being called out walking into rooms to talk with their recruiter. Where the hell is Collins? Looking at my watch, two hours sitting on my ass. Whew! Faces going in look concerned, a few seem resigned. Faces coming out mixed—relief, happy, a couple deeply troubled. Is this pass, fail or rejection?

Sitting here alone looking at the cracks in the wall, imagining it's a map of the world. I'm leaving in thirty minutes—fuck this waiting around three hours.

Thirty minutes is up.

Getting up and pacing—if I leave, what will the consequence be? I can see these assholes some other time—go talk to the Marine recruiters, they moved things along quickly here this morning.

"Hey, there he is," familiar voice behind me.

Nodding, doing my best to not be too pissed.

"We'd like you to do us a favor," impassive looking at him. "Sorry for the wait, I needed to talk to Major Andrews."

Shrugging my shoulders.

"We'd like you to take another battery of tests, you did really well on the standard tests and we'd like to see how you do on the advanced tests, there's a whole generation of new tech gear coming on line... computers, radars, the works. We need guys who can understand all this new stuff, you do well on these tests and you can write your ticket."

"What about the fact that I don't have a High School Diploma?" crossing my arms. What kind of bullshit story was I being fed?

"Well, your test scores put you in a category where that might be waived."

"Right," rolling my eyes.

"Come on back here with me," as he motions me to walk down the hall where all the other kids had come and gone, charming smile on his face.

A man sitting behind the desk rises up, same type of uniform—no stripes on his sleeve, oak leaves on his epaulets.

"I'm Major Andrews," he holds out a strong looking hand.

Firm handshake.

"Frank Caruso."

"Good to meet you, Mr. Caruso, please sit down." Taking a chair across from his desk—the office looks temporary, nothing personal from him or the Sergeant here.

"We'd like you to take another set of tests, shouldn't take long."

"Okay."

Passing me a set of folded papers.

"Can I have some work paper too?"

He nods and hands me a set of lined notebook paper and a No. 2 pencil.

If this is advanced stuff these guys are morons.

Basic calculus and trigonometry—this is easy beans. Double-checking my work. Looking up at the Major and the Sergeant watching me, scary these assholes don't have anything better to do. Passing my tests and work sheet back. The Major takes out a scoring template and goes over the test—flipping through a manual for the written questions.

Looking at the clock, the bland light green walls with what must be ten-year-old posters exhorting jerks like me to join the Army.

The Sergeant and Major looking at each other.

"How did I do?"

The Major takes a deep breath—no way I messed up on this one.

"Your ASVAB and Advanced Math scores put you way up into Officer territory," body shivering a little—unexpected. "These are some of the best I've seen. We just wanted to double check you know, make sure the ASVAB wasn't a fluke," he starts flipping through my applications. "You speak fluent Italian and Spanish?"

"Yes, Major," he nods.

"*How did you learn Spanish?*" he waits. Looking at him surprised.

"*I don't really know. I just have a good ear for languages. My mother made sure we spoke good Italian at home. I think that made it easier for me to pick up Spanish, you know, a lot of the same roots.*"

"*How's your vocabulary?*"

"*I speak mostly street Spanish, I can read some of the local newspapers, but it's more just to pass the time. A lot of my friends are from Puerto Rico and the Dominican Republic. Their families try to keep them rooted in their language, they like that I've taken the time to learn.*"

He nods, "*Very good.*"

"Normally with scores like this we'd be talking to you about going to Officer Candidate School," the Sergeant chiming in, he must be the bad news guy, "but given that you've not finished high school, we have a problem."

Passing the ball back to the Major.

"We'd like you to enter the Army and sign up for a six year program where you'll get a high school equivalency, do a technical training program with accelerated rank placement and as soon as you make E4, set you up for an Officer or Warrant Officer program, Mr. Caruso. How about that?"

"Hey that's a great thing, Frank," looking at the Sergeant, my new best buddy. "Warrant Officers get to fly the latest birds. I tell you, it's a fantastic gig."

Sitting back in my chair. This is not what I came for.

"Well?"

"This isn't what I expected. It sounds great. If this qualifies me for a shot at Ranger selection that's fine, but I want a contract guaranteeing me a slot in Airborne and then Ranger selection."

The Major looks at me, "Look, if you don't mind, I'd like to talk to you a little about the modern Army." He stands up—Collins backs up. Shifting restlessly in my chair—getting pissed, assholes wasting my time.

Detective Kelly's words coming back about characters I'd run into.

He's droning on about technology is the future, blah, blah, blah. How anyone can carry a rifle, the need for intelligence work, communications technology, and computers... "I think you can start to appreciate what an important role you, and people like you, can play in our Modern Army."

Looking at him, nodding like I've been paying attention.

Hands starting to feel cold.

"How about it, son?" said Collins, "it's a great offer, you work hard and you'll likely be wearing a bar on your collar in two years. Isn't that right, Major? An officer and a gentleman?"

"That's right, Sergeant," enough to accentuate the difference. "How about it, Mr. Caruso?" He sits down on the edge of the desk in front of me.

Unsettled where this is going. These guys are playing me, like they are my best friends. Why wouldn't I follow in my uncle's footsteps? All what they've said sounds good—there's got to be some bullshit predicated on their story they are not talking about. It sounds good though.

"Major, what you've talked about sounds really good, but that's not what I want to sign up for. I want to do what my uncle did. He was a Ranger, that's what I want to do. If that's not acceptable, then I'll go see the Marines."

He stands up, walks behind the desk and arranges himself.

"If you don't take this offer now, and let's say something happens where you don't make it... well, let's say it will be unlikely you'll still have this opportunity. Once you're placed in a given specialty, then..."

"Think about this, Son. It's not like school where you can change your electives later. You go this route; best case you'll get what you want. Worst case you'll be out walking the line bored out of your mind. Think about this, over seventy-five percent of the people that go through selection don't make it."

Nodding. These assholes don't understand. I'm not going there to try out. I'm going there to do it.

"So what happened? You were gone for a long time," Aunt Kitty calling out to me as I walk in the door.

"Hi, Aunt Kitty. Crazy day, they gave me all these tests and tried to talk me into going into a technology specialty, finish high school and they'd put me through a program which would lead to me being an officer."

"And you said?" she's wiping her hands on her apron.

"I had to threaten to walk out and said I'd go join the Marines if they didn't write me a contract for what I wanted."

She sits down. "Oh, Frank," looking at me, "I don't know if that was such a good idea. I mean, you were so concerned about your schooling, that seems like a lot to let go on something that's so," she's takes a moment. "That's so speculative I guess, I don't know." She looks around the kitchen. "Risky too, isn't that impulsive? You could have talked to us about this you know."

"But, Aunt Kitty," not knowing why she's changed directions on me. "I thought you'd be proud… all I'd thought through, came to a decision and all."

"Yes, but Frank, it sounds like you turned down something really good without taking a close look."

Nodding, "Maybe I messed up here, but it's too late. I signed the contract, well I guess I have an out," sitting back, "I still have to have Dad sign the agreement."

Looking at her, the terrible feeling of being off balance setting in.

Did I look the gift horse in the mouth?

Shaking my head—what would a stupid gift horse look like anyway, would the horse come with someone to shovel the horseshit?

Shrugging my shoulders.

"Well, there's one thing to say," she does her best to put on a smile. "You certainly are determined when you make up your mind."

"Is that so bad?"

"Well, I don't know, when you're dead set on something you kill off alternatives quickly. Who knows…" she smiles again, "let's get some food in you, I'm sure it's been a long day and your uncle will want to know all about this later."

She stops for a second, wave of sadness crossing her face.

"When do you leave?"

"Oh," getting the dates straight in my head, "the best schedule looks like going to Georgia for Basic in August and then transition into Airborne school with only a couple of weeks in between, after that it's the winter round of Ranger selection."

She's looking at me doing the math in her head—five months.

Sad smile.

She looks out the window.

"It's been really nice having you here."

Starting to choke up a little.

"It's feeling like home now, Aunt Kitty, it will be hard to leave."

"Oh you. Come give your aunt a hug," her head on my shoulder. "I'm really going to miss you."

Chapter 47

You promised yourself that you'd never come back here.

Doors pounding open, noise of pent up high schoolers released from class reverberating out into the busy street, a couple of the rich kids being picked up in cars.

"Heeey, Frank," from a posse of sophomore chickitas as they walk past on their way to 1st Avenue. Nodding and smiling, here come the party boys— Richard, Bradley and Corky surrounded by a gaggle of girls. Nina again, geez, she gives me a nice fuck you smile. Ah, it's good to be the king.

"Hey, Frank!" Funny, I've known Richard since kindergarten—I won't talk to him for weeks and then, snap, we'll be back in tune.

"What's up, Richard?" he's buzzed about something.

"Oh man, you gotta come this Saturday, it's a Rock'n Roll theme man, come as your favorite rock star man, it's gonna be crazy maaan," he looks at Allan who's just joined in and then moves closer to me, kind of imploring look on his face.

"Frank, not that I needed his suggestion, but my brother asked that I invite you. You know, keep things from getting too wild."

Laughing with Richard as he bubbles away doing some air guitar.

"Sure, I'll be there, no problem about your brother. He's what, heading up to Provincetown with his latest boy toy Ken or whoever?"

"Yeah, well," he looks away—like it's any secret his brother is gay.

Looking at him. Must be tough, parents dumped him down here so they can jet around the world. Still, he's got freedom most of the kids in school would die for.

"So," can't resist needling him, "breaking out the Elvis jump suit and glitter?"

"Hell no," he starts to get all worked up.

"Get them hips going, drive the girls all crazy 'n shit?"

"Nah."

"All right, all right… you gonna need me to make a run?"

"Oh man, that'd be great, everyone's got to pay twenty to the party kitty. It's going to be so much fun, man!"

"What are you going as, Brad?"

"Beach Boys, baby."

"That's pretty funny. You need to get a posse of surfer chicks too."

"I'm working on that," he wiggles his eyebrows and looks over at a gaggle of giggling sophomores. "Nina's going as her usual Mod Squad," he says looking at her, nice to see someone else needle her. "Hello, earth to Nina, all those Brit bands you love stole their stuff from Blues singers!" mimicking knocking on her head. "Ever hear of BB King, Muddy Waters, hello?"

"Oh, stuff it, Bradleeeey."

Cat and Julio walking out of the building together—insides going cold as

Richard's banter goes in one ear and out the other.

"Hey, I'll catch you later," looking back. "What time?"

"Eight, you can stay over if you like, you know, if you want to."

Like my aunt and uncle will let me do that.

Julio startled, "Julio, my man."

Cat stiffening, her shoulder turning toward me.

"Frank, I didn't... Thought we were going to meet on 72nd?" ignoring her. I know that look on Julio's face.

"Don't play me like that, Frankie." He looks hurt.

Looking at Cat, then looking at him.

"Hey, hey," from behind me, I know that voice—right on time, my good buddy. "It's Mister I-don't-have-any-place-better-to-go. Mr. Convict."

"Eat me, Leroy," looking at her. "You coming?" stepping between her and Julio, hurt look on his face, putting my arm in hers and walking west.

"Stop pulling me along, this hurts."

Crossing the street to Stuyvesant Park.

"Let me go dammit, Frankie." Walking quickly towards Stuyvesant Park as she tries to pull her arm away.

"Look, Cat," letting go of her arm as she rubs where I was holding her. "Let's cut through the bullshit. I'm not going to be a big, dumb puppy dog. I..." throat closing in, "I love you, but I'm not going to hang on here cause I'm scared of losing you." Looking at her, cars streaming down 2nd Ave. Wordless motion to her toward the nearest park bench.

"Cat, if it's over, it's over. The last few times we've been together... I don't know."

Sitting next to her, looking into the center of the small park.

Looking at her—she's staring out in space, her arms crossed on her chest.

"Talk to me, Cat, even if it's something I may not want to hear. As much as we've done together and been through together... at least let's be straight."

Nothing from her.

Park feels so empty. Looking around—sky is clear, pigeons waddling around looking for food, a few other school kids hanging out—a couple of seniors making out. This is the last time I'll be here.

When do you say goodbye to the old things you knew?

"I was thinking back on the time we went ice skating at Rockefeller Center last year. Man, was I spaz. You were skating circles around me, your little pink leg warmers around your lower legs, those nice, tight jeans, hm, hm, hm. There you were making fun of me, the little kids who could really skate were zipping in and out of slow pokes like me, people getting annoyed when I'd bump into them and shrug my shoulders... Your face was so alive. After finding places that were out of the way, we could kiss."

Bittersweet feeling running though me.

Sitting back on the bench, feeling the rough weathered wood.

"And here we are, Cat, on the other side of the world from each other. I don't understand, the up, the down. It's not making you crazy? It feels like we both know, but are too chicken to say it." She turns her face away.

"Say what, Frankie?"

"That it's time we split up."

"If that's what you want."

"That's not what I want, Cat!" Turning my body toward her. "That's not what I want, Cat. I want to fight through this. I want to fight through this with the girl I know who doesn't give up. Jesus! Why are we doing this?"

"I'm tired, Frankie," she sits forward, her long hair spilling over her hands. "I've been fighting everyone for so long. Maybe because we had something so strong, a connection that kept me going, you know. With my father always nagging and disapproving," she turns and slaps me on the shoulder. "And you going off all crazy. How's that supposed to make me feel, how am I supposed to trust you?" putting her face in her hands for a few moments. "What about what I need, Frankie?" She's looking at me. "It's not all about you, you know. I know you care about me, but when have you been here for me lately? You always want to talk about yourself and all the things you're doing, where's my place in all that? What am I supposed to do to help you? You never tell me, you never let me do anything. How do I know you need me? Tell me that?" her voice softening a little.

She looks at me.

"You hurt me," slapping at me again, softer. "I'm gonna have a bruise."

"Cat, baby, come here. I don't want to fight with you, but I will if that's what's got to happen. I been trying to keep this clean you know… keep the bad stuff away from you," looking at her. "You know deal with it, clean it up, not try to add more."

"But look you, you…" she's starting to come back, "if we are in this together, why aren't you letting me help you? Why do you keep on doing crazy stuff?"

Her arms crossed against her chest, she gets up and walks away.

Turning to me.

"How am I supposed to keep doing this, Frankie? I feel like everything's so great one moment, it feels like you're so good for me and then you're in these black moods. You say these wonderful things, talk about the future," her lips thin and pulled back. "How do I trust you, Frankie? What kind of crazy things are you going to go off and do next? And you'll be gone some place, God knows where. What about that?"

Standing up, extending my hand to her, she moves away.

"No," she holds up her hands.

Stopping, looking at her from a long way off.

"How am I supposed to take this, Frankie? Tell me. I mean it's not like I don't want to. I know how bad you feel about hurting your friend and all, that damn Leroy needs to take some of this too, he started all this shit. And now you have to go away, it's not fair to us."

Ask her. Ask her. Nervous.

Walking to her.

Ask her.

"Cat," softly to her. Coming close to her, "Cat, I want you to wait for me. I want us to be together through all this, in all that this means. Then after, I know I'll be a few years behind you, but just think, Cat. We'd be free of our parents... You know I didn't think about this till now, but imagine being able to go someplace warm, someplace wonderful were we can play on the beach all day, go out at night and have fun and then a place to ourselves when it's cool out. Think of having that freedom. We stay focused the next few years, just get through this."

Feeling her body soften a little.

Standing with her back toward me.

"Frankie," turning slowly to me, her head still down, her body looks like it's feeling the weight of gravity pulling her to earth. "How, Frankie? How do we make this work?"

Standing behind her, putting my arms around her—her body noncommittal, but not shrieking "no."

"We're smart, we figure it out. We could talk to my aunt and uncle, they stayed together while he went off to fight," the next thought coming at me like a ton of bricks. You had the courage to ask her—you can't stop now. Having to push the words. "We... no," taking a deep breath. "I talk to your father and come clean. Tell him I love you, tell him I want to marry you after we are finished with school, tell him I understand the stupid things I've done and that I'm going to change, grow-up." Her body starts shuddering.

Rush of elation going through me, cut short by her laughter.

Cold striking me—stepping back from her.

"Like that's going to work? Talking to my dad, right," her head starting to move side-to-side, "are you crazy?"

"Why not? It's the honest thing to do. If he says no at least we stood up for what we believe. After you're eighteen, it's your choice."

She's shaking her head.

"You know, you're so naive in some ways."

"What?" looking at her, stepping back.

She doesn't believe. Feeling my heart contract in my chest.

Frank you stupid ass, you stupid, stupid ass.

"Why are you looking at me like that, Frankie?"

"It's not your father," shaking my head, looking at the sky and taking a deep breath to keep from getting angry.

"You don't believe in me."

Stepping back from her and sitting down, not looking at her as she sits down next to me, but she doesn't have the nerve to say yes. Now she's all concerned.

Was I this stupid? Was I this shallow to be so enamored with her beauty, her popularity that I didn't see the person who won't take a stand for what she wants? She gets what she wants, but she sneaks around the things that pop up or gets away with things because of how she looks.

Oh God. Putting my face in my hands and rubbing slowly, you fool.

"What, Frankie?"

Looking at her—wanting to be pulled into those deep, wonderful eyes. Wanting to swim in them—regain that moment of perfect composure when we were together making love and drifting in daydreams afterward. Painful thought hitting me—I'm not the one she's going to make the stand for. Whether she's incapable or I'm not the guy, or I fucking blew it—doesn't matter. It's the same either way.

"Don't take it like that, Frankie," she puts her arm in mine. "I'm so confused. Don't jump to conclusions." Her head on my shoulders, "This is just so hard."

Wrenching myself back to the present, stepping back from peering into the dark river for moments. Forcing a smile on my face. Maybe there's a way back from all this. Shutting off the feeling in my gut.

"Okay, Cat, okay," standing up, putting my hand under her arm. "Let me walk you home, we can talk and just hang out, or we could go over to the pizza place on 1st, all your friends will be there."

"No," she shakes her head, "let's just take it easy, just take some time like all this didn't happen."

Faces on the crowded train.

Rocking with the motion of the car, the wheels squealing as we make the turn into the long tunnel under the river.

Was I right to fight with my father?

Was I right to stick up for my friends when he called them niggers and spics? Looking at people in the car.

This is my seventeen-year-old story—what's theirs?

Image of that night my uncle took me to see the abandoned children—walking through the entrance to purgatory in that drug warren.

Five months, Frank.

I know what I'm going to do with some of my time. Besides working out and getting into killer shape before I go into the Army, I'm going to see if there's something I can do at the hospital or the VA or something.

Quiet dinner.

Thankful Aunt Kitty isn't hounding me or getting mad like Dad would be when I need time to think and just dwell.

Tomorrow it's time to face my father.

Chapter 48

Muscles burning from the tough work out. Lungs have that wonderful tingly feeling after lots of air has been moving in and out for the past few hours. Skin on my hands feels weird after working the climbing rope at the YMCA gym.

Few people on the train into Manhattan.

Yawning and stretching—moving around a little.

Old lady sitting across from me lifting her feet up now and then so she can look carefully at each side of her shoes. My stop is next—time to transfer over to the BMT and get down to 22nd Street.

Long time since I've been at my father's shop. Insides hardening up in preparation for the insults that will be coming my way. Would I care if I never saw this bastard again? No.

Taking a moment to look at the plain, two-story brick facade.

Other than the big doors out back, no one would know anything was built here.

Deep breath—time to prepare for battle.

Walking into the front lobby—Margie working the desk.

"Hello, Margie," she looks up from the phone and her notes.

"Well hello, Stranger," she sort of smiles as she swaps papers around, punching in my father's extension. "I'll call your father, he's been working in his office all afternoon now and I don't know..."

Holding up my hand, "I'll wait, it's okay," nodding to her.

Stepping back from the desk, turning to look at the photographs on the wall from past shows and operas his company has designed and built, reviews of the shows, awards, letters from producers, years of history on the wall. Remembering back to some of the shows he'd taken me to during the final dress rehearsals and how he'd be talking about how all the machinery worked back stage, all the sequencing, all the work that went into the design.

This is his world. I'll never know if he was a big player, a small player or a buffoon who built stage sets for the powerful. He always bragged about how his shop only worked the major houses, how his designs and designers won all these awards.

At home it was always penny pinching and the constant drone of how I'm not good enough. Is that true? I've bought my all my own dive gear and such, but without Dad's connections in the Union, would I have gotten those jobs?

Margie's been working here for over ten years. He's got what, thirty guys working full time here and another bunch on the shop out in Long Island. To them, he's the Big Boss.

"Frank," her hand over the phone. She motions me in like she has some huge secret to tell then whispers, "You can go in now."

Walking through the thick glass door as she buzzes me in.

Passing the long front room where some of the designers are working away on big drafting tables, a mockup of a three-dimensional full stage design set on one of them. Sketches quickly water-colored on the walls, penciled in ideas, comments. I never knew Dad did these initial designs. Why would God give such a mean spirited man talent?

People I've met a couple of times, but don't know, talking, turning the model around, talking excitedly to each other. Pushing through the two big swinging doors to the huge, three story tall, main shop floor. Familiar smell of saw dust, paint and electrical grease coupled with the sounds of a busy shop—cutting, hammering, cussing, yelling and insults—some good-natured, most not.

"Hey look at what the cat dragged in," looking around. Catching Hermano's smile. Dad's lead carpenter, his right hand man on production.

"Hey, Hermano," he comes over and smacks me on the arm.

"How's the boxing going? When's your next fight?"

"This summer."

"You let me know, we'll come root for you. I bring the kids, we have lots of fun."

"Sure, thanks," as Hermano goes off and asks one of the guys why the fuck he's doing what he's doing.

Shaking my head—in Dad's shop, Hermano's one of his guys, the quality of his work is the number one thing in my dad's mind. Out on the street, to my father, he'd be just another spic. How the hell does that work? Bastard.

Walking up the rough stairs to Dad's work office—he's got a nice layout in front to meet with customers, but here's where he spends most of his time. Plans, phones, people, papers—pictures of Mom and us kids…

Reaching for the door, have to push my hand forward—checking that I have the manila envelope under my arm. Stopping for a second, looking down at the busy floor below me. The guys using one of the ceiling cranes to move a large piece.

Brusque motion to sit down, he's concentrating on the phone.

"I told you… you changed the motion requirements after the piece was built and I told you it was gonna cost you. Now don't come back and give me this shit that I'm fucking you over, Simon."

He nods into the phone.

"No, the price is the price. Go fucking get your next show built somewhere else. Oh right, the guys won't unload it cause it's not from my shop. Too fucking bad, maybe you'll listen to me when I tell you early on you've got an idea that won't work."

He waits for a second.

"Yeah, well kiss my ass too!" and he slams down the phone.

"Got to love Simon, been doing business with that Jew bastard for twenty years and he's still the same little schmuck, always trying to wheedle out of paying for the changes he's asked for and we've agreed on."

He sits back in his chair, smile on his face—he loves this shit.

"Well, well," he puts his hands together on his belly, "to what do we owe the pleasure?"

Opening my mouth.

"Wait, wait," he looks up at the ceiling, holding his hand to his ear. "What's that, Lord? No? I didn't think so either," he looks at me. "That was one of God's angels telling me that you weren't here to pay me the twenty-five grand I dropped to give that kid his face back and keep his mother from seeing your ass thrown in jail. Oh wait," he looks up at the ceiling again. "No Lord, no I don't think that's it either."

Feeling my insides start to simmer, familiar feeling of bitter bile starting to surface in my stomach, he just can't get by without a slight. We're going to be fighting like this until one of us is dead.

"Now what's that? No, he's not here to ask me what he needs to do to apologize for breaking his poor mother's heart. He doesn't care about how much she cried or how worried she was and how embarrassed she is that her son is living in a basement at his uncle's place. The Golden Boy, the Champion, let's see what the wandering son is here for?"

My jaw tightening.

"So, what's it going to be?" his eyes gloating. "You need something I can say no to, you want to apologize? Is that it? You're feeling bad? Oooh, too bad. No, you have no feelings! And besides I no longer have a son, so hey, what are we wasting our time for here!" His eyes flash on me. "GET OUT!"

Fists clenching and unclenching.

"I need you to sign this, then I'll go. If you refuse, I'll go to Mom. If she won't do it, then Uncle Vin will sign it."

"What, are you going to fucking sue me, you little prick?"

"Yeah like you've got anything I want, you…"

He's laughing.

That face, my insides starting to twist—that face, I want to punch it.

"Don't be so sure," he looks mean. "Ha, but you don't have to worry about that do you?"

"No, I don't, Father."

"Yeah, well that's the legal term. What new disgrace do you have for me?"

"I'm underage and need your approval to join the Army."

His face moves back like he didn't understand what I had to say. After a few moments he starts laughing uncontrollably. Laughing so hard he almost starts to choke. Holding myself in check while he wipes tears away from his eyes. Laugh till you choke you bastard.

"You?" He almost can't speak, he's laughing and pounding on his desk. "You, in the Army?" He starts rolling around on his chair. "Oh, this is rich," he's laughing so hard, people come in from next door. He waves them away.

He wipes the tears from his eyes.

"Oh this is rich, you Mister Wild Horse, doesn't like anyone telling him what to do, runs away when things get too tough, going in the Army. Oh God," he starts laughing again. "Ha, ha," mean laugh now. "I wish I could pay to watch that," he puts his head in his hands to wipe the tears of laughter from his face.

"If I didn't hate you so much. Hate you for what you've done to us, I think I'd keep laughing for the next few weeks," he sits back in his chair.

"That's great Pop, I hate your fucking guts too, you chickenshit bastard."

"Watch your mouth in my place you disgrace, you ingrate!"

His face starting to come back from the contortions of hate.

"You in the fucking Army, this is going to be good. I can't wait to get letters from you in the stockade, that's where they put guys who don't listen and do what they want to do."

"Just like you did Pop? You told me all the things you got away with..."

"That's different."

Shaking my head, putting the form on the table. He picks it up like it's a piece of shit, thumb and forefinger at the corner edge.

"You are going to be so miserable," he thinks for a second. "If only this wouldn't be another nail into your mother's heart. How she can still have any feelings for you after all that you've done?"

He signs the paper and throws it at me.

"You're going to be so fucking miserable. Good place for you with all the fucking losers and wrecks that can't make it in the real world. Go, go join the poor dumb fucks who have nothing better to do."

Standing there looking at him.

Holding up the paper, "I'm going to show you," holding up my left fist and shaking it at him. "I'm going to be the best fucking soldier they've ever seen. I'm going to go through college without you and all your bullshit and I'm going to be a success. You can't stop me! I'm fucking free of you!" People coming when they hear me yell at the top of my lungs.

Turning and walking through Dad's guys, they look concerned at their boss. His words bouncing off my back.

Storming down the stairs.

Cold wind coming up from the Hudson as I walk away.

I'm free of him, FREE!

Chapter 49

Long empty row of gray seats on the A train this morning. The subway car swinging back and forth as we pull out of the Aqueduct train station. Watching the structure of the racetrack receding.

Walking to the front of the subway car as it sways side-to-side.

Wide expanse of Jamaica Bay opening up in front of me—miles of tall green cattails swaying in the winds, the tracks heading straight out through the marshlands. Track ties blurring, changing from gravel and dirt here to open spaces above the blue green-water of the bay, then back again.

Lost in the motion of the train and the emptiness of the bay.

Noise of the train fading into the distance.

She's in school now. Image of her sitting in social studies class, her legs crossed, a couple of buttons playfully opened on her blouse to mess with me.

Feeling an open rift in my chest.

Losing the vision of her as we pass across open water again.

My words to my father replaying in my mind.

So this is what freedom is like? Alone, on a subway riding out to a dead and dying Rockaway.

Grandpa T's house out here burned down a long time ago. The big Mulberry tree we had in the backyard is gone too or so they said. Uncle Vin told me I wouldn't like what I see out here. He said all the stores I'd known are long gone, most of the houses as well. People squatting out there, a couple of new tenement buildings built up over the past few years on the bay side.

Train speeding across the bay.

It's first period now. Imagining people chattering away—who's dating who, who's breaking up, big discussion about some stupid TV show. I could be standing right outside the school. I could be right next to her, but I'd be miles away. Pushing down the feeling in my gut that it's over.

Body feeling a gnawing emptiness inside.

Dwelling on the places I feel really alive.

Out on the ocean—diving deep in the murky cold, having to think through the challenging situations, stay calm under pressure. Even though I was there for all the wrong reasons, when I was out on the streets—horrible as it was—it wasn't like dealing with the staleness, the tastelessness of my life at home. Out in deep woods with my dad and uncles.

Looking ahead as we pass across another patch of water. The beach is there ahead of me—miles of empty beach and boardwalk to run. I may have made a mess of my current life, there will be a new one starting soon—time to prep, time to be ready.

The cool smell of the ocean welcoming me back as the train pulls away at Beach 44th Street Station. I'm the only one here. Walking down the rusting steel stairway, down from the elevated train station. Stopping to feel the rough, pebble studded, concrete pillar supporting the elevated track fifty feet above me. Sidewalks cracked, long weeds growing up between them and around the pillars holding up the track.

Feeling the air being sucked out of my chest as I walk down Edgemere Blvd. Boarded up houses, burned out hulks of houses once alive during the summer months—areas where we used to play, the neighborhood kid's houses—all swallowed up by decay. Wrecked cars on the street, rusted out hulks on the vacant lots.

Beach 47th Street is gutted.

Jogging up to where our house used to be.

Uncle Vin was right. Ghosts wouldn't even come back here—all the things that once held them here are smashed, burned or decaying in a dull gray. You'd never know the world I knew as a kid was ever here.

Looking up and down the street, remembering the time I ran my tricycle into Mr. Wilson's new Buick Skylark and how pissed he was. The first time I heard Grandpa T curse. The time I lied to my parents to get a box of matches so we could light fires in one of the abandoned lots—oh, did I get a well deserved beating for that one. The laughter of the games of ringalevio with the neighborhood kids, the barbecues we had in the backyard, the blue claw crabs we ate by the pot after crabbing all morning, the time spent up at the top of the tree looking up at the summer sky—all gone.

Did it even exist?

This all was gone long before I came out here—sad this place will never be the same for other kids. A few black families still making a go of it—cars, junk piled up.

Do what you came out here for. Long distances to run. Run in the sand to work your thighs and burn your lungs.

Time to turn your back on the past and get going.

Will I need to do the same to Cat?

How do we pull through this?

There's got to be a way.

Getting my pace as I jog back toward Beach 44th Street where I'll cut down to the old Boardwalk. Time to make it hurt—five months to get into killer shape. Walk, run—toughen up my feet, work my upper body, work my core muscles. There's no going back.

Empty beaches.

Rock jetties thrusting out into the ever-present waves.

Body finding its rhythm as I run.

My eyes following the diagonal pattern of the boardwalk planks.

Energized by the ocean air, pushing my body to keep the pace.

Working to keep my breathing pattern, miles to go.

Images of Cat moving through my mind, the time we spent together. Remembering what it was like when I knew I was in love with her—the almost dizzy feeling pervading my being. Then, when she told me how she felt about me, how bright and full of wonder the world was. Pang of missing her hitting me.

Relaxing. Getting to the point where my body will just go on automatic and my mind will be free, time will suspend temporarily. Ramps that leads up to the boardwalk passing by.

Eyes relaxed, focused on the distance.

It will be sand in a few miles, then the bus over the Marine Parkway Bridge. If I'm not dead tired, hit a pick-up basketball game over by West End. Good ball players out here. Tough neighborhood, I ain't got shit to steal.

Settle into the rhythm.

Sweat running down into my eyes.

Thighs burning—legs feeling the welcome soreness of hard work.

Lungs burning as I push it through the sand.

Need to walk for a bit, feel like I'm going to puke. Man, am I going to feel this tomorrow. Hands down on my knees, fighting the feeling I'm going to throw up.

Keep moving, Frank.

Moving to the harder sand down by the ocean, slow jog. Smile breaking out on my face as I jump across the rocks at the base of the jetties buried in the sand.

Tying my sopping wet sweatshirt around my waist—cool ocean air feels good. People moving away from me at the bus stop.

Elderly black women avert their eyes, positioning their purses on the other side of their bodies, their bags between us. Imagining they are asking—who's this nasty looking white boy, all full of dirt and sand—what the hell is he doing here?

Long bus ride back over the tall bridge back across the bay. Looking down at a couple of boats heading out to sea. Standing up and stretching, calf muscles starting to cramp up. Need to drink more water when I do this, that last stop wasn't enough.

Feet feel raw. Man is this different running in boots.

Cooling down from good hard street basketball, my back on the chain link fence, sweat running down my face.

"Hey, good run, man," slapping Maurice and Felton five after winning our second three-on-three. Stretching to keep the cramps at bay, man I'm going to feel this tomorrow. Laughing at myself—overdoing it again.

"You okay there, White Boy?" Maurice popping a can of beer in a small brown paper bag neatly wrapped and folded down so the top is easy to drink from.

"Been running all morning to get in shape, legs starting to cramp."

"What? Summer league this early? You got a team you play on?"

"No man, got in trouble, got kicked out of school."

He looks at me—shakes his head, points his thumb at me talking to some of the other brothers hanging around "White boy over there thinks he knows how to cause trouble," guys laughing at that and getting the obligatory razzing.

"That boy don't know shit," chimes in Felton.

"Maybe, after I got my dumb ass thrown out of school, I got in more trouble. Judge told me I could enlist or go to jail. So, it's time to get in shape."

"What, Army 'n shit?"

"Yup."

"Sheeit, ain't getting my black ass in no Army," said Maurice.

"Sheeit, you keep getting your ass run off the court by a white boy like me, they wouldn't let your ass in," busting his balls. "They'd be sayin, damn, we thought that motherfucker was tight, but he was just too nervous in the service."

"Look at this motherfucker, talking all kinds of shit," some of the guys laughing, having fun. "Motherfuckin man telling me to go shoot some motherfucker, I tell that white man to kiss my motherfuckin black ass. Besides, what the fuck I got to go fight about? Niggers be comin' back from Nam all fucked up, ain't no motherfuckin jobs, just more shit piled on dumbass motherfuckers."

"You tell it, Maurice," said Felton.

"Sheeit, you a street kid. Got a little rhythm, not too much though," Maurice and Felton slap five. "What you gonna do when some lily white country cracker tells you to shoot some poor motherfucker just doin his motherfuckin thing? You tell them no, they gonna throw your white ass in with a bunch of niggers."

"Sometimes you gots to disobey," said Felton. "Man telling me to do this and do that. I been to fuckin history class, man. While you motherfuckers took our asses for a one-way ocean voyage, you were all cry'in and scream'in about liberty, taxation without motherfuckin representation, thrown' shit in the ocean and all. Y'all was a bunch of disobedient motherfuckers. Now you pull that shit, they gonna lock your ass up."

"So, what you gonna do with that shit?" Maurice animated.

"I did time at Rikers man, I got my ass thrown in the hole for taking down the prison badass. Guards beat my ass good cause I messed up their little system on the side, if you know what I mean. They put my dumb ass in a straitjacket, so I tell you, someone pushes me to the edge and it's someplace that's wrong... they can't do more than what's been done.

Longer maybe, but that shit doesn't scare me."

"Ha, I guessed this white boy's seen some shit, you got that edge."

"What would you fight for, man?"

"Me? Sheeit," Maurice looking down the court. "Some motherfucker come in here, Russian, Chinese, Mister Cracker Motherfucker in a white sheet, there are gonna be some badass niggers making things go down. Other than that, this country don't represent me. Some Vietnamese nigger wants to feed his family? We go bomb them? What now? You gonna get all stars 'n stripes on me?"

"Maurice man, what about all the fucked up shit that goes down in the world? Who's gonna stand up?"

"What about all the motherfuckin shit that ain't right here? You white boys want to go do all the Peace Corps shit, there are motherfuckers here ain't got food, ain't got a place to rest they motherfuckin head."

"I heard that," said Felton.

Nodding.

"That there is, that there is. Maybe I've to do my time and figure out what to do when I get out. I don't know. A lot of shit to figure out."

"Man, a lot of pussy to figure out too. Look at the shit."

Well-stacked sister walking down the street.

"Man that's some nice butter," checking out her butt. "Hmm, hmm, hmm."

Maurice and Felton look at each other and start laughing.

"Sheeit, listen to this motherfucker. That's some fine shit though."

"I heard that," said Felton.

Standing up, grimacing, feet feel raw.

"Good run like this every day here?"

"Pretty much, come a little later in the day and we'll have enough for good five on five full court. You get here, you ask for me, Mister Save the World motherfucker."

"Bet," he nods and goes back to drinking the wrapped can of beer.

Limping down to the D Train station.

Fewer people staring at me on the subway. Sweatshirt and hood on now to try and stay warm. Walking slowly, muscles and feet crying out as I make the last few blocks back to my uncles.

"Oh look at you," from my aunt as I come in the back door. "Yuck, get those into the wash, they'll mildew and stink up downstairs."

"Okay, okay, just let me die first. Oh, man do I hurt."

She's looking at me, "Get those off and get in the shower, I'll put some soup on for you," shaking her head, "my God, another crazy person in the house."

Warm water washing down my body feels like heaven.

Nice blister rising up on my right foot. I can feel it. Witch-hazel time.

Drying off, neatening up my living area in the dim light.

Taking a moment to photograph it in my mind. It will be gone soon.

"This is good, Aunt Kitty," hot minestrone, good olives, Asiago Fresco cheese—body feels like it's sucking it all in.

Deep drink of water.

"So, how was it?"

Putting my spoon down, breaking a breadstick in half.

"It was like Uncle Vin said, just so desolate," looking at her. "You'd never know that it was once such a happy place."

She's looking at me.

"Do you want to spend more time with Father Fiero? It might be good for you to have someone to talk to you during this period."

Looking at her.

"Why?"

"Oh don't give me that big Italian male I don't need nobody, eh?"

Laughing at her as she tries to put on a big goombah accent. Making fun of her, "Eh? Whaddaya mean, whaddaya know, eh?"

"I'm serious, Frank, you've had a huge rupture with your Father, that's got to hurt at some level," stopping, looking at her.

Focused on the food. Stamping down the images of my father's face. It would be so easy if they were only memories of us fighting, but there were good days too—summers in Rockaway, out diving in the Long Island Sound, the look on his face when I won my first boxing tournament. How proud of me he used to be. Deep breath.

"I hate him," more to myself.

"Don't let that turn into a cancer, talk about it. Your uncle and I are probably too close to you, but Father Fiero is a good man. He liked your spirit, Frank. Sometimes getting it out is such a healthy thing to do. Okay?"

Not looking at her.

"Okay, Frankie?"

Finishing off my soup. "Aunt Kitty, I can't lie to you… it just doesn't feel right," kneading my thighs. "I mean, why can't I just handle this?"

"Talking about what's going on in your head doesn't mean you're weak, Frank. You are a human being, body, emotions, mind, and spirit. All the things that have made us great, as well as the things that have made us beasts."

She stands up and takes my bowl to fill it up.

"That's why I worry about you going into the Army, you're such a strong man, so mature in many ways," she puts another bowl of soup in front of me. "Strength isn't brutality, yes, there are things we have to fight for, but I worry about you becoming inflexible…"

"Like my father?"

She looks at me.

"Yes, he's a very driven man. It's sad to see the... Well," she looks at me. "The things that made him successful, his drive, his creativity, his hunger to learn, his insistence on quality has turned into a stiffness. I don't know," she looks down at her hands. "A certainty about things, about people."

"He hates to be wrong," finishing the sentence for her.

"Can I tell you something, Frank? It may be hard for you to listen to now."

Putting my spoon down. Getting ready for another salvo.

"Sure, Aunt Kitty." Unsure, not going to give in.

"Sometimes it's hard to see the things we dislike most in our parents have taken root in us as well, not that we have to be like them, but we can't help take on traits of people we live with and are around."

Sitting back, feeling my face twist up—me, like my father? NO!

"Relax, Frank," her hands motioning me down, "it's just something to think about, you don't have to accept it."

"I'm not like him," feeling my grip harden on the seat of the chair.

"Shh, I'm not trying to tell you how to think or hurt you. I've learned a lot working with kids and their families over the years. Look, I wouldn't say this if I didn't care, okay? Capice?"

Her voice, her calm eyes helping me keep an even keel.

"I understand, Aunt Kitty... well, some of it, some is hard to, you know."

"I know, Frank," she sits back and then leans forward again, "I want you to be strong, flexible, able to think, able to deal with hard things, able to look hard situations right in the face and do what's right. Sometimes it's the hardest thing to do, to do the right thing when everyone else wants to do something else, cause they've been told to do it, or think it's the right thing or something. Have you ever seen the movie *Twelve Angry Men*?"

"Yes."

"Imagine that one man, he didn't know if he was right or wrong, but he stood up to eleven other men who thought the boy was guilty. To me that was a heroic act. Think about that, Frank, think about talking with men like Father Fiero as time to learn, to think about new things."

"No promises, Aunt Kitty, okay? But I will think about it."

"That's good."

Reflecting on her words.

Image of me standing with my sword drawn, barbarian horde ahead of me—walking slowly, shield in hand, locked in with my fellow legionnaires, sweat on my skin, smell of fear in the air. Can I do that? Would I have the strength to not turn and run? Mind drifting to the image of me standing before Alton—pride hurt, rage at losing the fight. Would I have the strength to accept an apology and apologize next time?

"Aunt Kitty?"

"Yes, Frank?"

"This Saturday, my friend Richard is having a party in Manhattan. Can I stay over and come back on Sunday? I've slept over at his place before; you can call and ask Ma. Well, truthfully, we didn't sleep much," flashes of trying to stay up all night, drinking cheap beer and watching crappy horror movies at four in the morning on TV coming to mind.

She looks at me, "Is your girlfriend going to be there?"

"At the party yes, but her dad would never let her spend the night out. It's a Rock'n Roll theme party; you know go as your favorite singer. I have no idea what to wear. But anyway, if you say no I'll understand, I just wanted to ask."

Nodding her head while she thinks.

"You've been good at building trust here with me and your uncle, Frank. If you promise me that you are not using this as a pretext to spend the night with your girlfriend, Catherine."

"I promise."

"Okay then, I'll double check with your uncle. Are there going to adults there?"

"No. Richard's brother is going away for the weekend and his brother told Richard that he'd like me to be there cause he knows that I'll keep a lid on things."

She laughs a little at that, "I can see that, so much the man already," straightening her dress. "Thanks for not lying about that."

She starts cleaning the table. Getting up to help her.

Chapter 50

"Hey look at you! That's pretty darn good, Frank!" Richard checking me out as he opens the door and I take off my long, dark blue wool coat. Music, conversations, laughter surging out of his apartment with such intensity that I can barely hear the tiny bells tied to my biceps with thin leather cords.

"Guys look, it's Jimmy Hendrix!" he's yelling out to no one in particular. It's too loud for anyone to hear him anyway. Stepping inside, lots of faces I know from school, lots I don't. Only a few got really into the spirit of things. Looks like we've got leather bound Lou Reed here.

"Looks like word got out," to Richard.

"Yeah man, this is gonna be a blast man!" he's rubbing his hands. "Best party of the year," he holds up for a high five. Politely slapping his hand—looks like he's had a few already.

"After the run I made yesterday we should be all set, right? We good?" bending down so he can hear me. He gives me thumbs up. Walking in, keeping my sunglasses on, letting my eyes get used to the low light—don't know how long this is going to last. Checking out the party, lots of 60's here so far.

"Cool digs, man," from Nolan talking with Mary.

"Hi Frank, wow, where'd you get all that?" she gives me a big smile.

"Hey, Mary," looking across Richard's large front room. The room's crowded with kids dancing, talking in groups—cigarette and wacky weed smoke hanging in the air. She looks happy to see me. Looking for Cat.

"I scoured all kinds of shops in the Village this week, took a while to find stuff that remotely fits," looking for Cat again, catching her eye, she looks annoyed that I'm not immediately fawning. "Let me guess," looking at her. "Carly Simon?"

"Close but no cigar, Bucko," her hands moving along her long plaid dress, hair blown out and tuxedo shirt, "Judy Collins silly."

Snapping my fingers, "Damn."

Nolan standing there annoyed like I'm butting in. Smiling at Mary, "Well, I'm going to mingle."

"Behave yourself now," giving me a little shrug. "She's over there," pointing to the dining room. She turns back to Nolan, looking pretty disinterested.

Breaking out laughing. Cat sees me and waves.

"Hey there, Elton!" loud over the noise. She's got these monster square glasses on, platform shoes and a big yellow top hat. Her little clique around her, some boys and girls I don't know.

"That's pretty groovy, Frank," smile on her face, no touching.

"Who are you?" one of the kids I don't know—good looking, wavy short brown hair, preppy clothes, ice cold blonde with him. Pretty, but looks like she'd have a conniption if she had to touch a cock.

"Cass Elliot," giving him a shit eating grin.

He looks at me, tries to figure it out.

"Nooo. Way funny. Morrison, Hendrix?" ignoring him. "That's it, Hendrix!"

"Hey Marta, you disco queen you," she's laughing in her tight sequined dress.

Leaning into Cat, she backs off a little. Trying to ignore the cold feeling that's running through my body. Urge to walk back out the front door and say fuck you to all this. What an asshole I am, hanging around with a bunch of high school kids.

"Where'd you get the crazy glasses?"

"Made 'em," she smiles, goes back to talking rapidly with Emily.

Okay—cold shoulder here. Time to get something to drink—still thirsty after my workout today. Felt good to get back into the 14th Street Gym. Walking to their big kitchen, brother handshake with Hector as Carlos Santana. Congratulating Nina on her Mod Glam Rocker outfit—she doesn't even know I'm busting her chops. Uh oh, there's trouble—Cherlyn in a tight black leotard top and tight jean dress, cowboy boots and hat with a feather in the band.

"Hey, Shorty," to her, she looks at me for a second and then gives me a sly smile.

"You were supposed to call."

Shrugging my shoulders, "It's been crazy... what, Eagles?"

"Sure, you're the first person who guessed."

"I hate them. Way to white for me."

"Look who's talking."

"Hey now," pointing to myself, "Jimmy can play the Blues."

She smiles.

"You going to get in trouble with your little Latin lady?"

"Not the way things are going."

"Don't be so sure," she puts her index finger on my lips, looks at my chest and arms, "you'd look good just in the vest," and walks back to a group dancing in the large family room back off the kitchen. Stay away—stay away. Shaking my head.

"Yo, Frankie!"

Turning around, "Hey, Julio," looking at him, he's a little uneasy, "I called a couple of time and didn't get you. Your moms tell you I called?"

"She did."

"I wanted you to know... I wanted to apologize for getting on your case the other day. What's gonna happen, is gonna happen."

Small smile breaking out on his face.

"Thanks man, you know I would never dog you."

"I know, I know, it's okay though. I don't think Cat and I are going to make it, things have been falling apart the last few weeks."

"Nah man, she talks about you all the time."

Shrugging my shoulders. Maybe she's just in party mode—she can get so wound up sometimes, like it's her world and we are just living in it.

"So, who'd you come as?"

"Shit, none of you fuckers know Tito Puente?"

"I was gonna order some food," laughing.

"Fuck you, man."

Julio putting on a big act like he's gonna punch me. Putting up my arms like Joe Frazier, getting in a crouch.

"Easy, Hommes, I'll grab you a beer," laughing.

"Make it quick, fool, don't make me hurt you in front of all these people."

Wading my way through a crowd of people at the huge double wide stainless refrigerator. You could fit a whole cow in this damn thing. Guy I don't know passing me a joint. Shaking it off. Reaching into where Richard and I hid the good stuff.

Popping the tops off a couple of Heinekens.

"Hey, where'd you get that?" some kid I don't know as I head back to the main throng. Shrugging my shoulders.

"Yo Julio, here you go."

"Thanks, Bro." Average White Band kicking loud on the sound system. Feeling tugging on one the strings of leather I'd tied around my biceps. Turning around. "Richard, what's up?"

"That jerk Carl is bombed man and he's bugging Yu Wen."

Rolling my eyes, "Doesn't that asshole have anything better to do?"

"He's a lame excuse for a senior," Richard looking antsy, his eyes moving side to side. Most of these kids don't know how to deal with confrontation.

"Let's go, I never liked that guy," and he's a bully. Following Richard as he works his way through the crowd—he's much nicer that I would be—impatient, taking the lead, moving through people in front of us. Richard looks at me sheepishly—he wouldn't do dick.

Getting annoyed seeing Carl getting right in Yu Wen's face and making squinty eyes. "What are you, some kind of funky Chinese hippy, maaan?"

Yu Wen standing his ground, his chest puffed up, Elise standing next to him looking nervous, her arm on his shoulder. She's as tall as all five-foot of Yu Wen.

"Carl!" loud. He looks, "Knock this shit off," holding up my hand as he tries to get his bluster up. He knows I'll kick his ass again. I got my first strike in Principal Richert's book for beating his ass when I was a freshman—say what you want, all the kids were rooting for me.

Keep your cool.

"Carl, have fun, let other people have fun, or get the fuck out. You dig?"

"He was dogging me, man."

"You heard the choices, make one, or I make one for you."

He looks at me for a second, backs off and wanders away mumbling.

"I not afraid of him," Yu Wen looking mad, pushing at me. "Why you butt in. I kick his ass!" he yells at Carl's retreating back.

Holding my hands up in surrender, smiling at him. "Easy there, Tiger. We'll go down to Chinatown later, go to one of those crazy basement restaurant places you love and have a hot chili pepper eating contest, okay?"

He snorts, pointing his finger at me, a tiny smile on his face, "I'm gonna make you cry, Big Boy," puts his arm around Elise and walks off. She turns around and gives me a little smile. I've always liked her. Not a real pretty girl, but she's always been solid—involved in activities at school, great sense of humor, not stuck-up.

Laughing to myself and calling out as they walk away, "You're on, man."

Richard and I start laughing. I shrug my shoulders.

"He owes you for letting him talk big in front of his girl."

"I don't give a shit. He's a good guy," I do like that little fucker, only kid that did as well as I did on the math SAT.

Stretching—taking a long drink of good beer.

I know this thirst, I better get a couple of glasses of water—hard as I worked out today, a couple of beers will put me under big time. Wandering back to the kitchen—taking down an old style beer stein from the top shelf. Cool water feels good. My throat raw from the heavy breathing earlier, too bad it wasn't heavy breathing with Cherlyn, body reacting to the thought of her, the way she moves...

Pausing, flashing back to the look on Gus' face when I told him I was joining up. He just sat there and looked at me, nodded, wrote a name on the back of one of his cards and told me to look him up after Basic. Said this guy runs a good boxing program in the Army and that I know his address when I get out. He waved off the thank you, but I know what that meant—I'm out of his inner circle, I'm not one of his guys anymore. I'm just one of the kids who comes to the gym and pays to work out.

Finishing my second glass of water, someone bumping into me, giving me a drunken smile—time to get back to Cat.

More girls crowding around her laughing, a different set of boys hanging on now. Makeshift dance floor crowded—Door's *LA Woman* playing.

"There you are you bad boy," she's a little woozy taking a big drink of some fruit punch looking thing. Someone lighting up a joint and handing it to her, she takes a big drag, holds the smoke in. Feeling my eyes open up wide.

"When did you start this?"

"It's maaarvelous," as she exhales. "I feel so good... so free."

Waving it off as she tries to pass it to me.

"Oh, don't be a downer man," from Allan, "this is good stuff."

"No thanks, I'm an athlete," he shakes his head.

"How do you know it's not good for you?"

"I've worked too hard to get in shape, I'm not going to break up my routine."

"Yeah, that's so important," Cat rolls her eyes, holds a slightly disgusted look on her face, like someone put a tiny cat turd under her nose. Cold shiver passing through me. Shrugging my shoulders. Man is she in a mood.

"Suit yourself," from Allan as Cat passes the doobie to Marta—she'll follow anything Cat does. Feeling the room go quiet for a moment—watching her face as she laughs and continues on about how much fun it's going to be this summer with her parents traveling in Europe. Marta takes big drag, passes it to Nina who handles the joint expertly, holding the smoke in. The preppy boy coming in for it next, his ice girl giving him a pee yew sign and walks off.

Slowly drinking my beer watching her beautiful face, her long slim fingers in almost constant motion as she talks about her trip to Yale, her beautiful neck. How can love be so far away at times like this? She doesn't even know that I'm here, doesn't care about how I feel. Last time we made love were in a kind of rage, like hungry beasts let out of our cages. Now it's like nothing's happened, the past has been wiped clean. How can she be like this?

Stepping back from her group, she doesn't even notice—pissed.

Looking around the room, fighting the temptation to go grab Cherlyn and get crazy. Image of looking into her green brown eyes, our sweat mingling flashing in, imagining her laying back on her elbows watching my slick cock working slowly in. She's moving her hips side to side, her curly pubic hair nice and juicy, my cock wet...

Shaking my head. No, that's not the way to do it.

Call Cat tomorrow, tell her this is over.

This is stupid to go on like this.

Walking away, painting a stiff smile on my face. Telling myself another story—there are going to be ups and downs, right? It's one of those nights. We'll be in different places next year, this summer, if I don't trust her, then what? Fighting off the disappointment. This could have been a lot of fun tonight.

Maybe it's me—it's right there, toke up man. Get high. Join the crowd. One little step—one step I know I won't take.

Watching Mary and Brad dance away.

Lisa coming over and jingling my leather straps, bells tinkling.

"Come on grumpy, let's dance."

Sly and the Family Stone *Dance to the Music* playing—at least it's something to move to. Getting into the music, time to have some fun. Moving with the group of dancers, some bumping into people on couches, Lisa falling over—reaching over to pick her up. Her big dashiki wrapped up in Elise's arm. Helping them untangle as Lisa laughs away, she puts her hands on my waist to get her balance and keeps them planted. Moving my body back a bit as she moves in close.

Taking a break from the dancing.

Lisa pounding down another glass of Richard's Sloe Gin Fizz punch—how all these girls can drink this stuff is beyond me.

"Easy there, kiddo."

She fans her face, her blond hair a little sweat streaked as she pushes it back behind her ears. She's a pretty girl.

"You feeling okay?"

"Just hot, can you get me some air?"

"Okay," making my way to the large open-air roof garden—must be nice living here. Cool outside, couples talking—others, well, some serious making out going on. Lisa downs her drink, falls into me and acts like it's funny—sloppy damn drunk.

"This better?" she nods, all of a sudden she's not looking so good. Her face starts to turn green. Her eyes start to move side to side quickly. "Breathe," holding her arm, "breathe Lisa. It's going to be okay."

"I need to sit down," moving her to one of the outdoor lounge chairs, squatting down next to her as she starts to fan her face with her hands.

"You okay?"

"My head's so dizzy, oh I'm sorry," she stands up, her eyes in a panic, rushes over to a big planter and pukes hard, her face all red. She retches again and again. Patting her back, holding her so she doesn't fall face first into her mess.

"Relax, spit it out. Breathe," she's crying, "easy, Lisa, easy there."

"I feel so stupid, Bradley won't even look at me and all. Nobody is nice to me except you, Frank." She tries to take my hands, her eyes closed.

"Yeah, well, I'm a regular saint," pulling it away.

"I'll get you some water."

Her head falling into her hands—Frankie C, ace nursemaid.

People talking to me as I pass by—bullshit small talk.

Girls who've had too much to drink starting to touch my chest.

Giving Lisa her water, making sure she drinks slowly.

"My head's spinning. I'm scared, Frank."

Holding her hand, "Easy now Lisa, take it easy," her skin feels cold and clammy.

"Let me lie down, oh God, oh God," her voice trailing back. Helping her lie back on the striped cushion of the lounge chair. Waiting with her while she calms down. People walking by and going "woooo," when they see me holding her hand.

She's finally starting to calm down, her eyes still closed, but she's not panicking.

Time to check in on Cat.

Moving through the drunk, thickening crowd. For all their needling of each other Allan and Nina are hooking up, arms around each other, sharing another joint. Yu Wen and Elise are slow dancing to Chicago *Color my World* amid the group of slow moving bodies. Sudden stop.

Cold feeling seizing my chest—Cat and Preppy Boy are dancing together. His arms around her waist grinding into her, she's grinding back. Feeling my face flush. Breath coming in slowly. She looks over and waves me over. Standing there for a second—the preppy boy not wanting to let go. Moving in.

"Go check on your sister," I hear her saying.

"Come here, baby, I missed you," her arms around my neck, hearing her laugh.

Weird mix of emotions hitting me—anger, desire, disappointed in how the evening is going, wishing I could tear through what's keeping us apart. She's not moving well—don't know if it's the weed, the booze or just the big shoes.

Closing my eyes, lost for a few seconds in the smell of her hair. Her arms around me, but there's no hunger in her, I could be anybody.

"You doin' okay, Cat? Hey, maybe you should take it easy."

She steps back her eyes coming out of a haze. She's starting to weave back and forth, her hand waving in front of my face.

"You know, I'm tired of all you people telling me what to do and all. I'm finally having fun and you're just another bummer. You're just like my father."

"What? Look, Cat," standing back, "don't be like that, I care about you, don't get like this."

"Don't tell me what to do! I'm so tired of all the dreary moods you've been in. I want to have some fun tonight. Go away, go practice being fun and come back when you can pass the test."

"I want to have fun baby, but look, you can hardly walk."

"Don't tell me what I can and can't do," she turns and storms back to her circle of friends almost falling into Marta's arms, pointing to me and making an ugly face—Marta, Emily, Nancy and the others talking and starting to laugh and joke as they make faces at me in unison. Feeling my cheeks start to get red—bitch.

Storming off to get another beer.

Long angry drink as I walk back outside to check on Lisa.

She's nowhere to be seen.

What a fucking night.

Standing at the railing, looking down 5th Avenue to the lights of Washington Square Park, people milling around the dry fountain, traffic along 5th Ave.

I'm not like the people at this party anymore—what the hell am I doing here? Looking back to the park, I'd rather be there.

Fighting the wave of wanting to put distance between me all these high school jerks. Thinking of all the guys I've been playing basketball with lately—man these guys have some shit to deal with. Fucking prissy white people back in there. Man I love Hector and Julio, but they have it pretty good. Missing Alton—we'd be bullshitting, busting on people in the party. He'd be charming the pants off Marcie, Janelle would be mad. Turning around as I hear jingling nearby.

Mary—oh no.

"Hey, stranger," trying to not like her standing near me.

"Hey, Mary," looking out at the cars moving down 5th Ave. toward the park.

"You don't look like you're having much fun."

"Let's see, between being the party policeman, managing a drunk Lisa Ames and seeing Cat get bombed and not want to be around me, I'm having a great time," emotion starting to run over me—recognizing what's been welling up. I want to go out and hit somebody. I want to go revel in a nasty street fight. I want to hurt somebody. Hating myself.

Looking down and shaking my head at sick feeling of recognition rising up in my stomach—this is how I felt before I got into it with Leroy and company. Holding my breath to push down the darkness. Am I destined to repeat this behavior? I can't escape.

"Fuck," looking down at my hands gripping the cold steel railing.

"Sorry to bother you!" hearing the edge in her voice.

"It's not you, Mary, sorry. I'm mad at Cat and recognized that… Well when I get like this and I don't get my head on straight, well," looking back down 5th Avenue at the cars and people moving down the street. "It's just…" looking past the tall buildings across 5th Ave. "Why do I feel so small at times, then so mad at others and once in a while there's this clarity? It doesn't make sense. There's so much to look at in wonder. The majesty, the worlds that are around us right now we don't even see. So little time," not looking out into the world, happier times playing in my head, reaching for them with paper fingers, "and we just don't know when it's the last you know. Like what would you do if you knew this was the last time you'd be with someone?"

"Talk to me, Frank," she's looking at me.

"It's hard, Mary."

She looks out across the wide gulf of 5th Ave.

Looking down at 5th Ave.

So easy to step over the railing and this would be over.

"You know, sometimes at school I can see a whole play in your eyes, passion, poetry," she stops for a second. "Yes poetry, I know it's not a guy thing, but I can feel it churning about there." Holding my eyes straight—if I turn now toward her now, one step to her and then... Keep looking at the street.

"I really liked how we talked when you took me to that little Italian place. It made me feel good to get a glimpse of what's been going on. I can't tell you how that makes me feel... so just, I don't know," her hands twisting back and forth on the railing, "so torn up. Like it's so unfair that you..."

"I've got to go inside, Mary."

"Well it was nice talking to you," she looks mad, I don't care. I can't do this now—breathing hard as I walk into the living room.

Bill Withers *Lean on Me* playing.

Eyes getting used to the dark, looking over to Cat's crowd—Marta giving me a funny look and then looking away. No Cat. Walking around the room—no sign of Richard or Bradley. The preppy girl talking to Hector—he's trying to smooth talk her. The party looks a little less frantic as people have settled into groups. Cherlyn's gone. Flipping over the album stack on the record player—crap, Rolling Stones are up next.

Putting the records down—this is wasting time—I don't care now.

Walking around, saying a few inanities to the drunks who are acting like they understand what I'm saying, still no Cat.

Feeling moving up my stomach—is she okay? Am I being stubborn, too proud? "Yo, Julio" as he's dancing away with some girl I don't know—kind a cute too—he looks over, "have you seen Cat?"

"No man, she was right there a little ago," pointing back to her group. He goes back to dancing. Worried now. Where is that crazy woman in her Elton John gig? Is she bombed out of her mind like Lisa? Moving to the dining room, walking around. Not here. Back through the kitchen, she's not in the hall bathroom either. Eerie feelings starting to creep in my stomach as I move toward the back of the large apartment. Maybe she needed to lie down. That's it. She wouldn't leave.

Opening a closed door—Richard and Maria yell at me. Stepping back—that's unexpected. What the hell's happening with Hector? Ice blonde?

Waiting for the bathroom door to open. Freddy coming our zipping up his pants—a group of kids in Richard's bedroom looking at albums, quiet music on in here—Crosby Stills Nash. Thick marijuana smoke floating around in the room, couples making out.

Walking further into the deep apartment. Guest bedroom door closed. Looking under the door—lights are out. Heart pumping. Reaching for the door.

"Don't go in there," Marta holding my arm, "please, Frank," almost pleading. "Let me go in okay? She's, she's not feeling well," shaking my head, pulling away from her hand on my arm. Something's not right. It's not been right all night.

Feeling like I have to push myself through a cold, thick barrier. Flipping on the light. Images smacking me—the preppy kid jumping up from the bed, snatching at his waist, zipping up his pants, Cat sitting up—closing up her shirt, shocked look on her face.

Standing there looking at them and feeling the life drain out of my body. Cold, feeling my fists turn to tight blocks of ice, heart pounding in my chest. Shaking in hurt and rage. Looking at her, looking at him.

How, how could she do this? All the pathetic images of us over the last few weeks dissolving into the snap image of her hands on his cock. Whip of anger shaking me.

"What the fuck are you doing with my girl? What's going on?"

"Get out of here man, this isn't your business!" indignant, embarrassed tone from the preppy boy. Something snapping inside me, stepping across to him—hard slap across his good looking face. Seeing shock and hurt registering. He backs away, starts to mouth something, Marta grabbing my arm. Easily shaking myself free, pointing at him.

"Get the fuck out!"

"What right do you?" CRACK, another hard slap for preppy boy. The look, the voice, the sneer replaced with him crying out in pain. "Owwwww, oooh," he's holding his face, stumbling back. Feeling the deep mean dark red start to rise up.

"Get the fuck out! Both of you!" looking at Cat, she's back off the bed now pushing her hair back, her eyes on the floor looking like how could this happen.

"How could you do this? GET OUT!"

Looking at her.

"Why are you doing this? You don't own me," she trips over something and falls across the bed. Heart ripping out of its socket, pain rending through me—worse than anything those fucks could have done to me in jail.

"GODDAMN YOU!" Picking her up roughly by the belt on her jeans and shoving her at Marta who comes over and puts Cat's arm around her. "You fucking bitch. Goddamn You!"

"You're something," Mr. Joy Boy looking at me. Getting to the edge, feeling the desire to go over and be free. Beat him, beat that pretty face into a pulp—make him ugly, ugly like me.

"You preppy fuck," grabbing him by the arm and squeezing hard, punching him in the chest, he shrivels, "if you say another word I'm going to break you up," punching him again, he starts to whimper. Remembering how good this feels.

Commotion spreading behind me, hearing Hector, "Yo Frankie, cool it man, cool it baby, we'll take care of Preppy Boy here."

"This prick was in here with Cat."

"Help me, please," he says out of breath as I swing him around, more of the kids I know coming in the room giving him evil looks. Cat sitting on the bed crying now, more of her friends coming in, hushed conversations going in the room. Putting their arms around her, helping her get her clothes straightened out again.

Pushing the preppy one to Hector and Brad—they escort him out telling me to keep cool. Feeling my hands reach up and grab my hair, pulling hard, wanting to yell. Face feels hot—I can't take this, I can't breathe, I can't take this—image of her, his little fucking cock in her mouth. "Rraaaah," yelling at her, people looking at me scared. Walking to the edge again.

No. Taking a deep breath. NO.

Looking at her, disgust, anger, hurt welling up.

"You couldn't even break up with me… this…" hands shaking in front of me, "for this, all that for this…" hands pulling my hair again, "you couldn't go someplace else away from here! FUCK," turning away from her, "and this is what love is? You can't even like me enough to…" kicking the bed, her little friends surrounding her to protect her from me. "Get out you fucking cunt bitch, I never want to see you again!"

Marta lifting her up, wave of anger and impatience rising up—picking up Cat by her belt again roughly, shaking her. People trying to get between us. Body shaking. I want to hit her. I want to hit her.

"No, Frank!" Julio butting in, trying to push me back, "I love you, man, but don't do it. You can kick my ass," his face torn, his eyes watering up. "I know I can't stand up to you, but don't do it…" Looking at Julio's face. Feeling hot tears coming down mine. Body engulfed in hurt and shame. Pushing him aside roughly, walking down the hall—ignoring people asking me what's the matter.

Noise of the party fading—yes that's it, that's it. Give into the blackness. Can't you hear that I've been calling you down to me? Yes, yes, it's time to revel in this. Time to find some gutter fucks and revel in the mud and slime—knuckles, flesh, teeth ripping muscles—black rage, punch, gouge, bite, kick.

Storming forward, mad at how much my aunt and uncle believed in me and here I am going off the deep end. Mad because I don't belong here anymore. Yelling at someone to get the fuck out of my face as they slink back, scared.

Pushing coats off the big table in the foyer.

Grabbing mine, people behind me. Looking at them, stifling the fuck you I want to hurl at them to try and bleed off some of the exploding well of pain inside my chest. How could she do this, something that was just for us?

Softening for a moment seeing Mary.

It's not just been Cat—goddamn this hurts so badly though!

I don't belong here. I'm the one that needs to get out.

Stepping out into the hallway. Noticing I'm breathing hard and shaking—taking a few moments to breathe, try and get my head back, get out of the crazy "you need to kill me to stop me" mood.

Pounding on the elevator button.

Impatient—taking the stairs three at a time.

Fifteen flights down, head clearing a little on the ninth floor. Stopping for a few moments, feeling the stabbing pain in my chest again. Walking down step by step slowly, wave of deep emptiness hitting me, looking down the center of the stairwell at the landing stretching down—deep quiet in here.

This is over now. I never want to see her again. Bitch.

Feeling the anger start to burn inside again.

Why not head to Washington Square Park—find some asshole that thinks he's a badass and beat the living shit out of him.

It doesn't matter if I win.

Stopping for a moment, cold thought stopping me.

What a pathetic piece of worthless shit, asshole, cocksucker I am. Here I am hanging on by a thread from going to jail, my uncle's reputation on the line to get me out of jail and here I am going off storming around like a big fucking baby. So what your girlfriend cheated on you? Like I'm the first asshole that's ever happened to? God, this fucking sucks!

Slowly walking the rest of the way down.

Echo of my boots on the worn marble steps is the only sound greeting me. Shakes, adrenaline shakes—breathe deeply.

Doorman looking at me strangely—cool night air feels good on my face. Rubbing my hands over my face. Staring out into the busy traffic on 5th Ave. All I have to do is step out in front of one of those cars. Feet moving toward me—snapping me out of my daze.

"What are you doing here?" to Mary as she comes toward me.

"I was worried about you, the look on your face," she's breathing hard.

"I can't take this Mary, I've got to go walk this off before I do something bad... I'm no good. You go back upstairs, have fun."

"I don't want to be there, I'm worried about you."

"You don't know me, Mary, you don't know how ugly," feeling my face contorted. She'll never know—shaking my head and walking away quickly. Got to get away.

Pile of taxis starting a honking match as an aggressive cab cuts across 5th to snatch a fare. Head down, blocks passing in a heated silence.

Anger slowly washing away, leaving the gaping sadness, the hollowness of the words we'd said to each other. It will be easier—the next few months will be easier.

How could she do that to me?

What a rotten fucking thing to do to someone.

You bitch, you fucking bitch.

Looking up as I pass 10th.

Shit, Mary is with me—this will take us right into Union Square. No place for her at this time of night. Why the hell is she following me? What am I some fucking freak show? Looking over at her, her arms crossed over her shirt, starting to shiver. Cool night for late April. Shaking my head—my nice little Mary.

"Here," giving her my long coat, putting it on her as she tries to protest, "stop it!" louder than I'd like as she wraps the coat around her body. "Let's get around Union Square, I want to say a last goodbye to school, then I'll make sure you get home okay?" After that I'll be free. Come back down here to the village. Go buy a quart of Colt 45, hang out, drink, go back to Richard's later, drink beer, watch TV, go boink Lisa Ames, she's been wanting it for a long time.

"Okay, Frank," as she pulls the coat up around, it almost drags on the ground.

"We must look like refugees from a Village People concert," taking off the carefully wound thin leather straps around my hair and arms and the costume pirate earring.

"You look cute like that, kind of like a Rock n Roll pirate."

Blocks moving by—fighting off the need to get mean.

"Yeah, a real odd couple, Jimmy Hendrix does Carol King," laughing, "sounds like a bad porno movie," embarrassed speaking that way in front of her. "Oops, sorry."

She laughs, "Don't be silly, that's kind of funny, kind of off the wall."

"Well you know…" shrugging my shoulders, "I'm hilarious."

Passing 3rd Avenue, ignoring people that stare. Goose bumps on my bare arms and chest. Slow pace. My mind drifting in and out of what I saw, trying to get it out of my mind. Embarrassment starting to set in—how would I show my face at school now? Leroy will have a good laugh when he hears about this. Fuck him, fuck all these people, I just want to be alone.

"You sure you don't want me to take you back to the party, Mary? I mean, I'm a real barrel of laughs here."

"It's okay, Frank, I'm not interested, I'm bored by the people there. I'd rather hang here… you can take me to the subway over at 14th and 1st later."

"No way, not at this time of night. It's a cab or company."

Slowly walking past dark three story brownstones and parked cars.

"Such a little hero all the time."

"Such a chump," looking ahead as we walk along 1st Ave. "Such a fool." 15th Street—it's quiet here. A few people hanging around the Beth Israel Medical Center, a few lights on in the school building. Standing there, held by memories.

"What are you thinking about, Frank?" her soft voice behind me. Like we've been walking together through a dark tunnel, realizing that she was invisible, but beside or behind me most of the way. Is she even here? Don't turn. Don't look.

"Seems so long ago now, the days when I thought I knew what I wanted, when I knew what was coming next." Taking a deep breath. "It's been like something cracked and all the pieces of what I knew started falling away slowly. I thought I could hold it all together, I thought I could figure it out. Bits dropping here and there that I didn't know weren't here anymore. Losing things, the more I move toward them, the further away they've moved, held like Tantalus, his sins so great to be held by what he wants and can't have."

"Yes," she says, "you know, most kids at school don't know that."

"I love myths, the stories, the things that inspired great people long ago."

"Dad talks about that all the time, where our ideas come from, why we hold certain ideas so dear over time. It's nice to hear you talk like this."

"What, jocks are supposed to be dumb?"

"Well, I know you're not dumb, it's not something I hear often."

Looking at the quiet school building. There's nothing here. It's a dead place. "I love to read Mary, I love to think and wonder about all those things. Not like it makes a fucking bit of difference now."

"It does, Frank, talk to me. What's your favorite?"

"You trying to talk me back from the edge?"

"Goddammit," she slaps her thigh, "why do you keep pushing me away? It's like I see all this depth in you... and you just play with me. Goddamn, you, Frank."

Feeling the thin, empty smile on my face. Like I'm seeing my face in spots on a smudged and dirty broken mirror. Clear at times, fuzzy and filled with anger in others.

"Orpheus is my favorite."

"Why's that?"

"The man who could move between the worlds of the living and the dead. The man whose music could let him move to places we'll never see," feeling dark, again, "or maybe that's just the situation talking," looking down at my hands. "A little while ago I wished I could have been dropped into a nice horde of ugly, smelly, barbarians with rotten teeth and bad accents." She starts laughing. Laughing a little with her. "You know, bad costumes, led by Woody Allen in this big fat Genghis Khan outfit, bad thin mustache and all running around with a thick Brooklyn accent... a hoase, a hoase my kingdom for a hoase," she's laughing and rolling her eyes.

I've seen enough of this old shell, this place. Looking once more down toward 1st Avenue. Heading to Stuyvesant Park.

"I'm gonna sit for a few and then I'll take you home."

"No more Gengis Moskavitz? No more trite references to Richard the Third?"

Chuckling, "The barbarians all left town. No, that's not true. They all fell dead at my feet from laughing too hard. In the Monty Python episode with the killer joke," pointing to myself, "there was a picture of me in the envelope."

Shaking my head, insides starting to churn remembering the feeling when Marta told me to not go in there, and there she was. My love. Is she okay, should I call her?

You bitch—fuck if I'm going to call you.

Chapter 51

Stuyvesant Park in hollow darkness.

Sitting on my favorite shitty park bench.

Feeling Mary sit down next to me. Unsure.

Moon behind rolling clouds.

Bare branches of budding trees framing the sky.

"And you know, for a little while, I really thought there was hope for us. Hope that we'd take something important and make it work through tough times. Not like it's some test to see who's the biggest masochist, but because you can make something." Feeling my blood start to warm up my body, fists shaking in front of me. "Something wonderful out of all this... No, that's not right, living life in all that it's supposed to be, embody virtue, be the things we strive for in our imperfections, our shallowness, our sadness, our anger. Pierce through the muck, the mediocrity. Take an empty space and fill it with form, words, passion, bodies, a home for people to grow, adventure." Looking up at the sky, the stars washed out by all the light from the City. "Be free in the full commitment of love, love beyond what's nice or what's easy or what looks good. Love that pulls us back from the blackness, but in itself is a crimson journey of pain, of wanting, what could be." Looking at my hands, flexing, clenching. "Are we destined to live these puny, little lives?"

Almost jumping feeling her hand on my arm.

"Sorry," from her softly, "I just," she touches my face as I look at her. "Just hearing you speak like that, I just had to... It's the poetry; the passion I know is inside you, Frank. You..."

Moving her hair from her face as she looks down at her hand on my forearm. Tucking her hair back behind her ear. Electricity moving through me as I take her hand, looking at our entwined fingers, then at her as my world explodes in the rich green depths of her eyes, her lips.

Savage energy coming from her thin body as she crushes into me.

Breathing hard, lips together, our mouths wide open—tongues exploring lips, teeth, gums—pushing deeper into her as she opens her mouth harder to let me in.

"Mary," breaking off. "What are we doing? Wait."

"Shh," she puts her fingers in my hair and pulls me to her, "I've wanted this for so long, you have no idea. I knew it would feel like this."

Locked in her embrace.

Uncomfortable feeling—pushing it away. Her hands on my leather pants, strong grip on my hard cock. Free in her shamelessness.

Uncomfortable feeling again.

Breaking off for a second and looking around the park, she's kissing my neck, her hand starting to move up and down my penis.

There, a shape that doesn't belong there.

Outline, putting it together—someone standing by the tree a few feet away. "Mary!" softly, brushing her hair back.

"What's the matter, Frank?" as I put my finger across her lips and stand up, uncomfortable with my condition.

"Stand behind me, if anything bad happens, run to the Medical Center across the street," pushing her behind me, her hands on my arms.

"What do you want!" menace rising in my chest, body ready. Relax, relax—tight muscles lose their power.

Breathe—be ready to bring it.

"What, Frank, I don't understand?" keeping her behind me.

"I said what do you want! I see you over there. If you have nothing to say, then get the fuck out of here!" feeling her body tremble behind me—she's looking around but doesn't see him. Stepping forward. "Get the fuck out of here!"

"It's a free park, man," tenor of his voice rising—he's tense.

"Free for you to go someplace else."

"Or what?"

Ugly laugh coming from my chest, "You picked the wrong night to be here and be fucking with someone," looking around, picking up a heavy wire mesh trashcan and throwing it in his direction. He steps back and jumps to the side as the can bounces toward him, running at him.

"You're crazy, man!" he takes off running. As he runs he drops something. Standing there breathing deep—body ready for battle, blood pumping. A few moments wishing he'd not run off. Hearing her footsteps coming toward me.

"What happened? What was he doing? Some weirdo?"

Pointing to the ground—jagged edges of a broken gin bottle.

"Jesus," she says, her hands and arms entwining around my right arm.

"Probably thought he could scare us, rob us for a few easy bucks, stupid bastard," body shivering with adrenaline, stepping to go after him as the rage rises up.

"No, Frank, don't go, don't let this…" looking at her.

My eyes moving to the beautiful outline of her lips.

"Wait for me there," pointing back to the bench, "I want to fix this," picking up the heavy can and walking it back, stepping over the fence and setting it down. Deep slow breaths to calm down. Okay, that's done.

Hands tingling—wiping them down on my suede vest.

She's standing back by the bench—she must be cold, she's moving around underneath my coat, bending over then standing up. Sweeping the park like I'm hunting. Looking for pieces of a body—things that are out of place here. Next time I'll… Knowing what comes next if I get my hands on him. It's dark here—I won't have to stop. Dusting my hands off on my used leather pants again. Shaking off the darkness. I need to get her home—it was stupid to bring her here at night.

Coming over to her and holding her, looking in her eyes, her eyes half closed but looking at me like she's looking at me from a distance. "Sorry, that ruined it all," looking at her, she's not backing away.

Lost in her look for a few moments.

"Shall I take you home?"

She's shaking her head her arms go around my body, her head in my chest. "I'm shaking, can you feel it?"

"Yes."

"You wouldn't have let him hurt me."

"No. This is crappy area to be around now," looking around the park, "I'm sorry, I shouldn't have brought you here, I'm sorry, Mary, I'm such a fuck up."

She shudders.

Lifting her head up gently with my fingers under her chin.

"Let's go."

She shakes her head.

"I felt so safe behind you, but such a... It's like your body gave off this charge. I feel guilty it was," her voice goes low. She moves closer, "Exciting, frightening," she runs her hand back through her hair. "I want you to kiss me like you did before, Frank. I've wanted to kiss you like this for so long, feel what you're like. I've seen you at school... like there's this smoldering fire in there looking for some way to express itself. And it's been out of reach for me too," tracing the outline of her face with my hand, she takes my hand wraps it around hers and kisses the back of it, holding it to her chest, stepping up on her tippy toes to bring her lips up. "I don't want to lose this moment."

Holding her eyes in mine. Slowly, deliberate, deep.

Sitting down on the bench together, coat unbuttoned, her hand on my chest and stomach, pulling her body into mine. She, brushes her hair back, straddles me, her hands running through my hair, thrilled by her touch, her trembling lips, the lack of hesitation as she opens up to me. Losing sense of time.

She opens my coat and drapes it out away from us, then around us. She pulls up her shirt and puts my hands around her warm waist. Moving her as she moves with me across the bursting erection in my pants. Stupid things are too tight.

She's fumbling with my belt.

Looking around, nervous now.

"Mary, this is crazy."

"Shh, I don't care, I want to live, Frank, like you said," she pushes my pants back, lifting us up so she can work them down a bit. Free, feeling her cool fingers touching, lightly stroking the side of my penis. She's rising on her knees, as her cool fingers guide me inside her.

Going in so easy, she's so wet. Wonder. Oh, wonder.

A soft deep guttural moan escapes her lips as she slowly sinks down on my penis. Enveloped by her wet warmth, feeling like shooting sparks are going off in my head. Her hands running through my hair, lips together, my tongue pushed deeply inside her mouth—she opens her mouth as far as she can. My hands on her bottom underneath the coat as she moves up and down—her body thinner than Cat's, but it's alive, electric.

Supporting her weight with my hands, moving her with me.

She's working all the way down on my cock. She won't accept anything else. Her lips on my neck now, her tongue in my ear. Up some, then pushing down again to get a little deeper, up again. Her lips by my ears, "This is sooo wonderful. Oh, I knew it would be sooo goooood," rotating her hips around in a circle to work my cock deeper into her pussy. She feels tense, trying too hard.

"Relax your body, good there, that's better."

Instantly opening up, moving to the full depth.

A deep "hmmmmmm," from her.

Her lips kissing my ears, my neck.

Moving faster now, she's pulling my hair, breathing faster.

Feeling the orgasm building deep inside my body.

Moments of deep passionate need channeling in to thrusting up with her as she moves down, positioning her hips so she can make good contact with my body.

"I can't hold off, Mary, oh God this feels so good."

"I want you to come, don't hold back, don't hold back, come Frank, I want you to come."

Biting my tongue to stop from yelling out. Her lips near my ear.

"I can feel that so deep," coming hard, violent waves shooting up, "so much need in you. I want this passion, I want this need."

Slowing down—so much pleasure as I move with her, painful waves of pleasure.

"I'm sooo close, don't stop."

Closing my eyes hard, doing my best to stay with her as she starts violently ramming down on me, moving her around in a circle as she pushes down, then pushing her back and forth when she's all the way down.

"That's it, that's it," dull cry coming up in her throat as she bites her fist, feeling the muscles in the walls of her vagina contract and throb, her body shivering, our heavy breathing almost in concert. Phase of hyper sensitivity over—moving inside her 'cause it feels so wonderful—moving with the need to make this moment last. She's moving with me. No hesitation in anything from her, nothing held back. Wonderful, raw, need for her rising, feeling another orgasm just below the surface.

"Yes, Frank, yes."

My God—how did I miss this?

Looking at her face twisted in a wonderful release, a wonderful openness.

"Oh, Frank," as her breathing starts to slow down, her left hand running through her hair as she starts to laugh softly. Laughing with her.

"This is insane," as she kisses me, sitting back on my lap a little, still inside her. She smiles—her face looks like there's a light shining from inside, "But it was so good, oh baby," as she kisses me.

Paranoia starting to settle back in, sweeping the park then looking back over my shoulder as far as I can. People in front of the medical center looking our way—it looks like they don't believe their eyes and are trying to figure out what we are doing.

"They are looking at us," she says teasingly.

"I don't want to move, it feels so wonderful being inside you like this. I wish we didn't have all this on so I could feel your full body near mine and do this again and again."

"Hmm," she kisses my nose, my lips, "we could go someplace?"

Looking back over my shoulders, the folks by the hospital are talking to someone else now.

"I think we should beat it."

She nods, pushes herself down and settles in with her whole body for a few moments, the wonderful mixture of our fluids slowly seeping out of her and down my balls.

Sound of her breath as she moves back and my still heavy penis slides out, leaning forward and helping her move to my side. She takes her panties out from my coat pocket and quickly and carefully puts them back on as I pull these damn tight leather pants back up, sliding my wet penis in and dressing right, then zipping quietly. Dammit, dammit, zipping down to release the pubic hairs I caught. Mr. Smooth.

Arm around her as we walk quickly west up to 3rd Ave.

Waving down a taxi—time to get the hell out of here.

Holding the door for her as she gets in—this is one of the new cabs with a barrier between the passenger and the driver.

"What are you some kind of Eskimo walking around at night dressed like that?"

"Right, how much to the North Pole?"

"Get the fuck out of my cab if you're just joking around, I got mouths to feed at home and they are not pleasant mouths at that. They get noisy when they get hungry."

"Corner of 76th and West End Avenue" she calls out.

He nods, turns the meter handle and takes off.

Mary collapses into me, putting my arm around her.

She tucks in next to me and puts her head on my shoulder. Smelling us on my right hand, basking in the musky, warm, rich odor. Taking my time to fully register the smell of her and link it back to what we just did.

"What are you doing?"

Turning my face to be near her ear so Mr. Comedy here doesn't hear anything. "I wanted to smell us together, it's wonderful."

Her body shivers slightly as she moves to bring her lips near my left ear again. "That's one of the sexiest things I've ever heard," as she puts her hand on my crotch and starts to slowly massage my cock and kiss my ear.

Sitting in our little cocoon—emotions rocking me. The hurt and shame of Cat hooking up with that preppy fuck mixing with awe at how good this feels—so warm, so open, so freeing. Mixing in with the guilt at how fast we hooked up.

"What are you thinking about?"

Shaking my head, softly to her, "What a night... From uninteresting, to disappointment, to I don't know, having my heart ripped out to, I don't know..."

"Tell me, tell me, I want to hear it," moving my head—her fine brown hair touching my lips, softly near her ear.

"Unexpected, wonderful, mind blowing at how just free I feel with you, how good this feels, a little guilty too—just rushing into, you know," her hand tightening around my cock as I talk to her, pulling her body closer to mine.

Her lips inches from my ear, "I've never felt this way before, Frank, my insides are just throbbing, my whole chest feels like it's just going to explode with emotion. This feels so right to me and I knew it. Just looking at your hands sometimes at school, I could tell how strong you are, scary strong because I don't think it's just brute strength, there's a deliberateness, a tenderness to you too, like you could focus all that like a laser if you concentrate and I'd be able to feel the heat. When you took me out to coffee a couple of weeks ago, it was like a door opened up to a wonderful place that I could see inside for the first time. You know when you know there's something there, but it's not till you see it that the ache of not being able to do anything with it sets in. And then now," she looks out the window. "I don't know what you think about me now. I don't want to be embarrassed."

"Shh," touching her lips, "Mary," looking at her, "I want this."

She nods her head, tucks herself into me.

Silent in the taxi as we speed through the 65th Street traverse through Central Park. Fishing for my wallet as we cross Broadway at 66th Street, lots of people out tonight at the outdoor cafes along Broadway—must be a big happening at Lincoln Center. Turning up 10th Ave.—looking up to the 50's, my parents are probably having a big party tonight. Bastards.

"Which corner you lovebirds want?"

"Near."

Light traffic, hitting a long series of green lights.

As he pulls over, "Here you go," handing him a five, for a $3.70 fare.

"You need any change?"

"Nope," as I hold out my hand for Mary to come out. He salutes and drives off as I slam the door shut, my body starting to chill out in the cool night in only my vest.

"You want to go someplace and talk for a while?"

She touches my face, so solemn for a moment.

"We can go up, my parents won't be back from the Island till tomorrow."

"You sure?"

"Silly," she takes my hand and starts to cross the street—pulling her back as she's not paying attention to another kamikaze cab driver speeding up West End, "We live right there."

"Oh," looking at the telephone booths on the corner, "I should check-in with my aunt... I promised I'd call."

"Really?" she looks at me.

"Really," digging my pocket for a dime. Glad these were a one-time gag, they are way too tight.

"What are you going to tell her?"

"The truth," smiling at her. "It took me too long to get them to trust me after all the, you know..." She looks wary, "Just not a lot of details, if you know what I mean."

"Wow, that's different than I expected."

Shrugging my shoulders. Dialing quickly.

"Aunt Kitty?"

"Frank," she seems surprised to hear me, "I'm glad you called, is everything okay? It sounds awfully quiet where you are."

"It's been a crazy night, Aunt Kitty, I needed to get out of the party for a while. Feeling uncomfortable with some of what was going on... kids smoking you know, marijuana, told them I didn't want any and all. Just got annoying. That wasn't a good enough answer for them. Catherine was getting high too, that's a mess, we had a big fight, and she did some... Anyway it's over, we broke up and I didn't want to be around those people for a while."

"Good for you, not bowing into peer pressure is such a hard thing. Are you okay? I know this has been hard on you both," silence on the phone, "do you want to come home? I can come pick you up."

"No thanks, Aunt Kitty, I promised I'd go help clean up tomorrow. I'll call Richard to see when things calm down and head back to his place."

"Okay, I want you to be safe okay?"

"I will, I promise."

"Bye then... Noon tomorrow? Call if you need anything."

"I will, Aunt Kitty," taking a moment, looking at Mary. "Aunt Kitty?"

"What, Frank?"

"Thanks for trusting me after all."

"Your uncle and I love you very much Frank, be good."

"Okay, bye now, Aunt Kitty."

"Bye, Frank."

Hanging up.

"Your aunt sounds like a neat lady," she has a different look on her face.

"This is your apartment building right?" pointing to the large awning, she nods. Breaking out in goose bumps in the cold.

Doorman opening up the main door and giving me a slow once over, "Evening, Miss Mary."

"Evening, Javier," he cocks an eyebrow at me she smiles and pulls my hand with her as we head to the elevator through the large marble encased lobby. Passing a huge mirror—we look in and make funny faces at our images, laughing.

Quiet ride in the old dark wood paneled elevator that clicks slightly as we pass each floor. Mary looking down, her hands clasped in front of her—smiling at her in my oversized coat. 10th Floor, out into a small hallway—surprised to see only two doors. She takes out her keys and opens the door on the left.

Dark as she walks in and turns around and looks back.

If I go in there, then anything with Cat is over.

A tit-for-tat's probably workable, but the way this feels.

That's stupid, Frank—what she did tonight was inevitable the way things were going. You were too weak to break it off yourself, so stop whining. Emotion of that thought hitting me—why can't I get over this feeling about her? Is that really love or am I just a big weakling? Am I falling into this because it's easy?

Her eyes questioning, the moments passing—would I leave her after this? Do I owe her anything? Is there a commitment I'm making by walking in that door?

More than there is now.

But the way she talked to me, the way she wanted me. The way I felt with her.

Her eyes holding mine, her face questioning, a slight concern shows on her brow. Isn't there something to be said for loving without reservation and not being afraid of passion, of putting everything you have into the moment? The few times we've talked together, I could tell her things that I could never tell Cat, or at least she wouldn't want to hear.

And then there's the sex. God that was so good.

Mary holds out her hand to me, time to choose.

Fingers wrapping around hers, following her willingly into darkness.

Lights gradually going on as we step into a large expensively laid out, but warm, lived in, room set out for comfort—lots of places to sit. This is so different than the expensive no one can sit in living room at my parent's house. Tall ceilings, walls filled with books, statues—a mixture of what looks like Greek, modern art and African—different abstract paintings. Wonderful carved dark wooden screens.

Wordlessly, we walk through the living room and through a long hall—passing two big bedrooms that look like they've been converted to offices; stacks of papers, books, typewriters, notes—the second is distinctly more organized than the first. Stopping to look at the second—great art on the walls—prints of Leonardo's inventions, Michelangelo drawing of hands praying. Walls full of books, a wonderful Arts and Crafts style desk chock full of all kinds of stuff—pictures, small ornate woodcarvings—tucked up against one wall.

"That's my father's office," she looks at me.

Looking at it, "Wow, lots of stuff packed in here," seeing a plaque with a Purple Heart and a Combat Infantry Badge. "Was he in the military?"

She nods, "Korea, but this is mostly for his work and research."

"What does he do?"

"He's a psychiatrist, so is Mom."

Looking down the hall—large black and white photographs of New York, must be Mexico, France—this one looks like Italy.

"He loves photography," she sees me looking at the photographs. "He collects the works of Paul Strand."

"He sounds like a neat guy," looking at her, "this is so different than my parent's place. Things are so cold, so formal there. Our living room has all this expensive furniture that no one is allowed to sit in..." stopping for a second. "You're not going to try and analyze all this are you?"

She laughs, "Good God no, and besides, who'd have the time?"

"Funny," slapping her lightly on the butt.

Giving her the hairy eyeball as she turns and walks down the hall opening another door. Wow, her bedroom is the size of our living room at home—stepping across the doorway. Big fish tank across from a queen sized bed, photographs of steep cliffs running down to the ocean, driftwood along a long beach with heavy fog hugging a line of mountains thick with tall green trees. Not a lot of teen things here—movie posters, *American in Paris, Singing in the Rain, My Fair Lady, Gone with the Wind, Key Largo*. Stereo system and records stacked up near her bed—TV in here too. Wow.

Lots of deep greens in here, bubbles of her fish tank are the only noise.

Smiling at her, uncomfortable moments of silence. She takes off my jacket and puts it over a chair by her desk, brushes back her hair and looks down at her tuxedo shirt—the tail still pulled out—slowly unbuttons her shirt and looks at me, her lustrous green eyes meeting mine for a few moments. Taking in the healthy glow of her fine white skin on her neck and chest. Her shirt slowly slips to the ground—fine patterned thin bra dropping next showing wonderful apple-sized breasts, small pink nipples. Stepping to her, her arms open up and come around my waist. Swaying together for a few seconds, teasing each other without lips. Her body feels so fresh, so healthy.

"These are really uncomfortable, you mind?"

"Take them off, silly," as she stands back, "I want to see you."

"You sure?"

"Are you a prude, Frank Caruso?"

"No," blushing a little. Things were so hurried with Cat. Taking off the second hand buff colored leather vest and then rolling down my pants—hard on popping out, no Joe Cool at half-mast here—big and pointing right at her. She's taking off her shoes, the long socks under her long skirt and then drops the skirt, laughing as she loses her balance a little kicking it off. Her little pink underwear coming down across her hips—nice calf muscles, thin thighs stretching down from her slim pear shaped hips.

Breathing labored, chest feels flush.

"Let me look at you for a moment."

Feeling shy as her eyes take me in.

Taking her in my arms, reveling in the wonderful tactile sensation of the full lengths of our bodies touching, the warm smell of our earlier sex surrounding us. She's kissing my chest and my neck, her fingers moving along the side of my erect penis. Running my hands up the full length of her back and down along the curve of her bottom, tracing the outline it makes at the back of her legs.

Burying myself in her neck, kissing, giving her small bites.

"I love how your hard penis feels on my skin," her words hitting me, jarring. "So warm, energy pulsating out of you, your hands, your muscles, wonderful. Here, feel here, feel how wet I am," taking my hand and slowly putting it between her legs.

"My vagina is so wet, so excited. You penis feels so good against me."

Feeling her, embarrassed at how she's talking, feeling my face flush. Her eyes closed as I bend her head back and kiss her neck, "Tell me what you like." Looking at her, body stiffening up.

"Silly man," she smiles and kisses me. "They are just words, talk to me, tell me how you feel. Tell me what you want."

"But yes, but... its, well. We... I never," struggling.

"You think about these words don't you?"

"Sure, but that's different," feeling my excitement level off—slightly annoyed she's letting the moment slip away.

Quiet distance growing in place of passion, what am I doing here?

"Talk to me, Frank, please"

Did I just get into another dead end?

Why is she doing this? I can't do anything right dammit. Hands down at my side. Looking past her at the photographs around her desk—*Bob Dylan, Carly Simon, Joni Mitchell*. Old style black and white photograph of a man I don't know with curly black hair, box weave sweater, cravat tied around his neck and a black shirt. Print of Van Gogh's *Iris* and other impressionist prints I don't know—a harbor, wonderful blue green water.

"What's the matter?" concern in her eyes, her head tilted slightly sideways. Stepping back from her, she bites her lips.

"Oh no," her voice low. "I'm so... it's just how you make me feel, so uninhibited, so..." She moves back and sits on her bed, pulls up her legs, crosses her arms and puts them around her legs. She looks at me, her lips pursed together.

Seeing how she feels hitting me.

Feeling stupid.

Sitting down next to her, she turns slightly away, her face resting on the top of her knees. Looking at her from what seems like a long way away. The quietness of her room settling in—no street noise here just the sound of a ticking clock and the bubbles of her fish tank. Putting my arms down on the bed and pushing down hard, flexing my triceps holding them—making them burn.

I guess what's left is to go.

Deep sigh going out of my body.

From where we were a little while ago—to this, dammit...

"Mary," she turns over and lies on the bed, pulling herself into a little ball. Moving down to the edge of the bed. Feeling my body sink down on the floor, the carpet feels weird on my bare butt.

What's left to me now? Empty trips out to run along a dead beach?

Working out every day till I go away?

Is this just another fucking prison?

Grabbing my hair and pulling—why did you do this to me, Cat?

Moment of clarity—there's no one to blame.

"It's a strange beauty," looking at her fish tank, "and it's just sitting out there, in the dark," my mind wandering out to the desolation out in Rockaway. "Places that once held so much that are just weathering away slowly, carelessly. Weeds growing, where children once played fiercely, their imaginations running wild. No one will ever know what that world was like. It's all gone. Their voices becoming the waves of small pebbles we used to throw into the calm marsh waters, the ripples of those days when everything was new and fresh now carried out to the deep sea and the land is empty, quiet again."

Mesmerized by her fish gently swimming in the tank.

"There are cool places underneath the boardwalk that are tucked away from the crowds of people... secret places where I used to lie in the cool sand and try to imagine the things I had no idea about. The unknown things that I'd want to feel with a woman, trying to sort out why looking at the girls started to make me feel something. I don't know, different." Pulling my legs up, closing my eyes and putting my head down on my arms as I cross them over my knees.

"Lying there in the cool sand under the boardwalk on my stomach, new feelings erupting in my groin as I pushed down in the cool earth. I'd roll over on my back, looking up at feet walking on the boardwalk. I could see just enough of the people passing above, watching the girls walk by... frustrated, fascinated," laughing softly. "I think you little monsters knew then that something was happening, that we'd changed, that you had a new wonder to us."

Hearing her move a little on the bed.

"That's beautiful... Frank, your voice carries through me," she's moving closer. "Why'd you become so cold earlier? I really felt oh..." I can hear her stretching back out on the bed, my body stirring to think of her naked a few feet away. "So exposed, so foolish for taking a step and saying what was burning inside me."

"I don't know, Mary," my eyes closed. "Too many things going through my head," letting the memory of the cool, dark gray sand take me back in time for a few moments, making the commitment to talk to her. "It was jarring to hear you talk like that, just threw me off. I felt embarrassed. We never spoke about our bodies. Sex or anything about sex was way off topic at home. Funny, sad really, how such a wonderful thing can be so twisted. Guys want girls who aren't ashamed to love it, but it's like got to be some secret that can't be let out, just how much we want it too. This titanic struggle between being so close to what we want, but never saying it, never being able to ask for it. How things can be dirty and wonderful. It's so weird. I can't say it without having my body react like there's something wrong. What a horrible sounding word too."

"What?"

Struggling, body cold, chest feeling compressed. Hearing a distant voice giving life to, "Vagina."

Low laugh from the bed, "Don't laugh at me, Mary O'Connor, or I'll..." Hearing her start to chuckle louder. She scoots her body around closer to the end of the bed, hearing her voice closer to me.

"Or you'll what, Bucko?"

"I'll, oh I don't know, drool on you or something nasty."

"Yuck," she makes a mock gagging sound.

"Come on, it's just saliva."

Feeling her get off the bed, the lights in the room going off.

"We can sit here in the dark and just talk, okay?"

"Gee, maybe I can go find my lyre."

"You're too tall and muscular to be a good Orpheus, although..."

Blowing her a raspberry. Relaxing a little more hearing her laugh.

"I was going to say before I was so rudely interrupted, sometimes hearing you talk takes me with you, makes me want to be close to you, be with you in some of the places you talk about."

"I just have to learn to talk about vaginas though."

"I have a very nice vagina, I'll have you know."

"Yes you do, Mary O'Connor," laughing with her. "What a funny name though… sounds like a technical name for a disease."

"Of course it is, look at how much craziness there is around sex, wanting to ignore it, control it, make it dirty, obscene, sinful. People don't talk about it. They sneak looks at the forbidden fruit in dirty magazines. Besides, Mom says it was a man that invented the term."

"So Mary don't take this as an insult, but who's this talking? I mean, how'd you come to know and think about all this?"

"My parents talk about subjects like this all the time, silly. On one hand it's amazing how horribly stupid we are about sex and then, on the other hand, how irresponsible people can be about it. We always used anatomically correct names at home here. When I was fifteen, we started talking about boys and what their bodies will go through, the biology of female bodies, sex, relationships," she rolls over on her back. "I talk to my mom and dad about all kinds of things, they don't want me to be naive or afraid of sex and at the same time, they don't want me to feel pressured into doing anything I don't want to do."

"Wow," shaking my head, "so different than my house. I imagine Mom having a conniption talking about anything related to sex. For her it always had to be some magical Hollywood or Broadway romance… and then it was sort of okay to refer to."

"Frank," her face is near my ear, "you have a very nice penis."

Laughing with her, trying to shake off the embarrassment of her words.

"What's a different word for you know…"

"You have to say it, Frank, don't be such a weakling."

"Vagina, vagina, vagina," laughing, but it still feels weird. Speaking in the dark, easier to talk. "Oh God, how am I going to look at you and not blush like a fool now?" Feeling her fingers on my hair, the light touch of her lips on my ear.

"Well, penis is a funny name too."

"Sure is," laughing with her. "Especially all the things we call it."

"Like what?"

Shaking my head in the dark "Dick, cock, one eyed monster, Big Ed, wang, schlong, willie, prick, weenie, wiener, Tiny Tim, my thaaang, snake, beef-cake, middle leg, peg leg, rod, sausage, pole, man-meat, member, tallywhacker," she's busting up.

"I like penis or cock, it looks like a little rooster don't you think, all pert and showing off?"

"You are bad, Mary O'Connor, looking so proper at school, so controlled."

"And here you are talking about sex with someone that loves you."

Breathing in at that.

"Did you hear me, Frank?"

"Yes, Mary, I heard the depth, the truth," my butt starting to feel uncomfortable on the bare carpet, "it's important for me to not say something that's convenient now. I feel so alive with you, I feel like I'm so free with you. I don't want to lie to you."

She rolls on her back. "You better not, Frank Caruso."

The bubbles of her fish tank filling the room for a few moments.

"It's been welling up inside and I needed to say it to you so you knew how I feel. Part of me wishes that we have some magic connection and you'd see that I'm the one you were meant to be with, but I'm glad you won't lie to me."

"I won't, Mary."

Standing up, and sitting down, laying back on her bed.

"Is this okay?"

"Sure, silly," her head down by my feet, rolling over.

Moments lying there with her, my eyes used to the darkness seeing the slim outline of her body as she lies on her back, her arms back underneath her head.

"Vagina, vagina, vagina. Hmmm, I think I'll use the word pussy instead. Soft, independent, wild, untamed, you do have a wonderful..." having to focus on saying the word, "pussy, or as the brothers would say pusssaaay."

She's quiet.

"So what would your parents think of this? Do they know you... ah have sex?"

"Mom got me a prescription for the pill last year, and yes. Especially once they meet you. I tell my mom everything."

"Everything? You're kidding."

"Sure, last summer in Italy, I met a boy a couple of years older than me, Marcello. We go to Florence every summer for a month. Well, last year we were there longer. I had such a crush on him."

"Wait, you were telling me you had a big crush on me."

She rolls toward me, "I'm allowed to have more than one you know." She lies on her back, "Well anyway, I talked to my mom about what it would be like and what should I do and all that."

"Are you going to Italy this summer?"

"Oh," she takes a moment, "yes, we'll be gone for a month, more if I want to."

"Oh," deflated, "I go away at the end of the summer."

"Well, what if I stay here?"

"Will they let you?"

"Maybe," I can feel her eyes on me, "is that what you want?"

"Vagina."

"You jerk," she slaps at me.

Taking a few moments, "Yes, Mary, that's what I want."

"Is that all you want?"

Turning to her in the dark.

"Time is what I want now, Mary," imagining that intent direct look in her eyes. "I used to think I had so much time ahead of me, but I really didn't and I can never get that back. Time with you Mary, time to get myself ready for who knows what will happen in the Army, time to get off my ass and help people," rolling over on my back, taking a moment. "My uncle took me to a place where men who were wounded or incapacitated in war, or just old now and need care. Spend time there or see if there's some volunteer work I can do at St. Anthony's Children's Hospital. Something, there's got to be something I can do that's good in these next few months."

Turning toward her, "And I want," taking a deep breath, "I want to feel your cool fingers on my body again, I want to feel the passion of my..." damn this is hard to say, having to push out the words, my voice not obeying my will and coming out softly, "being inside you, my penis," voice growing stronger now.

"My body inside you... your pussy. I'd like to make love with abandon, to see how far we could go if the fear of what our parents would like or wouldn't like was left behind. I'd like to..." damn, rrrrr this is frustrating talking like a little boy who's being naughty, "taste, taste your pussy, feel you come, feel your fingers running through my hair, pulling my hair," her hand on my stomach as she navigates her way to me in the dark. "Feel like we were on the bench earlier tonight," her leg coming up and over mine, feeling a tiny bit of fluid leaking from my erect penis. She's moving on top of me, feeling her wetness on my lower stomach.

"And I want to listen to you, hear about all the things you have here that I don't know about," her fingers lightly touching my face, my body starting to ache inside, breathing faster. "I want to write to you when I'm away, maybe take you places... that place of cool sand and desires I couldn't speak of, didn't..." her lips on mine, her legs stretching out, wrapping around mine, her leg muscles taut, her body warm and electric. Arching my back, supporting her as I flip her over.

Lips moving together, our heads changing positions every few seconds to explore new areas, putting my arms around her, her legs opening to me.

"Touch me here, Frank," as she takes my hand and guides my fingers down between her legs. Soft hair, warm rich, wonderfully fragrant moisture greeting my fingers as I move slowly around the lips of her pussy taking my time to part them and then move my index and forefinger across the warm center of her. Her hand guiding me, her breath quickening—kissing her breasts, her stomach.

Tracing a line down past her belly button with my lips, supporting my body weight on my elbows, my fingers clearing a way for my tongue to extend and lick up and down the length of her—shiver moving through her body. Her smell, her taste is different than Cat, fresh, salty like a clean ocean oyster. Excitement pouring through me at the way her body responds—less fire, more intense as I turn my head and move side to side to whisk my tongue across the top of her clitoris, my two fingers moving slowly inside her in circles, then massaging the roof of her wonderful pussy. Loving the taste of her, the excitement of her body traveling down mine to the tip of my penis.

Her fingers in my hair, pulling, pushing, circling.

"Oh yes, Frank, right there, that's so good, yes, yes…. oooeeerrrr, Ohhhh," her legs rigid, her back muscles lifting her pelvis up off the bed, the muscles in the walls of her vagina contracted and throbbing. "Oh, go sloooow, too fast," she's working to catch her breath, "too much, slow, that's it," my lips, my chin covered in the wonderful wetness of her. Slowly moving my fingers out, moving my body up.

"Hmm," she feels me moving up toward her and she starts to slink down. "My turn."

Shaking my head. "I want to be inside you," her lips on my neck, her hands moving to cup my bottom as I move between her legs, taking my cock and guiding it in with my right hand as I support my body weight with my knees and left arm, moving the tip of my penis along the outside of her wet pussy—the sensation of her is thrilling, doing everything I can do to move slowly, to let the fire burn.

Her legs spreading out, her pelvis tilting, a long "oooooo" coming from her, losing any sense of time, present in how wonderful it feels to be inside her. Her hands pulling me in, worried that my weight and size might be too much—resisting her going a little deeper each time, biting my lip, doing everything I can and not being successful at stopping the wave of energy building deep behind my testicles.

Rigid, pushing with everything I am.

"That's right, Frank, go baby, go."

Giving in to the building explosion, coming hard in waves, my body shivering, holding her hard, pushing my pelvis hard against her as my cock continues to throb—aftershocks, ejaculations—smaller waves of pleasure hitting me.

"Oh Mary, oh how wonderful," my penis too sensitive to move, holding her there as the tremors subside. Deep kisses, her legs wrapping around me, her body pushing back on me, pulling in all that I'm giving off.

Head clearing. Feels so good.

Starting to move with her slowly.

Not needing to tell her to stay with me, smile on her face, after a few minutes as blood returns and I hold her arms back, our fingers, our legs entwined looking into those wonderful green eyes, her body open, wanting. Cock thickening out, feeling her move with me.

Hard to go to sleep in her bed—going in and out of light sleep. Moments of guilt—I broke up hours ago with Cat and here I am, my body slathered in our sex. Reaching down and stretching out my penis to break through the tight, dried, thin layer of sweat, come, saliva and her bodies lubricating fluid—what the hell would you call that? Pussy lube. Sounds like some asshole motor oil commercial. Pussy juice? Not bad.

Looking at the ceiling and then the clock.

Do I deserve this? Am I some drowning man pulling at anything near to save myself? She's got her head together more than I do—but there's something so fresh, honest about her.

Looking at the clock—need to be out before her parents come home tomorrow and get back to Richard's. The skin on my penis feeling sore after all the sex we've had—last orgasm took so long to come, it hurt but felt so good, so deep when I came. Her arms and lips got tired, but she worked it, she wanted to make it happen. Shifting over to my side.

"Hmm," she turns over. "You okay?" her voice talking like she's a long ways away. "You move around a lot."

"Sorry," her hair draping over my chest as she curls underneath my arm.

Listening to her breathing softly and running back through each time we made love in my mind. Cat and I never had this—would things have been different if we did? Did I give up on her to quickly? Did she give up on me too quickly or are we just stupid kids playing at being grown up—stupid ideas on how we'd get to college and then get married.

Silence of her room settling again, bubbles of her fish tank.

To find this right before I go away.

Stomach tensing, slight sick feeling—the condemned man's last supper.

Why is she doing this? How could she say she love me—that's stupid, she doesn't know the storms that rage inside me at times, the blackness at times, the joy. So much easier to have just fucked Cherlyn's brains out.

But here she is, peaceful, totally relaxed in my arms. She'd do it again right now too. Feeling my cock start to rise up thinking about sex with her again.

Cold thought hitting me—in a few months she will be close to that Italian fucker again. Oh, maybe that's me, one of the two Italian fucks. Imagining him as she told me about him—different than my deep Southern Italian looks—a northerner, blond blue eyes—Joe bicycle racer. I hate him.

She's eighteen though—started school a year late.

My independent, passionate, curious, Mary O'Connor.

Closing my eyes, letting the musty smell of our bodies carry me away.

Eyes burning from lack of sleep.

Putting my face in the warm water running down from the showerhead. Her soapy hands on my legs and working their way toward my penis—still sensitive from all the sex we had last night but getting hard again. Her lips on my stomach, tucking her hair behind her head as she strokes underneath my cock, her wonderfully shaped lips, her tongue, her fingers moving in such a wonderful rhythm.

God I love how fearless she is.

Almost losing my balance in her shower as I ejaculate wildly, body shivering down to my toes. She's holding me in her mouth savagely, taking everything I can offer. Her fingers around the base of my penis.

"Oh God, Mary," bringing her salty lips to mine. "That was so good." If she's not afraid to do it and take it all when I come, I'm not going to be afraid to show her how much I love it, how good it feels.

"I was mad you didn't let me do much of that last night," she snuggles in close as I put my arms around her. "I love how hot and hard you get, oooh," she shudders a little. "You know what I like best about your penis?"

Smiling at her—I know I'm going to hear it.

"I love how thick it is, I love that you don't just slam me with it too," she starts stroking my back. "You make love to me, you just don't fuck with it, like you're trying to touch every part of me."

"Mary, you little…"

"What?"

Keeping the not funny dirty little whore to myself.

"You are too much."

"Why shouldn't I talk about it? Why are people so stuck up about something so natural, so wonderful?"

Laughing as the fire starts moving in her eyes.

"We are gonna get tarred and feathered if your parents come home and we're…"

She looks at me.

"Okay, okay," she's rolling her eyes. "Let's go if you are afraid."

"Buy you breakfast?"

A little smile from her as she's turning off the water.

"Eggs, to go with your breakfast sausage?"

"You know," her fingers touching my lips, "you could be funny if you worked at it," smacking her playfully on the butt as she steps over the lip of the large bathtub.

Quiet morning out on West End Avenue, fresh morning colors, feeling a lightness inside that's been away for a long time.

Walking up to Broadway, feeling last night. Tired, sore, fresh, the colors of the world coming back in and taking the place of the gray, dark shadows. Our arms around each other, her clogs click-clacking as we walk along with sidewalk, my hand down in her jean pocket.

Her face coming near my ear, "I'm not wearing any underwear."

"God, you are a wicked little thing!"

"No, I'm not," she looks at me, "I'm wonderful," standing up, stretching her shoulders out, her nipples standing out in her shirt as she walks braless, "I'm sexy and I'm happy."

Smiling.

"Me too, Mary, me too."

Chapter 52

Basking in the glow of her as I sit on the BMT downtown.

She has a phone. I can call her anytime I want to. She wants to meet my aunt and uncle—with Cat... Well my family was always an inconvenience. Looking at the tunnel lights flying by from 34th Street to 22nd Street. Well maybe a lot of that came from me. Talk to Aunt Kitty, Uncle Vin when I get back see if they'd like to meet her.

Lazy walk through Washington Square Park in the cool day, bright sun, lots of people out—rows of chess players on the MacDougal Street entrance, people playing Frisbee on the grass, a few elderly ladies sunning themselves with triangular fold out mirrors. People walking dogs, people yelling at them to not let their dog go right in the middle of the walkway. Like New Yorkers will ever pick up their dog's shit.

Congas and all kinds of percussion today at the fountain—guys jamming, drinking beer and whatever already, bogarting with the few young girls who want to play with fire.

Watching the floor numbers light up on the long quiet elevator ride up to Richard's apartment. Ringing the doorbell.

"You look good," to Richard as he comes to the door—tousled hair, wrinkled shirt, boxers and one sock. He stumbles as I come in.

Smells horrible in here.

"Let's get all the windows open, it stinks in here," looking around the living room—full ashtrays, wine bottles, beer cans, plastic drink cups with the remnants of his Sloe Gin concoction. I can only imagine what's in the back room. Hope these assholes at least flushed their condoms. He stumbles down the couch, swirling beer cans to see if there's any left and then looking in to make sure someone didn't put out a cigarette or a doob in it before drinking. Yuck.

"You have fun?"

He blinks, "I mmm, fink soo," he scratches his head. "Got to third base with Maria," he says after drinking nasty, warm beer.

"The world famous sixty-eight, eh?"

He looks at me cock-eyed.

"You know, you do me and I owe you one..."

"Shit, I think I hit the ceiling, oh man was she laughing I blew so hard."

"Right Mr. Moby Dick. Let's get this place cleaned up, I got stuff to do."

He stands up and looks at me.

"Sorry about last night man, that was pretty low of her."

"She's a cheating bitch," picking up an ashtray and going in search of a trashcan, Richard following along.

"I mean, right here."

"Richard," looking at him. "I was here, remember?"

"Oh, sorry man."

"She called a couple of times man," he stops. "I didn't know what to tell her."

Dumping the wet contents of the ashtray into a plastic lined trash can—man, just bring the can with you and dump them—stupid to bring them one by one in the kitchen.

"Hope you told her to go fuck herself."

"No!" he looks at me, "she's so…"

"What, beautiful?"

"Yeah, I mean, you know."

"Well anyway," shrugging my shoulders, feeling a creeping cold feeling—I'm going to have to face her and tell her it's over. What is she, some damn drama queen, after what she did to start calling and ask about me? Getting mad again, the image of walking up to that door, the awful cold feeling of walking through that door—like some part of my heart had a frozen dagger stuck in and seeing her… Stopping, taking a deep breath—I used the wrong words earlier, she's not a fucking bitch, she's a fucking cunt bitch.

Dumping ashtrays, empty cans, Richard finally getting off his ass and helping. "So what did you tell her?"

"Oh man, I told her it's crazy here and that I couldn't find you."

Elise comes stumbling out, her shirt a mess, she looks thirsty, her mouth and tongue trying to work some moisture up. She stumbles by waving a weak hi.

"Yu Wen here?" to Richard.

"Hell, I don't know. Lisa passed out in my room, barfed in my bed, what a mess." Fresh air starts to circulate through the apartment.

"Your brother's going to be pretty pissed" pointing to the leather couch. Some numb nuts spilled their drink on the leather.

"Shit, shit, shit," he's starting to wake up.

"Oh man, I got today and tomorrow, oh man."

"Call your maid, man! What are you waiting for, tell her what's up, offer her fifty bucks and tell her to keep this between the two of you."

"Oh uh, right, yeah, okay," he stumbles off.

Brushing the sweat off my brow with the back of my hand. Room starting to appear in some semblance of order. Lucky their maid Consuela brought in her sister, Miriam—they are working away. Now all I have to do is move the heavy stuff back. Richard's working to get Lisa out, her parents throwing a shit fit that she didn't come home—they didn't care enough to get their asses down here though and get her last night. Hands wrinkled from the soapy water as I help scrub out Richard's bathtub—man, did she blow chunks in here after getting started outside last night.

Coming into their big kitchen.

"*How's that horrible bathroom?*" Miriam asks while she mops, her fat body moving back and forth.

"*There was a dragon in there, I saved you from it,*" pinching my nose like something smelled horrible.

"*You're crazy cleaning up, we'll do it.*"

"*Ahhh and miss all this fun?*"

She waves at me like I'm a crazy man.

Washing my hands in cold water, running it over my face to rinse off the light sweat. Taking a cold bottle of root beer out of the fridge, walking into the living room, Richard feeding coffee and toast to Lisa. He looks impatient to get her out of here.

"You gonna be okay there, Lisa?"

She shrugs her shoulders. This must be more about not wanting to go home and face the wrath of her parents. Door ringing.

"I'll get it." Not going to say a thing to Lisa's parents about last night.

Stretching and yawning as I open the door—oh no.

Standing frozen in the doorway looking at Cat.

"What do you want?" hurt and shame from last night screaming back, no matter how much I try to push it down.

"Oh please, Frank," different energy than I've ever seen from her before, her hands shaking—first time, a slip in her self-control.

"I just… Look can we talk? Please?"

"Let me grab my coat."

Icy silence in the elevator down—what was worse, mopping up smelly vomit, used condoms, spilled drinks and such after a bunch of high school kids, or standing here? Hmm—this is much, much worse.

Nodding to the doorman on the way out.

Walking toward Washington Square Park.

"So, what do you want from me, Cat? I didn't think there was anything to say after last night."

"Don't talk to me like that, Frankie," she moves to touch me and I move away.

"You've made some mistakes, can't you forgive me?"

"You're going to put this on me?" Breathing to keep my head on straight. Looking away from her as we pass under the arch.

"No," she rams her hands in her coat pocket. "I love you, Frankie," her hollow words hitting me.

"Bullshit."

Big crowd around the dry fountain, conga drums are going, people moving to the beat, drinking beer, wine, smoking weed—the big impromptu party of the day. I need to get down here more often now that I have lots of time.

Taking a look at her walking a foot away from me.

Can't stop the bile "How can say you love me and then treat me like shit like you did last night? You wouldn't have anything to do with me, making fun of me in front of your little friends and then you hook up…" punching my fist into my left hand wishing I'd found that motherfucker when I came outside.

"I'm such a mess Frankie, this is tearing me up," she stops and shakes her hands up and down looking at me. People walking by starting to look at us, "All the things that have happened to us, it's making me crazy, I just needed…"

"Some release, too tough?"

"Don't put words in my mouth."

"Don't put other men's cocks in your mouth."

Slowly, the Cat righteous fire coming back "How dare you!"

"You wanna get mad, you wanna get good and mad so you can walk away and feel justified, then walk. Just walk!" spreading my arms and stepping to her. Turning away and walking away from the fountain. Mad because part of me wants to put this behind and feel like it was a few weeks ago. Was what we had meaningful because it was good or because it was the first— puppy love? Walking fast.

"Frankie. Please, Frank," feeling her hand on my sleeve.

Stopping. Turning. Pulling it back—looking for a place to sit down. Pointing to an empty section on the long park bench along one of the walkways leading to the fountain.

"You know, Cat, so much of me just wants to turn back the clock a day, days, what a couple of weeks? To feel like I did before, to have a vision of you, of us. Go back to that sacred place I felt I was in with you. But that's fucking ripped out of me and I'm mad because I want it back so bad."

"I want it back too, Frankie, please. I messed up, please."

Looking at her, like she'd never lord over my weakness if we got back together.

"No, Cat, this has been coming for weeks… we've been too weak, too sentimental to deal with it, hoping some miracle would happen," looking across the park. Colorful clothes, people hanging out talking, less conga music now—acoustic guitars out here and there. Staring off at the NYU Law building across from the park. "And I really hoped it would happen," more to myself.

Her body still, her eyes not focused at me.

Long chill settling in—ice forming from the lack of motion.

"And where were you last night?" she looks at me accusingly.

Fighting down the wave of guilt washing in.

"It's none of your business anymore, Cat, we are done, this is over," feeling my face turn hard while speaking the words I'd been so afraid to say. Maybe this thing with Mary's a naive fling—but I'm leaving soon and Cat and I left each other long ago. Damn, damn—feeling the emotion of her on my body, on my face.

"I hear you say that, but I know you don't mean that. I know you love me, Frankie."

"I do, Cat," mad cause my eyes are tearing up. "I really do, but if we get together again it's only going to delay what's coming. I..."

I need to say this—I can't just think this, the words coming out slowly. "I don't trust you." Taking a deep breath, "I'm not some plaything you turn on and turn off when it's convenient. I can't shut off how I feel or what I think because you don't want to hear about it. I mean, Jesus Christ Cat, we're supposed to be together and I can't talk about... What were we going to do when things got really tough? Get like your parents and act like nothing's wrong? Be a bunch of phonies?"

"I love you."

"And what does that mean, Cat? When things got tough you got blitzed, got high and took up with some fucking asshole you met. What an awful thing to do." She's silent. "The feeling of standing at that door and knowing you were in there with another man, the things that ran through my head. Do I leave the party and hang my head in shame, do I burst in there, do I go make a move and fuck someone else for some stupid revenge? It hurt so bad, I just needed to see it, just burn that in my memory..." stifling the other words like, you fucking bitch.

Evil thought coming into my mind. Just speak like it's an everyday thing. "So, you met him that weekend up at Yale right?"

"Yes, he was..." she's surprised at the words coming out her mouth. She looks at me hard and then hurt—her body sagging.

"I know you, Cat," looking at the elderly couple slowly sitting down across from us—he holds her arm so she can sit down. "You sneak around your parents with me. You say you love me, but you're too chicken to tell them. You say you love me but you sneak around with whatever his name was. Is that it, Cat? You just want things your way and don't want to deal with the consequences."

Feeling cold inside. Watching her knead her fingers together, her head tilted down. "But you know what we felt like together, Frankie"

"Yes."

"Can't that mean something? Look," she turns to me. "We're just kids, I made a terrible mistake, can't you let me learn? What if I change, Frank? What if I tell my parents I love you and we're going to be together no matter what they say? Can't you even accept an apology from me," that hurts as it hits home. "If you love me, Frankie, why can't you let me learn too? Why can't you forgive me?"

Slight wind blowing her black hair.

"You know, Cat, I was too mad at Alton, too full of hurt pride to accept an apology. I was wrong then." God this hurts as the memories of our years together boil and jump around. Things I didn't understand, the gut feelings that I shoved away as unimportant, coming clear. Uncomfortable realization that I know more about Mary in the short time that we've been together than I know about Cat. Have I been satisfied that she's such a force of nature, so alive, so beautiful and at times so attentive? Was I just lazy?

"I'm sorry if I'm not listening to you. I accept, Cat... I accept your apology. Look, I've made so many bad moves lately..." Holding her eyes as they get an expectant glow. Knowing deep down that I'll never live with myself if I don't tell her the truth.

Hesitating. Having to force the words out.

"We can't go back to what we had before, Cat. This has been coming for weeks. We've just not been honest with each other. It's over, Cat. I do love you, I won't lie to you no matter how much I want to just go some place and make love to you like we did. And I'm going miss you so much, Cat, your fire..."

Wrenching feeling in my chest as she looks down at her hands and gets up and walks slowly toward 6th Avenue, her head hanging down for a few moments, then gathering herself up, her pace picking up, brushing her hair back over her ears.

Turning the other way.

Biting my hand, fighting the need to go after her.

Chapter 53

Looking back at Manhattan now and then as I walk across the Brooklyn Bridge. Slow meandering walk home, my feet tired from the long walk in these stupid boots. Paying little attention to the joggers and bicyclists zipping by me now and then.

Stopping to look down at the nasty green water of the East River far down below as it slowly moves along. The tide is going out to sea.

For the thousandth time, it's over.

Did I just make the biggest mistake of my life? She had to know it too— I've never seen her defeated. I know if she really wanted this she'd have fought, like I'd have fought if I really wanted this.

Looking toward Brooklyn. Amalgam of scents coming up from the East River—none of them are pleasant.

Four months and change to go.

Fighting off the weight of all the shit that's been going down.

Image of those laughing, smiling green eyes brings a smile to my face.

Time to cast off all the trappings of my old life—it's all new now, baby, and who knows what the hell is coming. Stepping out with a lighter walk.

Yeah, got to get some good bop in my stride, baby.

Time to get in shape, be ready for Army life.

"I'm still in shock, Frank," said Aunt Kitty sitting across the table.

Stretching to get the long nap after last night out of my body, stifling the yawn brewing below the surface. Watching her, stirring her coffee, hands starting to feel a little sweaty. This is new—talking like this.

"I'm curious," she doesn't look at me, "is Catherine an only child?"

"No, she has a younger brother." Aunt Kitty nodding her head, stirring away while she thinks. She takes a sip of what must be ice-cold coffee. She makes a funny face and puts it down.

"So first, Frank, I'm really glad you dealt with this without giving in to the anger and hurt that must have been going through you. I could see it in your face while you talked. I don't know how you'll take this, but her behavior, while there's no excuse for it, from what you've told me, is unfortunately age appropriate. This has been a big event in both of your lives, especially since you were both conscious about being involved sexually as a part of a longer term relationship."

My insides starting to twist hearing that I fucked up again.

Putting my elbows on the table, my face in my hands, the lightness and joy I'd felt at walking home earlier being pulled into the mud.

"I can't do anything right. Jesus."

I can't see her, but I know she's looking at me.

"Frank, you have such a wonderful sense of responsibility and doing the right thing, but there are times where... Frank, you're seventeen. Look, you have the capability to be a fine man. If you stay this hard on yourself and you don't learn that you can't control everything in life. Things are going to happen and you have to deal with them. People are not perfect Frank, we all make mistakes, we do stupid things, we recover from the mistakes we make. I have a feeling it's going to take you a long time to understand this, but people are doing the best they can at any moment."

Body reacting instantly to her words, "No way, Aunt Kitty, look at all the mean, lazy stupid, hateful things people do. Is that the best we can do? Where's the honor, the integrity, courage in saying that? Do we all just give up and..." Looking at her, "We just accept mediocrity? No!"

"Doing the best you can doesn't mean accepting mediocrity, it means that you, Frank Caruso, have a capability to be a certain way at this time in your life. All those pushups and sit ups I hear you doing in the basement... how many can you do?"

"I don't know, at my best sixty-five at a shot now."

"If I told you to do a hundred, no two hundred, could you do it?"

"No."

"Should I get a nice fat razor strap and beat you because you can't?" she's smiling at me. "Should I call you a big Mama Luca because you can't, eh?" laughing with her. "You probably will be able to do some crazy number of pushups one day, but you can do what you can do now. The difference is that you are not satisfied with your sixty-five and have a goal, something you work on every day. I see all the books you come home from the library with and sit and read. That is stepping out of the ordinary and working, learning... be passionate, Frank, be yourself."

She takes a little break, her words filtering in.

"You have to learn to accept other people for what they are... some people don't have your drive, that wild hair of curiosity, the desire to learn. How you are will make some people crazy because, as you've found out, a lot of people want calm, secure happy lives. You need to be around people who are curious, motivated to learn and experience things, but give yourself and others a break, Frank."

Serious look on her face, "People like you can sometimes really damage themselves, they keep this Don Quixote like vision of perfection and end with something blowing out in them, ulcer, cancer, accidents, violent altercations... sound familiar, Frank?"

Remembering back to the morning I got into it with Leroy, Thomas Jones and Alton. Something was ready to blow that morning—I couldn't deal with it.

"Your friend Mary sounds like a very mature girl for her age." Aunt Kitty up, pouring out her coffee and getting another pot of water boiling for her French press, "I like that she wants to meet us and have you meet her parents. My advice, Frank," looking at me, "I know you'll debate this with me, so don't drive me crazy okay?" She sits back at the kitchen table. "Take it slow, you're going through a lot of changes now, emotional ups and downs."

Rolling my eyes.

"What?" she's looking annoyed.

"No, I was just agreeing, sometimes it feels like I'm losing it. I feel so down and then others it's like I can see how things could work and then I just bounce around."

"It's good that you are talking about it now, when you first came here you were wrapped so tight, it had both of us really worried. Look, " she gets up, "I have to go meet your Aunt Nancy," she rolls her eyes, "you know how I love that, but she needs some help. Vincent has reservations for us at Azzura at eight next Tuesday. Invite Mary, it will be good for her to meet us and see more of the family."

"Sure, Aunt Kitty, sure," helping her clean up.

Everyone is doing the best they can—looking at my aunt as she walks out of the room. I sure love her, but that's bullshit. Like my dad is doing the best he can when he used to humiliate my sister cause she wouldn't date boys? When he used to beat me? Fuck you, you evil little man. I'm going to show you.

Chapter 54

Feeling uncomfortable in my jacket and tie as I walk down West End Avenue. Pulling the cuffs of my white button down shirt below the sleeves of my navy blue light wool blazer. The flowers feel corny—fighting the urge to dump them at the next corner.

The rich deep blue and yellow of the irises standing out against the rose colored paper. Am I trying to kiss her parents ass? Why the hell do I do things like this? Why am I dressing like this? Noble gestures—nobody does this. It's too late, I'm right here, fuck it.

Night doorman giving me the once over, he must be trying to figure out why I look familiar.

"It was the costume."

He cocks his head and nods at me, "Oh yes, with Miss Mary a week ago."

"We are going out to dinner, do you need to ring me up?"

"No, go on ahead."

Holding the elevator door open for a woman in a full-length mink coat who reeks of perfume walking her little powder puff dog. She doesn't even say thank you. Frigging dog's in a little jacket and all. I get the once over and then the raised nose, the look of her seeing something cheap she doesn't like.

Giving the dog a little boot in the ass as it gets off the elevator behind her, she turns to look when it yelps and I'm back against the rear of the elevator looking up in the air. Bitch. Who would have sex with some painted up creature like that? Imagine how drunk you'd need to be to stick your dick in it, disgusting.

Enough. Shaking my body—got to get in a good mood to meet her parents. Imagining getting the third degree like I did from Catherine's parents. Oh how her father hated the fact that I'd have the balls to question or debate the great professor. Well, they can all go rot in hell.

Aged smell of the small hallway lobby on their floor—the carpet in the hall is well cared for and clean. Mind going the different places my friends live—Julio's, Alton's and Hector's almost slum level. You could probably fit all three apartments into Richard's place. Yu Wen, his family of three kids, two aunts, mother, father and a grandmother jammed together in the small three bedroom apartment down on Mulberry Street.

Pressing the doorbell, the flowers behind my back.

I should have chucked these.

Instant smile seeing her—surprised to see her answer the door.

"You look wonderful, Mary," and she does. She smiles—does a little show of her dark red dress. Cut just below the knees, still enough to show those lovely shapely calves—her dress square cut above her chest. Her hair

423

out—first time I've seen her in make-up—her eyes much more distinct. Wow.

"You look very handsome," coming over, looking behind her to see if anyone was there and kissing me on the lips—playing with my tongue, backing off and smiling at me.

"Come in," she closes the door. "What do you have there?"

"Oh," blushing a little, "I remembered the Van Gogh in your room, thought you might like these."

"I love irises," her voice perking up, she smiles taking the flowers. "That's really nice, just don't tell my parents how you chose though. Something I must have told you," she squeezes my hand, and comes close. "It's been a whole day now... I really missed you." She ducks in close to me, "I think the cough that kept me out of school the last few days is getting better," looking at me, her eyes relaxed, slightly closed. "You're a good doctor." Image of our bodies in constant motion flashing in taking me back to a wonderful place else for a moment.

Shaking my head, smiling at her, "You are bad, you know that."

She gives me a little smile and tugs me along into the apartment.

"Mom, Dad, Frank is here," she calls and takes my hand, walking me into the living room. Taking a few moments to get a closer look at a wonderful antique carved screen, months and months of work by a master craftsman—incredible.

"Well here he is, the young man himself," turning around to see a strong looking man with well groomed, graying hair checking me out. Very direct look but not calling me out. Breath shortening for a second as her mother comes in the room. My God is she beautiful—taller than Mary, similar build. She has Mary's eyes—a wonderful blue green—but her features are so finely chiseled, distinct, clear, regal. My mother is a beautiful marble statue—cold, delicate, distant. Mary's mother is living, moving... My God.

Blinking my eyes, deep breath—get back on track.

"I'm Joe O'Connor," he holds out his hand and we shake—firm, direct grip, not like some people who shake your hand and then push it away quickly. "This is my wife, Claire."

"It is good to meet you, Sir," completing our shake, turning to her mother. "Good to meet you, Mrs. O'Connor." Not sure how to make out how she's looking at me—mix of seriousness and questions brewing.

"Well, he doesn't look like a hardened criminal," she says. Shaking my head at that, not understanding, then she starts to smile. She's busting my balls, Curly of the Three Stooges running through my mind—back biter, rrrooffff, rrrooofff...

"It's after five now, union rules... we get to look like normal people after hours, no one wants to pay overtime nowadays."

"Oh, and he has a tinge of wit as well," as she steps forward and offers me

424

her hand. Firm handshake, quicker than her father's, Mary looks a little uneasy.

"We met last year," her father talking now.

"I'm sorry Mr. O'Connor, I don't recall?"

"City Championships, you played very well," remembering the game—one of those really good games when I was in the bubble. Man, Alton was so good in that game too—after the game, we were just trying to hang onto the glow, he was laughing and busting chops, his mom so happy, she looked so proud of her son. Nodding to him, feeling a pang—I'll miss that. Next year would have been our year to break out. Leroy would have been gone, Hector and Larry starting at guard. Julio sixth man, that sophomore kid Curtis coming along well.

Damn.

"Ah well, you were all so excited you probably don't remember."

"Sorry."

"Take a seat," pointing to the couch, Mary coming over with me. "Something to drink? Water, soda or something?" Looking at her, thinking about how she'll blossom over the next few years—when she gets herself set like she is, she's a beauty.

Imagine her in a few years. Ouch!

"No, thank you."

"He brought me these, I'll put them in a vase."

"Very nice," said her mother looking at me smiling but something else going on—oh, oh, she's starting to get a different look at me now that the niceties are done, like who the fuck are you and what are you doing with my daughter?

Comfortable couch.

"You were looking at the Venetian screen, what do you think of it?" her mother asks, direct probing look.

Looking back at the screen, "I was admiring the craftsmanship, it looks like very good wood, rich, deep, tight grain. Some of the furniture my Grandfather's family brought over from Sicily looks similar, wonderful scrollwork. He showed me these hand gouges to get the detail… Oh sorry to go off on a tangent."

Her father checking me out, "You appreciate craftsmanship?"

"Yes, Sir. My grandfather loved teaching us to work with wood, well, cooking too but…"

"Not very masculine is it?" her mother making a statement of completion.

"No, ma'am, that wasn't what I was going to say. My grandfather owned and operated a popular restaurant, I used to like to hang out and watch him work—he made sure everything got done just right. He used to have so much fun there," losing sight of her parents for a moment thinking of Grandpa T—that big smile of his.

425

"There we go," said Mary bringing the irises in a vase and placing them on the thick glass table in front of me. Sitting down next to me—taking my hand to claim her territory—her father watching her in an attentive, but relaxed manner.

"How's the grilling going?" Mary says with a smile.

"Oh, just starting," her mother quickly chimes in, "He's not even a little brown yet, we'll have to wait to flip him over in a little bit."

"As you can imagine, when Mary told us about your experience in school," her father calm, watching me, speaking slowly, "we were, as you might imagine, concerned"

Breathe—take another slow breath. Feeling the weight of silence growing in the room, both of her parents calmly watching me. At least he's direct.

Looking down at my hands. Tell it like it is man...

"I made some pretty awful moves," looking at them, looking down at my hands again. "It's funny, well, not really... I spent a lot of time blaming and making excuses about what I did, justify my anger and all. Maybe I still do, but I was wrong... I let a lot of people down," looking at him. "Even with all that, I mean, losing all the opportunities I had. I have to make something out of all this. The mistakes won't go away, I think it's only the things I do about them that matter now." Feeling Mary squeeze my hand. Sad smile at her, maybe she's too good for me.

Her father looks at me patiently, nodding his head.

"How did you know iris' are Mary's favorite flower?" her mother piping in to break the silence.

"Oh, school trip to the Met last year, I remember she was excited to see Van Gogh, they have a number of his paintings..." feeling stupid.

"Yes, I see." she says, dismissive tone. She knows its bullshit.

"Now, Mom," says Mary.

Her father relaxed, watching me—taking this all in.

"Mary say's you're going to Grotta Azzura for dinner?"

"Yes, with my aunt and uncle."

"I love that place," her mother pipes up. Uneasy around her.

"You are living with them now?" her father asks.

"Yes, he's a policeman. Detective Lieutenant," looking at them. "My aunt is the school psychologist at Brooklyn Academy." Looking at her mom—God is she a beautiful woman. Different than my mom—not a cold beauty, warm earth, she must even smell good. "I fit right in."

They give me a polite chuckle.

Mary moves a little closer to me, looking at her—fresh, open, happy look on her face—holding her eyes for a moment, can't help the smile that comes back to greet her. Catching her dad nodding his head, looking at his wife from the corner of my eye.

"So, you two should get going," he stands up, her mother looks a little miffed—she must have wanted to land a few more barbs. "In a couple of weeks we're going out to our place in the Hamptons, don't worry it's not fancy by any means, but we'd be glad to have you come along, get to know you a little better."

"The criminal as a young man?"

"And he's even read a little Joyce," he gives me a polite smile, "maybe there's hope."

"Oh Dad, that'd be great," Mary going up to him and kissing him, giving her mom a hug and a kiss too, "Frank loves the sea."

"You like to fish?"

"Yes, my uncle and I go after striped bass, blues and all out of Montauk."

He nods, slight smile, makes a calming motion to his wife.

"Well, be off you two."

Arms around each other on the way down, deep kisses—wishing I could pull the dress away and go for it right in the elevator.

"You did good there."

Smiling at her, "Does my back feel well enough done?"

Busy Broadway sidewalk, road thick with traffic.

"No!" she looks at me after telling her the story of my ride up with the old bat. "That's Mrs. Huntermeyer, she's a real piece of work." She starts laughing, "Oh my God, I wish I could have seen that, Dad would have laughed... Did you really?" as I'm signaling a cab.

"Sure as hell!"

Cab pulling up to the curb—opening the door for Mary, shaking my head as a well-dressed lady bolts right by Mary, crawls to the far door, sits there with her hands folded and starts to call out an address for the driver.

Leaning in, "Excuse me, this is our cab."

"No, it's my cab," she calls out. Mary looks bewildered.

"You cut in, now get out!" looking at her, the cabdriver impatient.

"Lady, this isn't your cab," he says to her.

"I'll call the police, you have to take me."

I've had enough of this shit.

Stepping by Mary, kneeling on the cab seat, grabbing her by the arm and pulling hard, "Help, help," she starts to yell and grab for the door handle. Getting mad—giving her a big yank that almost pulls her out on the pavement. She tries to hit me with her purse—easy to step away.

"Animal."

"Fuck you, lady, you tried to jump our cab," shoving her back on the sidewalk, people gathering.

"Police, police," she starts yelling and I hold her back with a stiff arm. She tries to move around and I grab the shoulder of her coat and pull her back.

"Get in the cab, Mary," trying to stay calm, the lady kicking at me.

"Maybe we should let her have it and take the next," she looks worried.

"No way I'm going to let her pull this bullshit. It's our cab!"

Mary getting in hesitantly—nervous look on her face.

The lady's hand on the door as I sit in the cab, she's trying to hold the door open while she yells for the police. Rolling down the window, reaching out, grabbing her wrist and squeezing the two bones together and twisting hard—her face goes into shock and she steps back grabbing her wrist, yelling in pain, yelling obscenities.

"Drive man! Corner of Mulberry and Broome Street," sitting back, body feeling the adrenaline rush, "man that was some pushy bitch."

Taxi pulls out into busy Broadway traffic—a chorus of horns blaring.

"Oh man, you ain't seen nothing!" the cabbie says laughing.

Mary looks at me then looks at him.

Busy streets as he heads down 72nd Street to take the West Side Highway. Driving past the docks—shiver passing through my body.

Mary sitting a few inches away.

"Never a dull moment," she looks at me then looks away.

"That made me really mad. I hate that "me first, I'm special, I get what I want no matter what" attitude. Probably a lawyer or something, too many nice people around, let them get away with that shit."

"First time that's happened to that lady I bet." The driver starts chuckling and looks back at us in the mirror. "You always this entertaining?"

"I'm working on it."

Mary looking out the cab window, her arms crossed.

"What if you talked to her more, what if she was standing there and we didn't see her?"

"Mary," patience, take a deep breath, "that's what she's counting on. She's a pushy New York bitch who thought she could get over on a couple of chump kids."

"How do you know?"

"I have very good peripheral vision, didn't see her anywhere near us. If she was there first, why did she duck in without saying anything? Plus, look how she acted in the cab. She moved all the way to the far side and she had her body hunched down ready for confrontation, she was holding on to the damn door even before I said anything. I mean Mary, give people the benefit of the doubt, but watch what they do."

"I don't know, Frank, you're so certain."

Looking around, looking frustrated.

"It's called street smarts, lady," the cab driver piping up. "That whole act was a con, I see people like that all the time. One time man, it was a downpour like you've never seen on 6th Avenue, nice middle-aged lady loaded down with shopping bags waves me down. So this Joe Brooks Brothers and his perfect blonde girlfriend cut her off and got in then wouldn't get out. They didn't give a good you know what about anybody else," he starts making girly waving motions around his hair and speaking in a high pitched voice, "Oh look, my hair, my hair," and shaking his head.

Paying—giving the driver a big tip.

"Here," he hands me his card. "Call if you need a cab." He winks then drives off. Looking at Mary.

"You okay over there?"

She nods, "Weird how nervous I got when you confronted her, my legs started throbbing and..." she looks around.

"Adrenaline started to pump, fight or flight."

"I wanted to say something but," she looks at me, "what do you do in situations like that? It happened so quickly..."

Shrugging my shoulders, "First is to learn to keep your head when your body starts getting ready for things like that, breathing is important, muscles don't work well when they are tense kind of like before a basketball game or before a boxing match," putting my arm around her as we walk down Broome Street. "My guess is that lady was counting on a surprise and her commitment to action... then us being young and not standing up to her."

"What if she had something in her purse, a weapon or something."

Laughing, "I'd a knocked the bitch out."

"No," she looks at me, horrified look on her face, "you'd hit a woman?"

"She's gonna hurt you or me?" stepping away from Mary for a second. "Mary, you crack me up. You call me a prude because I was embarrassed saying vagina!" saying it loud, people looking at me like I'm some crazed person, Mary shushing me with her hands, her face blushing a little, "Vagina, vagina, penis, pussy, cock," sticking my tongue out at a lady mumbling how disgusting I am.

Starting to laugh at myself, "And you think it's weird that I'd let you get hurt cause that skank was a woman... hey, equal rights in my book, baby," acting like a boxer talking to the reporters after a fight. "You know Howard, it was a tough fight. She had them mean pointed shoes on, but I knew if I cornered her, I knew I could knock the bitch out," Mary slapping at me and pushing me away.

Restaurant ahead.

"I'm sure Cat liked this side of you," impossible to miss the sarcastic tone. Stopping, good feelings deflating from that pinprick.

"What's that supposed to mean, Mary?"

She stands still, her fists clenched by her side, looking at the people inside the restaurant for a moment and then at me, "Why do you push things so far? We could have gotten the next cab, why's it always this big macho contest. I'm..."

"Not used to it?" taking a breath. "You need to improve your street smarts."

"And I suppose Catherine is?"

"To an extent yes, but she's pretty sheltered," looking at Mary, "look, do you want me to take you home?"

"What? Your uncle and aunt are inside," horrified look on her face.

"So what, if I've pissed you off and you don't want to be around me, then don't pussy foot around, they'll be disappointed, but I'll lay it out."

She looks hurt. "Don't you dare, Frank Caruso!" she looks a little mad. "Getting so thin skinned on me like that."

"Hey, you didn't have to do the sarcastic Cat comment."

"Well," she takes a breath, "maybe. But are you going to go around acting like some kind of wild man all the time?"

"Why should we let people push us around? Anyway, she started it."

"And you have to respond to every provocation? Isn't that what happened to you at school?" taking a sharp breath. "You were right, but look what happened?"

"So what you're telling me is, I'm not nice."

She looks at me, "Yes."

"Nice people are chumps, suckers Mary, I'm no sensitive James Taylor everything's beautiful…"

"Damn you, don't patronize me… Look, you stubborn man," she steps closer, "what if the so called skank, as you so nobly called her, fell hard when you pulled her out of the cab and hit her head on the sidewalk and was hurt or crippled or worse for goodness sake, it would be you who'd be in trouble again. For a cab, Frank, a fucking cab ride? You stood up to her, told her it was our cab, you told her to get out, you didn't cave in, but look at what you risked for that stupid cab," she stops to gather her breath. Opening my mouth to speak, she holds up her finger across her lips, "I'm not finished with you yet." Having to smile at her.

"What's so funny?" She spreads her feet wide, hands on her hips.

"I like seeing this side of you, it's tough for me to be around namby-pamby people."

"Well Mr. I'm-No-James-Taylor sensitive man, which is no great surprise by the way. I think," putting my arms around her, kissing her.

"Wait, I'm not finished."

"Yes, you are, I get it, Mary. You're saying be careful, don't paint yourself into a corner that will come back to bite you later," looking at her, "also known as, be mean and sneaky so you don't get caught."

She slaps my shoulders. "Would you be serious? Rrrgghh."

"Look, Mary," holding her, deep eye contact, my insides resonating with her fighting spirit, feeling good, starting to laugh inside from being happy. Deep breath of the car exhaust filled cool city night air feels really good.

"What?" I can feel her body starting to lighten up.

"I really like this, being with you, hearing you stand up for what you think."

"You really are horrible, Frank."

Moving my hips to sway her a little bit, she's relaxing and following me—ignoring the people walking by. My body remembering what it was like to be naked with her, my hands underneath her slim body, pulling her up into me—the smell of her skin, the feeling of her opening up with abandon.

"Someone's happy," she smiles as she feels Eduardo start to assert himself. "Shall we go in?"

She kisses me teasingly and steps back. She laughs as I take my sport jacket off and hold it draped in front of my stomach.

Crowded in here—people waiting, people talking loud, people smoking, drinking and eating. Looking through over to the tables as the maître d' looks at us, "Do you have a reservation?" comes with a snooty, dismissive look.

"*We are meeting my aunt and uncle here for dinner tonight, I think the reservation would be under the name of Mr. Vincent Caruso.*"

He looks at me, fumbling for words—chuckling to myself this guy doesn't speak Italian. With a big smile on my face in my most flowery Italian, "*My dear friend, you look like a man who was once a very well known fart jockey in Genoa whose job was to check the rotten asses of old ladies to see if they smelled like roses, is that right?*"

His face lights up in a huge smile, another waiter standing close behind him biting his lip to keep a straight face.

"*I guess you just look Italian,*" Mary giving me a little elbow and smiling. "My aunt and uncle should be here, Caruso, look through the book," I'm not going to take shit from this asswipe.

"Ahhh, here we are," he snaps his fingers, "Guillermo, please take them to table fifteen." A Southern Italian looking fellow in a crisply starched white shirt and black tie with a big white apron and red vest nods and motions for us to follow him. Walking through the crowded restaurant.

"*Your Italian is very good, I had to bite my tongue,*" said Guillermo, also known as William. "The Emperor can't speak a word of our mother tongue, yet talks and moans about the old country," in a thick accent.

"Oh, you mean Brooklyn?"

He gives a short laugh, a quick gesture with his hands and smiles as we come up to the table, my uncle rising, nice to see a smile on his face. He's been so stressed lately. The waiter gives me a wink and walks back into the fray at the front desk.

"Uncle Vin, this is Mary O'Connor," he reaches out a big paw, they shake hands. Mary very composed, calm giving them a nice warm smile, "Mary, Lieutenant Vincent Caruso and this is my Aunt Katherine," as she rises to meet Mary.

"Wonderful to meet dear, Frank's been telling us so much about you."

My face flushing a little, holding Mary's chair so she can sit down.

Settling in at the table.

"It's great to meet you both, thank you for inviting me to dinner. I hope this wasn't an inconvenience at all. My parents told me this was a fantastic place and I'm so excited to be here and to meet you. Frank's told me a lot about you too."

Surprised to see the maître d', the Emperor, hustling over—the Emperor, that's a good one.

"Ah, so you are all set Lieutenant?" putting us together with my uncle now, his eyebrows raised, his hands together. "I will make sure you have a superb dinner," now flourishing a semi-phony Italian accent. "Ah, here's Georgio now. Va bene, va bene," he waves the elderly waiter over who gives him a nonchalant look with his sleepy eyes. "We have a wonderful stuffed veal chop tonight, sage, Fontina cheese, prosciutto," he puts his thumb, forefinger and middle finger to his lips and kisses them to tell us how good the special is.

"Grazie, Mario, Grazie," my uncle in his deep authoritative Italian, and then ignores the unctuous Maître d' turning to Mary. "This is one of our favorite places," he says to her. "We've been coming here for over twenty years, is that right Mario?"

"Oh yes," he says and backs off as the waiter comes over. "Anything you need, just ask Georgio." He backs away and gives us a little bow—the people at the next table who must be getting ignored are looking over and talking to themselves.

"How are you? How is your family?" my uncle asks the sleepy-eyed man.

"I'm good, my family is good," he starts to warm up a little. "How are you tonight, Mrs. Caruso?"

"I'm very good Georgio," she smiles back, "Georgio, this is our nephew, Frank, and his girlfriend, Mary."

"Very good to meet you both." He produces four menus, "Not that you need these," and gives them to the ladies first with a nice flourish. "Shall I get you started with your usual Carpaccio? The Buffala Mozzarella is very good tonight, maybe make a nice Caprese salad?"

"Perfect."

Mary looking at him and my aunt not knowing what to say.

"So, Beauty," Uncle Vin leans forward smiling, "how is it dating the Beast?"

"Oh Vincent," my aunt says tsking, playfully slapping at him.

Mary starts to laugh—watching her, so different than Cat. If Catherine and I'd walked in together, people would have stopped and really taken time to notice her, watch her, maybe talk about her. Mary's easier to miss—but there's this delightful freshness about her. She's not waiting to be adored, she's out there—talking, laughing and asking questions. Feeling a smile come to my face.

"Frank... Frank, hello there..."

Looking at them, my aunt laughing.

"Hmm?" blushing a little.

"Some Beast," Uncle Vin laughing and sipping a glass of red wine that I didn't even notice get served.

"Mary was talking about her parent's invitation."

"Oh, yes, sorry."

"It's fine with us."

"Oh, okay. Hey that's great," smiling at her, at them. Uncle Vin rolling his eyes, "I'm having the veal special and if anyone orders pizza I'm going to call the police," Mary laughing with him.

"What do you suggest, Frank," said Mary holding the menu to me, moving closer, "There's so much that I don't know about."

My aunt and uncle exchanging quick glances and smiling.

"Oh," my uncle rolling his eyes, Aunt Kitty swatting at him. Uncle Vin calling Georgio over. Speaking in a low voice with Mary, "Are you a big pasta person or have you had gnocchi before?"

"What's gnocchi?"

"Oh," wiggling my eyebrows, "Do you like Gorgonzola cheese?"

She shrugs her shoulders, "I don't know"

"It tastes like blue cheese, strong flavor."

"I'll try it," she gives a little shrug, "I love new things." She looks at my uncle and aunt, "Frank took me to this extraordinary place for coffee and pastry. I couldn't believe how good the pastries were there and there were so many different kinds. I think I could have stayed there for a week and tried each one, Vinny-ero I think," my uncle and aunt smiling being swept up with her enthusiasm. She looks at me.

"What?"

Letting the Veniero's pass by. "Well the gnocchi are like a teaspoon sized potato dumpling made from flour, potatoes, egg, nutmeg and a little salt. They have a very light taste and carry the flavor of their sauce. I like them, we can share if you like or trade off if you don't like it."

"Okay," she puts her menu down, looking over at me, "Gnocchi with Gorgonzola and Walnuts it is."

"Hmm," looking at the menu, "I'm going to have the Veal Saltimbocca and the Tri Colore insalate," Mary nodding then looking over at my aunt.

"So Mary, tell me more about your trip to Florence, I just love it there, I can spend days at the Uffizi and the Galleria. Last time we went, we rented a Villa just outside of town," she leans in. "Vincent doesn't like being in the crowded city and I usually take my friend Madeline so we can go to the Palazzo and hit all the great places for shopping!"

Watching Mary and my aunt start to go into hyper speed girl talk.

Looking out of the corner of my eyes at Uncle Vin, he looks highly amused.

"Well," he says in a low voice, "They'll be going for hours."

"I heard that," says Aunt Kitty and then jumps back into her conversation with Mary without missing a beat.

"How did things end up the other day?"

"Oh," he takes a sip of wine. "What a mess," shaking his head. "From what I know, there's a real problem, greedy a-holes trying to get away with tearing down those building outside the channel. The fine they'll get slapped with plus greasing the right hands will be a lot less than what they can make on knocking down then selling the new buildings. I don't know if we'll be able to stop them in time. We'll get investigated for the riot. People will yell and scream about police, racism, you bet your know-what they'll have greased a couple of the local leaders who'll yell about us to deflect attention away from the real theft that's going on."

He drinks some sparkling water.

"I tell you kid, heaven help a lot of people if I ever get a star on my lapel."

Aunt Kitty looking over.

"Didn't you tell him, Vincent?"

"No, not yet," he looks at me. "Hey, he's so busy these days, when?" he makes a big play shrugging his big shoulders.

"What Uncle Vin? Is everything okay?"

"Hey, look at him," he's smiling. He tousles my hair.

"I got promoted to Captain, ceremony is next week."

Sitting back looking at him and feeling my mouth drop to the floor. Looking at Mary, she doesn't know what's going on but lights up with a lovely smile.

"Wow, that's great Uncle Vin, you going to take over a precinct?"

"Nope, something much worse," determined smile coming on his face, like he can see his adversary, "I'll be running a city wide organized crime task force."

"*Oh mama, I feel sorry for those poor sons of bitches,*" shaking my hands with my thumb, forefinger and index fingers together.

"Hey watch what you say, Cretin," he says smiling.

"What did you say?" asked Mary.

"I said I feel sorry for those sons of bitches."

She smiles, my aunt flattens out her hand and shakes like she's going to give me what for. Appetizers showing up, Uncle Vin ordering a bottle of champagne. Mary squeezing my hand under the table, my aunt catching that and gives me a little smile.

Uncle Vin looking at Aunt Kitty and Mary gabbing away, smiling, shrugging his massive shoulders, then looking at me.

"You made more fans down at the station last week, the guys were laughing their asses off about Miller getting ko'ed by a teenager. That SOB is in the middle of any protest, complaint, or anything. Son of a gun has got a VA pension for being wounded in Korea. He wheedled a government job, and surprisingly, he was injured on the job. The prick gets a pension for that too. Lives in a nice place, owes more people money than you can shake a stick at and is always talking about how the system f..., messed him over.

Oh, heck with him," as the champagne is poured, all of us raising our glasses.

"To Captain Vincent Caruso," says my aunt raising her glass. Uncle Vin smiling, his dark skin flushing a little bit.

"Congratulations, Uncle Vin."

No trouble getting a cab. Waving to my aunt and uncle as we drive away.

"Wow, they are really, really nice," big smile on Mary's face.

Feeling light, her eyes bubbling away, the city lights making a wonder kaleidoscope show on the taxi windows. Sitting close to her.

Strange to feel this good again.

"What are you thinking over there, you've been so quiet?"

Looking at her, those wonderful eyes, the finely shaped lips, her rich hair, "I hadn't realized how long it had been since I was really happy. It's been snatches of clear skies now and then, but I always came back to feeling like I had a sword hanging over my head, this horrible dread that something was going to go wrong at any moment. Seeing you be so free with my aunt and uncle, laughing, talking. They really like you, my aunt cornered me on the way out and told me to watch myself and to take good care of you."

"That's right, you better!" as she puts her hands around my thigh and pulls herself closer.

"All I need is a pushy lady to chuck out of a cab and life is good."

She pushes into me with her shoulder, "Watch it, Buster, I'll report you if you don't behave... I'm connected," she takes out my uncle's card with his private number and waves it in my face. "Remember, I'm the one he likes," laughing, putting my hand underneath her chin and lifting those wonderful lips to mine.

Standing by her door.

"Mary, you're crazy," she's listening in the apartment, "Okay, you go in, I'll act like I'm waiting for the elevator. I'll hang out ten minutes and then take off if you're not out." She makes a shh'ing sound, motions for me to wait, and quietly closes the door.

Body electric, my skin tingling.

This is going to be one titanic case of blue balls.

Headline in the paper—ocean liner sunk after running into a giant pair of testicles. Not bothering to look at my watch cause I know I'll wait longer than ten minutes. Elevator passing her floor going up, then dead quiet in the hall, nothing from the other apartment. Stopping for a moment.

Feeling like something is splitting open in me—a feeling hitting my heart like coming into the warm sun after being in the cold water for hours on hours. My heart feeling like it's growing larger, beating stronger—each pulse carrying an image to my mind of her—her laugh, her smile.

I love her, all the things she is dancing before me in a collage. The wonderful curiosity, the need to know things—the fearlessness of how we make love. Cascade of motions hitting me, stopping—looking at the painted plaster scroll work near the ceilings, the small cracks starting to show in one corner of the hall, the inlaid marble floor. Was it just infatuation, puppy love with Cat?

The door to their apartment opening carefully.

Looking at her slowly, letting how I feel wash over me like I'm bathing in light, standing in the most beautiful place I can be at this moment. She smiles at me, the colors in her eyes dancing around, her face seems to be lit from within, my heart warming, feeling like it's so full of life, my skin feels so sensitive, body alive—erection is part of the dance of the moment. If I can kiss you with my gaze, then let this be the moment, Mary. Can I reach you from over here? Is there some sign that I'm not alone in at this moment of wonder.

"What?" she says looking at me, motioning me come closer.

My fingers touching her face, her neck, taking a moment to breathe in the feeling of being close to her. Smiling at her, slowing down time to hold the moment, bathe in the intensity in every small movement.

"Mary, when you told me you loved me, I was ashamed. I was confused because of so many things going on that clouded my vision, so many mistakes I'd made. I didn't want to feel it because I was hurt or desperate or wanted to get back at…"

Lightly kissing her, body feeling like a cloud.

"But it just hit me right now, just the wonder of you, the wonder of how I feel with you."

Big smile breaks out on her face. Her arms around my neck, strength flowing through her arms to me. Feeling the radiant heat of our bodies.

"Let's go watch some TV in the den," she whispers. "We have to be quiet."

Her arm through mine as we walk in the house, her wet lips near my ear. "I've been in love with you for so long, watching you, seeing you so close. Wanting to reach out, having to live at times when I knew you just didn't even know I existed, that this existed. I'd imagine how intense this could be, how your hands would feel on my body. How shameless I wanted to feel with you."

"I know Mary, I can feel it now," as she closes the door to their den and turns on the TV—volume set very low, some Sunday night movie on.

Sitting down on the couch face-to-face.

She stops for a moment and listens.

"It hit me when I was waiting outside your door, it was like a curtain lifted to something that's been in the distance but frustratingly near. Like I can hear it, the sensation tingling on my body, but a mystery. You know, I don't know if you've ever been in the ocean long enough to lose core body heat, your skin is all goose flesh and is a bluish tone, your mind moves

436

slowly, like you have trouble talking, moving with any kind of coordination," looking at her as she places both hands down on my lap. "Then you come back on deck, take your wetsuit off and there's the life giving sun beating down on you with wonderful heat and light. It was like that, and I saw your face there…"

"Shh," as arms fly around each other, hard fast kisses, silent cries of passion. Feeling her unzip my slacks, she pushes me back on the couch.

Her warm, thin finger working me free—so hard, body burning for her. Biting my lips to keep my mouth shut as she takes me into her mouth.

Holding her hair to keep her from moving as my world fades from dark to light and then back to the feeling of her hands holding me as I come again and again, she's holding me there—not moving away. Starting to loosen the hold on her hair, she starts to massage my throbbing penis slowly, licking her lips, kissing my penis, slowly licking the tip as more aftershocks come up. Wonderful feeling flooding through my body—what wonderful care she takes of me.

Pulling her up to me, hugging her.

"Oh my, Frank, that was so intense," her voice shaking a little.

"My turn."

"Shh, let me go change into something quieter," kissing her deeply, her mouth feels hot and silky with a slightly salty taste—ignoring the initial disquiet at kissing her after I'd come—probing, reaching deep into her. She puts my shirttail over my penis and walks out quietly.

Skirt and big sweatshirt, cute white knee socks.

She sits on my lap, out toward my knees.

"Feel this," she puts my hand under her dress, "I came a few seconds after you did." She's stroking my penis again as it rises to her hand.

"I want it to be like this, Frank, I don't care what my parents think, I don't care if I only get to see you a few weeks out of the year, I want to feel like this," she positions her hips over mine and guides me into her.

"Mary," closely to her ears, "oh, Mary." Feeling the intensity of her body as she moves to take me in. Arching my back to move up inside her. Her head down, then back, then to the side as she moves her hips, her whole body alive with the moment of us.

"I love you, I love you, I love you, Frank," her body fully into the moment.

"I love you, Mary."

Riding the subway in a daze.

The car is almost empty.

Crumbling streets of Brooklyn look magically alive, like something wonderful could materialize from the broken streets in an instant, something

437

that was there all the time but I just couldn't fathom in the depth of the moment so it was quiet, waiting for someone living in a world of love to notice, to stop a moment and give life to the fearless need to love beyond reason.

Car driving by.

Walking through the dark streets near my uncle's place.

Stopping and looking up—imagining the vivid night sky when it's unmasked from the city light out at sea.

She'd love that—the deep blue and blacks, millions of stars in the night. Thrilled to think of being with her out on the sea.

Chapter 55

Hands still feeling the burn from rope climbing.

Looking at the rough pink of my palms.

Subway car rattling back and forth between 72nd and 79th Streets.

Frustrated at my lack of progress, still have to use my feet to make it all the way up on the tenth rep.

What if I go through all this and I don't make it? What if I don't make it through Ranger selection? Looking at the line of dim tunnel lights flashing by shaking my head. I guess I can always cook—smiling at the vision of me standing behind a steam tables which Grandpa T always hated, saying "Good morning, would you like some fresh garlic bread with that shit on a shingle?" He'd be so embarrassed at how I have turned out.

Snapping back to the car.

Kids running through the train car looking at people. Smacking at people's newspapers and then running away laughing. One of them giving me the finger after I try to trip him up—tempted to go run and beat their asses.

Train slowing down, picking up my shoulder bag and moving with the crowd toward the door, people filing off the train, people pushing to get on.

Slow walk up the wide staircase to Broadway.

Streams of people going in and out of the brightly lit Woolworth's across the street on the corner of 79th Street. Waiting for the light to change. Looking at the jam packed newsstand—*NY Times, NY Daily News, NY Post, Time, Life, Playboy, Hustler, Screw Magazine, Ebony, Cosmopolitan, Popular Mechanics, Popular Science, Time, Player, Esquire, GQ, Instinct, Men, Passport, Car and Driver*—what a mish-mash. Turning slightly from a guy giving me the eye as I glance over the men's magazines, covers filled with half-naked, washboard stomach, muscle boys. Time to go.

Walking on the slight downhill of 79th toward West End, dusk view of the Hudson ahead and New Jersey across the river, my weekend clothes over my shoulder. Yawning, stretching—body tired from the long workouts this week, thrilled by the thought of being near her. Laughing at myself—we'd probably be better off in the City sneaking around their big ass apartment, there's likely little room to be discrete at a small beach house.

Nodding to the doorman.

No weird look this time.

Nervous on the elevator ride up.

Just stay cool in front of her parent's man.

I wonder if she's said anything or they've asked about us sleeping together, wave of embarrassment coming over me. Silent lobby. Ringing their doorbell.

Opening slowly, "Yes, who is it?" through an inch wide crack.

"Avon calling."

"Oh, do you have anything that can help me, I've been so tense today?"

"Well, I think I can help you, Ma'am."

Door opening, Mary in a T-shirt and jeans, whoa, T-shirt and no bra—slippers on her feet, her hair tied back.

"Hey, I thought we were going to drive to the Island with your parents?"

She smiles and wiggles her eyebrows.

"What gives, Mare?"

She smiles at that, "I like when you call me that," putting her arms around me and pushing the bag down off my shoulder—her pelvis right up to mine, slightly rocking back and forth. "They went out today, we'll take the train out tomorrow and get picked up at the station."

"But…"

"They need time alone too."

"Do they know I'm here?"

"No, but they are not stupid."

"Don't ask, don't tell?"

"Something like that," she takes my hand. "I made us some dinner, come on in."

Following her slim little body into their kitchen—size of the kitchen and dining room in our apartment. Laughing to myself.

"What's so funny?"

"Oh, I was imagining a small beach house and your parents, you know, no kids. I imagine your brother isn't coming up from Swarthmore and all," my face flushing a little, still tough to talk about sex out loud. "The thought of naked parents running around is so weird, I mean, if they didn't get it on we wouldn't be here, right?" She's shaking her head as if I'm the biggest dope in the world. "I just can't imagine my parents you know, doing it," starting to bust up remembering my cousin Mikey talking about the hole in the sheet.

"What?"

"Hole in the sheet."

"Oh God, is that what you think it was like for them?"

"I don't know… Mom was always so proper, so uptight. She never farted or burped; she's a marble Madonna. I can't imagine her in a frenzy, who knows though," looking at her. "Your parents look more relaxed with each other." Thinking about how her dad actually touches her mom, massages her shoulders, pays attention to her. Image of her mom flashing in my mind, God, what a beautiful woman—from the way she reacts to his attention, she's got to like that he's treating her like flesh and blood. Imagine she smells strong, earth, tendrils reaching deep down.

"Relax, Frank, you can say anything to me," oh man, not going there.

"What's all this?" big production going on in the kitchen, something sizzling on the stove, pots, pans, plates all over the place.

"I made dinner for us."

Feeling my face break out in a huge smile.

"Mary, you are so crazy? Did you know your parents were leaving today?"

"Yes," she takes a covered sauté pan off the stove, "I didn't want you to lie to your aunt and uncle... plans change you know."

"You bad little girl," giving her a little spank, "can I help?"

"No you sit down, you can open the wine I bought."

Valpolicella—oh God, this is what people think is good Italian wine. Smile Frank, it's a gift—enjoy it. Coming up behind her, her jeans riding low on her body, wonderful curves, putting my arms around her and kissing her neck.

"Hmm," she puts her hands on mine for a moment.

Pouring some wine for us—getting the table organized, she has the forks and knives backwards. She's tossing a salad and putting a large wooden bowl on the table.

"Sit down now."

Kitchen smells of sizzling meat, steamed potatoes and butter.

Chew, Frank—smile and chew.

This is so undercooked. The pan must have been way too hot and the meat must have been really cold. She made it through—she took the time to plan this all out, smile and chew.

Holding up my glass.

"Thank you for dinner, Mare."

She gives me a distracted smile back, her mind going a thousand miles an hour over there as she's chewing and chewing away. Swallowing my steak—working on the overcooked green beans and the undercooked mashed potatoes. No salt. Poor thing—she really tried though. I'm going to eat everything here.

Looking at her lovely long fingers, she gave herself a good cut too.

"You okay, Mary?" she's quiet over there looking at her plate.

"It's not very good, is it?"

"It's fine, Mary. You made this, it's fine."

"But it doesn't taste very good."

Looking at her, trying to keep a straight face, she starts smiling.

"No," as we start laughing, she sticks out her lower lip like she's pouting.

"I tried so hard, I wanted to have a nice night together," looking down, her lip still out.

Walking over, kneeling down and putting my arms around her, "This is fine, wonderful, no one's ever done this for me before."

"But..."

"Look, I'm fine."

"But it's so tasteless! It's not even rare."

"I don't know what you have here, we could fix this up if you want to..."

441

make a nice sauce, cube the steak and let it simmer with some mushrooms and onions. I think the beans are goners. Can I look?" pointing to the fridge.

She nods.

Hmm, lots of nice fresh vegetables here—mushrooms, broccoli, asparagus—not a bad supply of ingredients.

Heating up the pan she massacred the meat in. Pouring in some wine to deglaze the pan. Stirring up the juices from the meat, adding olive oil, flour and then more wine.

"We get these all going and use the juices from the steak," she nods, sitting on the edge of their wide counter near the stove watching me. Stirring in more wine and tomato paste a little at a time, "Good thing you used a big pan, we should be able to get all this in there," as I put in a bay leaf and add some thyme and crumble up a little sage. Letting it reach a nice simmer and adding onions, garlic, mushrooms and covering the pan.

She's smiling at me, her legs kicking out and in slowly. Giving her a kiss.

Tasting the pan sauce—offering her a taste. Needs a pinch of kosher salt.

"Oh!" her eyes opening up, "that's good, Frank," she looks at me surprised. "I'm shocked, I'm impressed," looking at me.

"Hey, this is all from to my Grandpa T."

Dropping in the steak I'd cubed up.

"Needs a little more salt I think," putting in another pinch of salt.

"Why were you looking for that, we have plenty of table salt?"

"This dissolves faster, helps me taste where we are."

Stirring in a little beef stock, this is getting a little too thick, turning down the heat and covering the large pan. This was done bass-ackwards, but we'll have to see how this turns out.

Water for rice boiling on the stove.

Taking a drink of wine.

"This is so sexy," she looks at me. "You working away quickly, competently, concentrating," standing close, kissing her as she spreads her legs and I come in close, feeling the soft cotton of her jeans around my waist.

Panting, tasting our sweat, laughing like naughty school children.

"Are you uncomfortable bare bottomed on that cold stone counter top?"

"Hmm," her fingers moving through my hair as she looks and me, looks down at our bodies locked together.

Close to her ear, "I love it that you like to watch me being inside you."

"It gets me so excited, Frank."

She flexes her legs, pulling me close to her. Moving side to side to keep the good feeling going.

"Let's eat and then get on with the main course," wiggling my eyebrows.

"Okay, you have to leave your shirt off though."

Stepping back, sliding out of her.

"Oooh," she shivers, "I don't like when you leave."

"You think I could get a residence permit?"

"Let's see," she looks at the ceiling, while she crosses her legs, her finger tapping on her lips. "I think you'd have to apply for that and it's a very selective process you know." Bending down to kiss the top of her pussy—taking in the smell of our sex together. "Hmm, that will get you consideration though."

I feel like an idiot, my face hurting from kissing, laughing and smiling so much. "If your parents came home, we'd be so busted."

She hops down and pulls up her jeans, "Mare, I think that's so sexy that you weren't wearing any underwear, I could feel your body heat radiating out, hmm," she squirms her hips together.

"I feels so good, so silky with you inside me," as she uses her fingers to brush back her slightly sweat laced hair over her ears.

My body shivering a little.

Hungry—vision of her fine white skin before my eyes.

Serving her, kissing her on the cheek.

"Oh," she tastes some, looks at me surprised. "This is good."

Meat is a little tougher than I'd like, at least there's some taste.

Wine starting to make me feel a little buzzed.

Taking a moment to watch her, she catches my look.

"I feel so happy, Frank," big smile, then a wave of a different emotion washed over. "It's going to give me a lot to hang on to when you are away… a lot to look forward to when we are together," her face stern now, like she's scolding me. "You know, you better write, get me all hot and bothered like this."

"There you go, the condemned man's last wish before he's shot, make a beautiful young woman fall in love with me and then up and leave…"

"I'll up and shoot," she gets up, comes over and sits on my lap, her arms on my shoulders, "you better take good care of yourself when you're away, Frank Caruso."

Nodding to her.

"We have a lot to look forward to Mary O'Connor."

"Damn right," laughing with her arms around my neck.

Holding her close for a few moments.

"Mary, can I ask you something?"

"What, Frank?" she sits back a little. Smiling at her, looking into her wonderful green eyes. "What?"

"So you told me you told your mom everything"

"Right."

"And?"

She looks at me and starts laughing a little, her face taking on a more thoughtful cast now. She's looking at my face, my hair—her fingers on my lips for a few moments.

"I told her I was really in love with you, Frank. She knew I had a crush on you, but I'd never really talked about it much with her."

Watching her.

"What are you worried about, Frank?"

"Well, it's just..." looking down, "Cat's parents hated my guts. I just don't want that here. Well, if it's humanly possible anyway."

"Shh, you. You're beautiful." Shiver going up my body.

"Mom thinks you are very handsome and a little dangerous."

"Oh, so the desire to play with fire comes from her?"

"Maybe," she's nuzzling in close to my ear.

"What about your dad? He was just taking this all in when we met."

"Frank," she sits back, smiles at me. "Don't worry, I mean. It's touching that you are concerned. I'm not going to let them run my life. I love you, Frank Caruso, you are just going to have to deal with that."

Laughing.

"What?"

"Oh just, crazy running through my head."

"What?"

"German romantic movie."

"Frank, you are so weird sometimes."

Putting on my worst German movie accent, "I am Major Arschloch. You Vill Lof Me! Now, here are your orders. Ve vill schtup five times per day at the prescribed time und in the prescribed positions und ve vill like it."

Polite laugh from her, she wiggles her butt a little into my lap.

"Only five, Major?"

Lying in bed looking up at her ceiling.

Wish I didn't need to shower—want to keep the smell of her on my body. Forget about the shower, I wish we could stay here and make love all day. Hell with the beach.

"Hey, Sleepyhead," turning to her as she comes in with a towel around her hair, bathrobe and cute little bunny slippers.

"Hey, where'd you go earlier," hugging me, "I missed you." Putting out her lip to pout a little.

"Restocking the fridge."

"You didn't have to do that."

"Well, we went through quite a bit last night."

"S' okay," putting her head with the damp towel on my chest.

"Got some nice fresh croissants at Fairway and some stuff to whip up breakfast."

"Oh, I'm not much of a breakfast person, but okay."

"You go get dressed before I forget we've got to get to the station."

"Big meany," she sticks out her tongue and pinches me as she gets out of bed.

Quickly whipping up a nice scramble with ham, cheese, green onions, a touch of cayenne. Warming up her croissant—I'll warm that up okay. Looking at the clock—shit we need to get going soon. Bringing her plate.

"Room service."

"Silly," as I bring the plate over. "Oh, that smells good!"

"Eat, I'll jump in the shower."

"What about you?"

"I had a quick snack, we've got to go," tapping my watch.

"Oh, Frank," slight panic on her face. "You think we can make the train?"

"We've got to hustle," as I rip my jeans off. "We'll bribe the cab driver and get a wild ride down there."

"We," and starts to dribble a little of her food out of her mouth, using her finger to push it back in. "Hmm, oh that's good," chewing. Hopping into the shower—water is cold but I don't care. Washing my groin, butt, armpits—good enough. Quick shampoo—just let it dry wavy. Toweling off.

"That was fast," as I'm pulling on a clean set of boxers, jeans and a clean dark red rugby shirt, sitting next to her as she finishes her breakfast. "We can save some time if we buy our tickets on the train, the conductors will give us stink-eye, but it will save us time."

"Sounds like a plan," buckling up, checking my wallet, dirty clothes in my bag.

"Ready?"

"Sure, let me grab a couple more things," I pick up her plate—heading to the kitchen. "Meet me by the door, Mare."

World's fastest job of washing and stacking.

Quiet ride in the elevator down to the lobby.

"You look cute in that hat and sunglasses," she's got on a big dumpy sweater and jeans with her straw hat.

"Oh, this is my beach glamour look."

"Good thing I know what's underneath."

She smiles at me.

Hailing a cab.

"Whew, that was lucky," holding the door for her as she jumps in. "Penn Station, you make it there in five minutes you get an extra twenty," tires squealing as we get thrown back, I'm still holding up the bill.

"Hell, yeah," big black man driving the cab with a NY Mets ball cap takes the meter arm around with a smooth swing. Blasting up West End, honking, swerving around cars. Mary laughing as we get bumped around.

"Kind of like Coney Island," she says as he hits the brakes hard and comes within inches of an old couple that are yelling and smacking the cab with their canes. He shrugs his shoulders and jets off again.

"Here you are, man!" twenty-five dollar cab ride, we're doing okay.

Running through Penn Station, the sound of her thin sandals making slapping sounds as we run down the stairs to the main ticket area—looking quickly at the big board. Dodging the few people working their way around to look at the train schedules.

"There, the Montauk Train, track seventeen," pointing to the board, trains and destinations changing here and there with letters flipping over. Taking her hand to help her along.

"Give me your bag," as we run, taking the relay race baton from her. Down the stairs, few people at the station, a couple of men in blue railroad uniform walking the platform.

"Yeah!" as we step on the train.

She's breathing hard and starts to fan her face with her hat.

"Whew, I wore the wrong things," as we walk through the car—pretty full.

"Let's go forward and see if we can find one of these two seats facing each other configurations, stretch out a little."

"Okay," she waves, looks still out of breath.

"You doing okay, Mare?" stopping just as the train jolts forward, catching her wrist as she falls back.

"Let's find a seat okay?"

"Sure, sure," walking with her to an open set of seats, bags up top.

"Take the window," she sits down and is fanning herself, lifting her sweater up and out to get some cooler air underneath.

"Take it off."

She leans in, "I only have a bra on underneath."

Laughing at her.

"Stop," she smacks my arm, "I get cranky when I get hot."

Giving her a little poke.

"I'll kick your ass, Frank Caruso!"

Great fun.

"How about I nab a T-shirt out of your bag?"

"Okay," she keeps fanning herself. Unzipping her bag as the ticket guy comes in the car, taking the first T-shirt, dark brown with capital letters BROWN on it.

"Here you go," she tucks the T-shirt under her sweater, ducks under her sweater, pulling her arms in like a turtle—moving around underneath.

"Tickets," the guy looking at me.

"You have to forgive my wife, she's wrestling imaginary demons," making a circle around my ears like Mary's crazy.

446

"Ticket!"

"Two to…" looking at Mary, "what station do we get off at, dear?" elbow connecting in my side.

"Southampton you pain," muffled as she's pulling her sweater over her head.

"She's mean too." He's not amused. "How much?"

Giving me attitude as I open my wallet, "Seven bucks, funny man."

Taking a breath, stifling my snide comment—handing him fifteen. He takes out some long strips of tickets, punching holes in a couple of areas and moves on to the next seat.

"Oh, that's so much better," as Mary finishes takes off her sweater, blowing some of her loose hair out of her face, "What did I miss?"

"Well Honey, the ticket man doesn't think I'm funny," loud enough just to needle him a little.

"He's a smart man."

"Hey, no ganging up," holding up my hands like I'm innocent.

"I'm going to gang up on you for poking at me when I'm hot," as she jumps on me and tries to give me noogies.

"Hey, you're not noogie qualified."

"I'll show you qualifications," as she's laughing, trying to get at me.

"Do you two mind?" coming from behind us.

Looking back over behind us—bunch of uptight white people.

"Shall we," I look at Mary, standing up grabbing the bags. "You get the tickets."

Sticking out my ass to the couple behind us—patting it as we walk forward.

Sprawled out on each other in one of the cross seating rows as we come out of the tunnel, passing row upon row of two story houses packed right next to each other. Mind drifting along—images of last night filtering in, lingering in how much she works to take care of me, how that makes me want take her to a place where she's lost in passion. Was it the freedom that we have that pushes us to keep digging in deeper? If Cat and I had the time… She's so different though. Cat had the overt fire, but there was a place she wouldn't go—anything around her ass made her feel dirty. What is with Mary that makes me just want to be so free?

Shiver going through my body remembering waking her up. We went so long, it was almost like a dream watching her moving with me, the look on her face as she got closer and closer. Cock hard sitting next to her.

"What do you think it will be like?"

"Hmm?" coming out of my daydream, putting her hand down on my cock.

"Oh, I see what you were thinking about," she moves her thigh over on mine, "you think anyone can see us here?"

"Mary!"

"Chicken," she puts her sweater on my lap, reaches under and starts slowly caressing up and down the length of my penis through my jeans.

"Wait a second," bending over, standing up and slowly looking around. Not many people down at this end of the car, folded newspapers a couple of seats away, idea germinating.

"Here," giggling with her. "Let's try this," putting the newspaper up and folding it out so it forms some kind of barrier. Her fingers unzipping me under her sweater, she sits up in the seat and looks around.

Nervous, excited, lifting my right leg and putting it on the seat across from us, shaking—her fingers wrapped around the base of my erect cock. Hearing her laughing softly, kissing my ear, neck as she moves her hand slowly, "You've got the paper upside down."

"Oh, wha? Okay," flipping it over, realizing I had the stock market numbers. Opening up to beginning of the NY Times Business section. Her head on my shoulder acting like she's sleeping, turning to her, "I'm going to come."

Feeling her go deliberately slow, her other hand cupping the top of my penis. She ducks underneath her sweater, pulling the newspaper back to cover her as much as I can. Feeling the eruption coming from deep in my pelvis, her mouth moving slowly sucking hard, firm grip down by the base.

Feeling the paper shake, biting my lips as I come hard, trying to not lift my body up and push. She's holding my cock in her mouth while I ejaculate, pulsating again and again. Eyes closed, swimming in exquisite pleasure for a few moments. Feeling her move back, her hand still on my throbbing penis.

"Oh, Frank," she whispers in my ear. "You don't know how good that feels."

"That was so good, Mary. Let me take care of you, I bet you're really wet. I wish we weren't around any people so you could take your jeans off and I could lick your pussy for hours."

"You keep talking to me like that and I can come right here."

Acting like I'm showing her something in the paper, working my left hand down her jeans.

"You feel so warm, so wet, Mary."

Her eyes closed as I feel my way to her clitoris, her pussy so wet and wonderful. Getting hard again thinking about how good it tastes, how good it would feel to get her on top of me and just fuck like mad.

Moving in small circles then larger circles—slow then fast, changing direction. Taking my time, feeling her get close and then slowing down.

"I'm going to kill you later, oh..."

Smiling and laughing.

Putting more pressure, then moving down so my fingers can be inside her, then back to the top of her pussy. Working my pointer and middle finger to the side of her clitoris and gently circling the base—moving up to the top, going faster, harder. Feeling her body start to shake, her thighs crushing in on my hand.

She's laughing, and biting my ear.

"You make me so wild."

"Feel this, Mary," taking her hand back underneath the sweater to my still slick engorged penis.

"You just don't stop do you?"

Wiggling my eyebrows at her. "Pretty funny if we couldn't walk when we get off the train."

"Funny for you, Buster." She looks around, "I need to wash up."

"I can meet you in there?"

Smile from her.

Laughing as we come back to our seats. People have no clue or are too embarrassed to look at us. Folding up yesterday's newspaper.

"Good thing there's no quiz on this."

She puts her legs over my left thigh, her arms around my left arm and puts her head on my shoulders.

"I'm so in love with you, Frank. There's nothing I wouldn't do. I don't know, I mean, I knew how I felt about you, but this is just maddening sometimes. Like I'm stepping out of my body and just becoming this force that has to be close to you. A force that needs to feel you be fed by you and feed you too."

"This is wonderful, Mary," holding her green-blue eyes for moments. "I know I still get thrown about wondering what my life will be like in a year, how we'll see each other and all—but then coming to this clearing with you where the world just seems so full of the possible. I am fed by you, and…"

"What, Frank?"

Looking at her.

"I need this, Mary, I need you. I need the crazy wacky sense of humor. I need the insatiable curiosity. A couple of days ago when we were reading through some of your mom's books on sex, trying out different positions. What a wonderful culture India must be to have spent the time to document and invent such wild positions. Anyway, I digress. I feel so full of life when I'm with you. It's like I don't have to try to prove anything to you, there's no competition, and it's just this wonderful, intense, playful, attentive, smart, loving… I don't know, energy, music. I feel so alive."

She's smiling, looking at me.

"I also need the great blowjob on the train."

She bites my shoulder.

"I love you, Frank Caruso."

"I love you, Mary O'Connor."

Sitting there in the glow of being with her. Watching the landscape near the tracks shift from houses stacked right next to each other to smaller groups of houses interspersed with green trees.

"So, what were you going to ask me?"

"Oh?" she shakes her head a little. "Oh, I was wondering what you thought it was going to be like when you're in the Army? It worries me you know."

"Why's that, Mare?"

"Well, I wonder how it will be for you. What you'll be like a few years now. You're so impatient at times and I worry if you'll be really unhappy. It seems so regimented to me, everybody wearing the same things, doing the same things. People shouting at you, and well…"

"What, Mare?"

"How will you deal with all these people who aren't as smart as you telling you what to do all the time? I mean, look what's happened at school."

Nodding, looking at her for a few moments—the blue green eyes, her perfect lips, the fine chiseled features of a young woman's face blossoming into a beauty, fresh clean skin.

"I'm really going to miss you when I'm away, Mary."

Wave of sadness flashing over her face—she looks out the window.

"I wonder too," taking a moment to reflect on the different conversations with my uncle, Detective Kelly, some of the men at the VA hospital. "I could come back disfigured or crippled from a training accident. I've heard the fall-out from Ranger selection is pretty high just from injury. Or what if I don't make it and am Joe Infantry Man for four years… I guess. I don't know, Mary."

"I don't worry about that, I mean you failing. Though it would be weird if you were hurt bad… What would happen if you were successful though? Maybe all these stories of people turning into, I don't know, something hard, cruel are true. There's such a generous, warm side to you too. Is humanity crushed to create people capable of fighting in a war?"

Looking at her.

"What does that mean for us, Mary?"

"Oh geez, I mean, I don't know."

She's looking out the train window. The conductor walking by checking people's ticket stubs on the top of their seats.

"I'll always love you, Frank, you have to know that. I'll be there with you through this ordeal," she turns toward me. "I want you to know that, Frank. I will be with you through this. Okay?"

Feeling a wonderful warmth spread through my chest.

"Okay, Mary, you can be my connection to the world outside the military. Which god used to bring Hades' wife from the underworld to visit the rest of the Gods on Mount Olympus once a year?"

"Hermes."

"Well then, when she came out she brought spring with her, rejuvenation. Maybe going in and knowing what's here," touching her chest then touching mine. "Maybe knowing what's at stake, what is waiting for me as I do my service will help me maintain my perspective. Men have gone off to war or on long journeys and have come back. I think I'll have to call you Penelope and you'll have to learn to weave."

She's smiling a little.

"There's a risk though, Mary. It's the unknown, but wouldn't we be different in three of four years anyway? I guess it's up to us to figure out how to keep this alive through what's coming."

"I will Frank and I'm going to miss you so much too. Let's make the next few months magical, let's do all the crazy things we can think, let's talk about what we want to do over the next few years. You told me you'll get thirty days leave a year. There are places we can go; they don't have to be first class hotels. They can be ours."

"I like that, Mary." Sitting back and thinking. "It would be fun to go to Cape Hatteras. I've heard there's good fishing there. It will be close to some of the bases where I'll be training. I'd like to walk part of the Appalachian Trail or go see some of the places where Civil War battles were fought."

"That would be fun to go to the Appalachians in the fall. One of my favorite songs is Aaron Copland's *Appalachian Spring*. Do you know it?"

Shaking my head.

"I'll play it for you when we get back to the City. It's so beautiful." She snuggles up into me. "Will you build me a log cabin up there in the woods, grow a beard and love me like a mountain man?"

"What, can you make a baa'ing sound like a sheep?"

Slapping at me, laughing with her.

"I think those would be fun places to go with you, Frank. It doesn't even have to be anything fancy. Just find some nice place where we can sit and eat Chinese food naked like we did last week."

"Oh, so you like me eating noodles off your body?"

"Hmm," she pulls herself in.

"I may have to unfold that paper again."

She looks at me.

"I wonder if it will always be like this? Passionate, unabashed."

"I hope so, Mary. Anything to be unlike my parents or some of the other dreary old mom and dad types I've seen," body shivering when I think about Cat's parents.

"I caught them once you know," she says to me in a low voice.

"What?"

"A couple of years ago. I came home from school early. The place was quiet and I don't know why. I think there was mail for them or something." Her body going quiet for a second, "I came into their room and she was on top of Dad."

Image of her mother coming back in my mind, shiver running through me thinking about how beautiful she is.

"Oh my God. Did they know?"

"I stood there for a few seconds, it didn't register right away. But they were really going at it. Then Dad saw me first, Mom turned, her face was so ferocious for a second and then she saw me and hopped back pulling the sheets over them." Letting her be quiet.

"They were pretty calm though. Dad was laughing a little, told me they needed some time and that we'd be fine to talk about all this later."

"I can't imagine my parents doing it," shaking my head, sensations of going into my mother's closet to take my bankbook—the smells, the curiosity, the embarrassment of the situation reliving inside me for a moment.

"I don't think she likes me."

"Your mom?"

"No yours. I just get this uneasy feeling around her. Your dad seems great. I feel like your mom is probing, looking for something wrong."

Mary nodding, "She can be difficult at times, but I think you fascinate her a little, at least from what I've told her about you. All the things you've done in the outdoors, in sports and then being so smart and how off-the-wall you can be at times. I've told her how I feel about you too. For her..." she's looking out the window again. "Dad says she's a bit of a restless spirit, but I really admire how brave she is, how unconventional she can be at times. I mean our doctor was horrified when she talked with him about sex and wanting to get a prescription for the pill for me. She could have written it herself, but... Anyway, I think she likes you, Frank. I just think she's perplexed. She needs to figure things and people out."

"Oh, what about you?"

"I've got you figured out, Mister," she starts to rub her leg against me.

Smiling, "That you do, that you do."

"I don't think it will change me, Mary."

"What?"

"Going in the Army. There's too much I want to do when I get out. I mean, I'm going to go one hundred percent and do the absolute best I can, push myself beyond where I think I can go," looking at her. "And yes, that means keeping my big fat mouth shut at times."

"Oh, I'll believe that when I see it," she's rolling her eyes.

"Why, you little creep!" tickling and pinching her.

"Hey, watch it you big meany. You'll hurt my tender young flesh."

"What if you like it though? I mean, what if you want to stay in?"

"I hadn't thought of that," sitting back, letting my vision drift toward the window and the passing cattails whizzing by. "I guess that's a possibility.

How would you feel about that? I mean if we were together when you got out of school, it's likely we'd live someplace other than the City for a while. Could you do that?"

"I don't know, Frank. I think I could for a time, seeing new places, new people. It could be fun." She yawns, stretching out a little.

Nodding to her, thinking about Fort Hamilton and what living around there would be like. Not so good.

"What are you thinking about, Frank?"

"Oh, keeping my head on straight about going into the Army. It's not going to be the end of the world you know. It will pass."

"Yes, it will," she's closing her eyes and snuggling in. "I'll be there with you."

Waking up from a quick nap. Train coming to a stop.

Looking at her thin body, sleeping on my shoulder amazed at how resilient and flexible her little body is, how much she can take. Duh, Frank—they have babies in these things you idiot. Shiver going through my body remembering Jorge talking about his wife and going in the military.

"I don't want that for you, Mary. I'm going to make this work."

"Hmm," she gives a low mumble.

"Shh," as I drift back off to sleep.

Chapter 56

Train pulling away.

Stretching as Mary gathers up her bag and gives me a wonderful smile. Smelling the fresh ocean air—feeling the energy of the sea.

Maybe going in the Army is a stupid idea, but knowing she's with me...

Arms around each other walking down the long concrete platform, pulling her close for a few moments, feeling all the possibilities in the world when she smiles at me. Passing green weeds and cattails along the tracks waving at us as we walk with the few other passengers.

"Let's straighten up a bit," as she steps back and puts her sweater back on then looks at me and musses my hair a little. "You look like a wild man." Shrugging my shoulders. "And don't think I didn't see you giving those people behind us the kiss my ass gesture on the train, Mister."

Laughing. "Yeah, well," bopping along, throwing some wanna be attitude. "Fuck those cracker assholes."

"Easy there, Clyde," she looks out at the pick-up area. "There's Dad, let's go," and she waves and gives him a big smile.

Standing back, watching her run up and hug her dad, big smiles on both of their faces. Wave of sadness rushing over me for a moment, I can't remember Vicky and Dad ever hugging like that. She hates me cause I came along and was the apple of Dad's eye, she hates Dad 'cause he doesn't understand why she is who she is.

Shrugging my shoulders—got to shake this bad mood off.

Mary in the front seat of their old station wagon, listening to them rattle on back and forth from the middle seat after the obligatory exchange of conversation about the weather, the train trip, fishing tomorrow and big party tomorrow night.

Driving down Meadow Lane passing open lots, older houses, a couple of huge places being built up by the ocean.

"Wow Dad, the old Roberts place is gone. I really liked that place."

"Yes, I liked it too," turning to look—big house, columns out front serving no structural purpose other than to look impressive. Shaking my head, then looking forward. Mr. O'Connor looking at me in the mirror.

"You don't approve?"

"Ionic columns by the beach? They don't even bear any weight."

"You paid attention in Greek history class, I see."

"Oh, Dad," she turns to her father, "Frank loves myths, on the night... you know, when we met after that rotten party, we talked about Orpheus and myths, about movies," she gives me a smile, catching her dad looking at her and then looking at me—taking it all in. Uncomfortable silence while we drive.

"So, Dad, who's coming fishing tomorrow?" and they are off to the races again talking about people that are only names to me. Looking over at the long open beach—scooting over and rolling down the window to let the fresh ocean air in. Rough surf along the shoreline today—choppy, big waves, no jetties, looks good for body surfing but you're gonna take a beating if you don't time the shore break.

Pulling into a driveway swept with sand. Cozy, weathered wooden house nestled back in low sand dunes. Rich green ice plant and reeds growing here and there.

"This is fantastic!" looking over to the beach and taking a deep breath.

"You guys hungry?" her dad asks as we walk into the beach house.

"Oh, sure," she says, "we're famished."

Good catch, Mary.

"There they are," an elderly lady says walking towards Mary—long necklace of beads and turquoise stone set in silver, purple flower-patterned loose shirt, her silver hair pulled straight back. No attempt to hide her age, putting it out there.

"Mima, this is my boyfriend, Frank."

"Good to meet you, Mima," direct look from her, firm handshake then she turns, opens her arms to Mary and gives her a big hug, rocking back and forth.

"Oh, there's my favorite girl!" a very, very long hug.

Mary's mom coming into the small, sparsely furnished living room wiping her hands on a dish towel, then finishing off a glass of something light brown.

Shorts and short sleeve white shirt, beautiful legs like her daughter. Looking away quickly. She gives me a polite little nod and joins Mary and whoever the hell Mima is in a big hug. Guess I'm going to be part of the scenery for a while.

"Mima just got in this morning, isn't that wonderful," her mother talking to Mary, ignoring me, the three of them chatting away.

Awkward.

Looking at the room—well-crafted wood joinery on the simple, but well-made furniture—Shaker style, nodding to no one in particular. Bookshelves covering the wall, books stuffed in haphazardly, cut outs for artwork here and there.

"Everything from trashy dime store novels, to the crazy Russians my wife loves, to a few of my books as well." Turning, didn't even realize he was standing near me.

"Oh," looking at him. "These are Shaker designs, aren't they?"

"Very good, they are," he's calmly looking at me. "I like them because there's integrity to the design, how they are crafted, the idea behind the design." brief smile. "Why don't we unload the car and get the barbecue going? This is going to be a while," pointing back over his shoulder with this thumb.

"Sounds good to me," glad to be moving, liking her dad.

Fanning the charcoal.

"You drink beer?" he takes a sip of a bottle.

"Yes, not often though, my parents are red wine drinkers and even then, very little. My father has a couple of glasses and he's taking a nap on the couch. I'm afraid I inherited his alcohol tolerance."

He nods, "If you don't mind, I'll get things moving while you prep."

"Okay."

Dusk starting to settle in—deep, dark blues and purples in the distance.

Big back yard, sand volleyball court, hot tub, ping pong table warped from too much time in the sun, wood and stone hut set back away from the house and here I am, fanning away.

Imagining the conversations going on now, "Well, Mima," her mother in a hushed concerned tone, "Frank's the high school drop-out who's been arrested, spent a lovely couple of weeks or so in jail and who's joining the Army soon. Mary loves him very much so we're going to pack her off to a famous psychotherapist in Vienna on Monday to find out if she's capable of being saved from that beast."

"Oh you can't be serious dear, he seems like such a lovely man and look at those strong hands and shoulders, I imagine he's rather tasty."

"That's an itch I wouldn't mind scratching. If Mary were only after that…"

"How do you know dear, she's always been such an independent girl?"

Voice coming up behind me snapping me out of my daydream—Mary's dad walking over with a large tray covered in tin foil.

"Too much estrogen in there for me, how are the coals coming along?"

"I think we are about ready."

"Thanks, the quick light charcoal doesn't have the same flavor."

"We've never used them, this was my job out at Rockaway in the summer."

Taking the tongs and pulling up the large tin chimney I'd been feeding—nice orange coals tumbling out.

Grilling away as dusk settles in.

"How do you like your steak?"

"Medium rare."

He takes out a knife.

"Oh, you're not going to cut those open are you?"

"Sure, how else can you tell?"

"Can I show you a trick my Grandpa T showed me?"

He's giving me kind of a funny look, "Let's give her a go then."

"If you hold out your hand," holding mine out. "Go ahead, like this," he lifts his up. "Close your thumb up to the side and poke the fleshy area between your thumb and hand, that's rare," he's a little more interested now. "Touch lower, right here, that's medium rare, on the meaty part of the base of your thumb and that's medium, touch the base of your palm and that's well done."

"This way you don't let all the good juices seep out and dry the meat, here," poking the steaks, "these are pretty rare, this one's medium rare now. Give it a try."

Skeptical pokes at the meat and then his hand.

"Hey," a slight smile and a nod as he's working the grill.

"How are the men out here doing?"

"We are good, Claire."

"Oh, the Bridges called, they are stopping by at nine."

"One of those nights, eh?"

She shrugs her shoulders and places a large wooden tray filled with fresh asparagus, cut red peppers and open loaves of bread on the picnic table.

"Well, let's get to grilling these puppies."

Uncomfortable silence as we prep the food.

Night falling.

People I don't know coming and going, talking about other people I don't know. The small house is starting to fill up, Mary flitting around talking to different people, her parents talking to Mima. Folks show up for the impromptu party with bottles of scotch, bourbon, wine and beer. Now I know what that brown stuff Mary's mom was drinking earlier. People having more than a few drinks together and then moving on to someone else's house. Her mom keeps packing it away with each wave of guests. Lots of big words being bandied about—laughing to myself about the scene in Woody Allen's *Love and Death* where he's being accused of being jejune in the middle of a mock-philosophical conversation. I had to go look the word up; dull, of little interest, I had another good laugh at that.

Slipping out of the house—too much cigarette smoke in here, too many people I have nothing in common with.

Pissed that Mary ditched me.

Deep breath of clean sea air—rough sea pounding the shore.

Taking off my sneakers and shirt—toes in the cold sand.

Standing at the water line.

Lights in the distance from houses dotted along the beach—starting off at a slow jog, I wonder where Cat is tonight? Vision of her body appearing in my mind, someone else touching her, making love to her, her passion directed back at them, and I'm long gone from her mind. Body wrenching in reaction—running faster to drain the rush of regret, anger, frustration, loss and pain washing over me.

Nobody on the beach.

Nobody to blame.

Breathing hard, pushing to feel the pain, feel the burn in my legs to take my mind off Cat and what might have been. Focused on keeping my stride long, shoulders relaxed, pattern breathing. Chew up the beach.

Clear your head, run, breathe.

Welcoming the tired calm settling in.

Walking now—dark beach, sound of waves.

Terrible aloneness—remembering the things I've done, the places I've been, wave of feeling unworthy of her.

Sitting in the sand with my arms around my knees.

If I died right now, who would care? What if I come back from the Army like Artis? Why not? I'm not special.

Deep black pull of the deep rising up—what if I had jumped? I'd be out of the way people would be getting on with their lives. Raising my head up—long wave rolling in silver in the moonlight. Standing up, feet wet. Rolling up my pants. What if I keep walking?

Cold water around my legs, feeling the sand slowly being pulling out from under my feet, sea spray splashing up against my legs and stomach.

Maybe I am a bad apple—I mean how would I know? Look at what you do—I'm like this bad tempered badger walking around looking for anything to strike out at. Why was I even born if I was going to be this much of a fuck up?

Walking further in, cold water up to my waist as a wave passes and then back to my knees on the way out. Rocking back and forth with the surf, arms crossed.

Body shivering from the cold water.

Slow walk back up the beach, flinging a few rocks into the waves here and there. Stopping and laughing out loud—idiot, you don't know where their house is.

Up by the road walking slowly over rough broken sections of old concrete. House up ahead, heading away—get my shoes, socks and shirt.

What a dope I am. Great Indian scout I'd made—can't even find his frigging clothes. Taking my jeans and shaking the sand off, people coming up the beach. Snapping too and getting dressed again—buttoning up my jean shirt, realization that I'd been thinking like an idiot, Mary would care. Why the hell do I get like this?

"Hey, we were worried," said Mary's dad as they come up.

"Frank," she's out of breath. "Where'd you go? Are you all wet?"

"A little."

"Be careful out here at night, nasty undertow, nasty riptide at times," he looks at me, can't make out his look in the dark. "Let's head back, it's chilly out here."

"Your skin is really cold," taking my hand.

Her dad walks into the living room, leaving us outside.

"Why'd you go, Frank?"

"I don't know. I mean, I didn't know anybody, people didn't seem that interested in talking," shrugging my shoulders. "It was good to get out and get some clean air."

"You should have come gotten me, I missed you," she makes a playful sad face. Trying to smile, having a hard time pulling myself back from the edge.

"Are you doing okay?" a little more serious look from her.

Forced smile, sick laugh bubbling up at how insincere I must look right now. She takes my right hand and holds it up, blowing warm air and rubbing back and forth, "Come on, I'll make some tea, okay?"

Turning to the house with her, stopping for a moment under the fixed look of her mother from the front window. "It's okay," she says. "They were worried about you," as her mother turns away.

"I don't think they are worried about me, Mary." I've seen that look before.

"What do you mean?"

"Come on... I'm every parent's dream. The high school dropout, the trouble maker." Trying to stem the bitterness, mad at myself because her parents have been trying to be inclusive.

"Why are you doing this now? What's wrong, what did I do?" starting to hear the hurt in her voice as she pulls me to the side of the house away from prying eyes. Looking down at my feet.

"It's just," trying to search through all the words hitting me at once. "I don't know, look Mary... sometimes I just don't know where I fit in. I mean, what am I good for?" Another bitter laugh, "Well, other than yanking pushy ladies out of cabs, hmm, I wonder if there's a nice living in that. There you go, at career day my kids could talk about how I beat up old ladies for a living."

"Frank," she's shaking her head. "Stop it, stop it!" she takes a deep breath. "Why do you do this to yourself? We were so happy together this morning and on the way out here and now you're so... Far away from me, like you're so ready to chuck everything away when you get like this, don't do it," she stops. "Don't leave me like this, Frank... it," she takes another deep breath, "it hurts too much to see how wonderful you are and you don't know it." She shakes a little.

Feeling the ice start to melt.

"But, Mary," shaking my head a little to clear it. "What if I'm just not worthy?" looking at her. "What if I really am a bad apple and just don't know it? People in there talking about colleges, books, art, plays, writers I don't know anything about." Feeling welling up, "What if I'm just a bum?"

tears brimming a little bit, trying to pull back.

"Frank, oh Frank," she puts her arms around me—someone's here, stepping back from her. Her dad. Oh shit.

"There you two are, come on, I've got some warm cider on," he's holding the side door open.

"Be right there, Daddy."

He nods at her.

"Frank," coming close to me, "I believe in you," feeling her warmth. "Your aunt and uncle believe in you, I bet my parents will too, give this a chance. Don't put a wall up okay? Let people who care about you in, Frank. You're not alone. Some things take time to figure out."

Looking at her, wishing I could put this deep despair away someplace, lock it up, weigh it down, drop it into the deep cold ocean.

Warm kitchen—flexing my cold, sandy toes.

"This is good," looking at Mary, her hair loose, her elbows spread wide on the table. Soft jazz music playing in the living room—hushed sounds of conversation filtering in.

"Sounds like most of the movable feast have left."

"Hemingway," she rolls her eyes, "I get it."

"Me and my jejuneosity."

"What?"

"Oh nothing," swinging door opening, her mother precariously carrying a big tray of dirty glasses as she wobbles a little. "Ah, two more volunteers, let's go you two, time to help clean up."

She puts the tray down and takes another drink. One or two of those and I'd be snoring. Getting up to help, "I'll start on the dishes."

"And who says chivalry is dead," with just enough edge as she drags Mary out of the room. Deep breath, with Cat it was her dad, I guess it's going to be Mary's mom here.

Uncomfortable bed in the small guest room, hanging my wet dungarees up to dry—I have my boat shoes, knee length heavy shorts, sweat shirt and foulies all laid out for tomorrow. At least that will be something to do.

Mary's a couple of rooms away.

Lying on my stomach, pressing my raging hard-on down in the mattress reliving what it was like on the train out here.

Tossing back on my side. Taking off my t-shirt. Running my fingertips along my skin. Remembering how fresh her body smells and tastes.

In and out of light sleep.

Don't want to get up, but need to pee really badly.

Major piss hard on pushing out of my pajama bottoms.

Stumbling around in the hall, eyes having trouble focusing.

House seems quiet. Thank goodness everyone's asleep.

Blinking, not sure I see lights on or not.

Knocking, waiting, no answer.

Opening the door, stepping in, noticing the lights on. Blinking.

"Oh my," feeling the full rush of blood to my face, "Mrs. O'Connor, God, I'm so sorry," her mom naked, my eyes drawn to the patch of brown pubic hair. Pulling my eyes away quickly, she's looking down at my pajamas, then over my body.

"Shh, it's okay," slowly putting a towel around her body. "You can go use the bathroom at the front of the house," she's not looking away—shiver running up my body. She's looking right at me. Those eyes.

"Oh God, I'm so..." stepping back.

"Shh," she says. Body feels frozen, pulling myself back. Closing the door—wonderful breasts flashing up in my mind. Wonderful pink color, rich warm. Stop, stop, stop—shuddering. Maybe she thought I was her husband—I did knock, didn't I?

Cringing—good God, do I know how to fuck things up or what?

Mind running at a hundred miles per hour.

She's a doctor, right? She'll have had to gone to medical school—got to know about guys waking up with a big one. Oh shit, oh shit—walking in there with a big boner—moron, absolute moron.

Stumbling into the front bathroom, dick is so stiff that I need to bend over to pee at the right angle. Washing up and looking at my face in the mirror—idiot, moron, how could I have fucked up like that?

Walking back up the hall.

Body freezing, panic settling in. The door is slightly open again— catching an image of her shaving her long legs, can't help but look, rush of emotion holding me there. Oh God, she's looking at me. Her towel parted just enough. Held there for a moment in the swirling blue green depths of her eyes. She takes a drink from a small glass on the sink. Forcing my eyes away and walking to my room. Skin shivering in shame as I get under the covers. Is she setting me up? Imagining the conversation about how your boyfriend is a pervert, disgusting and all that.

Why was the door open the second time? I know I closed it.

Creamy skin, muscular calves, beautiful toes, she had dark red nail polish on her toes. Shivering again.

The look on her face though... How do I tell Mary about this?

Easy, you forget about it. You lock this away. It never happened.

Flipping over on my stomach.

Uncomfortable recognition of her spreading through me as a wave of deep prickly heat washes up through my body.

Fighting the pull of those eyes.

I'm just making all this crap up.

Cold chill running down my body, light footsteps in the hall.
Imagining them stopping by my door for a few moments, then passing.

Chapter 57

Gray fog rolling in from the sea surrounds the house.

Thank God the witch isn't up yet. Body still shaken from last night.

Helping Mary get her fishing gear together. Her dad in the kitchen getting coffee, toast and eggs ready for breakfast.

"You going to be warm enough in that?" looking at her thin sweatshirt.

Just focus on Mary's wonderful smile. No manipulation—clear, curious, intelligent. She cares about me. She loves me.

Sunday can't come fast enough to get the hell out of here.

Shiver running up my spine, there was no shame in her eyes.

She could have said something.

Shaking my head. Maybe it's just me making a big deal about this.

Angry thought surfacing—maybe she's toying with me.

"I have this knit fisherman's sweater I'll put on over," Mary gives me a little smile, coming close, "I missed you last night," listening in the hall, her door open—good, no suspicious action. Putting my arms around her and pulling her close—a few hot kisses, her leg wrapped around mine, letting last night melt in the feeling of her lips.

Mary pushing me into my room.

Clothes flying off.

Lost in the passion of her—attentive to every nuance of her body.

Sitting in the second row of their beaten up station wagon.

Sun coming up over Shinnecock Bay—passing stretches of state beach, stretches of well-appointed houses a few older ones mixed in, Mary and her dad talking about their last fishing trip. Nodding, answering polite questions here and there. Pulling up to a small harbor—feels good to be getting back to sights and smells I know. Pay attention to Mary today, last night was nothing—I'm being stupid.

Pulling in across one of the long docks.

"Frank, I'll grab the tackle, you bring the cooler, Mary, grab the bait buckets."

Making sure she's good before I carry the heavy cooler. Catching her dad watching me now and then. Did the witch tell him? Oh, how embarrassing.

Following him with the cooler.

"Hey, Fred," he calls out, a well-built elderly man waves back from what looks like a forty-four foot sport fishing boat.

"There they are, and there's my favorite girl," he smiles at Mary.

"Where are Scott and Harvey?"

"They'll be here in fifteen, who's the meathead?" he gives me a big smile.

"This is Mary's boyfriend, Frank."

Putting down the cooler, reaching out to shake a strong weathered hand. He nods, looking at me straight in the eyes—he likes the strong grip back.

"Good to meet ya," he gives me a once over.

"You spend time on the water?"

"Yes, Sir, my family has a boat out at Montauk. We're out as often as we can."

"Good, too many damn landlubbers on this boat for me. We'll have to see if you're any good. Come on aboard ya'll and get your gear stowed."

Car honking in the lot—Fred waving to someone, turning to catch a big Mercedes pull in next to Mary's dad's beat up old Chrysler station wagon.

"Like I said, landlubbers," he mumbles.

"Ah, well then Fred, they're here to have some of your old salt rub off on them," said Mr. O'Connor.

"I've got something for them two idjiots to rub off."

Mary starts to laugh as he makes an impatient "come on over" sign to the two guys getting out of the big car—all new fishing gear, clothes, all clean.

"You know how to rig a deep rod?"

"Yes, Sir."

"Good, get your butt working on these, we'll see if you're a lot of talk."

The two new guys haul their gear over, dropping things along the way. Captain Fred shaking his head, insulting them, Mary cracking up, her dad laughing at the expense of what I guess are two of his fellow doctors.

"Jesus H. Christ Joe, you need to teach these two how to dress, I'll get a bad rep you two numb nuts keep showing up like this."

"Frank, this is Dr. Scott Hanson," the taller of the two, striking red hair, weak jaw, clear blue eyes, soft hands, soft handshake.

"Good to meet you, Doctor."

"Likewise, Frank."

"And this is Dr. Harvey Holt, we work together at Columbia Pres." Harvey's the man driving the Mercedes—firm handshake, little eye contact.

"Hey, Captain Fred, check out this new Mitchell Garcia, it's sweet."

"Gear, gear, gear," he looks at them like they are a bunch of school children, "gear don't make the man," strapping on my belt with my marlinspike and fishing knife. Hanging my foul weather gear up on the rack with another well-worn set of foulies—putting my well-worn blue and gold 88th Precinct baseball hat on.

"Hey, Captain Fred," piping up, "you want this rigged for live bait high trolling or are we going deep?"

"We'll start high, see if we can catch any of them nasty blues. Water's been warm this year."

"Oh, I love them," said Mary as the four men wander off to look at gear. "They really put up a fight. I love smoked Bluefish."

"Yes, they do," as I finish tying off the leader, setting the weights light. "Where does he keep the tackle?"

"Here," a set of built-in drawers into the side of the lower deck of the superstructure. Taking a good hook—weaving, working a secure knot.

"What?" she's looking at me.

"I like watching you work, you're so intent on what you do."

"I'd like to be working on something else."

She starts fanning her face, "Oh, my," batting her eyelashes. "My daddy never told me about men like you."

"Men like what?" said Fred coming over.

"Oh, just joking around."

"Hey, this is my favorite girl, you mess with her and you'll end up in a lobster trap."

Ignoring the bluster, "Here's the rig."

He looks over it carefully, slight nod, "Passable," looking over my belt gear. "You know how to use that?"

"Yes, I do."

He turns, "Alright, get ready to shove off," out loud, the three men finish up getting their rods set, to me. "You know how to work deck lines?"

Nodding to him.

"Well get your butt over there and get ready to cast off then!" he looks all frustrated, but gives Mary a little pinch on the cheeks. "I don't know how you can stand being around all these incompetent men, my dear," as he walks into the wheel house and starts the engines.

The forward and aft lines are worn, but clean and in good shape.

"You gonna give me the good housekeeping seal of approval or cast off?"

"I'm ready."

"Cast off forward," Mary's dad gathering in the line, nodding to him as I move to the aft line. "Cast off aft," walking the line forward to the end of the dock as the boat slowly motors forward—stepping onto the deck, helping Harvey on the line.

Checking to make sure all the gear is secured for weather.

Taking a break, Mary coming over with a cup of something warm.

"I think he likes you," Mary sitting next to me, passing me a cup of coffee.

"Huh?"

"Fred, the Captain thing is a family name," she leans her head in, the wind starting to pick up a bit as we approach the inlet to the bay. Looking at her, looking back at the smooth water of the bay, the boat starting to bob a little more as we get closer to the open ocean. Squawking gulls, a few fat clouds out at sea.

"This is really nice," catching her eyes. "Something to hold onto while I'm away," she snuggles in a little nodding. "I'm sorry about last night, Mary. There's just so much to the world when I'm with you and then there are times where I feel so unworthy."

She takes a deep breath. Swells starting to pick up.

"Frank, if you could only see yourself how others see you."

"Like Leroy or Alton?"

"Maybe, but there are others too." Looking at her for a moment.

"We're gonna get bounced around today," looking ahead, catching her dad looking at us then going to back to talking with his friends. Coffee getting colder.

"You get seasick, Mare?"

"No way, we're sea faring folk," she points her thumb to her chest. Laughing.

"That's not funny, my dad likes to talk about his ancestors being sailors and fisherman out of Dundalk in County Louth."

"Where is that? Have you ever been there?"

"It's close to the border with Northern Ireland. Dad likes to say that we were reluctant migrants, as in wanting to stay out of British jails."

"Ah, the quiet rebel."

"I do what I like, Frank Caruso."

"I know, I know," smiling at her.

"We went there a few years ago, I think it meant more to Mom and Dad. I mean there are areas that are wonderful. Some…" she pushes her hair back. "Well some meant more because of old family. It was grand though," funny how her manner is changing a little when she thinks back, "seeing family I'd only heard about, places and all."

"It must have been grand," busting her chops a little.

"Mean," giving me an elbow.

Looking at the sea, "Hey, it's gonna get rough here, we should go take a nap or something, let our bodies get used to the motion."

"Ha," said Scott as I ask Fred where I can stretch out, Harvey rolling his eyes. Walking down to the main cabin, "I think he's worried about us sneaking off below deck." She shrugs her shoulders and yawns. Setting up a little area for her to stretch out on in the main cabin. Lying down across from her, letting the motion of the boat carry me off.

Speed change brings me back. Feeling refreshed after last night's bad dream. Stepping out on rear deck—big stretch. Lungs feel the energy of clean air. I must have been dreaming, that can't have happened, even if it did, who would believe it.

"Glad you could join us," snickers Harvey.

Four to six foot swells are going to make this fun.

"You want to get baited and ready, or just sit and jaw all day," from Captain Fred.

Walking back in to the main cabin. No one around, bending down and giving her a light kiss. "Hey, lady."

Sleepy eyes, "Hey yourself."

"Let's go catch some fish."

She sits up, stretches, rubs her arms with her hands and blinks, "Okay," feeling a moment of light in the lovely innocence of her waking up.

Feeling the skipper setting a nice trolling pace—getting her bait set, making sure the hook is set well, blue fish will rip right into this if they are around.

"Nice cast," she handles her gear well.

"Are you going to fish?"

"In a bit."

The other guys getting their lines out, Mary's dad coming over and casting his line as well, Scott and Harvey getting on each other's case—they've put together a hundred dollar pot to see who'll catch the biggest fish.

"You've got company," the end of her rod taking a dive.

"I bet it's a nice blue," her eyes light up.

"Next time it strikes, give a big yank," she nods, intense focus on her rod. The boat undulating up and down—if she hooks him, I can help her land the fish on the starboard side. A good-sized gaff and club set into the gunwale. Good setup.

"There," she yanks back hard.

Her dad all smiles, "That's good, Mare, take him, work him."

Her face intense, pretty good balance, helping for a moment when we come down off an awkward swell. She reels in.

"Wow," she blurts out smiling as the bluefish takes a nice jump.

"Keep good tension on the line, Mare," she nods.

She's intent as she works the blue fish to the side, getting a small gaff ready.

"Hey nice one," says Harvey coming over. "What, ten pounds or so?"

"At least," says her dad to the onlookers.

"Don't let him smack into the side of the boat," he says to her.

"Put a cork in it, okay Dad?" He's smiling at that one.

"Bring him over here, Mary, and I'll gaff him," holding her arm to help keep her steady. Beads of sweat breaking out on her forehead. Making a quick sweep underneath the Blue with the gaff. Jabbing the sharpened gaff hook into his gills, lifting the fighting fish up out of the water. Scott falls into me on a big up swell. Quickly regaining my balance.

"Nice fish, Mary." The others are clamoring around.

She's beaming, "Careful now," as I bring the thrashing blue on the boat, my right hand coming up underneath his gill slit, sliding out the gaff and handing it to her dad.

"I like to bleed them right away, makes them taste better, you good with that?"

"Sounds good to me," he says, reluctant. Imagining he's the one doing this most of the time. "Look at him snap away," says Scott regaining his balance.

Taking out my marlinspike, jabbing it down into the fighting bluefish's brain through the back of its eye socket—his body flapping hard then dying down.

"Let's get a weight on that Blue," says Fred yelling down. Mary watching me intently as I wipe the end of my spike and put it back in my belt.

"Here you go, Mare."

She shows the fish to her dad, "Well done, Mary, well done," he goes to his sea bag and fishes out a camera as she gets the blue on the hanging scale.

"Twelve pounds," she calls out.

"How much?" calls Fred down.

"Twelve."

"That's my girl, show these lubbers how to do it, ha!"

Bleeding him out then making quick work of the fillet—keeping the deep red outer muscles for bait, getting the rest on ice.

Big yawn from Mary as she reels in—big blue snatched her bait.

Getting my first line out. Playing it a little deeper than the others.

Feeling clear, feeling clean even though my hands reek of fish. Scott and Harvey starting to pay attention to what I'm doing after they both botched landing good-sized blues. Scott almost had his fingers taken off by an eight pounder. I quickly dispatched his fish, but he wanted to clean it. Nice big bandage on where he slipped up. Captain Fred yelling at him, calling him an idiot. Harvey is starting to get a little green. Mary's dad intense—he's landed three good blues so far, he wants another.

"I'm going to take a little break," she says.

"Make sure you take a big drink of water," over my shoulder.

Her dad working his line nearby. Nibbles, no real strike yet.

"I like how you look after her," surprised to hear him talking to me—there's been an uneasy space between us all day.

"She's really wonderful," looking at the sea, something nibbling at my bait. "That must sound trite, to you," looking at him. He's got that odd way of looking when he's paying attention, like he's weighing each word. "Funny that I've known her for three years and I didn't see..." looking out at the horizon, "I didn't see the depth, her curiosity, sometimes uncomfortable, her independence, her humor, her intelligence and to be honest, she's a little bit of a trouble maker."

He starts laughing. Boat slowing, Captain Fred changing course—maybe it's time for some bottom fishing.

"Yes, she is at that," he says looking out at the water.

Big strike, immediately jerking my rod back with all my strength.

"Good," he's excited.

"Doesn't feel like a blue, he's just sitting there."

Nodding to me watching the rod—letting up on the drag, line going out but not too fast. "Doesn't feel like a shark, though it could be a blue, too shallow to be a skate, could be a striped bass," he's nodding at that. Now he's fighting. Yeah!

"What's the lucky bastard got there?"

"He thinks he's on a striper," Captain Fred nodding.

"I'll work us back slowly."

Scott coming over, he's starting to babble bullshit advice—moving my body as the boat turns to keep the line away from the boat. Reeling in letting the fish tire some.

"He's not a monster," speaking out. "Maybe thirty five or forty pounds."

"Hell, that's a great fish!" said Scott.

"Speared a fifty pounder a couple of weeks ago free diving with my uncle."

"Bullshit."

"What's a picture worth then, Doc?" Asshole. "Hundred bucks?"

That shuts him up. He's starting to fight as I get him up to the surface—need to make sure he doesn't smack the line, "Can you tell how the hook set?"

Her dad looking over the side, "Looks good, keep working him, I'll get the gaff." Nodding to him while I work the tiring fish.

"What's going on?" hearing her voice from behind.

"Frank's on a nice striped bass," can't see her face, moving to the port side to keep from tangling up with the prop until I get him closer.

"I'll bring him starboard aft so you can gaff him."

Bugger's starting to smack around—easing up, playing him a little.

"Let me know when you're ready, Joe."

The stripper starts to smack around again trying to shake the hook.

"Ready."

Walking toward him, moving the fish carefully, rod bent at an extreme angle.

"Got him," triumphant look on his face.

Easing up as he hauls him up, "Jesus, Scott give us a hand here" as he slips and almost goes over the side. Scott gets his face too close to the bass and gets a fishtail smack that knocks him back. Left hand out to help them steady the net and bring it in.

"Hey," said Captain Fred, "nice work, kiddo," and he musses my hair.

Securing the big fish, strong hold under his gills as he fights. "What do you think Mr. O'Connor, on the grill tonight?"

"You bet your ass!"

Laughing with him.

"Get him on the scale," as I give the fish a quick coup de grace.

"Thirty-nine pounds."

Her dad gives me a big smack on the back. Mary looking at the fish—lifts the scale to see what its weight feels like. A slightly green Harvey comes out, looks at the fish, some of the blood running down and goes to barf over the side. Captain Fred laughing.

Helping spray down the boat in the late afternoon sun.

Finishing up stowing the gear and tackle we used.

"Hey," Captain Fred watching me, "you need to make some money, you come see me. I'll put you to work. Nice to see a kid who knows his way around a boat."

"I will Captain Fred, thanks for a great day."

"Hell, you did half the work, if I was a generous man I'd give you a tip, but I'm not a generous man," he starts laughing and I start laughing with him. Satisfied looking at the clean boat, Mary and her father waving over by the packed car.

"See ya, kid," he gives me a big handshake.

"See you, Captain Fred."

"Get going, you got a great girl there, remember, lobster trap."

"I get it, I get it."

"You better, I'm not as nice as those city boys."

Big yawn from Mary, "Dad, I'll sit in back," putting her wrist over her mouth to cover a yawn.

"Okay, Sweetie," he looks at me, "why don't you grab the front seat."

Feeling the long day, eyes have a salty slightly burned feeling. Looking behind at Mary, she's conked out across the bench seat. Smiling at her. Mr. O'Connor always watching.

"I have to be honest with you," as we drive slowly along a long stretch of beach road. "Part of me would rather have you as a fishing buddy than dating my daughter." Here we go. Taking a deep breath, at least he's being honest.

"Another part of me sees how you take care of her, it's really touching. Another part of me lauds the questions you are asking," he looks at me, "I couldn't help overhearing you talking to Mary last night, well that's not true. I listened in."

Blur of the road passing.

No idea where he's going with this.

"Viking boys used to go through a stage called lying in the ashes, the adolescent stage. It's a difficult stage, something we don't really celebrate or approach purposefully in our culture. I think the Jews do it better... coming of age, recognizing a change. Not only that the boy is now a man, but in how their family and friends should look at them, how they treat them, what they expect from them."

He looks at me briefly.

"Lying in the ashes, living in a grey world, lots of things changing. The fires of childhood burning out, fires of manhood starting to set in, body changing, brain changing."

Not understanding the words.

Image of my father flashing inside—curtain pulled back for a moment.

"Sometimes the Viking boys would lie at the bottom of the huts for days at a time, that's the lying in the ashes bit. That's where the fires burn at night."

"It's about parents too," absent-minded.

"What's that?"

"It just hit me, it's like my dad and I have been locked in this battle. Like he can't see me or won't recognize…" Swirling thoughts, hard to speak, "I'm not that kid he was so proud of, I've changed and then, well nothing's good enough anymore. Like tearing me down is going to bring back something." Taking a deep breath, feeling like my body is a couple of pounds lighter. "Hell of a way to get there," to myself.

"The road less traveled, young man."

Looking at him. What is this now?

"What do you mean, Mr. O'Connor?"

"Some people get along on an easy path, high school, college, jobs, marriage. They may or may not be faced with situations where they have to question themselves, ask important questions about who they are, what they believe, why they believe and then test those answers in the world where there really are no black and white answers to these questions."

Driving, watching as scenes of the long bay change and morph from clear open water, old decaying boats here and there, houses with expensive boats docked behind them.

"You, my young friend, for better or worse, have put yourself in a position where you are going to have to start thinking through and answering those questions. It's a path I wish more people in our society would go through, life is becoming so much easier," looking at me. "Not that I think people should suffer for suffering's sake, but when things become too easy, we lose the understanding of what it costs, the value behind it. You could appreciate that Venetian wooden screen, one of my favorites by the way, because you have a background that lets you see the master craftsman. Most people look at it for a few moments, comment on what a wonderful antique and then move on wondering how much it cost, not because they are shallow, well, not shallow purposefully, but they don't know what it takes to produce the work."

He digs a stick of chewing gum out of his jacket pocket.

"Out on the boat today I imagined you as a young Jack London—wild, untamed energy, intelligent, having a hard time fitting that into the things most kids your age do. I get the feeling that your family has had you out doing things most city kids have long forgotten—you showed real skill today, not just catching fish—all the little things that years of experience brings. Fred was impressed and he's a hard man."

Letting the road pass by for a few minutes.

"He's one of my favorite writers."

"What?"

"Jack London"

"Ah ha, *Call of the Wild*?"

"When I was younger yes, but in the past few years books like, *Martin Eden, Sea Wolf, People of the Abyss.*"

He's nodding and chewing away, the smell of spearmint mixing in with the smell of the day's fishing.

"Who else do you like to read?"

"Steinbeck, Henry Miller, Larry McMurty," looking out across the bay again, feeling a weight of failure talking about people who'd done so much. "Others, probably the only good English literature class I've taken," image of Mr. Emerson flashing up. "Our teacher, Mr. Emerson talked about the *Paris Review*, where writers were interviewed and talked about the writers and people that influenced them. I followed the people the writers I liked read," you're talking too much Frank. I must sound like an idiot here.

"Those are good writers, they write about strong people, strong situations."

"When I read," looking out across thick layers of tall cattails bent by the wind coming on shore, "it's like the pages disappear after awhile and I'm there, sometimes after my father and I would go at it, that would be my refuge or getting into the ring during Golden Gloves tournaments and getting it…"

"Were you good in the ring?"

"Yes, in the ring anyway," laughing to myself. That prick Leroy beat me though. He is a crafty man. Smiling to myself… here I am, Ajax, the strongest of the Greeks whipped by the crafty Ulysses. "Outside of the ring, well, I don't think I'm doing so well."

He starts laughing. Turning around to check out Mary, tension leaving my body for a moment seeing her sleeping there peacefully.

"My father was a good middleweight, helped get us all over during the famine."

Looking at him, "You follow the sport?"

"Yes, Claire hates it, but I like getting out with the two you met today and a few others seeing a good card and then going over to Dempsey's for some good red meat. I'm not much of a fan of heavyweights, I like the lighter, faster fighters, the ones who can't be sloppy and rely on size and strength to get a knockout."

"You'd like Gus, he runs the 14th Street Gym. That's where I used to train…" deep breath. "Before I messed things up, he had high hopes I'd be ready for the next round of Olympic quals, I wasn't good enough for the last one."

He nods.

"Gus is always talking about speed, skill, conditioning, timing… yeah, he's something else."

"I've heard about that place."

"I bet he'd have heard about your dad," brightening up.

Watching Mr. O'Connor drive—he's off in his head probably thinking about his father. Boxer, geez, I wonder what he was like. I bet he knows how to take a punch. Shifting around in my seat, clothes sticky from all the salt air and spray—hands still smell like fish and will for a few days. Thinking back to being with Mary out at sea, smiling to myself—she did really well, was right in the thick of things. Not afraid of fish guts or getting her hands dirty, Cat would have never done that...

"The Army will change you."

Sitting up snapping out of my reverie.

"What's that, Mr. O'Connor?"

"The situations, the people we are around, the different cultures we live in change us. We adapt, sometimes unconsciously to our surroundings, even the strongest do that, Frank."

"I, well," taking a moment, "I don't understand why you are telling me this."

"I spent some tough times close to the front line in a mobile unit and, it's not like that inane movie MASH. During the war, well," he's quiet for a few moments. "A lot of the questions I was talking to you about earlier started bubbling up, as they have consistently as I've grown older and had new experiences, marriage, kids," he looks behind him and smiles. "If you find situations you want to talk about or write to about, I'd be glad to write back. Put some of what's gone in to earning these gray hairs to use."

"I'll do that, my uncle said the same thing. He was a Ranger in World War II."

"Ah," he nods. "Mary had a good time at dinner with your aunt and uncle."

"They've been," reacting to the emotion of my words, "they've been lifesavers."

He nods again and keeps driving.

What does that mean—men need to learn to treat the young men differently? What does that mean for the young men to treat their family differently?

"Why did you say the Army will change me? Do you think I'll have problems there?"

He never answers right away.

Hum of the tires on a rough section of road, the day settling into dusk.

"It's a different world, Frank. Different language, different rules and they don't take a lot of time to orient you kids... you get men who are very good at getting under your skin in your face right away and you are in it. In boot camp you'll be thrust right in, sink or swim, kiddo. During the last war kids would be off the street and in the jungle fighting for their lives in a few months," he shakes his head. "Stupid." He moves in his car seat a little. "And then when they were done, dump them right back on the street, more stupidity. I understand what they need to do, get you guys ready to go under tremendous physical, emotional and if you will, spiritual stress... you might be called upon to kill someone in a different uniform who's just like you, could be your age or younger. Could be a kid or a woman in some cases. They've got to do that in a few months, so it's repetition of tactics that make no sense to you but will be lifesavers in combat."

He takes a quick look at me, then back to the road.

"I'm not a pacifist by any means, though I continue to hope we'll learn to use war as a last resort. I want our young men to serve, serve well and then able to regain a good productive place in society afterwards. Our society is blissfully ignorant of what happens during and afterwards, what it does to some people. There's a point where all the training in the world doesn't matter, you have to do it, you have to step out, but I'm a firm believer in preparation, careful deliberate preparation. Getting a bunch of gung ho kids... Well, anyway."

He looks over his left shoulder for a couple of moments.

"My uncle took me to volunteer time at the VA," shaking my head remembering the people, the smells of the place. "It was... I don't know, so disjointed from what I thought it would be like. I mean my dad and all my uncles served, so I had... I don't know. I didn't think there would be so much anger and disappointment from guys who served in Southeast Asia. And then other guys who retired are proud to have served and all. It really made me think... I've been going back there to help out, lot of the guys there are pretty lonely and all. Not many people say thank you."

He nods—a sad look on his face.

"I'm beginning to really like your uncle, sounds like he's a man who wants to cut through the window-dressing and get to the meat of things."

"Yes he is, Mr. O'Connor," laughing to myself.

"Well, if anything, that's good preparation. You can see the possibilities; people like your family came through. I did, but truthfully with a lot of help from my peers afterwards and a great woman. You've seen others who maybe feel something has been stolen from them. I can tell you something I've learned," he looks at me for a second. "It takes a lot of strength to look at humanity, that includes ourselves, and not be trapped by the depth of ugliness and tragedy that exists. Fixating on the good or the evil in this world is a luxury you may not have, being able to see the good and bad in all of us takes a resilient, strong spirit. It means you don't give up looking for the good in life, but you remain careful, observant if you will. I think you know from your time on the street that there are predators out there... you'll find plenty in the military. I'm sure you'll find dedicated, brave men and women too. It will be a search for you to find the best and stay away from the mutton heads," he laughs at that. "There are plenty of them in the officer and enlisted corps."

Letting the road hold my attention.

"Can I ask you a question?"

"Sure, Frank."

"Something struck me as you were talking. My uncle's talked about it a few times, you mentioned it again," shaking my head, trying to get my thoughts together.

"Just relax, Frank, you're asking the right questions. Give your brain a chance to pull things together. I see so many of you kids be so hard on yourself."

Calming down.

"What about the journey back? One of my favorite movies is the *Searchers*. At the end, the Ethan character played by John Wayne stands outside the house while the whole family walks inside. It's like he's gone so far that he can't re-join those he loves. You said earlier the Army would change me... So, how do we come back?"

"We may have to drive around for a while to get to that one. It's a good question, a deep question."

Catching a glimpse of their beach house in the distance.

"Is Mary still asleep?"

Looking behind me, then nodding to her dad.

"Let's take a short drive then."

"Everything we do in life changes us Frank. The fishing trip this morning, you can never do that same fishing trip again."

"I don't understand."

"Let's say the weather and everything else is the same and all the external and environmental stimulus remains the same. The difference will be you. Today you've been in a new situation your experience of the situation has produced a change in you. So, for example, you can't go back to not knowing Captain Fred, right? You could forget him over time, but for now at least, you've met him, acted a certain way, observed what you could observe."

"Sorry, what do you mean, observe what I could observe?"

"Well, unless you'd spent years out on the ocean, how would you have known to help Mary land that big blue? Scott and Harvey were standing there watching and it's not like they didn't try to help, they didn't have the experience to understand the consequences of what was happening at that moment. In five years, they may have the knowledge to do what you did. It doesn't mean they are any smarter or dumber than you are, they just didn't have the common sense you have about fishing. It takes time to develop real learning—you can study something in a book and may or may not be able to repeat it, but real learning takes months and sometimes years of practice to become fully embodied, actionable."

He looks at me for a moment, "I'm of two minds on this, and I go back and forth. For example, our school system wants you kids to learn by studying lots of facts and figures, the raw elements of information. Yet at the same time, to me it's not knowledge, because you are not taught how to think with these facts and figures. There's no relevance to your life, the things you are being asked to do. Yet without a basic knowledge of the fact and figures… So Mary's told me you are very good at math. Is that right?"

"Yes," wary.

"Imagine if you were dropped into Calculus without the background of algebra and trigonometry."

Frustration of 6th and 7th grades comes into focus for a moment.

"I was so frustrated for a time." Looking out the window. "I couldn't understand why they wanted us to memorize all the theorems, it just didn't make any sense. When I got to Trig and then Calculus, it was like a light went off and I was able to move through material easily. I was so mad though, if they'd shown me what they were after, man I could have been so…"

He's nodding his head slowly, "You have one of those brains that's always trying to put things together," he's nodding his head. "I'm starting to understand more about why you are where you are. And I don't mean that in a pedantic or patronizing way. Unfortunately our systems, mostly our educational systems, are designed to address the bell curve. You understand standard deviations?"

"Yes."

"Imagine how you'd design a course for students whose intelligence, not that there's a really accurate way to determine that because there are so many different types of intelligence, but anyway that's a different topic. Let's get back to the bell curve, so if I have a general population group whose intelligence is in the third or fourth standard deviation, schools like you're in now probably go out to the fifth or sixth standard deviation," imagining the curve. "The coursework is designed to deal with the maximal area under a given range of standard deviations. If you're at either end of the spectrum in terms of intelligence or physical capability, you'll likely be frustrated. Maybe your intelligence puts you out at one or two standard deviations beyond what the general population is, you might not be challenged enough. People express that frustration in different ways as I think you've experienced. We humans absorb things at different rates. We learn things at different rates. The things we learn enable us to observe different phenomena. You and I may look at a boxing match and see the years of skill and training that went into the fighter being able to box at a given level of expertise. How they jab, how they defend, how they deal with pressure and all. Other people see people whacking away at each other, they don't see the speed and skill. They don't know what it takes to develop the skill. People see what they can see, Frank. Unless they've walked a mile in your moccasins, they have no idea what you've seen, what you've learned and how you've changed."

"Jesus Christ!" sitting back looking out the car window.

"Something there?"

Shaking my head, body cold, thinking of how mad, how frustrated I was with Cat that she wouldn't listen to me. Looking out the window, deep wave of sadness washing over me understanding how naive I was with her—I let her walk away.

"I was thinking how stupid I was."

He's quiet.

"I think Mary told you that after I got in trouble, well... My dad and I were at a breaking point and he didn't want anything to do with me, so I landed in jail."

"Yes, she's told us."

"When I got out, I was mad at people close to me because they didn't understand, or worse, I thought they didn't care," shaking my head, looking down at my hands. "I made a hash of things going in, then another one coming out. Idiot!" hands clenching into fists and then unclenching, trying to squeeze out the horrible feeling creeping up inside.

Fighting off the feeling that I'm going to mess this up too.

"You know, Frank, there's no way to know the future. Life is imperfection and one of our big challenges is learning to look at our own imperfections, learn about ourselves, learn how to deal with who we are. This may sound namby-pamby, but you have to accept that no matter what you do in life, you are going to make mistakes and that you have to accept yourself for what you are and what you can do at this moment, right now. Who you will be in the future is based on who you are right now, the small things you do right now to learn, to make different choices. Otherwise we just keep on making the same mistakes over and over again and then blame life that it isn't fair. Look, we all don't start at the same place. Life is not a level playing field. You were born with the particular set of genes and family history that makes you what you are. Like it or not, it's what you've got. You'll never be a jockey and it's likely you'll never be a concert pianist, you may have the coordination, but you've not been playing the piano every day for four hours since you were five. But, we all have tremendous capability to take this plastic, this imperfect form that we are, and shape it to what we want."

"You can beat yourself up for all that you don't think you are or you can get on with what you want to be. In my book, that's the dirty little secret of free will. You come in with a stacked deck, biology, the culture of the time, your family. But then, unless you're mentally handicapped at birth, what you make out of this soup is up to you."

We start to near the house again.

"Or as a very wise man once said, you can either make chicken salad or chicken shit. The choice is up to you."

He's smiling at that.

"But let me tell you something I've learned, these things take time, Frank.

The wheel of life grinds very fine, but it grinds very slowly."

"Well anyway, enough of me rambling on," he takes a deep breath. "You get to face another challenge tonight, few of the people at the party tonight would have any interest in a conversation like this. Come find me if you get bored, we'll go have some beers, I'll show you some of the projects I'm working in the Horrible Shed, as my wife calls it. You know that hovel in the backyard," he's smiling thinking about this work there. "I don't have the skill to build things from scratch, but I'm a damn good at restoring them."

"People too?"

"Even better at that." Smile on his face.

Opening the door, kneeling down, speaking softly, "Hey, Mary." She's curled up on her left side. Shaking her shoulder—she's conked out. "Mary," shaking a little harder.

"Hmm, go away," she waves at me.

"Come on, we're back at the beach house," shaking her again.

"No hmm."

"I'll get something cold."

A little louder, "Nooo."

She sits up smacking her lips like her mouth is filled with cotton and blinking her eyes. Big yawn. Holding out my hand to her, warm thin fingers entwined in mine. Holding her eyes for a moment.

Please God, give me the strength to walk with her through life and not make a mess of things.

"You look so sad, Frank, what's the matter?"

"Oh, thinking about how stupid I've been. How wonderful this is and hoping that I don't mess this up."

"You can't silly. I love you. I'll take care of you. I'm your guiding light."

Smiling at her, stepping back holding her hand as she steps out of the car.

Chapter 58

Amazed at how many people can fit in this little house—crowd spilling out toward the makeshift bar stacked with whatever people are bringing over to share in the backyard. Filling Mary's glass with ice, staying away from the punch they made for us kids and filling her glass with some ginger ale. I guess what they don't know won't hurt them, since the wise-guy neighbor kid Mark poured a full fifth of vodka in when no one was looking.

Weaving my way back to a section of the living room.

Waving my hand in front of my face as some lady exhales a big cloud of smoke as I walk by. Mrs. O'Connor waving me over.

"Frank, this is my good friend Donna Markov, she's published a wonderful book on Dream Analysis. It's gotten great comments from the community."

"Donna, this is Mary's new boyfriend, Joe thinks he's wonderful," she takes a quick sip of her drink, her comment left hanging there. Nothing about what she thinks about me. Too bad she didn't marry Cat's dad. What a great combination. Quick recognition, in the bathroom last night, she was drinking in there too. She'd just put it down when I came back the second time. Push it away. I don't want to remember how I felt.

"Pleased to meet you Miss, Ms. or Doctor?" putting on a nice face.

"I see he's trained."

"We're working on him," they turn slightly away—I guess the pleasantries are over for now.

"Well, as long as I don't have to be locked in a closet."

Her friend gives me a strange look, tilting her head a little. Mrs. O'Connor looks impatient. "The Peter Sellers character in *What's New Pussycat?*" looking at them, raising my eyebrows—they don't get it. "The psychiatrist character locks what he calls "naughty patients" in a closet." Looking at them, shrugging my shoulders. "Well I guess you haven't seen it. Funny, funny movie, I think it was one of the first screenplays and direction by Woody Allen."

"When you see a movie, how much of the dialogue do you remember?" her friend asks.

"Almost all of it, the story, what people say, music too. Probably why I pick up languages quickly."

"What do you speak?"

"Italian and Spanish."

"*So if I were to speak to you like this, would you know what I'm saying, or are you just trying to make pleasant conversation? I think my friend Claire is not sure if she likes you dating her daughter, what do you think of that?*"

"*I think you speak with an awful accent, and I can understand that she's concerned about Mary,*" looking at her, seeing the horrified look on her face, "*Just kidding, just kidding,*" holding up my hands in mock surrender. "*It's quite good. It's usually my accent that Italians make fun of. My father's family is all Sicilian which, is quite different than the formal Italian my mother spoke and taught us at home, but my father and uncles all like to keep up with Sicilian, reminds them of where they come from. So it makes some Italians crazy trying to figure out where I'm from."*

"Well, you two are really going strong," her mother looks a little miffed at being left out.

"He's a character this one."

"Well, I must hurry up to deliver this," holding up my glass.

Dodging a man with paint splashed all over his T-shirt and dungarees.

"Wait, wait, you're the guy that stole Jackson Pollock's jeans."

"Yeah, well," he looks down and starts laughing, "bite me, Funny Boy," as he turns around and heads outside to the bar.

Walking back to the living room—Mary waving me over. People sort of dancing, more like moving near each other to some pretty way out jazz—bodies moving in rough synchronization, drinking, smoking.

She's standing up holding her hands out—people sitting on the floor grooving to the music or whatever the fuck they are doing, parting in front of her. Maybe I should call her Moses.

"Come on slowpoke, it's our turn," rolling my eyes—more charades as a competitive sport. Sitting down next to her. Put a smile on your face Frank and don't be a douche bag. Mary's picking a category from the straw hat we've put categories—thank goodness we are doing movies. Our two mostly not paying attention teammates look at the folded scrap of paper—they're having fun as they are going to be "actors" when they get older.

"It's your turn, Mare," as she elbows me.

Martin, one of the artsy neighbor kids leans in, "Oh, oh, do the keffiyeh thing, I'm sure no one has ever heard of *Lawrence of Arabia*" as he starts making wrapping movements and his younger sister Helena pulls his arms down and smacks him—he punches her back.

"Easy you two," she sticks out her tongue at her brother, then in Mary's ear. "Gee it's fun having newly minted teenagers on our team."

She gives me nice, "Shh."

"Okay, make way you losers," as she moves through the opposing team—a little older, but pretty bombed on the spiked punch, laughing and being silly. The occasional glare from one of the not too drunk parents quiets them down. The glares are coming less frequently.

Mary holds up two fingers.

"Two words," she nods.

Acting as though she's bicycling like crazy then she reaches behind her back and picks up something and puts it quietly in her pocket looking around to see if anyone is watching.

"Bicycle Thief."

She points at me, smile on her face. "Yes! Are we good or what?"

"Damn," Maile, the cute little blond from the other team puts down our score. "Well you guys are really ahead, let's take a break, I want to dance and play," she puts her hand on her boyfriend Ben's lap.

"Okay, as long as you admit defeat," says Mary, rubbing it in.

"Alright already," Maile's boyfriend, "Man, this is getting to be a drag."

"Loser," Mary laughs.

"Oh yeah, let's get out on the volleyball court later, we'll show you."

"You're on," and she pats me on the shoulder. "See you suckers later," as a bunch of kids wander off into the mass of tipsy, try to be cool adults.

"Hey, you," she smiles, looks around and kisses me.

"Hey, yourself," smiling at her, we duck back behind one of the big stuffed chairs. Her arms around my shoulders, "I had so much fun out fishing today. Wouldn't that be exciting to have our own boat," her eyes flicking up to some of the paintings on the wall of the sea and ships mixed in with various modern originals, probably from a lot of the drunkards here tonight.

"It would." Holding her close, her skin still tasting a little of salt. "We wouldn't get much fishing done though."

She wiggles her eyebrows and rests her head on my shoulders.

"I'll be right back," she hops up and is gone.

Lying back against the wall—glad most of the competitive charade players have moved on. Living room filled with people grooving away to some other abstract jazz saxophone, their still bodies going all sorts of ways out of time and out of sync with each other.

Four months.

Waving in front of my face as a big cloud of cigarette smoke wafts over— couple of people getting together on the chair, looking up at them—man they are getting at it here. Looking around—nobody paying them much mind, lights being turned down, music slowing down.

"So, Frank man," Martin sitting down next to me.

"What's up?"

"Man, Mary's mom told me you were going in the Army."

"And?" giving him a hairy eyeball.

"Just, don't hear many people doing that."

"Marty," shrugging my shoulders, feeling like I'm becoming the object of curiosity here. "It's a party, aren't there better things to talk about?"

"Hey, if you don't want to talk about it."

"Marty, I've been attacked by people who think I'm joining the Nazi party. I've been told the military is a place for losers. I've seen what happens to people who serve who've been disfigured that nobody wants to acknowledge. I've talked to kids who are already married and they are going in because it's the best opportunity to get ahead... So, what's to talk about?"

"Geez, I didn't mean it like that... What I mean is I've got friends who did a couple of years in Peace Corps. I can set you up with them if you want to change your mind. There's so much that needs to get done in the world and all. Look at how rich we are here, a family in Bangladesh could live for a year on what we consumed tonight."

"Hey man, I don't see you saying no to all this."

"So, doesn't mean I can't do anything about it. At school, I volunteer to help raise money for the flood victims. I met this guy that's started a micro Bank, they make loans to families and small farmers. It's amazing it's putting money to work right where it needs to be. There are so many things we can be doing man."

"I'm signed and sealed, Martin."

"Nothing's final, man."

Shrugging my shoulders.

"You got that right."

"Look I'm not bugging you, it's just I don't run into many guys... You know."

"Chumps enlisting on their own?"

"Not like that. Hey man, my dad served and I'm not a bleeding heart. There's so much that needs to be done you know and," he looks at me, his eyes moving around for a few moments. "Like how will change happen unless we do different things? Can you do something different? Can you make a difference?"

"I'm not following you, Marty."

"Look we pour all this money into the military, but how much goodwill does that get us? I mean, this may sound stupid but if we took all the money we spent on the Vietnam War and worked from the bottom up. Like help everyone there build a house, have access to clean water. Help them buy pot-bellied pigs, chickens and what not. How different would things have been? Why do we have to start bombing first? Look at the billions in aid that were spent that was just squandered by corrupt governments. It just bothers me man, sending good people off 'cause we do things the same old way with the same results. It's nuts man. It's such a waste and then the people at the bottom just, I don't see their lives getting any better this way."

"That's a pretty good one, invade by moving van."

"I mean I know it's not practical, but we're such good builders. Why not put all this energy to work making the world a better place. If shit happens, then it's time to bring out the big stick. That's what I like about the Peace Corps, basics man, is what my friend Rick told me. Water, sewage, electricity... teaching people to read, raise food."

"How long did he stay overseas?"

"He did two years, then he came back finished medical school and is going back to the Amazon with the Red Cross. He loves it there. There's so much to do man."

"He sounds like a good man."

"I could hook you up with him. Mary say's you're smart, good with your hands, good with languages. Lots of things you could help with. Rick might be able to get you into something really cool. The things he tells me about the Amazon… what a place."

"What about you, Marty?"

"Well, I graduate from University of Pennsylvania next year. I'm thinking I'll go over with Rick for a couple of years then come back and go law school or something. That's what my mom wants me to do."

"Sounds like a great adventure."

"What about it, man? You don't have to do the Army thing."

"I'm signed up Marty, maybe that would have been a good thing to do a month ago, but it's too late. Besides, there's a part of me that really wants to see if I can do it. Go through some of the toughest training around."

"But, Frank man, isn't there a price you pay for that? What if it's not worth it? What if you could take all the energy you put into being this hero guy and make a difference somewhere else? What if you don't make it? Then what?"

"I've met guys who've been through it. My uncle and some of his guys."

"But what if they are the few that can really deal with it, man? What about the others who don't come out so well? I'm not trying to be negative and all, but what if you've only seen the small percentage? My dad…" he takes a deep breath, crosses his legs. "My mom told me he really came back different. She said it was like something was seared shut. He never talks about it… you know the war. Distant when I was growing up." He looks at me, and then looks off through the crowd. "Just makes me wonder if there's a better way. No Nixon lying. No Johnson's brash belief that he could fix everything. No Ford bumbling around."

He's looking down at his hands.

"But how do you know what's right, Marty? What if we did screw up in Vietnam… does that mean we should retreat from our place in the world?"

"You think we should be the world's police force?"

"I don't know, Marty, after all the death and terror of World War II to then have the fucking Russians annex half of Europe and bring an even worse scourge. What if we'd stood up to them and just kicked their asses? No Berlin wall, no Prague Spring. You talk about people on the bottom getting screwed."

"What if we'd lost? What if we'd won? Do we take on China next? When do you stop, man?"

"Isn't that the risk you have to take?"

"Well, man. I don't know. I don't want to be a bummer, like you said it's a party, man. Don't let them change you. You seem like a good dude. I've known Mary since we were little. She's great. She really likes you."

"I bet she was a hellion."

"You said it. Hey, I'm going to go grab a beer, you want something?"

"No thanks."

"Okay, I'll come back. We can rap some more. Think about what I said. There are always options. My father's a doctor, who knows maybe you fell, your equilibrium is thrown off and you can't serve. There are always choices, man."

Nodding, moving so he can get by.

Chair behind me shaking as it feels like two bodies plopping down.

Seeing Mary's shapely leg in front of me, she's holding two paper cups and hands them to me before sitting down. Looking at the light tan liquid at the bottom.

"What's this?"

"I snitched some of Dad's good stuff."

"Mary," giving her the joking hairy eyeball.

"Well, it's a party, besides Mom's having a good time as usual and Dad's out there lying about all the fish he caught," she takes a little sip. Following her lead—burning, bitter—a sort of sweet after taste.

"Tastes like seaweed," licking my lips like I've been given nasty medicine. The alcohol making my mouth, throat and stomach feel warm. "What is this?"

"It's Irish Whiskey, Jameson. Dad's favorite. Well Mom's too."

"Oh, this is what she's been knocking down," taking another small sip. Yuck. "She seems to drink a lot of this stuff?"

"They joke about the Irish thing," she said taking a sip and making a face. "You like it?"

"Not really, but I want to be a big girl tonight."

"You start smoking and I'll sock you one, Mary O'Connor."

"Eccchh, I hate that."

She takes another drink, smiles. Another couple of sips and I'm starting to feel warmer, the cigarette smoke and all the people become less present. Less noise, more Mary as we snuggle into each other.

"Let's take a walk on the beach. I feel cooped up."

"Okay," she smiles one of her mischievous little smiles.

"What?"

"Walk, sure…" she's giving me a mocking look. Shrugging my shoulders. "We shouldn't duck out for too long though," as she walks close to me.

Strong wind blowing in from the sea. Little light coming in from the thin sliver of the waning crescent moon—dark sky alive with stars. Cool air, feeling her arm around me, my toes in the sand, walking silently away from the house.

Peeking around the small dunes to check the angles.

Giggling as we take our clothes off. Laying out my jeans so she's got a little something between her and the sand.

Cool wind circling up from the sea.

Lips connected, she's giggling a little.

Lying on the hard sand, losing myself in her.

Insane heat and pressure inside my body—trying to contain it.

"Go baby, go all out," she calls into my ear.

My body plunging in, taking her with me, moving her.

"Oh, oh," on each sinking, probing thrust.

"Yes, I can feel it Frank, I want you to come."

Body losing all control, shuddering, jerking inside her as she holds me close to her. "Yes, oh you feel so good," hugging me, kissing me.

"I," talking to her from a place a long way away, "I can't believe how good this is, Mary, how good that felt." Catching my breath, "I feel almost selfish."

"Shh, you feel wonderful," pushing her hips up into me. "Hmm, so connected to my body." Softly, "the rush of warmth inside me when you come is so intense."

Kissing her, my body responding to her words, my cock moving in her warmth slowly reaching for her, bringing her to where I'd been.

Filling a circle in my heart.

Taking a long circle around the house.

"Let's split up," she squeezes my hand, still feeling the sand between my toes. "You go around back and see if there's a volleyball game going. I'll move through the front."

Wind against my back from the sea.

Looking at her as we walk—I don't want to go back in there. Mind flashing to us going our own way—go hang by the beach all night, get a couple of sleeping bags and zip them together. Turning, damn, waited too long—she's off. Breathing in the sea air. Smell of her on my fingers, closing my eyes, trying to live in the intensity of what I feel when I come—what she feels like.

Music from the house spilling out into the crowded backyard, people laughing and cheering on the young fools out on the sand volleyball court.

Stopping by the makeshift bar, filling a paper cup with water—downing it and filling it again. "Hey, get in here," one of the kids waving to me, taking my shirt off and getting on the court. The lady Mrs. O'Connor introduced to me giving me the once over along with a couple of the local girls—ignoring them.

"Where do you want me?"

"Down front," he looks across the net. "Time to even things up now, heh, heh."

Serving, moving.

Not going too hard on them. Waving to Mary as she comes out.

Her dad making the rounds.

Her mom fluttering around—man she's hitting the booze pretty hard as she knocks down another glass of whiskey. Laughing away with her friends. Maybe she was bombed last night. Maybe she won't remember.

"Your serve, Superman."

"Okay, Freddie."

Easy serve over the net—bumping the weak spike up, the neighbor girl, Nancy misses an easy one.

"You'll get it next time," as people start grousing about her missing again.

Laughing as Mary gets down on the other side of the net across from me like a football player.

"I'm taking you down, big boy," she yells, people are laughing.

Not too hard spike past her.

"Hey," she wags her finger at me, "I'm gonna get you for that, Buster."

Taking a break from the game—party starting to slow down. Kids are back to coupling up and getting into groups they know. Mary talking to some of her friends, stretching, hungry—need to pee. Feeling a little woozy from the last glass of scotch that Mary sneaked for us—don't know why people like this stuff, stomach feels acidic. Mouth watering for some food, too bad this pack of wolves took apart the fish we caught.

Rummaging around in the kitchen.

Pickles, American cheese slices, white bread, some milk—yuck. Keep looking—eggs, onions, some old Parmesan cheese. Time to whip up a quick scramble and some toast. People cruising in and out of the kitchen.

"Smells good," some guy I've not seen before, short well cut black hair—button down shirt, jeans. He looks at me, a little long. "Hi, I'm Scott, you did that well," now he strikes a pose, his cologne reaching over. I get it.

"I'm going to eat this before it gets cold," getting some polite space between us.

"Where has Claire been hiding you?" he starts to act cute.

"My first time here," taking a mouthful, stomach feeling calmer, "Mary invited me, we go to high school together."

"Oh, God," he moves back, "you don't look like a high schooler."

Shrugging my shoulders.

Not meeting his eyes, ignoring him while he's checking me out.

"Well, if you want to play, come find me," he wiggles his eyebrows.

Polite fuck you smile as he leaves—fat chance, ass-master.

Cleaning up after my snack—body feeling better, stomach less acidic, head clearer. Putting the big frying pan away in the pantry, drying it off. A crowd has moved back to the kitchen. Stepping out of the small pantry, Mrs. O'Connor and a couple of her friends talking and smoking—opening up cans of Planters Mixed Nuts, pouring most of them into a bowl.

"Oh, how sad and he seems like such a nice young man."

About to turn around and head out the side door.

"The Aaarmy of all places, what a boorish thing to do. What's Mary thinking? She's always had such good taste."

"Maybe she'll get over him when he's gone."

"What do you think, Claire?" standing in the shadows, stomach starting to boil.

Fucking bitches.

"Well, you know," she shrugs her shoulders like she doesn't care. "Love me, love my dog, I guess."

Shaking my head, repeating what I heard to myself. Body reacting. Her Freudian book friend touches her on the arm and motions toward me. My face flushing, hands flexing into fists. Her mom looks at me as shame moves through my body.

"What a horrible thing to say about someone."

"Frank, look now," she blinks her eyes.

"I'm a boor," looking at her uptight, prig friend, "why because I don't sit around and write books about why people are afraid of sex... Jesus lady, when was the last time you even saw a cock?"

"That's enough!" Claire's body moving from an anxious pose to indignation, her friends looking embarrassed.

"I may come from a working class family, but goddammit, when we don't like someone, we tell them to their face, not the big smile and..." she's pushing her friends back to the party and stepping toward me. She backs me up away from the crowd. Her friends looking over their shoulders—horrified.

"Enough of this! Don't you know when to stop," she pushes me back toward the pantry away from everyone else, her face on fire.

"I don't know when to stop?" breathing hard, fire burning in my chest meeting the fire in her eyes, I can't stand the hypocrisy. "Like maybe you'll leave the door open again tonight?" Her eyes opening wide in shock, furious look on her face. Slap stinging my face.

"You beast, you animal," her face red, enraged, "get out!" hissing at me. Cheek smarting. Import of what I'd done hitting me. Jesus Frank, you fucking blew it! Looking up at the ceiling, taking a deep breath—what an hour ago I was with her near the sea, and now look at what I've done. I just couldn't let them have their little...

Fucking shit. Fucking cunt bitches.

Frank, oh you stupid, stupid man.

Putting my shirt around my neck.

Walking through the crowded hallway, head down, sound of the party muted.

What, do I pack my stuff and say goodbye to Mary? See her in the city if she'll still want anything to do with me? I'll walk the miles to the train station. Closing my eyes as I step in the room—looks like people have been in here. The bed all messed up by a quickie.

Staring stupidly at the guest room.

We never know the last time do we, Frank? Moments ago the world was so full of promise and then I can't keep my mouth shut. Smelling Mary on my skin.

Losing track of time in the disgust of the moment.

Fuck, fuck, fuck—how do I recover from this?

Door opening behind me.

"Mary, it's not..." turning around, what the fuck am I going to say? Shock, feeling my body turn rigid for a moment—her mom, "I'm..."

Door closing, she's leaning back—her hands on the doorknob.

Her face reddened—tense. Wordless torrid silence.

Anger, frustration, pain welling up inside me—voices fighting to get out. Body shocked by the feeling of her across the room—like something from the deep earth rising up inside me from her, warm earth smell, long roots reaching up from within the rich fragrant earth.

Standing there locked in her eyes.

Blushing at the reaction to her.

"You need to learn when to shut up," it feels like her legs are parting slightly.

Feeling dizzy.

Keeping the words inside locked up. Do I shut up now? Do I say there's a heat coming off you that's slowly filling the room, making it harder for me to breathe?

Just watching her, if she reached out and touched me, I know I couldn't resist. Feeling my head slightly spinning. I won't move though.

"That's..." she looks down, her toes stretching and gripping the carpet, her body tense for a few moments, "sometimes we say things to mask what we don't want to acknowledge, I'm sorry you heard that no..."

She's breathing slowly but with more effort.

Body feels like it's rooted in the ground I stand on—petrified.

"I'm sorry I said that and that's going to have to be good enough."

Moments passing, the clear blue of her eyes rising up like a giant wave and crashing into me, I can see us in my mind—her body flashing in from last night, the rich pubic hair—the earthy taste of her, our bodies moving with abandon, knowing how she'll surrender to it, how we'd revel in it.

Hands sweating.

The door closing behind her as she leaves.

Sitting down on the narrow bed, cold shiver going through me.

Her words, "It's okay, my friends won't say anything, they know me."

Confused, disgusted, angry...

What if she's just fucking with me?

Drunken witch who likes to play with fire.

What a bitch! What horrible people!

Wishing I could just vomit them all out of my body.

Clean air hitting my face—noise of the house fading in the low ocean roar, sand crunching under my feet, Mary telling me she'll meet me down here in a few minutes.

Shaking my head—she doesn't even know.

Does her dad know?

My God! What fucking assholes.

Stretching out my stride. Clothes off quickly and dumped in a tangled pile like seaweed cast out at high tide. Cold, cold water and sand suspended in the shallow water hitting my face—welcome shock to my body as I wade in. Running again, knees pumping high to get over the water—strong current pulling out after the last wave.

Free for a moment diving through the next wave—needing the body punches as I'm thrashed by the powerful wave. No jetties here to break up the flow—full force.

Yes!

Up, strong strokes out to sea. Dive under the next wave—room to swim now. Shaking the water out of my hair, toes touching the sandy bottom—turning and looking toward shore, treading water. Light of their house in the distance—empty beach.

Breaking into a strong crawl stroke parallel to the shore, body rising and falling with the waves.

Stroke after stroke—knowing my distance perception in the ocean is off at first, what feels like fifteen minutes is just a few minutes, settling for a long swim. Driving my muscles to squeeze out the shame.

Fuck, here I am, and I can't stop thinking about this—asshole.

Swimming harder. Out of breath, treading water. Shit, I've vectored out to sea. Kicking up and then stroking up with my arms as I surface dive feet first—toes touching down, probably fifteen feet of water. Floating on my back my tippy toes out of the water. Floating into the rolling waves out here beyond the break line—catching my breath looking at the sky.

I want this to work with Mary.

If her mom raises a shitstorm, then so be it.

Calm spreading through me, scrubbing my face with cold salt water. I'm not going to quit. Fuck that witch.

Relaxed pace back to shore.

Letting time pass. Not feeling anything close to the bottom yet—looking up, shit, long way to go. Doubling down—swimming harder.

Breath starting to come harder—looking up, what the hell is going on? Keeping my head out of the water while I do some strong breaststrokes—going backwards. Panic rising as I start to tire, mouth starting to water, head spinning—acidic juices spreading up.

Throwing up—inhaling water, coughing, throat stinging.

Spitting out—deep breath, dive under the water. Cold feels good, strings of mucous washing away from my mouth.

Fucking rip tide—stupid, stupid.

Flipping over on my back, worried at how much energy I'd expended stupidly. Floating on my back, cold shiver starting to go through my body. Sculling on my back—let this carry me out. Breathe—panic now and I'm dead meat. Recoup what you can. Swim parallel to the shore, relax you can make it.

Lights along shore receding, teeth starting to chatter.

Thirty yards or so to go, body knows it's in a death struggle—I won't give up. Switch to sidestroke—move parallel to the shore, maybe slightly back toward land. Moving easier now, muscles sore, tired, cold. Arms slapping at the water versus strong strokes—switching between crawl, breaststroke, sidestroke as each muscle group tires. Calf muscles starting to cramp, curling up in a ball, grabbing my toes and pulling up, massaging as pain ripples up.

Ragged, stumbling in the rough surf, puking up raw stomach acids. Blackness creeping in—my vision starting to recede into the distance. Surge coming up from my stomach.

"No," coughing, punching the water.

"No," kicking hard toward the shore.

Wave pounding me, rolling me over, feet touching the bottom, lungs screaming for air—insane thrust up, face breaking out.

"No!" Another wave of nausea grips me, acid bile spitting up.

"Rrrrrrrr," pushing forward and cupping water in my shivering hands. Washing my mouth out with sandy water, spitting it out. Waves pushing, then pulling me back out, losing my balance. Rolling, holding on.

Pushing forward again. I fucking want to live!

Crawling on to shore—chest heaving trying to force oxygen into my raw lungs, lying back on the cold sand—body shivering, teeth chattering, eyes closed.

Sick laugh pushing out into the dark night.

Warm. Need to get warm.

On my stomach, crawling to a semi upright position.

Reeling like a drunkard.

Jesus is this even the right way.

Blinking my eyes—ocean on the right, okay.

Arms crossed on my chest—dick like a little shriveled peanut pulled way up in my body, chest and stomach matted with sand. Teeth chattering, stumbling along, hands rubbing hard on my arms and chest.

"Mmmorron," can't even fucking speak.

Feel like I'm walking through sloshy Jell-O.

People up ahead.

Keep it together man.

"Hey," calling to me, waving now.

Uneven steps forward—kid from the party, Marty.

"We've," he comes jogging up. "Oh, no way man, that's crazy!" blinking to get him in focus, walking to where my clothes are piled up—got to get something warm on. Ignoring him as I walk forward.

"You went swimming out there?"

"WWhhat, ittts looks like."

"Here," he's waving to another sets of douche bags, "I found him!" looking over for a second, back to finding my stuff.

"Mary's all worried, she brought us out."

"Ggg-go fffind some mmatches or ssssomething… sstart a fire out here."

"Cool," he's still waving, idiot.

"What's going on?" Carly, Darren and a wave of bozos come toward me while I try to find my clothes. There—finally. Walking—pain shooting up, stubbed my damn toe on a big piece of driftwood. Shaking trying to put my pants on, hopping around like an idiot, knocking as much sand off as I can, kicking my underwear away, gift to the beach gods. Sand in the crack of my ass feels like sandpaper rubbing around in there. Shivering as I put on my shirt. Rubbing my arms and legs as hard as I can.

People's voices becoming distinct.

"Pisser, a beach fire."

"Get more driftwood," said Marty as he comes back arms full. Kids starting to fan out as more come down the dune from the house. Hands shaking as I break up smaller pieces of driftwood—jokers have brought too much big stuff. Fishing my small pocketknife out of my pants, blade locking in—be careful Frank, this sucker is sharp. Shaking while I shave off uneven bits of wood from what looks like an old fence post, lucky the wood is soft.

"DDddon't," as Carly drops a log on my small pile of shavings. "Nneed smaller, kkkay?" Building up the teepee of shavings and smaller splinters.

"You don't look very good."

"Mmmorning person," as I break up inch thick tangles of trees— throwing the damp in a different pile. Think that's Calvin starting to help out.

"That's not funny," said Carly.

"Jesus Frank! Where have you been?" catching Mary's outline.

"Occceannn, bbbad idea."

"You sure have a keen sense of the obvious, it's dangerous out there, bad rip tides this time of year," she puts her hands on my arms and then my face. "You're freezing!"

"Fffire."

"What do you want me to do? I should get you back to the house get you in some hot water."

"Nnnno, the, this wwill be okay, mmatches?"

"I got some," must be Marty, can't really see.

"You, you guys lie down, bbblock wwind."

They look at me, pointing to the ground in front of the fire, getting worried that I can't even strike the matches. Lying down, cradling my hands, striking three paper matches together bringing them slowly to the twigs—flickering out. Moving closer now—blinking my eyes—moving some of the larger kindling aside to cup the really small stuff. Tiny flame sprouts up. Protecting it from the wind, carefully adding larger kindling to the fire. Warmth dancing in my eyes but I can't feel it—flickering light shows Mary's outline.

Slowly putting more wood on, laying thinner pieces across in a box pattern now that I have a little going. Shit too much. Leaning in, blowing low on the fire—got to fight to re-ignite the flame, put too much on too fast. Smoke rising, lucky finding a few shavings to bring in—my hands should have felt the heat from that. Nothing.

Flames sprouting up again, head dizzy from all the blowing. Ignoring the comments behind me as the fire starts spreading quickly—relaxing a little. Rubbing my hands and putting them near the flame. Totally focused on the life saving flames dancing in the ocean wind.

"Mmary, that's good," taking my eye off the fire for a second. "Can, can you get a bbblanket or something?"

"Don't you go anywhere, Mister," outlines of a worried look. More kids bringing wood over, getting a couple of big ass logs in place to serve a base over the small fire—shit, wrong direction, moving them around—people annoyed that I'm moving them around. Laying more wood on top, flames catching and climbing, steam starting to escape from the core of a couple the thicker pieces. Warmth starting to creep in, feels almost painful, kneeling and sitting upright to capture some of the flame.

Good blaze going, rubbing my arms and chest—sand stuck to the peach fuzz on my chest feels weird underneath my damp shirt, standing up now to get my legs exposed to the heat—turning around, just like basting a big Italian turkey.

Marty handing me a bottle of something.

Yuck, strong taste—shitty whiskey, stomach warming though.

"Thanks," wiping my lips with the back of my hand and giving it back.

"Take another drink man."

"No, it will come back up."

He shrugs his shoulders and sits back down leaning back against a log, Mary throwing something on me—thick, rough.

"That's good," sitting down wrapping it around me. She's pulling it tight around me, putting her arms around me.

"Don't do things like that, Frank... you," she grabs a handful of hair and pulls it a little bit, pulling me to her face, "you really had me scared, I was about to get my dad and everyone."

Fire roaring up—lots of kids tending to it now. Still shivering, slowly warming up, radio turned on, couples dancing by the fire, beer and bottles of whiskey being passed around.

"Just needed to…"

"What, Frank?"

"I don't know, seemed like a good idea at the time."

"Man, you're lucky," said Marty taking another swig from his pint.

"Yeah," said Freddie and his blonde little girlfriend nodding. "Guy fishing the shore break last year got pulled out, caught in the rip, never found him."

"What a way to go," his little blonde shivers at the idea.

"It's a nasty rip, had to swim out then down a hundred yards."

"You are so lucky, man," said Marty. "You want another?"

Shaking my head.

"I'll warm up faster if you're in here," looking at Mary.

She looks at me and starts patting my arm to lift it up so I can make room. Body feeling better—warmth settling in.

"What am I going to tell my parents?"

Shrugging my shoulders, running through some sick ideas—gee Mom after you made a pass at him a cold shower wasn't enough and he almost drowned. Shaking my head.

"What? Is everything all right? We had such a good time you know and now you seem really distant."

"Just cold, Mary, it will pass, lose too much body heat and things really slow down. Stupid of me to worry you like this."

She snuggles in, putting my arm around her, face feeling flushed from the fire. Kids passing around various bottles snatched from their houses or Mary's house. Most of the kids up and dancing around the fire, being ignored feels good. Sand kicked our way by accident by Marty and Kevin as they wrestle around.

Looking out to the cold, clean ocean, the moon reflecting in the waves coursing toward the shore, breaking on the beach, leaving thin sheets of water to push up and then fall back to the sea.

"Tell them we had a good fire down by the beach."

She moves away, looks at me. Not buying it, but not pushing it.

"Things went too fast this weekend."

"Nice if it were only us out here."

"Hmm," she pulls herself in.

"Keep this between us Mary, please."

Letting the vision of her witch mother get pulled down into the watery depths, seaweed tendrils wrapping slowly around her as the warmth of Mary's body spreads through me.

Early morning LIRR train in the distance.

Checking to see if her dad can see us from the car.

Hugging her again, she looks down at my waist and smiles.

"I'll see you in the City tomorrow, okay Mr. Strong Silent type who almost drowned himself," turning to the side a little, she rubs her hip against me, "I'll be home alone till nine or so," she smiles.

"Okay, Mary," she turns a little, catching her arm, pulling her back to me—putting my hands on her bottom and pulling her close. Looking into her wonderful green blue eyes for a few moments, so much of her mom—unspoiled, fresh, the deep smell of sex awakening in her, I wonder if she'll live in the same dangerous passionate place. Shaking my head to keep the vision of last night from coming back.

"It's going to be so hard to leave at the end of the summer," she's nodding along with me, "I..." rush of emotion, it's up to me not to let what almost happened ruin what can really happen.

"What, Frank?" a wonderful freshness in her eyes, her face.

Kissing her lightly on the nose, her lips.

"I'm really falling in love with you, Mary... deep, hard. At first I didn't know what this was other than it felt really good, but now," looking at her, lost for words.

Standing on her tippy toes.

"That makes me feel so warm inside, Frank," she looks down for a moment, her arms around my shoulders, "it used to make me hurt inside seeing you at school."

"Thank you for believing in me, Mary."

"I love you, Frank, of course I believe in you."

Chapter 59

Tough body check inside—trading hard elbows fighting for the rebound—just quick enough, whipping the ball down the court, Ivan going up for a smooth layup, slapping him five on the way back.

"Good break."

"Good pass, Doc."

"Ten-two," he calls out to the court.

"Fuck you man, it's ten-four," Mr. Big Mouth getting the inbound pass and talking more trash. Shaking my head.

"Four my motherfuckin ass," said Ivan getting pissed—I get it, this dipshit has been pulling this all day.

"You scored one, this dude scored one, that's all," backing up Ivan.

"You calling me a liar," he's looking mean at me.

"I'm saying you can't count for shit, take it from there or shut the fuck up—this ain't no score by powers of two game my man," as I backpedal down the court to get back on defense. He's grumbling calling for the ball—I've played Ray before, he's gonna try and post me up—then pop out to try a quick jump shot.

"Quit pushing me," the big mouth is dribbling around with guys open.

"Pass the ball, man," from Antwan as he cuts down the lane.

"Shut up and play nigger, you get your ass open, I'll hit you."

Ivan needling him, pushing him back to maintain position.

"You couldn't hit shit you Helen Keller playing motherfucker."

Guys on the court and on the sidelines breaking up at that.

"Man, fuck you!" he's trying to juke Ivan off balance, he turns his back—burst of speed toward him, he's still not paying attention to anyone else but Ivan. Batting the ball forward, he tries to grab at me, pushing it forward full speed, spring down the smooth asphalt court—big step beyond the foul line, feeling free, big leap, ball high in the air—moments of joy, hard slam dunk. Guys on the sidelines waiting for the next game or watching start holding their heads, calling out "oooooo", slapping five, talking trash.

"That's eleven, Mr. Math," said Ivan. "You can walk your ass off the court."

"Fuck you, I was fouled, it's our ball."

Chorus of bullshit coming from on the court and from the sidelines, I'm waving my hands, yelling, "Next." Guys telling him to sit down, stop the punk train, walking up to me and slapping me five, Mr. Big Mouth's own guys are waving him away. Seeing Hector walking up to the court.

"Who's got next run?" Joaquin yelling.

"Yo, Antwan," his strong shoulders turning toward me, sweat running down his face, his bald head, "good game, man!"

"Good game man," brother handshake.

"I'm done, I got to go," called Peter.

"Ah shit man," said Ivan, as Peter starts to towel off.

"Yo Ivan, pick up Hector, he can play," he nods.

"Pick me up, I can deal," said Mr. Big Mouth.

Ivan shaking his head, "Hector, you ready to run?"

"Man, pick a brother," said Mr. Big Mouth.

"Shiiiit, pick a motherfucker who can't play and can't pass. That'd be the shit."

"Man, fuck all y'all!"

He storms out, guys laughing, telling him goodbye sweetie and shit.

Feet feel raw, body tired—sweat pours down my body.

"Damn that was a close one," sitting down and leaning back on a bowed out section of chain link fence next to Ivan and Hector—he's rubbing his ankle, slight grimace on his face

Looking at him work his leg, "That was a hard fall, good thing the season's over. Coach would be pissed if you got laid up playing street ball." He puts a towel on his face.

"I thought Julio was coming down, man."

"Hell Frank, he's you know..."

"Hey, I'll catch you bitches later," said Ivan getting up. "Time to go make some money."

"See you later, you elevator operating motherfucker," to Ivan as he heads out. Hector laughing, giving me five and loose shake with a flash of his white teeth.

"Man, just cause you can play doesn't mean you can talk shit."

"Hey man, I learned from The Master," pointing at him, he laughs.

Feels good hanging here—like time and all the bad things I've done have rolled back for a little while. If only Alton and Julio were here, we would be the team ruling the courts. Well, most of the time anyway.

"So what's up with Julio, man?"

"Mira loco Frank, think man, for a smart dude, you're pretty..."

Looking at him. No. Shaking my head.

"You're kidding?"

"He's scared of you, man!"

"Fuck that bitch!"

Hector shrugs his shoulders.

"I'm a have to call that young man, I'd rather be tight," shaking my head. "If he wants to deal with all her bullshit..." twinge inside me, "well, that's his business."

"You sure?"

Another argument breaking out on the court—guys crowding around two guys playing the dozens. Older guys starting to show up after work—the half courts further up the park are filled up now.

"I'm sure," looking into his jet black eyes for a minute. Hector shrugs and watches the court action for a few minutes.

"What's your thing with Mary?"

Listening to a couple of good your mother's so fat, she gets a cut, she drips gravy and your mother's so stupid she got fired from her job at the sperm bank for drinking on the job.

"Man, it's crazy, it's different," stretching my legs out. "She's got so much more freedom than Cat. Man, like we've been going at it after school, her parents go away for the weekend sometimes... I like her Dad and all, her mom..."

"She on your case?" he gives me an elbow. "Got to protect her daughter from the bad street boy?"

"Sheeiit," uncomfortable feeling spreading over me, "got to protect me from her. There was some weird shit that went down man. Her mom's been weird since."

Hector looking at me, "You're fuckin with me, right?"

"This is no bullshit, man," checking him out. "You ever seen her mom?" putting my thumb and forefinger together and slowly shaking it back and forth. "Que bella," image of her long legs flashing up from the depths. "It was crazy man," looking out at the game.

"You gonna leave me hanging?"

"You can't talk about this at school," looking at him. "Man I'm serious, you tell little Marta there, she'll blab all over school. I will fuck you up."

"Nah man, I promise"

Taking a deep breath, "So dig this, I needed to get up and take a piss the first night I'm there. So it's quiet in their house, I walk to the bathroom near the room they put me in. Man I was still kind of groggy but I knocked on the door right? Nothing. I walked in," images of her body flashing in my mind, "I was hot and all so I had my pajama bottoms... I step in and there's her mom getting out of a bath, I don't know if she thought I was her old man or something, but I'm standing there with this big ass hard on pushing out my pj's like a fucking tent pole, and this bitch is looking at me, checking me out."

"Oh, man," his body starts swaying side to side.

"So I got embarrassed, mumbled about being sorry and backed out, but man... For having two kids and all, what a beauty, rich skin, breasts and all. And she wasn't shy, she was looking right at my dick man, then at my chest, she was checking me out man."

"Oh shit," he cringes.

"Right, so that could happen man, right? Dude makes a wrong turn, you apologize and you back off right? No harm no foul and all that bullshit."

"Sure man," he shrugs. "So what's the deal, mano?"

"So I went to another bathroom, right. Check this out, when I left her I know I closed the door and backed out."

"So?"

"When I walked back past the bathroom on my way back," shudder going through my body. "She'd opened the door like that," holding my fingers a few inches apart. "She was there, shaving her legs, her coochie hair just visible enough, she saw me looking and looked back, man, seconds, but it seemed like…"

"Man, Frankie, how you get in these fucked up situations, man?"

"I'm a shit magnet or something," frustration boiling up inside.

"Magnet for crazy bitches who want some of that hot Italian," he's laughing, nudging me with his elbow, other guys looking over to see what Hector's onto. "So if Mary's not in the picture, would you have done her? Gotten some of that nasty Mrs. Robinson action 'n shit?"

Thinking about the witch when she came in my bedroom.

"That would have been a dangerous place to go man… witch woman like that, man," shaking her out of my head. "You do crazy things, think crazy things," watching the action on the court, another game starting up. "But it's like I'm not going to trade something good with Mary for some crazy shit like that." Need to get up and walk, shake off the image of her mom.

"Let's walk up to the neighborhood and get something cold to drink."

He's still thinking, getting up slowly, his sleeveless sweatshirt soaked, putting on his headband and wristbands. "Man, I'm not going to be able to check out her mom without acting funny."

"I will fuck you up, Hector!" smiling seeing if he's jiving.

"Got to catch me first, fool," and he starts dancing around like Ali. Laughing feeling lighter about the whole thing.

"Hector, man, let's go fuck with Julio."

He starts laughing, "I'll get him to come out, you're there acting all mad," he's laughing. "Got to give me some skin on that."

Feels good to be walking my old neighborhood with Hector.

Sidewalks busy. Jiving with people we know here and there.

Turning east. Kids playing stickball in the street stopping and giving the finger to car that dares interrupt their game.

Voices in the narrow hallway, Hector jiving with Julio.

"…they're not going tonight. Anyway Mom's working, I'll hang…" Julio turning and stops dead when he sees me.

"Julio, my man!" standing up, acting all amped up, waving my arms back-and-forth.

"Oh shit man, oh man," looking at Hector like he'd been stabbed.

"It's not right, man," surprised at his face, "I ain't gonna run."

"Time to come clean," acting hard.

Looking at him, he's really upset his body trembling—adrenaline must be kicking in. Fighting off the urge to keep pushing it, he's really squirming. Taking a breath, relaxing my body.

"Julio," breathing to stay calm, this still bothers me that he's picked up with Cat. "Hector told me," smiling. "Look man, we've been tight since IS 44, I'm messing with you." He looks unsure. "I'm done with Catherine, don't..." his body relaxing a little, looking at Hector suspiciously, "don't let it mess everything up we've been through as friends, okay?"

He nods, pushes Hector, "You maricon motherfucker," who stumbles down the step and lands on this feet in front of an old lady pushing a cart. She whacks at him with her purse—Hector starts laughing, Julio and I laughing at him while he ducks away from another swing of the killer purse.

"Yo, you missed some good run today," said Hector as we head uptown. "All worried 'n shit about getting your ass busted by Mr. C. here."

"Man, fuck both a you!"

Feels good being with these two geniuses. People weaving around them as they do a mock boxing match, shouting curses at each other in Spanish and laughing.

Good feeling lingering, body feels cold as the sweat dries off—people staying away from me in the subway when they get a good whiff of my nasty, sweaty body, car too crowded for them to move away much.

Tomorrow those two will be in school—Julio will be with Cat, twinge of missing her. Mary will be there too—I'll be doing what? Working out—doing chores and then off to the library until she gets out of school.

Watching Mary study at her desk in my shirt that's almost long enough for her to use as a robe. Her legs looks fresh, her foot dangling down over her leg crossed underneath her body, lightly swinging back and forth.

Staring up at her ceiling.

Invitation to a boxing match at the Garden with her dad coming up tomorrow. Do I go? Staying away, acting guilty—taking a deep breath. Just 'cause this is tough doesn't mean that I'm going to give up. I've put the witch in a big trunk, put chains and locks on it and dropped it into the deep ocean. This is real. This is what I want.

Cat so fiery, so fierce at times then unwilling to take the step to get what she wants. Maybe she didn't really want it? Uncomfortable feeling coming over me—maybe I was too impatient with her. Was that it? Did I blow that up?

Mary's so calm on the surface—underneath though flexible spring steel, not afraid of what she feels, not afraid to need, to want. Maybe Cat's so used to being the object of desire, always being chased, she doesn't have this—but look at Mary's mom, probably hounded after too, but the hunger there.

How am I going to leave this behind?

Chapter 60

"You've sure been chipper lately."

"What?" snapping out of pulling up weeds mode.

"You," said Aunt Kitty as the outline of her standing with her hands on her hips comes into focus.

"What's that, Aunt Kitty?" shaking my head.

"You've been happier lately," she's smiling standing there in her gardening outfit—a mishmash of old comfortable clothes, scarf over her head, smudge of dirt on her nose and well-worn work gloves. "It's nice to see."

Nodding to her, smiling.

"Well, we've got all those ratty old tomato plants out."

"It's nice to see you smile again, Frank," she's looking at me.

"What?"

She's rolling her eyes, and laughing, "She's good for you."

Feeling my face flush. Wiping the sweat off my face from working in the warm early summer sun, smell of earth on my hands, body feels good doing a good job here for my aunt.

"She sure is," looking at the clean sky over the neighboring brownstones.

Looking around at the yard.

"This what you wanted?"

"Yes," she's looking pleased. "Vin's been holding this over my head for weeks now."

"He's hardly…" looking at her.

"I know, he's so busy with his new job. It means so much to him." She takes a deep breath. "Well, I have my favorite nephew here, I guess that will have to do!"

"You have your best nephew here!" smiling as I dodge her glove.

Picking up my shovel, the thick rusted steel rake and the hoe.

Door open to the garage—the little area she'd given me to work on some of Grandpa T's furniture is nice and clean. Putting the garden tools away and moving to the coolness of my little work area—at least my prick father let me get my tools.

Running my hand lightly over the last coat of shellac I'd put on the card table. Nice and smooth, kneeling down to look at it from different angles. Grandpa T would like this. My eyes wandering over the precision of his work—the finish even in the areas where no one would look was done to perfection. That was his way—make everything the best.

Dad used to be like that.

Is that one of the things that's been nagging at me? All the things he used to tell me about quality work when I was a kid, how good it used to feel to work together. My uncles laughing at me with my little tool belt—trying so hard to do good woodwork, Grandpa T yelling at them telling them I was the only craftsman in the house. Has that been nagging at him all this time? What he's compromised to make ends meet? The fast work his guys turn out… But that's their business—shows have to be ready by a certain date, the audience can't see what's behind the set anyway. Maybe he misses the clean feeling of…

"Come in the house, Frank, I'm making some lemonade."

Garage snaps back into focus.

"Okay, Aunt Kitty," looking my work over. This is ready.

Carrying the table into the house.

"I think this is ready."

She's already changed into a light summer dress—she must have some I-Dream-of-Genie power, snap she's fresh, either that or I'm a space case.

"Oh," she looks at me, "your uncle will be so happy. He loves the old pieces from his father."

"It feels good to give something back, he's always so, you know looking out for everyone else, so busy."

"Shh, this has been really good for him, to have you here, to see you getting yourself together."

Cold, sweet, tart soothing my throat, "That's good."

"Have some more, you worked hard out there."

"You sure you're Italian, Aunt Kitty?" smiling, I know this will drive her crazy. She throws a rag at me.

"I'll show you Italian," giving me what for.

Few people on the midday train out to Rockaway.

Standing up front next to the conductor's booth, eyes fixed on the stretch of open water ahead of us. It would be so cool to be able to open the door and lean out into the wind coming toward us, letting the wind hold me up. Letting the loneliness of the train heading out over Jamaica Bay fill me.

This is my world.

Adjusting the backpack with my boxing gear and two five pound bags of sand. In another two months, I'll be able to do my long loop out here with twenty pounds. Looking at the calluses showing up on my hands from all the rope climbing and bar work I've been doing. Outside shot repeatability going to hell—but I'll be damned if I'm going to fail the Ranger qualification cause I can't do enough pull ups. Making sure my boots are tied snug—wiggling my toes.

Rockaway rising up in the distance.

The long boardwalk up in my vision—three miles and then into the hell sand then take the bus from Riis Park over to Coney Island.

Later tonight, I'll be back with my aunt and uncle—this will all be gone.

Closing my eyes—holding Mary's lovely eyes in my vision, wishing I could take her with me. Imagining her in class—let's see two o'clock, what, that's social studies today. The classroom coming into vision, where I used to sit—seeing the cocky fuck I used to be making fun of people.

Invigorating beach air.

Running by the slowly decaying beach houses. Stopping here and there to throw some combinations—elderly couple slowly walking down the aging boardwalk looking at me like I'm nuts.

Sweats drenched. Sprint to the end of the boardwalk.

Into the sand, baby.

Slowing my pace a little, staying in the deep sand as long as I can, running till my thighs and lungs scream. Make it hurt—I'm going to be in the best shape of all the guys showing up for basic. Body screaming in pleasure at how much this hurts and how much I've gained over the last couple of months.

Last look at the ocean, jogging in place—head swimming a little. Heading up along the road along Riis Park to catch the bus over to Coney Island.

Shoulders burning, rushing to the bathroom as my stomach retches up. Hand over my face to keep it down, eyes watering.

"Damn, boy," as I throw up. Another heave.

Breathing, heart pumping—flushing the nasty toilet.

Washing my mouth out in the sink, spitting out. Looking at my face in the dirty broken mirror—skin flushed, hair still flecked with specks of sand.

Back into to the musky, sweaty long gym hall.

Taking a short drink of nasty water.

Sitting on stool, elbows on my arms, feeling like Gumby with my training headgear. Looking up at the clock—5:20, shit need to get going. Brother I was sparring with calling me over.

"Yo man, you gonna be here tomorrow?"

"Sure will."

"In the ring man, bet," he holds up a taped fist, smiling big hole where he's missing a tooth, his bite plate in his locker.

Tapping his fist with my glove "You got it, Big T."

Ribs feeling his hard shots, he's better than me, older than me—but that's the only way to get better. Keep showing up; keep working hard with better fighters.

Wringing the sweat out of my T-shirt.

"What the fuck you got in there, man," one of the trainers picking up my backpack.

"Bags of sand, man I know told me it was good training."

"You crazy? Boxers don't train with that shit," he's shaking his head, muttering something. Shrugging my shoulders—Detective Kelly told me to get used to running with weight on my back. Besides I'm not a boxer—I never was.

Chapter 61

Hard walk back up these stairs.

Slow steps. Stopping at the landing.

Familiar sounds and smells—all the times I've been here over the years. Grim smile, I'll never be able to go back to the good times.

Knocking on their door, wishing they weren't here so I could just leave a note. I know that I'd wait here though. I'd come back. They are leaving this summer—North Carolina, just a place on the map to me, kinfolk for Alton and Mrs. Brown. Looking down at my feet on the worn welcome mat.

Her eyes calm, distant as she opens the door slowly, her housedress neat as always, "Hello Frank," she doesn't invite me in, she stands at the door protecting her domain.

"Mrs. Brown. I... Well, I got this for Alton," holding out the new basketball. "Can I... Well, I just wanted to stop by and give it to him."

She stands back a little, slight nod of her head.

"He still tires easily, you be patient now."

"I will, Mrs. Brown, I promise."

Looks like the packing has started already—school's almost out for them all. Mary will be leaving for Europe with the witch soon. Hector and Julio will be hanging out here in the City working during the summer, playing summer league. This is the time the four us would be getting ready for summer leagues together, together...

"You have a deep sadness look in you."

Looking at her, nodding slowly, "Lots of... I don't know how to say it. It's regret, but it's more than that. It's knowing that I can never go back to the way things were," having to take a deep breath to control my emotions, feeling my throat choke up. "It's more than knowing I need to say I'm sorry. I thought I had so much figured out and then," looking at her. "I was found wanting. I was tried and I failed. So much to think about," looking at my feet, eyes watering up. "And it's not that I messed things up for myself," blinking my eyes, stopping speaking to stay in some semblance of control. "The worst part is what's happened to the people who, love..." can't say it.

"It's okay to talk how you feel, honey."

"Who loved me," looking away, eyes sweeping the threadbare carpet, the simple Formica steel dining table, the repaired couch, the uneven bookshelves filled with text books, novels, scrap books. Pictures of her family going back generations—strong, intense, intelligent looking black men and black women.

"That does you well."

She's looking at me now, like she's searching for something.

"You still got such a long way..." she's nodding, searching in my face, speaking in a hushed tone "I feel sad for you, Frank. It's like you've got so much unhappiness to go through till things become clear and even then.

People like you, I don't know where to start. It's like there's a cursed invisible hand that touches with beauty and power, makes them different, leaves a mark. Most people can't see it, some can feel it..."

"I've tried so hard to be different than my father."

"That's not what I'm talking about, honey, but it's got to be the time it takes," she takes a deep breath and looks away. "Let's go see my son, okay?"

Not following her, trying to put her words together, like she was speaking from a long way off. Last time I felt like this... I was up in our tree in Rockaway. I'd climbed as high as I could and watch the sun, sitting there for what felt like hours.

"Come on, Frank," she's calling. Shaking my head to get back here.

Down the dark hallway to Alton's room—she let him have the room that has the view out to the Hudson River. Squeezing my fist as he stands up— he's lost so much weight. His face hollow, the natural grace he had on the court looks lost for a time. His mind knows what he has, but his body is still weak. He doesn't say anything. Boxes in his room. A few posters still on his wall—Walt Frazier, Willis Reade, Oscar Robertson, team pictures. He sees me looking and steps back—sits on his bed.

"I got this for you."

He's looks at me and then looks away. Mrs. Brown stepping out of his room. Deep quiet in here—sitting on the floor.

"It took days and days of showing up at the Garden after the Knicks home games." More sadness coming over seeing that he was looking through old yearbooks. Imagining the pictures of us clowning around in there.

Forcing myself to talk to keep it together.

"Friend of my uncles got me back near the runway to the Knicks locker room. I just asked every time I saw him. Finally he asked me why. Why was I standing there with the little kids? So I told him it was for a friend who loved watching him play, loved his game, a friend who was in the hospital getting better. Frazier came by... he was calling me a chump," smiling as best I can. "But Earl finally signed it, see," holding the ball out to him, the big signature of Earl the Pearl Monroe and get-well Alton on top.

Some life coming into his eyes, "It's for you, something from the City and all," standing up and handing him the ball.

He takes the basketball, holds it weakly and keeps looking down.

"I go away in a few months," sitting back down on the clean but worn parquet wooden floor. "So different than I thought it would be. Things I thought we'd be hanging out doing, getting ready for summer leagues and all now."

Legs crossed, elbows on my legs, head resting in my hands. Hearing the door to his room open for a few moments then close. Time passing in silence, street noise filtering in, day getting hotter.

"Does it still hurt? Is there anything I can do?"

Nothing, he shifts and sits on the floor too.

Looking under his big long desk, "I remember when we'd make those all those crazy paper airplanes and fly them out your window. How we'd sit underneath your big desk trying different things out from that book your mom bought. Your mom getting mad cause people on the street were complaining about them crazy boys."

"Remember at the pool up on 60th, I never laughed so hard in my life. I was crying… my stomach hurt when you were standing behind that guy who was yelling at me for splashing and jumping around. You were mimicking everything he did. He was so pissed cause I couldn't keep a straight face. All of us were laughing."

Taking a deep breath.

"Man, was he pissed."

"You have that gift with people, Frank."

Nodding, not wanting to look up. Hearing the rich tone of his voice. Closing my eyes hard to shut out how I remembered his voice from that day right downstairs.

"When I was on the street…" going to talk about my fan club, people who'd pay to see me fail, but it doesn't sound funny anymore, "so, when do you get fit with the face protector so you can play?"

"Few more months now, probably have to wear it next year."

Sneaking a look. His body turned at a right angle from me facing the window.

"What do you think it's going to be like down South?"

"Man, I remember visitin 'n all. Supposedly the best program's where I'm going. NC State does a lot of local recruiting."

"I bet they'll move you to guard, your jumping and shooting ability will have you skying over those guys. They won't be able to hang with you."

"Maybe," he nods slowly, "going to have to change my game…"

"Mary told me you'd finished honors this year, I'm…"

"She's a good girl," his voice jumping up.

"Yes, she is."

"Jenelle still getting chased off by your moms?"

He gives a weak laugh, "Devil woman, she's got to save me from her you know." He looks at me for a second—then his face goes back to being silent. Nodding. Looking out the windows up into the light blue sky framed by Brownstones on the other side of the street.

"What you been doing?"

"Just working my conditioning. My game's gone to shit. Well, my jump shot anyway, funny my speed and jumping ability have gotten better as I've learned to stretch. Anyway… I go away in a couple of months and want to be ready for what's ahead."

"Can I ask you?"

"What, Alton?"

"You afraid of what you might become? I mean I seen you on Leroy... Mom says all these crazy things sometime but, I seen you, man."

Looking at him, our eyes meeting for a moment.

Letting the high clouds move by.

"Part of me is excited. I've been doing a lot of reading and studying the history of what folks like my uncle went through. Some of the things I've read, well, I didn't have much of a perspective to understand. Probably still don't..." Taking a deep breath. "On the other hand, I wonder if I have what it takes to keep cool when things get tough. When I got put in solitary confinement, I could feel a deep meanness coming on. Like a junkyard dog whose got to bite 'cause they hurt so bad inside."

Mad because I keep talking around the real answer.

"I do worry though, Alton, cause deep down inside I know I couldn't handle the pressure off all the stuff going on at home and school... I blew it. And look what's come of all that."

His head nodding slightly, he looks down at the new basketball.

"Man, Earl the Pearl." Smile on his face for a moment.

"He was so cool when he signed it."

"You know, you remember those games we got to see at the Garden when he played for the Bullets? He was like magic, him and Frazier battling it out. Earl so smooth, faking, spinning, Frazier think he's have him boxed in and all, and then bang," smiling, seeing some life come back to his face. "Long shot, swish."

"Your style will be more like Big O, but maybe more mobile, more speed."

"You think?"

"Man, you'll run rings around guys in NC, you'll be too fast, too strong for them to hold you. Plus you got that strong D. You keep working that explosive first step like Coach had you doing..."

Slight smile comes to his face again.

"Next year would have been our year, man."

"It sure would," rush of emotion coming up my chest, "I wish I hadn't blown it for us. I'm sorry about that every day now, Alton. I'm sorry that I couldn't listen."

Our eyes meet for a second. Slight nod.

"What does Janelle say about you leaving?"

"Oh, man," he shakes his head.

Quiet settling back in his room, tracing out the lines of the parquet floor as if they were the map of an ancient city.

"You want me to go?"

"Getting kinda tired, man."

"Okay," looking over at Alton. "You good if I come back?"

"What, you gonna bring a ball signed by Frazier next time?"

"Chump," smiling at him.

"Army chump."

Nodding at him. "That I am. A chump in a green uniform soon."

"But still a chump."

"Better than a non."

"Oh man, don't even be starting with me," weak laugh. He gives a quiet cough.

Sitting in the silence of a few moments of good feeling, not shying away from the recognition about how much I'll miss him and all the good times we had.

"You feel strong enough soon, you want to go work some easy ball?"

He's looking at me for a moment, looks away out the window.

"That's been awhile man."

He won't look at me. I should have known, dumb to ask.

Getting up. Quick look around, pushing down the words I want to say.

"This was nice man, the ball 'n all."

"I'm going to miss you, Alton."

He looks at me then looks away.

"Sometime soon, be good... You know, go out, 'n take a few shots."

"Sure will, Alton, sure will."

Chapter 62

Stomach growling—hunger eating at me.

Looking out over the Hudson, the setting sun reflecting against the white stone of the Soldiers' and Sailors' monument. Why the hell I wanted her to meet me here I'll never know. My hands resting on the cool, roughly hewn, dark grey granite stone making up the thirty-foot retaining wall above lower Riverside Park. In the distance, ships are moving down the Hudson.

Imagining that I can feel her before I can see her.

Essence of her body carried by the wind—her molecules carried over time mixing with mine, moving through me? I can't smell it, but it feels warm, luxurious, smooth—that moment after we come together, our bodies entwined, pushing, reaching and then moments where there's a clarity.

"Frank," she's laughing, snapping out of my trance, smiling at her.

"Wow, you were really spaced out."

"Hey, Mary," bringing her close to me, holding her as slowly as I can, smelling the freshness of her. Taking the moment that may never come again, stretching it out, hoping for eternity.

"Are you okay?" She's moves her head back to see me.

Eyes still closed, "Lead me some place," waiting for her. "Not too difficult to walk with my eyes closed though," smiling, closing my eyes. Feeling the contact with her.

"I don't…"

"Just take me some place, I can't see, all I have is your voice in the darkness." Imagining her looking at me with that funny tilt of her head. Feeling her arm wrap around my left.

"Hmm, well, okay. This is kinda strange," she's quiet. Trying to remember which way I'm facing—I was looking out toward the Hudson, turned left—I should be looking parallel to Riverside Drive, one of the old cannons to my left, benches a few feet away between me and the cannon.

"Step with me."

"This is so weird," walking, fighting the desire to either stop or open my eyes. Stepping in rough concert with her. She's turning me around—must be heading uptown now.

What's up this way? Oh, it's walkway down to the lower park greenway.

"We're going to turn left."

Bumping into the stonewall, "Ow."

"Sorry, here step to your left, we'll turn then I'll tell you when to step down."

"You had to pick stairs," shaking my head.

"Well."

God this is hard, feeling like I just want to inch forward.

"Relax, Frank," she puts her right arm around my waist, her left through my arm, "I'm stepping down, you follow okay," relief flooding through as my toe touches the next step.

"Again."

"Again."

Imagining the long walk way down—two or three steps before it drops to the next level. "Are we near the bottom?"

"Silly... we're not even halfway."

"This is so weird," following her body, fighting my instinct to lead—how can I now, I can't see a damn thing. Time moving so slowly, I can hear her breathing; I can feel her concentration—her grip on my arm.

"Okay, we're going to walk down a slight downhill now."

"Okay, wake me when we get to the greenway," her fingers digging in to try and tickle me. "Hey no fair, tickling a blind man, there's got to be a law against that or at least a sticker I can put on your back, you know, kicks helpless people when they are down."

Losing track of where I am, taking a step at time.

Feeling like I'm floating with only her touch keeping me present.

"Feels like we've reached the bottom."

"Just a few more feet."

Smell of the river and the parkway, relaxed steps.

"There's a pothole here, step to the right, okay, now back to the left."

"Let's find a bench."

"You going to tell me what this is all about?"

"What? Letting my love lead me out of darkness is not enough. Sheesh."

"Okay, you can sit down."

Off balance for a second, so weird not being able to see.

Sitting next to her with my eyes closed, warm sun bearing down on my face, sounds of a few birds, more sounds of cars racing along the Henry Hudson Parkway, people walking by talking.

"Frank, what's going on in that little pea brain of yours?" she says as she's tucking into me.

"Me Cro Magnon man, mighty hunter, take club, hit woman on head and drag her off to cave. Hmm, have woman, trying to figure out where to find club, hard problem for man with pea brain," sitting like the Thinker. "Hmm, must invent ax first, that solution. Cut down tree, make nice club and then I hit woman on head, then life be good."

Sitting with her, sun feels good.

Time to step off.

"Mary?"

"What, Frank?"

"I've been thinking about this so much lately, I wish there was. Well..."

"What, Frank?" hearing a little concern in her voice now.

"It's hard to say, to put into words."

"You're getting back together with her!" she jerks away from me. "I know you told me she's been calling you, she's been getting in my face at school how I butted into something that wasn't anything of mine, how she wants you back."

"Mary," reaching out with my hand, finding her arm waving around, working my way up to her hand, taking it, "no, nothing like that."

Holding her hand.

"I'm not afraid of her you know."

"Mary, I love you, I know what I want out of life. It's not Catherine. It's you. I've been thinking how easy it's been for me to think things are going to keep coming my way because I'm special, so easy to overlook the things that don't come often or even again. The things that open for a time and then are gone, and if we don't take them, they may never come around again. And when they open for that brief time, we've got to take them, we've got to step out, be brave and step into the unknown, take the chances that come with it."

Feeling her body move away a little bit.

"What are you trying to tell me, Frank?"

"Oh," swallowing hard, "I," feeling my brain swirling around, "Mary I want this to... I want us to be together, you know, promise to each other that we'll be together." Opening my eyes, the bright light, strong greens of the park, light reflected off the light stone too much for my eyes for a moment. "I'll be away for a few years but we can make that work like we've talked, going places together, being together. You'll be almost done when I get out, but that's okay, I can catch up. I want this to be here through all that we go through. I want to promise you that I'll be here for all that. That you'll be with me," looking at her, wary look on her face.

She looks out across the river for a few moments, her lips tight.

"Are you asking me to marry you, Frank?"

Sinking feeling in my stomach.

"Mary, we've told each other how we feel, how much we love each other right? Isn't this the natural way to go? I mean, not now but shouldn't... When people feel like this, shouldn't they say it? Say what they want?"

"Yes but, so soon," she looks at me, moving a little further away on the bench, "I mean I'm, flattered, but we are so young, it's not that I want to see other people, but can't we promise to be together, get through college, you the military and finish up school first? Then we can go live," she shrugs her shoulders. "Go see the world. Find some little island where clothes are optional."

"But cause you're married doesn't mean you can't do that. Look at Jack London and I don't know, his second wife, they built a sailboat to go off and sail around the world together. Doesn't finding the person you fit with so well mean that all those things are better cause you've made the jump, cause you've made the promise in front of your family and friends?" Looking at her, hoping she'll look in my eyes and feel what's inside trying to break out. "Where it's not like something that comes and goes, it's something you tend to, something you fight for?" she won't look at me.

Feeling the happiness I'd discovered the other day slowly dribbling down a hole opening up inside me.

"Frank," she's trying to make this okay now, putting on her game face, "I do love you. This is so sudden, look…" she looks at me for a moment and then looks away. "Could this be that I'm going away soon for a month and then you'll go away later this summer? Don't you trust me that I love you?"

Putting on my game face too. Just need to look away for a second.

Letting my eyes follow the long span of the George Washington Bridge across the river to the green cliffs of New Jersey.

"Frank," coming back to her lovely face, "I don't know," she looks away for a moment. "I feel like you're feeling desperate, no sorry." She must be seeing my reaction in my face. "I didn't mean it like that. You've been through so much and I want to be with you. I do, Frank. I think we're too young to be jumping in with our eyes closed. Please trust me, Frank."

Looking down at my hands, realizing how tense I was. Relaxing, wiggling my fingers. Leaning forward, elbows on my knees, chin resting on my hands.

"I do, Mary, I trust you, that's why I could close my eyes and know that you'd take care of me. But look at me please," sitting back up, her eyes on mine, trying to reach out to her from what I feel, my chest so full of love wanting to burst out, oh if there were only the words. "Mary, when you… No, no it's not you. To love," closing my eyes for a moment, taking her hand, wrapping my fingers in hers.

"To give life to this wonderful freedom inside, to know that here is the person you want to be with, isn't that something precious, something to care for?" opening my eyes. "Like a flame that's kept inside when we're apart, that leaps out and joins with you when we're together, where we can let it rage and revel in the flame together," taking a second, she's closer. "Then we let it be calm at times, a light to guide us, a place we tend to, a place our children can come for warmth and love." Feeling the hole inside me close up, the fire for her, the passion to hold her building again.

"Isn't that worth taking the step when you know it's what you want?"

Her face seems pulled in different directions. Long silence.

"I don't know, Frank… can't we take our time here, talk this through? I do love you, Frank, we're so young, how do you know that this is so real?"

Pinhole opening up again, fighting to keep from letting the reality of her saying no drive me to close the door. "There's so much we have in common, movies, books, writers we like. Crazy kind of humor, desire to do new things and try new things. I mean, a woman who likes to go deep sea fishing, what's not to love about that?"

"Yes, but why now Frank, why the rush?"

"Is it a rush to behold what makes the world… No, that's not it. That changes my world from a small place of dull grey frustration to something spacious, a place filled with colors, sounds, where possibilities are bounded only by our imagination."

Looking at her.

"No?" Feeling the moment passing. "Isn't that something to stand for, Mary?"

"Yes, no, I don't know," she looks out at the river squeezing my hand, lifting our entwined hands up and then bringing them down on her thigh a few times.

People pass walking their dogs.

Looking out across the Hudson "I can't believe I said behold... that's such a funny word, like some biblical prophecy's going to spurt out of my lips. Here he is live from Riverside Park, Frankadamus..."

Nothing—no reaction.

That's not true—it's not nothing, it's no.

Feeling the joy deflate in my body.

Standing up, letting our hands part, walking across the small green square, remembering what's underneath here, the dark train tunnels I used to walk in. Standing by the stone retaining wall at the edge of the greenway, river moving slowly inland now. Stop it Frank—you sprang this on her out of the blue. Don't get all down in the dumps. Don't start this.

She's leaning on the wall looking down at the river.

"You can trust me, Frank, I'll be here for you," she's touching my arm. "You don't need to go to the extreme, we're so young... I promise I'll be there for you, Frank, I think we should wait till you're out of the Army and I'm done with school."

Feeling my lips purse, nodding with her.

"Look, don't tell your parents I asked, okay?"

"Sheesh, like that will happen. Mom's been so confrontational with me lately, so pushy." Rolling my eyes at that—like I have no idea what that's all about, right.

"I understand, Frank, I'm," she turns back to the park. "I want to figure this out too, I hate the timing and I can only imagine what it's going to be like to not have you here. And I know we'll talk and write," she looks at me a little laugh. "You better write too," then back following something in her vision. "I don't know. It's like something I'm starting to rely on and need is getting pulled away. It's unfair," she leans into me. "Oh Frank, Frank, Frank," quiet for a few moments, watching the cars drive by below me.

"Maybe you're right, this is what we've been given, things quickening... It's scary for me to think that things could change so quickly and..."

Looking at her, she meets my eyes.

"I guess I understand a little of what you've been going through, things so abruptly changed, tossed up and you're being so brave facing it, trying to keep yourself together."

Brushing the small tear coming down her face with my thumb.

"Shh, Mary," pulling her to me, "we'll figure this out, I guess we have to stay at it," turning and walking with her back toward 79th St., the way to her parents' house.

"To be honest, I sure wish you'd said yes, though it scares the hell out of me to think about what we'd do if you'd said yes."

"I didn't realize this was a time based offer... I might say yes."

"Mary," stopping and looking at her, "no you wouldn't, and it's okay, it was a wild crazy idea, maybe I am being desperate, like Tantalus grasping for things just beyond his reach."

"You already have them, Frank," as she walks close to me.

"Okay, Mary," putting my arm around her—silence surrounding the ebbing of the flame doing my best to ignore the feeling of losing something here. Watching her walk, it's not the end—why do I put myself into these all or nothing positions?

"You'll keep thinking about this?"

"Yes," she smiles, "Of course I will."

Flame taking a little jump in my chest.

Even if I know it's not true.

Chapter 63

Telling time by the improvements in my charts—rope climbs, pull-ups, push-ups, sit-ups, distance and time all heading in the right direction. Smiling to myself for a moment remembering how we were joking on the phone about how I'm developing the Popeye like wrists that will match the calluses on her fingers.

A couple of weeks till she gets back from Italy—I can't wait.

Chapter 64

Long silence on the phone filled in by the background hum of the overseas line. "But Mary, there's got to be a way," breathing, thinking this through. "What if you just come back... for God's sake, you're eighteen now," feeling another wave of anger rise up in my stomach focused at that fucking witch, that fucking cunt witch bitch. "What if I buy you a ticket back to the States?"

"No, I mean I want to," hearing her start to silently cry again, "I can't do that to my parents, this has been so hard."

"But, why can't you tell her no thank you, why now?"

Another silence.

"Is there something else?"

"No, no, Frank, oh no!"

"God does this suck!" My aunt walking by trying not to look but seeing the concern in her face, waiting for her to move through the hall.

"Why now, Mary? This is intentional, it's just to keep us apart," looking around, wanting to hit something.

"No," long distance line humming away. "I don't know, it's been so weird here between them, I want this all... Frank, it's not like you're going away forever you know. We can see each other around Christmas time, you've told me you'll get time off, I can come see you."

Image flashing in my mind of the cheap, shitty motels around Fort Hamilton, feeling like I'm deflating, losing the fight—she's not coming back.

"Cheap motel sex at Christmas..." Shaking my head. God does this suck. Why isn't she fighting for us? Isn't this when love's supposed to triumph—when things aren't easy, when you have to go against the grain?

"Oh," hearing her take a deep breath.

Another long pause.

Searching for ways to break through.

"Mary, look I don't know..." got to be the right thing to say, somehow—coming up empty, frustrated with my stupid brain, "I don't know how all this works yet, you know leave, what I'll be doing. I'm assuming that after basic training I'll go to airborne training and after that, if I make the grade then I'll go through Ranger selection, but when, where... I mean what if things don't go that way. Given all the other bad luck, maybe I'll end up peeling potatoes for four years," throat feels a slight burning sensation of helplessness. "Mary, what do you want?"

Silence punctuated by the hum of the long distance line.

"I want to be there, you know how much I've missed you. Your letters have kept me going. It's been so hard here at times, it's like she's looking for things that are wrong. Dad and Mom have been at it too."

"It's not you, Mary."

"I don't know, Frank."

"It's not you, whatever is going on with your mom, whatever's crawled up..." catching myself, "well, it's not you."

Crushing silence.

"Mary, look what if I go down and buy you an airplane ticket back, I bet you could stay with one of your friends or I bet Richard would let you crash at his place. Is it money? I can wire you money, right?" Feeling like possibilities exist while I talk to her. "What's going to happen next year when you go away to school? You'll be free, take that step now. This trip was supposed to be four weeks, why not hold them to that?"

"I can't Frank, I tried."

"Why won't you fight for us?" seeing my aunt walk by again.

"I can't explain this any better... Can't you see my side in this, I feel like you're making me the bad person here. Isn't it reasonable for Mom to want spend our last summer together doing something we both love? Don't I have a responsibility to my family too?"

"I don't know, Mare," body slouching down in the chair now, closing my eyes, trying to picture her face. "It's been just so, I don't know," gray fog is all I can see. "Before you left it was like we had such a good thing going, we were so in tune. Yeah your mom was acting weird and your dad was concerned we were moving too fast, but," deep breathing to try and catch some of my energy—mad that I'm giving up, mad that I don't know how to fight. "Isn't that something to fight for?"

"I don't know, Frank. I'm so confused."

"Mary," choosing carefully. I have to say it, "Come back to me, come back and be with me, please. Please, Mary. I know it's tough to make a move like this."

She's sniffling a little.

"I can't Frank, I love you, I can't do that to them now. She means well, she really does." Pressure building in my chest—what do I fight here? How do I fight this?

"Frank, we can make this work... I love you. I love you so much. We can make this work. Okay?"

"Okay, Mare. I love you too."

Hanging up the phone—dejected, angry because I know all the cheering up she tried to do is a bunch of goody two shoes bullshit. She had to choose and she chose. Angry with myself for playing along, like any of that will matter, there will be some other excuse later this year.

Sitting down in the dim living room, distant sounds of my aunt puttering around in the kitchen. Feeling my world become empty again, the light of her face draining out of me.

Maybe it's better this way. Bullshit.

The yelling rising up in my head—I miss her—I miss her body, I miss her wacky sense of humor, her curiosity—those moments when we can be lost in each other after sex.

Why couldn't I tell her this? Well I did, but I didn't say it like this. I said it like I was mad, like I was owed something.

I need to write her—I can't let this sit like this.

Chapter 65

Empty subway out to Rockaway Beach is my daily life.

Standing at the front of the train and letting the wide expanse of Jamaica Bay fill my vision in another vain attempt to take a bite out of the emptiness inside. Relaxing into the rocking motion of the subway.

Rain clouds in the distance.

Wishing there was a way to let the rushing wind slowly carry away each molecule of this terrible sadness.

I must have been cursed to have beheld the wonder in her eyes and then be cast away without the voice to speak these words to her.

Monsters should not dream.

A handsome face given to grotesque reanimated life has no right to a soul.

Carefully walking down rusted steel steps toward the cracked pavement. Weeds growing up in the sidewalk move with the wind coming in from the sea. And yet she loved me.

Eyes brimming up—is this the curse of the fallen, moments of heaven held just beyond our reach, our cries falling on deaf ears? Ghosts that sometimes can be seen then disappear and stand in scattered ruins, invisible, isolated in their silence, held captive in the distance of remembering those moments of wonder when we were lost in time together.

Monsters should not love.

Is that what makes me all the more grotesque, that through some miracle I could be normal after all?

And now I run with weights strapped to my back through ruins.

Miles of empty beach my home.

No weight that I can take off will ever free me of my guilt. Fools—to think we could cheat the world. I, that the fallen can lay claim to love. She, that love can breathe life into an empty shell of clay.

Pathetic boy. Once trapped by anger and pride, now unable to stop the daily mark and measure of my time that masks the pain and having to look back to that day when I knew she loved me.

Run, monster, run. Run to oblivion again that you may feel something other than she is gone and what you had will never again be.

Run through the anger.

Run till your vision blurs and time suspends.

Run you monster for this is all you will ever feel.

Stagger, breathing through burning lungs. Vision swimming.

Face feels like it's burning.

Sinking, knees in the wet sand.

A moment of her smile.

Distant blackness calling.

"Is he dead?"

"We should call the po-lice."

"I seen him, crazy white boy running like a wild man talkin to his self."

Shapes in the distance.

Must be the daily crowd of ladies who try to stay as far away from me as possible. What an asshole I am, getting all worked up. What, I'm the first jerk whose girl got taken away by her family? Why do I do this to myself? I can't even be depressed like a normal person—I go out and run till I pass out. Probably puked on myself. Blinking my eyes.

Sandy hands, body wet from lying who knows how long in the light rain.

"You need us to call someone?"

Sandy lips, I must have passed out face down.

"No. I'll be okay, just give me a minute."

Head dizzy as I sit up, resting my head on my knees.

Some fucking monster—moron more likely.

"Musta come from one of them places fo crazy people," as I hear them walking to the arriving bus.

Seagulls chattering and fighting over something on the nearby jetty, brushing the wet sand from my hands, the bus is long gone.

What a mess.

Standing up—leg and back muscles screaming.

Taking off this stupid backpack.

Sitting at the lonely bus stop bench.

Eyes drawn to the sea.

There's a whole world out there, Frank. God, will I miss her. God, do I miss her. Sick laugh rising up—who would have thought the Army would be a relief after all this?

Fucking loser.

Letting the view across to Coney Island from the top of the Marine Parkway Bridge fade. No way I'm going to be able to do anything in the gym today.

Go home, go read, go sleep. Tonight you're heading over to the VA with Uncle Vin. You can complain all you want Frank, but she's still gone and you go away soon. Don't be such a big fucking pussy.

Bus stopping and starting as it makes its way along Flatbush Ave.

I could call her—I could call Cat. I could tell her all the things I understand now that are too late. We'd meet and talk. We'd end up going at it like two crazed people out for revenge the way she's been carrying on lately.

That's really smart, Frank. Take a mistake, compound it with another mistake, and then throw another few at it. Hey, while you going… Moron.

"Oh, Frank! Look at you!"

Damn, I thought she'd still be out. Cringing at the through of another long talk about how I shouldn't feel sorry for myself.

"You look terrible. Shake all that off outside. What did you do?"

Standing there looking at her—shrugging my shoulders.

"Another crazy person," she's smiling, still concerned. "Go get changed, I'll make us some lunch."

Stopping in front of the wall of family pictures on the way to my basement room. Yellowed, black and white pictures of Uncle Vin, Dad, Uncle Michael when they were kids dressed up in sailor outfits, wedding picture of my grandparents. Trying to imagine what it must have been like for their families—to lose everything, move here from Sicily with little money, speaking little English and start from almost nothing. There they are getting married at Saint Martin's, the now springing from that moment.

Looking down the long wall of framed photographs.

Shiver running up and down my spine. My great grandparents started with nothing when they came here. Looking at the stoic faces of pictures from back then. Determined, solid—no whining, no looking back. Aunt Kitty was right—I was acting like a big baby. Take a deep breath, let it sink in and own it.

Stopping by the photos of Uncle Vin and Aunt Kitty at their wedding, Dad in the wedding party. He's a bastard, but look at what he's done. His company is a foundation a lot of people's lives depend on.

He built it from nothing.

Fighting off the uneasy feeling in my stomach.

Moving down the wall.

Uncle Vin dirty, unshaven standing in front of a captured German concrete bunker with some of his fellow Rangers. Smiles, grim faces, weapons ready. They look exhausted, a few bandaged up. How many of his friends died that day?

Hearing Aunt Kitty puttering around in the kitchen.

Looking back into their living room. Smile on my face seeing that Uncle Vin has put a couple of Grandpa T's pieces that I've refinished in there. Feeling inadequate at what I've given back to them.

I'll be alone on a train heading down to Georgia in a few weeks.

So much to do before I go.

Now that I see it, so much I can do before I go.

There are people at the VA who look forward to me coming by every week. I have a wonderful woman to write to. Closing my eyes, taking a moment to remember our last night together. We'd stayed up all night—it was the early morning. We took a cab down to South Street Sea Port and watched the sun rise over the masts of the old sailing ships; huddled up together drinking coffee, doing our best to stretch each moment.

Remember that Frank, hold it. You never know the last moment.

Make each moment matter.

I have so much to do before I go.
I have a man to prove wrong.
"Frank, are you coming up?" smiling to myself.
I have so much to be thankful for that I didn't known I had.
Shiver running up and down my spine.
The man I am starts now, not in a month, not in a year.
"Be right there, Aunt Kitty."
I have a friend to help heal.

About the Author

Steven Farnworth was born and raised in New York City. In addition to his work as an author, entrepreneur and engineer in Silicon Valley, he has started two high technology companies and holds multiple patents. He served honorably in the US Military and is an avid archer, free diver and outdoorsman. He lives with his wife and family in Northern California.